The Monopoly Murders

by TOM J SANDY

The Monopoly Murders

©Tom J Sandy - 2006

Hardback edition published by Eye 5
ISBN 0-9546897-6-3

Published 2006 by Eye 5.
Text © Tom J Sandy. The moral right of the author has been asserted.

A CIP catalogue record for this book is available from the British Library

The Monopoly Murders is a work of fiction. Any resemblance between characters living or dead is entirely coincidental.

Published by: Eye 5, 148 Godfrey Way, Great Dunmow
Essex CM6 2SQ, United Kingdom
www.eye5.org.uk

Typeset by Eye 5

Printed and bound in the UK by Bath Press

Charles B. Darrow, an entrepreneur from Pennsylvania, is
credited with inventing Monopoly.

American game manufacturers Parker Brothers
originally rejected his game, claiming it had
more than fifty basic errors.

They reversed their opinion in 1935. Since then more
than 200 million sets have been sold.

✝

Thanks to Karla Mahar and Mark Chapman,
and to Jojo Kate for the cover

+

Those who eat fugu soup are stupid.
Those who don't eat fugu soup are also stupid.

Japanese proverb

The Monopoly Murders

✝

CHAPTER ONE

✝

Dearest Edgar
I do hope you don't mind me calling you Edgar?
Tough if you do.
Well, have you got it yet? I don't think so, somehow.
I'll be in touch again soon. Won't say when, I'd like
to keep you on your toes.
Best wishes as ever
Jake T J

DETECTIVE INSPECTOR Rory Alexander must have read the note a dozen times that morning. He was still clueless as the last lunchtime before Christmas beckoned.

He was ready to enjoy as best he could a four-day festive break, JTJ permitting. At least now he had a first name to work with: Jake. But was Jake his real name? Highly unlikely. And Edgar. Why Edgar?

He examined the brown envelope one more time. It was addressed 'personal' to DI Alexander; printed from a personal computer, just like the words on the sheet of plain A4 copier paper inside. All very personal. Except there were no signs left by the person he wanted.

Plain tap water had been used to seal the envelope. The only prints found on the note belonged to the inspector. Two other discernible prints on the envelope needed checking, but Alexander would wager his mortgage – when he got one – on them belonging to postal staff and the sergeant who handled the internal mail deliveries.

If Jake had timed this note to ruin his festive break then he had timed it with unerring accuracy. It was genuine, of that Alexander was certain. The Met had kept JTJ out of the papers.

Jake. Jake. Who the hell are you Jake? He wracked his memory and could not come up with a single Jake. A few Jacks stumbled through his grey cells, some lingering longer than others. He had played football, badly, with a Jack at college; in his teens a Jack had lived a couple of doors from the family home; and he had put two Jacks behind bars. Both of the latter were still doing time so he could rule out them. Anyway, burglary to murder was a long hop. Alexander could picture a couple of Jacobs, too. But no Jake. He knew no-one who went by the name Jake. Except Jake The Peg from a long ago novelty song.

And TJ? Would he have to wait for more murders before this joker enlightened him further? Joker. Joker! Joker? Could the second 'J' be for Joker? Three murders, strange sense of humour this joker. He was getting a headache. Time for a pint and then some brisk, last-minute Christmas shopping. His Christmas shopping had been last-minute for as long as he could remember. Had Jake done his shopping? Alexander shut that thought out of his brain, as he knew it could only serve to worsen his headache.

✝

CHAPTER TWO

✝

HE REALLY wasn't paying too much attention. Until she started laughing at him. "Ha-ha-ha. Poor Jake. See you in a little while."

Rory Alexander shot bolt upright; his eyes suddenly wide open and staring almost maniacally at her. "What was that? What did you say? What ...what did you call me?"

There was urgency in his voice, an urgency bordering on panic. His face was flushed. The other four people round the table stared back at him. Their stares were more of bewilderment.

"What did you call me?" he repeated, his voice lowering from a fevered squeak to a more manly growl.

She began crying. "You're hurting me."

"Rory! Rory what the hell's wrong? Take your hand off Katie."

Alexander looked up at his brother Kyle who was tugging at his shoulder. He hadn't realised he was gripping his niece's arm. "Sorry, sorry ...I'm really sorry Katie ...it's just ...I think I need a glass of water. Oh Christ! Sorry."

Alexander rose from the dining room table and staggered in a semi-daze through the newly-decorated archway and into the kitchen. He was filling his second glass from the tap when Kyle and his wife Jade joined him.

"Christ Rory! What was all that about? It's only a game, you silly bugger — you've scared poor Katie out of her wits."

"She'll have a bruise on that arm in the morning," said Jade, arms folded and eyes breathing fire and brimstone at her brother-in-law.

"Sorry folks. I've been feeling a bit off, work and all that. I'll just apologise to Katie and I'd better be on my way. It was a lovely meal, really it was. Thanks."

Jade left the kitchen and returned with Katie and her younger sister Judy. Both

3

girls were clutching their mother's floral frock and looking warily at their uncle. Katie had stopped crying, thankfully. Mum, too, seemed calmer. She obviously hadn't noticed the mark Rory's hand had left on the archway's peach paint. Rory was now composed; the colour of his face back to its pale normality.

"Hi Katie. Silly Uncle Rory didn't realise he had hold of your arm. Can you forgive a silly policeman? Please?" He kneeled for effect and looked the eternal penitent. The girls began to smile as he bowed down, rested his head on the kitchen linoleum and came up with a small teddy bear hanging from his teeth.

"This is for you, Katie. I'll try and remember to bring one for you Judy next time I come round. Am I forgiven? Please? I need a hug."

Katie left her mother's side and slowly approached the kneeling giant. He was still an inch or two taller than the 12-year-old girl. She wrapped her arms around Uncle Rory and after a tentative few seconds told him this was her biggest, bestest, squeeziest hug, and she took the bear.

Rory waited a few more seconds, trying to smile his avuncular best and holding Katie at arm's length so he could look into her eyes. Then he began laughing gently. "What was that silly name you called me in there?"

"What silly name?" Katie looked puzzled.

Rory laughed some more, praying it did not sound as false as it felt. "That name, in the game?"

Katie frowned and tilted her head.

"Jake," chipped in Judy. "Go to jail, Jake." She was almost singing, though to no tune Rory could recognise. "Go to jail, Jake – do not pass 'GO' – do not collect 200 pounds."

"Oh, Jake The Jailbird!" remembered Katie. "Poor Uncle Rory landed on 'Go To Jail'. Ha-ha-ha."

"Oh yes, right!" He felt his heart thump. "Well, well. I never knew the name Jake. Is that what they call him? Jake The Jailbird? Ha." He was laughing again and striving to conceal his excitement. His stomach turned over; his mouth, despite two glasses of water, suddenly felt very, very dry. He helped himself to a third glass.

"I guess it is something they picked up from my sister's children in Baltimore. Monopoly was about the only game they decided they all liked when we went there last autumn, or Fall as everyone insisted on correcting us." Jade's fire by now seemed to have been dampened. Alexander tried to keep his eyes away from the archway.

"Jake The Jailbird was arrested by Edgar The Cop," said Judy, still in her singsong voice.

"Edgar The Officer! Not cop," snapped back Katie, showing off now and apparently recovered. Rory laughed a little louder and smiled at his brother.

"Jake The Jailbird and Edgar The Officer; we live and learn, eh Kyle?" By now he was sure even the neighbours could hear the rumbling from his belly and the pounding in his brain.

"News to me, too, Rory. Not that I was ever allowed to play." He began mock sobbing, which made the girls giggle.

Rory was pleased to be saying his farewells on a lighter note. His brain was a whirl of emotions, though his insides had settled. He had shocked himself by grabbing hold of his niece. Disgusted himself even. In truth, he hadn't even realised he had a hold of her until Kyle had shook him. How could he have done that; grabbed hold of his little niece and made her cry – without even noticing what he was doing? He washed the memory from his mind as he smiled all the way to the front door, kissing the girls and shaking hands with his brother. He once more profusely thanked Jade for a wonderful Christmas dinner, patting his stomach for effect. He smiled even wider as Kyle gave him a brief hug and told him not to work too hard and not to take all the crazies personally. He was sick of smiling and glad for the shock of the outdoor air.

There was a chill wind blowing idiotically as he walked the three miles home. He enjoyed walking any time, any weather. He needed the walk this evening.

Jake The Jailbird. Edgar The Cop, or Edgar The Officer, not that it made much difference. American Monopoly. Did the British version use names, too? They wouldn't be Jake and Edgar surely? Was the killer a Monopoly freak? Why use those names? Monopoly? Surely not. But. But. But it figured; or at least it fitted in with what scant evidence they actually had.

Alexander decided he would go shopping the next day. Last minute Christmas shopping, and now shopping on Boxing Day – definitely a first for him. American and British versions of Monopoly on expenses would probably be a first in The Met, too.

He'd wished he had been paying more attention to the game at his brother's house. By the time he reached The Crown And Anchor, half a mile from his home, he had recalled most of the property sites in the game. Luckily, there was no-one on the streets to witness his mutterings. He was missing one station, one brown, one light blue, one purple, two of the bloody oranges and one of the yellows.

The Crown was doing a decent trade for Christmas night. Unusually, blokes outnumbered women customers by around five-to-one. Unusually for any other time of the year, that is. Many pubs up and down the land closed after lunch on December 25th. The other four on Highgate Hill had, hence all the drinkers had flocked to The Crown. There were a few youngish couples sitting at tables, but the clientele consisted of primarily single men like DI Alexander or men just desperate to escape the banal domestic festivities for an hour or so.

Alexander was pleased to enter the warm pub. He took off his spectacles and wiped away the mist before propping himself at the bar. He preferred to stand and used the stool to hold the small plastic bag which contained the gifts his brother's family had handed over. He had already forgotten what gifts he had received, or given for that matter. Bloody Christmas.

The top quarter off his pint of Bass disappeared in a single sup and Alexander examined his change – £2.40. Sneaky bastard Robin! When had he put up the prices? Robin Jackson wasn't around to answer his query. The not-so-affection-ately branded 'Robin Bastard' had hired staff for the night and was probably snoozing his head off upstairs in front of the TV. Money for old rope the pub business, thought Alexander; he could handle the easy life – beats chasing serial killers for a living. He was still pondering the price of beer and Monopoly colours when he heard a glass plonk by his left arm. He looked round to see the toothy grin of Trevor Taylor. The grin looked the same but Alexander had to make a double-check at the outfit – he'd never seen the plumber dress so smartly.

"Evening Trev, and all the bloody festive greetings to you. Christmas presents, are they?"

"Just the shirt, officer. And I would guarantee bought and paid for – our Janice's not one for your knocked-off East End clobber."

"Nice shirt, Trev. Used to have one just like it before my old man got a job."

"Very funny. And how was your day? Did we go to church this morning?"

They both laughed. "Funerals and weddings, Trev. Funerals and weddings. But if I had my way I'd avoid those, too."

"Well, why am I not surprised? Does the lucky Lucy know this? Is she expecting a walk down the aisle?"

"She knows she can have one if she wants. I'll go along for the ride."

"Still on course for next summer? Can't beat a good summer wedding. Both mine have been summer jobs."

"Yeah. Maybe early July then we can have a honeymoon before the little buggers get let out for the summer and start clogging up the airports."

"She not joining you tonight?"

"Nope. She's gone north to see her folks for a few days. I've been round our Kyle's."

"Glad to escape by now, eh? I was. Turkey and TV are a lethal combination."

"Not much TV. Thankfully his kids aren't totally hooked. I played Monopoly for the first time in ages."

"Now that is what families should do at Christmas. No such luck with my lot, though. TV's been on since first thing this morning. Another pint?"

"Twist my arm."

Fresh pints appeared promptly and Alexander smirked as he caught Taylor counting his change. "I remember when ..."

" ...you could buy four pints, four bags of crisps and have change from a fiver."

"And enough for a bag of chips on the way home."

The men supped in silence, examining the proud profile of the pretty barmaid. Alexander nudged his drinking companion. "Too old for me, never mind you, you dirty sod. Quiz time: a large Scotch says you can't tell me the name of the guy in jail in Monopoly?"

"Name? What d'yer mean, name? 'Go To Jail', you mean?"

"Yeah. The guy behind bars on the board has a name. I never knew until this evening."

"Not a bleedin' clue, Rory. New one on me." He took a large sup of his pint and then thought a moment. "Ronnie? Reggie? Charlie?"

Alexander grinned as his pal rattled off the names of the Krays, London's most notorious gangsters from the 60s.

"Jack," interrupted a voice two barstools away. "The Yanks call him Jack; not sure if we have a name for him."

Alexander recognised the face as a regular but could not put a name to it.

"Not bad, pal. But it's Jake, actually. So my little nieces tell me."

"Jake, yeah, right." The man nodded, scratching his head. "They have a name for the cop, too ...escapes me."

The detective let him think for a while but came to the rescue just in time to prevent him scratching away half his scalp. "Edgar. Let's all have a drink to Edgar The Officer. My shout."

Alexander shook his head and once more grimaced at the small change; it was a joke that would never wear thin. The newcomer joined them in discussing the greatness of Monopoly for half an hour. They discovered they all had a liking for the green property sites; and his pals also helped Alexander recall the names of those properties which had eluded him on his walk to the pub. At the back of the detective's mind was JTJ, and that was where it would stay for now, even when Taylor asked how work was going.

"Criminals don't take Christmas off, do they? Surprised the force can do without you."

Taylor, like many Londoners, easily made light of serious issues. Trench humour saw them through to the weekend. Three murders were not going to upset the routine stoicism of the capital's citizens: the Blitz spirit still reigned.

The Germans, the IRA, the Krays (well some still regarded those days with a disturbing affection) and not even Osama Bin Bag could rattle a Cockney, so what hope a killer with three notches on his belt?

"Any closer to nailing the nutter?" asked their still unnamed companion without too much enthusiasm. He was 'pal' or 'mate' or 'that guy with the funny beard' and his name could be revealed if and when or not at all. Nobody cared much as long as he filled in the gaps with something remotely resembling interesting conversation. That was the essential beauty of blokes and pubs.

"You'll read about it when we do get him," was all Alexander would reveal. "They always make mistakes – without fail."

The drinkers took the hint that was the end of that conversation, though Alexander had hardly sounded at his most convincing – not to himself and probably not to his companions. They discussed the following day's football programme until closing time. Only Mr Anonymous was a serious football fan, but Alexander could hold his own in general company.

Pubs have an anorak for each and every occasion and topic. Barroom experts made their worlds go round, more reliable than any encyclopaedia. Alexander glanced at a table in the far corner from the bar. Three single mid-20s men had claimed their usual spot. The detective hardly knew them, certainly not their names, and often wondered what they did for a living. One thing he knew for sure, he had never met football brains like theirs. Not only could they tell you who won the FA Cup Final in 1897 or whenever, but they would know the goalscorers, times of the goals, and could have a damned good stab at the starting line-ups. More than just a game, some people claimed. Monopoly was more than a game to someone, too.

He was drifting in and out of the conversation. The crowd was thinning out and he was ready to do the same. One for the road, a large Scotch thrown back in one to brace himself for the chill outside. He knew Taylor would not be long after him. Such a polite plumber listening to Anonymous rambling on about

Chelsea's chances. The wind had whipped up and Alexander considered heading back indoors for another shot of whisky. But he was eager to get home. He fastened the top button on his light-brown suede jacket and hugged himself tight as he mopped up the half mile to his flat in record time. The wisdom of sharing his newly-discovered Monopoly knowledge with the pair at The Crown sparked a shiver but he shrugged and marched on.

The streets were calm for 10.20 at night. Very quiet. Alexander noticed some of the shops had even switched off their neon lighting for the holy day. His flat was a hundred yards off the High Street, the top floor of a terraced house on the neat, tree-lined Annandale Avenue. He broke into a gentle trot as he approached No. 29; the wind was more vicious down Annandale.

Kettle or heating? The usual dilemma as he climbed the stairs. The kettle won by a matter of seconds. Alexander took off his jacket and rubbed his arms and shoulders as he waited for the kettle to boil and the heating to bring warmth to his tidy flat.

He was a man of habits, and it was his habit to always turn off the heating if he expected to be out for more than a couple of hours. It kept the bills down but by Christ it was cold! He took off his shoes and socks, another indoor ritual, and jogged on the cold linoleum for a minute, listening to the radio for company rather than to catch any particular programme. A quiet Christmas Day around the United Kingdom, it appeared. The Queen's Speech, the Pope's message, a customary domestic tragedy: a family of four killed on a motorway while travelling to relatives. He was sure the media actually relished relaying those stories at this time of year. Somewhere the story probably cheered up some poor soul. The north-east of Scotland had been the only region to enjoy a white Christmas, though a particular harsh cold snap had hit most of the South and Midlands. Didn't he know it.

Brief news and weather bulletins were followed by a review of the best-selling festive albums. It made a pleasing background drone as Alexander settled himself at his desk with his coffee and a folder. He opened the brown cardboard folder and took out several dozen sheets of paper – photocopies of items filed at the station.

The 35-year-old detective inspector did not really need to examine the contents; he knew them off by heart. The locations, the times and the three victims. He merely wanted to confirm what had already struck him in his brother's kitchen. He had managed not to appear startled at the realisation that JTJ was Jake The Jailbird and that his killings had taken place on or near sites on a bloody

Monopoly board. Alexander shook his head. It couldn't be that, could it? Crazy. Absolutely crazy. He wanted to pass on his discovery. He was almost desperate to. But to whom? Who would scoff loudest and longest? Maybe they would just humour him? But Alexander convinced himself he was right. Thank you, Katie. Sorry if you have a bruise in the morning.

Two strangulations.

The first was a 22-year-old single woman found three months ago in Whitechapel, the infamous stomping ground of Jack The Ripper. Alexander had at first wondered whether the initials were done by a dyslexic.

Victim number two was a 19-year-old male Korean student five weeks later. The pathologist insisted the student had been dead at least 72 hours before the body was discovered under a pile of rubbish bags on Regent Street.

Jake had struck again two weeks ago. A 72-year-old widow had been suffocated and her frail body left to rot for several days at her flat off Vine Street, a strange central London home for a lonely old lady.

The homicide squad had been unable to unearth any link between the three victims except the initials JTJ scratched, not too deeply, into the lower arm. One on the right, two on the left. No pattern there, then.

Alexander had spearheaded the public appeals, appearing twice on national television. He assumed his most recent appearance had prompted the teasing note from Jake TJ. Now there was another clue: Monopoly. He shook his head again and rose from the table to make more coffee.

His flat was very tidy, disturbingly so, some might claim, for a single man. But it had always been that way, even before Lucy had arrived on the scene two years previously. The bedroom was just about large enough to accommodate the double bed she occasionally shared. The spacious lounge enjoyed a comfortable sofa – Alexander's biggest household expense – TV, stereo unit, computer and a solid bookcase which dominated the room. Non-fiction these days outnumbered the French classics from his days as a modern languages student at King's College. The living room/kitchen was tiny in comparison. A solid pine dining table served as a desk while the cooking and washing facilities could just satisfy the needs of a bachelor. A shower-room completed his abode – not bad for 600 quid a month. Well not bad at all by London standards. He would miss the old place when he and Lucy moved to the suburbs after their impending marriage.

Warm at last, Alexander took off his sweater and sat back down with his coffee. He stared at the papers without needing to read them and decided he would bide his time before informing the Gasbag. He would go shopping, however; his mind was made up on that. Before making a proper fool of himself he would check out his nieces' information, even though he was already convinced. And that was half the battle for a natural cynic.

✝

The driver was flustered. Just over 20 minutes to go. He hurriedly parked up and whipped off his seatbelt, not noticing the figure emerge from the shadows as he opened the car door. "Hey!" yelled the driver, grabbing his leg.

"Watch where you're going, mister," snapped the hooded figure without turning round or breaking step. The figure turned a corner and once behind a wall took off the hooded jacket, stuffed it into a duffel bag and left it behind a waste bin.

Three minutes later the figure was back at the car. "You OK, sir?"

The driver was outside the car and holding onto the door, his head bowed as though he was about to vomit.

"I'm just feeling a little bit hot – just a funny turn. I ..."

"Here, you look like you could do with a drink."

"Thanks," said the driver and took a few hurried swigs from the bottle.

"Are you sure you're OK? Would you like me to get some help?"

"No, it's all right. I ...I'm sure I'll be fine. Thank you."

"OK. Take it easy now. I'd sit down in the car and catch my breath if I was you."

"Yes, I will. Thanks again."

The driver was in the car an hour later when the figure returned, back wearing the hooded jacket. He was slumped rather than sat in the driver's seat. A scratching noise startled the hood, who was relieved to spot a stray dog sniffing round a trash can. There was no-one in view so Jake checked the passenger door. Good, it was unlocked.

Jake slipped into the seat and immediately noticed the driver was still alive, barely breathing, though. Minutes left at most. He'd made a bit of a mess down his front. At least the driver's eyes were closed so he could not see the initials being scratched onto the inside of his left arm.

"Wonder who he was?" mused Jake, strolling unhurriedly out into the daylight.

✝

CHAPTER THREE

+

ALEXANDER woke in the dead of night, sweating and desperately in need of water despite the coldness of his bedroom. He had turned off the heating a minute before diving under the duvet. He had not drunk too much that evening. So it must be the nightmare. Why did nightmares usually make people sweat so much? He was unused to them so he could not decide from experience. Yet twice now within less than two hours he had woken and had to rub his eyes and shake his head to erase the vision of screaming Katie clutching a bent arm, broken by the fierce grip of a monster yelling 'What did you just call me?'

This second awakening he needed to towel himself down before climbing back into bed. He slept fitfully for a few more hours; the vision staying away from his mind at last. The detective was tired but pleased to get up and shower at seven o'clock. The heating was still gurgling into life as he clicked the kettle into action for his regular morning fix.

Bloody nightmares! He wondered whether or not to call his brother and check on Katie. 'She'll have a bruise in the morning.' That was what Jade had snapped. Kids were resilient and he was sure Katie had forgiven her silly uncle. Alexander did not scare easily. But the incident had scared him more than it had scared Katie, he assured himself and decided against the call; no need to make a drama over it.

Shopping on Boxing Day. He would walk into the city and join the throngs of bargain hunters. Opening the curtains, he peered out at a bright day with a hint of a slight wind: a good walking day.

Alexander quickly brushed his not-too-short brown hair backwards as usual and puffed out his chest; yesterday's feast was not discernible on his 13-stone, six-and-a-bit-foot frame. It was five miles to the West End from Highgate, a pleasant enough trek on a fine day. There were some dreary stretches where he could step up the pace as he knew he would later idle through Camden Town, browsing at the market stalls and fighting the urge to buy some piece of bric a brac just for the hell of it. Those urges were becoming less and less frequent, especially when he was ambling without Lucy, as his flat simply could not cope.

Books he could never forsake, but other trinkets had long ceased to hold any fascination for him. One day, when he had his palatial spread in the sticks he would go to Camden armed with a big, fat cheque-book and spend, spend, spend to his heart's content. That skull preserved by Tanzanian pygmies would look grandly macabre on a chunky mantelpiece. That grotesque Victorian – or was it Georgian? – ornate plant pot featuring scantily-clad Polynesian maidens would take pride of place by his water-lily pond. Future dreams.

He took a detour through Regent's Park, managing to avoid being trampled by the scores of joggers, before landing on Oxford Street mid-morning.

It was too much to ask. Much too much to ask of any reasonable man to join in the mayhem before he'd suitably refreshed himself. He avoided the temptation of finding a pub as he planned a session later that day. Instead he plumped for his favourite coffee shop.

You could hardly walk a hundred yards around London these days without stumbling across a coffee shop. Alexander preferred Prêt A Manger. Not cheap, but not bad by city centre going. And fresh food, always very fresh – the signs around their cafes let you know they prided themselves on that. The coffee was something else.

The shop by Soho Square was enjoying brisk business. Alexander ordered a double macchiato from the smiling girl sporting the barista badge, and took it outside where he managed to nab the one vacant table. The world bustled by with bags and bags of bargains as the detective sipped and smoked and studied the faces. His leather jacket was fastened tight to keep out the cold. It was a little milder than the previous day, and so relaxing he treated himself to another macchiato and 20 more minutes alone with his thoughts.

Suddenly he jumped up and slapped his legs: action stations. Just Monopoly, just Monopoly, he repeated the drill to himself as he prepared to weave into the mass of humanity. He removed his wallet and keys from his trouser pockets and ensured they were well zipped up inside his jacket. He hoped his fellow shoppers were aware this was a prime day for pickpockets. But statistics told him many of them were not.

Alexander noticed he was in a minority; not many single people were out on the streets, if you discounted the occasional beggar. Couples, families, groups of youths, several Oriental tourist parties and two sets of football supporters killing time before kick-off; but not many singles. He backtracked to Regent Street and soon realised that was a no-go zone. The queue waiting to simply enter Hamleys – London's self-styled 'most magical toy store on earth' – was daunting. No matter how huge the discounts, Alexander would not be joining the line. He would rather walk, browse and hope.

Both sides of Oxford Street were covered in about an hour. He'd bumped into people at frequent intervals; possibly pickpockets, it was hard to tell. Still, he automatically patted his jacket after each encounter.

By chance, having ambled down a side street for respite, he happened upon an unassuming little shop on the fringes of Soho. It was double-fronted with a brown door separating two large wood-panelled windows.

There was nothing special about the shop, nothing at all; it blended in with many others to be found off the main drag. Yet today it stood out for the simple reason that it sported not a single sticker proclaiming 'SALE!' No garish 'HALF-PRICE' stickers, not even '25 PER CENT OFF'. Nothing at all to lure the casual passer-by in and hunt a bargain.

The slightly fading sign, italicised gold lettering, proclaimed this was 'The London Board Games Store'. Alexander felt as if he had been lured there by a spectre. There was a dim light on in the shop, and the sign on the door said 'open' yet Alexander saw no sign of shop assistant or customers.

The windows appeared to have been cleaned recently, though like all others had attracted a small film of overnight grime from the streets. The goods on display were dimly lit. Alexander spied a Monopoly box plus a few other games from his childhood: Cluedo, Scrabble, Go! And games for younger children tucked away at the back: Snakes and Ladders, Ludo.

Chess and draughts dominated the display in the second window. There must have been at least a dozen chess boards set out, ranging from the simple to the elaborate. Many were too gaudy for Alexander's taste.

"Well at least I shouldn't have to wait to be served," he muttered as he entered, the doorbell making a louder ring than he expected.

The shop's interior was larger than one would have judged from the outside. The floor was polished wood, oak and probably original, Alexander guessed. There was no pretence at festive marketing, no Christmas promotions, though a display in the centre of the floor contained games he had never heard of and a folded black card with 'Latest Editions' hand-written in gold lettering.

In both front corners of the floor space stood two tables with chess sets laid out. Both had two chairs by them, ashtrays and drinks coasters, which suggested visitors were able to sit down for a game. Unusual, he thought, but a nice touch. He saw the table to his right appeared to host a game in progress.

"Please don't touch," said a voice from behind the counter. Alexander turned sharply; he hadn't heard footsteps. A casually-dressed man was approaching him, smiling.

"I really should make a note of the positions, just in case they get disturbed. Alfred and George would be distraught. Do you play, sir?"

"Hello," said Alexander. "No, I don't play, sorry." He was not sure why he had apologised. "Well, I mean I can play – badly. It's a pleasant gesture, allowing customers to play."

"Oh, not customers really. A few friends and regulars – for the price of a coffee. It makes for company, even silent company, and does make the shop look active. Alfred and George are two pensioners who just can't keep away. Take their chess very seriously. I would think a full half crown rests on the outcome of this one." He chuckled.

Alexander smiled. "Are you the owner?"

"I am indeed. John Forsyth, grandson of the shop's founder." He held out a hand. Alexander shook it warmly.

"How can I help you?"

"I'm just browsing, actually. Fascinating shop you have. But one thing I definitely need is a Monopoly set please."

"Ah." John Forsyth looked disappointed as if he was expecting something more challenging. "A belated Christmas present is it?"

"No, no," said Alexander, again almost apologetically. "I was playing yesterday for the first time in years and just thought I would like one of my own. I would like two, in fact. My nieces played the American version on a recent visit to relatives and I was hoping to find one to send them as a gift." A small white lie. But maybe he would pass it on to the girls after he had finished with it.

"I see, well we shall have to narrow it down. I assume you want the traditional British version?"

"Traditional version? Yes, I assume so."

"There are so many these days it is impossible to keep track. So many people and companies seeking customised sets."

"Really? I thought it was just a board game."

"Just a board game! Dear me. Look around you, sir. There is no such thing as just a board game. People take their games very seriously, you know. And some treat Monopoly just as seriously as Grand Masters treat chess."

I know. I know, thought Alexander. Deadly serious, some are.

"As you can see, over here," Forsyth waved his arm to the left of the shop, "are all the different types of chess sets I stock. Not a bad selection but it pales in comparison to some of the specialist chess stores. "And here," wave to the right, "are the traditional board games, as I call them. But that is just to differentiate them from the modern games which I keep on the next floor. Keeps the clientele distinct, too. Don't want the youngsters disturbing the thought processes of my Alfreds and Georges. Ever noticed how so many of the modern games seem to involve violence? Quite sad, really."

"No, I hadn't. Bit out of touch with games to be honest. Got bitten by the Monopoly bug yesterday with my nieces."

And Monopoly in its current guise was more violent than the 40-some shop owner could ever imagine.

"Right, here we go. The original British Monopoly – the usual London properties – £39.99. Just the two sets left."

"Yes, I'll take one, please," said Alexander, even though the price temporarily shocked him. Not that he ever had any price guide in mind.

"Fine. Good. And an American version, you say?"

"Yes, please." Alexander was already browsing through the shelves and now comprehending what the owner had meant. There must have been at least 50 different versions of the game, even a Star Trek version. Whatever next?

"Hmm, the Americans seem to bring out new versions at a remarkable rate. Do you have any idea which version your nieces played?"

"Not a clue, sorry. Is there an original one? Same as our London version?"

"You mean the Atlantic City one?"

"Atlantic City?"

"Yes, yes Atlantic City. The game was invented there – or the inventor lived there. Some fascinating books on Monopoly down on the next shelf. History, strategy, that kind of thing, if you're interested."

Alexander kept his surprise to himself. He had always considered Monopoly a very British game. "Terrific. The original Atlantic City version, please. Even if it is not the right version at least I can claim to be passing them an authentic piece of gaming history."

He smiled and bowed down to check out the bookshelves. A few moments passed in silence as Alexander leafed through the books. He replaced most but put two to one side.

"Disappointing," muttered the owner. "I'm afraid I can't find a new one. I know I have a second-hand one upstairs. Would that do?"

"Sure, no problems. Oh, as long as it is complete, though."

"I'm sure it will be. Second-hand is third floor. You mind keeping an eye on things while I go upstairs?"

"Of course, not. You're being most helpful." And it wasn't as if the shop was inundated with customers or potential pilferers. Alexander settled down at one of the chess tables and began reading the history of Monopoly. He was intrigued by the legal battles concerning claims to the game. Yes, he'd take this book, too.

He wandered around the shop floor, examining other board games. He could see beyond the counter into what looked like living quarters in the back. There was no noise coming through so he hazarded a guess that Forsyth lived alone with his games. Shame; a bloke like him should have had dozens of kids scurrying around. Five minutes later Forsyth re-appeared.

"Here it is. I've wiped off the dust. Now as far as I know it is complete and in reasonable condition. I also discovered this – one of the first European versions. I can let you have both for, say, £20? If you are not happy you can always return them for a full refund."

"Deal. And I'd like these two books, please. They look very interesting. May read them myself before passing them on," he winked.

Alexander carefully pocketed the receipt, thanked Forsyth once more and wished him a happy and prosperous new year. Within a few minutes he was transformed from the otherworldly atmosphere of the 'The London Board Games Store' into the modern chaos of the shop-til-you-drop West End of London. No desire to hang around, Alexander made a beeline for the Tottenham Court Road Tube station. It was on the Northern Line and a direct route home to Highgate. Direct, but that was all it had in its favour.

He had to stand for the first few stops as the train was crammed to bursting point. Eventually, he managed to find a seat for himself and his three bags. He wondered what his fellow travellers would think if they knew this detective inspector had been shopping for Monopoly games to help him catch Britain's most wanted man.

Alexander was tempted to grab a quick pint at The Crown; shopping was such thirsty work. But he realised he would have to explain away his purchases so he headed straight to Annandale. He nodded at a couple of neighbours and bade them season's greetings but walked briskly on.

Once inside the flat and the kettle ritual duly performed he took off his shoes and socks, and settled down at the table to examine his purchases. The booklet inside the American version was on plain off-white paper, not the semi-glossy material favoured by many these days. He assumed 1953 was the date of manufacture; not bad condition at all for more than half a century's gaming. He wondered how many children had derived countless hours of pleasure from this particular set.

Atlantic City. New Jersey, he discovered. Well here was another fact to test the anoraks down the pub. Doubtless some bright spark would know – Mr Anonymous perhaps. Alexander was warm from his exercise, so he changed into his customary lazy-day-at-home outfit: baggy tee-shirt, baggier jogging trousers. His bare feet were cooling on the linoleum. He even turned the heating down a notch. His blue-grey eyes ran round the board.

The names meant nothing to him, except The Boardwalk, that is. Was this the famous Boardwalk that The Drifters crooned about? Some of the squares were familiar: Go! Free Parking, Go To Jail, Just Visiting Jail, Chance, Community Chest and the utilities.

The board was shiny, a few dents and marks but smooth to the touch mainly and Alexander let his right hand glide across it several times in circular movements as if he was cleaning it – or was he trying to divine some hidden meaning? Or assistance? Guidance? Could the board put him in contact with his new tormentor? Christ! It's a not a Ouija board, you stupid sod. Still he was mesmerised by it. He was discovering Monopoly existed outside inner London.

He played with the dollars, fiddled with the houses and hotels, and tumbled the dice. He was surprised to find ten metal tokens. Most were familiar to him but he could not recall the horse or the wheelbarrow. One book informed him that the first games produced in 1933 did not contain tokens but that players were expected to use coins or buttons as their individual markers.

Subconsciously he had chosen The Car. He was rolling the dice and moving The Car around the board as he leafed through the books, discovering new names and places. Rich Uncle Pennybags was the name of the top-hatted character synonymous with the game. Edgar The Officer had a surname – Mallory – yet Jake The Jailbird did not. A psychiatrist would have had a field day with Detective Inspector Rory Alexander of New Scotland Yard's Serious Crime Directorate this Boxing Day.

He interrupted his reveries to rustle up a hasty stir-fry to line his insides for a night down The Crown. Stir-fries were his specialities: quick, easy and tasty. The bonus was just a plate, wok and chopping board to wash up afterwards.

Alexander was drying himself after a shower and listening without much attention to the sporting results on the radio as he tidied away his new toys. A French horse had won the King George at Kempton, England's cricketers were holding their own Down Under. Three internationals had been cited for violent conduct following a brutal Rugby Union encounter in Bath. Glad tidings to all men. Arsenal and Chelsea were keeping up the pressure on Premiership leaders Manchester United. All suitable topics for The Crown.

He laid out a long-sleeved white shirt and a pair of Levi's – traditional denim for a man his age; none of this fashionable faded and pre-torn nonsense. Some cretins actually paid an extra fiver for the rips. Would you believe it? Black or brown shoes? And he had just three pairs plus some trainers. Now he knew why women took so long to dress. Brown as he would wear his suede jacket. The trill of the phone jolted him back into the real world.

"Rory? Christine here. Hope you're not busy. There's been another one."

"Another murder? Our Jake?"

"Looks that way. Just took the call five minutes ago. The scene is pretty chaotic by all accounts. Two traffic bobbies found the body in a car park used by football fans heading for Highbury. They're having to let cars go otherwise there'd be a riot. They're keeping behind a few vehicles on the same level."

"Which car park? You have the address?"

"Yes, a multi-storey. Corner of Baron Street and Pentonville Road."

"Pentonville? Bit of a trek from Highbury isn't it?"

"I'm not familiar with the area. Can you get there smartish, Rory? I mean like NOW!"

"I'm on my way. Few miles across town from here – be there in 20 minutes, traffic permitting."

"Good. Get it under control and let's hope the yobs haven't destroyed any evidence. See you in the office first thing."

"Will do. Want me to call you later?"

"Only if you think it's necessary. Oh, and Merry Christmas."

"Same to you."

Pentonville Road. Alexander was pretty sure but just wanted confirmation before dashing out. He ripped open his brand new British Monopoly set and flung the contents onto the kitchen table. Confirmed: Pentonville Road, one of the light blues. At least his childhood memory was intact. Bastard Jake. He could murder a pint; he could murder Jake The Bleedin' Jailbird.

Alexander decided his Crown clothes would have to do for work tonight. Within five minutes his lime-green Vauxhall Astra was heading east. Twenty minutes was really hoping for too much good luck at junctions at the best of times. With shoppers mingling with football traffic it took him three quarters of an hour to reach the multi-storey car park.

✝

CHAPTER FOUR

✝

"DR MCMILLAN'S phoned to say she's on her way," the PC informed Alexander as soon as he arrived at the scene. There was police tape cordoning off an area of about four yards around the blue Mercedes. A few people sporting Arsenal Football Club regalia were hanging around, some smoking, some with hands in pockets, some just kicking the dust off the ground.

"Dr McMillan?" queried Alexander, quickly taking in the scene.

"Home Office. She's on Christmas duty for the prof so it appears."

"Right, thanks. Don't think I know her."

There was another PC idly guarding the taped area, within which three white-suited scene of crime officers were at work with their bags of tricks. Boxing Day so a skeleton squad. The third officer on the scene approached Alexander and thrust out his hand. "Inspector Rogers. I'm second in command match days here," he explained.

"DI Alexander. So what have we got?"

"Those two over by the wall reported the body. They were returning from the match and noticed the bloke slumped in his seat. They tapped on the window to see if he was all right. There was no response so they tried the door ... and then they phoned in."

"Bit far from the ground aren't we for football traffic?"

"The club provides this for about 70 executive season-ticket holders who normally use an official car park at Highbury. Some redevelopment's going on so the club's leased this level and puts on a minibus every half hour right to the ground."

"I thought they were moving ground anyway?"

"Eventually, so they claim. As for now it's important to keep the big season-ticket holders sweet."

"So these were all local fans, no outsiders? Who were they playing by the way?"

"Middlesbrough. Won 3-1. Yes, all Arsenal fans on this level. I've kept behind the occupants of the six vehicles closest to the deceased's car; thought it best to let the others go to keep the relative peace here. The PCs were smart enough to grab around 30 number plates if you need them."

"Good. I doubt it, but you never know."

"No-one claims to know the bloke or to have seen anything suspicious. You want me to keep them here or can I let them go?"

"You can let them go inspector, once you've checked the drivers against the vehicles. I just need to speak with the people who discovered the victim."

Alexander took out his mobile phone and tried to ring DC Mike Burns.

"You'll have to go outside the car park to make a call; can't get a signal in here."

Bugger it. Burns may as well enjoy the rest of his Christmas. Alexander had only considered calling him as insurance. Better to have two minds on the job.

"So, you discovered the body, then?" Alexander said to the two men Inspector Rogers had brought towards him.

"Davey did," said one, tilting his head towards his friend. "He had my dad's ticket for the day. Dad took mum shopping in town."

Lucky, old dad, thought Alexander.

"So Davey, tell me exactly what you saw, please?"

Davey sniffed. "Just the guy with his head in the steering wheel – looked ill or something."

"So what did you do?"

"I tapped on the window. Was just gonna ask if he was OK. No response or nothin'. Scott came over and tried the door. It was unlocked so we opened it."

"Scott opened the door, that right?"

"Right," said Scott. He was tall and slim, smart but casual. Slacks rather than denims. Mid-20s. A faded 'Gunners Champions' scarf was draped over his shoulders.

"Then I shook his shoulder," added Davey, less smart, same age range, annoying sniff. "He didn't move so I shook him again and he toppled over."

"We couldn't phone from in here, so I went outside and called 999," interrupted Scott.

"And you watched the car, Davey?"

"Right. A few people stopped to see what was happening."

"Touch anything? Did anyone touch anything? Anything at all inside the car?"

"I didn't touch anything. Well just the guy's shoulder. No-one else did, 'cept maybe the outside."

"I need to be clear on that, please Davey. No-one touched anything inside the car? Not the steering wheel or seats?"

"No, just outside. Scott opened the door."

"Two PCs were here within ten minutes of the call," said Inspector Rogers.

The rest of the fans had been sent home by now. They could be called for questioning later, not that Alexander thought that would be necessary.

"You were the driver, Scott? Which is your car?"

"That one. Dad's car, actually." He pointed to a well-polished silver Lexus – very nice. And pricey.

"Listen, can we go yet?" asked Davey, shifting on his feet. "I'm bored and cold and I've gotta go out tonight."

Alexander turned abruptly and glowered at him. The look in his eyes seemed to scare Davey and he took a step backwards.

"Oh, dreadfully sorry, Davey. Bored are you? Pining for the pub? Listen you fuckwit, I'll tell you someone who's bored. That poor bastard in there is dead bored right now. He's seen his last Christmas, missed his last bloody Arsenal game ..."

Davey stared down at his feet while his pal blushed.

"You selfish cretin. He could have a wife, kids; ever think of that? Or does your brain just extend as far as your next pint?"

Davey muttered something which may have been 'sorry.'

Christ! Some people! Davey hung his head, in shame or perhaps to avoid Alexander's scowl. Inspector Rogers was surprised by the detective's outburst but silently applauded. Alexander was considering giving the young man another mouthful when a yellow Fiat Punto swung round a corner of the car park and drew to a halt in the middle of the lanes. A slender woman got out. She was clutching a black bag. "Dr ..." Alexander struggled to recall her surname.

"Helen McMillan, Home Office."

They shook hands. "DI Alexander, and this is Inspector Rogers." He turned to the two fans. "Wait over by your car, please. I'll let you know when you can go."

They shuffled over to the Lexus about ten yards away but didn't get in. Scott seemed to be chastising his friend.

"Anyone touched anything?" asked the pathologist.

"Not inside, as far as we know," said Alexander.

"One of my lads," corrected Rogers. "He saw ... so we contacted the Yard."

"Just the one body, I believe?" Was that disappointment in her voice?

"Yes, no idea who yet. Here for the game we believe."

"How long's he been dead?"

"That's what we're hoping you can tell us, doctor. Don't think we have met before; you work with Professor Carmichael?"

"That's right. I'm standing in over Christmas while he suns himself in The Canaries. Right, let's have a look then."

She donned the suit provided by one of the scene of crime officers. She declined the gloves, preferring a pair of her own from the black bag. The boiler suits had finished working inside the tape and had now fanned out to see if there was anything else worth collecting and bagging. It was a thankless task and they were clearly just going through the motions while they awaited Dr. Death.

Alexander let Dr McMillan go about her work. "I'd better go and make the peace with those two," he said to Rogers. "We have all their details?"

"Yes. Checked out."

"You can go home now lads, thanks for your assistance." He placed his hand on Davey's shoulder. A moderately firm grip. "Listen, Davey. Sorry if I snapped back there. Just try and spare a thought for the poor sod, eh?"

Davey nodded and muttered another feeble apology.

"Thanks for calling us. I mean it. The quicker we get on murder cases the more helpful it can be."

"Murder? He was murdered?" Davey and Scott both stared at the detective, wide-eyed. "How do you know he was murdered?" said Scott.

"I know," nodded Alexander. "We'll be in touch if we need your prints. Safe journey home, lads. And have a pint for me and him, eh."

Such a diplomat, he thought as he watched the Lexus slide away. No point in rubbing up the public the wrong way. He took out a cigarette, and offered one to Rogers. The two officers puffed away in quiet for a few moments.

"Who spotted the signature?" Alexander broke the silence.

"The initials you mean? PC Collins; he's the only one who's been inside the car."

"Who else do you think he's told?"

"He'll have told Aberly. And, of course, I told the Super."

"Which Super?"

"Chief Superintendent Simpson; he's in charge here on match days. He rang The Yard and I guess that's how you came here. Connected to the others is it?"

"Yes, I think so. All I can say for now. Listen it's imperative this doesn't get out, OK? I mean really imperative."

"Gotcha. No worries here. Copycats, eh?"

"I live in daily dread of them. I need to speak to the PCs, make it plain to them, too."

Alexander took out his notebook and jotted down a few lines — names mainly — while Rogers went to call over the constables.

"You were the only one to enter the car, Collins?"

"That's right, sir."

"Can you recall exactly what you touched?"

"Well, the door was already opened and one of the men was standing by it — Davey Harrison. I leaned in, shook the body a bit. I would have touched the steering wheel, driver's seat, maybe inside driver's door. I checked for a pulse and that's when I noticed the scratches. They looked fresh, and the watch had been moved up."

"The watch had been moved up? What do you mean?"

"The deceased's watch appeared to have been rolled up his arm slightly …as if to make room for the initials."

"Fine. I'll check when the doc's finished. Now this is very important, who did you tell about the initials?"

"Just PC Aberly here, then of course Inspector Rogers."

"No-one else? Be frank, this is very serious."

"No-one at all, sir."

"And you, Aberly? Told anyone?"

"No, sir."

"Good."

"PC Collins, could Davey or anyone have seen the scratches while you were examining the body or afterwards?"

"I very much doubt it, sir. My body would have shielded it from anyone outside the car. I made a point of rolling back the sleeve before leaving the car."

"Very smart. Good work constables. Now I cannot stress how important it is that you tell no-one about those marks. I'm sure you know why. Got it?"

"Yes, sir." They both nodded vigorously.

"Thank you." He turned to Rogers. "I just need you three to hang around and make sure everything's all right until we move the body. Shouldn't be long."

The pathologist was still poking around in the car. Carmichael didn't usually take this long; what was she up to?

Alexander looked around the car park. This level had been cleared now. What a depressing place. The grey concrete walls contained patches of graffiti — at least that brought a little colour to the gloom. The smell was getting to Alexander, too. Grease from discarded fast food packaging fought with petrol fumes for control of the atmosphere. Worse than the bloody Tube. The bins were overflowing and a few plastic boxes wafted across the floor by the far wall. He lit another cigarette, moving well ahead of his allotted daily quota.

Two in two weeks, Jake. Stepping up the pace my boy. Or did Jake just have it in for Christmas? He cast his mind back a few hours to his entertaining outing in the city. John Forsyth's world in 'The London Board Games Store' – surely that was the Christmas spirit, not this sordid scene? He could murder a Prêt coffee or a pint of Robin's ridiculously expensive Bass right now. He did have some sympathy for Davey. Not much, mind you; the insensitive little toad. Fuck diplomacy. If only …

"All yours, inspector."

Dr McMillan had left the car, crossed over the police line and was taking off her gloves. She straightened her red pleated skirt and shook a few wrinkles from her matching jacket. Wonder what she had been doing when she took the call, thought Alexander.

"Poor chap missed a decent game," she said, perhaps reading his mind.

"You a Gooner?" smiled Alexander, using the nickname preferred by Arsenal's deadly rivals, Tottenham.

"Oh yes, indeed. Just missed a handful of home games in a dozen years."

"I see, hence the red and white outfit."

"My match day attire." She curtseyed.

Alexander studied her as he stepped into a white suit. Late 30s, wedding ring – the essentials for most men. Straight brown hair just touching the shoulders and covering her ears. A touch of make-up around the eyes and lips, just enough to meet Alexander's approval. Happy blue-grey eyes. Almost laughing.

Dr Helen McMillan had absolutely nothing in common physically with her superior – the lugubrious Professor Edward Carmichael. The Canaries, had she said? Alexander could not imagine the senior Home Office pathologist getting his kicks anywhere never mind those fun-packed holiday islands.

"Give me a couple of minutes, doctor, then I'd just like to ask a few questions if that's all right."

"Certainly, inspector."

"Rory, feel free to call me Rory."

"Good, I'm Helen," she smiled a smile worthy of a toothpaste advert.

Alexander leaned over into the car from the driver's side, got out again and moved round to the passenger door. He got in, gently lifting the left arm and letting it flop onto his lap. He rolled up the sleeve and turned the arm round. The initials were faint but seemed to leap out at him and drill into his brain.

The PC was right; the watch did appear to have been edged up the arm. There was JTJ scratched into the skin just above the wrist – lower down the arm than on any of the previous victims. He wondered if there was any significance in that.

Was Jake in a hurry? Been disturbed?

Alexander noticed that the scratches did not seem as deep as the others, not quite as deep anyway. All the markings had been slight, just enough to be visible and as if they were meant to last just until the bodies had been found. Jake had a light touch. Significant? Alexander doubted it.

No wedding ring. No jewellery at all, apart from the watch. He was no expert but guessed a medium-range one. It looked heavy. He tried the glove compart-ment – locked. He checked the ignition for keys, looked on the floor and eventually found them clutched in the victim's right hand. It took a little uncom-fortable prising to wrest them free.

A manual for the Mercedes S320 – basic rate about fifty grand Alexander believed – a few maps, codes for the radio and alarm, a hip flask and a passport. Unusual to keep your passport in the glove compartment, thought the detective. He took it out: Derek Chisholm. He'd turned 49 last month. The photo showed a serious face, white shirt, dark blue tie. He bagged the passport and popped his head out of the car.

"Here's our man," he shouted over to Inspector Rogers. "Couple of a contact addresses. See if you can get confirmation, would you?"

Rogers leaned over to collect the bag and informed Alexander the details matched those from the vehicle check.

Alexander returned to his perusal inside. Chisholm's eyes were closed; he looked at peace. He was wearing dark greenish cords and a thick, lined brown jacket – stained now. Something had made him ill before he died. An Arsenal scarf was tucked into the left pocket. He wore a green polo neck under the jacket – suitably weather-proofed for watching football in December.

The trouser pockets yielded a handkerchief and a few coins, the inside jacket pocket contained a very thick wallet: almost £300 in 20s and 10s, driver's licence, bank and credit cards, phone card, a clutch of business cards – seems he worked in the financial sector – and finally, his Arsenal season-ticket book. The ticket for today's game against Middlesbrough had already been torn out and was lying loose in the book.

Two box files lay on the back seat. Alexander flicked through them: business stuff, confirming Chisholm was an accountant with a City firm.

He sighed, had another glance at the initials left by his tormentor and then left the car. Once back over the police line, he arched his back and stretched his neck for a moment before taking off the suit.

"Over to you, boys," he nodded to the three waiting scene of crime officers.

"So, doctor …Helen, what can you tell me?"

"I'm really not sure yet, Rory. I need to get him back to the lab. Is first thing in the morning OK?"

"Sure. At least we can rule out strangulation, couldn't see any marks round the neck. Looks like our Jake suffocated him, then?"

"I don't think so."

"Really?" Alexander looked genuinely surprised which seemed to amuse the pathologist.

"This is the first body I have personally examined, but Professor Carmichael has shown me the previous victims. But I think you have a different MO here."

"Why's that?" Alexander was all ears.

"First of all I couldn't see anything he could have been suffocated with …"

"Jake could have taken it with him?"

She ignored his remark. "I saw no sign of fibres by the mouth or nostrils. I could, however, discern a faint smell by his mouth. Not just from the vomit, but a strange smell. Not like any food or drink odour I could place; more like a, well, like a medical smell. Plus, he wouldn't have vomited if he was being suffocated. I really do need to have him on the table before I can say for certain."

A serial killer with three different MOs, strange, unusual and very disturbing.

"What about time of death? Can you confirm that, Helen?"

"Yes. He's been dead around six hours, say eight maximum, which would figure if he was on his way to the game."

"Yes."

"No obvious signs of violence, blows to the head or wounds …that sort of thing."

"OK. Without putting you on the spot, what would your money be on?"

"You mean cause? I would say heart attack."

"Heart attack?" Alexander again sounded surprised.

"Yes, but of course you are more interested in what caused the heart attack, aren't you? That I do not know and hope to find out tomorrow."

"Thanks doc …Helen. Here's my card; be grateful if you'd ring my direct line as soon as you have any information."

"You won't be popping by for the PM?"

"Not my scene, unless of course there is something you think I should see. I'll have a light breakfast."

"I'll bear that in mind," she said, a half-smile creasing her face. "Tomorrow then. Goodnight."

"Night." Now for the really shitty part.

Inspector Rogers had confirmed the address and personal details of Derek Chisholm and had insisted on accompanying Alexander along for the really shitty part. After Alexander had made a quick call to the media department, they made small talk on the drive to Elstree on the northern outskirts of London, neither man wishing to discuss one job all coppers hated: breaking the news to families that they had lost a loved one. It was never easy at the best of times. It was worse when murder was involved. Small mercies that it wasn't a child.

Rogers had phoned the local station and they had arranged for a WPC to be ready to join them. "As far as we know he did not suffer. Remember that if she starts asking questions," Alexander informed WPC Samantha Forbes.

Forbes was 22 and had been on the force ten months. She was doing the whole Christmas shift for the overtime. The stocky blonde didn't appear too disturbed at being hauled along for the shitty part, rather she was ecstatic at having the tedium broken by involvement in a murder case, no matter how minor her role. She managed as best she could not to let the case-hardened inspectors see her excitement. She'd seen Alexander on TV and paid most attention to him.

They pulled into the large driveway of the Chisholm residence: a five-bedroomed detached house on a small executive estate. A large garden and seven-foot hedge ensured the Chisholms enjoyed privacy.

"Wife Susan, kids Marie, 24 and still at home, Thomas, 26 and married," said Rogers as the trio approached the door.

Susan Chisholm looked surprised to see her three visitors. Her mouth dropped as Alexander produced his warrant card.

"Thomas? Is it Thomas? Marie? What's happened? Oh God!"

The inspectors spent ten minutes consoling Mrs Chisholm, now widowed and weeping hysterically. Perhaps there was an element of relief that it was her husband and not one of their children.

As soon as decently possible, Alexander and Rogers left WPC Forbes to look after Mrs Chisholm, to rally round family and friends and make sure the kids heard the tragic news from police officers. Marie was out with friends and due back later that evening. Thomas lived with his wife and six-month-old daughter four miles away.

"Been to worse," said Rogers as they drove away. Alexander nodded.

They continued in silence towards Rogers's Muswell Hill home, soft classical music playing in the background. Rogers bought Alexander a pint at his local before the detective thanked him for his assistance that day and insisted he had to get back to Highgate.

He parked the Astra untidily, didn't bother to change but legged it to The Crown. He was desperate for a few pints and some light relief.

The Crown was heaving; much busier than the previous evening and a more assorted crowd. Alexander was enjoying his second pint of Bass with Trevor Taylor and another regular, Jim Johnson – a Highgate estate agent – when a commotion from the backroom grabbed their attention.

A breathless Robin Jackson suddenly appeared. "Rory, give us a hand to sort this lot out, please."

"Fuck it!" He slammed down his pint glass and slowly walked through to the back. Two overweight, tattooed men – old enough to have some sense – were wrestling with a pool cue. A broken ashtray had spilled its contents onto the pool table. There were fragments of glass scattered around from two shattered pint pots. Curses filled the air. Some girl he didn't recognise was holding a bar towel to a man's face as blood trickled down his cheek and onto his yellow shirt.

A small crowd surrounded the tattooed two, wary of entering the sweaty, heaving, swearing fray. The landlord was bouncing around on his toes, warning them to stop it or else.

Alexander did not recognise either man, clearly outsiders. Muscly but not up to much. He considered putting in a call to the local station. "Fuck it!" he snarled again. He took a firm grip of their necks and thrust their faces together; they were almost kissing. "Don't finish yer drinks; just fuck off or I'll call the cops. Don't want you round here again, ruining good people's Christmas." He pushed their faces more tightly together and made a rubbing motion. A couple of youths in the crowd started laughing. Suddenly Alexander yanked back their heads, the pool cue fell to the floor, and he pushed the men to different sides of the room.

He stood back, waiting anxiously to see their reaction. He tried to look his meanest, which wasn't that mean with his Michael Caine glasses and twinkly blue-grey eyes. Robin Jackson stuck out his jaw in a pathetic attempt to signify defiance. Still it seemed there existed some brain among the fatty brawn. The men glowered at Alexander before picking up their jackets and scurrying out of a side door.

"Thank heaven for that," said Taylor. "I was right behind you just in case. Fat lot of good I would have been - not had a fight since school."

"Nor have I," said Alexander. There was sweat on his brow.

The pair returned to their corner of the bar and their pints.

"Sorry about that, people. They aren't from round here," announced Jackson to all his customers. He moved over to Alexander and his co-drinkers.

"Thanks, Rory. Now drink up, lads. Next one's on me."

"Christ! It really is Christmas," said Taylor, racing to finish his pint before the landlord changed his mind.

✝

CHAPTER FIVE

✝

ALEXANDER alerted his inner team before he left for work. He made no apologies for ending their Christmas break early. No rush, but be in the Murder Room by 11.30 latest; he'd fill them all in on the details then.

He'd slept well, five solid hours and no nightmares; probably the walking round the shops had helped. He showered and felt fighting fit, ready to go Jake hunting with a vengeance. Notes he had left scattered around the kitchen were collated as he drank his second cup of coffee; food would come later.

The detective paused before folding the sheets of paper containing his Monopoly doodles. Was he ready to run his theory past CS? He persuaded himself he had no choice. Nothing so strange as real-life murderers.

For once he managed to sit down on the Tube to work. He even found a parking slot for his briefcase. Most days he would clutch it to his body with his right hand, his left holding onto one of the ceiling rails as the train rattled through the underground tunnels.

The manic early morning rush-hour was not his most enjoyable part of the day. No matter what the weather outside, the carriages always seemed too humid and too smelly. People grumbled, but no-one acted.

Today was more like late night travel, minus the drunks. He guessed most of his fellow travellers were either tourists or day-trippers.

Alexander was in good time so he disembarked at Westminster and enjoyed a leisurely stroll along the Thames Embankment before heading back to Parliament Square and north to Broadway and New Scotland Yard.

He had rarely seen the streets so peaceful. None of the shops were open save a corner coffee house which had one customer. Two of the pubs displayed signs proclaiming they were closed for the Xmas Break. The sun peaked through the clouds, there was no wind; it was crisp and ideal for an invigorating walk by the coast, Alexander thought as he mounted the steps to The Yard. He didn't know them, but he nodded at two uniformed constables. They returned his greeting.

Empty and eerie, the Murder Room was as he had left it a couple of days ago. It was several rooms, actually. The investigation had spread out after the third killing revealed they were dealing with a serial. It would be hard to demand more floor space in the already crowded building.

Detective Superintendent Christine Stevens had yet to report in. Alexander went to buy a coffee before unlocking his room and powering up his computer. He stared out of his window at the street below as his computer flickered into life. His dark blue jacket was slung on the back of his chair; he settled down, lit up a cigarette. Then he decided to do his report in the Murder Room; that way he could check on arrivals.

He had a desk there and now powered up his other computer and began typing notes on the murder of Derek Chisholm, family man, City financier and keen Arsenal fan.

Susan Chisholm had not really been questioned. Alexander had seen no point in it, plus she was far too distressed to think coherently. He had managed to persuade her to hand over a couple of recent photos of her husband – one sporting an Arsenal shirt and one from last summer's holiday in Sicily. A local CID man would go round later and do the formalities. Alexander knew, though, that this was just another random killing by Jake. He was certain of that above all: Jake cared not a jot who his victims were; they just had to be available. Did they carry signs: available for slaughter?

Poor bastards. Nothing in common, just there, somewhere, anywhere, at the wrong time. The wrong time being the time Jake was there, playing out his twisted game. "I'll get you. I swear I'll get you, you sick fuck," Alexander mumbled to himself as he typed away two-fingered.

Now and then Alexander would look up to check the sound of footsteps. Officers seemed to be tip-toeing along the corridors. Voices seemed muffled. He checked his watch: 9.17. On a normal weekday the place would be alive with the sounds of modern humanity, voices that didn't seem to know the meaning of the word whisper, office machinery whirring incessantly. Some laughter, lots of shouting and the constant electrical buzz from the multitude of computer terminals. But not today. No, today it felt more like a mortuary than a Murder Room. Suddenly, all that started to change.

DC Mike 'Rab' Burns was the first to breeze in. 'Rab'? Well he was Scottish, wasn't he, and why stray from the obvious. Burns lived closest to The Yard — a one-room apartment in the Barbican: pricey but handy for the City, especially during his days off. The 26-year-old bachelor had been unpacking when he had taken Alexander's call almost two hours earlier. He'd flown down after a whirl-wind Christmas break back with his folks and friends in Dundee. Seventy-two hours had been more than enough.

True, he loved his parents, could just about handle his sister's amorous meanderings, but he discovered his true friends were thin on the ground these days. Most had either flitted away to Glasgow or Edinburgh, some had got them-selves wed, the silly buggers. Some had started families, the even sillier buggers. There had been a haphazard reunion of old school and college pals down at The Whistle on Christmas Eve but once they had exhausted 'old times' most discovered they had little in common.

"Wakey, wakey. Rise and shine."

Alexander looked up and smiled at the constable who was scratching his head through his wavy black hair.

"Cockney phrase-book for Christmas I deduce."

"Ach, sir. Makes me ever-so 'umble to sit at the feet of a master of detection."

"Morning, Mike."

"Mornin', sir. Such a nice one I decided to walk. Doesn't look like I'm late."

"First one in, which makes you teacher's pet for the time-being. Give me a few minutes to finish this and I'll be with you. Why don't you grab yourself a coffee?"

"Sure. Want another one, sir?"

Alexander winked. "You're a quick learner, Mike. White, no sugar."

Burns had been in The Met for four years. A solid, popular worker with a keen brain and a fair wit. His accent had softened a shade, primarily during a four-month stint south of the river in Brixton. Alexander was pleased to have him on board. The DI was reading his two now printed pages of notes when Burns returned with the coffees. He passed the notes over to his colleague and sat back to enjoy his drink.

"Cause of death, sir? You don't say how he died?"

"Well done. And that is because I don't know yet. The pathologist wasn't sure but ruled out strangling and suffocation."

"Really? He's getting a different kick then?"

"Seems that way. She wasn't sure but thought maybe a heart attack. Wonder if she's onto the post mortem yet?"

"By she I guess you mean Dr Helen?"

"That's right, Helen McMillan. Know her?"

"Attended one of hers once. Some tramp got done over last summer and the prof let her do the PM. Quite a cutey ...for her age." Footsteps could be heard coming down the corridor leading from the entrance. Louder, quicker footsteps than Alexander had heard all morning.

"Do I smell gas?" said Burns.

"Watch it, Mike! Not in front of your superiors."

Detective Superintendent Christine Stevens had arrived. She looked a little flustered. "Bloody M25! Morning Rory, Mike."

"Morning, ma'am," they chorused.

"Bad traffic today?" said Alexander.

"Roadworks and shoppers. Recipe for major delays. I should have known. Must have been a three-mile tailback heading to that new retail park. The time people will waste hunting down a cheaper settee."

Nods and sighs of sympathy.

"Well, it's nice to see you two in. The rest on their way, Rory?"

"We had three scheduled in to man the fort anyway, but I've called Pierce, Peters and Gough. They should be en route. Told them 11.30 in here. I thought we could have a talk first."

"Good. Yes. Give me five minutes and then my room OK? Perhaps DC Burns could rustle us up some coffee?"

"Sure, ma'am."

"We've all played tea-boy once upon a time," Alexander said to Burns as the superintendent bustled off. He was tempted to ask where Burns ranked Stevens on his cutey scale but thought it unbecoming. Maybe one for The Ferret later, assuming The Ferret was open.

"Could you scan these in while I'm in with the boss," he said, handing Burns the two photographs borrowed from Susan Chisholm.

"So this is the poor bastard. Two kids, you say?"

"Yes, about your age."

They waited in silence until Alexander rose. "One sugar for the Super, I think. You know my order." He dug a two-pound coin from his pocket and handed it to Burns. "Get yourself one, too." He gave thanks for subsidised office canteens; City coffee prices could break the team, the amount they drank.

Christine Stevens was a medium-build, fair-haired 41-year-old mother-of-two. Not in bad shape at all ...yes, possibly a cutey once upon a time. Her initials earned her the nickname CS Gas, some preferred CS Gasbag or plain Gasbag, claiming she talked too much, which was a little unfair as Alexander knew many coppers who could bore the backend off a cow more quickly than Stevens.

Alexander had never worked with her before this case, but found her efficient and polite. His overall verdict was pending for the moment, though. She'd come to homicide seven months previously, but still found herself bogged down with paperwork and queries from past cases. She needed to dump the baggage quickly. That wasn't always easy with the drawn-out cases the Serious Crime Directorate dealt with.

She lived out west, Aylesbury, a bit on the expensive side for Alexander and Lucy. Some days she drove to work; others she took the train. Her greeting more generally than not consisted of the details of her trip: not bad or lousy. Alexander hoped she had recovered from her journey and that he would be able to grab her undivided attention as he strolled to her office with an armful of files and a rather weird theory. Would she buy it? He took a deep breath, here goes ...

The door was open, he didn't bother knocking.

"Sit yourself down, Rory. Burns on his way with those drinks? I'm gagging. Bloody traffic. Lousy, absolutely lousy."

"Won't be a minute, Christine." Christine for private chats and when she was in a good mood, ma'am in front of senior officers.

"Definitely our man again?"

"Yes. No doubt about it."

She sighed. "Why can't murderers take Christmas off and leave us to mop up the regular thieves and villains?"

"Maybe Jake doesn't have a family and was at a loose end." Alexander surprised himself. He hadn't thought of that yesterday; everybody had family at Christmas.

"I've seen last night's Press Release; short and sweet. Smart move."

"Thought it best to avoid labelling the death suspicious till we'd talked."

Burns entered with the drinks.

"Thanks."

"Thanks."

He knew not to linger.

"So, run by me what we know."

Alexander told Stevens all the details he had managed to pick up yesterday.

"A different MO. Strange. Can't think of any serial killers with three different styles."

"Dr McMillan was most insistent: definitely not strangulation and no signs of suffocation. I'll put a call through in an hour or so. Give them time to get going."

"You're certain just a random victim again?"

"Certain as I can be. As I said, the car park is not normally used for football traffic. So I don't think we should go chasing someone who hates football or Arsenal."

"Yes, I agree. What shall we do about the Press today, then?"

"I don't think a conference is in order. I'd like to wait until I have more information from the path lab and then issue a statement, hopefully in time for the evening bulletins. People tend to pay most attention then, though half the nation seems permanently semi-pissed at Christmas. DC Burns is scanning in a couple of photos I got from the widow. May jog a memory or two — there were plenty of vehicles in the car park."

"OK. Show me the Press Release before it goes out. What about the family?"

"I was just going to let local CID handle it. You think one of ours should be there, too?"

"Yes, I do. Even if it is just random, as you say, I'd be happier with our own report — just for consistency if nothing else."

"Fine. And it's not as if we are swamped with leads."

A brief pause then Alexander coughed. He coughed again as if clearing his throat. "There's one more thing, Christine."

She could sense he was uneasy. "Well?"

"I know this is going to sound bizarre, but I think I've found a link."

"Really?" She leaned forward. "Don't be bashful then; let's have it."

He coughed again. "Monopoly."

Stevens had her chin resting on her fists, her elbows propped up on the table. He waited for the word to sink in.

"Monopoly." Not really a query but Stevens raised her eyebrows and stared at him, indicating that the word had at least arrived even if it hadn't quite sunk in yet. So Alexander told her of the game at his brother's on Christmas Day and his discovery of Jake The Jailbird and Edgar The Officer.

Stevens did not scoff; she seemed fascinated. She didn't tell him that she had spent breakfast alone in her kitchen on Christmas morning, drinking coffee after coffee and filling more than a dozen sheets of paper with possible meanings of Jake TJ. She had been doodling so intensely that she hadn't heard the children rising to see if Santa had visited yet.

"Whitechapel, Regent Street, Vine Street and now Pentonville Road. All places on the London Monopoly board."

"Yes, yes." She paused momentarily. "Brown … green … orange and light-blue, right?"

"That's right. You a player?"

"Oh, haven't we all been at some time or other? Children love it. Mine have just graduated from the kiddie version. Kids just love playing with money. Money and fire. Fascinating, Rory. Bloody amazing. Bloody hell!"

"That's what I thought." His fears of embarrassment had now vanished.

"And you say your nieces heard of Jake and Edward when they played in the States?"

"Yes, and it's Edgar not Edward. Edgar Mallory to give him his full name."

"Edgar, of course. The notes. Bloody hell!"

"Question now is: how far do we let this theory go? If you're happy, I plan to tell the rest of the team this morning."

"I think we have to, as long as we stress it does not leak out. No pattern, is there? I'm just trying to picture the board; there's no pattern in the places he has chosen?"

Now Alexander felt free to tell Stevens about his shopping expedition.

"I had the boards out in the kitchen yesterday. Funny, I was messing with them when you rang. No, I can't think of a pattern, but to be honest I wasn't really looking for one. Sad to admit, but I was simply wondering where next. Shall I put one of the team on it? I can see if any of them have a penchant for puzzles."

"Yes. No stone unturned, please. Fascinating. Right, let me know as soon as you have any news from forensics or the path lab. I said I'd file a report for the Assistant Commissioner this afternoon."

"The AC wants a report? He requested one?"

"Yes, Rory. We've spoken." She looked at him as though disappointed that he had to state what she felt would have been blindingly obvious. Mind you, Alexander was a detective. Bloody good one. He had time on his side before the higher world beckoned. Too much of her time was wasted – in her opinion – keeping superiors abreast of her movements. Why couldn't they just read the damned files like everyone else?

"I'll get cracking then." He walked out, trying to summon from his memory bank the reason for his abrupt dismissal of any pattern yesterday.

The Murder Room was buzzing when he returned; possibly due to the arrival of DS Caroline Peters. Hair unkempt as usual, probably another night on the tiles. She had organised a card game to see who would do the first coffee run.

Burns was sat smugly with his arms folded. He had won, so it wouldn't be him. Alexander nodded greetings and let the game unfold. DI Keith Blake appeared from down the corridor. The last of the day's intended arrivals.

"Wanna join in, sir?" said DS Ian Walters. "Need to if you want a coffee?"

Blake and Walters were seconded to the team from Whitechapel as they had investigated the first murder.

"Let me take off my jacket first, eh? Three-card turnover?"

"Yeah."

"OK. Deal me in."

A few more hands flew across the table until Blake was left out on his own.

"Nice start to the day," he grumbled as DS Peters started writing down the order. Alexander smiled at Blake. The two men got on well, Blake having no problem playing second fiddle to an officer equal in rank. It was common knowledge that Alexander's chief inspectorship was merely awaiting signatures. Though the Gasbag was titularly in charge, this was Alexander's team.

They waited for Blake to return with a fully-laden tray before gathering round Alexander's desk in a huddle. He reserved his office for more private one-on-ones. The efficient Burns had already started a new notice board, pinning up the two photos and Alexander's notes which would be replaced by updated versions throughout the day.

"First things, first," announced Alexander. "Seems our Jake has no respect for our skeleton squads – everyone had just left for the day when yesterday's call came through. So from now on, 24-hour manning. Twelve-hour days, eight till eight, 13-hour nights, giving us a half hour overlap. Overtime has been cleared."

Smiles from most of the faces, especially the single officers.

"Can you work out the rotas, Keith?"

A nod. "Two at night OK, Rory? Just from the inner circle"

"Yes, two I think should do it for now. Feel free to use the outsiders, though. Up to you."

"Right, I suggest me and Craig handle the first couple of nights." He glanced at DC Craig Gough to see if there was any dissent. Gough merely nodded.

Alexander then talked his officers through the latest killing, and then his Monopoly theory, his mind reinforced by his meeting with Stevens. He still drew a few quizzical looks.

"Now, who fancies themselves as good with puzzles?"

"Crosswords and stuff, you mean, sir?" asked DC Vicki Jobson.

Before he could reply, three fingers pointed towards DC Martin Wright who tried not to blush.

"Been known to tackle a few crosswords in my time," he shuffled in his seat.

"Come on, Brains. Still in Mensa, are we?" said Caroline Peters. "What's your record for the Rubik's cube?"

"Mensa, really?" asked Alexander, impressed.

"Doesn't mean much, to be honest, sir. I just took a few tests – must be eight or nine years ago now."

"Grand. Job's yours for today then, Martin. I want you to go and buy a Monopoly set – now make sure you get the London one …Mayfair and all that. See if you can work out if Jake is operating to any pattern. Get a snapper to photograph the board, too. I'd like a decent sized blow-up on …" he looked around the room, "that wall over there. It's a little hidden from anyone who may pass through and might think we're all madder than we really are.

"I haven't really looked for a pattern myself, and off the top of my head I can't envisage one. But you never know. Any clue as to where he might strike again would be a Godsend."

"Right, sir," said Wright. It sounded like a strange but interesting day's work. Bang up his street.

"DS Walters and DC Jobson can go and interview Derek Chisholm's widow. We think it is just another random murder but best to have our own people there. Check with local CID to see if they want someone along. They were keeping a WPC at the home overnight, not sure how they've left things this morning. The widow knows we are treating the death as suspicious, but you'll now have to inform her it's our serial killer. See if I can get a cause of death from the path lab before you head off. Look busy. Keith can I just have a word before you head back to bed?"

They retired to Alexander's office.

"Thanks for that Keith. Listen, if it doesn't suit your domestic arrangements let me know, but would you mind taking charge of all the night shifts while things settle down? Four nights at least, five if you want the overtime."

"Great minds. Sorted, Rory. I'll take five – Sunday to Thursday. Spend some quality time with my family. I'll share the others around the sergeants. Could do with New Year's Eve off, though. Wife's booked a baby-sitter."

"Excellent. I must admit I thought it was a bit Mickey Mouse we had no-one here yesterday when the call came in. Try get some shut-eye and I hope we'll have a few more details when I see you later."

+

"She's just scrubbing up, want to hold while I see if she's finished?"

"Will do, thanks."

A few seconds later, Alexander's call was put through.

"Dr McMillan, I…"

"Helen, please."

"Ah, yes. I was just wondering if you had anything for us yet, Helen?"

"I've just finished a preliminary examination. But I need to run some more tests. I have an acquaintance coming round in an hour or so to have a look. Very kind of him at Christmas."

"Oh. Why more tests? You mean you can't tell me cause of death yet?"

"I can tell you cause of death was as we suspected. Heart attack, by a whisper."

"By a whisper?"

"Yes, his heart packed up just before his respiratory system was about to. There was an internal race within the poor man's body to see which could kill him first. Very messy, not seen anything quite like it."

"Can you explain?"

"Not in exact detail until I have had the benefit of my friend's opinion. He's an expert in tropical medicines and toxins. Lectures at quite a few London colleges. But it is safe to say the victim was poisoned."

"Poisoned? Well that is a departure from plain throttling."

"Indeed. Remember I said I could discern a faint smell by the mouth?"

"Yes."

"Well that came from the corrosion of the lungs. His insides were rotting, basically. But, as I say, the heart won the race. Blessed relief, too. From examination of the body and internal organs, I am of the mind that he was paralysed by some agent."

"Paralysed? Christ, this is off the MO!"

"Paralysed, but pretty alert. He would have been in great pain for maybe an hour, inspector …Rory."

"The other deaths were fast, no-nonsense. You're saying this one lingered?"

"Not for too long, an hour, two at most. Maybe he actually died during the match, not before as I suggested yesterday. But he was incapacitated and beyond help."

There was quiet as Alexander tried to imagine poor Derek Chisholm slumped in his car, willing his own death as his lungs and heart fought to kill him.

"Any idea how he was poisoned?"

"I've found several traces of highly toxic substances, others I want help with, hence my call to Professor Whittow. He was intrigued and is on his way now. I can say for certain that barium chloride, lead chloride and formaldehyde – all lethal in certain dosages. Lethal and nasty. There are also signs of a neurotoxin – never seen it before."

"Some bloody cocktail!"

"Some bloody cocktail indeed. I am at a loss as to why so many different toxins should be in one body. But I can safely say the combination was deadly and very painful, even if for just a short time. Listen, you there all day?"

"Yes, may pop out for lunch but take my mobile number …any time, day or night. Like murderers we never sleep."

"Be in touch, soon hopefully. Bye, Rory."

There was something about the way she said his name that unsettled him. Maybe he had just become accustomed to the more formal approach of Professor Carmichael.

Alexander spared a thought for Derek Chisholm before heading off to update his officers. He warned Walters and Jobson to just let the widow know that he had died of a heart failure brought on by the attack. "Keep it as vague as possible," he stressed. "No word of poisoning …enquiries ongoing etc."

Alexander had had nothing to eat that day, but skipped lunch. Just a quick pint with two of the team. Thoughts of poisoning and internal battles between lungs and heart had dampened his appetite.

He and DS Peters pored over old files, searching for clues and any links with the latest victim. Anything they might have missed first time around. They made calls to families and friends of past victims to see if the name Chisholm rang any bells. Other officers would be dispatched on door-to-door enquiries later in the week. Deep down they knew it was a fruitless task, but one that had to be done – you just never knew.

Alexander broke the monotony by preparing a Press Release, which he had sanctioned by Det Supt Stevens before passing to the Media Office.

'Police are treating as murder the death of an Arsenal fan on Boxing Day. They believe the killing of father-of-two Derek Chisholm may be linked to three earlier murders in the capital.'

Photos, details of time and place followed and witnesses were urged to contact The Met. It was just after 5pm when the call came from Dr McMillan. "Sorry it's taken so long, and I'm afraid I won't have anything for you until the morning."

"Oh." Alexander didn't try to hide his dismay.

"Professor Whittow says he has a few suspicions but didn't care to share them with me yet. He's taken a sample and several readings. Said he would be in touch with a few colleagues around the globe tonight and let me know soonest. Best I can say."

"He could not enlighten you then?"

"Well," she hesitated. "He did say one thing."

"What was that?"

"He wasn't sure but ...just between us until it's confirmed OK?"

"Sure, Helen, just us."

"Venom. He mentioned venom."

"As in snakebite?"

"I guess so. But, listen, this is all just speculation. I know you're eager for clues but just let it take its course, please."

"Will do. Thanks for letting me know, anyway. Goodnight."

☩

Lucy was lying on the sofa and watching TV when he arrived back at his flat a few minutes before 9pm. "Hiya, honey. You're late; this new murder is it?"

Alexander threw his jacket over a chair in the kitchen and walked through to the lounge. He bent down and pecked his fiancée on the cheek.

"Hi darlin', when did you get back? Nice visit? Yeah, another bloody murder."

"Been here a couple of hours. Made myself some pasta, not that you've got much else in. Some left; just needs a couple minutes reheating. Come and join me. This is almost finished."

She was glued to a BBC historical drama, lots of stiff collars, powdered wigs and plunging necklines. Alexander soon settled down next to her with his tray of pasta arabiata, barely reheated. He wolfed it down in no time, not really caring what it tasted like. His stomach had been craving food and this was his first proper meal of the day. He knew not to speak until the credits rolled. Thankfully, they weren't long in coming.

"Somebody was hungry," Lucy said as she tucked her left arm behind him and nuzzled his neck.

"Filled a hole," he said, rubbing his slightly-bristled chin against her forehead. His finger toyed with her brown hair which fell just a couple of inches down her back when she didn't have it tied up for work. He preferred it this way, more natural; and often told his pretty, slim fiancée so.

"All well and happy back home?"

"Yeah, not bad. Duty done for a few more months. All looking forward to the big day. And how was Christmas here? Cut short I hear. Care to tell me?"

"You heard the news then?"

"Yes, it was on TV a couple of hours back. Very sad."

"Another poor bugger bites the dust – no rhyme or reason. Tell you in the morning. Now I need a shower, and ...." He winked and flicked his head towards the bedroom.

"Mmmm, I'll be ready and waiting, Alfie boy."

Alfie boy, he thought as the power shower refreshed his tired limbs. Should I change the specs; did I really look like Michael Caine?

They made love – passionate and quick, and then rapidly fell asleep in each other's arms. She was exhausted from seasonal excesses and travel, he from chasing a serial killer – he didn't seem much further along the way to success.

✝

"Inspector Alexander, please."

"Speaking."

"Oh, hello, Rory. Helen McMillan. Got something for you."

"Morning, Helen, you're bright and early. Let me get a pen."

"Pufferfish."

"Pufferfish?"

"Pufferfish, blowfish, globefish, swellfish – it goes by several names. The deadliest food known to man."

"Fish? The victim was poisoned by a fish? That what you're telling me?"

"The scientific name for the poison is actually tetrodotoxin. It's a very potent poison, producing death in a matter of minutes sometimes. Professor Whittow emailed the test results to several contacts and one in Tokyo came up trumps."

"Please thank Professor Whittow on my behalf. Any idea how the poison was administered? Is it easy to get hold of?"

"Professor Whittow says it is not a common commodity here, not anywhere in Western Europe. We believe it was probably part of the overall cocktail and administered orally."

"You mean the victim ate something; his food was spiked?"

"More likely a drink, but it could have been food. Did you find any signs of food?"

"No."

"Didn't think so. The stomach contents didn't reveal much. Looks like he had had a light breakfast and possibly a chocolate bar later. It was chocolate that was down the front of his coat. Chocolate has that effect, especially if one wolfs it down without chewing properly."

Alexander thought he would be skipping breakfast again.

"The pufferfish is a fascinating creature," continued Dr McMillan. "The Japanese catch them and produce an expensive delicacy called fugu. The organs of the fish – liver, ovaries and gonads – contain this lethal neurotoxin. Only expert chefs who have passed a course are permitted to prepare fugu, even so there are several fatalities a year even these days in the Far East. The chefs are supposed to top themselves if one of their clients succumbs. Don't think they do, though. Honour isn't what it used to be."

"Shame. Is it on sale here?"

"I don't think so. Professor Whittow said he sampled some once in Tokyo at a seminar. His hosts insisted. Ever seen the memory of a meal make a grown, well-educated man shiver? He said it was the most exciting and scariest meal he had ever had."

"I'll stick to Italian and Chinese, thank you. Mind you, I may give Chinese a wide berth for a while."

"Don't blame you. The professor may be getting in touch with you. I think he wants to do a paper; when all this is over of course. For now his lips are sealed."

"Does he know it's the serial killer? Has he told anyone?"

"No. No. Of course he knows it's a murder, but I made sure he didn't see the marks on the body. He wasn't the slightest bit interested in the outside of the body anyway.

"Incidentally, I made a second examination of the body this morning, and I discovered the tiniest of pin-pricks on the right side of the body, hip-level."

"And you think…"

"Not sure what to think, actually. There is no way of telling for certain, but it looks like he could have been injected with something. There is a faded red mark, five-mill diameter at most and almost invisible now, around the hole. Not big enough for a hypodermic needle, but maybe there was an attempt to inject a small amount of poison. Impossible to tell, but thought I should mention it."

"Thanks. You've been most helpful. Anything else?"

"I'll prepare two reports now: one for Professor Carmichael and another for the police minus all the medical jargon. I'll do yours first and email it before lunch. Want me to post the printed version or can you send someone round?"

"I'll pop over myself. Say just after one?"

"That'll be fine."

✝

CHAPTER SIX

+

Dearest Edgar
How was your Xmas? Get any nice presents?
Mine flew by me. I'm not really one for all that
false bonhomie and tinsel. I did enjoy
Boxing Day, though. A wonderful day for
blowing away the cobwebs. I took in some sport.
Invigorating.
Love to Christine and all the gang.
Jake TJ

DI Keith Blake had recognised the typing on the envelope within seconds, even though he was coming to the end of a quiet night shift and thoughts had turned to bed. He'd bagged the letter and left it on Alexander's desk.

"Didn't bother phoning, Rory, as I guessed you'd be on your way."

Alexander had summoned an officer from forensics to open the letter for him. The boffin merely placed the envelope under a kettle. Christ! I could have done that, thought Alexander. So much for Hi-Tech Crime Units. The boffin had prised the single sheet of paper free with a pair of tweezers, scanned the image and taken the original back to the laboratory. There would be no prints, Alexander knew.

He had four copies of the note printed out. One was pinned next to the first note on the main white notice board. He and DI Blake were examining another copy.

"Same paper, same typing, same font," said Alexander to no-one in particular. He rose and took a couple of paces forwards and then backwards before leaning over to peer at the sheet again. "See anything I don't, Keith?"

"I see bugger all except someone who's trying to take the piss out of us."

"Glad you said 'us'; I was beginning to take it personally."

"The Gasbag will be delighted to get an honorary mention. Guess he picked up her name from the last Press Conference."

"'Sume so. Get yourself off to bed, Keith, see you tonight."

"Right-O. Report's over there, thin reading, was dead as a dodo here. I left a note for DS Peters. Her contact called to confirm today's meet."

Alexander pointed to the letter on the notice board as officers drifted in. Now he had copies of both letters spread before him on his desk. Beginning and sign-off the same, but this second seemed even more personal somehow. Probably just the chatty Christmas jibe. Did Jake really not have much time for the festive season or was that just his little joke? No mention of 'have you got it yet?' Did Jake know he was onto him and his Monopoly game? Surely he couldn't?

"Ah, Christine! Morning. We need to speak."

"Morning, Rory. That urgent is it?"

"Pretty much so. Jake's sent his love."

+

Lim Man was a busy little man, even at 11am with no customer in sight. He barked out orders in Chinese now and then before turning to address the two CID officers in English. Not grammatically-perfect, but a shrill, chirpy English picked up over 55 years in the London restaurant trade.

Second generation British, he had been born into the trade and taken over the family business when his father retired some 30 years previously. He had added two more restaurants on the outskirts of London, but the Ding Ho in Soho's Chinatown was the centre of his empire, and highly profitable year round.

"Fugu? What the fuck you want fugu for?" Lim Man looked insulted as he stared at them with his hands clasped and leaning on his paunch.

DI Charlie Ormesby let DS Caroline Peters answer. Ormesby had been going to the Ding Ho since he was 18. Thirty-one years later, and nearing retirement from the force, he was a regular diner and a firm family friend. He and Lim shared a passion for Tottenham Hotspur Football Club. They also enjoyed a gamble, though Ormesby played for minor stakes and mainly at weekends.

He had been shocked a couple of years back when Lim had invited him on one of his 'business trips' to the Orient: a two-week jaunt starting in Hong Kong where he met several generations of the Man family, and ending in Bangkok where the volume of money Lim fluttered away genuinely shocked the copper.

"We need to know how easy it is to obtain fugu in the UK, Lim. This is very serious so any help you can provide would be most appreciated."

"No-one will know anything, Lim. This is just between us three," added Ormesby for reassurance.

"Crazy Japs. Fucking crazy Japs. Fugu: only for crazy people. Fucking kill you."

"Exactly," added Peters. "And that is why we need to find out who is bringing it here. I'm sorry I can't tell you any more. But we really do need your help."

The Chinese had used to eat fugu, but not Lim's people, he insisted. And hardly at all these days. The diminutive restaurateur took off his glasses and studiously began wiping them. "I don't know I can help. I will ask around, OK. No promises. Crazy fucking Japs. Maybe someone at the markets will know."

"Thanks, Lim," said Ormesby offering his hand. "Probably see you at the weekend. Give me a call if you hear anything."

"Or you can contact me here," said Peters, handing over a card and shooting her colleague a frosty glance. My case, not yours – and don't you forget it inspector. She thought he had got the message.

"Lim will let us know if he uncovers anything. Trust me; he is sound."

They were outside the restaurant, standing idly as pedestrians skirted round them. "We could try a couple of Japanese restaurants now if you like?" suggested Ormesby. "I can't claim to be well in with the owners, so we'd need to make it official like. Best to go outside Little Tokyo."

"Sure, might as well while we're here. Lead on."

Chinatown was starting to get livelier. Ormesby loved the area. Even though he had policed it most of his professional life, he still frequented the streets on his time off. There was crime for sure; plenty of it. Some of it was organised and bloody. But drugs were less of a problem these days as the triads had spread their wings following two successful busts five years back. The drugs squad were fully aware they had shuffled the problem elsewhere.

Honour killings had been a major cause of concern at the turn of the Millennium. That was a tricky subject as the Chinese clammed up; even Lim had been unable to help him. Friends and relatives mysteriously died. Police knew the deaths were almost certainly related to assumed tarnishes on the family name; and improper relationships.

Gambling dens sprang up quicker than the police could close them down. Even the liberalisation of the gaming laws seemed to have little effect. Outsiders were welcome, as long as they left penniless.

Ormesby guided Peters confidently through the colourful streets which even the gentle grey drizzle failed to diminish. He nodded greetings, with no hint he was out to impress the sergeant with his local knowledge and acceptance. If he was, it wasn't working. She wanted in and out with no fuss; a no-frills, no-nonsense detective Caroline Peters.

The 30-year-old had served her time with the Hertfordshire Police, joining The Met a few months after her divorce two years ago. Thankfully, there had been no children to complicate matters. The skinny, 5ft 7in brunette had split the proceeds of the terraced house with Peter Brookes and escaped as soon as possible after one drunken row too many. Her drinking, his arguing. She had reverted to her maiden name, was still drinking more than was good for anyone never mind a woman her build. Bundles of nervous energy kept her weight down.

She could handle her drink as well as most men, and she was purely a social drinker; no hidden stashes of the hard stuff at home or at work. She drank for company or purely because she found pubs the most fun-packed places on Earth. Natural intelligence and a dogged attitude towards police work earned her a growing reputation with The Met, and promotion to sergeant had been swift.

"Distinct worlds," said Ormesby as they walked, trying to keep undercover. "Japs and Chinese, rarely mingle. The cuisine is worlds apart, too. They share a lot of the same suppliers, though, more so these days than they used to. Big, big market oriental cooking. Cook much yourself?"

"Naah. Eat, drink, don't cook. No time for it."

"You should try it. Lim's given me some great recipes – better than the usual stuff found in books. He showed me round the kitchens once. You wanna see those guys work!"

"Raw fish, isn't it? That's the big Jap deal? Sushi. Tiny portions all dolled up and designed to rot your guts. Not my cup of tea. Eight or nine pints and I'm happy with a red-hot Indian."

Was she trying to impress Ormesby now? She silenced him for a few minutes at least. Peters suddenly realised they were walking along Wardour Street. "Not been here in a few years," she said, looking around. "Used to hang around a couple of bars close by. Can't think of their names."

"Probably changed hands and been done up. Change for change's sake seems to be the motto with many joints these days. Hundred yards or so on the right,

Harita's; we can ask there. And then there's Enoki about a quarter of a mile away. Never been in before but I am told it's the rising star of Japanese dining."

The proprietor of Harita's, the eponymous Harry Harita, was most deferential and eager to please. He could buy as much fugu as they wanted – or could afford – from Japan, but he was not allowed to import it into the UK. Sorry, he knew no-one who smuggled the fish in. Of course, he would keep his ears to the ground. He had tried fugu in his native Osaka and if the officers were ever there he recommended they try it – it truly was delicious.

"Would you eat it?" asked Ormesby as they headed for their last port of call.

"Sure. Try anything once, especially if I was pissed or someone dared me. Mind you, I wouldn't be paying for it myself; not on a sergeant's salary."

Ormesby smiled, "Yeah. How much you say it cost?"

"I read you could pay a hundred quid for a four-pound fish. Hardly the sort of fodder you chuck in a vindaloo." She smiled at her guide. "Would you try it, Charlie?"

"No way. Give me Lim's any day. You should try his deep-fried chilli beef strips if you're a hot girl. Won't find better this side of Watford."

"Oh, I'm a hot girl all right." She laughed so loud passers-by glanced at the couple. Charlie blushed.

Enoki's was the least rewarding of the restaurants they visited. The owner seemed to have a permanent frown. He was nervous, too, constantly checking over his shoulder or looking beyond the officers as if to see what was happening outside.

He had opened the upmarket Sushi bar two years ago; he'd never tried fugu, had no intention of trying it; and most definitely had no idea where it could be bought, certainly not in London. But he did nod assent that he would ask around, and took their cards.

"Not sure if these last two was a good move," mused Peters as they headed back towards Ormesby's station.

"You mean word getting about?"

"Yeah. Too bloody shifty the lot of 'em. Something about their eyes; wouldn't like to play cards against them."

"I know. Look, I can vouch for Lim one hundred per cent. He'll be discreet and pass on any information he gets. Wager a month's pay on that. The other two …sorry I really don't know."

The streets were getting busier as restaurants began opening for lunch. Boards appeared on pavements advertising special business lunches. They were great value for anyone who fancied three courses at such a ridiculous time of day for eating, thought Peters.

"You've been a big help, Charlie. Thanks. I'm gonna hop on a Tube here. Keep in touch."

"You're welcome. Soon as anything crops up I'll let you know. Happy New Year."

"Right. Happy New Year to you and yours, too."

✝

Alexander had tilted his leather swivel chair back and was lying with his feet on the desk, his hands on his chest. Every now and then he would unclasp his fingers and drum them together. He stared at the 3ftx3ft Monopoly poster on his wall. "Sleeping or thinking?" said Det Supt Stevens.

Alexander swung round his chair and brought his feet to the floor. Stevens was standing in the doorway, left hand on hip, right propped against a wall.

"Hello, Christine. I suppose I could just about plead thinking. I very much doubt my thoughts are worth too many pennies, though."

"You've a meeting planned for this afternoon, I hear?"

"Yes. Just an end-of-year brain-storming session. Let people air their thoughts and theories – want to earwig?"

"What do you think?"

"Up to you, of course, but maybe best not."

"With you, don't want to spook anyone. They're your boys and girls, Rory. It's good timing, too. Out with the old and all that."

"Yes, I thought so, too. Get it all off their chests before they head for the boozers and get wrecked."

"Good idea. Let me know if anything interesting develops. Who's manning the fort tonight?"

"Couple from Paddington." He checked some papers on an untidy pile on his desk. "DS White and DC Reynolds. Volunteers, God bless 'em."

"You've sent quite a few home recently. Was that wise?"

"I couldn't see much point in keeping them any longer. They went back on the understanding that I can request them at a moment's notice. Their stations seemed happy with that."

"As long as you know what you're doing. I don't want any slip-ups because of under-manning."

"Christine! Did you see the place on Tuesday? There was no room to fart never mind sit. Keith had to call on two sergeants to help him sort the rotas and allotments. We had four on night shift; they took five calls between them. Pity the poor sod who had to handle two. Ninety officers. They were going round the houses for the third time, just to keep warm I reckon."

"Well, well. A memorable day in Metropolitan Police history: Detective Inspector complains of too many staff."

They both smiled. Stevens knew what Alexander meant. The inquiry had grown to monstrous proportions. Paperwork had piled up, too, as friends, relatives and possible witnesses had been re-interviewed.

A little late in the day, Alexander had made it the responsibility of individual officers to check original notes and add updates where they deemed fit and necessary. Each victim now had their own individual database, stored on a separate computer in the Murder Room. Some information made it to the Police National Computer; some remained within The Met. Once upon a time a buff folder would have sufficed. Now it was database upon database. Cross-references were the new buzz. No piece of information, no matter how apparently useless, was to be overlooked.

DS John Hodges was in charge of compiling a complete file of all victims, edited down so that detectives had quicker access for cross-checking. He'd needed three constables to help him but was satisfied it was now up to date. Until the next time. That was what had been puzzling and worrying Alexander when Stevens disturbed his thoughts. Next time. Would Jake ring out the old year with a bang; ring in the new with another killing?

It took five minutes for the crowd in the central Murder Room to loosen up. DS Stuart Pierce had done it. "I think Caroline's blow-job – I mean blowfish – is our best lead," he'd said to uproarious guffaws. True to form, Caroline Peters had not blushed.

Pierce himself had discovered the previous day that the tetrodotoxin from the blowfish had almost certainly found its way into Derek Chisholm's body via the tiny hole on his side.

Forensics had found a minute trace of the toxin on his trouser pocket during a UV scan. They were puzzled as to its origin until checking with Alexander and hearing of the results of the post mortem. Dr McMillan had informed Alexander that, yes, the tiniest amount of the toxin could cause death. A single fish contained sufficient poison to see off 30-plus grown males. That explained the pin-prick, then. "So, for now, let's assume he was pricked with a small amount of this stuff and then the other poisons entered his system afterwards, while he was fighting for his life," said Alexander. "He could have drunk them willingly or Jake could have forced them down him."

"You think he actually met Jake then?" asked Vicki Jobson. "You think Jake was in the car with him?"

"That's possible. Yes, that's possible."

"Could Jake have been masquerading as a car park attendant or something?" Pierce again.

"I've spoken to all three attendants. They saw nothing suspicious," said DC Curtis Maynard, a 29-year-old from Enfield.

"The fish poison would have killed him eventually," said Peters. "So why administer the others? The chlorides? That puzzles me."

"Maybe he was in a hurry and wanted to be quick?" said Maynard. "Or he didn't really know what he was doing and just bunged him up with a few chemicals he could get his hands on," suggested DC Craig Gough.

"I'll go along with that," said Peters.

"Could be, could be," said Alexander. "Dr McMillan's report says the body contained sufficient poison to see off up to a dozen average build males, over a certain time and if untreated."

"The chlorides are not too difficult to obtain. Licences are needed for larger quantities but they are pretty much readily available. So we're back to Caroline's blow …fish. We need to know how Jake got hold of the stuff."

"Working on it. No response from the streets yet. Best bet is a restaurant owner in Chinatown."

"Give it another week then perhaps you may need to press harder, Caroline," said Alexander.

"I was wondering if we had any cops we could call on to help out?"

"Any cops? Call on any bloody cops you like, Caroline."

"Sorry, boss, I meant any Chinky cops. You know, blend in better; maybe have a scour around some of the wholesale markets?"

"I know there are two Chinese on the drugs squad. Wouldn't say I know them personally but they came to Enfield on a job once," said Maynard.

"I'll have a word with the Super and she can request them from the AC if we feel the need. Yes, I am thinking this poison is our lead hope so far. Anything from Mensa?" Alexander looked across the room to DC Martin Wright.

"Mensa's brain hurts," said Wright, clutching his head. "Blank I'm afraid boss. If there's a pattern there it beats me. I started off by thinking someone might be playing a game. You know, rolling the dice and killing wherever their piece landed. Roll a three and fine: Whitchapel Road. Then came Regent Street. No problems again if they don't take any action when they land on Community Chest or Chance. But then all the way round to Vine Street? Possible but unlikely."

"You'd think he'd make it easier for us by going round the board in order, wouldn't yer?" said Peters.

Mensa continued: "Then I considered maybe two people playing. Hard to see a pattern unless the dice favoured no-go areas. I've tried colours, numbers, names – nothing. I even considered one of those random number selectors, similar to the lottery, and, sure, one of those could be used but that proves nothing we could benefit from."

"No stations or utilities yet."

"Nothing on the red and yellow side, either."

"Too many places to choose for a surveillance job, boss?"

"Don't be daft."

"Where could he hit for the Chance and Community Chest squares?"

"Income Tax. Go! Bastard's spoilt for choice, ain't he?"

The comments started flowing thick and fast. Some intelligent, some quips, some mumbles. At least they were airing their opinions. Mensa's was not the only brain hurting. The murder sites seemed as random as the victims.

"Could be more than one person playing. In fact there could be more than one person involved in the killings if not actually taking part at the sticky end."

"Do we think he actually chooses a spot? Or does he just roam the Monopoly streets armed and ready to pounce whenever he sees a suitable victim?"

"I've wondered that and, to be frank, I would have said he's a roamer – until the last one. That seemed planned, but the victim chosen at random. And if he failed he could always move on. As DC Gough says: he's not exactly lacking choices."

Alexander caught DC Sarah Hughes shifting uncomfortably a few yards away. She looked down as their eyes met.

"What was that, Sarah?" he asked.

"Nothing, sir, didn't say anything," she replied, sheepishly.

"I must be hearing things then."

"There is one thing, sir."

"Please share with us. No matter how useless it's still worth a drink on me in The Ferret afterwards." Gently, gently. Poor girl was a newbie and a little on edge among the murder vets. The 28-year-old blonde picked up a piece of paper from the desk on which her right buttock was perched.

"Just a doodle, really, but I found this on the desk when I came in this morning. Free Parking stroke Pentonville Road and several question marks." She passed the sheet via a few hands to Alexander.

"Thank you, Sarah. That's one of the desks the night boys use, right?"

"Think so," said a voice from the back.

"Anyone recognise the hand-writing?" he held up the sheet.

"Probably DS Walters," said Pierce. "He uses that desk. Significant, you think?"

"Not a clue, but I didn't see anything in the night-log. Listen everybody. I know you feel like we're looking for a needle in a haystack. But we'll get there. Trust me, we will get there. So anything – even doodles like this – don't keep them to yourselves. I'll decide whether or not it's important. You all know the score – 99 per cent of our information proves useless. But it's always better to have than have not."

Cross-references were the new buzz. He stressed that once more before pinning the sheet on the Chisholm board. "Right tidy up, let's leave this place spick and span for the new night crew. Four to hang around till they arrive – sort it out among yourselves. Anyone cares for drink I'll be in The Ferret in an hour."

Peters was already shuffling a pack of cards before he had turned for Det Supt Stevens's office. Good team player Caroline Peters; you wouldn't find her pulling rank for a coffee run or an extra hour or so down the pub. Maybe that's why she was so popular. He knew many a senior officer who could learn a lot about respect from Caroline Peters.

+

Alexander put a friendly arm around Sarah Hughes and guided her to a quiet corner; well as quiet a corner as you could find in The Ferret at 6.30pm. He was surprised to see the pub so busy, imagining most would have been scurrying home to prepare for the biggest night out of the year: New Year's Bloody Eve.

"Didn't mean to embarrass you back there, Sarah."

"That's OK, sir. I was…"

"Rory, it's always Rory in here."

She smiled and tried it out: "Thanks, yes. Rory." It sounded strange. She felt her face redden and stared intently down into her vodka and orange.

"But perhaps you needed embarrassing. You're a key member of a big team, Sarah. You come highly recommended. You wouldn't be here otherwise. But I don't do shrinking violets too well. I've no room for them on board. Not on a murder inquiry. A very big murder inquiry. OK?"

"Sorry, I …I just didn't want to land anyone in it."

"Bloody hell, Sarah! You haven't landed anyone in it. Think about it: DS Walters was probably just doodling away during the wee hours. The night shift's hardly been inundated, and he'd only had a few hours kip before covering for Keith. He's an experienced cop. I'm not going to bollock him; I'll just give him a gentle nudge, a reminder to put everything in the log, even his doodles. He won't take offence."

That seemed to have eased her conscience.

"OK now?"

"Yes, thanks."

"So anything at all. You can come to me, Stuart, Keith, Caroline. We won't ridicule you. Well, Caroline might." They both laughed.

"One thing. Just one thing I'd been wondering."

"Yes, go on."

"London Monopoly, but the name Jake; you think our man might not be a Brit? Maybe a Yank?"

Alexander took his arm from around her shoulder and rubbed his chin.

"Clever, Sarah. I like that. Not saying I agree, not saying I think much of Free Parking or Pentonville, but it's another piece for our jigsaw. Now a clever detective would pop back into the office and make a note about that. Copy for yourself and send one to DS Hodges. He's up to date with his filing. Give him something to ponder over his morning hangover."

She was smiling broadly, while Alexander looked a million miles away as they moved to mingle with the throng of laughing policemen.

Do as I say, not as I do. It had crossed Alexander's mind that Jake was a Yank name, based on a Yank game, so clearly the killer could be a Yank. So why hadn't he made a note on file? Too many bloody pieces in this jigsaw.

✝

CHAPTER SEVEN

+

THREE WEEKS LATER

"BANG GOES your theory, then," Det Supt Stevens greeted him. Not 'Good morning inspector', not 'Hello Rory'. Not even a cursory 'Hi'. Just 'Bang goes your theory, then', delivered as a statement of fact; an admonitory opening gambit if ever he heard one.

Alexander skipped a beat before replying: "Good morning, Christine. Have I time to grab a coffee before I discover how my theory has gone 'bang'?"

"Sure. OK. Be an angel and grab me one while you're there. Two sugars today; I need sweetening before I see the AC."

Alexander darted out of her office and hurried down the corridor to the canteen. The Gasbag seemed frosty even by her erratic standards. Sweetening? She could start by easing off whatever pills she took that made her appear so jumpy some days. He wanted to like her; he did like her most days. But other days …his verdict was still out.

Bang goes my theory, not 'our theory'. What did she mean? Had there been another killing? He joined the five-strong line for hot drinks at the canteen and grunted a few replies to colleagues who greeted him. He, too, needed sweetening today. Looking around the freshly-painted canteen, he spotted the usual suspects occupying a dozen or so of the 26 larger tables. Night shift workers tucking into huge fry-ups before heading home for welcome shut-eye, day workers kicking off their shifts with coffee and a cigarette and perhaps a slice of toast. The exception was a table hosting six burly CID officers – all male – preparing for the day ahead with enormous plates in front of them. The plates contained residue of British breakfast fare, reds, yellows and browns mingled with congealing grease. Now the silent sextet was piling into two mountains of toast in the centre of the table. DS Pierce was diligently mopping up the egg yolk from his plate when Alexander walked past holding his two coffees.

"Take your time," he whispered. "I'm in with the Gasbag. Shouldn't be too long as she's off to see the AC this morning. My office in, say, half an hour. Bon Appetit."

"Mornin'. Sure thing boss." Pierce barely looked up before reaching for his fourth slice of toast.

"There you go, pretty sure that's the sugared one." Alexander sat down opposite Christine Stevens and placed his cup on the table. "Now ...bang goes my theory?" He stressed the 'my', held his arms open wide and looked intrigued; studious rather than perplexed.

"Well, don't say I wasn't a little dubious from the start," said Stevens. "Thanks for the coffee. Ahh. Needed that." She handed Alexander a print-out from her computer. "Our JTJ has been at it again. Two days ago — in Berlin."

"Berlin? Berlin, Germany?"

"Congratulations inspector. Your hearing is as acute as your geographical knowledge. Berlin, the capital of Germany. Somewhere I've never been and somewhere I've never had any particular desire to go. No sun, no beaches and, to the best of my knowledge, nowhere to be seen on my Monopoly board."

Alexander studied the print-out. White female. Aged 27. Believed strangled. JTJ scratched into inside of the left arm. Nothing believed stolen. Danish passport, though someone had scribbled four question-marks alongside that. Did that mean they weren't sure whether the passport was Danish or whether the passport didn't belong to the victim? Hotel Bogota on Schlüterstrasse, district Charlottenburg-Wilmersdorf. Meant nothing to him. He'd check soon as he was out of here.

"Hmmm. Strange, very strange." Alexander rubbed his chin, scratched it and rubbed it again.

Stevens handed him another sheet of paper. "These are the details of the officer you'll be liaising with. I'm told his English is first-rate. How's your German?"

"Pretty much non-existent. French and Italian with a smattering of Spanish, but never touched German academically."

"Well, he'll give you everything they've got and naturally you'll reciprocate. I'll try and raise it with the chief, but for now it's between our two offices. Until JTJ strays further afield. Just do us all a favour and don't go blowing Herr Vonderheid's Teutonic brain with your Monopoly hunch, eh?"

"Sure. Fine. OK. Yes, of course not." Alexander was still rubbing his chin.

"Right. Get cracking. I've a few items to sort ..." Her words faded away as Alexander rose and left, clutching his two sheets of paper. He slouched along two corridors at snail's pace, studying again the scant details of the Berlin murder. He retraced his steps and headed back to the canteen for more coffee. DS Pierce was just leaving the smoking section. "On my way, sir."

"No rush Stuart. Give me another 20 minutes OK. Make yourself useful by checking all flights to Berlin from London for the past fortnight."

"Eh?"

"London, capital of the United Kingdom, to Berlin, capital of the Federal Republic of Germany. All flights from all London airports. We don't need passenger details – not yet, anyway – but just details of regular flights."

Dubious from the start? Bloody liar – she had been hooked as soon as he told her. Covering her back more likely. Preoccupied, if he was feeling generous of spirit. It didn't take Alexander long to locate the Hotel Bogota on Schlüterstrasse once he'd settled in front of his computer with his third coffee of the day; and it was barely light outside.

The hotel was just 20 yards off Kurfürstendamm. Bang goes my theory, eh little miss Gasbag? DS Pierce caught his boss smiling to himself.

"Care to share the joke, sir?"

"No joke, Stuart. No joke at all in fact. Suitably refreshed are we and ready for a long slog ahead?"

Pierce let out an involuntary belch. He apologised and blushed before both detectives dissolved into equally involuntary giggles. A very masculine thing, or schoolboy thing. Even the word belch could crumble the solemn visage of many a respected figure.

"And thank you for sharing your breakfast with me. Now I shall be able to survive till lunchtime without snacking. Berlin flights – sorted?"

"Well I wasn't exactly sure what you were after, but I've checked and basically you can fly from any of the big three London airports or City Airport to any of three Berlin airports. Any time from dawn till dusk, and any price you want really. The cheapies start at just a few quid plus taxes and the business suits can splash 600 quid-plus. Takes an hour or so; about the same journey time as flying to Glasgow, say. Care to fill me in?"

"Jake's been doing his dirty work over there." He handed Pierce the sheet of paper to read while he busied himself copying details of the Hotel Bogota.

"Christ! Berlin! But ..."

"That's not on your Monopoly board, right?"

"Well, sir, I was just thinking he's playing some distance away from home."

"No need to be coy, Stuart. I've already had the piss taken out of me by the Super ...bang goes my theory, she seemed pleased to inform me."

"Oh. How was she then?"

"Thankfully, less chatty than normal as she has other things on her plate this morning. The chief wants an update on that corruption case she was working on. It seems to have hit a brick wall. So she had a minor snap at me – very minor, but unlike her all the same."

Then he leapt to his feet, finger pointed to the ceiling professorially. "Now, my trusty sergeant, should I inform her before she dashes off to see the AC? Or afterwards? Hmmm, tricky one?"

"Inform her of what exactly?" Pierce's mouth was slightly curled to the left, he realised Alexander had something up his sleeve. He occasionally ponced around like this when he did. Very unbecoming in a senior detective. Still, as prima donnas went Alexander was well down Pierce's list.

"Well, I wouldn't expect you to know, but what does Kurfürstendamm mean to you?"

"Nothing, in a nutshell. Putting on my best detective's head and taking in what I have learnt this morning I would hazard an informed guess at – Germany? If you asked me to narrow it down I would probably plump for Berlin."

"Bravo indeed. Kurfürstendamm is their Mayfair. Well, not quite. I have no bloody idea what the street is like, but let me inform you that it is the highest valued property on the European version of Monopoly. And like our beloved Mayfair it occupies one of the dark blue slots on the board.

"I have discovered that the Hotel Bogota is within spitting distance of Kurfürstendamm; world-championship spitting distance perhaps, but spitting distance all the same."

The rather tired attempt to mimic the saintly Sherlock seemed to have tired Alexander and he slumped into his chair, smiling faintly.

"You're saying Jake flew to Berlin on a jolly and decided to commit a murder based on their bleedin' Monopoly board? Sounds a bit far-fetched."

"I know. I know. Don't think I haven't asked myself a hundred times a day these past few weeks whether or not I'm barking up the wrong tree. But I have yet to hear anyone else in this investigation come up with a more sensible lead, or even a half sensible one."

"So what's the plan of action today then?"

"Well I intend to check a few things here before ringing this Ralf Vonderheid chappie. Don't suppose you can shed any light on any of those abbreviations by his name?"

"Sorry, sir, all Greek to me." He couldn't resist a chuckle.

Alexander frowned. "Right, now you can go shopping and find us a decent street map of Berlin. And don't come back with one which has a bloody big wall running through the middle of it. Then you can run a check to see if our boys have anything on the Danish passport. And finally you can prepare all the official case notes in some semblance of order and chronology so I can email them to Germany this afternoon. See you in The Ferret for lunch – one o'clock on the dot, OK."

"Sure." He clicked his heels together sharply, turned and left.

Alexander returned to his computer and searched his 'favourites' for the Monopoly website which had details of the European version.

"Koenigsallee! That's it! Koenigsallee, the other dark blue property." He slapped his thigh and then rang reception for the international code for Germany. The female receptionist at the Kriminalpolizei branch office took a second to switch into very passable English.

"Good morning Inspector Alexander. How may I help you?"

"I wish to speak to Ralf Vonderheid, please. I believe he is expecting my call."

"One moment, please, I will transfer the call to Inspector Vonderheid."

"Thank you. Herr Vonderheid is an inspector?"

"Yes, that is correct. I am transferring you now."

"Morgen, Vonderheid." Slight cough and background of paper being shuffled.

"Inspector Vonderheid, my name is Inspector Rory Alexander from New Scotland Yard. I am conducting the investigation into—"

"Ah. Very good morning to you sir. How are you and how is London?"

"I am fine, sir. As for London, well the best I can say is that it is not raining."

"Ha-ha. Very good. I have been twice to your grand city and twice it rained cats and dogs. Big cats and dogs. And one time we had a real pea-souper. Humph. I must come again in the summer. Please call me Ralf. May I call you Rory?"

"Sure Ralf. Sure." Alexander relaxed. Clearly the German was enjoying practising his English.

"Now, our mutual friend JTJ. We are to share information. I will have some more news to send you perhaps this afternoon. Can you send me your information, please?"

"Certainly. My sergeant is preparing the notes now and I can send by email if that is fine by you. I assume you have a secure server?"

"Yes, yes, certainly." The detectives exchanged email details before Vonderheid filled in some more background for Alexander.

A colleague had attended a Europol meeting recently in Strasbourg. Though Europol's main concern was terrorism and major international crimes such as drug trafficking and people-smuggling within the European Union, the London serial killings had been discussed and the JTJ signature cropped up. It was now logged on an obscure database. Vonderheid was surprised to discover that the killer had been in contact with DI Alexander.

"Jake, you say. And what about T and J? You have any clues?"

Alexander resisted the obvious temptation to blow his Teutonic brains with his Monopoly theory and obeyed the Gasbag. "We have a few ideas. As soon as any-thing is confirmed I will let you know. I assume you haven't mentioned JTJ to your newspaper people?"

"No. No. Nothing at all. I have decided not to mention the possibility of the London killer until I have spoken to you. I will let you decide."

"Thanks, for now I would prefer no mention at all of JTJ or any links with our murderer. Can you agree to that, please?"

"Sure thing. No problem."

"Now, I noticed on the fact sheet you sent that there were question-marks by the Danish passport. Can you explain those?"

"Yes. Now we know the passport was stolen. We have found another address in Berlin that the murdered woman was using. It is clear she was a small thief; we think part of a gang from Poland. There were several more passports in the second apartment and many purses and handbags. The information is being looked into and I will send what I can later today."

"Great, thanks. Just one more thing for now: how far from Kurfürstendamm was the body?"

"You know the Ku-damm? Well the body was very close, hidden beneath some garbage down an alley – ten metres at most from one of our busiest avenues. I will be happy to show you the scene of the crime if you come to Berlin."

"Thanks Ralf. Maybe I will do just that. Goodbye for now."

Alexander was just packing up for the day when he was summoned to Christine Stevens's office. "My turn for coffee I think. White, no sugar, right?"

"Yes that's right. Thanks." She seemed in a good enough mood as she phoned the canteen and asked for a handy DC to ferry two cups down.

"You bloody knew, didn't you? You bloody well knew."

Was that a smile he had glimpsed?

"Knew what Christine?"

"Monopoly. European Monopoly. You knew soon as I opened my big mouth this morning. Well I guess you have checked it out now, and …?"

DI Alexander was blushing slightly and shuffled position in his seat.

"I was going—"They were interrupted by DC Craig Gough. "Should be warm enough I hope – end of the pot. New brew's on if you fancy another cup in about 20 minutes."

"Prompt service, DC Gough. You missed your calling. Thanks, we'll let you know. Close the door on your way out."

"I was going to tell you in the morning. I had no idea from the print-out. How did you find out?"

She laughed out loud. "The Assistant Commissioner!"

"The AC? How did he know? How did the meeting go?"

"Oh the meeting was splendid. He loves me and it seems he loves you, too. Welcome to the cuddly club. The Wilkes case is well and truly off my back; he is satisfied the notes I handed over to that useless tosser Havers were accurate and complete. I am now fully-fledged homicide with no back catalogue. I do hope the sleazeballs are gentle with Havers, poor man."

"Glad to hear it. I could sense it was bugging you, if you don't mind me being frank."

"Course not, should be your middle name. Anyway after we had pushed the councillor and his greedy chum to one side – and I really did my utmost to avoid landing Havers in the shit – we were enjoying a delicious selection of sandwiches and I mentioned Berlin."

"And?"

"And before I could suggest that scuppers our Monopoly lead he said: 'You're saying our chap is now playing European Monopoly?' I almost choked."

Stevens was laughing again and shaking her head. Alexander wasn't sure why, but he covered his mouth to mask his mirth.

"His wife had bought the Rowley children a European version for Christmas; thought it would help them understand the EU and continental geography as well as providing entertainment. I didn't know where to look. He asked if you had traced the location yet. I tap-danced and said you were working on it."

"Wow. Do they have the new version in euros?"

"What? New version?"

"Well mine's an old one I picked up second-hand," he said without hint of embarrassment. "You play in ecus – remember the old commercial European currency? Bankers and the like used it before the euro became the rage."

Stevens rolled her eyes, threw back her head and laughed even louder at the ceiling. "This becomes more like a madhouse every day."

Both senior detectives were almost in tears of hysteria. An observer would probably have thought he was watching a cop comedy on TV rather than the epicentre of a serial murder investigation at work. If Jake could see them now.

"Never did come to terms with hard and soft ecus," said Alexander deadpan as the laughter subsided.

"OK, come on now. Frivolity's over. What have you been up to while I was tap-dancing?"

"Well as you guessed I did check first thing after we spoke, and the victim was found just a few yards from Kurfürstendamm – the European equivalent of our Mayfair. I spoke with Inspector Vonderheid. We seemed to hit it off. I was surprised to learn JTJ had been mentioned on some Europol database. Who decides these things? I thought we had decided the fewer in the know the better?"

"News to me. I can only assume it came from the AC's office, though I am sure there will be the usual warning flags. This Vonderheid and his team are keeping it out of the German media, I hope?"

"Yes. We agreed no details at all of links with our killings for now. He invited me over to view the scene and body. What do you think?"

"Why not. Should only be a 24-hour job? Fancy taking your Lucy for a week-end maybe?"

"Might just do that, thanks."

"Anything else?"

"Pierce has checked London flights – far too many to go chasing passenger lists. Even if we knew for certain that Jake had flown direct from London to Berlin we'd need to narrow down the timeframe to a few days to make it worthwhile. It could have been a one-off away-break or it could mean our Jake does some form of European business travelling. Keeping options open as usual.

"Inspector Vonderheid sent me updated details and I emailed him all our files. ID on the victim has yet to be confirmed; seems she was in a gang that robbed tourists. They have found several passports, two of which have her photo in them. He hopes for more info soon. Strangulation confirmed as cause of death by Berlin path lab. Considerable amount of alcohol found in the system – a pretty mixed cocktail. Looks like whoever she is she had a happy last night out.

Also some traces of recreational drug use – marijuana and cocaine. No news on Japanese killer fish."

"So she was not poisoned, merely pissed and stoned out of her brain when murdered. Same as …"

"Victim number two, the Korean student in Regent Street."

"And we believe the alcohol and drugs were self-induced?"

"No reason to suspect otherwise. No hint of drink-spiking. The Korean's pals say he was a pretty straight guy when he arrived the previous year. Developed a liking for the London highlife, drank modestly but it was alien to him and a few drinks would get him pissed. He'd share a casual joint, no serious drug problem and no evidence of needle-usage picked up by the path department."

"So our Jake picks out helpless targets. That it?"

"Basically, yes. The Whitechapel woman wasn't exactly helpless but not in the best of physical condition either. Anorexic and suffering from a heavy cold or flu, but no evidence of alcoholic or drug intake."

"Christ! Are we any closer? Our Oriental friends delivered yet? Anything forensic to report?"

"Still working the Chinese markets – proving slow-going. DS Dhiang is assisting DS Peters but they can't find anyone who'll admit to importing the stuff or willing to talk about anyone who does.

"DC Gough is having fun collating all the fibres, more than four hundred bits and pieces from various items of clothing. No matches between scenes. They could belong to anyone, friends, relatives or just casual passers-by. Still, they are being kept and logged for possible future matches."

"Future matches – so we wait until Jake strikes again and hope we get lucky. Not ideal is it?"

"Sorry. Reminds me, I must ask Ralf for their fibres."

"Ralph?"

"Inspector Ralf Vonderheid; we're on first-name terms."

"How cosy." She looked earnest. "Seriously, that's good. Oh, and I forgot to say the AC says if we need extra resources I don't need to ask. I told him you had enough for now but might need more if we have to go door-to-door again. Take that on board – an order."

"Good, always sensible to have a woman in charge of the purse strings. Hope that didn't sound sexist."

"Ha! How about you let this old woman delve into her purse and buy you a drink for the road?"

"Deal. A few of the team should be in The Ferret. Shall we join them?"

"Why not? This purse is positively bottomless." She moved for her coat.

+

Detective Sergeants Pierce and Caroline Peters and DC Mike 'Rab' Burns were stood at the semi-circular bar of The Fox and Ferret. The pub was a half mile from Broadway. There were boozers closer to New Scotland Yard but here they didn't stand out as coppers. Or didn't think they did.

The pub was enjoying its busiest time of day. Office workers piled through its revolving doors from around 4.30 and this time, two hours later, was peak business. Within the hour people would start drifting off to catch the rattler home: to the outer reaches of London or the leafier towns and villages of the Home Counties. The trio were startled to see CS Gas accompanying their boss. All managed not to show it, except Peters who spluttered some of her pint of lager onto the bar floor.

"Evening boss, ma'am. What's your pleasure, passion or poison?" said Pierce.

"These are on exes ... I mean on me," winked Stevens at the trio. All shared her joke. She was all right, they supposed. Standing your rounds was a solid sign of all rightness.

"Nice to see you here, ma'am," said Peters, now recovered. "Welcome to The Met's finest drink and think tank. I'll have a lager, please. Foster's, best thing to come out of Oz since Skippy."

"On pints I see Caroline. Watch that figure now. You know what sexist pigs male cops can be. And please drop the 'ma'am' in here, eh? Me and Rory are into first name terms. You may call me Chris or Christine. I prefer Christine, dislike CS Gas and would consider Gasbag a disciplinary offence."

Alexander shouted up the drinks as the thought sunk in that their superintendent actually had a sense of humour and just possibly a personality.

"Cheers Chris!"

"Cheers Christine!"

"Cheers Christine's expenses!"

Trust Burns to be all too forthright. All had noticed Alexander slip the receipt to her. Alexander just raised his pint at Stevens and smiled.

"Christine's been having cucumber sandwiches with the AC today. He's right behind us all the way; absolutely all the way. But a few more leads would be welcome. That about right?"

"More or less; except the sandwiches were smoked salmon." She licked her lips.

"Where's Goughie?" asked Burns. "He was supposed to be joining us."

"Loitering in the canteen last I heard," said Alexander.

Right on cue DC Gough joined the team. He'd spotted Stevens with them and merely twitched his mouth; not quite a smile. He ordered a pint of Bass and was surprised to see the Super stretch over to pay. She didn't bother with the receipt, fearing for her reputation. "Cheers all!" Gough supped and raised his glass.

"Cheers Thread!" rang the refrain.

"Fred?" queried Stevens.

"Thread," replied Pierce. "Craig's on fibres."

"Almost enough now to make a half-decent jacket. You perky lot will be sorry when you see it."

"Thread. I can think of worse nicknames."

Gough coughed and tried not to blush. The others just laughed.

"See the note I left on your desk, Rory?" said Pierce.

"No, came straight here. Important?"

"Not really. From your German chum. Seems the Danish bird is a Pole."

"Right. I think I can make sense of that."

"Is it right what Stu says, this bastard's now playing Euro Monopoly?" said Peters.

"Looks that way. Only bloody link I can find. Open to offers, folk, no matter how daft. Remember: what happens in the D-and-T Tank stays in the D-and-T Tank until I say otherwise. Or tonight, as she has a one-day membership, until Christine says otherwise."

"I'm still going for a single white male, late 20s, early 30s. Has an older sister who always cheated at the game." The deduction of Caroline Peters which she was happy to share once again.

"I can't figure out whether he likes the game or loathes it," said Gough. "Which side you on boss?"

"Still on the fence. All I know is that it means something to him. Means a lot to him. Enough to unhinge his mind and send him on this spree. Why now? Who knows?"

"Pathetic. Clever. Crazy. Squeamish." Burns offered.

"Squeamish?" chimed in Alexander, Pierce and Stevens in not quite perfect harmony.

"No blood," replied Burns. "Just struck me earlier in the canteen, so I wonder if our Jake is a little squeamish."

"No blood?" asked Stevens. She was still finding her feet among Alexander's cosy team and made a mental note to refrain from asking too many questions – in public at least. She was wondering whether this gathering was just a little too casual. For now she'd defer to Alexander's style. Actually, she found herself rather enjoying the company.

"Well I don't know about Berlin yet. Any blood there?"

Alexander had quickly realised what Burns was babbling about. "No, no blood in Berlin to my knowledge. Strangulation again. Isn't it a big leap to say the absence of blood makes our Jake squeamish? Good call though, Mike."

"Yes, good one Mike. Here's to the D-and-T Tank. My shout."

"Oh I should be ..."

"Tut, tut, Christine. After we have allowed a Super honorary entry into our inner sanctum. You can risk one more, even if you're driving."

"Go on, then. I'm not driving home tonight so no worries there. And I am interested in your D-and-T Tank theories, so keep them coming."

The pub crowd was starting to thin, but the noise was still raucous enough. Yet Alexander was always sufficiently alert to potential eavesdroppers. Not that anyone happening to pass by would have the foggiest what this group was rambling on about. He wanted a quick getaway tonight, having promised to be in for dinner with Lucy. Still, be bad form to leave before Stevens.

"No blood; never thought about that before. No sharp weapons either, eh? Nor any blunt objects. In fact the bodies are left pretty tidy, considering. Worth running by the shrink, Rory?"

"Sure Caroline. Why don't you fix it up in the morning?"

"I'm going shopping again. Can you get someone else?"

"Hey! Did you get me those spices?" asked Burns.

"Rab, I have enough spices to cook a feast for an emperor; several emperors. Better than the stuff our supermarkets sell, according to my Chinese buddy, and a damned sight cheaper. Some bloody mark-up. I left them on a table in the canteen – free for all. If you missed out it's just tough."

"Any of his signatures draw blood?" asked Stevens.

All eyes turned to Alexander.

"Not that I can recall, though I didn't attend the first scene. Just pretty light scratches, really. One of them was barely visible, like Jake was in a hurry maybe."

"The one that puzzles me is the old woman," said Gough. "No fibres found 'cept from her own stuff."

"And?" asked Stevens, forgetting her mental note.

"Just unusual, that's all. You'd expect some from the woman grabbing at a coat or something. Or even from whatever was used to pin her down. There was no cushion or nothing on top of her when she was found. She was just face down in her own sofa."

"No-one seems to have got to grips with Jake," Alexander said to Stevens. "Nothing at all found under any of the victim's nails; no skin, no blood, no fibres. Hence the helpless victims theory."

"Meaning someone being murdered would usually put up a fight."

"Yes, unless they were physically incapacitated. Mind and body impaired through either drugs, drink or just plain frailty. Or fish poison."

"I wonder which will let down Jake?"

"Christine?"

"Drugs, drink or just plain frailty? Which will be Jake's undoing? Right, now I really must be off. Thanks for the company. Bright and early in the morning."

+

Burns yawned and cursed. He didn't dare open his eyes yet. He arched his back slightly and stretched his arms wide, yawning loudly this time. "Christ!" He shot upright as his arm touched bare flesh. His eyes were wide open now, yet it took him a few seconds to recognise the form of Caroline Peters.

It slowly came back to him. They had moved on from The Ferret to two other pubs on the way back to his flat in the Barbican. Lights had come on as they had staggered drunkenly and noisily along the hall, spilling grease from their Indian takeaway.

His mouth felt like the bottom of a birdcage. Drink, man needs drink. He turned away at the sight of half-eaten meals in the kitchen. Drunks were always less hungry than they imagined. He downed a good half-litre of grapefruit juice straight from the container in the fridge.

Peters's snores were making him laugh, despite his thumping head. He checked the kitchen clock, took a felt-tip pen from a drawer and went back to bed. Twenty minutes later, there were signs that the sergeant was awaking from her slumber. She began shuffling position and ended up facing Burns when she opened one eye; a half smile. She closed the eye and opened the other. Was she checking that both worked?

"Mornin' tiger," she croaked, tracing a finger down his chest.

"Tiger? Was I?" he smiled.

"As if I can fuckin' remember!" she laughed aloud now, yawned and stretched. She shuffled again and ended up on her back, both eyes open and staring blankly at the cream-coloured ceiling. Her arm was irritating her and she began rubbing.

After a few seconds, she sat up and looked at the red marks she had left from rubbing. "What the …what the fuck!" She turned to look at Burns and he was grinning like a schoolboy.

"You fuckin' idiot! You stupid, fuckin' Scottish idiot! That supposed to be funny?"

His face was bright red. "Sorry. Just a joke."

"Joke? Excuse me while I piss myself laughing. Get the fuck out of here."

"Caroline …"

"Now! Just fuck off."

"Look Caroline—"

"I said NOW!"

"Caroline …this is *my* flat."

Her breathing seemed to have slowed.

"So, it is," she smiled at the ceiling. "So it is. Jeeze, Rab, you have a sense of humour, all right."

"Sorry."

"OK. OK, let's just forget it, eh?" She shook her head and punched him lightly on the arm. "Now, where's your shower? And why isn't the bloody kettle on?"

Stupid Scottish bugger, she muttered in the shower, the letters JTJ fading away as she scrubbed at her arm.

+

CHAPTER EIGHT

+

SARAH HUGHES had been fascinated. The last few weeks had opened her eyes on how a major Met investigation was conducted. A far cry from Clapham and a conveyor belt of burglaries. She knew her role was minor in the great scheme of things, insignificant maybe. But she knew she was a good detective – everyone told her so, everyone whose opinion mattered to her at least, and promotion to sergeant couldn't be too far away.

Even the profiler's abrupt dismissal of her own theory that Jake might possibly, just possibly … perhaps be a foreigner hadn't unsettled her that much.

She wanted to say something, but wasn't sure what. She sensed, accurately, that Stuart Pierce had not been as enraptured by the trip to the sticks as she had been. Rather than make small-talk for the sake of it, DC Hughes contented herself by staring out of the window. Still green, so much green and yet London lurked a few miles away. Raindrops trickled down the car window and she entertained herself with the tried and tested childhood game of guessing which drop would reach the bottom first. She won four out of seven before becoming bored with the game and quit while she was ahead.

Traffic was light, but would not stay that way for long. Spray squirted onto the windscreen as they cruised past a long line of lorries, probably heading for the channel ports judging by their number plates. French, Belgian, Dutch, Spanish and a couple of nationality marks she did not recognise; perhaps from the old eastern bloc, or the Balkan states. They were becoming more and more frequent these days.

Pierce was drumming his fingers on the steering wheel of the Mondeo estate. It was a smart, comfortable car. BBC Radio 4 hummed stately as only Radio 4 can, more background than anything else. Hughes sighed and turned to look through the windscreen, Pierce glanced at her, correctly sensing the blonde DC wanted conversation.

"So then, Sarah. Let's hear your first profile of your first profiler."

She shifted in her seat. Good, he had broken the silence. She didn't want him filing her under 'chatty type,' Gasbag's younger sister, knowing Pierce's piercing wit. Pierce was a top notch detective and decent enough bloke if you could kick through the chauvinist crap.

"Very interesting," the 28-year-old replied, deadpan. "Must be some money in that lark; unless that place was paid for by a rich hubby."

"She's not married, never has been to my knowledge. Rich aunt died and paid for that place, I believe."

That place was a five-bedroomed mock-Georgian detached house in half an acre of well-manicured grounds. The lawn would have made a decent putting green for four or five holes, thought Pierce. The trees were neatly trimmed, surprisingly so for January. A hired gardener, he guessed, though he had no idea whether Sheila Forbes-Hamilton had green fingers. She just didn't look the type. It was his fourth visit to her Hertfordshire home-cum-office. Or 'surgery' as she preferred to call it, giving it a self-important medical moniker.

"Two grand she'll charge," added Pierce. "Two grand at least for that little consultation."

Hughes whistled. "Beats working for a living."

"Yeah, a day, two at most, to read the edited files and then Hey Presto! Here's the guy you're looking for. Notice how she kept saying 'of course, this is just my opinion based on the data provided.' Money for old rope. But, come on, I want to hear what you think."

"Well, she was a little pompous for my liking, but she seemed thorough and professional. Good grasp of her subject. I had noticed no ring on the left hand, but many women are like that these days. The latest trend."

"Ha! You think Dr Forbes-Hamilton follows fashions? My old mum wouldn't be seen dead wearing her kinda gear."

"But your old mum's from Essex, different style in Herts didn't you know."

"You leave Essex out of this. God's country," joked Pierce. The 31-year-old stocky bachelor was a product of Harlow, a new town on the Essex-Hertfordshire border. It served as London overspill, relatively cheap housing and all modern architecture. Home to Pierce, but he was growing tired of it and planning to exchange his three-bedroomed semi for a flat in central London.

"You aren't miffed that the quack dismissed your theory?"

"My theory, is it? Dear me, now I am honoured. DI Alexander has told us all – every little bit helps form a bigger picture. Don't be shy in coming forward. Maybe I should get some badges made up."

"Did you like her?"

"Respect more than like. Too stuck-up as I said. Wouldn't say posh, but–"

"Full of self-importance. My thoughts exactly."

"But she has a good record?"

"Jury's out. Her reputation's built on one solid profile, serial rapist stalking the leafy Hertfordshire villages. She's come a little close a couple of other times; I'll give her that. But–"

"Nothing that hasn't been mulled over at the station or in the Tank?"

"Exactly."

"All those books; the titles blew my mind. I'm sure the actual contents would send me straight to the funny farm."

"Yeah. Scary stuff. Half those bloody authors should be behind bars. In fact, I think half of 'em have been behind bars."

"Her reasoning seemed sound."

"How? Come on, I'm interested, really. What did she actually tell us that we didn't already know?"

"It's not a case of that, is it? What she did – what I imagined her job to be before we came out – was to piece it all together and formulate a considered opinion, an expert opinion."

"She's won you over then I gather."

"Look at all the opinions we had. I had mine, you had yours, Rory had his, Caroline hers …and I bet the Gasbag shared her opinion with the inspector if not with us minions. Swamped in opinions. Now we have an expert one."

"So-called expert one. Free tip: don't take it as gospel. They always cover their backsides. More get-out clauses than a Labour Party manifesto."

"Cynic."

"Ouch! Straight to the heart."

"Scoff if you like. Maybe I should profile you?"

"Whoa! No thank you. Back to Jake. You go along with all of it?"

Almost certainly single and male, Sheila Forbes-Hamilton had said. Educated, probably to university level, maybe even post-graduate. Yes, Pierce was right; a good few options left open even in her précis.

Lived alone or with a single relative, was hard to say whether male or female relative but if pushed would go for mother.

Aged at least 30, would pitch for late 30s early 40s. British, not American. You could tell that by the style of the letters. Forbes-Hamilton claimed to know of Jake The Jailbird and Edgar The Officer before reading the files – and she was pleased to inform the detectives that she was thoroughly English. Jake was British, but Forbes-Hamilton was most assuredly English. Strange that.

Monopoly had played some pivotal role in his life. You didn't need to be Stephen Hawkings to work that out, Hughes had to admit. Knew London well. Was mobile. Chose victims carefully if randomly, hence the absence of witnesses. No significance in the blood-less nature of the murders, except to emphasise a tidy mind. Plus, blood could get on clothing; make detection easier, wouldn't it?

The poison? Now that had intrigued Forbes-Hamilton. The nature of the cocktail in the car park killing suggested someone with a little knowledge of biology and/or chemistry rather than an expert. Hadn't the pathologist said something similar? Maybe Pierce was right, money for old rope.

Hughes turned her gaze left and began studying the raindrops again. "I'm writing up the report then?" she asked without looking at the driver.

"Yep, you sure are. Just to supplement the expert ramblings of our resident shrink. Show me before you file it, then I can sanction it with my 'total bollocks' stamp."

She put her hands together as if in prayer. "Oh one day maybe, if there is a God, I will be a sergeant and such a cynical bugger."

"Not something you can get on prescription. Maybe I should give lessons? I've learned from some experts myself."

+

Lucy Laing was a true diamond. Alexander hadn't felt like playing, but she had insisted. He was The Car; Lucy was The Shoe.

She was a 32-year-old Human Resources manager with an expanding fast-food chain. Their coffee was second-rate, Alexander delighted in informing her whenever she tried to drag him into one of their shops, waving her staff discount card.

Not quite Yorkshire, not quite Geordie. Lucy had a pleasant northern accent which she owed more to a four-year course at York University than to the many hours spent behind the counter at her parents' Post Office in Darlington.

They'd met by chance one Friday night at The Crown. The slim brunette with smiling green eyes had moved into her own flat in Highgate after the house she had rented south of the river with three co-workers had been bought by a developer. Highgate was closer to work and within her price range – just.

A few chances encounters at the pub and on the street had led to Alexander one day suggesting a meal. They'd been going steady more than a year now, by some distance the longest of the detective's relationships. Lucy had almost taken up permanent residency at his flat since Christmas, though she liked to have at least two days at her own place to keep on top of maintenance. Her flat would be going on the market soon when they planned to start looking at houses in earnest. Alexander thought part of her decision to spend the odd night away was a desire to keep their relationship fresh. He knew many couples who had lived together for years and shown no signs of getting hitched. Lucy, he knew, was very keen on formalising their union – desperate almost.

She had treated him to a low-level coffee table from the New Year sales. It was placed in the middle of the lounge and now they were engaged in their nightly ritual: a game of Monopoly. A reggae CD by some band Alexander had never heard of danced softly from the speakers in the corner. The couple tapped their feet subconsciously.

The coffee table had been bought to bring a semblance of tidiness to the lounge after Lucy got fed up treading on houses and dice and metallic tokens.

"Instead of you just brooding over the bloody thing why don't we have a game?" she had suggested about three weeks back. "Might help you think?"

They could not escape Monopoly these days; even when watching TV. Alexander had arrived home one night to find Lucy watching a Poirot video. Agatha Christie's Belgian sleuth and Captain Hastings were playing Monopoly. It was February 1935 and Alexander refrained from informing his fiancée that was several months too early for the London game to be available. Lucy had a crush on Hastings, giggling with childish abandon each time he uttered an 'I say!'

Alexander rolled a three and a two and moved his token to the Electricity Company. "I say! Buy it," he announced, counting out the notes and hoping for a reaction to his Hastings impression which never came. He'd already acquired the Water Works. Lucy would have to pay him double rent now if she landed on either.

The utilities were puzzling him. The tax squares were puzzling him. Jake had hundreds, possibly thousands, of potential targets. Stuart Pierce had compiled a list of the most high-profile ones, totalling 80. Some joker had drawn a smiley face by the Inland Revenue departments. For once, Alexander's black humour had deserted him and the offending item replaced.

Needle in a haystack. Jake went for soft targets anyway, not high-profile ones. Would they finish their game before he caught Jake? Impossible to say. Lucy had a more balanced property portfolio; some on each side of the board. The yellows were the prize, each property now hosting a little green house. Alexander had more cash in hand, a random selection of properties, including Whitechapel and Vine Street – two of Jake's haunts.

She'd been in jail twice, he once, reminding him of Christmas night at his brother's. He hadn't felt like playing this night, but Lucy had insisted.

"Fancy a weekend in Berlin?" he suddenly asked, completely out of the blue, his bare foot stroking her knee.

"Berlin?" she stopped shaking the dice in her hand. "Berlin? Why Berlin?" So he told her about his day.

"Berlin, Jeeze! Couldn't he have picked somewhere more romantic: Venice, Rome, Athens …oh, sorry, not something to make fun of, is it?"

"That's all right. Happens every day. Keeps us all from going crazy. Anyway, Athens isn't in the game." He spoke without humour. Lucy stifled a laugh.

"Lots of history Berlin. Not sure about the clothes shops, but steeped in history. Up to you, love. I can wangle a weekend if you like. Don't worry; we won't be breaking into the wedding fund. I'd need half a day tops for police work."

"Sounds great, darlin'. I'm sure I could occupy myself for a half a day even without shopping. When you thinkin'?"

"This weekend too soon? All you'd need is permission to leave work a couple of hours earlier on the Friday. Regular flights from any airport. Heathrow looks best if The Met's paying."

"Yeah, let's do it."

She threw double two and landed on Fleet Street. She had two of the reds now.

+

Uncomfortable as hell, but he tried not to show it. Christine Stevens was all poise and purpose, yet Alexander knew she was uncomfortable, too. They had wanted to delay the Press Conference until after the weekend. Until Alexander had returned from Berlin. Assistant Commissioner Joseph Rowley had listened to their arguments. He had listened politely as was his manner. Listened and then ignored.

"Pressure from all corners," he had said. He meant the Commissioner. And that meant someone was leaning on the Commissioner. Politics, of course. Bloody politics, Alexander had muttered as he and Stevens left the AC's office.

"Lunch with some suits in Whitehall yesterday," Stevens informed him. "A quiet word in his ear, passed down the line from the Home Office. We live in a political world," she had agreed.

That was about as close Stevens usually got to letting down her guard in Alexander's presence. When it came to power politics, the detective inspector knew she could play the game. Was quite handy at it by all accounts.

Never call a spade a spade when you can get someone else to do it for you. He hoped he would never have to join the ranks of the fawning politicos in order to get promoted. Impossible, cynics would say. Haroldson, Alexander would reply, tipping his hat to the legendary Met Commander. Haroldson was retired now. His legend lived on. A dogged murder investigator who brooked no fools.

Alexander had been a rookie DC on one of Haroldson's investigations about nine years ago. A middle-ranking Home Office minister had wandered into the Murder Room during a Haroldson briefing.

"And who the bloody hell might you be? And what the hell are you doing in my Murder Room?" Seconds later, the Home Secretary had popped his head into the room, followed by an entourage of suits ...and the Commissioner.

"Oh, sorry, sir. We'll put the murder investigation on hold while you do the tourist thing."

Alexander could still vividly recall the look the Commissioner had given Haroldson. Hands stuffed into jacket pockets, Haroldson had returned the look in trumps. A Home Secretary for once showing signs of sense had defused an explosive situation by putting a hand on the Commissioner's shoulder and guiding him back the way they had come. "The officer is quite right ...can't interfere ...work to be done ..."

Police had moved on, politics had moved on; Alexander was fully aware a Haroldson wouldn't last a week in The Met these days. The Met's loss.

Stevens read the statement, Alexander took most of the questions. It was more than a month since the previous conference. There had been bulletins, yes there had been bulletins galore; sometimes two a day. They had gone as far as issuing one bulletin informing journalists that the Press Bureau would not be taking individual inquiries on the case. The Press and Media Liaison officers had complained that they felt under siege.

A sergeant from the Press Bureau sat alongside Stevens and Alexander. His job was to keep the throng packed into the hall in order. He would point at figures, giving them permission to ask a question. As hands shot up from the reporters, the officer tried to keep track, his hands and fingers working overtime to let them all know he had noted them and they would be called in some kind of order.

Stevens's statement had revealed just one new fact to the Press mob: police were looking into the possibility that the latest victim may have been poisoned. All very vague, but it made ears prick up.

Derek Chisholm, smiled down from a large white board behind the podium. He was wearing his Arsenal shirt. His was the largest photograph, being the most recent victim. Smaller photos of the others surrounded him. The one of the old widow disturbed Alexander. It was the only picture they had been able to uncover from the last ten years of her life; taken at an old folks' party a year or so ago. Her features were barely visible. The lab wizards had done their best blowing it up but it was fuzzy as hell. So that is the story of the last decade of her life, poor, poor bugger, thought Alexander. He knew too well that there were thousands like her in the capital. Thousands of old folk unloved and unwanted. All just waiting to die.

Alexander tried not to think of Berlin. Just a few more hours and he and Lucy would be far away from this madhouse. The AC had been most insistent: Don't mention Berlin. Not yet anyway; wait and see how the trip goes. And we'll need to time the announcement with our German friends. Can't go upsetting them.

So why couldn't this bleedin' conference wait till then? Politics, bloody politics. Though the AC would never admit it.

"No, I'm afraid we cannot go into details about the poison, it is just one line of inquiry we are pursuing."

"No, madam, we are not aware of any links between the victims. We are of the firm opinion that the killings are totally random."

"What about the people you have been interviewing?" asked a bespectacled man from the centre of the crowd. "Any firm suspects? Any charges imminent?"

Alexander coughed. "Several people have come forward. Four people have been charged with wasting police time; two others have been put into custody pending psychological reports. None are suspects.

"I would warn people against wasting the time of myself and my officers. It is an offence The Met takes very seriously. But please let me stress: if anyone has any information, any information at all, please come forward.

"Take a few minutes to look at these photographs. If you saw any of these people on the dates in question we wish to hear from you. The police are here to help and protect you. You have nothing to fear, all information will be treated in the strictest confidence.

"We are aware that some people may wish to remain anonymous. You can ring this number …" he pointed to a freephone number in large black type on the board behind him. "And one of our officers will speak with you.

"Any information at all," he again stressed. "It may not appear to mean much to you right now, but every little piece helps."

Reporters began folding notebooks; they knew the cops were getting desperate. This was an appeal, not a Press Conference. The seasoned hacks felt a shade cheated.

Stevens thanked them for their attendance and invaluable assistance and wound up the meeting. Reporters and photographers began racing for the door. Despite lugging large, heavy cases the snappers always seemed lighter and quicker on their feet. Deadlines, deadlines. Reporters from the dailies hung around muttering, grumbling, putting cigarettes in mouths ready for the great nicotine fix that awaited them outdoors.

"Poison; that will make a decent line."

"Doubt it'll make the front page."

"They haven't got a fuckin' clue."

"Why all the fuss over a bastard Arsenal fan?"

Laughter.

"Swifty?" Supping motions.

"Yeah. Which boozer? Don't know any around here."

"Four hundred words of this shite then a good few swifties for me I reckons."

"Ronnie's – hour from now. Synchronise watches gentlemen …"

✝

Curtis Maynard was just two hours into his first night shift and already feeling fidgety. He'd read the day's updates; that hadn't taken him long. Over in the corner, tucked away from the eyes of casual visitors, a Monopoly board had been set out. Craig Gough's idea. While away the hours yet keep night workers focussed on the task at hand. Who knows, it might even stir some grey cells into action. The game had been set up for just two players, using The Car and The

Iron. The latter was in case any of the ladies happened to find themselves on nights, said DS Pierce to a mixture of snarls and sniggers.

Officers spun a coin to choose pieces at the start of the shift. They played whenever they felt like it, some showing more interest than others.

DC Maynard had landed The Iron this night. He was pacing round the room, waiting for DS John Hodges to return from the loo and take his turn.

Outside noises – too muffled to make out – reminded him that The Met, like crime, never slept. Tonight was chillingly quiet, though. One call so far, another nutter. The dull buzz of the phone didn't so much make him spring into action as stretch and reach a lazy hand across two desks.

"Good evening, DC Maynard speaking."

"Hello, hello, I want Caroline. The woman. Sergeant Caroline."

"Who's calling please? Can I help? I'm afraid DS Peters has gone home."

"I am busy right. I want Sergeant Caroline."

Oriental. Lots of voices in the background.

"Thank you for calling, sir." Slowly now. "Sergeant Caroline is not here. Can you please tell me what this is about?"

The man seemed to have taken his mouth away from the phone and was yelling something in Chinese. "Lim. Tell Sergeant Caroline, Lim Man."

"You want Sergeant Caroline to call you back, sir? It will be tomorrow morning, OK?"

Maynard noticed DS Hodges had returned and was smiling at him. A puzzled smile.

"Yes. Yes." More background shouts. "She has number OK. Ding Ho. Lim Man."

"Ding Ho, sir?"

"Yes. Yes. My restaurant. She has been. I have to go."

"Thank you, sir. Will Sergeant Caroline know what this is about?"

"Fugu. I found her fucking fugu. Gotta go."

"Eh? Oh ..."

The phone was dead.

"And what was that all about, pray tell? Sergeant Caroline?"

"Fugu, John. Fucking fugu to be exact. Some Chinese guy has found our Sergeant Caroline's fucking fugu."

✝

CHAPTER NINE

✝

LUCY LAING was agog; the four Germans around the table were in stitches.

"Encore," clapped Ralf Vonderheid. He was almost in tears. His wife was laughing more out of astonishment, as were her sister and her husband. All spoke wonderful English; not quite in Ralf's class but sufficiently fluent to shame their guests.

"That's basically the sum of my repertoire," said Detective Inspector Rory Alexander, trying his best to keep the British end up.

"One more time then, please. I need to write this down," said Inspector Vonderheid of the Berlin Kriminalpolizei.

Alexander and Lucy had landed in the German capital early evening, checked into their hotel and were now finishing dinner at a quiet Italian restaurant. Art and food, that was all the Italians had over the Germans, Vonderheid had told his London counterpart. Cars, suggested Alexander. Didn't the great Schumacher drive an Italian car? He was laughingly informed that the Germans had kindly bestowed honorary nationality on Ferrari.

Vonderheid had agreed to give up his precious Saturday morning to go over the case with Alexander, but pleasure before business. They had polished off the tastiest and biggest meal Alexander had had in years and were sipping their coffees and liqueurs when Frau Katarina Vogts had asked if he minded her saying something.

"What? Anything. Sure, fire away."

Fire away? Did she know what he meant?

"It's just that you look very much like the British actor."

Alexander laughed. "Oh yes, people do tell me. Michael Caine right? It's the glasses."

Smiles around the table. They all knew Sir Michael Caine. "Funeral In Berlin," said Herr Vogts, nodding. "Long before our city was reborn."

"I don't do that one," said Alexander, rising to his feet. Was it the drink? What the hell. He twiddled with his glasses, coughed, as was his nervous habit

"Oi! You're only supposed to blow the bladdy doors off."

Puzzled looks, then giggles. Lucy wondered what on earth her fiancé was playing at.

"The Italian Job," informed Alexander. "Ever seen it?"

Vonderheid was chuckling now, his hands clutching his belly. "Oh yes. Is that from the movie?"

Alexander nodded, shuffled his feet, coughed again as if to clear his throat. "Oi! Don't throw those bladdy spears at me!" He was pointing at nothing in particular. The women appeared to be trying to hide their faces behind napkins.

"Zulu. A very British movie." Alexander shrugged and sat down, his lines from Michael Caine movies exhausted.

"What's It All About, Alfeeee?" sang a voice from a table about five yards away. Alexander turned to see a rosy-cheeked man holding up his glass as a toast. His hosts applauded as Alexander sat down.

"Well, I am amazed," said Lucy. "Where did that come from?"

"Stuart. DS Pierce. Christmas Eve down The Ferret. He was pissed out of his brain and wouldn't let me go until I'd performed. Seems he's a big Michael Caine fan; takes all sorts."

They discussed favourite movies, actors and actresses as they finished their drinks. Vonderheid settled the bill, dismissing Alexander's proffered credit card with a flick of his hand. He flicked his hand a lot.

"And now, let us find you a taxi to your hotel. A strange choice the Hotel Bogota." He looked knowingly at Alexander. "Tomorrow, nine o'clock not too early?"

"Nine will be fine. Thank you for a splendid evening."

Alexander walked off the evening's feast on a clear but cold Saturday morning. He had woken Lucy gently to inform her he was going for a stroll. "Go back to sleep, love."

A forced march to start with; he strode down Kurfürstendamm without paying much attention to his surroundings until he reached Koenigsallee. His only reason for going there was, well, to say he had touched base; actually set foot on 'the other' dark blue one on his European Monopoly board. He felt a little like those anoraks who visit all 92 English football clubs just for the sake of saying they'd done it. They were like mountaineers, or explorers, or vain tourists. Another notch on the belt. One night a week shortly after the Berlin killing he had studied the European board and decided that maybe one day he would make a grand tour of all the sites.

It was just turning six o'clock when he hit Koenigsallee. There were a few signs of life, and he had nodded at a few strollers, replied 'morgen' to casual greetings. He could pass as German so long as no-one asked him the time or what he thought of the weather.

Once over the road, he turned back and started walking much more slowly up the Ku-damm, glancing left and right to absorb his surroundings. The road markings weren't that difficult to comprehend thanks to his English map. Traffic was light by London standards for this hour, but he noticed the cars were predominantly smarter. Mercedes and BMWs stood out still in Britain; here they appeared commonplace. Ralf Vonderheid would later explain to him that the actual prices were about two-thirds of what the cars cost back home. Even cheaper when you considered German wages were higher. He tried not to linger at the murder scene, preferring to wait for Vonderheid's official tour in a couple of hours.

Lucy was still fast asleep when he arrived back in their room. He took off his suede jacket and realised his shirt was clinging to his back. He emerged from the shower to find Lucy sitting up in bed, rubbing her hair.

"Garlic," she grimaced. "Chuck us a fruit juice from the fridge, would you?" She gulped down the pear juice – the picture on the can looked like a pear, so they determined it was pear juice. Lucy's tastebuds could not confirm it.

"Ahh. That's better. Why is it all good food comes back to haunt you?" She ran her tongue over her lips. "Any chance of another?"

The Hotel Bogota was comfortable. It reminded Alexander of one in the west country where he and Lucy had spent a weekend last summer. So, this was where Jake's Danish/Polish victim had spent her last night.

They studied the map over coffee. "One o'clock," repeated Alexander for the umpteenth time, pointing to a spot near the railway station.

Lucy nodded, her mouth hanging slightly open. "Yes master," she drawled slowly as if in a trance. "One ohhh-clock …there." Pointing at the spot his finger had just left.

Alexander shook his head, finally understanding she was mocking him. Lucy laughed. "Treat your officers as cretins, do you?"

He put up his hands in surrender. "OK. OK. I just wanted to be sure you could find it."

"Can always ask a policeman if I get lost." She jumped out of bed, flinging her arms wide. "Hello world. Good morning Berlin."

"Right. I'll go and wait for Ralf downstairs. One o'clock then."

"One ohhh-clock." She had her arms outstretched, like a zombie. "Caf-fay Ray—"

He flung his towel at her and headed out of the door.

Alexander was sitting in a comfortable armchair in reception when Inspector Ralf Vonderheid breezed through the entrance.

"Morgen, Rory," he thrust out his hand.

"Morgen, Ralf." Alexander rose, folding the paper and placing it back on a table.

"Berliner Zeitung. I am impressed. But it is not my paper."

"I understood perhaps one word in fifty. Nice pictures, though."

"Dear me, I should have asked you to bring some newspapers. Is The Sunday Times still this thick?" He held his fingers several inches apart.

"Yes. The paper boys need to get a union."

"Did you sleep well? Lucy?"

"Yes splendid, thank you. I decided to skip breakfast. Last night's meal is still here." He patted his belly. "It was delicious. Thanks very much again."

Vonderheid raised his eyebrows as Alexander informed him of his morning stroll. "Exercise. Yes I think I can remember exercise. Not at six in the morning, however." He smiled a toothy smile.

Vonderheid looked four or five years older than Alexander. He was slightly shorter and had closely-cropped fair hair; not quite short enough to be classed as military-style. His paunch revealed signs of maybe too many good Italian meals. He could walk, though. Was this his natural walk or was he in a hurry to get back home and enjoy the rest of his weekend?

He was out of the door and guiding Alexander to the murder scene without checking to see if the Englishman was following.

"Here," he said as they stopped a few yards from where Schlüterstrasse met Kurfürstendamm.

Alexander examined the alleyway. There were no signs that anything untoward had taken place recently. The narrow alley separated the shops on the Ku-damm from the start of Schlüterstrasse; a car could just about squeeze down it.

"The body was found against the wall by a workman." Vonderheid shrugged as if to say "That's it. That's all." No blood, but Alexander knew that.

"The body was hidden by rubbish bags?"

"Yes, but it was not a serious attempt to hide. You know …three bags were just left on top of the body. The workman said the legs were clear, from the knees. And that is how it looked when we came. Does this look similar to London?"

"A little. Well, two of the killings …bodies have been found off main roads …down alleys something like this."

"Shall we continue? One more short walk and then I can drive you to my office."

The Berliner was off without awaiting a reply. He took Alexander on a 40-minute round-trip, stopping outside three bars which they believed the victim had visited that fateful, fatal night.

"This is the last bar," said Vonderheid as they stood outside the Hard Rock Café on Meinekestrasse. "One of the staff remembered her speaking a mixture of German and English when ordering her drink. He thinks it would have been around 11pm but was not certain."

"She was alone?"

"He thinks she ordered two drinks, but could not remember seeing anyone with her. They were very busy at that time, he said. You see, a foreigner would not stand out there. You will find as many people speaking English as German. But that does not mean they are English. The universal language of travellers and tourists, right?"

"Yes, that is why we are so poor at learning other languages I guess. Any idea when she left?"

"No. But we are sure this is the last place she visited. Well the last public place."

"Time of death was between one and three o'clock?"

"Yes, and the body was reported at 6.25. My car." Vonderheid pointed to a sparkling green Audi; a more discreet green than his own Astra.

Alexander tilted his head in appreciation. "Your own or a police car?"

"My weekend car. I sometimes use at work on Fridays; just to fill up on gas and have it cleaned." He winked.

Alexander wagged his finger. "Don't tell the tax-payer."

The Audi cruised along some minor streets effortlessly, though Alexander sensed it would rather be tearing down an autobahn. Even Audis needed exercise. Immaculate for a weekend car, with not an item out of place except for a raincoat and a briefcase lying on the back seats. Even they looked like an interior designer had positioned them. Alexander deduced that if Vonderheid had children they were either grown up or did not use this car. Alexander diplomatically made no comment as Vonderheid slipped in a CD of some German crooner warbling through classic ballads.

The parking space was tight yet Vonderheid managed it in one; he looked competent and at ease behind the wheel.

"This is her other hotel. We found more passports, five thousand euros in 50 euro notes, several hundred in smaller notes …and an address book."

"The address book helped you wrap up the gang?"

He shrugged. "We arrested six, charged five and sent the other back to Poland. It will not stop more coming."

"Her Polish passport was genuine and the Danish one false? How can you be certain?"

"We have checked with Polish police in Cracow. Yes, she is definitely Felka Babinski. Felka means 'lucky.'"

Alexander thought better of stating the obvious.

"We have little idea what the Danish passport was for," continued Vonderheid. "We are thinking it was easier to use that for checking into hotels. Few people speak Danish, and it would not be as suspicious as a Polish passport. The Poles have a poor reputation here."

"Your guess is that Jake picked up Felka at the Hard Rock, left with her and then murdered her?"

"Or they met soon after she left the bar."

"And your pathologist is certain she was killed in that alley?"

"Yes, why?" he frowned.

"I mean, she wasn't killed elsewhere and then her body dumped there?"

"There are no signs of that. Has that been the case in London?"

"No, no. I was just checking."

Vonderheid pulled out of the parking slot. "The police headquarters now, OK? You can see our files."

"Fine."

Vonderheid would make an excellent taxi driver. He appeared to know all the short-cuts, rarely using the main roads. Berlin was wide awake now, noisier and dustier. Alexander wound down his window, which surprised his driver. "Just trying to get a feel for the place, you mind?"

Vonderheid pretended to shiver but signalled assent with a slight curl of his mouth and eyebrows. A fruit and veg market seemed to have been set up in the middle of a smart residential area. "Illegal, but no-one seems to care," he said. "All foreigners who don't pay taxes. They make a better living than me."

They appeared to be shouting in a mixture of languages. German and probably a Slavic tongue, thought Alexander. People poured in and out of an S-Bahn entrance. It seemed as busy as the London Tube at rush hour on a workday.

"Special parking for our wonderful detectives." They had a choice of half a dozen vacant spaces. The dozen or so vehicles in the car park were all immaculate, and higher range models than you would find in a British police station. The same could not be said of the HQ. New Scotland Yard was pristine in comparison. Vonderheid snapped out an order and the receptionist produced a leather-bound book from under her counter. He rapidly scrawled an entry and, without speaking, passed the book for Alexander to sign.

"My office." He was off again, through a door which buzzed noisily as he entered his card. Alexander did not have time to assess the offices and rooms which branched off a long corridor.

By now he had realised Vonderheid was not in a hurry but that was his normal manner of doing things. Quick, quick …quick-quick, quick.

"I shall order some drinks. Coffee or tea with milk?" he smiled.

"Coffee will be fine. Milk, no sugar. Thank you."

"An English version, specially prepared for our friends from the Metropolitan Police." He pulled a thick folder from a drawer and dumped it loudly on his desk. "You will have seen most of it, but maybe there is some more detail. I don't think the Polish thieves are of interest to you. But there is a full interview with the barman at the café, the autopsy, some more of Babinski's family background. Please, you can take that with you."

"Great, thanks. Now, you have some questions for me? Anything you did not understand in our reports? I have one or two officers who could do with English lessons." Alexander smiled.

Vonderheid returned the smile, but it did not linger long on his face. He was studying his guest. "Let's wait for the drinks. Then maybe you can tell me about your last email. I am intrigued, yes? Intrigued is the word?"

Alexander nodded. He leafed through the files in the folder while waiting for the drinks. A stern-faced, uniformed female officer appeared after a few minutes. Biscuits, too. Good, he was starting to feel peckish now after his morning exercise.

Assistant Commissioner Joseph Rowley and Detective Superintendent Christine Stevens had sanctioned his request: he could reveal details of their leads to the Berlin force on the strict understanding that they were not to be made public without London's agreement.

Assured though he was that his Monopoly theory was accurate, Alexander felt more uncomfortable spelling it out for the Berlin detective than he had a few weeks back in the Gasbag's office.

Vonderheid did not take his eyes off Alexander until he had finished speaking. His face could have been a mask. Then he rose from the desk and walked to the window. He could just make out his car, maybe a hundred yards away across a lawn which needed trimming. The lawn — or his Audi — held his gaze for a few moments before he abruptly spun round, his hands pressed together almost like he was at prayer.

Vonderheid was about to speak when Alexander plucked a sheet of paper from his briefcase. "That is a photocopy of Jake's first note. And this ..." he was rummaging in his case ..."is the second. You may keep them, but please, for you and your superior only. My chiefs are most insistent."

"Your secrets are safe, Rory. No-one here will believe them anyway. I am joking, OK?"

"No problem. You are not the first to find it ludicrous."

"Ludicrous?"

"Unbelievable."

"OK. Thanks. Yes, it does seem ...ludicrous. But we are detectives; we deal in the unbelievable, the ludicrous. You heard of our cannibal? Well that is ludicrous, eh?"

"Too true."

"Of course, I know Monopoly, but I myself have not played the game. You say Ku-damm is on a German game?"

"Not German, European. Kurfürstendamm and Koenigsallee."Well, it could be on a German game. Alexander had not considered that, and more disturbingly neither had any member of his team.

"Amazing."Vonderheid paused, tapping his finger on his chin. "European game, you say. Hmm. Munchen; Munich as you say. Hmm. Yes, I do believe our game is from Munich. But I do believe there are games for other cities. Anyway, now you think he will kill on Koenigsallee?"

"No! No, no, Ralf. Not at all. We discussed that and obviously we would have contacted you immediately if we thought there was an imminent threat. We have no idea why he killed in Berlin. But from the London killings ...well, they are just random."

Alexander carefully explained the lay-out of the London Monopoly board to the German, passing him a folded A3 print-out which he studied with a fierce intensity. "Whitechapel, Regent Street, Vine Street, Pentonville Road," said Alexander pointing to the sites. "No pattern that we can see."

He could see Vonderheid appeared to be counting. He shook his head after a while. "Have you shown this to a numbers man?"

"Numbers man? You mean a mathematician?"

"Yes, that is it."

"No. My officers and analysts from our Hi-Tech Unit have examined so far. We do not wish to seek expert help from outside. There is too much risk of the details spreading. Already too many are in the know."

"I see. Yes. So you have no idea where the next killing will be? You are expecting more killing?"

"Yes, sadly we are. But we have no idea where. He is spoilt for choice in London …or in Europe. We have no idea yet why he was in Berlin. I mean he could be German, but we think not."

Alexander took a sheaf of papers from his case. "This is the only other information I have for you: a profile of the possible killer from one of our psychologists."

"But it could be Koenigsallee?"

"Yes, it could be. It could be one of a thousand places. But we think London. You see, we have no idea when or where. We have discussed possible surveillance, but there are too many options. We hope that perhaps closed-circuit cameras may pick something up, but that is just a hope."

"So you would not advise me to order look-outs on Koenigsallee?"

Alexander held his arms out wide. "Ralf, that is up to you. But look at the dates in London. No pattern. He could kill tonight, he could kill next month. He could kill in London, Brussels, Paris, Rome, or, yes, Berlin."

"It is hard, but I think I agree, I will have to see what the director says. Is there anything else?"

"I don't think so, Ralf. Unless you have any more questions for me? You can always email or phone me – any time, day or night. You have my home number and mobile."

"Yes, we shall remain in touch. Now, can I take you back to the hotel?"

"No, thanks. I am meeting Lucy in the centre. Point me in the right direction and I shall be fine. You know the Café Regensburg?"

Lucy spotted him striding across the square, sending pigeons scattering before him. "One ohh-clock, master. Caf-fay Ray-gansss-burgg."

Heads turned from tables to check out the strange voice. She smiled and lowered her arms; gave her fiancé a kiss on the cheek.

"You can stop that right now," he wagged his finger at her as heads returned to their own conversations. "Been here long?"

"Ten minutes."

"You broke your promise," he said, pointing at the bag by her feet.

"Nothing for me, darling." She drew out a football shirt. "For Gav, he's into this sort of thing. Are they any good?"

"Hertha Berlin, dunno. You're asking the wrong guy. I once got Halifax confused with Huddersfield and was suitably chastised by the anoraks down The Crown. I'm sure your brother will love it."

"Fruitful morning yourself?"

"Yes, worthwhile. Always nice to see how our allies operate. Some things I needed to tell him in person, too. I wanted to see how he'd react. Can't do that via email."

"Good. Drink, then let's play tourist, eh?"

"Sure. And I'm glad you went shopping."

"You are?"

Alexander managed not to blush. "Yes, because I need to do some myself. It can wait. But if we happen to pass a decent toy shop ..."

The top deck of the tourist bus was empty except for the two hardy British tourists. Hardly surprising as it was January and bladdy nippy, as Sir Michael Caine may have said. Lucy was clutching Alexander's arm and nestling her head on his shoulder. She was still smiling at the private impersonation he had just given. Maybe people from the upper flats along the route had seen him.

A bitter wind was keeping Alexander awake now. The weather was deceptive; just a few feet above ground level and the wind was biting into them. But they would rough it out. Upstairs provided a grand view of the Berlin sights. Building sites, more like it. Two colleagues had told him what to expect. The city was nearing the end of the biggest rebuilding operation since the end of the War. Old East Berlin was being transformed into an area suitable for its affluent twin.

"Allegedly, this line is where the wall was," said Lucy, reading from her guide book. The bus driver had given them headphones and pointed to the dials to turn for English language, but neither had bothered with them after a few minutes.

"Checkpoint Charlie." He nudged Lucy and pointed down to her right. "Is that it? How disappointing." He had hoped to see a few sinister Cold War characters lurking in shadows, surrounded by an overwhelming bleakness. This looked like a portakabin in the middle of a housing development.

The Brandenburg Gate was most impressive; Unter Den Linden pretty and maybe worth a stroll later. Alexander was fascinated by history, walking for hours and hours round ruins and buildings, reading inscriptions of the famous and infamous. Today, he could not get one infamous character out of his brain, a fictional villain come to life. Lucy seemed happy, though, which made him glad he had suggested a trip together. A slight drizzle was falling as the tour bus arrived back at the square. Alexander tipped the driver five euros and then dragged Lucy back to the Café Regensburg. The few tables that had been out front under the awning had been folded. A canvas fence had shielded customers from the elements but Alexander had still been surprised to see people sitting in the open air, coats or not. They sat snugly inside the Café Regensburg, drinking coffee and brandy for an hour, discussing options for their evening's entertainment. Alexander fought the urge to suggest the Hard Rock and a few other bars by their hotel. He smiled. Whatever you want Lucy.

✝

The weekend had been a success. More than sixty hours without speaking to anyone from The Met – very rare.

Two people had seemed about to leave messages on his ansa-machine but decided against it. Alexander had been relieved to avoid a customs spot-check. No drugs, no firearms, just 200 cigarettes and, ahem, two German Monopoly games. Ralf Vonderheid was indeed correct: the traditional German game was based on Munich. But a Berlin set had been produced more recently, and not surprisingly Kurfürstendamm was Berlin's Mayfair. He would email Ralf and post notes on the computer log, just to cover his back.

Where the hell next, Jake?

The taxi dropped off Lucy at her flat before heading for Annandale. Before catching their flight they had decided Sunday night was best spent alone so they could catch up on their chores before returning to work.

Chores rarely took Alexander long. This weekend he had heeded advice dispensed long ago by a fellow officer and travelled in clothes he was ready to discard. He had ditched a battered pair of boots, socks, tee-shirt and tatty pullover in Berlin. After unpacking at home he threw away another pair of socks, underpants and a one-time favourite shirt whose collar was starting to fray. He added a couple of towels to his washing to make up a decent load. He listened to the radio and the rattle of the machine as he typed out his report at the kitchen table. The trip had been worthwhile, he concluded, but he didn't expect much to come of the Berlin angle. He deleted the last part, replacing it with confirmation that he would keep in contact with Ralf Vonderheid just in case there were further developments in Germany.

The Crown sounded inviting as there was often a decent crowd on Sunday nights, but he wanted to be fresh in the morning. Nothing on the television could sustain his interest for long and after 20 minutes channel-hopping he skimmed through the two Sunday papers he had home-delivered. Both contained updates on his investigation, but no fresh news for readers who had been following the murders carefully. Good; no news was definitely good news for the time being.

Eventually he settled on the sofa, feet up as one of his free newspaper CDs span soothing tunes around the cosy lounge. Lights were low and dim, fire burning orange and red – an ideal setting for a romantic evening, but Lucy was a mile away and Alexander was busy with his thoughts.

A cursory glance at the CD cover informed him that he was listening to Sibelius, though he couldn't be bothered discerning which opus. He sipped his Lagavulin. At the price of the single-malt Islay Scotch, sipping was all that a detective inspector could afford. Now if he'd been a Hollywood heartthrob ...he glanced at the newspaper cutting she had sent him and he had taped to the bottle. An interview with actor Johnny Depp in which he claimed: "I don't drink hard liquor anymore, but I sometimes order Lagavulin just for the smell. It's so good. It's unbelievable."

That must require considerable self-discipline, Alexander mused. To smell but not to taste. This particular bottle had been opened 18 months ago. He had waited a few months out of embarrassment. It was a parting gift from a girl he had dated briefly without too much enthusiasm. He had been quite relieved when she had informed him she was returning to her native Kelso. Alexander gave her a book of French poetry and his best wishes. The Lagavulin went straight to the spot; yes, he had come out on top in that bargain.

The folder lay open on the floor. He picked it up and leafed through it again to remind himself of the contents. "Money for old rope. Total bollocks but here's the profile. Didn't bother having it shrink-wrapped. Ho! Ho!" Stuart Pierce had chuckled as he dumped the folder on Alexander's desk. "Holier than the Vatican; more get-out clauses than a Labour Party Manifesto." Pierce had trotted out his customary jokes for his own amusement if no-one else's. One day Alexander would get around to asking him what he had against profilers.

He started making a list. When they were children, Alexander and his brother

Kyle loved to sit with their mother at the dining room table and watch her making her interminable lists. Often they would join in. Not just shopping lists; Ivy Alexander had lists for each and every occasion. It was as if she could barely function without them. The boys were allowed to add one item each to the weekly shopping list. Rory would go for savouries, usually crisps (salt and vinegar please, added in parenthesis) but now and then he would request sausage rolls or pork pies. Kyle had the sweeter tooth: chocolate, always chocolate and no need for additional specifications. Mum could buy plain, milk, white, nut or fruit-and-nut – as long as it was chocolate Kyle was content.

Mum also had TV lists, and she was fair to a degree of which Solomon would have approved. If there was ever a disagreement over their evening viewing, she would devise a game to determine who had first pick. The boys liked the holiday list the most – what toys to take, which places to visit, which rides they planned to go on. When mum ran out of practical lists, she was a dab hand at conjuring up others. They played Desert Island Discs and discovered that mother was partial to really old men singing really old songs. They would list their heroes – for some baffling reason mum now favoured women, including that French one we burned as a witch. They would list their favourite movie stars, football players. They did meals one time and, naturally, Kyle's always concluded with chocolate.

Alexander was doodling on his pad, and smiling to himself as he recalled the evening he and mum teased Kyle for naming Jimmy Carter in his top ten famous Britons. At bedtime Kyle admitted to his older brother that he had jotted down Jimmy Carter because he had been struggling to think of any more famous Brits, and there was a Jimmy Carter in his class, wasn't there? And all the boys were always ribbing Jimmy Carter.

Alexander looked down and studied the list he had made this evening:

Single
White
Male
30-45
London / Britain
Mobile
Fit
Games / Monopoly

He put a circle around 'single' and drew a line to the side of the sheet, adding two question marks. Then he turned to the profiler's report.

Single. Sheila Forbes-Hamilton had written plenty on this but without a great deal of explanation; or any explanation that to Alexander seemed copper-bottomed. She suggested a loner, someone with few friends – if any – and someone who perhaps liked to keep secrets from friends. Someone who lived alone or possibly with an aged or infirm relative. She preferred the aged/infirm relative option, possibly a domineering maternal figure, and the killings were Jake's escape from his daily grind. Alexander took another sip of Lagavulin, lit a cigarette and thought a moment before adding a third question mark alongside 'single.' Underneath 'single' he wrote:

Bachelor?
Divorced?
Widowed?

He felt pleased with that and hoped mum was smiling down on him. The team had discussed it, of course. They had discussed it in ever-increasing circles. But for some time now it had been fixed, with no dissenting voices, that they were hunting a single bloke. Alexander could not recall whether it was Jobson or Hughes who had suggested a jilted saddo whose girlfriend had run off with his Monopoly board.

White. That didn't take him long to ponder and he flicked a tick by 'white.'

Then – hang a on a minute! Single was bugging him. He drew hard on his cigarette, drawing every last gasp before stubbing it out in the ashtray borrowed from The Crown – borrowed not by Alexander, officer, but by someone who attended the party he hosted last summer. Another sip, another question mark by 'single' and then another cigarette from his packet – his quota was well and truly scuppered, but Lucy wasn't there so who was counting?

Single. Single. Single. He was speaking aloud and adding question marks each time the word left his lips. Shipman – the devil's doctor was married. Sutcliffe – the Yorkshire Ripper was married. He lit his cigarette. Then his face contorted and he coughed two clouds of smoke towards the ceiling. The Wests! Rose and Fred West, probably the sickest of a diseased bunch, were actually a married couple. Rot ye in hell. By the time he was ready for another draw on his cigarette he noticed the top half of his sheet was covered in question marks of varying emphasis.

Male. Pause. Tick. Pause. No, leave it.

30-45. he returned to the profile. To be fair to Ms Forbes-Hamilton she readily conceded this was a shot in the dark, though in words more befitting a psychological profiler. 'As traditional board games are not the current vogue among the computer generation,' she intoned, 'it is reasonable to assume the game has some nostalgic connotation for the perpetrator.'

Alexander skipped three paragraphs of infant psychology which looked as if they had been lifted straight from a text book. He was intrigued by what Ms Forbes-Hamilton remarked next. 'Judging by the grammatical accuracy of the notes, we can probably deduce that the perpetrator (how she loved that word) is educated to a reasonable standard ...'

The CD had finished. Alexander grunted as he shifted position in order to reach over and press restart with his big toe. The fire showed more red than orange now but he refused to apply more coal; the Scotch was working its magic on his body if not his brain. He took his last sip of Lagavulin, corked the bottle, noticing a third still remained. Time for the cheap stuff. He rose and ambled to the kitchen, head down, shuffling and muttering.

Returning with a ten-quid supermarket special he settled back on the sofa and flicked a page on his pad. He began writing, not so much a list this time as random musings. Education, he wrote; does this rule out couriers, van drivers, taxi-drivers? He tried to drag from his brain the name of the cabbie who had won 'Mastermind' but it eluded him as successfully as Jake was doing.

As he was lighting another cigarette, Alexander flicked back to the first page and instinctively placed a firm tick by 'games/Monopoly.' That was bloody obvious, wasn't it? Pause. Wasn't it? Of course it was, so he managed to resist the very minor urge to add a question mark next to the tick.

His eyes wandered up the page, settling on 'fit.'

Fit. Tick. No Pause. If Jake turned out to be wheelchair-bound, Rory Alexander's resignation would be immediate, regardless of pending promotion and adverse effects to his pension.

Mobile. Laugh. Tick. Ms Forbes-Hamilton had penned 12 paragraphs describing to the incognoscenti just how jolly simple it was to get around London these days. Twelve paragraphs and all without a mention of the congestion charge.

London/Britain. "Correct!" Alexander raised his glass and toasted the room. London was indeed in Britain, but he placed an asterisk beside it, flicked the page over and returned to the profile. He had never seen so many possibles, maybes or perhapses on three sheets of an official police document — almost a match for the question marks on page one of his pad. DS Pierce had grunted something about England and Britain but whether or not his comment had held any significance was beyond Alexander. His memory — long or short-term — had witnessed better days.

Jake could be a Londoner. Jake could work in London, full-time or part-time. Jake could have a job which involved occasional trips to London. Jake may have studied in London. Jake could have friends or relatives in London. Or a girlfriend. Perhaps Jake followed a London football team. Ms Forbes-Hamilton went on and on. By the time he had finished his scribblings, the second page contained as many question marks as surrounded 'single' on the first.

Alexander flicked the pad and poured another Scotch. This would be his last as a glance at the wall clock revealed it was approaching a quarter to one. So much for an early night. Last Scotch, two more cigarettes. He nodded three times for his brain to acknowledge the message.

White
Male
Mobile
Fit
Monopoly

These, he had now determined with the assistance of Scotch, Sibelius and Benson & Hedges, were the definites. He placed double ticks alongside each before throwing his pad on the floor.

Alexander never got round to that second cigarette. He drifted off thinking of his mother, thinking of Jimmy Carter and thinking of his father, Roy, who had never been one for lists. Dad had always been too occupied in his shed to be bothered with lists.

✝

The alarm jolted him out of the most delicious dream. He had been nibbling Lucy's neck as she read an article to him from one of those magazines he could never understand why people bought. It was an article on lists. Celebrities had been asked to name their favourite words.

'Goal' said a footballer. Boring. 'Nibbling' said a drag queen. One-nil to the drag queen. Alexander had begun nibbling Lucy's shoulder.

'Medal' said an athlete; 'gold' said a swimmer. A dull draw.

'Cabinet' said a politician. Yawn.

'Scandal' said a BBC executive. 'Salacious' claimed a former tabloid editor. Alexander judged that one slightly in favour of the tabloid editor.

'Unbuttoning' said Chief Inspector Morse. Who? Morse? Alexander stopped nibbling and looked over Lucy's shoulder. "Well the photo is of John Thaw but it says Morse," said Lucy. "Unbuttoning. Dirty old devil," said Alexander. "Damned good word, but I'm more of an unzipping man myself."

He had returned to his nibbling. Then he was flapping his arm where the alarm clock should have been. Strange, it didn't sound as loud as usual. He realised he was on the sofa, creaked himself upright and shook his head. The fire had gone out and his lounge smelled worse than the pit at The Crown. Cramp delayed his stagger to the bedroom. He gave the offending clock a hefty whack and moved to the kitchen where he forced down two pints of water, cursing himself for failing to take a pint before he fell asleep. He hadn't nodded off on the sofa since his pre-Lucy days. His head felt fair enough, a dull fog at worst, but his mouth required a cleansing of Augean proportions.

Ten press-ups, ten sit-ups, ten back-stretches then a shower and he was pleased to learn he felt better than he should have – physically-speaking. As he was brushing his teeth for a second time he switched on the kettle, quickly followed, with some trepidation, by the radio. He drank his coffee as the news-readers poured out their litany of bad news. It was bad news for many – particularly for those with stakes in High Street retailers – but nothing to cause Alexander professional concern. He brushed his teeth a third time before he dressed and packed his briefcase, pausing to scowl at a packet of cigarettes on the table by the sofa. This would be a good day to quit. He shrugged and stuffed the packet in his jacket pocket.

Sensibly, he took the Underground to work. It was packed, too packed for him to contemplate reading his Berlin report to remind himself what he had written yesterday. He eased the irritation by thinking of Lucy's neck, and his five favourite words which had earned him a playful dig in the ribs: Nicked. Guilty. Beer. Lagavulin. Home-time.

"Home-time," he had added, "is definitely hyphenated so counts as one word. And, of course, home-time means I will soon be in the arms of my precious fiancée." He mentally erased 'nicked' and 'guilty,' substituting 'nibbling' and 'unzipping.' He was certain he would stumble upon a better word than 'home-time' by the time it was in fact home-time.

✝

"Hello, sir. How was Berlin?"

"Gut, sehr gut. Danke schon."

The desk sergeant beckoned down the corridor. "Well, welcome back to the real world. Something on your desk for you. Your pal."

"Jake?"

"Yes, sir. From Berlin, of all places."

Alexander quickened his step, almost running down the corridor to the Murder Room. It was busier than he expected for 8.30. DS Caroline Peters was wearing a raincoat and collecting papers from her desk. She looked about to scurry off somewhere.

DS Hodges and DC Maynard were dressed for the outside, too. The night shift, he realised, surprised they weren't already on their way home. DS Pierce had a tray in his hand, about to head for the canteen. Four officers were at their desks, heads down; two others were examining a map on a far wall.

"Morning all. Nice to see the place looking so busy. Something I should know? Letter for me I believe?"

"Morning."

"Morning."

Nods and muttered hellos.

"Bagged and in my top drawer, Rory," said Pierce. "Postcard, actually. Forensics are waiting for it. I said you'd want to see it first. Coffee?"

"Yes, sure, the usual please."

Alexander opened Pierce's drawer and took out a polythene bag. It had been sealed. He recognised the postcard, having seen hundreds similar to it in Berlin. One of the pricier ones, featuring a raised plastic casing on the front side, supposedly containing fragments of the old Berlin Wall. But it was the rear side which attracted his attention. Handwriting! At last, something to go on? All eyes were on him as he read; they already knew the contents of the card.

Dearest Edgar
Missing you, missing London.
Managed to entertain myself last night. I do
prefer the London nightlife, though.
Probably be back before this arrives.
Stay warm.
Best wishes as ever
Jake T J

Postmark the day after the Ku-damm killing. The writing looked strange, even at first glance. He read it again several times. Blue ballpoint. The pen was either running out of ink or the author had not applied much pressure when writing.

"Looks like a child could have written it," said DS Hodges.

"I need a snap of it – better have both sides. Then off to forensics." He looked around the office and handed the bag to DC Vicki Jobson who appeared to have been studying the wall with no apparent purpose. Look busy, even when you're not; who had advised him of that years ago?

"Have to dash boss, DS Hodges will explain."

"So, where is our Caroline in such a hurry to get to?"

"Chinatown," said Hodges. "A possible lead on the fucking fugu. DC Maynard took the call."

Maynard took Alexander through his phone call with Lim Man. DS Peters was on her way to meet DI Charlie Ormesby in Soho and then they were heading for the restaurant.

"It's all in the night log, Rory," said Hodges. "This isn't, though. Came through about 20 minutes ago on the fax."

The sergeant handed Alexander two sheets of paper. One was a cover sheet, the other an entry form: To the South-East District Monopoly Challenge.

✝

CHAPTER TEN

+

BUSINESS was slow, Lim Man glumly informed the two detectives. He was thankful that February and the Chinese New Year celebrations were on the horizon. Plenty of colourful carnivals meant plenty of customers for the Ding Ho and the multitude of smaller establishments dotted around Chinatown.

"Even my good friend Charlie doesn't come to see me in January," said the Ding Ho owner, and he wasn't smiling

"Let's all shed a tear for the richest man in Chinatown," said Ormesby, reminding Lim that he had dined there with a few friends just a week ago. He turned to DS Caroline Peters. "I should point out sergeant that what Lim means by slow business is that the restaurant is not for once jam-packed with people tucking into his most expensive banquets. He is never happy unless there is a waiting list at least 45 minutes long. Sometimes inscrutable, often miserable."

"Pouff! Bills, Charlie, bloody bills. Council tax!" He raised his eyes.

"What year is it?" asked DS Peters, going along with the small talk but eager to get to the point of her visit. Very eager but aware not to rattle Mr Man.

"Horse. Year of the Horse."

"Maybe I'll come along. I know a few of the crew like a good banquet."

"Book early. Yes book early. Not many spaces left. Very popular Chinese New Year."

"Now, Lim, why we're here ...you have a name for us?"

Phew! Peters sighed inwardly. They'd been there ten minutes and Man had appeared uneasy about broaching the subject. The restaurateur looked around him sheepishly. He edged his seat closer to the large round banquet table and leaned forward, facing slightly more towards Peters than his friend from the local station.

"I don't know if any use, but I heard a name. Down by Docklands market."

Ormesby knew the market. Not so much a traditional British market, more a collection of old warehouses with a few stalls set out nearby. Some big companies were trying to get footholds into the lucrative Asian food business but were having to locate their premises well away from the ethnic ones in Docklands. The gangs made sure of that.

Close by were small shops selling spices and frozen foods at a fraction of the cost the big stores charged. Communities basically kept themselves to themselves, but often Chinese, Japanese and entrepreneurs from the Indian sub-continent did mingle, putting aside their regional and business rivalries for once.

"Ashihei Takeuchi." Man had a stab at spelling the name, then decided to write it down.

"He deals in fugu?" asked Peters. She, too, knew the markets from her brief trips with the Chinese detective. But not the one Lim Man seemed to be talking about in his hushed tones. It was as if he feared his own staff overhearing him.

"He deals in anything. Be careful, dangerous man."

"Dangerous?" interrupted Ormesby.

"Can be very," shrugged Man. "Best just ask for information. You try to arrest and ...dangerous."

"Have you done business with him, Lim?"

Lim Man reacted as though Ormesby had just asked if he declared his Hong Kong property portfolio to the Inland Revenue. He gave the detectives an address and directions then excused himself to prepare for the lunch trade. "See you new year, Charlie."

"Sure, Lim," waved the inspector. "Might try and drag Sergeant Caroline along."

The diminutive Chinaman was muttering to himself as they left. Fucking fugu. Fucking Little Tokyo.

+

They found Ashihei Takeuchi doing a brisk trade, money changing hands at a rapid rate. He didn't bother to count the notes, just grabbed them from outstretched hands and handed over boxes from behind him. He had one assistant whose task seemed to be ensuring the heaps of boxes remained at a comfortable level for Takeuchi. The Japanese trader seemed to know which box the customer had requested without turning round completely. Peters and

Ormesby watched from a distance at first. People paid them a little attention, though not enough to make them over-wary. Whites were outnumbered at least 15-1, guessed Peters. Ormesby seemed the more at ease of the pair, having visited a similar wholesaler's with Man a few years ago. There was a long row of warehouses, all with their huge gates wide open. This was a part of Docklands still untouched by Yuppiedom, the buildings probably early-Victorian and in need of considerable repair. The outsides were, but Peters glanced inside a couple as she and Ormesby casually strolled along the quayside. Inside the walls had been plastered and painted or whitewashed. Spotless. The floors showed some signs of wear, scuffs where trolleys had been dragged, dents where heavy pallets had been stored. Scraps of paper and plastic wrapping wafted about. Not much dust, though, unlike her home.

Huge white signboards were covered in Oriental writing. Men were wiping the boards and constantly changing the contents. It reminded her of the bookies at the racetrack. Yes, must be market prices. After a while, she began to feel conspicuous and voiced her concerns to Ormesby.

"Yeah. They probably think we're from the Health and Safety. Best buy something to blend in a little better."

They had reached the larger warehouses now. One, displaying an anglicised translation alongside Japanese, consisted of several vast four-storey buildings. There must have been at least a dozen lorries outside waiting to unload. Japanese workers, dressed in just jeans and tee-shirts despite the January cold, scurried to and fro loading crates onto forklift trucks. Around one side of the building, more frantic workers were loading crates onto other lorries ready to carry the goods to all corners of the United Kingdom.

"Don't mess about, do they?" said Peters.

"They sure don't. Bit different in the afternoons, though. Most shut up shop by noon. Don't think there is much else down this way — just more wholesalers. Round the bend there are the Chinese ones. Same as this really, just a hell of a lot more of them. Fascinating place."

They backtracked and had walked fifty yards when Ormesby pointed to a small building. "Just buy some stuff here. Want anything?" She followed a couple of paces behind. Perhaps the locals would appreciate her deference.

A sign said 'supermarket', but that was the sole nod to the mother tongue. The symbols surrounding it meant nothing to the officers. Inside was like no supermarket Peters had ever seen. Nothing like the ones DS Dhiang had taken her to. No bright lights, no colourful packaging, no massive notices proclaiming special offers. And just a tiny counter by the entrance. A bespectacled old woman was behind the counter, reading a Japanese newspaper.

Peters couldn't tell if she was sitting or standing. Four aisles confronted them. Shelves – five high, held cardboard boxes, their fronts roughly torn open to reveal the contents. The pricing – or what they took for pricing – was all in Japanese.

Ormesby nodded to the old woman, took a basket and began strolling down the aisles, Peters once again trailing in his wake. He was on his second aisle before he reached into a box and plucked out a jar, grinning as he passed it to Peters. "At least the label's in English," he said.

Peters had never heard of wasabi and pulled her face.

"Delicious," was all Ormesby said.

Teriyaki. Yes she had heard of that. "Get one for me, too. You never know when it might come in useful. It's going on exes anyway. All part of the undercover op, boss."

Ormesby grinned at DS Peters. She was all right, he supposed. The inspector added a few more bottles, jars, packets and sachets to his basket before heading back to the counter. He recommended some for Peters to take for her colleagues.

Eyes were raised from the newspaper, a sigh and then deft fingers ran over the keys of the till. The old woman did not utter a single word. She pointed to the LED on the till and Ormesby handed over a £20 note. He considered asking her if she stocked fugu, decided against it and took his change with another nod of the head. I can play the silent type, too, Madam Butterfly.

They took two plastic bags for their purchases. "Now we really look the part," said Peters without hint of humour.

"How you want to play it?" asked Ormesby.

"You reckon he'll be winding up in an hour or so?"

"I would think so. Or he'll collapse if he keeps going at that rate for much longer." Takeuchi could be seen in the distance, arms still darting forwards and backwards.

"He's more likely to talk when he's finished business, right?"

"There'd be less risk of prying eyes then, too," said Ormesby.

"Might be best if you do the talking. I get the distinct impression that women are an endangered species around here."

"I think that sounds smart – not being sexist myself, of course."

"Ground rules: we don't tell him anything. Not even the vaguest hint what it is about. And we stress he is in no trouble if he co-operates. If he doesn't, well he may get visitors. OK?"

"Sure."

"Now, I suggest we just let him know now that we will want a word when he's finished flogging his salmonella. Give him something to think about. And then I'll buy you a coffee while we're waiting."

Takeuchi had not even deigned to glance at Peters. The whirlwind Japanese trader had spun round when Ormesby had placed his hand on his arm and asked for a word, please.

He had waved a handful of notes at Ormesby and spat something in Japanese. They were almost certainly not the kind of Japanese words used by the emperor, Peters guessed. A police warrant card did the trick. Takeuchi peered at it closely, then blew out his cheeks. "What you want? Can't you see – busy now."

His accent was an improvement on Lim Man's, though the Chinaman had the edge on vocabulary, especially of the four-letter kind.

"Nothing to worry about, sir. Nothing at all. We need your knowledge and help, please." Ormesby had tapped his own head for effect. All the while smiling his most reassuring smile. "We'll be waiting over there. Thank you."

Takeuchi had glared at him for a moment then resumed trading; with a little less speed and confidence this time. His customers had caught the scene and some had stepped back a pace or two.

Within seconds, though, trade was back to normal, but Takeuchi kept stealing glances at the English couple. Dangerous, Lim Man had said. He looked wary and worried rather than dangerous.

They had visited the market's equivalent of a burger van. Comprehending nothing on the menu, Peters had slowly requested two coffees, pointing at a large tin of Nescafe on a shelf. It was difficult to ruin a cup of instant coffee but the van owner had done his best.

Now they were sat on two metal mooring posts by the quayside. Ormesby declined the offer of a cigarette. Peters finished her coffee and sat as if examining her shoes; Ormesby's eyes flitted along the upper storeys of the warehouses. Havens for illegals, no doubt.

He noticed how the buyers didn't seem to walk; they ran like they were in a desperate hurry to get somewhere. Maybe in fear that their purchases would go off.

The crowd was dwindling, but Takeuchi showed no inclination to pack up shop. He attracted a few more customers with his sales pitch, which was a very shrill sales pitch. Finally, another glance at the two detectives and then some words whispered into the ear of his assistant. He could have screamed at him, the detectives would not have grasped a word of it.

His assistant began taking crates back into a warehouse. Takeuchi took off his overall, revealing a bright, red woollen pullover. He rubbed his hands vigorously on the apron and then wiped it across his forehead several times.

Sweat had reappeared on his forehead by the time he had slowly ambled across to Peters and Ormesby. Peters was feeling the cold but steeled herself not to show it. "Licence. I have licence," he said, pulling a tatty sheet of paper from his trouser pocket and holding it out. He was addressing Ormesby.

The inspector decided there and then against introducing DS Peters. He smiled his most reassuring smile again, and again it had no effect on the Japanese man.

"It's not your licence we are here about, sir. We think you can help us. Just some information that is all."

"Eh? Information? What information?" Takeuchi was glancing around to see if anyone was watching. His fellow traders were too busy packing away their wares. Sounds and smells from several thousand miles away filled the air. Peters noted the traders were dutiful about collecting the scraps of paper and boxes that blew along the quay.

"Fugu. We hear you can get fugu."

Takeuchi threw out his hands and began shaking his head from side to side. So violent were his movements his head looked in danger of toppling from his neck.

"Not allowed. No fugu. Not me."

"Please listen Mr Takeuchi, you are not in any trouble, OK?" Ormesby spoke slowly, though both officers knew the trader had a pretty good grasp of English.

"Course no trouble. I have done nothing wrong. I am good businessman."

"Yes, of course, sir. But let's say someone wanted fugu; you could get some, right? You can import the fish from Japan?"

"Nooooo." It was long and drawn out.

Peters was back to examining her shoes. Ormesby continued pressing Takeuchi gently, more reassurances. Without warning the sergeant raised her head and grabbed Takeuchi's pullover, dragging him closer to her.

"Don't fuck us about, we haven't got all day. You can tell us here or you can come to the station."

At last, a different reaction; one of shock, disgust, possibly contempt. But a little fear lurked at the back of his eyes. Fear or discomfort. Peters preferred to think fear. It gave her a tiny tingle to know she had rattled him. He had understood completely. "Answer a few simple questions and we will be on our way. You will never see us again, got it? GOT IT?"

He waited a moment before nodding meekly.

"Someone asked you for fugu recently. Who was it?"

He glanced around furtively before replying: "Two customers. I …I sometimes have people send from Japan for them. Maybe five, six times a year."

"Two people buy from you? Two people in London?"

"One has people in Manchester. They like fugu. Other …yes …London."

"When did you last buy any for them?"

"Manchester …maybe two months. London …few weeks."

"Your London buyer, what does he do?"

"Do? You mean business?"

"Yes."

"Chef. Good Japanese chef. He has special clients."

"Special clients?"

Takeuchi nodded. "No fugu in restaurants."

"You mean he prepares fugu, but not for sale in restaurants?"

"Right, yes. For business people …parties. Fugu good to impress, OK." Oh, yes, they were impressed by the qualities of fugu.

"Did he say who wanted the fish a few weeks ago?"

"New client, he said. Could I do special order? He paid extra for two weeks. Usually three, four weeks get here."

"Did he tell you the name of this client?"

More violent head shaking.

"But the chef has a name. We need the name of the chef and your friend in Manchester and we will be on our way."

Takeuchi again glanced around him. The sweat was pouring from him now; down his temples, forehead and cheeks. He gave them the names, and snarled his annoyance at Ormesby for checking the spelling. Before the officers could thank him he had turned and was striding to the warehouse.

"I suppose I should now commit hari kiri," said Ormesby. "Isn't that what the Jap blokes do when they lose face?"

"Good job you're not a Jap bloke then, isn't it? Buy me a pint and it can be our little secret."

"Deal. Then we can visit Mr Ichisake Kimiyama and see who he's been cooking for."

"Sounds more like a motorbike than a bloody chef."

+

The extension was smothered in hanging baskets. Perhaps when spring came and their contents were in bloom the two-storey building would look less incongruous. It had been an essential addition to the 17th century cottage, though. Irene Montgomery and her late husband, Arthur, had had it built in the mid-70s to host their ever-growing hoard of Monopoly memorabilia.

At first, they had plenty of room to spread out their collection. Now it resembled a grand, old junk shop. Irene had taken a breather when Arthur passed away of a congenital heart ailment almost a decade ago. She had considered selling off their collection at first; it was too painful for her to even look at the stuff. Within seconds of walking into the extension she would be weeping for her beloved. Then one day, the tears stopped. A friend had popped by to ask if she would still be running the annual South East District Monopoly Challenge. It was what Arthur would have wanted, wasn't it?

Yes, of course, that was what Arthur would have wanted. It brought Irene back to life. And it had brought Detective Inspector Rory Alexander and DC Sarah Hughes to Eastbourne. Alexander was enjoying the guided tour; Hughes was bewildered. What a bloody hobby, she was thinking.

"Ted Heath," said Alexander. "You know him?"

Mrs Montgomery did not know the former Prime Minister personally, but was pleased to inform Alexander that the photograph showed him playing the first Russian version of the game. Dozens of photographs adorned the walls, most housed in modest steel or black wooden frames.

DC Hughes pointed out TV host and politician Gyles Brandreth; a European champion, said Mrs Montgomery.

Bleary-eyed and laughing, a group stood outside a pub the constable seemed to recognise. Mrs Montgomery could be seen peering between two strapping young men clutching pints. They represented Eastbourne's team in a Monopoly pub crawl around London. "We didn't do too well, but the boys had a grand old time," chuckled the old lady.

"These five people," she said, pointing to a photo of three men and two women who looked to be in their mid-40s, "they're from Brighton. They went round the world in 80 hours, playing Monopoly in all six continents. Got the strangest looks in Peru …I think it was Peru, they said?"

The first room on the upper floor contained hundreds of games, at least as many as Alexander had seen on Boxing Day at 'The London Board Games Store';

the main difference being these were ALL Monopoly games, no aliens allowed. Printed, laminated cards identified the versions. The largest section contained novelty versions, including a replica of a set commissioned by Alfred Dunhill comprising golden hotels and houses. It had set the designer back £20,000. An even more luxurious set had been made, featuring diamonds, said Mrs Montgomery. DC Hughes's ears pricked up. At least she hadn't nodded off, thought Alexander.

Some of the sets were housed in glass-covered cabinets. Alexander studied a 1930s American original; a simple white box, corners a little frayed but the board and cards seemed to be in excellent condition for its age.

"Missing one house; great shame," tutted Mrs Montgomery. "Great shame."

Alexander knew the names of the properties off by heart, but was reluctant to admit it. He browsed a while longer before noticing their hostess was standing by the entrance to the final room. She seemed impatient, but her mouth was twisted in a smile of sorts.

She wasn't impatient to get rid of her guests; no, she was merely keen to unveil the exhibition's piece de resistance. A gigantic table, supported by 16 sturdy legs dominated the room. Again, it was glass-covered.

Alexander let out a soft whistle as he peered at a huge papier mache model of London, featuring all the Monopoly properties suitably highlighted in their respective colours. A plaque read: Designed and created by Arthur Montgomery and James Hetherington 1962-65. Special adviser Irene Montgomery.

"Special adviser," she clucked, shaking her head. "That means tea, biscuits, encouragement and sympathy."

Alexander noticed tears welling up in her eyes. They were happy tears of happy times.

"Those boys had so much fun. Every spare waking hour they sweated long and hard: a true labour of love. Thirty-two months it took them; they were like two poor lost souls when it was completed."

Alexander put a comforting arm around the woman's shoulder. "It is wonderful, absolutely wonderful. You must be very proud of your Arthur."

She looked up at the inspector and beamed.

"Wow! It's as big as my lounge," said Hughes, suddenly finding her voice.

"It's as big as my whole flat," laughed Alexander, giving Mrs Montgomery a gentle squeeze before releasing his arm. The trio examined the model in silence for a few moments. It truly was of epic proportions. Then Alexander turned to face Mrs Montgomery, a hand gently back on her shoulder.

"Now, Irene. Is it all right if I call you Irene? We have a few questions we think you can help us with."

"Irene is fine; everyone calls me Irene. I'm not Victorian you know; just Mrs Montgomery on all those damned bills which seem to arrive more often than they used to."

"Thank you. Now how about we go downstairs and maybe Sarah here could make us all a cup of tea?"

"I am more than capable of putting the kettle on," she replied, leading them out. "The conservatory if you wish to smoke …it's the only room I allow smoking."

"Wherever you wish Irene. The kitchen is fine by us."

"Oh." She sounded disappointed.

"Or the conservatory if you prefer," replied Alexander, feeling puzzled.

"Well, I was just hoping one of you smoked. I mean a lot of police officers do, don't they? I mean, I wouldn't mind one myself …seem to have run out."

"The conservatory it is."

Alexander took out a crumpled packet of Bensons from his inside jacket pocket, opened it and offered them around.

"Very kind of you. These days, well I can make one packet last a whole week, sometimes two. Never could pack in for good though. Arthur, well once upon a time he was like a chimney, till the doctor warned him. Then he stopped overnight. Just like that! He claimed he never felt any pangs. So I tried …to give him moral support. But I had to nip out now and then, while he was distracted."

They were all smoking, and ignoring the two huge plates of biscuits and homemade cake. Alexander would ask to take some for the journey back, just to be polite.

"Now about the fax, Irene." He moved his armchair so he could face her without twisting his body. "This is secret, between us, please. We are looking for someone who has been wasting police time – a lot of police time."

Mrs Montgomery shook her head as if horrified that anyone could do such a thing.

"Phone calls to companies, hoax deliveries, that sort of thing. We had a boy turn up once with a dozen pizzas." He laughed. "It's funny in a way, but not funny deep down, you see."

He's a convincing liar, thought DC Hughes. She would have believed him.

"Well I just received a phone call last night. About eight o'clock, it was; and she gave me that number …I thought nothing of it."

"She?" shrieked Hughes, before checking herself and pretending to cough.

"The caller was a lady?" said Alexander, all smoothness and calm.

"Yes, yes. South African woman."

"Did she tell you that, or did you guess from her accent?"

"Both, I suppose. It was a poor line, but I could tell a foreign accent right away. I think I had just pinpointed it when she said something about having to catch a flight to Pretoria early in the morning."

"Strange time to phone, wasn't it? Eight o'clock on a Sunday evening?"

"Yes, I suppose so. But she said she had been having problems with her computer. Chris Hetherington does that for us, James's youngest boy."

"You mean a web site?" asked DC Hughes.

"Yes. Amazing and all beyond me."

"James would be the man who made the model with your Arthur?"

"That's right. Two lovely boys he has. Allan's got two children, just started senior school I think. Chris is still at home. He plays now and then. Wouldn't call him keen, but he kindly offered to make the web site and he and his father try and keep it up to date."

Hughes yielded ground for Alexander. "We may wish to speak to the father and son, Irene. Perhaps you could let us have a contact number before we go."

"Of course."

"Now, can you please try and tell us everything the woman said last night."

Mrs Montgomery paused before continuing. "Well, she said she was not able to get the entry form from the computer. I forget the words she used ...not one for computers and that mullarkey. Anyway, she was ever so polite. Then she asked if I could kindly fax a form and one of her team members would fill it in and return. That was when she said she would not be able to do the form now as she was off to Pretoria."

"And so you faxed the form to the number she gave you first thing this morning?"

"Yes. I can just about work one of those things. Chris is always popping round to fiddle with the knobs, though. He says I must be pressing the wrong buttons. I would have tried to send it last night but I was watching a detective serial on the television. Don't think I shall see it through to the end; I have trouble with the Newcastle accent."

"Did she give her name?"

"Yes, yes. I wrote it down." She pointed to a telephone, sitting on top of a small wicker table in the adjoining room. "Would you mind?" she asked Hughes.

The constable returned with a small pad and showed it to Alexander. Mrs Montgomery had written down the Murder Room fax number and the name Mrs Jacques. Alexander studied the pad, his eyes catching his colleague's. Very funny indeed, they were both thinking.

"Thank you, Irene. Can you remember anything else Mrs Jacques said?"

"Hmm. Not really. She thanked me, said she and her team looked forward to meeting us all at the championships."

"Well if you do think of anything else, don't hesitate to call. Here's my number, if I am not in one of my colleagues will help. Thank you for you time, Irene. You've been most helpful."

"But you haven't had any cake?" Mrs Montgomery seemed distressed to be losing her company.

"Oh. I don't suppose you have a bag, do you? May I take some for the journey?"

"Of course, of course." She rose and hustled off into the kitchen, returning with two large freezer bags.

Alexander smiled as she used the tongs to place two slices of cake in one bag and a selection of biscuits in the other. "May I be very cheeky and ask for one more piece of cake, Irene? I have a sergeant who possesses a very sweet tooth."

He winked as she added three more pieces of cake to the bag.

"You know you remind me of someone," said Mrs Montgomery, escorting the detectives to the front door. "That actor ...whatsisname?"

"Brad Pitt. Yes, quite a few people tell me that. Many thanks again, Irene." He took her hand and kissed it ever so lightly, causing her to blush mischievously as she waved them off.

+

"Mmmmm."

"Mmmmm what, Sarah?"

"Mmmmm Brad Pitt."

They laughed and drove in silence for a while. Hughes was pleased with the morning's work. Pleased that DS Pierce had been out of the office and she had been able to accompany the boss on an outing. And she was pleased that – one silly yelp apart – she didn't think she had cocked up anything. She felt her career advancing.

"What do you think, sir?"

"I think, Sarah, that I should maybe get some contact lenses."

✝

Mid-afternoon, a whirlwind whistled down the corridor into the Murder Room. Caroline Peters was disappointed that not one officer looked up from their desks. A dozen or so of her colleagues all otherwise engaged. She loudly placed her handbag on her desk and strode the few feet across to DI Alexander.

"Hello, Caroline. Won't be a minute. Sit yourself down."

"It's a woman, Rory. We're looking for a woman."

"Yes, we know. South African woman."

"Oh! Aussie woman I was told."

✝

CHAPTER ELEVEN

✝

DS CAROLINE PETERS was typing away furiously. DI Rory Alexander placed a coffee on her table and stood sipping his, watching over her shoulder.

"He swore blind an Aussie. Said he'd worked there for two years – cheffing in Adelaide. So he knew Aussie accents."

Alexander turned away and strolled round the room. He had four officers on the South African angle, checking with the embassy, checking international companies – especially those with offices in London, Pretoria and Berlin – checking flight times for London to Pretoria, on the very unlikely chance that the woman had been telling the truth.

He knew several officers had overheard DS Peters's comments and were now perhaps not working with the degree of enthusiasm and diligence they should be. The word of an old woman, who admitted the phone line had been a bit dodgy; the word of a frightened Japanese chef who specialised in preparing illegal and potentially lethal dishes. Was one of them telling the truth? Or were they more games Jake enjoyed playing? Too many dead bodies told Alexander this was no game. No matter what his personal beliefs, angles had to be pursued.

Forensics had drawn a blank on the postcard from Berlin; so the fax and the fugu were the remaining hopes of progress.

"Back in a minute, need a piss," he told Peters as he poured the dregs of his cup into a plastic wastebasket.

His ears pricked up at the sound of a newspaper being flicked through in one of the cubicles. Smoke wafted over the top. Not one of his boys, he hoped.

He took off his spectacles and splashed water over his face. Edging closer to the mirror he examined lines around his eyes and mouth. Were they laughter lines or his first wrinkles? His brain felt tired but at least his eyes looked clear, the grey perhaps stronger than the blue. His cheeks were just the right side of rounded, without looking flabby. Maybe contact lenses would suit him. He put his glasses back on and stepped a couple of feet backwards, tilting his head from side to side. Michael Caine, indeed.

DS Stuart Pierce burst in, clearly desperate. "Who's a pretty boy, then?" he gasped without breaking stride. "Ahhhh, that's better."

"Hello, Stuart. No joy at forensics then."

"Nope; not that we expected any, right. Just another fibre for Thread's collection. Tiny one under the stamp – no match. How was the south coast?"

"Come back into the room and I'll fill you in."

Peters didn't seem to mind having another bloke standing over, staring at her computer screen. Her fingers were fluent, her typing amazingly accurate, even though her mouth was operating a few seconds in advance. It puzzled Pierce how she managed it. They were hearing her story before she had written it. Sarah Hughes came over to join the group, though she stood a few feet behind the men. She had just finished editing Alexander's report for the composite database: the one used primarily by the people on high, the Commissioner and the Assistant Commissioner and possibly a few suits from the Home Office. Special Branch dipped into their files now and then, just to check if any inquiries were stretching into their sphere of operations.

"That's it," said Peters, folding her arms. "I'm sure he's on the level, Rory …for the very simple reason that he was scared; shit scared that his boss would find out. It was Inspector Ormesby's suggestion to wait until he'd finished his lunch shift, which was a smart call. I don't think we'd have got anything out of him if we'd dragged him out of the kitchen.

"Once I'd assured him we'd no intention of telling the owner if he told us the truth, it was hard to shut him up. It all poured out too fast to be made up. Either that or he's a bloody expert story-teller."

"I don't doubt you, Caroline. I'm swaying towards the idea that the accents are part of the game. A 70-odd-year-old woman and a Japanese chef – it wouldn't be too difficult to con them would it? You think his description is reliable? Spoke to graphics?"

"I wanted him in with graphics this afternoon, but he is back in the restaurant at five. He's agreed to come first thing in the morning. I thought that was fair enough?"

"The sooner the better. Make certain he's here tomorrow then, without fail. It's not our job to worry about his bloody boss." Alexander adopted his most commanding voice. Peters immediately absorbed the message.

"Sure, boss. I just …"

"I want a picture of this bitch, Caroline. Disguised or not, I want a picture."

"You think this is Jake, then?" said DS Pierce.

Alexander nodded. "I know what you're thinking Stuart. But, no, I am sure this is Jake."

"Enlighten the rest of us ignorant sods, Stu?"

"He's wondering if this woman is an accomplice, am I right?"

Pierce made the faintest signs of assent with his face. "But …well …"

Alexander interrupted again. "But you and DC Hughes here went to see our psycho-star, and her expensive, expert verdict was that it was obviously a bloke, almost certainly a British, white, single bloke."

"Right again."

Alexander slammed his fist on the desk. "Going outside for some fresh air and a fag." Now that was statement in need of psychoanalysis.

"Join you," said Pierce. "Can I scrounge one, boss? Seem to have run out."

"You mean you seem to have run out *again*. Come on, then."

Outside actually meant a walk to St James's Park or Parliament Square. They didn't like to loiter close to the Yard.

Alexander started heading for the park. Pierce caught up and they strolled side by side in silence, Alexander not getting out his now seriously crumpled and depleted packet of Bensons until they were in the park. His second cigarette of the day. The park was busy but peaceful, a haven from the mechanical whirrs a few dozen yards away. Tourists stood examining maps, pointing this way and that; regulars bustled off, their destinations clearly fixed.

"Everything all right, Rory?" Pierce ventured to break the uneasy atmosphere.

"Yes, suppose so."

"I thought you'd have been a bit more upbeat – about the new leads and all."

"I am, really I am. Bit pissed off at myself to be honest."

"Why's that then?"

"The woman thing – none of us got it, Stuart. Not fucking one of us. Not me, not you, not Stevens, not even fucking Rowley. You ever work with Haroldson? No, he'd be before your time. 'Rule nothing out, nothing at all; until you have disproved it to complete satisfaction.' We ruled it out without pausing for breath, Stuart. And we are supposed to be London's finest. Christ! Fuck it!"

"No good kicking yourself, Rory. History. Time to move on. And if I had a penny for every time you brought up Haroldson …" His words drifted away as he realised his boss was in no mood for levity, showing no outward sign of even hearing him.

"You know what Lucy said to me in Berlin? We were in a café, just a few hours after I'd left the German cop …and she says to me: 'How can you be so certain it's a him?' What did I do? I gave her all that shitty shrink crap."

"Rory—"

"And then she says: 'Oh, all right darlin'. Just seems strange writing Dearest Edgar. I mean girls write 'dearest', but blokes?' And what did the great Detective Inspector Alexander do? He tickled her under the chin and said: 'Perhaps he's gay.' And then the great soon-to-be-DCI Alexander laughed his bleeding head off."

Pierce smiled. "Some girl your Lucy. Best of British to both of you."

"Yeah, she puts up with a lot. Come on, let's see how many pigeons we can kick on the way back."

✝

Four was definitely a crowd in Alexander's office. Ideally, there would have been five but DI Keith Blake was off for the day. Alexander had walked and smoked his anger out of him and had summoned his available sergeants to a private meeting. He berated himself initially and then his closest aides for dismissing the possibility of a female killer all too swiftly before he pressed on.

DS John Hodges was given the thorny task of recalling 30-plus officers from the outposts to join in the tomorrow's no-stone-unturned inquiries.

"Anyone gets prickly, John, just mention it is sanctioned by the AC." Alexander stood up, clapped his hands together and walked to his window, turning round to face his colleagues. His hands were pressed against the windowsill and his feet stretched outwards. "No decent leads and then suddenly two appear together."

"Like London buses," said DS Pierce. "Not that we should complain."

Peters and Hodges smiled; Alexander's facial muscles showed not the faintest twitch.

"We can now assume our Jake is a female. We can assume that, but we will not rule out the outside possibility that this woman is simply an accomplice. She could be a willing accomplice or she could be unwilling."

"Unwilling, sir?" queried Hodges.

"Duped, John. Outside chance, I know, but Jake could have persuaded an acquaintance to make that telephone call, and even to go hunting bloody fish for him."

"Taking it one step further, Rory, could even be two women?" said Peters.

"Indeed, Caroline. Let's keep that in the back of our minds."

He rose from the windowsill, edging closer to the three sergeants. Now he stood with his hands in front of him, clutching the back of his chair.

"The accents: South African or Australian, which I would say includes New Zealand?"

Faint nods from the group.

"Again, at the back of our minds. No barking up wrong trees. I'm no expert, but I would have thought it was pretty simple for someone with modest skills to fake an accent on the phone, or to fool someone for whom English was a second language. But at least we know we are looking for a woman now, right Caroline?"

"Oh yes! Mr Kimiyama seemed impressed. 'Pretty but real crazy,' to quote him. They met twice. Once in the street close to his restaurant. He had spotted her as he arrived for work; she was outside telling one of the waiters it was a shame they didn't have fugu on the menu. So he followed her, made his pitch and they fixed a date for three weeks later. Second time was at a friend's flat where the exchange took place. She was dressed exactly the same on both occasions."

"This friend's flat; why did they go there?"

"Kimiyama lives with his girlfriend. Got the impression it was a one-room fleapit. Says he only does blowfish to save for a bigger place when they get married. He borrowed a friend's place for a couple of hours for the demonstration."

"Demonstration?" said Hodges, turning to Peters.

"It's in the report, but, yes, she wanted a demonstration. She handed over two grand for four blowfish – well over the going rate. Well, the going rate in Japan. Her line was that her husband was a big businessman with connections in Tokyo, and she wanted to prepare a special meal for some very special Japanese clients."

"And he believed that total shite?"

Peters shrugged. "Like I said, he thought she was crazy. All he was concerned about was the cash. Now he's worried, and nervous. He doesn't know why we are looking for the woman, but I did tell him he was in the clear if he co-operated.

"He didn't say it in so many words, but I'm pretty certain he's not licensed to make this fugu; the Japanese authorities are very strict about licences. Chefs need to pass some kind of exam to obtain the licence. Don't try this at home kinda thing. Woe betide anyone unlicensed who does. If the fish don't kill yer, the law will.

"He says he saw a master chef back in Japan make it on several occasions. So he used one fish to show the woman which parts were safe and which weren't. She took that one, warts and all so to speak, and the three whole fish."

"So, we're looking for some woman with the deadliest freezer in Britain," said Pierce.

Alexander managed his first smile in several hours.

"Sounds like my 'ex'," said Hodges. "What would you like tonight, love? Pizza? Or shall I rustle you up some fugu?"

"Right," said Alexander. "I need to see if Detective Superintendent Stevens is back before I head off. Tomorrow, if our chef pal isn't here smartish you go and get him, Caroline. Prompt Gough that you may need him. I want to sit in with the artist, too."

"He'll be here, sir. Last thing he wants is us lot crawling round his work."

"John, I still want the Pretoria angle pursuing. But I also want a list of all official British Monopoly organisations – and their members. If you need more bodies, just get them. DC Hughes is right now working on Internet sites; she should be able to point you in a few directions."

"Stuart, soon as we get this photo-fit I want it round the key witnesses of all the victims – discreetly, though. As many bodies as you need. Now, I'd better warn the powers that be."

＋

Alexander got off the Tube a few stops early, wanting a walk for exercise and for thinking. He'd decided against going to The Ferret, the crowd of officers there was dwindling anyway, mainly as a result of the longer hours the inner circle was putting in.

He wasn't one to keep strict tabs on his colleagues, didn't mind them popping out for a drink now and then. But the whole atmosphere had changed over the past fortnight certainly. Suddenly they had seemed short on conversation. Officers would down their drinks speedily and then make some excuse for having to go back to the office for a few final calls, or to check their reports, before heading home. He didn't want to lose The Ferret gatherings and logged a mental note to invite the crew there himself.

Christ! Was it only yesterday he'd been in Berlin? The off licence stocked it, the Italian white wine he and Lucy had enjoyed last Saturday night with their German hosts. He bought three bottles. They could have one tonight; rare on a Monday but what the hell. A few glasses in front of the TV and he could apologise to Lucy for mocking her.

She beat him to the flat by two minutes. The sound of the key in the door surprised her, as did the broad smile and the plastic bag held high.

They were sipping their second glasses of wine and staring aimlessly at the TV screen when the phone rang. Alexander rose, stretched and drowsily ambled into the kitchen.

"Yes," he growled, not giving his name or number.

"Sir? Is that you, sir?"

He recognised the voice. "Alexander speaking."

"Sir, King's Cross. Looks like Jake again."

"DC Hughes, that you Sarah?"

"Yes, sir. I was just leaving and the call came in literally a minute ago."

"Bloody hell! Can you get there? Is DS Pierce there?"

"I think he mentioned a quick one at The Ferret then he was going home. Want me to try his mobile?"

"No, I'll try for him. Who else is there?"

"Just the night crew, minus DI Blake. He called in saying some family illness."

"Get a uniform to drive you over. I'll meet you there quick as I can."

"Yes, sir. By the way, it's platform six."

+

The young man barely noticed the figure standing by the train door, reading a paperback book. Five minutes from London, best to have a pee now rather than pay at the station.

He had just entered the small cubicle when the door crashed into his back with a sharp crack. It sent him hurtling forward and his head smacked against a bar above the window. Before the curses had left his mouth, an excruciating pain shot through his knee and up his leg to his groin, forcing him to lose balance.

Spinning his head round, all he could see was the hugest pair of sunglasses staring down at him. Then something blurry came down over his head and round his neck. He was kneeling now, on his right knee while one hand clutched his left knee, exacerbating the pain. Pain he had never felt before in his 23 years. The other hand was grappling with something which was tightening round his neck.

His eyes were wide open but he could focus on nothing. His mouth was wide open but no sound could find its way out. All he could hear was the rattle of the train. He found himself being raised by the thing around his neck; raised and twisted round so he was facing the toilet bowl. Then something pressing against his back, forcing his head down. It felt like a boot.

Now the man's arms were grappling aimlessly, clawing with little effect at his neck, chopping powerlessly at the foot on his back, and then switching to support his knee. His neck, his knee, his back – his brain could hardly cope with the multi-targetted assault. Life and strength were ebbing rapidly out of his solid frame. Suddenly his face was drenched; the toilet had been flushed. He felt pieces of paper stick to his cheeks, toilet paper was being rammed down the bowl, forced into his mouth and making it even harder to breath. The toilet flushed again and he blacked out.

She kept twisting and tugging on the belt. She was now standing on his back with both feet, pushing one of his shoulders into the bowl, too. She flushed the toilet twice more, though little water appeared. Then she placed one foot on the floor and one on the back of his neck. With a sudden violent movement she jerked on the belt, throwing his head back and out of the bowl. She heard a crack. Only then did she release the pressure on the belt, slowly twisting it free.

Her hands were red from the exertion. She studied the palms, knowing blisters would appear by the finger joints soon. She was breathing heavily and felt clammy. The muscles in her forearms ached.

The rattle of the train had changed pitch, and she could hear voices and scuffling noises from outside. The train was pulling into the station and people were collecting luggage, dragging bags along corridors and preparing for speedy disembarkation.

Jeeze! She hadn't locked the door. She hastily flicked down the latch. Then she flushed the toilet one last time – more of an instinctive reaction than for any particular reason. She knew the unknown young man was dead.

Lucky escape there. Clumsy job, too. Clumsier than she had expected. She should have realised water didn't stay in the bowl on train toilets. Yes, poor planning.

Never forget the detail. She took several deep breaths to try and compose herself. That had been a physically draining couple of minutes. Ah! but it had been different, a new experience. Another step along the extreme edge. She was amazed how quickly her heartbeat slowed. Her face was a mask as she scratched her calling card into the man's right arm.

The train screeched to a halt; she could hear the sounds rising and then diminishing as passengers poured out into the great city of London. She counted to a hundred slowly.

A final check in the mirror, minor adjustment needed to sunglasses, and then her movements were swift, confident and composed. Out through the door, closing it behind her. Onto the platform and a brisk step until she reached the stragglers.

Then she stopped, glanced behind her. No-one there. She looked up at the sign displaying destinations for the train on the adjacent platform. The Cambridge train was due off in two minutes.

Bowing her head, she took off her sunglasses and placed them in a case. Both case and gloves went into the right pocket of her coat. Then she took off the coat and placed it over her arm. She turned round and jogged to an open door.

"Can I pay on the train? Didn't want to miss it?"

"Course you can love. Settle yourself down and we'll be away in a minute."

"Oh thank you. Thank you, " she said, breathlessly.

What a lovely Irish lassie, thought the guard. Bet she has a beautiful singing voice.

+

Alexander arrived a good 15 minutes after Sarah Hughes. She was pacing around on the platform, three uniforms close by; one was her driver, the others from the transport police. She seemed relieved to see her boss.

"I've had it cordoned off best I could, sir. Both corridors inside, and here as you can see."

"Good," he said, though he had seen much neater work.

"Professor Carmichael and the woman doctor arrived just a minute ago. They're in there now. That's the woman who found the body. A cleaner."

Alexander looked towards a bench further up the platform where another uniform was consoling a woman.

"You spoke to the cleaner?"

"Not yet, sir. Thought it best to wait for you. I've told the others no questions until you got here. We're just making sure she is all right."

"And is she? Fit to talk?"

"Very shook up, not surprisingly. But we can give it a go."

"Let's do that. I'll just make my presence known to the professor."

"There's the two transport bobbies, sir. They've seen the marks. That's how the call-in got routed through to us. I've told them not a word, but you may wish to emphasise the message."

"Yes, of course." He rubbed his chin, worried. The circle of information was growing wider. Victim number six: how many knew about JTJ now?

"Inspector. Now why do you save your juiciest killings for Dr McMillan?" Carmichael was easing off his gloves.

The cleaning woman had been unable to shed any light on the murder. She had found the body about ten minutes after the train had arrived. Her screams had brought colleagues running to her.

Now the detectives were standing outside the train toilet. The space was cramped, and forensic officers were hanging around, eager to get on with their work. Alexander introduced DC Hughes to the two pathologists, realising he himself had not seen Professor Carmichael since before Christmas. Helen McMillan smiled at him, but she seemed a shade more reticent than at their previous meetings. Carmichael could be an imposing figure.

"Nothing so fascinating as blowfish, I am afraid," continued the senior pathologist. "Common and garden strangulation on first examination. I am hoping we can find something on the slab."

What a strange breed, pathologists. Common and garden strangulation: that should make the relatives feel a whole lot better. Alexander was wary about revealing the new information to the pathologists, and had primed DC Hughes.

"Jake again for sure?"

"Yes, he chose the right arm this time."

"We may get something from the fingernails. Some signs that there may have been a struggle."

"More for the forensic boys than us, Helen," said Carmichael, peering down at her.

"As you can see, we haven't been able to examine the body properly yet," continued Carmichael.

Alexander was leaning to look into the toilet. It was difficult without touching anything. There appeared to be a thick object in the victim's back pocket. Probably a wallet. He was tempted to try and take it out, but was wary of entering the cubicle. Something at the back of his mind told him this was different, maybe, just maybe, forensics would find something.

"That is how he was found? With his head down there?"

"Yes. You can just see the marks on his neck. Considerable force was used by the look of them. Shall we let the photographers get to work? I was planning to go to the lab early tomorrow, so I can get started first thing. That OK with you Helen?"

"Sure. I'll be there for six."

"DC Hughes?" Alexander moved to one side, making room for the constable to view the scene.

Sarah Hughes was transfixed, but masked her fascination well and was beginning to understand how the vets operated emotionally. She was once again working as Alexander's oppo as Stuart Pierce was out of reach. Stuart Pierce: the most cynical and heartless of the bunch. Yes, she could learn from Pierce.

This was the first scene she had witnessed in the flesh, though like all her colleagues she had pored over numerous photographs time and time again. Her murder experience stretched to two banal cases: a domestic love triangle and a business dispute over a few grand. Knives used inexpertly and messily on both occasions. This was something else.

"What do you make of all the paper, sir?"

"And the soaked head …looks like the loo was flushed. Maybe sh …aaaa-choo."

Alexander had almost given it away. Almost said SHE. And even after labouring his point to DC Hughes that they keep the docs in the dark for now. Slipping old boy, he scolded himself.

"Bless you, sir. That cold's still lingering."

"Thank you," said Alexander, wiping his nose with his hand. "I was saying maybe Jake was attempting to suffocate or drown this bloke. Let's not try second guess our medical experts for now." He nodded at the pathologists. "Come on, nothing else here for us. Let the SOCOs in."

Alexander offered to buy Hughes a quick drink at a nearby pub, while the forensics worked. Then he would go back and search for an ID before returning to his patient fiancée. She gladly accepted; nothing to go home for, home being a one-bed flat south of the river in Clapham.

"Didn't look like the work of a woman, did it, Sarah?"

"Not unless she is a Russian shot-putter."

"Or used poison again? A crowded train, I don't get it. Would you call that stupid? Reckless?"

"Or cocky. I wouldn't call Jake stupid, but the fax and now this …"

"Maybe, yes makes sense." He sipped his pint, a bit too warm for his liking. "Now, Sarah, where next? That's what really bugs me more than the why. Where the fuck is this bastard, male or female bastard, going to strike next?"

"That's what the crew do back at the office."

"Eh?"

"Stare at that photo and wonder where next." She reddened before continuing. "There was going to be a sweep, till someone said that was too sick."

Alexander half-smiled. He had played a few sick games in his early days. Wagering small amounts with senior officers as they headed for murder scenes. A quid for guessing closest the victim's age, marital status …he had to admit it helped many get through the daily grind in their murky world.

"I tried working backwards once," Hughes added.

"What do you mean?"

"I tried to decide which would be the best one to leave until last. I thought Mayfair would be a fitting coup de grace. Then I thought about second last – that was the end of that thought process."

"Well let's hope we get lucky before Jake decides the game is over. The mortuary would run out of space."

Hughes was just about to ask if he'd like another drink when the inspector's mobile rang. He quickly silenced the musical chimes from some 70s classic.

"Finished here, sir. You wanted another look before we had it removed?" It was Warfield from forensics.

Hughes had to break into a trot to keep up with Alexander as he marched the short distance back into the vast railway station. Crowds had gathered by the entrance to the platform, trying to get a peep at what was occurring beyond the police tape. Four uniforms guarded the area from ghoulish eyes.

Alexander and Hughes slipped on the gloves offered by one of the white suits. There was now a rucksack sitting in the area by the cubicle.

"It was two carriages down that way. One of the transport cops claims to have touched it," said Derek Warfield. Alexander had met Warfield at numerous murder scenes, and they had spoken on the phone. Yet the detective had no idea what the man was like under his work outfit.

"Have a flick through the rucksack, DC Hughes." Funny how he could switch like that, she thought. One minute it's Sarah, next minute it's DC Hughes. It felt to her like he had been programmed.

Alexander made straight for the victim's back pocket. Sure enough, a wallet. It contained a fair amount of cash, 300 pounds and as much again in euros. Large denominations. Some credit cards and an ID card favoured by continental Europeans but not the Brits — yet.

Dutch, 23 years old, name of Ruud Koeman. Alexander checked the other pockets of the victim's jeans and jacket. A discounted ticket from Edinburgh to London, some coins, a scrap of paper with the name and address of a London hotel scrawled on it. The inside pocket of the jacket yielded a handy-sized map book of the UK.

"Camera, clothes and a couple of books," said Hughes, raising herself up from the rucksack.

"Take down the details from his wallet and get them back to The Yard."

The body was being carried out on a stretcher before the two detectives had reached the end of the platform.

"My car's that way."

"Right, goodnight, sir."

"Yes, goodnight, Sarah, and good work tonight."

"Happy to tag along, sir."

"I mean it — good work. And it's late, have an extra hour in bed in the morning." He walked to his car knowing full well she would probably be back in the Murder Room before him the next day. Give her six more months before she began to lose that breathless exuberance.

＋

CHAPTER TWELVE

✝

IT WAS boredom that did it, if Antonia Helm was honest with herself. Not love, not remembrance, not sentimentality, and not even a false sense of revenge.

Of course, she had tried to convince herself it was all of the above in some measure. How she pined for her beloved, saintly Robert Allan Abrahams – the flower of his generation. Her first soulmate; her one, true soulmate and almost certainly the only soulmate she was destined to have.

Memories of their two glorious years as inseparable as Siamese twins often made her weep. Helm sobbed herself to sleep frequently; too frequently a counsellor would have claimed, if she had ever bothered to seek assistance. After all it was seven years now.

She was weeping and pining and reminiscing that mild September night in London, and she was mightily bored. Did the boredom prompt the tears? That was something she had never asked herself. Boredom was not something she was ready to confess to.

But some virulent concoction of emotions triggered a reaction beyond comprehension; a reaction which set the 30-year-old American on her perverse and wicked course of action.

She'd walked to Whitechapel in a trance. Hours later she could not recall why she had chosen Whitechapel or why she had walked rather than grabbed a taxi, or why she had chosen that particular young woman. Maybe it was because she had looked so sickly and seemed such a soft initial target.

No, hours later, Helm had absolutely no idea why she had done what she did. All she knew was that she was still high on the buzz of it all as she paced around her hotel room several miles across town.

Helm hoped and prayed that Rob had witnessed it all from on high.

"Whitechapel, Rob. It's one of the brown ones on the British game. Remember how we used to dream of coming to London together? Well, I'm here now, my shining star. Here for both us. Goodnight precious."

She moved the small Monopoly board off her bed, noticing that her token was on Whitechapel. Of course, that was why she had gone there. Of course.

Helm could not sleep. A large brandy from the mini-bar had been downed in one gulp to settle her nerves as soon as she was safely behind her hotel door, sweating and wide-eyed after her exertions.

Now she had exhausted the four sachets of instant coffee, didn't feel like tea and was way too wired for bed still. Champagne! Yes, a toast to us, Rob.

The half bottle from the mini-bar was uncorked and two glasses poured: one for me and one for you, Rob. She sipped hers slowly, letting the bubbles tantalise her tongue. Then she downed Rob's in two swallows before sliding between the sheets for welcome sleep.

✝

SEVEN YEARS EARLIER

The meal was frightening, horrifying. But it was also exhilarating. Antonia had come to realise this past year what life was all about. She was slowly losing Rob and was desperate to taste life at all its extreme edges. Extreme was almost a 100 per cent Rob word, extreme edges a certain 100 per cent Rob phrase.

Atlantic City had whetted her appetite. The first murder was not really a murder. No, not really a murder. The second had been Rob's idea and had scared her at first, until Rob had talked her round. His logic was beyond reproach. Why not? he had said. People murder every day, for the most ridiculous reasons. So why shouldn't we murder for pleasure? Life's extremities, he had explained. Life is all about extremities, experiencing them, enjoying them.

She locked her bicycle to a drainpipe and bounded up the steps to the flat. Rob was already there, sitting in the living room with Juichi Baisotei. They were drinking *sake* out of blue Japanese cups.

The two men were enrolled in the doctorate programme at Harvard's Law School. They all knew Rob was unlikely to see graduation. He looked fine this evening, though. His face was deathly pale as usual, but there was fire and life sparking from his eyes. Yes, his eyes were most definitely alive, and so was his brain – the keenest, finest, most brilliant brain Antonia Helm had ever encountered. "A drink for my rose queen, please Juichi. Then let's eat. Don't know about you two but I am positively famished." His laughter was feeble, but Helm beamed at him. She had just about come to terms with the tragedy of his life and no longer wept in his presence.

Rob was a haemophiliac. Eighteen months ago he had been pronounced HIV positive following a blood transfusion after cutting himself on a tiny fragment of broken glass. Doctors said any infection or virus; any serious loss of blood could prove fatal. Rob's heart and lungs were weak, too. The medical experts could not be certain whether the causes were hereditary or a result of too many childhood pranks and tumbles. Fate had dealt him a poor hand: a brilliant brain and a body growing more pathetic and wretched by the week.

Rob had just two friends in the world. He had plenty of admirers, of course, though perhaps jealous scholarly rivals would be a more fitting description. People looked up to him for the ease with which he grappled with the trickiest of legal issues. Riches and perhaps one day the Supreme Court would have beckoned for a man with a reasonable life expectancy.

He had known of Antonia within a few days of commencing his undergraduate course. She was difficult not to spot. Tall, athletic, fresh-faced and always smiling – the prettiest by a country mile of their law class, and very popular.

She had known of Rob, too. He soon stood out as by far the most academically bright. But it was only in their final year that they really came to know each other. A chance gathering at a café near Harvard Square – a meeting to run through a projected legal debate their class was slated to produce for the whole Law School. People drifted away, leaving Antonia and Rob silently stirring their drinks. Antonia lingered at first out of pity for the frail genius. Words came in fits and starts from her, but they flowed from Rob. Not just legal jargon, course work, but any word he seemed to utter took on an almost lyrical resonance to her ears.

He was fun, too, she quickly discovered. A devilish sense of humour. Two hours later, after discussing Shakespeare, Wilde, Roman architecture, Renaissance art and, naturally, baseball, Antonia had blurted out an invitation to dinner. He had politely accepted, insisting she allow him to bring the wine. They spent ten more minutes discussing his passion and knowledge of wine. She hadn't touched a drop of alcohol but she walked back to her flat more than a little light-headed. Dizzy on the word webs this spidery guy had spun.

Their friendship grew and grew; they became an item – though never in that sense, they insisted on telling anyone bold enough to ask. She visited his parents' humble home on the northern shores of Lake Michigan. Mr and Mrs Abrahams were overjoyed that their only child had a girlfriend, such a pretty girl, too. He sufficed to introduce her as a very dear friend from college.

He spent a weekend with her family – a more well-to-do home with a swimming pool on the outskirts of Providence, Rhode Island. Her two younger sisters had looked quizzically at the strange creature Antonia had brought home. He certainly had a skill at making the girls laugh, but he didn't look the type for their all-action big sis.

Antonia managed a modest law degree and then decided to apply for a postgraduate course at the Business School. Rob and Juichi Baisotei were the only two of their class to successfully apply for the law doctorate course.

Juichi had been satisfied playing second fiddle to Rob – a distant second. People were jealous of Juichi, too. How could a Jap score such high marks? He didn't even speak English properly, for heaven's sake.

Rob and Juichi became close, academically. They would compare notes, work out problems together, and occasionally watch baseball on TV. But Juichi was never really allowed into the other, private world shared by Rob and Antonia.

Until this night.

Juichi had wealth behind him, and an overbearing father who wanted nothing but the best for his son. Mr Baisotei was a senior partner in a lucrative law firm in Sapporo, the administrative capital of the island of Hokkaido. To celebrate his son's acceptance for the doctorate, the father invited him on a business trip to Tokyo.

They had a round of golf at a very exclusive and expensive course in the Japanese capital. Just the nine holes thankfully as the father had clients to meet in the afternoon. Juichi had no love for the game, and certainly not much ability. But it made his father happy to be out in the open air with his son, and Juichi was grateful for the exercise.

In the evening, Juichi was invited along to a celebratory dinner. Father had concluded contract negotiations between two electronic firms. His clients were delighted with the deal.

Like all Japanese, Juichi had heard of fugu and the deadly blowfish. But he knew no-one foolish enough to have actually tried it. Now his grinning father – he'd never seen him so excited – was asking him to taste some. Not asking, telling.

The other four men around the table in the back room of an unassuming restaurant stared at the young man, their eyes all laughing in unison.

Were they making fun of him? Was this a joke? Some middle-aged suit's practical joke? A test? To the father, it was a ritual, bringing his son into the world of business he hoped he would one day dominate. A ritual, a coming of age. This is what wealthy businessmen do. He decided against adding 'and then we go gambling and whoring.' Maybe when his son had completed his doctorate.

Juichi could not lose face, not in front of his father and most definitely not with all these powerful men watching him with their narrow but excited eyes. He braced himself, smiled and stuck his fork into a thin slice of fish. He had no idea whether or not there was etiquette supposed to be involved in this culinary death-wish. His tongue rubbed against the fugu, the texture was pleasing. He chewed and rolled it around his mouth, swallowed and then smiled approval at his father.

"Better than McDonald's," he said.

Oh how his father laughed. "Better than McDonald's!" He slapped his thighs, slapped his son's back, a little too hard. He was laughing so hard Juichi feared a heart attack.

Wasn't *that* funny, father, he thought. But he noticed the guests were acting as though they had never heard anything so hilarious in all their lives. Then they all started tucking into the delicacy with a surprising gusto. Not one showed any element of fear. More dishes and wine and *sake* flowed.

Juichi managed to glance at the bill before his father whipped it off the tray, throwing it back with his credit card and waving away the offers from his clients. The offers were not serious. Juichi noticed. They were gestures, gladly withdrawn with a shrug and a smile of thanks to their host.

The son could not believe the figure he had just seen: 41,000 yen. Six men had just eaten a meal which cost 41,000 yen? Almost 400 American dollars a head? The wine and *sake* were the best quality, but 41,000 yen?

Rob had been enraptured by Juichi's story. He had never heard of fugu, never heard of blowfish. A week later Rob knew more about the delicacy than Juichi.

He had ransacked the vast libraries of Harvard University for books and magazine articles, and spent hours using online facilities.

He shared his new knowledge with Antonia, of course.

"A new extreme, a new edge for us. We must get some, my rose."

She, too, was entranced by the story. And, yes, they needed to try it. That was only natural. Any sense of wariness one would have expected in a normal girl had ceased to exist for Antonia. Life on the edge with Rob was what mattered. Few could even begin to understand the ecstasies they reached.

If only their colleagues could have seen them that day at Bleecker's Rock, standing on the precipice sipping pilfered Bollinger from pilfered 200-dollar flutes and knowing that one-and-a-half paces forward meant plummeting 900 feet into hostile waters. "I think we'll give the extreme edge a miss this day," Rob had laughed into the wind.

If only their colleagues could have seen them that day at Portland, Rob at his tattiest, looking barely able to stand, with a walking stick in one hand and a book in the other. He was reciting passages from Moby Dick and collected 57 dollars and 34 cents for his efforts.

Juichi told his friend not to be ridiculous. It was almost impossible to find fugu outside Japan, and stupid to even try. He reminded Rob of the dangers. More than 100 deaths in Japan last year. Yes, said Rob, he had read that and, yes, he knew all about licensed chefs. Only the stupid died, those who weren't trained how to prepare fugu. But the U.S. Food and Drug Administration had granted certain restaurants licences. Surely we could persuade someone to sell us a fish?

"Why don't you go to one of those restaurants then?"

"Hardly the same is it?"

"What's not the same?"

"Don't you want to see a whole fish? To look at a fish that can poison up to 30 men? Don't you want to touch it? And then …to eat it? Doesn't it simply thrill you?"

"We aren't trained, Rob! You know how long those chefs have to train to get a licence?"

"But, you see Juichi, I have found the preparation details."

One night, about three weeks after Juichi had told him the story, Rob invited his friend back to his apartment and showed him the Internet site. Juichi browsed through the Japanese version, studying the detailed graphics accompanying the words informing the viewer how to make fugu and survive – hopefully. The site should have carried a health warning, but it didn't.

Juichi shook his head, said no, no, no, definitely not. Please stop being silly, Rob my friend. But Rob would not stop. Hardly a day passed without him cajoling Juichi, nagging away, imploring at times until one day he agreed. He agreed to try at least. Yes, he would try.

No promises.

In fact, some of Rob's sense of adventure had rubbed off on Juichi. It became a secret binding the two friends closer together. A fortnight later, Juichi bounded up to Rob who was sitting on a bench reading a law journal.

"I think I can get some!"

"Hello, Juichi. What was that?"

"I think I can get some blowfish!"

Rob flung down the journal, paying no notice as two loose pages fluttered free. "Really? How? When?"

A friend knew someone who worked at the Japanese consulate in Boston. For the right price he would agree to ask a chef he knew down in DC. He would tell him it was for a scientific experiment. He would agree, he was certain. Always best to keep on the right side of useful consular officials. For the right price he could get some. The right price was $1,000. Rob looked crestfallen, no way did he have a grand going spare. No worries, insisted Juichi. He was well in control of his generous allowance, plus his father had made emergency provisions available. Juichi did not like to boast, but a thousand American dollars would not be missed from the account.

Now, there it lay in the kitchen of Juichi's apartment – a thousand dollars of fish. It was hard to believe. The table was in the middle of the kitchen and the three friends peered down at it.

The fish was dead unfortunately. Rob had ideally wanted a live one as he had read that they were meant to be killed as soon before eating as possible. They were very lucky to get a whole blowfish. Normally they were killed and cleaned before export to the handful of American restaurants licensed to sell fugu. Still, here it was, on the kitchen table before a trio of crazy Harvard students.

The blowfish was about 18 inches long. Almost 60 dollars an inch, Rob informed Antonia. Luckily, a fair proportion of it was edible. He pointed out the underbelly to her. That was the part that swelled when the fish felt threatened, earning it the alternative names of pufferfish or swellfish. The eyes were big and dark. The mouth looked small, though it was difficult to tell as it had been sewn shut. Fishermen did that to stop the fish from killing each other after they had been caught. Three of the fins were silvery coloured. The rear one was brownish, matching the skin. Spots and scales reminded Rob of the fish his father and uncle had caught on Michigan.

Antonia thought the blowfish was ugly, and it didn't look like it would be attractive to the palate either.

Juichi unwrapped a thick cream-coloured cloth that was on the worktop by the shelves: brand new, glittering sushi knives. They looked chillingly sharp.

Pots, pans and dishes had already been prepared by Juichi who seemed keen to impress his friends, especially Antonia. He had only exchanged the briefest of greetings with her in the past.

"Shall we commence?" said Rob, feeling they had stared long enough. His friends continued to stare for a few more seconds before nodding in tandem, as though controlled by a puppeteer.

"First the fins," said Juichi, reading from the notes the two men had prepared earlier. The fins were soaked in *sake*, more part of the ritual than adding any distinctive flavour to the drink. Rob did the fins then handed over duties to Juichi whose hands were the steadier.

Now Rob was reading, and looking up to watch Juichi at work. He cut away the skin slowly. Very slowly. It was possible to eat the skin, if the scales and spikes had been removed, but Rob and Juichi had decided this was maybe just a little too tricky for them to attempt. Even Rob knew some limits.

The blowfish's head was chopped off and discarded without much ceremony.

"Starting to look better already," laughed Antonia a little nervously.

An hour later, Juichi had removed the most lethal parts – the liver and ovaries which contained the tetrodotoxin. The organs were placed on several sheets of newspaper. "I read that the poison is a thousand times deadlier than cyanide," said Rob, smiling at Antonia.

Once satisfied that all the edible parts had been safely removed, they began the meal. Rob insisted they count to four and then all tasted the first mouthful in sync.

This was *fugu-sashi*, informed Juichi. He had bought a dipping sauce called *ponzu* from a regular Japanese supermarket. The slices of white fish were so thin they were almost transparent.

They ate in silence, standing in the kitchen. Nervous eyes darted from one to the other. Gradually, smiles appeared. No-one had died yet. They drank the *sake* afterwards while Juichi checked on the stew which held the remaining fish.

"My mouth is too numb to taste anything," said Antonia.

"That is to be expected," said Rob. "It is caused by a tiny amount of the poison which seeps into the flesh. Don't worry, it's not dangerous. We'd be writhing in agony or dead by now if it was."

Few words were exchanged during the rest of the meal. Nervous giggles, but hardly any words.

"Well that was a pleasant change," said Rob as they sat in the living room afterwards. In fact, it was probably the biggest meal Rob had eaten in months, if not years. He would usually just nibble, often and at the most unusual times of day, but Antonia could not recall him ever finishing what she would class as a hearty meal; a banana was a meal to Rob.

Juichi just looked at his friend with a radiant smile. If Rob was happy, Juichi was delighted. Thousand dollars be blowed.

Antonia was smiling, too, but part of her was alert to any sign of after-effects. There were none and she grew more and more calm, then more excitable.

"We did it! Do you think we are the first Americans to prepare our own killer fish?"

"Should I class myself honoured to be labelled American?" said Juichi.

She blushed, then they all laughed some more, delirious that they had danced with death and survived.

Later that night she lay in Rob's arms back at his apartment. They hugged and talked. Hugging was as far as they ever got, it was like an unwritten rule between them. Their affection was on a higher, purer level, Rob claimed.

"Ever been to Atlantic City?" he asked her, completely out of the blue.

"No, never. Why?"

"I need to go. I need to play poker; a proper game of poker, with real people in a real casino. I need to, before I die. Atlantic City's closer than Las Vegas. Would you like a weekend break there, my rose?"

✝

They went right to the very edge and beyond in Atlantic City. Not that they had planned to. The murder just happened. They were on The Boardwalk, staring out across the Atlantic Ocean and dreaming.

Rob had $550 in his wallet, safely tucked inside his inside jacket pocket. Fifty of the dollars was profit, not a great profit — just ten per cent of the stash he had saved over three months, being thriftier than ever with his small allowance.

But the money hadn't mattered to him. He had considered blackjack, having heard the legendary tales from the gangs operating out of the Massachusetts Institute Of Technology. They had beaten the odds, beaten the system, taken casinos across America for several hundred thousand dollars. The MIT gangs were so good they could count cards in their sleep; multi-deck cards. But they had big-money investors behind them. Rob was a relative pauper and the multi-million dollar establishments would go unscathed from his visit. Proving himself against serious gamblers was what had mattered to Rob.

He had practised and practised. He had practised by himself, he had practised online and then he drew in Antonia and practised playing against her. That had been all too easy. They had played with Monopoly money. Monopoly was a game he had enjoyed since childhood. Not being physically able to join in the more robust pastimes of his contemporaries once haemophilia had been diagnosed, he played board games. Chess, checkers and Monopoly.

The Monopoly set had accompanied him to Harvard and took pride of place by his rows and rows of legal tomes. Taking Monopoly money off Antonia had been amusing; but Rob developed an itch for the real thing.

Ten per cent was his goal, and ten per cent had been pocketed after two days and around seven hours of gambling the smallest stakes possible. Antonia had watched him from a distance. Occasionally she had tried the slot machines, dabbled at roulette, and even tried blackjack, though card-counting held no attraction for her. She swore to him hand on heart that she was about even, maybe a couple of dollars ahead. She was thrilled by the brightness of the casinos, the jingle-jangle noise, the people. There was no dress code and after a while she found it impossible to determine the minnows from the whales. She had spent an hour gazing starry-eyed in wonderment at a craps table at the Tropicana. The sheer intoxication of the dice rollers was infectious, though she had not been brave or foolhardy enough to try the game herself. She found it baffling.

They had walked to the end of The Boardwalk. "Europe, 3,000 miles that way," said Rob, pointing out across the cold, grey sea. "Let's go to Europe." He turned to face her. "If I make it to next summer, let's go to Europe, my rose."

She fought back tears, knowing the odds this time were very much against him. Recent medical tests had revealed a weakening of the muscles around the heart; what should have been a minor cold had flattened him for a week. He had struggled to rise from his bed to go to the bathroom, having to linger longer than normally necessary before being able to make the return trip.

He sensed her discomfort and smiled. "Do you know the English have a different Monopoly set to ours?" And then he rattled off the names of all the places he wanted to visit with his rose ...if he made it to next summer.

They dreamed and schemed, she looking a million dollars in her red dress which the wind wafted against her lightly tanned legs, he looking like a shabby old man – a brittle old man – in his off-cream suit.

For some inexplicable reason, one that Rob could not later explain, he took out his wallet and began counting the money. He just heard the whoosh of the roller-blades in time. In time to see the black youth screech to a brief halt beside him and snatch for his wallet. It was no contest.

The youth had the wallet and was away. He had gone three yards at most when his left knee buckled under a ferocious kick from Antonia. She swung out her handbag and the strap became wrapped around the fallen mugger's throat. She squeezed and twisted and yelled for all she was worth. And she cursed. Words poured out that Rob would never have dreamed of hearing from her lips.

Pure outrage that anyone would dream of doing such a thing to any person, never mind to her Rob. Then she squeezed and twisted some more until, after a while, she felt Rob's hand on her bare arm.

"I think that's enough," he said softly. She turned to see Rob looking paler than ever before. He seemed scared – and she had never seen him frightened. No fear, not even a little bit – that was her Rob.

"I think …I think he may be dead." They both looked down and saw a face contorted in terror, eyes wide open, mouth twisted. One wrist was bent back more than ninety degrees. The mugger had broken it when he fell.

"I killed him. Jeeze, I killed him."

Rob took hold of her by both shoulders. "We have to go. We have to go now."

He drew her gently away. She stopped, feeling the tug of her handbag. Slowly she unravelled it from around the dead man's neck, only then realising just how tightly she had pulled it. Rob stopped to collect his wallet before leading her away.

He looked around. There appeared to be people to the south of them, so he steered her north. It was the opposite direction to their cheap motel but they could worry about that later. They walked for two miles or more, heading inland and then making a U-turn back towards the bright lights. Rob felt safer the brighter the lights. After a while he hailed a taxi and used $20 from his profit for a ride back to the motel. They didn't speak until morning.

✝

CHAPTER THIRTEEN

+

SARAH HUGHES beat DI Alexander into work by two minutes. She had slept soundly for five hours or so and looked her usual smart self.

Alexander looked a little ragged at the edges. He was, once again, pleased that his glasses masked the heaviness of his eyes. Not being able to sleep, he had left Lucy in peace for a couple of hours and brooded over endless coffees and cigarettes in the kitchen. She commented on the smokiness of the flat as she was getting ready for work. What had happened to his enjoying a ciggie every now and then on social occasions?

He was off and away before her, just catching her comments that she may spend a couple of days at her own place as she guessed he had a busy week coming up.

"Morning, sir, coffee?"

"Morning, Sarah. I could murder for one, as they say." He was nodding to officers as he took off his jacket. "Get someone else to go, Sarah. I need you to write the report. Think I've damaged one of my typing fingers."

DC Hughes blushed, feeling embarrassed to ask a colleague to do the coffee run. Caroline Peters came to the rescue. "Give it here," she said, reaching out her arm for the tray. She picked the coins off the tray and told Hughes to put them in 'the box'. Then she turned to DI Alexander. "I'm going, you're paying. Six in the round so a fiver should do it."

Alexander grumbled but dug into his pocket for his wallet.

"Careful with that typing finger now."

It had just turned seven o'clock, close to shift change-over. Alexander could see DC Curtis Maynard was hovering, wanting his attention. He had phoned Maynard late last night and given him plenty to keep the night crew busy.

"Be with you in a minute, Curtis." He summoned Hughes to his desk.

"I'm going to be tied up this morning so I need you to write our report. Use my computer. File it on the desktop and I'll check it later. Everything from the moment you took the call. You know the score."

The night crew had been thin on the ground last night. DI Blake had cried off, DS Hodges had gone off chasing what turned out to be another hoaxer, which had left Maynard and two other DCs manning the fort – all well-trained and highly capable officers; all grounded and highly recommended.

Alexander had tried to play fair with the pressured outlying stations, but now – six murders. SIX. He may have to take his superiors up on their promises and request more full-timers. See how today pans out he told himself. He preferred tight ships, another Haroldson trait. And more bodies meant more paperwork. He had attended a conference two years previously where some Chief Superintendent from Coventry had produced statistic upon statistic, accompanied by state-of-the-art computerised graphs. He left fully confirmed in his own mind if no-one else's that more bodies meant more paperwork – very impressive paperwork – but not necessarily greater clean-up rates.

"Curtis," he said, turning round.

"Sir, I hope we've managed everything you wanted." He held several sheets of print-outs. "CCTV footage should arrive this morning. Nothing from the platforms, though, just the main concourse."

Alexander took the paper and flicked through the sheets. Statements from the transport police who called in the killing. Name and address of the cleaner who found the body. The inspector didn't think any of them would need interviewing, but he would send officers out just in case.

Then a list of the train's itinerary from Edinburgh to London. It had stopped at Newcastle, Darlington, York and Peterborough, before arriving at King's Cross approximately one whole minute ahead of schedule.

The final three sheets interested him most: lists of all those who had reserved seats or had paid by credit card. The dead Dutchman was not on the list, but Maynard had highlighted three names of people who had reserved seats in the carriage where his rucksack had been found.

"DC Devonshire contacted the Dutch authorities, sir. The embassy and the police in Utrecht. Told them probably a mugging gone bad. They were sending someone round to see the family and said one of their officers would be in touch today. They have emailed three hi-res photos of the victim."

"Fine. They seem on the ball. Thanks."

"And Detective Superintendent Stevens called about an hour ago, sir. Said she'd be in 10-ish and you were to make yourself available for a brief chat."

Alexander checked his mobile: two missed calls. Must have been while he was on the Tube.

"I hope she stressed 'brief'. Right, home time for you boys. See you later."

DS Peters was handing round the coffees. There were grumbles from new arrivals.

"Five minutes everybody," Alexander stood to address the room. "Then I want your undivided." He realised he had nowhere to sit, having settled DC Hughes at his own computer. He pulled up a chair by Peters.

"When are we to expect our killer chef? Thanks for the coffee by the way."

"You're welcome. The change is in the box."

The box was all-embracing, but generally used for buying gifts or cards for colleagues. If it got too full it was emptied for a round of drinks at The Ferret – a quorum of five being required. Alexander gave a grunt of approval.

"If he isn't here by nine I send out a search party. I gave him explicit directions so he's no excuse for getting lost. Fun last night?"

"Bags of it. Looks like a busy day ahead. The path lab was planning to start early, and now I hear Christine wants to see me."

He spotted DS Pierce and beckoned him over, informing his two sergeants of the latest killing before rising from his seat. He raised his voice for attention.

"As you all should know by now, number six came in last night. Looks like a strangling. We should have details soon.

"Young Dutchman travelling to London from Edinburgh. We have details of around 50 people who were on the train; some shared the same carriage. I want them all checked thoroughly. Anyone who caught their attention – especially a woman, possibly with a foreign twang to her accent, possibly wearing sunglasses. Absolutely no mention of any connection to the other five until I say so. None at all." He looked around the room to see everyone understood.

"DS Pierce will sort out the names for you. Photos of the victim are being processed. Remember, this could be our best lead yet. The killing was by someone on that train. Don't rule out the killer being a man – some force was used – but concentrate on suspicious females. Someone on that train; narrows it down considerably from someone in 20-odd million. Get cracking."

Detectives began walking towards Pierce but Alexander held them back with a wave of his hand.

"Call up the cavalry, Stuart. No locals on the interviews unless necessary. People may have been heading off to catch other trains, or to airports. But everything within reasonable distance we handle."

"Sure."

Alexander moved to check on DC Hughes's progress. Occasionally he would signal approval, occasionally suggest amendments.

"Elaine Pascoe's ready and waiting, sir," shouted DS Peters from her desk.

Good. Alexander had requested Pascoe if available. She was a senior graphic artist working for the Directorate of Forensic Services. He'd worked with her before. The only person missing on the scene was the killer chef. Twenty-five minutes before they went hunting for him. He arrived with eight minutes to spare.

He was escorted through by a uniform. Peters was right; he looked so nervous you'd have thought he was about to be charged with multiple murder.

Sod's law, two officers were trying to attract Alexander's attention. Phone calls for him. Hughes, too, held a receiver up expectantly.

"Take messages," he barked. "Back as soon as I can."

DS Peters made the introductions after thanking Ichisake Kimiyama for his presence.

"You can take down your hood Mr Kimiyama. No-one will know you are here. Trust me."

The chef was reluctant to obey, raising his eyes to get a better look at the inspector from underneath the grey hood of his fleece jacket.

Alexander offered his hand, receiving a clammy and light handshake. He placed a hand on Kimiyama's shoulder and steered him along a corridor and up some stairs. They had climbed one floor before the hood was lowered, revealing a thickish mop of jet-black hair. The chef was short and skinny. He gave his age as 28.

Fortunately, Elaine Pascoe had her own office, so Kimiyama managed only the fleetest look around the vast open plan graphics room, crammed with computers and walls covered in pictures and posters.

Pascoe was in her mid-30s. A mother of two, slightly overweight, tinted glasses. She was prepared, having sketched a rough outline from the verbal description the chef had provided DS Peters.

"Drink?" she said once Kimiyama had settled himself in a chair by her screen.

He nodded. "Coke?" he mumbled. The detectives were fine, thank you.

She picked up her phone and requested a coke and a tea, milk, one sugar, for herself. Her soft voice informed Kimiyama to take as long as he needed. It was very important they get the photo-fit as accurate as possible. So soothing she could have been a doctor, or a priest. Peters and Alexander watched in silence.

"Let's start with the sunglasses. You told Caroline that this woman wore sunglasses every time you saw her?"

A nod.

Pascoe clicked and suddenly the screen split into two. Down the right were images of dozens of pairs of sunglasses. She began slowly scrolling down. "Stop me as soon as you see a pair like the ones she wore."

She had scrolled ever so slowly past 50 or so pairs of shades, most looking like refugees from the Terminator. A grunt.

"Pardon? This pair here?"

Kimiyama pointed at an image above the one Pascoe had highlighted. Pascoe dragged the image to the other side of the screen.

"Let's keep looking. You may see another pair similar."

A few more grunts, followed by shakes of the head and shrugs. The coke arrived and seemed to lubricate the chef's vocal chords. Images of different styles were now appearing. Kimiyama brought Pascoe to an abrupt halt by touching her screen and indicating his first choice. "Yes, that one. She wore like them."

Pascoe enlarged the main photo, and corrected the size of the sunglasses so they sat neatly on the face.

"Does that look something like her? Is the face about right? Not too fat? Too thin?" She played around with the face image to indicate what she meant.

The witness made more vague reactions then said: "She wore a hat. All the time she wore red hat. Very red."

"OK. Let's leave the face like that for now and try and find a hat."

Pascoe knew from DS Peters's report that the detective had been unable to get a reliable description of the hat from the chef. The face now disappeared and the screen was split into several sections. She closed down the folders containing men's hats. She doubted the woman would have been sporting a bowler or a trilby. Kimiyama shook his head when a series of caps appeared. He indicated that the hat was wider. Ten minutes later he had pinpointed a fedora-type hat, only narrower.

The chef's eyes opened wider as Pascoe began altering the colour from black through various shades of red. "Yes," he said, touching the screen again. Pascoe hated fingers on her screen but would let it pass. Now the hat joined the face and the shades.

The nose and the mouth proved trickier; they usually did, especially when glasses were involved. Eventually, Pascoe had created a photo-fit that Kimiyama claimed looked like the crazy, crazy woman who had come to him for some blowfish.

"Are you sure, Mr Kimiyama? Is there anything you would like me to change?" her most soothing voice possible.

Alexander decided to speak. "We are in no rush, sir. You are being very, very helpful. Would you like another coke?"

The chef hadn't looked at his watch, but Alexander knew he would be thinking of getting to work for the lunch shift.

"No," he said. "That is good. That looks like her. Crazy woman. Crazy woman."

They thanked him, reassured him there was nothing to fear, checked he had their cards and phone numbers and was to get in touch if he remembered anything or if the crazy woman contacted him again. He was given a gentle warning that it would be inadvisable for all concerned to import further blowfish into the UK. Unless, of course, the crazy woman requested some. Then he could promise her the earth …so long as he let them know. DS Peters escorted him out, uttering more reassuring words and checking he fully understood this meeting was private and he was not to mention it to anyone.

"Ten minutes to clean this up and then you can have it," said Pascoe.

"Thanks," replied Alexander, checking his watch and remembering Det Supt Stevens was awaiting him.

The timing was bad, she said. When was a good time to get oneself murdered wondered Alexander. He had brought her up to date on the killing of the Dutchman before she explained why the timing was bad.

Detective Superintendent Christine Stevens had been granted an audience with the Assistant Commissioner the previous afternoon. He bore salutations and instructions from on high. The Metropolitan Police Commissioner Norman Brook wanted a reshuffle – or had he said re-organisation? – of the investigation.

Naturally, Alexander had his complete backing; he was a first class detective inspector, soon to be detective chief inspector. He would, of course, understand why the actual promotion was being held up until this investigation had been resolved. Wouldn't look good in the media, would it? Not with a serial killer still at large.

But, you see, what the Commissioner wanted was a little more gravitas – that was the word he had used – yes, a little more gravitas brought to the head of the investigation.

So, Stevens was to adopt a more hands-on approach, and a commander was to be brought in to act as liaison with AC Joseph Rowley, the head of the Serious Crime Directorate.

"Liaise? Is that what you said, Christine?"

"Listen ..."

"You mean the Commissioner thinks we are making a pig's ear of it so he wants to bring someone in above our heads. Meanwhile ...naturally ...obviously ...of course ...we have the Commissioner's complete backing. In a nutshell?"

"You think I am happy about it?" She slammed the palm of her hand against the top of her computer monitor, making the whole table shake. Alexander waited.

He waited for his own body to calm down, and for Stevens to sit back down. "And which commander are we getting?"

"Jonathan Marshall. I've worked with him before – decent enough bloke, not that I'd personally trust him. Has a reputation for being Rowley's eyes and ears."

"And a reputation for fraud and computer crime, if I am not mistaken. A bloody good reputation, but when the fuck was the last time he was on a murder inquiry? He's coming here to spy us on us, right? Let's not beat about the bloody bush."

"He'll report direct to AC Rowley, yes. But Rowley's just doing what the Commissioner's told him to do."

"Because some nosey bugger in the Press or some paper-clip in the Home Office has been chewing his ear. Christ!" Alexander rose and paced the room. He knew there was little he could do but accept the situation.

"Sit down, Rory. It's up to us to make sure he's kept at arm's length."

Alexander sat down. "I'll swing for him if he comes the paperboy with me. I'm a detective not a bloody pen-pusher."

"Well you be a good boy and I'll keep him off your back. You may think I'm a bloody pen-pusher, too, but I'm still a detective. So get used to seeing more of my pretty face in the MR. I'll leave it up to you what you tell the team. Maybe best to say nothing unless asked."

"Sure, Christine. Didn't mean to have a go at you."

"I should hope not. Now, AC Rowley wants you to call him when we've had our chat."

+

Alexander had a habit of snapping when he was tetchy. That was a sign that his brain was overloaded, Lucy had told him. Think before you speak, but don't go for that counting to ten nonsense. Think of something calm and soothing, like an ocean or clouds.

Oceans didn't work for Alexander; he had tried, but waves hundreds of feet high sprung into his brain. The waves were submerging New York, just like in that movie. Clouds were OK, most of the time.

He was thinking of clouds now, peaceful fluffy clouds in a summery blue sky. Then it started raining. The sky turned black and it was raining Monopoly pieces …and huge bloated spiky blowfish …and heads wearing sunglasses and red hats.

He was spoken to before he had a chance to speak.

"Path lab's been on, prelim report's filed: strangulation, no sign of poison, but lots of signs of bruising – knee and middle and lower back." Alexander gave DS Pierce the faintest of nods.

"Press Bureau's going crazy, sir. Want to know when they can expect a statement."

Another faint nod to DC Vicki Jobson.

Rowley could wait. Rowley would bloody well wait. He was a detective inspector running a multiple murder inquiry. Deep down, though, he knew the AC was right. The team needed beefing up at the top end of the sharp end. DI Keith Blake was proving little use. Alexander wondered whether his family problem yesterday was connected to the separation he had mentioned last week.

Blake had confessed to hitting his wife during an argument and told Alexander they were having a trial separation. Alexander expressed sympathy when what he really wanted to say was something much more brutal. Broken police marriages were hardly a surprise. A senior officer feeling sorry for himself was no use to Alexander.

He sat and thought for a few moments before turning to his computer and browsing for the pathologist's report. He struggled to concentrate; his brain was well and truly overloaded. The fax, Eastbourne and Mrs Montgomery's shrine, the chef, the Berlin postcard, the poor Dutch bugger, and now more gravitas required – all in just over 24 hours.

"Rowley here." Alexander sat up in shock. He must have been on auto-pilot when he picked up the phone.

"DI Alexander, sir."

"You've spoken with Christine Stevens?"

"Yes, sir. I was about to call you; I just have a report from the path lab to check through."

"Yes, bad timing. Bad timing. Change of plan. Meeting my office lunchtime. I'll have some sandwiches sent up. One o'clock sharp. All right?"

"Certainly, sir. One o'clock."

Bad timing, good timing. Change of plan? Alexander wasn't sure if he ever knew there was a plan.

✝

Commander Jonathan Marshall had a brilliant record and had risen through the ranks rapidly. He was just four years older than Alexander but looked considerably more. His face was paler, too, caused by too many hours hunched over piles of paper or computer screens, tracking trails. He had been around the globe many times, usually without leaving London. Along the way he had made friends in high places, both home and abroad. He had led the Americans to break up a drug-running operation in Florida while his main intention had been to hunt down dirty money from the Far East. A Chinese counterfeiting ring proved difficult, but the then Chief Superintendent Marshall stuck doggedly to his computer and traced several million euros to the Middle East and then to Kiev and from there to a printer in Shanghai.

Marshall was roughly the same height as Alexander, but a few pounds lighter. His hair showed flecks of grey. He wore thin wire-framed spectacles which made him look like no movie star Alexander could conjure up.

The two men shook hands and smiled. Stevens was there, too, and sufficed with a bow of the head in Alexander's direction.

"Help yourself to sandwiches," said AC Rowley. Then, without further ado, he launched into business. "The Press. On our backs. I am not happy and nor is the Commissioner. This is no reflection on you or DI Alexander." His last comment was directed to Det Supt Stevens.

"But we need to take the initiative. Yes, initiative."

Alexander hadn't really been listening. He was weighing up Marshall and wondering when was the last time he had seen action in the outside world. When was the last time he had seen daylight or fresh air? The same could be said of Stevens, and certainly Rowley for that matter. It wasn't jealousy. He did not envy them their seniority. To be fair to Stevens, he had seen her work the interview rooms. Top notch she was, too. A keen mind ready to pounce on any verbal slip.

"DI Alexander?"

"Yes, sir. Yes … errrm … the Press. I do think another conference is in order. The issue now is how much do we tell them."

"We have little time to play with," said Marshall. "The South London gangs have called a ceasefire it appears and now the Press buggers are back on our case. A Royal scandal would help but that lot seem to be heeding sound advice all of a sudden. This Dutchman doesn't help. Bad timing for us."

Bad timing. Was it a sound bite they learned higher up The Met ladder? Bad timing for the Dutchman, too, Alexander felt like interrupting. Pity about the South London gangs. Marshall was about to continue, but delayed too long. Were his thought processes simply slow? Or was he attempting to parade himself as a deep thinker? Maybe he was thinking about asking the Brixton boys to stir up the South London gangs.

"Well DI Alexander has several leads he needs to explore, so we planned a brief conference and statement later today." Good lie, Christine.

"We were planning to release the victim's photograph and ask for anyone on that train to come forward. DI Alexander's team has already started contacting those who booked their seats with credit cards."

"But don't you think it is now time to widen the appeal? We now have the photo-fit, don't we – must admit I am surprised it is a woman."

"That is what DI Alexander wanted to pick your brains about, sir." She stressed the 'your' and directed her comments to AC Rowley, deliberately ignoring Marshall. Is this what she meant by tap-dancing? Is this how she had earned the nickname Gasbag? She seemed good at it.

"We didn't have time this morning, so I suggested he raise the issue with you and seek your opinion, sir."

"It's not something we wished to rush into, sir." Alexander joined in the soft shoe shuffle.

"Of course," said Rowley.

"Now, I would suggest we wait until the weekend, collect our thoughts and see if we make any progress on the leads. As DI Alexander says we most definitely must not rush. The Press are ready to pounce. What we tell them must be carefully considered. DI Alexander and I have already rejected any mention of the Monopoly link. Imagine the chaos that could cause!"

Det Supt Stevens was really moving now.

"The main issue is whether or not we release the photo-fit to the Press."

"Katherine Hepburn."

"What? Commander Marshall?"

"Katherine Hepburn, sir. The photo-fit looks like the actress — Breakfast At Tiffany's."

Rowley gave him a puzzled look and then returned his gaze towards Stevens. She was raising herself out of her chair. "So, sir, if it is all right with you, DI Alexander and myself shall keep the newshounds at bay today. Can we arrange to meet on Friday to decide about the photo-fit and any further information we wish to divulge?"

"Friday? Hmmm. Friday it is unless you hear otherwise from me. Let's say morning. Won't you have a sandwich before you go?"

"Got a bag, sir? I'll take lunch over the path report; only had time to glance at it so far."

"Could have been a lot worse," said Stevens as they walked down the stairs to her office.

"Marshall seemed a little too eager to impress, desperate to say something but all he proved was that he isn't up to speed on the case is he?"

"Katherine Hepburn!" laughed Stevens.

"You'd think a commander would know when silence was a virtue." Alexander shook his head. "Always getting her mixed up with the other one, Audrey."

"So was Commander Marshall. Did Sir Michael ever work with them?"

Alexander punched her lightly on the arm. "I wouldn't know. But I hear he's now working with Ginger Rogers."

"Practise makes perfect, Rory."

+

CHAPTER FOURTEEN

✝

THEY DIDN'T speak much on the Greyhound back north. Antonia stared out of the window; Rob stroked her arm. Every now and then he would whisper in her ear. "You were brilliant. You saved me. You saved us. You're wonderful."

She didn't feel brilliant or wonderful. She had killed a man and she felt numb all over. Too numb to think. Rob no longer looked frightened.

They met the following day in the late afternoon. Rob walked to her flat, half a mile from the Law School. He could walk fine most days. There was nothing wrong with his legs; he could walk fine, even for long distances. But he was slow, stopping sometimes every hundred yards to catch his breath or calm his heart-beat. Then he'd be off again.

Colour had returned to Antonia's face he was pleased to notice. He kissed her cheek and reciprocated her smile. Their eyes were different, though – his twinkling as normal, hers dull and lifeless.

"Now, my rose, I do so hope you're not fretting over a minor accident of life?"

"A minor accident?" Her voice was steady and low, betraying no sign of emotion. "I killed a man, Rob. It was murder, not a minor accident."

"Oh no, no …no …no! Most definitely not murder. Self defence. We were being mugged."

"I killed a man."

"And I envy you …"

"Envy?"

"Yes, envy." He took her by the shoulders.

"Rob …" she gave a little shrug but let his hands remain on her shoulders.

"And now I must join you. I must join you on that far edge."

"What are you talking about?"

"I need to kill a man."

"Rob, stop being silly. This is not one of your games." Her voice raised a notch, a tiny notch. More animated.

"Oh, but it can be. Don't you see?"

"I can't see anything …except the face of a man I killed."

"Now, ask yourself this, Antonia dearest: are you distressed because of the man? The mugger? Because he is dead? Because he may have friends and family who are wracked with grief? Or are you distressed because you are feeling sorry for yourself? Because you have some false sense of guilt? Because you fear the police?"

Too many questions for her to respond to a single one of them.

"Let's settle down and have a drink." He took a bottle of red wine from his satchel: Chassagne Montrachet grand cru, an expensive vintage Burgundy. Of course, it had been pilfered. Rob adored fine wine, but he could never dream of affording to maintain his passion on a struggling student's budget. Petty theft, as he called it, was another one of his pleasures on the extreme.

The wine had little effect on her at first, but her smile gradually grew warmer and more like the Antonia he knew and loved. He spoke softly and calmly. They nibbled at a salad he threw together from items in her fridge. The wine was finished and Antonia was coming round, speaking more, and moving her body less jerkily.

He returned to the kitchen to make coffee. Then he produced a bottle of Hine Cognac from his bag. There was about a third left.

"I need to go shopping again soon," he said with a sigh and a sly, knowing tilt of his head. They sat side by side on the sofa, barely touching.

"Atlantic City. I shall kill a man in Atlantic City."

"Rob …please …"

"We have to go back, my rose. We certainly do have to go back. You know when you fall off a bike? The first thing they say you must do is climb back on: to conquer any fear of cycling again. So we must go back to Atlantic City. And I must kill a man there."

She slurped her coffee, sipped the brandy. It was smooth and warming. Relaxing. She laughed for the first time since that terrifying moment on The Boardwalk.

"You couldn't kill anybody Rob. Come on."

He feigned surprise and dismay. "Why ever not? Is it beyond me?"

She touched his hand and turned to face him, smiling. "We both know, dearest, that you are not built for mortal combat."

"Ah! So I need the strength of an ox to kill a man, do I? How you have disappointed me."

"You are my star and I love you. You have the brain of a thousand men, but—"

"The body of a mouse. I know. I was not planning to kill by brute force." He flexed his feeble biceps. She laughed again, louder this time.

"You know what the existentialists say? Life is to be lived in all its extremities to be understood. You must taste all the pleasures to live life to the full. You must go to the edge and look over the precipice. You have been closer than me. Now it is my turn, and I shall not rely on brute force."

"What then? A gun? A knife? I cannot picture you holding either, dearest."

He paused, swilling the Cognac around his glass and staring into the mini whirlpool. It could be hypnotic.

"Poison," he said after a while.

"Poison? What? Cyanide?"

"Tetrodotoxin."

"Rings a bell, what is it?"

"I will forgive you and blame the wine and brandy for your appalling memory loss. Tetrodotoxin is the poison supplied by our beloved blowfish."

"You can't be serious! You are going to ask Juichi to buy some more fish? You know how much that cost!"

"No need. I already have some. A tiny white lie; I told Juichi I had disposed of the organs, but I just happened to have kept the liver. Now it is carefully sealed and concealed in my freezer compartment."

"What? Really?" She was laughing now at the sheer craziness of her friend. The most brilliant and craziest friend anyone could ever have. "I just don't believe …you never cease to amaze me. Is it safe?"

"Oh yes. Don't worry, I have nothing else in the freezer compartment – not even ice."

She expressed doubts, fears, guilt still lingered; he soothed her with words as usual. He philosophised on the concept of murder. His arguments were extreme, but that was just how he liked to live, and for how long he was not sure, though he knew it was not that long.

Rob stayed the night, drifting off on the sofa in the early hours of the morning after the couple had talked and conspired for an eternity. He knew he had convinced her to join him once more in taking another trip to the farthest boundary of his bizarre world. Once the subject had been raised and Antonia had virtually sanctioned approval, Rob let it drift. It drifted for six days as their lives returned to academia and outings to cafes and parks. He spent more time at her apartment than his own. They idled rather than attacked life with their former joie de vivre. Pranks – no matter how daring – were tiring for Rob. These days his exhaustion matched the exhilaration.

Then he decided to show her the liver. It would make a splendid line in a movie. 'Would you like to come up for coffee? I can show you the most poisonous liver in the world. It's in my freezer?' And there it was now, still sealed but on the kitchen worktop.

"OK, so we go to Atlantic City and you persuade some cretin to eat this? Right?"

The old Antonia was back. Lively and laughing, and excited and game for anything. She had read scant details of the murder of a young black man on The Boardwalk: police were appealing for witnesses but none had come forward. It would soon be filed with the other cold cases, Rob informed her. If they aren't important figures or from wealthy families the cops don't give a hoot.

"It only takes a tiny amount. I could slip some in a drink or on some food. Or I could inject it."

"Inject?"

"A pinprick would kill a man, or so I have read. Takes anything from a few minutes to a few hours. I am not certain, but I guess it depends on the level of dosage and the weight of the person. I have a few ideas I am still working on."

Legal studies had taken a backseat these days. When he wasn't staring at the blowfish liver in his freezer compartment and pondering how to deploy the poison, Rob was online practising his poker with a greater intensity and pondering the wisdom of increasing his profit target to 15 per cent.

One day it hit him: he would kill a man at a casino. Any man would do, but he would have to be gambling and winning. Yes, what a way to go – with a pile of chips sitting in front of you and a large whiskey in your hand.

Days went by with no further mention of their scheme. Not the Atlantic City scheme at least. Rob had other things to keep him occupied; one of which was stealing some jewellery for Antonia. He planned it meticulously and emerged from the jeweller's with a $5,000 ring pocketed and a cheap fake in its place. It joined two books and a photo of the couple in a shoebox hidden in his apartment: his bequest to her.

His 23rd birthday was looming – February 27th, a Saturday. They decided that would be ideal for their next visit to Atlantic City, putting off a trip home until the following weekend. His parents were disappointed but pleased that their son was keeping so busy in his dying days.

Rob kept his experiments secret from Antonia. That was difficult as she was popping round his apartment more and more these days, not just in the evening, but at any spare time of day. One morning, when he knew she had course work she simply could not skip, he bought a rat, a hamster and a guinea pig from a pet shop three miles away. Then he purchased several items from a hardware store. His shopping was not heavy but it was cumbersome. He was sweating heavily and breathing in short gasps when he reached his rooms.

After resting for the best part of an hour, he went into his kitchen and began to work. He wore huge rubber gloves and a face mask as he dealt with the liver. His parents would have died of shock; a fugu chef would have died laughing. The liver had defrosted overnight and the plastic bag had been placed inside a larger, stronger bag. He doubted biochemists conducted their experiments this way, but he had discounted seeking help from other students. He knew none outside his immediate circle.

The liver turned paler, more brown than red. He squeezed the liquid through a funnel and into a sturdy plastic cup. There was surprisingly little liquid. He fastened the screw top as tight as his hands would allow. Then he rested for a few more minutes.

He had four brown eye-dropper bottles of varying sizes on his kitchen table. One was empty; the other three contained various levels of a weak sterile saline solution which had been carefully measured using the eye-droppers.

The cup holding the lethal juice was no use for the next stage as the eye-droppers would not reach the liquid, so he had to pour it into a more shallow container. Then, a little shakily, he began transferring the liquid.

One bottle contained 20 drops of pure liquid, another 20 drops mixed with 20 drops solution, another 20-40, and the last one 20-100. There was still some liquid remaining; that would be enough for his next experiment, utilising a child's chemistry set, if this did not work.

In all honesty, he was not too sure of his experiments. He had tried to investigate, but his serious attempts at acquiring scientific knowledge had ended at 13 years of age. Now he needed to rest again, checking his pulse and finding it high; it was the excitement rather than the exertion.

He wished he had bought more animals, a fourth at least. They were all different species, too. Was that a good idea? No. But it would have to do. He chastised himself for a poor piece of planning. Next he selected four pins he had fastened onto the ends of chopsticks with glue and strong tape. They were all the same size. He placed each inside the bottle holding the weakest solution and then set his stop-clock, the kind used by chess players and a 'gift' from one of the science labs at the chemistry faculty.

Not rushing, but with trembling hand, he started the clock and began counting inside his head. He picked up one chopstick, poked it through the bars and gave the guinea pig a sharp jab, retracting the chopstick immediately. He laid the stick down on a sheet of polythene and repeated the action with the hamster and the rat. Thirty-seven seconds had elapsed when he sat down and waited. An hour flew by, Rob's eyes flicking between the clock and the caged animals. They appeared to suffer no reaction, adverse or otherwise.

He reset the clock and repeated his experiment using the next strongest solution, two parts saline, one part poison (or liver juice as he called it). He made himself a cup of herbal tea as he sat down to wait again.

Nineteen minutes and about 30 seconds later – judging by the quick glance at his clock – things started to get interesting. He noticed the hamster first; it was trying to poke its head through the bars. Its face seemed contorted. Liquid was oozing from its mouth. Less than two minutes later, its legs had given way and it was splayed out on the floor. He could see something was still throbbing beneath its fur so he knew it was not dead.

Rob turned his gaze to the other animals, something was happening to them, too. The rat was moving, but slowly. The guinea pig seemed rooted to the spot. Their faces looked strange, too; though how he could not guess, not being well versed in the physiognomy of tiny creatures.

Ratty interested him most, moving as if it was on the moon or wearing lead-filled boots. Suddenly it toppled over and lay on its back, again the teeth were bared and there was foam-like substance around the mouth. The guinea pig had still not moved, but now its eyes were closed.

He wished he had more equipment, more scientific know-how. He wondered what was occurring inside the bodies. How did it feel? Were they in pain? How much pain? There were no noises for him to gauge. What was happening to their brains? Their hearts? Their other vital organs?

Between 35 and 36 minutes into the tests, he noticed the rat's heartbeat seemed to have ceased. Hamster's was barely discernible; guinea pig still upright. A minute later, he was certain the rat and the hamster were dead. But what had happened to the guinea pig? He gave it a gentle prod with an untreated chopstick and it toppled over, stiff as a board. There was no sign of any heart beating beneath the animal's coat. He stopped the clock. Forty-one minutes and 27 seconds.

He sat down, smiled and studied the dead animals for half an hour, sipping his lemon and ginger tea which was cold by now but still refreshing. It worked! He discarded the weakest bottle of poison, pouring the contents down the sink and leaving the tap running. He poured the remaining untreated liquid into the first bottle. Then he taped together the bottles, using a strong parcel tape.

He ran the tape round them and over the top, so the lids were as tight as he could manage. Each had already been labelled. He placed them on the top of his shelving, out of sight. He threw the chopsticks into the sink; he wrapped the remains of the liver in polythene and placed it inside a plastic bag. Satisfied the pins had been cleansed, he broke up the chopsticks and they joined the liver.

The animals felt heavy but truly lifeless as he plucked them from their cages and dumped them into a large black trash sack. He tightly wrapped the sack in tape and placed it inside another black sack. He considered trying to sell the cages, but decided to break them up. Soon all the remains of his experiments were tightly packaged and placed inside one black sack.

Then he scrubbed his kitchen spotless, using the strongest bleach stocked by the local store. Not that he thought he may have spilled any poison, he just wanted to be sure. It was cleaner and more germ-free than the day he moved in.

+

Black and green bags were piled up high by the incinerator, a mile from his apartment. The men were enjoying a smoke and had their backs to him. He threw his sack straight into the inferno. It reached – just about – clipping the lip of the four-foot high container before toppling into the flames.

"Hey, buddy!"

"My girlfriend's cat," said Rob. "Got run over and she didn't know what to do with it so …"

"Yeah, yeah. Think those bags there are waiting for Christmas? You're supposed to leave your rubbish there, man."

Rob apologised and handed the man a dollar, explaining he was a poor student but thanked the men for understanding. His girlfriend's cat, you see.

The man pocketed the dollar without a word and returned to his cigarette and his companion.

Rob waited until he and Antonia had dined that evening before telling her about his experiments. They were cross-legged on his floor and playing a game of Monopoly. She had long since finished flinching whenever one of them landed on The Boardwalk.

His parents gave Rob $1,000 for his birthday, suggesting he book into a 'nice place' for his weekend break with 'that lovely girl'. They got a large twin-bed room at Bally's for $250 at the last minute. Rob earmarked $250 for travel and other expenses, adding the rest to his gambling fund which now stood at $1,300.

Bally's was too close to home for their mission, though. They spent the Friday night roaming the casinos. Despite not being able to concentrate 100 per cent on gaming, Rob managed to clear $85 profit. African Queen – a new one on Pacific Avenue – attracted their attention. Building was being completed on their previous visit; now it had been open three weeks and was doing brisk business.

Rob insisted they end the evening with a stroll along The Boardwalk. He hugged her a little closer as they walked past that spot. Antonia shrugged. "Scumbag deserved it," was her only comment.

Saturday night, she was wearing red again and they were trying their best to look like two weekenders just mooching around the African Queen. Earlyish, so we can have a gamble later, Rob had suggested.

Too good to be true. A middle-aged man in a Hawaiian shirt was making a lot of noise by a roulette table. The shirt was short-sleeved and the man had a monstrous pile of chips on the table in front of him. He was rubbing his hands and laughing – laughing loudly. A waitress stopped at his side. "Another Jack rocks, honey." Just like Rob had envisaged – Jack Daniel's. Too good to be true.

Rob retired to the men's room and returned to Antonia a few minutes later. She was leaning against a slot machine and watching the roulette table. Rob was careful to stand well away from her as he handed over his jacket. He was wearing a blue and white striped long-sleeved shirt, a New York Yankees baseball cap and a pair of Antonia's sunglasses. He had cultivated a moustache for the occasion. She glanced down at his left arm and a shiver of excitement rippled right through her.

If anything, the man's pile of chips had grown by the time the waitress returned with his drink, a very generous measure. He handed her a five-dollar chip as a tip. She smiled and wished him luck. Odds-evens, high-low, red-black. Rob was checking the board showing where the ball had been landing on recent spins. Winning is not part of this particular exercise, he told himself. Killing is.

Rob took a deep breath and sauntered over to the table. He leaned very carefully over the man's shoulder and placed a ten-dollar bill on odd numbers.

"Money on table," said the croupier. A dour-faced pit manager gave the bill a quick look. The target had chips all over the table, favouring high numbers, reds and the top six.

"No more bets." The croupier waved an arm over the table. Eight pairs of eager eyes watched the ball spin round and round and round, willing it to stop on one of their squares.

"Woo-hoo!" The man was clapping his hands above his head even before the croupier spoke.

"Thirty-one black." The croupier began dragging away all losing bets. Mr Hawaiian shirt didn't mind waving goodbye to the red bets; he had more than doubled his stake on the high numbers.

Rob waited until the croupier had finished settling all winning bets. He picked up his $20 and turned to leave.

"Hey, watch it!"

Rob spun round and saw Mr Hawaiian shirt holding his right arm.

"Oh Jeeze!" Rob looked at his own left arm. A pin was sticking out. "I'm real sorry, man. New shirt, musta missed one."

"No worries, just a scratch. Be lucky."

"You, too," said Rob, ambling away.

He barely acknowledged Antonia as he took his jacket and a small satchel from her and headed for the men's room.

Once inside a cubicle, he pulled a pair of black leather gloves from the jacket pocket. He gently removed the pin, wiping it clean with toilet roll. He flushed the paper down the pan. Next he took off his shirt, and then the surgical sleeve which embraced his arm from the elbow to a couple of inches above his wrist.

Underneath the sleeve was another sleeve – this one made of quarter inch thick rubber. Jeeze it was tight! It took Rob several seconds to prise it off. He rubbed his arm to get his circulation flowing properly.

He put on a blue Yankees tee-shirt from the satchel. His striped shirt joined the pin and the sleeves in a plastic shopping bag. Finally, sunglasses and a Panama hat completed his outfit. He tried not to rush, though he was desperate to join Antonia. He wrapped the plastic bag tight and placed it in a waste bin, knowing the casino cleaners emptied them regularly.

"Anything?" he asked Antonia, joining her by the slot machine, a comfortable 15 yards or so from the roulette table.

"Nothing yet," she replied, turning to waste another two quarters in the slots.

"Try not to stare," she whispered. "Been three more spins since you left and he's still winning and throwing back JD."

Rob started pacing around, hands stuffed in pockets and a tuneless whistle emanating from his thin lips. His eyes never left the roulette table. And then …

Then, four spins later, the man bowed his head and put a hand to his mouth. He turned to one side and Rob and Antonia could see liquid dribbling between his fingers. Then a coughing noise, followed by a terrible retching sound. Fellow gamers were staring at the man; one woman placed a hand on his shoulder. The croupier called for assistance. A floor manager rushed to the man's side; the croupier made a drinking motion with his hand to another suited figure sporting an African Queen badge.

"That's right; blame Jack Daniel's," laughed Rob inside, though outwardly his face was frozen. He noticed Antonia was glued to her spot, staring wide-eyed at the scene.

The floor manager was trying to usher the man away from the table, but was struggling. Two waitresses appeared. One was dispatched to find more help. Within a minute two security guards had appeared, closely followed by a cleaning lady who stared with disgust at the mess the man had made. The croupier was pleased that his table had been spared. He shrugged at the other gamers, then turned to a pit boss. Rob guessed he was asking what to do with the guy's chips, or when he should restart the wheel.

The Hawaiian shirt was almost completely surrounded now; it was difficult to see what was happening. Suddenly all moved away except two security men who were holding the man under his armpits. He was of average build, but the muscled guards seemed to be struggling to help him walk. The floor manager seemed in a hurry to get him off the gaming floor as quickly as possible. Lost time meant lost money. Scenes were not good for business. Suddenly, his legs gave way. One guard lost his grip, then the other and the man tumbled to the floor.

Gasps then screams. Not full-throated screams, more like minor shrieks as people saw the prone figure, his face turned to one side, eyes open and liquid dribbling from the corner of his mouth.

"He's dead!" yelped one woman, causing more gamblers to turn away from their tables to see what the commotion was all about.

Rob tugged at Antonia's handbag. "Time to go." His eyes were more alive than she had ever seen them.

Five weeks later Antonia found Rob's body. He had died in his sleep. There was a brandy glass by his bedside table, a little liquid left in the bottom. On the floor was a book – The Myth Of Sisyphus by Albert Camus. In the middle of the room, lying on a tatty rug, sat the Monopoly game they had started last night. Rob had already bought The Boardwalk and Pacific Avenue.

✝

CHAPTER FIFTEEN

✝

THE POSTCARD came a day later than expected. It came from Cambridge, which also took DI Alexander by surprise. And, as expected, forensics said the writing matched the Berlin postcard sufficiently to claim the same hand. Almost certainly a right-handed person using the left hand had done them both.

Nothing surprising there, then. The content, however, seemed more taunting – and more threatening

Dearest Edgar
Your media appearances are becoming a trifle dull.
Are you scared of letting the Press
know about our little secret?
It is our secret now, isn't it?
Surely, you have got it? You must have by now.
The woman officer amuses me. Christine is
your boss. You mind that? Do you fancy her?
Our friend's birthday is approaching.
I shall smile and be happy, and I shall
try and give you something special
to excite your taste buds.
Best wishes as ever
Jake T J
xxxxxx

"The kisses are new. What do you make of them?" said Det Supt Stevens. "Six kisses, six victims?"

"Yes, I'll go along with that," said Commander Marshall.

Wish you'd go along somewhere else, thought Alexander. Marshall was dead wood, contributing nothing, demanding lots. Lots and lots of paperwork. He tied up two detectives for a complete day's shift, printing out page after page of interviews, pathology reports and photographs. So much for the paperless society. Alexander wondered whether Marshall had required print-outs of the massive volumes of documentation that had accompanied most of his fraud cases. He shed a silent tear for the rain forests.

Christine Stevens ignored Jake's attempted jibes at her expense. "Our friend's birthday; does that mean anything to you, Rory?" She emphasised 'Rory,' knowing the use of Christian names irked Marshall. That was something he and AC Rowley had in common.

"Nothing, nothing at all. I have people working on it, but a big blank so far. They have checked out a few key figures, politicians, celebrities …that sort of thing. Nothing."

"It's gone for psychoanalysis now?"

"Yes." Alexander hadn't shared his contempt for profiling with Stevens, but the grimace on his face told her he wasn't expecting much joy from that quarter. Officers were on their way to Cambridge, armed with several dozen copies of the photo-fit.

Two passengers on the King's Cross train had recalled seeing a woman similar to the photo, but they hadn't spoken with her and could not recall her acting suspiciously. People were still being traced and questioned.

Alexander did not expect Cambridge to uncover any fresh leads. He was certain Jake would not be a resident, or a student. Jake was not that careless. Still, he had to go through the motions.

"I'm worried about the poison," he said after a brief silence. "I mean why go to all that trouble to obtain it, use it once and then go back to strangling – a not too clean strangling at that? Doesn't make sense to me."

"Perhaps she used up all the poison?"

Alexander looked hard and long at Marshall before replying. "There was sufficient poison in those fish to kill a hundred people. It's all in the reports." He stopped himself from adding 'all the reports you have had printed out,' but Marshall got the message.

"As you say, Rory, a lot of poison; and why this particular poison? There are plenty of others around, easily obtainable and pretty damned lethal."

"My guess is that it's a personal thing. No connection has been found with

Monopoly. Open to offers." He stole a quick glance at Marshall, who was staring at the ceiling, or was it into space?

+

Alexander took the call from the journalist as the Press Bureau had been most insistent. Ben Simmonds would not reveal anything over the phone, suggesting a meeting at a pub not frequented by The Met's finest or Fleet Street's finest.

They met later that evening at the Black Horse, opposite Hyde Park on Bayswater Road. Alexander had been cautious when he arrived, spotting a host of cameramen a hundred yards from the pub. He soon discovered they were hanging around Lancaster Gate waiting for a footballer to re-appear after his personal hearing into a serious disciplinary charge. His antics on the field of play would have seen him arrested several times if repeated on the streets.

The bitters on display did not appeal to Alexander so he ordered a pint of Guinness and settled himself at the quietest and most discreet table he could find. Simmonds arrived a few minutes later. He was drenched, even though the Tube station was just a matter of yards round the corner.

"Good evening. Just bought yourself one, I see." Alexander nodded; the hack could buy his own bloody drink. The Daily Herald crime reporter shook out his umbrella before approaching the bar and ordering a lager.

"Cheers! How's the world of detection?"

"Cheers. We keep busy and try our best. You need a new umbrella, by the way; more holes in that one than most of your stories. Now, why'd you need to see me so urgently?"

The 31-year-old reporter swallowed a good third of his pint before taking the papers from his briefcase and handing them to Alexander. Simmonds was a 31-year-old Mancunian who had been plying his trade in 'The Smoke' for four years. He stood six feet tall in his thickest soles, wore expensive-looking, loose-fitting suits – almost but not quite designer. He had thick, fair wavy hair and a light, permanent tan. He drank and smoked, but jogged and worked out, too. More footballer than traditional reporter.

"Came yesterday; thought you might be interested."

Alexander was holding a roughly-opened envelope, typed, posted in East London. The single sheet of paper contained one type-written paragraph.

"They say people who write in caps are angry people," added Simmonds. "This place has gone downhill." He was taking in their surroundings while finishing his drink. "What say I get us another, then we can have a little chat?"

Alexander nodded.

NEXT TIME THERE'S A PRESS CONFERENCE, MAYBE YOU COULD ASK THE INSPECTOR IF HE PLAYS MONOPOLY?

The note wasn't signed. Alexander had folded it by the time Simmonds returned from the bar.

"Assumed it was another Guinness. So …care to enlighten me?"

"Arrived yesterday, you say?" Alexander was striving for time. To think.

"I was out on a job and opened it just before lunch."

"Who has seen it?"

"Me, the editor, news editor — that's it. Been through a few mitts if you're wondering about prints. And the envelope could have been handled by all and sundry."

"And you think this refers to me?"

Simmonds was already halfway down his lager. He studied the detective over the rim of his glass.

"If you want to play silly buggers I can just go ahead and run the story."

"What story?" Alexander tried to smile.

Simmonds held out his hand for the papers. "Silly buggers it is."

"Sit down. Let's say I am intrigued."

"Thought you might be. Would it help you decide if I mentioned that yours are the only cop conferences I've attended this year? And I borrowed a neighbour's Monopoly game last night — must be 16 years or more since I last played; forgotten what a fascinating game it could be."

Now Alexander knew Simmonds had put two and two together and come up with a number very close to four. Not bad arithmetic for a tabloid reporter.

To be fair to Simmonds, he could have run a speculative story. Alexander could see the headlines: 'Monopoly Link To Serial Killer' or 'Kill Again And Do Not Go To Jail.'

"Listen, Ben." First name and a conspiratorial whisper. "I need to have this examined. Sit on it for now; would only cause panic otherwise."

"Whoa! No—"

"Tomorrow? Can we meet tomorrow? I'll have something for you. I promise."

Simmonds had finished his drink. Alexander pointed to the empty glass: "And I'll get you the pint I owe you, OK? Say I call your paper about 11-ish?"

"Eleven? Fair enough, I suppose. Can't promise how long my boss will be prepared to sit on it, though. Editors, you know."

No, Alexander had not met any editors.

"Good. Tomorrow, then." Alexander offered his hand. Simmonds shook it.

"We're on the right lines, though, aren't we?"

"Maybe. Maybe." Alexander took his coat.

Home or The Yard? Home. Lucy was still at her flat so he would be able to work in peace. He was in a hurry and decided to hail a cab — be at least 15 minutes quicker than the Tube now that the rush-hour traffic was easing.

Christine Stevens's daughter took the call and shouted to mum, who was dozing in her armchair in the lounge. "It's a man from work, mum!"

Pray God not another one, she thought, taking the receiver and shooing Hazel back into the lounge. She listened to Alexander for a minute, and thought for a few seconds before replying.

"Eight o'clock, my office. Oh, and I'd best invite Marshall. Sorry. Goodnight."

+

"Berlin."

"Berlin?" Det Supt Stevens asked.

"Yes, Berlin," repeated Commander Marshall. "Inspector Alexander can square it with his German chum, and then let this reporter have Berlin."

"He means the murder not the whole city," said Alexander deadpan. Crack open the champagne, Marshall had contributed. Not a bad call, either.

Alexander had considered Berlin last night. Berlin and a great many other possibilities. He had been wracking his brain and had slept light and short, waking at the crack of dawn and going for a jog to clear his head. Why had he held out a carrot for Simmonds? Stupid. Stupid to promise him anything at all. He could have asked Rowley to warn off the editor.

"Yes, sir. I think that is a good option."

Stevens checked to see if Alexander was choking. "How will you play it, Rory?"

"Hmm ...tell Simmonds this morning, and call Inspector Vonderheid tonight. I'm sure the Berlin police will play ball. They've kept the London link out of the Press so far — on our wishes. I can tell him we're revealing Berlin at a Press Conference tomorrow. That fair enough?"

"And Simmonds? If he gets quizzed by the rat pack?"

"He can say he got the story from Berlin — a freelance or something. We could do with something else for a Press Conference. Something to keep the rest of them at bay?"

The meeting had commenced at 8.15. Stevens and Marshall had looked immaculate as usual, Alexander had shaved and showered but there were rings under his eyes. Again he was pleased the heavy spectacle frames masked them. Michael Caine was proving useful these days.

Silence. Three brains were working silently. Stevens suggested more coffee and phoned their order to a constable.

"Maybe next time we should meet in my office? I have a machine – a gift from some American contacts. Makes excellent espressos, lattes or cappuccinos. Three's not quite a crowd for the jug, but four is." Marshall was waffling to break the silence. The coffees arrived and the commander pulled his face.

"We let them know we're looking for a woman," said Alexander after a couple of sips. "No photo-fit, not yet anyway. We just tell the Press we wish to speak with a woman who was seen on the King's Cross train. We can say she was wearing a hat, possibly reddish, and sunglasses."

He had the edge on his colleagues. His brain really had been through the mangle that night. "We can flesh out Berlin, too. Let's say I give Simmonds the briefest info; we can then tell the Press more on the murdered woman's background. False passports, gang of foreign thieves. I think it will work. They can squabble about the Berlin leak to the Herald in private."

Marshall and Stevens nodded approval. "Call it for early morning, I would suggest," said Marshall. "Soon as the Herald hits the streets the Press Bureau will be hounded."

"Ten o'clock," said Stevens, making a note without waiting for agreement.

"I plan to let Berlin have the photo-fit, too. I'll emphasise not for media release. Any objections?"

"It's going on the database soon?"

"National and international. I think it's best to wait until after tomorrow's conference, then at least we don't upset the Germans. I really think I should prime Inspector Vonderheid first."

The databases were an essential facet of modern policing, allowing senior investigating officers access to millions of files maintained on computer by police and civilian staff at The Yard. It had proved invaluable, especially when officers wanted to track down criminals operating outside their known area. Alexander knew Marshall was one of its biggest fans.

"I can't decide about the bloody blowfish."

"What can't you decide?" asked Marshall.

"Whether to make the details available. Is it a key factor or a red herring?" Alexander reddened momentarily at his own pun. "I mean, one killing in six. Hardly a pattern of poison."

"And it's unique to this case as far as we know?"

"Yes, sir. Nothing has been found in any other files elsewhere."

"Let's keep it quiet for now. Finally, I think we need to issue a warning to editors. Make them aware that any information which could lead to copycat killings will be highly irresponsible and frowned upon."

"Frowned upon. That should scare the living hell out of them." Marshall smiled at Stevens. Her riposte was a frown, which while not quite scaring the living hell out of him at least made him avert his eyes.

"Perhaps you could issue the warning, sir? As the senior officer."

Stevens signalled an end to the meeting by rising from her chair. She had tight, very level lips.

+

The Press went crazy for a few days: 'Berlin Link', 'Mystery Woman Sought'. Most of the dailies sent teams to Berlin and ran stories about the Polish gang targeting tourists. The stories were a real mish-mash, part murder background, part tourist alert.

There was no Valentine's Day Massacre – the smart money had bet Jake would strike again that day. Some claimed that was the 'special birthday' mentioned in the note to DI Alexander.

Officers slowly tracked down more train passengers, but the interviews yielded no fresh news. The photo-fit had been shown round hundreds of cafes, pubs and hotels in Cambridge. No-one recognised the face.

Alexander re-read files he now knew backwards. DS Peters gave the Japanese chef Ichisake Kimiyama the shock of his life by turning up unannounced at his flat one early morning, just passing by and wondering if he had been able to remember anything else from his meetings with the crazy woman? No, he hadn't, goodbye.

What did he want? Lucy asked Alexander one night at his flat. He was paying virtually no interest in the property brochures they were leafing through. Lucy's flat was on the market and she was hoping for £30,000 profit. Not bad on an

£80,000 investment less than 18 months ago. Alexander had an insurance policy due for maturity next year. Unless there was a savage stock market crash he would pocket at least £40,000.

Lucy's money would act as their deposit, and they would mortgage themselves to the hilt so they could afford a three-bed semi-detached 25 miles or so outside the city centre. They had decided on north of the river, Lucy claiming it would be more convenient for her occasional trips north to visit her parents. Essex and Hertfordshire were now vying for their hard-earned money. Lucy couldn't decide; Alexander didn't really care.

She took the Essex property magazine from his hands and threw it on the carpet on top of a pile of other papers. He'd been staring at the same double-page spread for five minutes. All the properties had been well beyond their reach.

So, what did he want? Would he be happy if the killings just stopped? If this Jake suddenly called it a day and toddled off to his or her farm to grow organic vegetables? No, that wouldn't do at all, said Lucy.

"You have to catch the criminal, don't you, Rory? It's not just enough for the murders to cease, is it? You need someone to blame."

"It's called justice," he muttered.

"Is that what the people want? The people who pay your wages? Would they be happier if the killings stopped, or if there was another slaying so you could edge maybe just a little closer to catching the killer?"

"Serial killers don't stop, that is the problem. Sometimes they go months or even years, and then suddenly something makes them start all over again. People would live in constant fear, even if Jake took out a whole page advert in The Times and said 'that's all folks.' The fear would never go away."

"So you want another killing?"

"Christ, Lucy! I'm not saying that."

"Ok, sorry. Let's say you *need* another killing."

Alexander knew she was probably right. He rubbed his eyes. "Maybe. Or a mistake – could be the simplest thing. What brought this on Lucy?"

"Try a ten-minute attention span for starters. When was the last time I had your undivided attention for more than ten minutes? Ask anyone who was in The Crown on Saturday. You were so vacant, Rory. Glazed eyes and it wasn't the beer."

"Sorry, love. You're dead right, it is bugging me." He took hold of her hands. "I just want you to know I do love you."

She smiled for the first time that evening, kissed his cheek and ruffled his hair. "Bloody coppers."

"Just do me one favour, darlin'."

"What's that?"

"Buy a bloody house. Any house you like – you know the budget. Wherever you're happy, I am happy."

She knew he meant it, too. "That is a deal."

Now it was his turn to smile for the first time that evening. He picked her up and carried her into the bedroom. "Ten minutes undivided, you say? Can't promise ...but I'll try."

✝

Antonia Helm had had two boyfriends before she met Rob. Nothing to do with love, she just wanted to see what all this fuss about sex was. Her friends were talking about it all the time. She knew a few who had tried it at High School. The second boyfriend lasted a day short of four weeks, which was ten days longer than the first. So that was what sex was all about, a lot of fuss and mess for a few tingles. The outside was all-American good time girl; the inside was all-American weird, even before she went under her soulmate's spell.

There had been plenty of dates and dinners since Rob's death. But no romance. She did wonder if she would have landed the Paris post sooner if she'd accepted the sleazy advances of the vice-president's greasy son. But she was pleased she had earned it on merit alone.

European Consultant, her business card said, most definitely not sales person, though her role did involve promoting the products of Immediate Software Solutions around northern Europe.

Her Parisian apartment was up for sale as she now spent most of her time in London. Immediate Software Solutions' success in the UK was primarily down to Helm. Since landing in the Old World two years ago, she had maintained old customers and attracted a handful of new ones. The feather in her cap was a several million dollars a year contract to supply and maintain computer hardware and software for a major pharmaceutical player with its HQ in London.

ISS had a tiny office in London. It was central but shabby. It was more a mailing address than office. There were two tiny rooms, neither of which was suitable for inviting clients. Helm was the only person to use it, and that was seldom. Now she used it to store her very special things. Four-star hotels, on expenses, naturally, were her chosen abode. She was in London for a fortnight now, before a whistle-stop tour of the Benelux countries. Yes, she really did need her own place in London. Nothing too grand, just somewhere she could call home, where she could have maybe one of those compact hi-fis, and a bookshelf; and somewhere she could lay out a proper Monopoly board.

Time to play. She got up from the bed and walked to the wardrobe. Hidden among her underwear was a travelling Monopoly set, one of those magnetic ones. She always made a note of the positions anyway, just in case the pieces fell loose during trips.

She took a few swigs from her bottle of water and then threw herself back on the bed and began toying with the dice. Rob's turn, wasn't it? Yes. Rob's turn didn't count but he had to have a turn. Nine. She moved The Shoe – Rob had always liked The Shoe – from the Water Works to Park Lane.

Her turn now. Helm took her time shaking the dice in her right hand. "Where shall it be? Where shall it be?" she chanted softly, her eyes taking on a hypnotic stare. Five. She moved The Car from King's Cross to Just Visiting Jail. Now wasn't that simply hilarious! Oh how she wished Inspector Alexander and that Stevens woman could have been watching. A jail ...could she? Helm lingered a moment before dismissing the notion.

Rob again. Six this time. The Shoe passed GO! on its way to Whitechapel but did not collect £200 as they weren't playing with money. What was the point?

"Where shall it be? Where shall it be?" The mantra of murder. She threw double four and landed on Malborough Street. Lucky Malborough Street! Doubles didn't count; it was where you landed at the end of your turn that mattered.

Seven next. Helm sat up and clapped her hands. Leicester Square. A yellow – she hadn't done a yellow yet. She liked Leicester Square, too. Wouldn't it be exciting, Rob?

She got up and walked the room for a few moments, pleased with the luck of the dice. She took a sheet of paper from the hotel notepad and jotted down the positions of the pieces for next time, folding it inside the game and returning the box to her underwear drawer.

Leicester Square was a mile away at most. She would go for a bite to eat and a recce tonight.

It was four days till Rob's birthday.

✝

CHAPTER SIXTEEN

✝

SHE HAD been watching the two men at the bar for about 15 minutes. Either one would do. Her table was hidden from their view in the crowded Knights Of St George. She preferred the one on the right, having heard him say he was in the city on business. The other guy looked like an office worker, refreshing himself before heading home. Helm made her move when her theory proved correct.

"Oh, I am sorry. So clumsy of me – been one of those days. What is it?"

"No problems, love," said the businessman, wiping the beer from his sleeve.

"Please, I insist. Especially with the damned prices they charge in this town."

"American?"

"How'd ya guess?" She laughed.

"Well, I'll have a bitter then, thank you kindly. Anything to oblige and maintain diplomatic relations with our greatest ally."

Helm smiled again and ordered the drinks. She could tell the man had already sunk a few pints; this was her first taste of alcohol that day, having stuck to water while assessing potential victims.

"The Queen!" said Helm, raising her martini.

"And your president!"

She apologised once more and made to return to her table. "Jeeze! Would you believe it? A girl can't leave her table for two seconds."

"You should take a leaf out of the Germans' book and leave a towel."

"Ha! Ha! Yes, I have heard about the Germans on holiday."

She looked around, knowing full well that tables were at a premium.

"Looks like I'm gonna have to stand. Just like one of the British blokes. Ha! Ha!"

"Is it really that bright in here?" The man tilted his head towards her sunglasses.

"Eye drops. Some kinda infection the doc said. I think the cure is worse than the cause." Yeah, he's game.

"Business or pleasure?"

"Why I'm in London? Pleasure, most definitely pleasure."

So she spun him her yarn, as the British say. The trip had been booked last summer. A couple of weeks before Christmas she'd split up with her boyfriend – he was a slimeball anyway – but she'd thought what the hell; why waste a trip that was paid for? Now here she was, having a great time but couldn't you do something about the weather?

"This is mild for February. Another drink?" He'd finished his pint and saw her glass was almost empty.

"Hmmm, twist my arm. Is that what you say?"

He laughed again. "Yeah, that's what we say."

"Just one more, then I really should go and eat. I am absolutely starving. This tourist thing sure takes it out of you." Come on, pal, take the bait. He didn't let her down.

"Me, too, wouldn't mind a bite. Been dashing here and there all day. You sometimes forget how big this crazy city is."

She toyed with her drink before replying. She tried not to sound too coy. "Well, I spotted a terrific looking pizzeria I was going to try—"

"You mind if I join you? Diplomatic relations and all."

She thought for a moment. Don't sound too keen. Then …"Hey sure. Why not? Diplomatic relations. Cheers!"

Helm tried to pay some degree of attention as he unloaded his business problems, but inside her the excitement and tension was mounting. She had to force herself not to rush the drink.

Good, there was a free table by the wall.

"By the way, I'm William."

"Like the prince? Nice name."

"Always been William, never Bill. My parents hated Bill. Always wonder why they named me William, then. And you?"

She looked at him for a moment, then reddened or tried her best to. "Parents! God bless them. I hate my name."

"Why's that? Come on, tell me."

Helm leaned forward. "No, you have to guess."

"Well, I mean, how many girls' names are there? Give a poor guy a clue."

She took hold of his left hand, having noted his right was his drinking hand. She took a pen from her pocket and turned his hand over so it was facing palm upwards. She tried not to press too hard but wanted to make an impression that would last a while. JTJ she wrote in blue ballpoint.

"Now, the surname is easy. But, tell you what, guess any of the two Christian names and I'll pay for the meal."

The waiter interrupted them and they ordered pepperoni pizza with side salad. He suggested they share a bottle of red wine. Even better. Excellent, in fact. Her mind floated back to Atlantic City and the poor victim throwing back Jack Daniel's. Then the guessing game commenced. The businessman, from Birmingham he'd said, was loving it. The wine arrived and they toasted diplomatic relations once more. Henry Kissinger couldn't have wished for a more cordial tête-à-tête.

After five failed attempts at both initials she said she needed the bathroom and left him scratching his head. She was loving it, too. This was easily her most exciting outing to date. The name thing had just hit her. Brilliant. You are so clever, Antonia. Rob had told her that often. She could see Rob smiling down.

The gloves were worrying her now, though. What if he said something about the gloves? She could hardly claim to have a skin infection as well as an eye one. Fashion. Yes, the gloves were a fashion statement. All the women wore gloves in New York. No doubt the craze would hit London before the Second Coming. You are so clever Antonia.

The bottle was tiny and nestled neatly in her right palm. She had practiced many times in the ISS offices but she performed the exercise a few more times to relax herself, deftly unscrewing and rescrewing the lid.

Two huge pizzas and one large bowl of salad were awaiting her return. Before sitting down, she leaned across the table, her left hand reaching over, hovering a second before she flicked at his shoulder.

"Fly," she said. "I think I got it. Cheers! Any more names for me?"

He took a slurp of his wine and began slicing his pizza. "I'll leave the Js for now. Not that I can think of many more." They were both smiling and chewing. He took another good slurp, draining his glass. He began pouring the wine and guessing.

"Theresa? Tessa? Tanya? Trudy?"

She shook her head and laughed. William bit into a slice of pizza. He wiggled his eyebrows as he chewed. "Tara? Tonya? Tina? Ta ... Ta ..."

A cough to start with, then napkin to mouth, initially out of embarrassment she thought. Then, hand to throat. More coughing followed by a horrendous sound from deep within. He turned to face the wall, one hand resting on it for support as he threw up by the side of the table.

The sounds had attracted the attention of fellow diners. Helm rose from her chair and placed her hand on his shoulder. Then the man's legs gave way and he fell into his chair, almost toppling himself, the chair and the table over.

"Darling! Darling! Darling ...waiter!"

An anxious-looking waiter was already approaching the table.

"It's my husband ...his tablets. He's left them in the car." She was fumbling in her pockets. "Watch him, please. I need to get his tablets."

As she was dashing from the restaurant she turned and shouted back in her best Irish accent: "Water! Get him some water!" William fell off his chair.

Outside, she tried not to rush. She glanced back once. No-one had followed her outside. She turned a corner and walked as calmly as possible to another pub she had been in earlier. She made a bee-line for the toilets. Hat, sunglasses and coat came off quickly. Then the blouse, shoes and skirt, just to be sure.

She let down her hair, pulled a pair of tatty denims over her tights. Then a green tee-shirt, green socks and a pair of trainers. A hooded fleecy jacket completed her change-over.

Before leaving the cubicle, she checked the tiny bottle. It was empty – she had poured the whole lot into his wine glass! A whole batch of poison! I hope that guy knew how much I paid for those damned fish, she chuckled nervously. She flushed the toilet, rinsing the bottle in the gushing water. A whole bottle!

Her gloves remained on until she had disposed of the bottle in a bin by the washbasins. Then the gloves joined the rest of her original outfit in her bag.

She quickly left the pub and made a slow circuit of the square before entering a pub 50 yards from the pizzeria. Helm ordered a large Cognac and coke.

"Coke in a bottle please, I'll pour it myself."

Luckily, there was a free stool by the window. The windows hadn't been cleaned too thoroughly, but that was a welcome sign; she wouldn't look too obvious as she stared across at the pizzeria. People were leaving now, and they did not look as though they had enjoyed their meal. A waiter and a flustered man in a black suit – the owner probably – were hanging around outside, looking both ways.

Two uniformed police officers walked quickly – but not hurriedly – towards the restaurant and were waved inside by the black suit. Two minutes later, one of the officers and a waiter returned to stand outside the restaurant. They seemed to be informing potential diners that the restaurant was closed.

Helm noticed her brandy glass was empty. She couldn't recall drinking a drop. The coke tasted sickly, but Helm did not want to draw attention to herself by buying another brandy yet. She drank slowly from the bottle.

Fifteen minutes later, with no further action taking place across the way, she asked a couple to watch her jacket as she went to the bar, returning with another large brandy. This seat she did want reserving. Her whole body was tensed. For some unfathomable reason she felt like a cigarette, even though she had smoked less than 20 in her life. She fought the urge and kept watching and waiting.

A further 30 minutes passed, and she was on her third brandy and coke before more people began arriving; a police car – flashing lights and all – dropped off a man and a woman she took to be detectives.

Alexander's arrival almost caught her by surprise. He stepped out of the driver's side of an unassuming green car. Bright green. Yucky; she expected him to have better taste. No-one else appeared to be in the vehicle so she guessed it was his car. All of a sudden there was a crowd. She couldn't keep abreast of the situation. The biggest crowd in one of central London's busiest squares was congregating outside the Italian restaurant.

More uniformed officers were winding tape across the whole restaurant facade, a van deposited a bunch of people in white suits, an elderly man and a younger woman arrived by a taxi. The police officers seemed to know them.

So many curious passers-by had gathered around the pizzeria now that her view was completely obscured. Finishing off her brandy with a gulp, she collected her things and headed outside.

Even standing on tiptoes she wasn't able to see above the throng and into the pizzeria. She got close enough to memorise Alexander's number plate, however, and made a note as soon as she was a safe distance from prying eyes. She'd also caught the sign in the rear window. That may come in useful.

The two bobbies had done their best once they arrived, but the damage had been done, and Alexander could hardly blame the owner. Infuriating but totally understandable. Most of the diners had left as soon as they realised there was a dead man slumped at a table. He'd been vomiting, too. Twelve tables still held half-eaten meals.

A middle-aged couple and a party of four had stayed behind to help, or was it out of ghoulish curiosity? The bobbies made them wait for the detectives, and they all seemed happy to stick around.

The party of four yuppie types had been at the table closest to the dead man. They were celebrating a promotion and had been too busy drinking, cracking jokes, flirting and telling tales to pay much attention to the victim and his girl-friend. Possibly an American accent but then she had shouted something as she left and sounded more Irish, or Welsh maybe.

All the waiter could remember was a red hat and sunglasses which she kept on. No, he could not tell what sort of accent she had, but they spoke English. The older couple could not add anything; the woman saying the first time she paid them any notice was when she heard the man being ill.

All six of the diners, the owner and two waiters were in agreement once they had seen the photo-fit, however. Yes, it was a fair likeness of the woman who had shared the table with the dead man. Drink seemed to be wearing off for the yup-pies and the two women began sobbing into napkins; the middle-aged couple stood in a shadowy corner holding hands.

At least Professor Carmichael seemed happy. Dr McMillan was with him again. Was it coincidence or were they Siamese twins? Lovers even? Hardly.

"No outward signs," purred Carmichael. "Judging by what the waiter says it sounds like poisoning. Quicker we get this chap on the table the better. You seen the hand, inspector?"

Dr McMillan held the palm upwards so Alexander could see the writing.

"A significant departure, Rory?"

Carmichael raised his eyebrows at hearing his colleague refer to the detective by his first name.

Alexander looked around for some latex gloves. The junior pathologist handed him a pair and he took hold of the hand, leaning close enough to lick it.

"Strange," said Helen McMillan. "Don't you think? Surely it would take just as long to write as to carve it?"

"Thereabouts," Alexander replied after his close-up scrutiny. "So there must be another reason. Not the most discreet place to try and leave a signature, especially when your dinner partner is throwing up."

They both glanced at the mess left by the victim around the table, down the wall and on the floor. This was much messier than the Arsenal fan. His shirt and suit were covered in vomit, too. His eyes were still open; his head tilted back but at least liquid had ceased dribbling from his gaping mouth.

"Finished, inspector? Let the forensic chaps do their stuff then we can get cracking. I'd like to work through the night on this one."

"Yes, professor. Can you give me a ring soon as you're done, or maybe a few minutes in advance? I'd like to come over. Doesn't matter how early."

"Certainly. You can pay for breakfast."

Pathologists! How could they do a job like that? How can I do a job like this? Carmichael was often keen to stick in the knife, but this corpse had whetted his appetite more than usual.

Alexander was heading out of the pizzeria when he checked himself and turned back. He'd hardly acknowledged the presence of his two officers. He mumbled a thanks to DS Hodges and DC Hughes for arriving so promptly – he knew they'd been having a cosy drink at The Ferret – and left them a few instructions.

The uniforms did their best to clear a way for him through the crowd still hanging around outside. He headed home knowing once again he would sleep little.

It hit him at a few minutes after 2am. Too wired to sleep, he forced himself to at least lie down on the bed and close his eyes. Images flashed behind his eyelids, the businessman most prominent. Alexander had seen many a gruesome murder scene; lots of blood and gore and mutilated bodies. Victims battered beyond recognition. Old victims, young victims – some mere toddlers. Yet he found the Jake murders more chilling. It was the poison that frightened him most. Too clinical, too easy almost.

But why the pen? And why on the palm? He shot up in his bed. Of course, so obvious. She wrote the initials with the bloke's blessing. She wrote while he was still alive, before he had been poisoned, before he was clawing at the wall and gasping for his dear life. Had to be that way. Like kids often did with phone numbers. Now why didn't you leave your number, Jake?

The night's events had now convinced him that Jake was a woman and probably working alone, not as an accomplice. Maybe he would discover in the morning if they were much closer to nailing the bitch. Sleep. For now he must try and sleep.

+

Commander Jonathan Marshall won the day. He had not been seen before the 10am briefing in Assistant Commissioner Rowley's room, not even dropping by to say 'good morning' to the senior investigators.

Alexander argued that the woman was obviously disguised when she killed.

They had no idea of her hair colour or style, and no information on her eyes. The sunglasses covered almost half her face. Think of the top half of someone's face. How dominant it is. Look around this room, look at OUR faces. Do you concentrate on the bottom of the nose and the mouth? Or on the top half: the eyes and the hair? To make his point, Alexander grabbed hold of Det Supt Stevens and turned her to face away from the two senior men. She looked startled. He asked Commander Marshall to describe her mouth.

Marshall smiled at his little trick. "We're not saying your point isn't valid, inspector–"

"And then there is the Japanese chef; he was stabbing in the dark when he and Pascoe discussed the mouth. The sunglasses – he said he stared at the sunglasses."

Rowley stood up to speak. "All valid points, Inspector Alexander. But, you see, we are simply asking people to come forward if they have seen this woman." He held up the photo-fit. "Clearly she has to get into her killing garb somewhere and sometime along the line. The only sightings we have, she has been wearing this outfit." He waved the paper with distaste. "We don't know whether she dresses like this all the time – when she goes to work, goes out to dinner or the cinema …or whether it is reserved for murdering innocent people."

Rowley let the sheet flutter onto his desk. "But it is the only image we have." He prodded the face. "The only artist's impression. Give me a photograph and I'd use that. I'd love a photograph, and I'm sure we all would. For now this is the image we will use. This is the image you two will give to the Press today. Got it?"

"Yes, sir."

"You've called it for noon?"

"As you requested, sir," said Stevens.

"Good. The Commissioner wants it in tonight's papers if possible. Might make the final editions, I hope. He told me Mrs Brook and their children have dined at that place. Supposed to be jolly good, too – if you like Italian."

Even Marshall had to find a spot to study now. Anywhere but Rowley's eyes.

"Everything should be on the database by now, sir." Alexander interrupted his ramblings. "Photo, details of the poisoning, the signature. We might get a match."

"Good. Yes, let's hope so."

"DI Alexander quite understandably fears information will start leaking out now, sir. So I am preparing another note to the media. I'm quite happy to send it, unless you feel it should bear the hand of yourself or the Commissioner?"

"Thank you, commander. I'll get back to you on that."

"Right. We'll keep you informed of any developments, sir." Stevens brought the meeting to an end as she often did. Gasbag was rather a cruel tag. She sensed the AC's mind was wandering, probably trying to recall if he had forgotten any of the Commissioner's instructions.

✝

Standing room only. The Murder Room was heaving with bodies; very busy bodies by the look of it as Alexander and Stevens returned to check progress. They had but a few minutes to spare before preparing to meet the Press pack. DS Hodges and DC Hughes arrived together, confirming to Alexander that they were now an item. The two officers had stayed behind at the pizzeria, garnering any further information they could from staff and the six diners. They had been thorough. A sizable file had greeted Alexander that morning: approximate time the woman and the victim entered the restaurant, what they ordered, precise timing of call to the police – by the owner. The woman had dashed out claiming something about getting her husband's tablets from the car. No-one could remember if she had mentioned what the tablets were for. No-one had heard her speak, though one of the diners heard laughter coming from the table. A waiter said he had seen the woman go to the toilet. The victim had ordered the food and the wine. They had seemed to be happy and enjoying themselves until …

Until the man started throwing up and rapidly dying from blowfish poisoning. A massive dose of poisoning, according to a breathless Professor Carmichael four hours earlier.

Hodges and Hughes had also ascertained names and phone numbers from the owner of four men who had made reservations. Officers had already tracked down three of them that morning. Birmingham officers had broken the tragic news to the wife of 39-year-old William Munroe. "Another cow he was screwing, was it?" had been her immediate reaction. They had no children. Small mercies.

"All up and running and winging its way round the globe, Rory," said DS Pierce, turning away from the row of computers that were reserved for the national and international data collection.

"Let's hope it rings a few bells somewhere."

"And you asked me to remind you to email Berlin before you forgot."

"I had forgotten so thanks for reminding me."

"That doesn't make sense. If you've forgotten, he's reminding you AFTER you forgot, not before ...Oh never mind. I must have caught Rowley Ramblitis."
Stevens smiled faintly.
"Be careful, Christine. You'll be getting yourself a nickname. Let me just rattle off a courtesy note to Ralf. Let him know what's happened."
"I'll wait in my office."
Alexander beckoned DS Pierce towards him after he'd finished typing.
"Keep an eye on DI Blake for me, Stuart. He's not been feeling too well."
"Problems at home I gather. Shit happens."
"Word's going round, is it? Always does somehow. He's sorting out the photo-fits for the extras – I want everybody re-interviewed and shown that picture, Stuart. EVERYBODY."

✝

Antonia Helm sat on her hotel bed. She was nursing a hangover and had cancelled her scheduled business meeting, blaming the English weather for her rotten cold. *Jeeze, Rob, that was some party! I musta drank enough brandy for both of us and half of Harvard.*
After leaving Leicester Square she had stopped in two more pubs on her walk back, then a nightcap – or maybe two or three – at the hotel bar. A business suit had tried it on, but she hadn't been that drunk. *I've just killed one of your kind so watch it!*
Breakfast had been two bottles of water from the mini-bar. The third and last sat half empty on her bedside table. She was holding a cup of black coffee and staring at the TV screen.
Her laptop computer was open by her left side but all she had written was 'Dearest Edgar.' The words would simply not flow this morning.
Behind Alexander and that superintendent woman was a huge photo. The artist had done a decent job; it did look somewhat like Jake. Such a shame Jake now had to die. He could hardly complain, not with such an exciting six months under his belt. She would dispose of the outfit before the day was out.
Helm raised her cup to the screen, toasted Rob and Rory. She toasted diplomatic relations and laughed. *Welcome to March ...meet Jake The Second.* She put down the cup and lay back on her bed, laughing harder. Her head was clearing.

Another hour and she would face the world. She closed her eyes and wondered what kind of outfit Jake The Second should wear.

+

CHAPTER SEVENTEEN

✝

DETECTIVE SERGEANT Stuart Pierce was on his feet as soon as he spied his boss enter the MR.

"Some days I think it'd be easier to get an audience with the Pope."

Alexander's look told Pierce humour was not the order of the day, but he could not help himself at the best of times

"Six o'clock. Six oh-fuckin-clock. Yes, Stuart, very kind of you I'd love a sandwich." The inspector ran a hand through his hair, threw his briefcase onto his chair and placed his dark blue jacket over his computer monitor.

"Vicki!"

DC Vicki Jobson jumped out of her seat like a frightened rabbit.

"Our leader would like something to eat. Be a darlin', would you. Two of those chicken stick things and two coffees. Thanks. Oh, get me a bag of crisps, too. Any flavour; surprise me."

"Christine around?" asked Alexander.

"Mr and Mrs Gasbag left about two hours ago."

"Mr Gasbag?"

"Marshall. Don't think he's said two words to the crew since he's been with us. You OK, Rory?"

"Bloody knackered, Stuart. But thanks for asking. You were chasing me?"

"Yes indeed. Something you should see. Something you will want to see."

"Two minutes to freshen up – be right back."

A shower. What he really wanted was a shower, a long, hot as hell shower. They had showers on the next floor. He made do with a sinkful of warm water, plunging in his face and just standing by the washbasin feeling the best he had all day.

The Press Conference had dragged on longer than he anticipated. Stevens had been brilliant, the Press Officer pretty damn useless. Alexander felt he had handled it OK. Would AC Rowley pull him up for mentioning that the woman in the photo-fit was obviously disguised?

Three hours with forensics. THREE HOURS! All for nothing except a few more fibres for 'Thread' Gough's collection. No prints: not on the plate, the cutlery …not even on the bloody wine glass. Gloves, forensics had said. Smudges indicated gloves. Made sense, Alexander could not picture the woman wiping her prints off knives, forks and glasses as her victim was throwing up. The image again made him shudder and he pulled his face out of the water. He drained the basin and then filled it again.

The carpet revealed plenty of footprints, none of which had been clear enough to prove much. Maybe she had been shuffling her feet under the table? Nothing in the ladies' loo. Too many smudges round the washbasins, assuming the woman had taken off her gloves to wash her hands. Sorry, Alexander had told the smiling scientist, I have no idea whether or not she is a hygienic serial killer.

Then the nauseating smells and sights of the pathology lab. Sicilian red, a full-bodied Sicilian red. The poison had been administered via a moderately-priced wine from Mafialand. Helen McMillan was certain of that. She and Professor Carmichael had worked all night. He had retired to his London apartment; she had grabbed a few hours in her room at the lab before delivering a sleepy lecture to even sleepier students. Her eyes looked worse than his, thought Alexander when they had met a couple of hours ago.

Samples from the scene had been tested and found to contain high levels of tetrodotoxin – much, much higher than had been the case with Derek Chisholm. By samples Alexander knew she meant vomit scraped from the wall and carpet of the pizzeria, provided courtesy of the forensic department, always happy to give the medical experts first call.

The body had been examined thoroughly, and no sign of puncture wounds had been found. The stomach was virtually empty but there were further traces of tetrodotoxin. Professor Carmichael had been puzzled by traces of marine bacteria he was not familiar with, though he believed them linked to the poison. An educated guess was that a chemist had not prepared the poison and that the bacteria were from the blowfish. Dr McMillan had emailed her specialist friends again for their expertise.

Alexander dried his face. He looked cleaner, and he even felt a tiny bit more alive. A chicken and sweetcorn baguette was waiting for him. Ripping off the wrapper at an indecent haste, he began chomping like a starving man. He gave

DC Jobson the thumbs up.

"Ready?"

"Sure. What you got?" he asked Pierce between mouthfuls.

"Took a call just a few minutes after the Gasbags had left. An American cop had seen our info and dug out some stuff from one of their unsolveds from seven years back. Guy died in a casino from, wait for it ...bloody fugu poisoning."

Pierce was clicking away at his computer keyboard as he spoke. His sandwich lay untouched; Alexander's chewing had slowed.

"The cop, a ...Lieutenant Dirk Preece from Atlantic City Police Department ...was tied up for the rest of the day but thought we should look at this."

The sergeant turned his monitor so Alexander had a better view. A video began playing, just numbers at first.

"This is a police composite taken from three separate security cameras at the African Queen casino. The casino had only been open a few weeks."

Alexander pointed at the screen and dropped his sandwich. "Yesterday," he blurted, sending pieces of sandwich from his mouth. "February 27th – our friend's birthday is approaching. The note, the last note."

"Indeed. Now just watch this."

DS Caroline Peters had come to watch, too, standing a yard behind Alexander. All watched in silence as the drama unfolded. Nothing too noticeable at first as the camera focussing on the roulette table concentrated on the players and where they deposited their chips. Next, the croupier's hands came across, pulling away losing bets. Winning bets were paid out and then nothing for a moment until a new scene appeared – a separate camera. A figure in a baseball cap and a striped shirt, viewed from the rear was walking away. He took something from a woman and carried on walking. The camera just caught him turning round a bank of slot machines.

Then, another different angle. A man in a loud shirt was clutching his throat. The roulette table was just behind him and people had turned to stare. People tried to help the man who appeared to be vomiting and staggering. Two minutes passed as more people gathered round the scene, and suits tried to wave them away. Another angle, no it was the second angle. The woman in the red dress was still standing by the slot machines and had been joined by a man wearing a brownish jacket.

Camera three again, two beefy guys were trying to help the loud shirt away. His end looked almost comical as he slipped from their grasp and fell to the floor. Camera two again, the couple by the slot machines were walking away arm in arm. "So that's what it does to you," said Alexander, subconsciously pushing the remains of his sandwich into a bin. "Let's see it again, Stuart."

DS Walters and DCs Burns, Gough, Hughes and Jobson, sensing the interest, joined the audience for the second showing. Pierce had seen the video half a dozen times already, once with transatlantic commentary from Lieutenant Preece.

"This is a five-minute edit of a 35-minute video in real time, according to Preece. He said this is the only version available in digital format. The other doesn't add anything ...more before and after, more of the roulette table, a lot more of the guy dying, but mainly backs of bodies. No better shots of the couple by the slots."

Pierce took a pencil from his drawer. "Now this bloke here is the victim. Nice pile of chips, he's winning pretty big. Then, this guy in the baseball cap leans over and puts down a ten-dollar bill. You can do that, I'm told, though they prefer you to use chips. No good view of his face, unfortunately.

"Game over, both guys have won. Stripey picks up his winnings and then, look, something happens as he turns to leave the table. Something scratches Loud Shirt's arm and that is how the poison gets in. Loud Shirt holds his arm and Stripey seems to say something. All ends in smiles. The peak of the cap hides his face.

"Stripey walks away, takes jacket and bag from woman without a word it seems. Now, and this is roughly eight minutes later, Loud Shirt is in trouble. The casino told the cops they thought he was just drunk; said he'd been throwing down Jack Daniel's like he was attempting to hike the share price. Takes him 13 minutes or so to croak.

"They assume the guy now standing with Red Dress is Stripey, having done a quick change in the toilets. Now he's wearing shades just like his fancy woman. Big shades for both of them but not quite as our Japanese chef described."

Pierce offered no further comment as Loud Shirt's life ebbed away before their eyes. There was no sound to the video, the silence making it seem more sinister. Lieutenant Preece had also provided still photographs: blow-ups of the couple by the slot machines. Pierce showed Alexander the one he considered the best – three times the original size, the images blurred, but revealing some detail of their clothes if not their faces. The shades and the headwear made the faces pretty unrecognisable, anyway.

"I have an email address and a phone number. Preece said best to try and call him tomorrow 3pm our time. He's out of the office all day today but can be contacted on his pager if we need to speak to him desperately."

"Good to know that some people are watching that database. He just stumbled across our case?"

"Like us, they have guys daily checking updates, others checking keywords and stuff. He spotted our Jake himself. Their material isn't on the database but this Preece worked the case a few years back. I didn't get much time to speak but he seemed a decent bloke. And he insisted on informing me the weather there was worse than here."

"Right, I need to go to my office for a few minutes, better send Stevens a note while I'm there. Can you run a few copies of the video and photos onto disc, Stuart? Say three for now."

"You're thinking that could be …"

"I'm thinking, Caroline, that I am gagging for a pint and ready to adjourn to The Ferret if anyone's up for it. I'll need a guide; seems ages since I was there. Give me 15 minutes."

Once in his room, Alexander emailed the American cop, thanking him and promising to call at 3pm UK time. He copied the message to Detective Superintendent Stevens and Commander Marshall.

He flicked through the online news sites; some of the international news agencies were showing details of the Press Conference and featuring the photo-fit. Sunglasses apart, it bore no resemblance whatsoever to the woman on the video.

Ralf Vonderheid had emailed. Berlin police had found one barman in a cafe who recognised the photo-fit but could provide no more information. His team should brace themselves for many such reports over the coming days, he suspected. He placed one of the video discs in his briefcase and had the others sent to his superiors' rooms.

The photo-fit was staring at Alexander in The Ferret, too. Several drinkers were reading copies of the London evening papers, or had discarded them on tables and chairs.

Pierce and Peters had accompanied him, others coming as soon as the shift turnover had been completed. Alexander's first pint barely touched the sides. He ordered a second for himself while his colleagues caught up.

"Vicki's upset," said Pierce after a few moments of silent drinking.

"Oh yes?"

"She'd narrowed it down to Elizabeth Taylor or Paddy Ashdown in drag. She's been working on February 27th birthdays."

Alexander smiled fleetingly.

"I don't suppose you've been able to check Loud Shirt's birthday, Stuart?" said Caroline Peters, finishing her pint and waving the empty glass under Alexander's nose.

"There's a brief biog on the disc." He looked to Alexander. "But, no, can't say I noted his birthday. Guy was a salesman from Philadelphia; he was alone and celebrating the end of a successful business trip along the east coast. Case was filed after about eight months. About all I know."

"The bloke interests me. Stripey." Alexander looked at Pierce. "Did you notice how he was holding his chest when he returned in his new gear? Like he'd just done a bloody marathon."

"Probably keen to hurry back and view the results of his handiwork," said Peters. "How old would you say?"

"Impossible to tell from those images – 18 to 48."

"You need to be 21 to gamble, and they're pretty strict on ID if you look even the teeniest bit close. Youngish I'd say, judging by the shape of Red Dress. Nice figure."

"Getting off on serial killers are we, Stuart?"

"Just red dresses, Caroline. There is no known cure. I don't suppose you've got—"

She gave him a playful shove. "Well Stripey did nothing for me, if you want to know. Prefer a man with a least some meat on his bones."

"Seems I have timed my entrance to perfection," said Craig Gough, puffing out his paunch.

"Immaculate timing, Thread." Alexander held up his near-empty glass.

Jobson and Hughes were a few seconds behind him, chatting away conspiratorially as only women can do. Bound to be some bloke they're discussing, thought Alexander. Possibly DS John Hodges. He caught Pierce's eye and knew he was thinking along similar lines. They exchanged knowing looks; honorary women for a fleeting moment.

Rab Burns arrived. Gough organised a whip-round as he shouted up the drinks. All the officers handed him a fiver which he stuffed under an ashtray on the bar. A trusting lot, coppers. Order your own drinks from now on and put in another fiver when the guilt hit you.

"Happy birthday." Burns toasted Jobson.

"Very funny."

"I've got first call on the Liz Taylor interview," said Pierce.

"As long as she's wearing a red dress and shaves off fifty years and a good few pounds, eh?"

"Red dress?" said Burns. "My mum's got at least three red dresses."

"Keep her away from our Stuart then," laughed Alexander, now more relaxed than in days as he shouted up another pint.

"Ah! The video woman. Got yer. Quite a cutey, wasn't she?"

"Did you know the casinos out there have more than ten deaths a day due to gambling?"

"Ten a day, Thread?"

"Oh there's more to me than just fibres. Just had a quick surf over the ocean. All the casinos are required by law to employ medical staff 'cos of all the old codgers keeling over. It's mainly retired white blokes having heart attacks brought on by gambling. Ten a day."

"Those two guys trying to hold up Loud Shirt didn't look like nurses to me," said Burns.

"That's because they thought he was just pissed."

"Come on, Stuart. Ever seen anyone behave like that when they're pissed? I know from experience."

All laughed, even Alexander who had seen Caroline Peters drunk a few times but never seen her keel over.

"Wonder what happened to Loud Shirt's chips?"

"A Jock whipped them away while no-one was looking, Rab."

"There should be a law against slandering a whole nation," he sighed.

"You think Red Dress and Stripey are here working as a team, Rory?" asked Sarah Hughes, bringing the laughter to a juddering halt.

Funny, Alexander thought, since the video had appeared there had been little mention of Jake. Now it was all Red Dress, Stripey and Loud Shirt. He wondered what AC Rowley and Commander Marshall would make of their nicknames.

"We rule nothing in ..."

"...and we rule nothing out." A chorus of four.

"But, yes, I am eager to know about Stripey ...and the date."

Alexander was not contributing much to the drink-and-think tank this evening. His mind just needed clearing and the beer was doing its medicinal best. If he stayed too long he knew his mind would be so open that lateral thoughts would pop out like a scattergun. He preferred those thoughts in private.

Part of him had contemplated calling Lieutenant Preece's mobile, but then he considered how he would feel if he was out working a case and a foreign cop rang him for information on a seven-year-old unsolved. Six pints in 90 minutes, which was some going for him these days. Alexander pushed a ten-pound note under the ashtray and headed for the door, waving to jeers from his colleagues in the background as he bumped into a table.

He felt fine outside. Absolutely fine. But he hailed a taxi, knowing the best thing for him now was sleep. Back at Annandale he wolfed down a sandwich. Cheese and ham were the handiest items in the fridge, so cheese and ham it was. He took his cup of coffee and cordless phone into the lounge and turned on the CD player. A Rachmaninov compilation – free with one of the Sunday papers – was still in from a few nights ago. Lucy answered after four rings.

"When did you start wearing mascara?"

"What love?"

"I saw the Press Conference – your eyes looked terrible."

"Thanks for that – I feel a whole lot better."

"But your voice was pretty yummy."

"How was your day?"

"Terrific. And guess what? I've got a buyer for the flat – asking price and no chain. Brilliant, eh?"

"Hey that's great." Alexander put as much enthusiasm as he could into his now not-so-yummy voice. "Coming over Friday?"

"Yep. You can have me for the whole weekend. Now don't get stressy, but I need you to run your eyes over half a dozen houses I've earmarked. Just in the brochures, love. Any we agree on I'll make appointments for myself next week. OK? Take you five minutes, probably less knowing you."

"Sure. Sounds exactly my kind of house-hunting. Gonna try for an earlyish night. See you Friday."

"Love you."

"And you. Goodnight."

✝

Alexander was biding time; at one point he was actually twiddling his thumbs. He had slept seven hours solid. Over his first coffee of the day he had listened to the news on the radio while watching the casino video on his computer. Shave and shower and back to the video. It was noon now and he knew the Loud Shirt's death scene by ugly scene, off by heart in normal time and in slow motion. Det Supt Stevens had wanted to watch it twice in her office. Then Commander Marshall arrived and watched it.

Marshall was on his third viewing when Alexander offered to go fetch more coffee from the canteen. He needed a change of scenery. He declined lunch invitations, and sat at his desk in the MR reviewing interviews and surfing the Net for background on Atlantic City. Half a dozen homicides a year; he'd expected more for an American city. Then he noticed Atlantic City's population was just 50,000. A quick calculation told him that was the equivalent of 2,000-plus murders a year in the London area – a statistic to send a shiver down the Commissioner's spine.

Even though it was miserable and raining outside, Alexander strolled down to the Thames for something allegedly called fresh air.

Having dried himself off, he grabbed a coffee and sat at the desk in his own office. His neck felt uncomfortable, even though he rarely buttoned up his short-sleeved working shirts. A tie was kept in his jacket pocket for occasions which required one. Why was he so eager? What did he expect to learn?

On the dot of three o'clock he punched the numbers with more force than usual, as if his phone needed the extra power to stretch across the sea.

"Yeah, what is it?"

"Lieutenant Preece?"

"You got him."

"Hello lieutenant, this is Inspector Rory Alexander from—"

"Hey buddy! Sounds like you're in the next room."

"Yes, it's a good line. Someone here must have paid the bills."

"Hang on a minute, buddy. You wouldn't believe the mess around this desk." Alexander hung on and studied his own neat desk.

"Yep, I got it. African Queen, the casino not the movie."

Alexander warmed quickly to the Yank. There was a friendly air to his voice. He could picture him with his feet on a desk, probably smoking.

"Seen your artist guy's picture – you think that is our Miss Scarlet?"

"Miss Scarlet? Oh, right, yes, the woman in the red dress in the video?"

"The one and only."

"Miss Scarlet, I like that. Afraid we have been less imaginative and have tagged her Red Dress."

Christ! Monopoly and now Cluedo. That's going to blow a few minds.

"I'll tell you all I can, buddy. I was a rookie on that case and we got nowhere.

Zilch. Seems like little Miss Scarlet O'Hara and Babe Ruth just disappeared into thin air."

Alexander paused. OK, so the guy was not talking Cluedo he was talking Gone With The Wind. He was lost on Babe Ruth, but assumed he meant Stripey.

"Babe Ruth is the guy in the striped shirt, right? The actual killer?"

"Uh-huh, yeah. That's right, least I think he was wearing a striped shirt before he changed."

"That's right. Then he changed into a blue tee-shirt."

"He sure did. A Yankees shirt, but maybe you Brits can't tell that from the video. He had on a Yankees cap at the roulette table, too, then he changed into that white Panama. We flooded New York City, New York State. But jeeze buddy, Yankees fans are everywhere. You can even buy their gear in London these days."

"You worked the case for eight months, I believe. You pick up any leads?"

"Nope. Nothing much, anyway. A few suckers in the casino could recall the red dress but that's all. Nice touch that dress, gotta hand it to Scarlet; she took the attention away from her face."

Alexander thought of DS Pierce ...and men all over the world. He wondered whether Lucy had a red dress.

"The casino put up a big reward – two hundred grand. They were new, you see, and were worried about the bad publicity. They shouldn't have bothered. All the ghouls came out. The joint was packed; everyone wanted to see that table, play at it if they could. Some folk, huh."

"What about the victim? Were you able to find out much from that side?"

"Joe Bloom aka Jack Daniels to the casino staff. Problem was we didn't find out until late Monday that he had been murdered – even then it was a lucky break."

"Monday? Two days after he had died?"

"Yep. See, the casino just assumed another heart attack. Witnesses said he'd been at a blackjack table for an hour or so and downed maybe four JDs. The roulette croupier said he'd been playing and winning at his table for at least two hours. The security videos backed that up and showed he'd had seven drinks. Two waitresses said JD was the only drink he ordered. And those casinos, man, they don't serve half measures; they want you at 30,000 feet and higher when you're at their goddamned tables."

"So they just assumed the drink made him collapse. His collapse looks pretty spectacular on the video. I'm surprised no-one spotted anything suspicious."

"Yeah! I know. But, you see, their eyes are on the tables. They're more worried about tricksters pulling strokes than a few guys dying. The top man was unavailable till he discovered we were investigating a murder."

"And the mortuary was closed for the weekend I guess."

"No way – 24-7 those folk operate. He just joined the line. His turn came up Monday and was going to be filed as another cardiac until a young guy discovered the poison and traced it back to the scratch on the arm.

"They roped in some college professor who identified it as tetrodotoxin from this pufferfish. Well that got plenty of folk off their backsides. Was like a medical convention around here for a while. Media went crazy, even CNN ran a piece on it, man. Crazy – for a week. Like I said, that brought the ghouls out, too."

"You get anything on the guy – Jack Daniels?"

"Nothing. I was on that side, checking out his background. We thought it might have been a hit. But the wife was clean. Sure, JD had messed around with girls now and then while on the road, but there was no lover, nothing like that. He was a good husband and father back in Philly by all accounts. Business was steady. He did all right for himself. Insurance paid out just enough to keep wife and two kids comfortable. Just an average Joe."

"Sounds familiar."

"After a while there was nothing for us guys to do. No more leads, no more similar cases – zilch. The case died a natural death. Now, I gotta ask you, buddy …"

"Fire away."

"See, we thought just a couple of crazies – homegrown crazies. But I saw yesterday your information about South Africa and Australia. You got any more on that?"

"No. No. I wouldn't read much into that. We think the woman has been faking accents."

Alexander told Preece about the Japanese chef and Mrs Montgomery and her Monopoly memorabilia. And then about the Monopoly connection with the London killings.

Silence. Then …

"Is this for real?"

"Seven dead bodies says it's for real lieutenant."

"Dirk. The name's Dirk. But never Dick."

"Rory. Rory Alexander. But I can get used to buddy."

"Well you got me, Rory buddy. You sure got me now. Monopoly. You know that game started here?"

"I sure do. That's two connections we seem to have."

"You're thinking American, right? Scarlet and Babe Ruth."

"Could be. I admit I am leaning that way after seeing your video. Babe Ruth puzzles me. We have nothing on a man. Our most detailed information comes from the pizzeria a few days ago. A woman matching the photo-fit poisons a man and then makes her escape, claiming she has gone for his tablets. The diners at the four tables closest to the victim's have all been accounted for. We're also fairly certain the woman was alone in Berlin."

Oh fuck! Now Alexander had to explain the Berlin Monopoly connection to an incredulous Atlantic City lieutenant. Hardly pausing for breath, he told Preece about the notes and Jake TJ, ending with the final one and the special birthday.

"I know it seems hard to believe, Dirk, but trust me, we've been through it time and again here. Give me an hour and I'll email you more detailed files, OK?"

"Sure. Sounds like fascinating reading."

"Thanks for all your help. Keep in touch."

✝

Sheds were for old men, he laughed. They needed a garage, the bigger the better.

"You mean a dumping ground," retorted Lucy dismissively. "Unless, of course, you mean to take up car maintenance." She made a point of keeping her head down as her eyes scanned the property page of an Essex newspaper. It was the third paper she had studied over breakfast. She was still in her dressing gown, drinking coffee and trying her best to abide by her promise.

Lucy had girlfriends who had been known to spend hundreds of pounds on household goods without seeking approval from their husbands or partners. Sally, a girl on the secretarial staff at work, had breezed in one Monday morning and gaily informed all that she had bought a new car that Saturday – a brand new Escort. She had owned the car for more than 36 hours now and Bryan still hadn't asked the price. But a house? Lucy was too embarrassed to ask any of her friends or colleagues if they had been granted sole discretion to purchase the marital home. It wasn't as if houses were a gender thing. Her mum had always chosen the curtains and bed linen, but Lucy was certain dad had a hand in wallpaper and carpets. She had watched him decorating the back room at the post office once and he asked if she approved of the colour.

Alexander had caved in. Well he had given a little ground and agreed to drive out to Essex. Not to check out properties, but just to get a feel for a few villages and have a pub lunch.

Lucy was well armed with details of train routes and timetables to London and distances to nearest stations.

"Well, yes," Alexander conceded eventually. "You know, somewhere to keep stuff; garden stuff if you insist on having a garden." He looked away. She knew full well that he desired a garden as much as she did. "You know, lawn mower and spade and all that; and a toolkit."

"Toolkit!" She could not stop herself from looking up now. "You're not telling me you have a toolkit?"

"Well, not yet – but maybe one day."

She smiled, shook her head and returned to the paper. "I shall look for one with a shed and a garage."

"If we have a garage we shouldn't need a shed, should we? I swear my old man spent half his leisure hours in his bloody shed. Old men and sheds. Stuart said his dad would head for the shed whenever Coronation Street was on. He knew there was no chance of his wife disturbing him so he could enjoy half an hour with his smokes and his men's magazines."

"And your dad? Did he have a secret porn stash?"

Alexander laughed. "No! Not dad! Well not that I was aware of. Dad was a tinkerer – the original Mr Fixit. If it was broken he could fix it. If it wasn't broken he had to pull it apart and put it back together again in case it ever did become broken. Anything mechanical or electrical. I never could see the fascination."

"Useful sort of father."

"Yep. We had the best-maintained bikes in Streatham." He got up and put on his jacket. "Come on, get yourself dressed and we'll go find us a shed and a garage, preferably one with a house thrown in."

+

They arrived back at his flat a few minutes before 6pm, happy with their excursion.

"For you," said Alexander, putting down two bags of groceries to collect a letter from the mat inside the doorway. He stuffed it in Lucy's coat pocket and they hauled the bags upstairs. Alexander began putting away the food and clean-ing products – shocked at how run-down his kitchen had been.

"Wonder why anyone should write to me here," said Lucy, tearing open the letter. Alexander barely heard the strange, strangled cry. He turned to see Lucy propped against the wall, her eyes and mouth wide open in terror. The envelope was in her left hand, a sheet of paper on the kitchen floor.

"What is it? What's wrong, love?"

He picked up the note and read. His mind went haywire. Somehow he managed to quell the bile rising in his throat. His brain wasn't sure whether to inform his face to register horror, shock or fury.

Are you looking after him, Lucy?
He looks dreadfully tired some days.
Jake TJ
xxxxxxx

+

CHAPTER EIGHTEEN

✝

YES, seven kisses. He could count and saw there were seven fucking kisses. Yes seven bodies, too. He was well aware how many fucking bodies.

"My fiancée and my fucking flat. That's what I am concerned about right this fucking minute."

Assistant Commissioner Joseph Rowley's office looked and felt strange. It was two years since the head of the Serious Crime Directorate had last been there on a Sunday.

It looked strange because three of his senior officers were dressed in denims and tee-shirts, even Detective Superintendent Christine Stevens for heaven's sake. He had seen Commander Marshall in his leisure clothes of choice before on a visit to his home. Detective Inspector Rory Alexander was the youngest of the trio and reminded him of his sister's latest toy boy.

It felt strange because the most junior officer was pacing around cursing and slamming his hand against the furniture. He'd let it pass for now. It wasn't every day a serial killer hand-delivered a taunting note to the girlfriend of one of his men.

Stevens placed a hand on Alexander's back and applied gentle pressure, enticing him to sit down. He eventually obliged. Alexander glanced around the surface of the desk as if he'd lost something. He picked up a paper clip and began unbending it.

"Smaller than this," he told the room. "He, she or fucking it could have killed Lucy with something smaller than this."

"Please try and calm down, Rory."

"Calm do—"

Stevens placed a finger over his lips. "She could have killed you; she could kill anyone of us. She could kill anybody ...the Prime Minister, a member of the Royal Family ...anyone. We all know how lethal that stuff is. That is why we are here. And first we have to decide what to do about you and Lucy. We need to decide that calmly. Lucy is safe and being looked after."

Lucy had been close to becoming a nervous wreck. Until anger took over. Alexander was grateful for that. Lucy's anger was a rare sight to behold; now it had its advantages. Two unmarked police cars had stood outside his flat all night. A doctor had been called and Lucy had firmly declined his offer of something to help her sleep. She had cried and she had raged. Now Lucy was at New Scotland Yard, in the canteen with two detectives. Alexander hoped they could persuade her to eat. He knew he, too, would have to try food sometime today.

"Quite right, Christine." Rowley had figured the Lord's Day was a day for Christian names. He was very much old-style; 48 years old, 12 of which had been with The Met since moving from Swindon. Once upon a time he had been a workaholic, then a young wife had appeared in his mid-30s, followed a few years later by children, and now he preferred regular hours. He stood an inch taller than DI Alexander but weighed in two stone heavier, the result of too many business lunches since his promotion. He ran his hand through his grey, thinning hair before addressing the junior officer again.

"Now, Rory. We have house-to-house going on now. Your street, surrounding streets, pubs and any shops that are open on a Sunday."

"Sir ...come on ...we all know she will look nothing like that photo-fit if she has any ounce of sense." Alexander had calmed. He appeared drained.

"Let me finish. They are checking the photo just in case; and they are asking if any stranger stood out. If anyone saw anyone acting suspiciously. They are checking all premises that use CC-TV cameras. We are doing all we can until we have any further information.

"You have no idea how this person knew where you lived or about your Lucy?"

"Not a clue. I thought about it all night. Few outside The Met would know: family, a few friends, a handful of locals. To the best of my knowledge we aren't on any database as a couple. I mean we don't even have a joint savings account yet. I can only assume this creature conned someone who knows me into handing over details. But I can't think of anyone who knows me who would do such a thing."

"I don't like to say this," said Marshall, "but do you suspect it could be anyone inside the force?"

"Can't say it hasn't crossed my mind. But I refuse to believe anyone would do it knowingly."

"But unwittingly is a possibility. That would be my bet. Someone rings or calls in person, urgent parcel for DI Alexander ...you've just missed him ...oh but he has to have it today. Choose the right moment and you'd be surprised what supposedly private information people will divulge."

"You could have been followed, Rory," said Stevens. "Your face is well known these days. Anyone could follow you from here."

"I've been through all that and, yes, I can think of ways someone who really wanted to could track me down without a great deal of difficulty. But Lucy? How the hell would they find out about Lucy?"

"Jonathan, that will be your priority," said Rowley, taking charge of a conversation that had been up and down a few blind alleys in the 20 minutes they had been in his office.

"Inspector Alexander ...Rory, now I have to decide what to do with you."

"Do with me?"

"Naturally. First, do you wish to stay on the investigation?"

"Of course, I want to bloody stay!"

"Sit down! Or I won't even consider it an option."

Rowley was composed and fixed Alexander with a steely gaze; a gaze that could have been moulded from purest Haroldson. Alexander was not aware of the phone calls and conversations that had taken place during the previous evening and before he and Lucy had been escorted to The Yard.

The Commissioner was in Holland attending a conference on Internet crime. Norman Brook and Rowley had spoken for half an hour last night with the AC being granted complete control over decision-making and resources. Brook had phoned Alexander at his flat to offer sympathy and support.

Rowley had canvassed Marshall and Stevens in separate calls. Both were of the opinion that Alexander should continue as normal if he wanted to and if he appeared emotionally able. Marshall had been quite firm on the issue, more so than the shaken Stevens who had been unable to mask her distress.

"I shall think about it, and I want you to think about it very seriously. Discuss the matter carefully with Christine and Jonathan; and with Lucy, of course. We shall meet here in the morning and decide. Ten o'clock."

Alexander nodded.

"Good. Now your home is under round-the-clock surveillance. Where are we moving you to?"

"The flat just off Smith Square, sir," said Stevens. "It's being prepared now.

Security is good already in that area but we will have two officers guarding the flat itself. We will have someone contact Lucy's work tomorrow and explain a family illness."

"I don't think she'll want that, Christine."

"Will she not?" said Rowley. "Well let me remind you, my job …our job …is to protect the people of London whether they like it or not. Of course, we can't prevent people behaving stupidly. But we can try."

Rowley picked up the paper clip Alexander had been playing with. He held it between his thumb and finger while not taking his eyes off Alexander.

"If your Lucy makes a fuss I suggest you show her a video recording. You know the one I mean."

+

Super Tax, Community Chest and finally Electricity Company had led to Antonia Helm paying the north London suburb of Highgate a visit. But it was chance that had saved one lucky resident from certain death.

Just a day after the resounding success at the pizzeria, Helm had returned once more to her Monopoly board, hungry for more action. She landed on Super Tax and didn't bother paying the dues; her turn again and now Community Chest – someone was playing hard to get. She threw the dice for Rob, a little impatiently, anxious for her turn and the luck of the killing ground. Now, at last, six and four: Electricity Company. She had made no plans for what to do with the utilities. In truth, she had no plans at all. Should she skip the utilities, too? Helm was about to roll the dice again when it came to her. She rifled through her belongings scattered along the sideboard until she found the notepad. Detective Inspector Alexander's number plate plus the sign in the back of his little green car – Highgate Motor Auctions. Yes, they must surely have electricity in Highgate, she giggled. There was a fair chance the policeman lived nearby if he'd bought his car from there. Wouldn't it be simply wizard, as the English say, to go to work on his doorstep?

Friday morning she arrived early by Tube, played the tourist by visiting Karl Marx's tomb at the cemetery, and then went hunting the murder scene, though, of course, only she knew it was going to be a murder scene.

Electrical goods shops had been discounted, but a sub-station would be fair game. There was one about a quarter of a mile to the right off the top end of

High Street, according to her maps.

Helm was wearing her hooded fleecy, new tight-fitting denims and trainers; she blended in nicely with the locals. The sub-station was fenced off and the only door was padlocked, warning signs hung from all four sides. The pathway was narrow and led from High Street to a 1960s housing estate. Only maintenance workers were permitted vehicle access. Lighting was ideal: one post outside the sub-station with the next ones being at least a hundred yards either side. Plenty of shadow in the night. She could wait or preferably follow a lone walker down the alley, feign she needed help with directions and then pounce when the victim had turned. Yes, ideal. Might as well return tonight.

Pure chance. She returned to Highgate by car and parked a mile away. It was a few minutes after eight o'clock. She had walked once through the alley into the housing estate and then round via the main roads. If possible she would exit via the estate, fewer people out at that time. As a last resort, if she discovered people approaching from both directions, she could skirt round the fence and make her escape across a small playing field.

A small group of trees on the opposite side of the road from the alley and about fifty yards closer to the centre of town provided shelter as she waited and watched. She noticed that people carrying bags and packages from fast food outlets were using the alley. Two couples came onto High Street, heading for a night out.

Then, the laughing couple caught her eye. Maybe it was the sound of their voices carried on the wind that made her turn round. It could be him! Impossible to tell from this distance and in the dark, but it looked like him! Detective Inspector Alexander was walking along High Street towards her. A woman was hugging herself to him. He was talking; she was laughing.

As they suddenly turned and entered a public house she knew it was him. He was wearing a suede jacket with the collar turned up. That was the jacket he had been wearing when he arrived at the pizzeria.

What should she do? It seemed too good to be true: a murder committed by Jake a few yards from where the investigating officer was enjoying a few pints of ale. She had to stop herself from laughing.

Excitement grew inside Helm as she waited, thinking now rather than paying attention to the alley. Beneath her fleecy, she was wearing her new Jake outfit. Once again her hair had been done up tightly; a floral headscarf instead of the red hat. Her earrings were a matte green, to avoid glittering too brightly. Heavy red lipstick and eyeliner aged her by a good ten years. The purple pullover was pulled up close to her chin. The pleated skirt was a lighter shade of purple. Tights and practical black shoes completed the changeover. She looked nothing like the real Antonia Helm – whoever that was.

She was ready to kill, but she wanted to know more about the inspector. She wanted to get close to him. She wanted to know more about the woman, too. That surprised her. Helm was happy just to poke fun at that woman officer who sat on the conferences with him. But this woman had been hugging him, and they had been happy and laughing. Helm wasn't jealous. It was silly to even think that she had any designs on Alexander. It was just that …it was just that it could have been her and Rob. It should have been her and Rob.

Jogging back to her car, she wished she'd brought some poison with her. But the last two bottles were being saved for special occasions. That would be the icing on the cake, killing him in his own pub. Then she realised a Highgate pub wasn't on the Monopoly board and that wouldn't do at all. She had to play by the rules, her own rules as handed down from on high by Rob one warped night while she had been sleeping.

Two makeup wipes did the job. She studied her face in the rear-view mirror of her Ford Escort. No smears. She took off her pullover to reveal a light blue plain tee-shirt. Pulling on the jeans wasn't easy in the confines of the passenger seat. Her hair she fixed with a band and tucked it down the back of her tee-shirt.

What jacket to wear caused her most consternation. She was playing at being Antonia Helm so Antonia's cagoule was the correct choice. By the time she had finished she could have been that bright, wide-eyed girl who skipped to her first day at Harvard all those years ago.

Heart thumping, she turned round the Escort and parked by the trees. Satisfied no-one had seen her she got out and put on the cagoule and walked to the pub. She took a deep breath and entered The Crown And Anchor. It was packed with people as it usually was on Friday nights. Heads turned to look at the newcomers – nothing to be concerned about, just an ancient British pub tradition. No eyes lingered. They had drinks to be drunk.

Alexander and the woman were stood close to the bar, merrily chatting away with another couple and two men. She forced herself to look away. There was a clear spot by the bar about ten feet from the inspector's party. In between was a hatch for bar staff to move from behind the bar into the lounge. She knew it was strictly against pub etiquette to block that hatch

"What's yer poison, luv?" The barman's words startled her. She must have looked shocked, too, before she could manage a smile, realising what he meant.

"A Perrier, please." She spoke ever so quietly. Would he catch an American accent? Her own accent was safest, especially in a pub.

"Ice?"

She shook her head, paid and said "thank you" to his back. Her back was turned to Alexander. She listened intently as her eyes scouted around the pub, trying not to stop on any particular spot. People were talking all at the same time but she picked up pieces of the conversation. "Cheers!" seemed to be the most common word in the English language.

Wedding …houses …Essex …Lucy ….July …flat sold, fingers crossed. She put snatches of conversation together and guessed Lucy was Alexander's girl-friend and they planned to wed in July. Someone accused Lucy of robbing The Crown of a good man. Then loud laughter. One of the group seemed to be called Terry. There were lots of 'mates', 'pals', and she thought she heard a 'Janice'. They talked of house prices and cars and football and summer holidays.

She finished her drink and left. Outside she checked her watch, 10.15pm. Last orders was 11pm in British pubs and people started drifting away a few minutes afterwards. Would Alexander stay till closing time? Would they go elsewhere afterwards or straight home? Would they go to his place or hers? She recalled hearing talk of flats and sales.

An inviting McDonald's across the road made up her mind. She ordered a Big Mac and chocolate milkshake and sat and watched the pub from a bench by the window. Three couples entered but she saw no-one leave. At 11 o'clock she walked to her car, glancing back at the pub door now and then.

Alexander and Lucy left at 11.25 with three of their drinking friends. The trio turned and headed towards Helm's car, the young lovers going in the opposite direction. She waited a few seconds after the threesome had passed before starting her engine. Alexander and his fiancée were still in view but soon turned down a side road. Helm followed and slipped into the first parking space she saw on the street. She just caught sight of the house they entered. Two minutes later she drove past, checked the number and then headed back to her hotel. The alley lay unmolested that night. Pure chance. She could have done it. Of course, she could. But after discovering where the detective or possibly his girlfriend lived Antonia Helm was far too excited. She had other plans to make.

Helm was back in Highgate by mid-morning the next day. She'd taken the Tube and was pleased to see shoppers were out in force. A jogging outfit was her chosen attire for the job – a good excuse for being in a hurry.

McDonald's was doing a lively trade, it looked as though The Crown And

Anchor was about to open, people were pouring from the alley. Doubts appeared again as she approached Annandale. They had first come when she was typing the letter: what if someone opened the door as she was about to post it? Chances were slim but the fear gnawed at her insides. Then it was subsumed under the rush of excitement; a bigger thrill than any roller-coaster.

She turned to look down the street as she was crossing the road. No car! His green car was missing, and she was certain it had been there last night. That sealed it. Helm walked along to the next street before turning. It was best to walk round and then come down Annandale from the opposite direction so she would end up on the crowded High Street. A few yards before entering Annandale, she started jogging, stopped to open the gate, two strides to the door of number 29 and noticed there was an upper and a lower flat. No time to think, she thrust her gloved hand into the letterbox and was back on her way, jogging a little quicker now until she reached High Street.

That was fun, she thought to herself on the Tube back into central London. But her features looked glum, knowing the best part of her day was over.

✟

Lucy was bearing up very well in the circumstances. Alexander thought she was taking it better than he was. She knew the secure flat made sense; she even joked about how much a place like that would cost. He hoped she would feel the same after being cooped up there for several days, possibly weeks.

An hour before dusk Alexander persuaded Lucy to go for a walk with him. He was concerned she may develop a phobia of people and places. He had known it to happen.

"We'll be safe, love. Our own private bodyguard ...and we'll steer clear of any places with a Monopoly connection. We need to go out, really we do."

Monopoly connection. She could tell by the look on his face that he was being serious. She wasn't housebound, but don't go near anywhere with a Monopoly connection – in London? Lucy now hated the game.

Without letting Lucy hear, Alexander informed one of their plain-clothes guards of their intended route. He was to stay ten yards behind them.

"Are we safe down here?" The mock tremble in her voice could not disguise her true feelings as they walked around Smith Square. "You've got to catch this bastard, Rory. We can't live like this."

"We're doing everything we can, darling. And I'm convinced we are getting closer. She's getting cockier, making mistakes. It's not going to be easy for any of us, especially you."

"OK. Let's give it a week, eh? Then maybe I could go and stay with my parents? Or friends? Away from London."

"Maybe, we'll see. But please trust me on this, Lucy. I'm going to The Yard tomorrow and may be able to pick up more information then. Have you thought any more? Can you think of anyone acting strange?"

She shook her head.

Alexander was calm when he met AC Rowley the next morning. He had his speech prepared and it did the trick. He knew the case better than anyone, Jake was targeting him for his taunts – what was to stop him or her focussing on another officer if he was taken off the case? The Press would want to know why. All very sound arguments along the lines Commander Marshall himself had expressed to Rowley. DI Alexander was happy Lucy was safe and he was convinced he was mentally up to the job.

"Good. Get on with it then." Rowley took hold of Alexander by the shoulders and held him at arm's length. "But anything you need – and I am talking personally now, not professionally – you let me know immediately. Got it?"

"Yes sir. Thank you."

Expressions of shock and sympathy were getting on his nerves within an hour of him settling at his desk in the MR. He addressed the team, thanking them and insisting the best way to help Lucy put this behind her was to nail this sicko.

"Don't get sidetracked by the letter at my flat; that is just one of Jake's diversions. It seems she likes to play games with me because I am the most visible officer. If there is anything to be found in Highgate, it will be found. But we have many other lines to follow. We're getting closer. I know it is slow and painstaking, but we ARE closer. Believe me."

He stumbled through the day, an outward façade of competence. Jake was right he did look dreadfully tired these days; he felt it, too. Thank heavens there was no Press Conference on the horizon.

DS Pierce was a Godsend, subtly taking command of many of the details. Stuart Pierce and Rab Burns were to be his shadows for as long as necessary, Det Supt Stevens had insisted.

Commander Marshall dropped by to sadly inform him that Highgate had drawn a blank. No-one saw anything or anyone out of the ordinary. None of The Yard's duty officers had noted any requests for personal information.

He returned to the flat earlier than normal and was pleased to find Lucy asleep on top of the bed. Fully-clothed but sleeping and looking so peaceful. He joined her, closed his eyes but could not find the blessed release of sleep.

✝

Antonia Helm had never had much problem sleeping. After killing the mugger in Atlantic City she had been haunted for a few days but had always slept. She had slept well on Monday night after a boring but busy day meeting clients and handing out brochures of the new ISS products. More than just an upgrade, she had been adamant. Tuesday was spent on the phone to clients up and down the UK, on mainland Europe, and HQ back in good, old Kentucky.

The office had been the best place to change into her Jake outfit, the hotel being too close to home for comfort. Her first red one tonight – The Strand.

Once again the bottles lay untouched in the fridge. For a few fleeting moments she had contemplated doing the reds in one hit with the poison. She could manage it easily: a nice walk along Fleet Street, The Strand, ending up at Trafalgar Square. Killing would be easy, leaving her signature maybe not so easy. It was against her self-imposed rules, anyway. Obey the dice. Obey Rob. She had lost track of how many times she had been round the board; she had thrown at least three doubles, hit Community Chest and Chance several times. But she had always obeyed the dice.

The Strand was not too far from Leicester Square; maybe she could go for a pizza afterwards; a private, sadistic chuckle bounced back at her off the walls.

Dark and quiet with the added bonus of no residential properties nearby. Helm prided herself on choosing her locations well, though the train had been hairy. This was most suitable – a short, narrow street of office blocks. It could act as a shortcut to The Strand from the north or to Trafalgar Square to the west. She had seen one man doing just that.

She chose the side where several offices had inset entrances suitable for laying a body. Her first walk had shown her that no tramps were sleeping there. Now it was just a case of waiting. Five minutes later she heard quick footsteps heading in her direction. A furtive look both ways revealed the coast was clear. She looked up when the woman was a few feet away.

"Excuse me; I wonder if you could help, please. The White Lion pub, do you know it?"

"No, I am sorry, I am a stranger around here."

English with an American accent, but the woman was clearly foreign. Smartly-dressed with a tan a shade darker than Antonia's.

"Oh dear. I was supposed to meet my husband there ten minutes ago, I was sure he said Tavistock Street."

The woman looked about to walk on, but suddenly stopped. "Here, I have a map somewhere in my bag ..."

Perfect. A hefty kick to the back of the knee, the leather belt lassoed over the stooped head. The bag fell from the woman's grasp as her hands flew to her neck and began grappling with the belt. Helm pulled sharply backwards, forcing the woman's legs from under her.

Helm dragged the victim back into one of the office alcoves, dodging the right hand which struck back at her a couple of times. Twenty more seconds should do it, but the woman was surprisingly strong and putting up a good fight.

Suddenly a click followed a second later by a searing pain in her left thigh.

"Sonofabitch!" shrieked Helm, releasing her hold on the belt and stumbling onto her right knee. Now the woman was on her feet, rubbing and stretching her neck. Helm saw the glint from her left wrist; a short blade was protruding from the woman's watch. She coughed but said nothing. Helm was attempting to get back on her feet when the woman's boot smashed into the side of her face, sending her toppling over.

A mixture of anger and contempt was etched into stern features. Some strange curse hissed from her lips before she turned away and started jogging towards Trafalgar Square.

Helm forced her upper body upright and lay against the office window. She felt the side of her face with her hand; it was numb and something was probably broken. But it was her leg that was causing her to shake. Blood was pouring from an inch-long gash. Helm knew the gash was deep, too, as the woman had used maximum force.

Police would be here soon. Jeeze! It was agony to move, but she had to.

The leather belt, which had proved so lethal for some, was fastened as tight as possible around her thigh, and she managed to haul herself to her feet. Pain shot through the leg and up to her hip as she hobbled up the street, leaving a trail of blood in her wake. Tears streamed down her face and she tasted the hideous makeup.

By the time she had turned a corner the flow of blood seemed to have eased to a trickle. That was one good sign – the tourniquet was working. She hauled herself into the shadow of a group of bushes and lay down, panting and fighting back tears. Think! Think, don't just try to run. She managed to stifle her sobs as a couple walked by, too ensconced in their own world to notice the prone figure just a few yards away.

Hospital was the sensible choice, but surely they would alert the police. The police! How long would it take them to arrive? Trafalgar Square – easy to find a copper there. That woman was strange, and her watch; Helm had never seen a watch like that. A very handy watch for a girl to have.

Gritting her teeth, she pulled her jeans from the rucksack and began slowly pulling them on over her shoes and tights. When she reached the gash she gave a loud yelp at the faintest touch. No-one came running to see what the noise was. One-two-three, she clenched her teeth so hard she expected them to crack as she quickly hauled the jeans up to her waist.

Panting, groaning, crying and feeling desperately sorry for herself, Helm lay there unable to move. Gradually the pain eased and was replaced by a numbness. The left side of her body felt paralysed.

She was amazed no police had arrived yet. How she managed to get upright she will never know. But she was able to stand and shuffle along; not for long, though, before she needed to rest. She was fifty yards at most from the scene of the attack.

A lamppost acted as prop as she waited. There was no other option. Ten more minutes passed at an agonising crawl. Still no police. Why on earth not? But, at last, a taxi. And, joy of joys, it was available.

She didn't care whether or not the driver believed she had fallen, she just wanted to get back to her room. At least her brain was starting to function again and she wiped the smeared makeup away as she sat in the back of the taxi.

The walk was going to be hell, but she told the driver to drop her off at a hotel round the corner from hers. When he had driven away, Helm hobbled to the hotel wall. It served as a crutch as she made slow progress. Stopping for breath, she took off the headscarf. Next stop she took her fleecy jacket from the rucksack. Now she looked something like the Antonia Helm that hotel staff would recognise.

Same story; she had tripped and fallen. No, she didn't need any help, thank you. She would be fine once she lay down.

Thank God the minibar had been replenished. She grabbed a handful of spirit miniatures before collapsing on the bed, the movement sending more pain through her leg. Three bottles of brandy later, she eased off her jeans as far as her ankles. The pillow was so soft and soothing. She lay there and wondered. She wondered why no police. She could only assume the woman hadn't reported the assault.

Someone tries to murder you in central London and you don't tell the police? Very weird. Very lucky.

✝

CHAPTER NINETEEN

✝

ROB CAME to her in her sleep as he often had done for the past seven years. Surrounded by clouds. The clouds suited his pallor. Haze made it difficult to see clearly but the faintest of smiles showed he wasn't angry with her. But he was chastising her again. Clumsy, poor planning, what's gone wrong, my rose? Then concern. Does it hurt? Have you lost a lot of blood? Thanks heavens it wasn't me – I would have bled to death. Ha! Ha! Ha!

His full-throated laughter woke her. She shot up and felt the pain within seconds – first the face and then the leg. She stared at the bloody mess. More blood had seeped out during her few hours of sleep and had left a five-inch stain on the duvet.

Rob was right – he was always right. He had ticked her off after the train killing, and she hadn't learned: it was important to plan the place and study the victim. Hadn't she done that in Regent Street? In Leicester Square? Certainly in Berlin. Even Whitechapel had an element of subconscious planning.

Throbbing. Her thigh was throbbing now. She lay back again, exhausted.

Bad thoughts came to her. Bad thoughts about Rob; the first bad thoughts she had ever had in her life about her soulmate. It was all right for him, wasn't it?

Who had he ever killed with his own hands? He'd scratched a drunk in a casino – big deal! But she, Antonia Helm, had felt death at her hands. She had squeezed the last breaths out of fellow human beings. She had touched them as they breathed their last, too weak to even beg for mercy. Not just feeble old women either. What about the Dutch guy, Rob? Could you have handled him? No way.

Dry sobs followed by convulsions. She had no tears to shed – it was as if her ducts had dried up in the night. She was shaking, making the bed heave and causing the pain to intensify. Now she begged Rob to forgive her for thinking ill of him. Then she begged him for help. What should she do? Guide me, please guide me. Eventually she drifted back to sleep and did not wake until gone 10am. Rob hadn't come to her that time, but she felt better, more relaxed and beginning to think straight. Her leg was still throbbing but the pain was more a nag now. Maybe she had just become accustomed to it.

Helm could not recall the last time she had taken a bath – must have been in her early childhood. Certainly since High School she had been a shower girl. But now she wanted a bath. Part of the reason was practical, of course. There was no way she could stand in a shower.

Reaching the bathroom was her private Everest, and achieved in stages. Clinging onto furniture, she first reached the table with the telephone. Work! She realised she had missed a 9.30 appointment.

Could she trust herself to speak? She had to. She rang head office in Paris: a bad fall, she could hardly walk and would probably seek medical attention later today. Could someone apologise to her clients?

Hop, hop, hop to the wardrobe, causing the flimsy door almost to break away as she supported her weight. Two more hops and she was sat on the side of the bath, running the water. She took two painkillers while the bath was filling, then she slid in, keeping her injured leg above the water at first and then ever so slowly easing it under the foam.

Ahhh. Warm with a minor tingle. The pain seemed to flow away but the water was turning pink. She was losing blood again. The wound was wider than expected, she could now see. It needed stitching, to heal properly and lessen the risk of infection.

She lay in her dark pink sea for 15 minutes, trying to relax but thinking, all the time thinking. Helm had almost forgotten about the woman, but now she reappeared. Had she told the police? Was anyone looking for a woman with a leg wound?

Forget the woman, her leg required urgent treatment and had to be her immediate concern.

Dare she risk a London hospital? She could call hotel reception and say she'd had an accident in the bathroom. Would any of the night staff be working still? They would remember her coming back last night complaining of a fall.

Or a hospital outside London? But how the hell would she get there? Stumbling around her hotel room was an ordeal.

She sat in the bath as the water drained away. Ripping a long strip off a bath towel, she fixed it tightly round her thigh to stop the blood flow. Then she used the hand shower attachment to rinse her body of the pink hue. She was happy she had a plan. Not a perfect plan, but a plan.

One: she would phone reception and ask them if they could find her a walking stick.

Two: she would have them order her a cab for Heathrow.

Three: she would grab another cab to take her to a hospital. She would check a map but knew there was a good choice of sizable towns not too far away.

Four: she would tell the hospital she had fallen last night in, say, Paris. Yes, Paris. She had banged her face heavily on a wall and then landed on a piece of sharp metal. She had done her best to clean it up for the journey but now she was in pain.

Unless Rob came up with a better plan in the next few minutes, that was what she would do. She threw her essentials into her small rucksack, knowing she had probably seen the last of this hotel room.

✝

The Israeli Embassy is the most heavily fortified in London, for good reason. Car bombs, letter bombs, protestors storming the gates – the building at Palace Green close to Kensington Palace is a popular target for pro-Palestinian groups and assorted left-wing activists.

One car bomb had been so massive the explosion had shaken the walls of the nearby palace. The Israelis had a long-standing disagreement with the British Government about security, wanting permission to deploy their own armed guards around the perimeter.

Inside the fortress, the Israelis could do what they wanted. Outside, the British Government provided more seen and unseen surveillance than even the American Embassy was granted.

DI Alexander was being driven there by Sergeant Alex Langhurst of Special Branch. His shadows, DS Pierce and DC Burns, were in the back of the car but had been informed by Langhurst that they were not invited into the embassy. It would take time to have them checked out and added to the list, so they would have to wait with the car.

Langhurst reminded Alexander that they would be on Israeli territory as guests of Aral. They had no legal jurisdiction.

The mysterious Aral – Langhurst did not know if it was his first or last name but that was what everyone in Special Branch knew him as – had phoned a contact in the intelligence services early that morning, offering possible information on the London serial killer. Several calls later, Aral had agreed to meet an investigating officer. Special Branch were along out of the usual courtesy to foreign embassies. Alexander was unsure what the usual courtesies meant and didn't really care. He was intrigued by the call and keen to hear what this Aral had to say.

Aral did not look mysterious. He was about 60, wiry with olive skin and a warm smile. The cardigan made him appear like a favourite uncle. His room was Spartan, though Alexander guessed it wasn't his actual working room. There was a desk with no drawers. No computer. No filing cabinets. Not even a photo of an Israeli hero or politician on the walls. This was a room for meeting guests. Quickly and with the minimum of fuss.

After handshakes and greetings, Aral waved to a tray of tea, inviting his guests to help themselves. No time to waste, the tea had been prepared in advance. He apologised for his rush but he had an important meeting scheduled and could give them 15 minutes at most.

Straight to business. "One of my colleagues was attacked last night, inspector. She considers herself fortunate to have escaped."

"Is she all right, sir? Where was this attack?"

Aral held up his hand. "Yes, thank you, she is recovering. Her neck and throat are very sore; this attacker was quite brutal. It was on a street off The Strand at approximately 8.50pm. Here, Graveson Street." Aral handed Alexander a map with the street highlighted and a red X two thirds of the way down. "Please let me tell you what I know and then if you have any questions I will answer them as best I can.

"It was on the left hand side heading towards Trafalgar Square. An American woman asked my colleague if she knew of a pub nearby. She forgets the name of the pub but says the woman said she was due to meet her husband there. The pub almost certainly does not exist. It was a ruse.

"My colleague was trying to help, looking in her bag for a map when the attack happened without warning. She was kicked in the back of the leg, she fell and felt a belt around her neck. Well she says it was a belt, probably of leather and dark in colour.

"The woman was quite strong and was squeezing very tightly. My colleague stabbed the attacker in the leg rather severely – there would have been a lot of blood. The woman fell, my colleague kicked out at her, hitting the left side of the face – this will probably be bruised badly. My colleague ran for a taxi and came back here.

"While she was being treated for the abrasions around her neck she stated what had happened. This was brought to my attention. I am aware your serial killer has been known to strangle people, so here we are."

"Why weren't the police called last night, sir?"

Aral held up a hand. Langhurst coughed. Alexander assumed the code to mean 'forget it.'

"I can tell you that the attacker was about five foot nine, slim but athletic and strong. She was wearing thick red makeup around her eyes and lips. She had on a dark knee-length coat and a headscarf. My colleague remembers flowers, and blue being the dominant colour. She had a dark-coloured sweater and a slightly lighter coloured skirt. She did not get a good look at the shoes."

Aral had been reading the description from a sheet of paper. "Does this sound like your killer? We think it was too amateurish to have been a deliberate attempt to murder an embassy employee."

"It could well be, sir. The details are most helpful. Is it at all possible to interview your colleague?"

"That is not possible, I am afraid."

Alexander did not like that one little bit, but he had heard Langhurst cough again. He must brush up on Special Branch codes.

"But she is certain the attacker spoke with an American accent?"

"Absolutely. They had spoken briefly before the attack, and she screamed 'son of a bitch' when she was stabbed; not a common phrase outside the United States."

Alexander had seen the brown, unmarked envelope lying on the desk. Now Aral handed it to him. "Blood samples of the attacker, taken from the knife. They may be useful to you."

The Embassy staff were efficient. As well as a sealed bag containing a piece of what looked like gauze with a red patch in the centre, there were details of the blood type plus a DNA reading. The inspector had questions, quite a few questions, but …

"I hope I have supplied all the relevant information, inspector. Now, if you would excuse me. Naturally, if we can be of further assistance don't hesitate to contact me." He nodded towards Sergeant Langhurst. "Special Branch have the numbers."

They shook hands and Alexander looked into Aral's eyes. He saw nothing mysterious, nothing dark, nothing sinister. They were indeed the lively eyes of a favourite uncle.

On the drive back, Pierce and Burns were eager for information but Alexander silenced their probes with a look. His own personal code. He wanted to make the most of his time with Langhurst.

"You know Aral well, sergeant? Is he all above board?"

"You can trust the information he has given you if that's what you mean. As for being all above board, he's a spook. They live well below board level."

"I admit I'm impressed with the information, the detail, the DNA – and less than 15 hours after the attack. Would have liked a few minutes with the woman, though. Would I be right in assuming she was here illegally?"

"Possibly, though I doubt it. If Aral is involved, it's almost certainly Mossad. London's one of their biggest playgrounds outside the USA."

"Secret Service – you think that explains all the detail?"

"Yes, sir. You'd hardly expect a clerk to note so much detail if someone was trying to murder them. Your attacker is lucky."

"Lucky? In what way?"

"If the agent had wanted her dead, she'd be dead."

"And why isn't she dead, then?"

"That I am not sure. Mossad does try to behave these days after all the bad publicity a few years ago. But if the agent had sniffed Arab, the attacker would have died. Swiftly.

"Maybe the agent was concerned about being spotted there and needed to make a hasty getaway? Maybe she really did think it was a mugger? Maybe she didn't want to kill an American? Maybe she was frightened? Even Mossad agents must get scared sometimes.

"One thing's for certain: as soon as she reported the incident the Embassy would have had people out there. Within half an hour of the attack, I'd say."

"Wonder what they found?"

"It's fair to assume they didn't find the attacker. The body would now have been disposed of if they had. But you can bet your mortgage that her report and all those details were in Tel Aviv before midnight. She'll have been checked out. Someone will have decided to contact us. But she'll be on their files – till the day she dies and probably a good few years afterwards."

"They contacted us pretty quickly. That surprise you?"

"A little, yes. But they never sleep. They will have had people on it all night.

The MO will have convinced them it was not a professional hit. Trying to kill a Mossad agent with a belt? Probably gave some of them a good laugh."

"So, the bottom line is, I am to trust everything Aral told me?"

"I have no reason to doubt his information. If you catch this woman and she is the killer, don't be surprised when it leaks into the papers that the Israeli Embassy helped. Always striving to present a helpful face to the locals."

The car was pulling into Scotland Yard. "One final thing worth bearing in mind, sir," said Langhurst. "There could always be an ulterior motive."

"Meaning?"

"Games, all spooks like to play games. War by deception is the Mossad motto. Just something I was taught many years ago. Take Aral's word as truth, but keep it at the back of your mind. Here's my card if you need to contact them or us again. Don't try and call Aral yourself, please. That wouldn't go down well on high. Not well at all."

Alexander didn't think this Aral — a man with no known job description — was playing games. Jake was the one playing games. The Strand — his first red one.

Pierce and Burns were bursting for details of the interview. They had picked up bits from the conversation between their boss and Langhurst.

"I need to see Christine first. We'll meet in my room afterwards."

He passed the map to Pierce. "Get this copied, Stuart, and two officers out there now. They're looking for blood on the ground. Lots of blood I believe. The smart money says it's our Scarlet's blood. Any area they find, I want sealed off."

Detective Superintendent Stevens was anxiously awaiting his return. "Well? Well? What did they have for us?" She seemed to have been taking lessons from Pierce and Burns. "Wait, better see if Marshall's around."

Stevens and Marshall listened patiently, not interrupting once.

"Aral; not seen him in years. I needed a Special Branch escort, too. He must be pushing 60 now." Marshall added that the Israeli could be trusted — he had helped enormously on two of his paper chases. A veteran of the Entebbe raid, he added. Rumours wafted about that he was involved in the forged British passport rumpus a few years ago but nothing the spooks could ever make stick. Nothing much stuck to Aral.

A knock at the door disturbed them. DS Ian Walters poked his head round.

"Thought you'd want to know, sir. DS Peters is at the scene, says the pavement and road are splattered with blood. SOCOs and uniforms are on the way."

"Right. I'm on my way. OK, Christine?"

"Yes, best thing. Let us know when you're back and we'll reconvene here."

He brought Pierce and Burns up to speed on the morning's events as they made the short drive to The Strand. They beat the forensics van by thirty seconds.

Uniformed officers were busily erecting long lines of crime scene tape. As usual, crowds were gathering. DS Caroline Peters was standing outside one of the office blocks – Sir Robert Peel House. She explained that DC Hughes was visiting all the offices to the east, informing workers to use the back entrances; three PCs were assisting her. Alexander glanced upwards and saw dozens of faces peering through windows. Not much work would be done in the next few hours.

"Some clever bastard decided to scrub the stains away from here. You can just see faint marks. This looks like where the attack took place." Her right arm pointed the way the trail led eastwards, away from Trafalgar Square. Overnight frost had caused the stains to fade but it was clear which way the woman had walked or crawled.

"Must have been some wound," said Burns.

"If you were being choked to death it's a fair bet you'd stab the attacker pretty damned hard," said Alexander, slowly following the trail – now surrounded by tape. Four white-suited scene of crime officers were poised for instructions.

"As you can see, the trail comes round the corner here. She appeared to have stopped by these trees, probably to rest. The blood is much thicker. Then to the kerb where it ends. My guess is she hailed a taxi – or someone picked her up."

"Sorted, I hope." A breathless DC Sarah Hughes had joined them. "I could swing for some people. 'Oh is it something to do with all that blood outside? Wondered what all that was about.' Fucking amazing, isn't it? All this blood and not one bloody person thought to call the cops."

Except our Israeli friends, thought Alexander. Was this Jake's big mistake? A Mossad agent? He signalled for the SOCOs. They could start work; not that he expected much with all the busy bodies walking by since early morning. Too busy to phone the cops and report a suspicious amount of blood splattered by their office.

"We have a blood sample we need to check against the blood here. Your best bet may be by those trees."

Peters and Hughes were instructed to stay at the scene until he could organise relief. He wanted both – Peters in particular – back at The Yard.

On the drive back he wasted no time running through tasks with Pierce and Burns. All hospitals to be checked. All. Work outwards. All taxi firms. Yes, all; he knew there were dozens. Tell them to wake up any drivers who were out last night between seven and 1am, say. Limping woman in The Strand vicinity, bleeding badly from left leg. That will do for now.

They clicked into gear as Alexander headed for Stevens's room again. He felt time was pressing. Act fast. All that blood lost. Maybe Jake was bleeding to death somewhere? If not she would need medical attention. What if she was a doctor and could fix herself up?

Good, Marshall was still there. He had been drafting a Press statement with Stevens. Even better. It wasn't a bad statement, either; senior officers had some usefulness. Alexander suggested a few amendments, pros and cons flying back and forth in healthy argument.

Ten minutes later they had agreed. There would be no conference, just a state-ment and a polite request to editors to give it prominence. Initially, Alexander was reluctant to say it was in connection with the serial killings but his colleagues persuaded him otherwise, citing maximum exposure was essential.

It was on its way to the Press Bureau by 1.30, and with luck would make the later editions of the London evening papers. Then the tea-time TV and radio news programmes.

Metropolitan Police urgently wish to interview a woman who was injured during an incident close to The Strand last night.

They believe she may have information vital to their inquiries into the London serial killings.

The woman suffered a severe wound to her left leg which would require medical attention. She may also have bruising to the left side of her face.

The woman is described as being around five foot nine inches tall, and of average build. She may speak with an American accent.

Members of the public are advised not to approach the woman but to inform police of any sightings.

The final two points had caused some disagreement among the detectives; Marshall won the debate by persuasion rather than rank. If badly wounded she was unlikely to employ her fake accents. If they didn't warn the public and some-one got injured or killed the serious shit would hit the fan. Part of Alexander was actually warming to Marshall, as a copper if not quite as a drinking buddy yet.

+

The nurse at Slough General Hospital did not believe Antonia Helm for one minute. The junior doctor had been too busy to either notice or care. All he saw was a wound that needed stitching quickly and a woman who needed a blood transfusion before she became his first fatality of the day. Stitches first, he told the nurse before dashing to another room.

Driver 147 of Airport Cars thought he was about to have his first fatality ever as he caught occasional glimpses of his passenger through the rear-view mirror. The Yank woman was close to collapse, no wonder she wanted a hospital. Helm had wanted to go to Reading after checking her map in the first cab. Reading was a reasonable distance from central London. But she had felt herself growing weaker and weaker as she stood in the short queue. She checked her map again and asked Driver 147 for the casualty ward at Slough hospital: a strange drop-off point for a passenger from Heathrow. Not much luggage for a Yank, either, and she took her time getting in the seat.

Driver 147 did not spot the blood on his backseat until he was collecting his next fare back at Heathrow. It would have been his next fare if the couple had not turned away in disgust.

Helm had to sign forms as she was being checked out: liability waivers for foreigners. She paid them no attention as she scrawled her signature.

The needle hurt, but kept her from passing out. Yeah, right honey, a metal railing in Paris. Whatever you say. The cut was neater than you'd get from your average brain surgeon. Yeah, and you banged your face when you fell. Whatever, honey. A Sister popped by to examine her handiwork. Staff Nurse Motril kept her thoughts to herself and kept the stitches nice and deep and tight as the doc had requested. The staff room would soon hear of the poor Yank with a nasty piece of work for a boyfriend.

Helm finally dozed off a few minutes after the transfusion. She was lifted into a wheelchair, her leg supported at a 90-degree angle, and she was left in a recovery room with a group of fellow patched-up people, sporting an array of plasters and bandages.

She woke two hours later. Scared at first until she realised where she was and what had happened. Her leg felt tight and she glanced at the heavy wrapping. A porter kindly fetched her a cup of water as she gradually came round, feeling different somehow but a damned sight better than she had that morning.

After a few minutes she tried to haul herself out of the chair. It took her three attempts to get upright but she found she could stand fine as long as she kept her left foot off the ground. Her walking stick had been left by the side of the wheelchair. She picked it up and, taking slow steps, walked out of the hospital and into the fading sunlight.

The hotel was out of the question, but she needed to go to the office. She could figure out a plan on the way there. Maybe Rob would come to her.

"Sorry, love, I'm waiting for someone. Want me to ring for one?"

Yes, she did, and sat on a bench until her taxi pulled up.

Rob didn't come to her as she closed her eyes in the back of the taxi. Helm was all on her own. She heard the news on the radio in her office. If she hadn't used up all her tears last night she could have cried.

+

CHAPTER TWENTY

✝

BY LATE afternoon the phones in the Murder Room were going crazier than ever. The noise, while not quite deafening, was most annoying to the frayed nerves of detectives working flat out while struggling to hear themselves think.

DI Alexander had a hand over his right ear as he spoke to Ralf Vonderheid, informing the Berlin inspector of all the latest leads – apart from the Israeli connection, naturally.

He spent longer on the phone with Lieutenant Dirk Preece. Yes, they had good reason to suspect they were hunting an American, probably Scarlet O'Hara.

Zilch on Babe Ruth.

Preece promised to do all he could at the Atlantic City end and informed Alexander that the FBI was now sniffing around the case. The manner in which he spat out FBI and some curse on the Feds told Alexander it was not an ideal working relationship.

Then the taxi drivers, pulling up in random order but ready and willing despite the chances of a decent tip being non-existent. Driver 147 was first, and he was still in a foul mood having lost an afternoon's trade because of that American cow's bloody mess on his backseat.

Yeah, that's right Slough General. Yeah, she had a bad leg – too bloody true she had a bad leg. She owes me fifty quid for the valeting. Looked like death warmed up she did.

Then the owner of a string of black cabs who patrolled the West End. One of his guys had collected a street fare last night. She looked rough, he said, and he dropped her off at the Watson Hotel in Holborn. The good thing about the taxi firms, all the callers shouted, making themselves easy to hear above the din.

Alexander was assimilating as best he could the morass of information when

DS Pierce shouted to him. Slough had turned up trumps. American woman treated for nasty leg wound, given stitches and blood transfusion. She walked out without a word of thanks.

"Taxi boss is checking with his drivers now."

Pierce returned his attention to the receiver. "You have an address? I need the address, please."

Alexander walked over to Pierce's desk and tried in vain to eavesdrop; the owner seemed to be yelling instructions and directions to his drivers at the same time as he was talking to the detective. Soon Pierce pointed to his notepad and began scribbling.

"OK. Thanks, sir. Got it."

Pierce turned to Alexander. "There, not long after four o'clock this afternoon. It's off King Edward Street by St Paul's. Woman was American, had a walking stick. Driver said was a business street rather than residential. Woman seemed to go into a property to the left of an estate agent's; right-hand side heading towards the cathedral."

"Four o'clock – almost four hours ago." Alexander paused, thinking. He didn't take long before making up his mind. "Let's go." The urge to do something positive combined with the need to escape the unholy clatter of the MR.

Already officers were on their way to the Watson Hotel, others to interview last night's cabbie. Slough hospital staff were being interviewed by phone and being informed local CID would soon be calling. Staff Nurse Motril was most detailed, down to the make and size of the woman's shoes.

The Hotel Royal Gardens was slow to respond. It was only when the night porter caught sight of the London evening paper a couple of hours into his shift that he informed the night manager that that pretty American woman on the third floor had come in last night claiming she had injured her leg in a fall.

None of the day staff were present, the woman was not in her room, so Night Manager Jason Harris rang the home of the day receptionist to discover Antonia Helm had asked for a walking stick, and then a taxi. He dithered, wondering whether or not to seek advice from higher up. The decision was entirely his own, and he needed a drink of water after making it. Helm was a valued visitor, and she had attracted many ISS customers to the Royal Gardens.

DC Hughes and DC Maynard were next door at the Watson Hotel – a newly-converted block of flats and offices now named after Sherlock Holmes's admirable assistant. Black and white stills from old Basil Rathbone movies dominated the walls, interspersed with autographed portraits of Nigel Bruce,

Ben Kingsley, Edward Hardwicke and several other actors. The detectives were examining guest lists and quizzing puzzled young members of staff, who had almost certainly never seen a Rathbone film, never mind read a Conan Doyle book, when the call came through.

An excited Maynard almost dragged Sarah Hughes from the reception desk. "Next door. She's been staying next door. DS Peters is on her way but we're to go there now."

Alexander was being kept up to date as Pierce drove, fast but not recklessly. Lights lit up St Paul's. The cathedral was being restored and the lights were more to protect the public from the construction fences than to highlight the magnificent 300-year-old domed edifice.

"On the right. Look for an estate agent's sign."

They parked 50 yards away on the opposite side of the road. The three detectives waited, studying their surroundings. The street was lit but not too brightly. About 100 yards to the north was a pub with a red and yellow light beaming outwards, painting the pavement with a warm glow. It looked inviting. A couple walked by, then a man in a dark business suit. So well did he blend in with the street that he almost escaped their attention. Traffic, thankfully, was light. All they had seen were three cars heading in the direction of the cathedral.

Alexander was first out of the car, followed by his colleagues. They stood look-ing at the four-storey block of terraced buildings opposite them. As they slowly crossed the street Alexander felt a tingling creep through his body. More light; ideally he would have liked more light.

Display lights shone on outrageously priced business properties in the estate agent's window, but that was all from the buildings. There was no other sign of life in there. In fact there was little sign of life or light in any of the windows; no keen business type staying late. Business must be good in these parts.

Pierce pointed to engraved mock-golden placards advertising the businesses inside the building joining the estate agent's. This particular block hosted six businesses; four of which had intercoms. Alexander went through them slowly, receiving not a solitary response.

"Back to the car," said Alexander. "Try the pub, Rab."

Alexander was about to ring The Yard when he was beaten to the punch.

"Rory, we have a name. Antonia Helm. Hotel-Echo-Lima-Mike." It was Christine Stevens. "She's been staying at the Hotel Royal Gardens in Holborn. DS Peters is being let in to her room now."

"American? Who does she work for? We're outside a block of offices on St

Norbert's Street now."

"Immediate Software Solutions. Yes, an American company, based in Lexington, Kentucky. We're trying to raise people this minute."

Burns was outside the car, a tall suit beside him. "We have a key, sir. Mr Worthington shares the building."

"We're about to go in, Christine. All the usual channels …"

"Done as we speak."

Usual channels: airports, ports, car hire firms – anywhere identity was required to travel. He felt obliged to check, even with a senior officer. The walls were tightening.

"I just have a key for the front door," spluttered Mr Worthington, a skinny, bespectacled suit standing a good three inches taller than any of the detectives.

"What's all this about our Antonia? Hear she may have hurt herself?"

"You know the woman well?"

"Nodding terms I suppose. We've had the odd drink at The Wren." He pointed to the pub up the street.

"Seen her today?"

"No. I did hear her, though. Late afternoon, but I was tied up on the phone. Her office is just across from mine."

"Which floor?"

"Second. Hers is on the right."

"May I have the key, sir? Why don't you just wait by the car with DC Burns."

Mr Worthington jangled a heavy key ring before finding the one he wanted: a Yale which he displayed to Alexander. "But her office is bound to be locked."

Alexander had ceased listening and was approaching the building with Pierce. He opened the heavy door and looked for the light switch. He flicked a switch and the staircase was flooded in the brightest light imaginable. "Christ! No wonder the bitch wears sunglasses!"

All element of surprise vanished with Pierce's cursing. They knew no-one was home but crept cautiously up the steps. A small, square white sign told them they were about to break into ISS, UK.

Alexander knew she wasn't there, but his heart was pounding all the same. He kicked open the door with one hefty crash of his foot. The light switch was on the right. He flicked it on and entered, keeping his back to the wall. It was less well lit than the staircase.

Desk, computer, telephone, fax, filing cabinet, and another set of drawers by the window. All very tidy with just a few folders to the right of the computer.

Neither he nor Pierce spoke as they edged towards a second door. Alexander turned the handle slowly and pushed open the door. He flicked the light switch to reveal a smaller room. It looked like a storage room. There was also a side worktop with a microwave oven, a kettle and a radio. Beneath the worktop was a fridge.

"Give Rab a buzz to let him know it's all clear. Tell him to get the forensics and some local CID here. We'll be down when we've had a quick look round. I'll do the other room."

"Oh, Rory!" Pierce took a pair of latex gloves from his pocket.

"Oh shit! What have I touched?"

"Door handles, wall, lights. No sweat."

Alexander was grappling with the computer's Internet connection when Pierce shouted to him. Pierce was more the computer buff – quite an expert – and should have been in Alexander's seat.

"You need to see this."

"What is it?" said Alexander, walking back into the storage room.

Pierce had the fridge door open and was holding a piece of paper which looked to have been torn from a notepad.

Is it you, Edgar?
You must be thirsty so I've left you a drink.
Go on, it's only coke. Honest.
Jake TJ

In the middle of the fridge was a small glass containing a dark-coloured liquid. "No kisses. Maybe she doesn't love me any more." Alexander shivered.

They were on their way back to Scotland Yard. Alexander had handed over the computer to Pierce and watched his sergeant's stubby but nimble fingers fly over the keys, extracting a few pieces of information that may prove useful before the SOCOs had taken the machine apart byte by byte.

"Lucy! Look at the bloody time! I'd better phone her."

His fiancée was not worried by his absence; instead she sounded in a state of considerable excitement.

"It's OK, love. I know you've been busy. I'm glued to the 24-hour news channels. You're close, aren't you? You're going to get her, aren't you?"

"We're close, Lucy, very close. That's all I can say for now. Are you OK? I mean really OK?"

"I'm fine, honestly."

"Listen, I'm planning to stay at The Yard tonight. Want me to send a WPC round?"

"No, don't bother. I've two strapping constables outside if I need them. I'm really fine."

"Try and get some sleep. I'll see you tomorrow."

"Get her, Rory. Just get her, but do take care. I love you. Goodnight."

✝

All is lost. Situation hopeless. We attack.

Antonia Helm liked to think they were the last words of an American hero, a Civil War commander. But she recalled some yarn about a British general defending some god-forsaken faraway part of Queen Victoria's Empire. Whatever. She agreed with them partially while still clinging to a slender chance of survival. The news on the radio had alarmed her, but now she had calmed down and decided: She would attack.

Worthington made her rush; she didn't want him popping his head in, asking if she fancied a cuppa or maybe a drink at the Sir Christopher Wren later.

Now she wasn't sure which was the greater handicap. Her leg was no longer causing her the excruciating agony it had last night or that morning. But, even gritting her teeth and tensing her body as hard as she could, a couple of normal paces was the most she could manage before breaking into an obvious limp.

No bone was broken in her cheek she now assumed. It, too, had ceased throbbing but the swelling had not gone down and the slight bruising had turned a deep purple. She checked herself in her compact and thought she looked like the Elephant Man's uglier sister. No makeup could mask that, but at least it was mainly towards the jaw. The headscarf would have been the sensible option, but she had left that at the hotel.

Her tartan scarf would have to do. She wrapped it round her face, as high up as possible without appearing like a bank robber. She pulled up the collar of her coat and went to brave the outside world. The world that was hunting her down, or trying its damnedest to.

It was cold outside, but not that cold that one needed to wrap up for the Arctic. She knew London well enough to realise that people had to look determinedly outrageous in order to attract attention at rush-hour. Workers were dashing everywhere, especially to the pub or to catch the train. It didn't matter who got trampled underfoot. They were British, but none of this women-and-children-first nonsense – not at going home time.

But self-consciousness is impossible to shake off. So she limped along, trying to stick to shadows and stopping occasionally for a breather, using a map book as a prop. Normally, she could walk to St Paul's Tube station in five minutes; this evening it had taken at least three times that. Having bought a railcard, she positioned herself by a wall on the platform. She was nervous about getting on a train. They were so bright inside. They would be packed at this time. People would be reading newspapers. People would be looking around; someone was bound to spot her face.

Situation is hopeless. I attack.

"Excuse me, sir. Would you be knowing if the next train goes to Euston?"

The man was engrossed in a paperback novel. He looked down and saw a smiling face. He didn't notice it was tilted slightly to one side.

"Errm, yes. But you need to change …change at Tottenham Court Road. Yeah, Tottenham Court Road."

"Oh, thank you, sir."

She stood by his side until the train pulled in. She had known he wouldn't be Irish. She had never met a black man who was. He was a good prop.

Euston wasn't really necessary. It was a spur of the moment thing based on the miraculous freedom from pain a few neat stitches could bring. The tightness in her leg was quite reassuring. It told her the wound was slowly healing, though commonsense told her she must support it whenever she found a private spot. That may be some time.

Helm cursed the myriad of walkways in the London underground as she made such slow progress. All the time she was thinking. Would they have found out by now? Yes, she was sure. The woman kept appearing before her. Who the hell was she? One of the taxi drivers must have reported something strange, especially the poor guy with blood all over his seat. But who knew much about her? Did the hotel know about her office? Yes, they did. The car hire firm knew, too. In a day or two I may be able to drive, she thought.

It was almost three hours after she had left her office before she found a suitable pub by Euston Square. She sat down on a wall a few yards away – to catch her breath and compose herself. She had bought some cigarettes at a shop in the station concourse.

Situation is hopeless. I attack.

She walked up to the bar and ordered a half of Guinness, though she really wanted the largest brandy possible. The packet of cigarettes came out after her second gulp. She leaned across a group of men to a guy who was smoking.

"Do you have a light, please?"

The man flicked his lighter. She nodded and exhaled before returning to her drink. Three more quick gulps and she walked out of the bar. Once outside, she stubbed out the cigarette and headed for the taxi rank. No-one would spot her bad leg in the queue. She was tired of walking. She prayed for an Asian driver.

She'd never met an Asian who spoke Irish.

+

A DC whose name he was struggling to recall stood by Alexander's desk. He was on the phone and stooping to make notes. Commander Marshall and Detective Superintendent Stevens had taken over the desk immediately to the right – DS Pierce's desk.

Marshall was working the international angle, using his chunky book of contacts in many walks of law enforcement to track Antonia Helm's history. Stevens was doing her best to keep pace with the flood of London sightings.

The DC – Clive Hadshaw – had taken down a brief report from Caroline Peters. A bloodied duvet but little else in the hotel room. She was on her way back and forensics were working the room now.

"Right, Rory. Here goes." Stevens straight down to it. "She took a taxi to the Hotel Watson, walked the few yards to her own hotel, Royal Gardens, told night staff she had fallen and hurt herself. Next day she asked for a walking stick and a taxi to Heathrow. The owner of the firm they use says he cannot contact the driver, probably gone out on the piss as he now has a few days off.

"She caught another taxi at Heathrow. Driver took her to Slough General where she had her leg stitched up. They reckon she left there sometime around three. Taxi took her to her office. No sightings since."

"I saw a walking stick at the office, so it looks like she's hobbling around on her own. Forensics emailed anything yet?"

"A bunch of stuff for your attention has just started arriving, sir," said DC Jobson. "Number four of six is here now."

"What's this, Rory?"

"Some files from her office computer. They're for DS Pierce really. He asked forensics to send as soon as they'd given the computer a once over."

"Address books, letters – that sort of thing, ma'am." Pierce was scouting around for a nearby desk to commandeer.

"Use mine," said Alexander, taking the hint and dragging up an extra chair. The chair belonged to a WPC who had been doing runners for Stevens and Marshall. She returned with a tray laden with as many coffees as it could hold.

"Would you three like–" She had no need to finish her question as Alexander, Pierce and the still standing Burns gave her the thumbs up.

"Paris, she operated out of Paris," Marshall had finished his call and was addressing Stevens. "Hello, Rory, I think we're beginning to smell her. She has an apartment there and a car. I've several names and numbers to call, and I'll get the Sûreté on it. She could be heading there. Rory, if you're free could you check with the Americans for an update?"

Before Alexander could speak Marshall handed out two sheets of paper to two DCs. "Americans working for ISS in Paris; everything they know about Helm. You got their numbers from …Henry Chartis, head of personnel Europe.

"FBI have set up shop with your pal in Atlantic City for now – best to ring him."

"Some French email addresses going up, sir. No details, just emails." Then Pierce turned his monitor round for Alexander. He had found email addresses for three Helms – two had more details in the address book.

Alexander rang Lieutenant Dirk Preece and was transferred to a different office.

"Hey buddy!"

"Hello, Dirk. Any news on the family?"

"Getting there. Jeeze this place is crawling with Feds. We got a mum died 18 months back, cancer. Dad moved from Rhode Island soon after. Feds are chasing him around Baltimore, seems he has a brother there. Two sisters, both younger, seem to flit around–"

"I've got a Joanie Helm, address book says 177a, Fourth Street, Milwaukee. And a Susannah Helm, 26 Cypress Avenue, Westchester, NYC." Alexander gave Preece the email addresses and a phone number for Susannah.

"Nothing on the dad as yet. But we have about 50 American email addresses, most look like organisations rather than friends. We'll send the lot to you. What about the company? ISS? We have people working the Paris end."

"Feds should be there now. They're playing it by the book and refusing to hand over information on the phone."

"Don't they fucking know this is a serial killer we're after?"

"They know something like that, and that is why the bastards are covering their backs. Feds tell me this Antonia Helm is responsible for some mighty fine deals."

"Some mighty fine murders, too, Dirk."

"Yeah, I know buddy. We'll get there."

"Anything on Babe Ruth?"

"Not yet."

"OK. I'll be here all night – anything you get give me a call."

Burns attracted Alexander's attention as he was taking the call. "Three guys croaked in a pub by Euston Station an hour or so ago. Early reports say they started throwing up one by one and then collapsed. Locals have it sealed."

Within minutes DI Keith Blake and DC Martin Wright were on their way to Euston. Alexander was barking out orders: taxi drivers again, train departures. He knew Euston served the North-West and he told Pierce to check the computer addresses for anyone that way. He soon came back with a handful of clients: one in Birmingham, two in Manchester and one in Glasgow.

Had Helm caught a train to one of the main northern cities? Was it that obvious? Was Heathrow a trick? Paris a trick? He tried to keep his mind free. Within a couple of hours the day's last trains would have departed.

Alexander was expecting the call to be from Blake at the murder scene, but it was Lieutenant Preece.

"Babe Ruth is dead, and has been for seven years or so. We just got it from one of the sisters. I'll send you the details as soon as I've typed them up. But it looks fair to assume she's on her own. Sister said she knew of no boyfriend in Europe, and no close girlfriend that had been mentioned."

"Thanks, Dirk."

Marshall's French connections now had the Parisian end under wraps, he informed. The flat was being examined, her workmates traced and questioned.

An hour later, DI Blake reported in. "Bloody traffic! Looks like Jake, but no signatures that I can see. Not on the arms anyway. Reagan's the pathologist – young bloke I ain't seen before. McMillan's on her way from out west but we can't get hold of Carmichael. It's a bleedin' mess. Seems they were staggering everywhere."

Where are you Jake, alias Scarlet O'Hara, alias Antonia Helm?

Where are you going?

+

CHAPTER TWENTY ONE

✝

ANTONIA HELM was arrested thirty yards from the taxi rank outside Edinburgh's Waverley Station at 7.30am. She did not try to resist. In fact, she did nothing but smile. In the back of the police car she sighed and closed her eyes.

As soon as the arrest was confirmed, DI Rory Alexander, three of his colleagues and The Met's solicitor were on their way to the Scottish capital, catching the first available flight from Stansted Airport.

It was a slip of the tongue. She had been dozing on the train from King's Cross to Aberdeen, her leg resting on a seat opposite. The young man asked her to move it so he could get through to the next seat. If she had remembered she was Irish she may have got away with it.

She went back to sleep and did not see the nervous man jump over her leg a few minutes later. Transport Police boarded the train at Newcastle. The news was greeted with a flurry of calls back in London. Bruising, leg, American accent – they were sure it was her. Edinburgh police were primed to board the train when it next stopped. The plan was amended as she joined the rush pouring out of the carriages.

Once she was in a clear area, four anxious detectives pounced. A pin prick could kill you; be careful. One thrust both her arms up her back, another cuffed her, a third checked her hands before wrapping a heavy tape around them. The fourth rifled through her bag. Two uniforms appeared and stood menacingly, stun batons held aloft. Passers-by stopped and stared; some hurled abuse at the policemen for what appeared heavy-handed tactics to arrest a slip of a lass. Cops poured out of two unmarked vans to prevent an incident. Helm had grimaced as her left leg buckled, but she had not cried out. And then she had smiled at the policemen.

An American consular official and a young lawyer hired by ISS were already at the police HQ when The Met team arrived. Somebody's quick off the mark, thought Alexander.

"It is my duty to protect the rights of American citizens," spluttered the consular official. He looked embarrassed.

"I insist on being present during any interviews," said the solicitor trying to sound authoritative. He looked more nervous than embarrassed. All interviews must be recorded, he said loftily and received dismissive glares from the detectives. He was probably picking up the biggest pay cheque of his career; his brief simply to ensure ISS came out of this mess as clean as possible. Not an easy job when one of your employees is about to be charged with killing up to a dozen people. Alexander barely glanced at him.

There was paperwork to be dealt with. Whose side are we all on, thought Alexander as he signed here, there and everywhere The Met's own solicitor pointed.

He wanted so badly to see Antonia Helm but was managing to hide his anxiety as he was taken through to another room and shown her belongings, which comprised the contents of a medium-sized blue rucksack with a flexible frame, plus a scarf and a dark raincoat. A small brown bottle was sealed in a plastic bag. "Has anyone touched this?" asked the London inspector.

"No, sir. We have a pretty good idea what it is. It was already in that plastic bag."

Her purse contained the usual assortment of credit cards, £235 in three denominations, six business cards, and a top-up card for a mobile phone – yet there was no mobile phone, and they'd found no details of any accounts on her computer.

Three changes of underwear, a couple of tee-shirts, two books …and a small case. Alexander opened the case and stared at a magnetic Monopoly board.

"Do you wish to see her, sir?"

Alexander waited, still gazing at Antonia Helm's belongings. He picked up one of the books. The Myth Of Sisyphus; he had copies in French and English 'To My Rose, Love Always Rob.' So, Babe Ruth had enjoyed French philosophy.

"Wouldn't mind a coffee first, and I'm sure my colleagues …" He waved to the silent trio a few paces behind him: DS Peters, DS Pierce and DC Burns.

Alexander first set eyes on her at 1.17pm precisely, according to a digital wall clock behind the suspect's chair. Nice of the Scots to give her a room with a clock.

Antonia Helm looked so normal. So wretchedly normal. The victim of a mugging, or a domestic assault. More an unfortunate crime statistic than

Britain's most wanted. Her brown hair was flowing down, rat's tails in need of a good wash. Her clothes were crumpled. The tee-shirt had a stain where she had spilled some coffee. A pullover was lying by her feet, next to a pile of magazines the uncommonly civilised Edinburgh officers had provided.

He studied her face, trying to gaze intently into her brown eyes to fathom what lurked there. What was behind her murderous spree? But his eyes kept being diverted by the huge purple bruise which stretched along the lower jaw and halfway up her left cheek. The Mossad agent had indeed given her a hefty kick.

"If she mentions Lucy, hold me back," he had told DS Pierce outside the room, quickly adding "Only joking, Stuart." He wiped his spectacles for longer than they needed, then in they trooped.

An Edinburgh WPC stood a few yards from Helm's chair. She was dismissed as Pierce, Peters, Burns, a local chief inspector, both solicitors and the consular official entered the room, shuffling along the sides to find space where they could hug the walls. No-one seemed keen to get too close to the wraith-like figure in the chair.

She spoke first, looking up from her magazine and smiling. "We having a party, Rory? You sure brought enough people for a party."

He let her croaky chuckle subside. She was amusing no-one but herself.

"Miss Helm, I am Detective Inspector Alexander of The Metropolitan Police."

"Oh! It's a formal party. Wish you had said, then I could have dressed for the occasion."

He wasted little more of his breath. She was under arrest, he and his colleagues were here to escort her to London where she would be formally charged with several counts of murder. She did not have to say anything but it may harm her defence …

Helm wasn't listening to a word of it; she was laughing her head off now – maniacally. Alexander turned to leave.

"Hey!"

He turned his head but not his body. She was holding the magazine out. "It's his birthday next week; March 14th. I wonder if he knows he used to look like you?"

Laughter filled the room. One woman's terrible laughter.

Once outside the room, Burns was first to speak. "Pathetic. Creepy, very creepy, but pathetic."

"Off her bleedin' rocker," said Caroline Peters when they had walked down the corridor and into a large open room where officers were manning phones and generally looking busy. "You know what's going to happen, don't you? She won't

Tom J Sandy

serve a fucking day in a proper nick."

"As long as she never sees the light of day I don't care." Alexander's face was like granite.

"Give me the fucking key and I'll gladly throw it where nobody will find it," said Pierce.

Burns was by now engaged in conversation with Chief Inspector McGee. He turned to inform his colleagues: "We've got the first carriage of a train tomorrow morning – 8.30 from Waverley, gets in King's Cross 12.50."

Alexander nodded. The train had been his favoured option. That way the consular official and the solicitors could join them if they so wished.

"Two transport police officers either end of the carriage," continued Burns. "And Chief inspector McGee has been instructed that two of his detectives should accompany us. They'll be in the next carriage back. We'll be driven directly onto the platform; no-one will know anything about our plans."

"Fine. Better safe than sorry. Nobody's going to try and spring her, though. She's alone …all alone and has been for a long time."

Alexander stretched. He did not feel tired, despite having a sleepless night. He felt at a loose end. Her look, her laughter had unnerved him. The room had felt claustrophobic, and he had previously determined that a formal caution would suffice for the time being – unless she wanted to make a statement. Less than a minute in her company convinced him no useful information would be forth-coming that afternoon.

"Chief Inspector. Thanks for everything. Just to check, she'll be kept in one of your cells here until the morning?"

"Yes, that's right. Just down past the interview rooms. Private cell, obviously."

"Tomorrow morning then. We'll be here before six."

There was little else for four London detectives to do in Edinburgh, so they ate and drank. They all felt at a loose end and probably looked it as they tramped from pub to pub without much enthusiasm. Rab Burns had to act as interpreter in a couple of hostelries where barmen scowled. They were happy to take their money but not their accents. It had been Burns's suggestion to avoid the tourist traps.

It was time to dine after Pierce had almost started a fight. "Bit effeminate that," he said to a 40-something suit, "pouring water into a single malt."

"It's common practice in Scotland," said Burns, squeezing his body between the two and regretting his earlier idea.

"You mean it's OFFICIALLY effeminate," roared Pierce, clutching his sides.

They were in the Chinese restaurant before seven and out by eight. All four detectives were tucked up in their separate beds by nine. "This is going to have to be kept very quiet," said Peters as she bade her colleagues goodnight. "Bed before nine! Think of my reputation." Burns wondered if she would like some company, but maybe this was neither the time nor the place.

Alexander was glad of the late afternoon session. The beer helped him enjoy his best night's sleep for several weeks. He helped himself to another 20 minutes under the warm, scented duvet after the alarm clock woke him at 4am. He had showered and was rallying the rest by five. They would walk the mile to the police station, grab a bite at the canteen – open at 6am according to Burns – and go through the day's plans. The case was as good as over for him and his team. But he would not rest until this killer was under lock and key in London.

"How's our guest been?" Alexander asked the desk sergeant.

"Good as gold, sir. Muttering in her sleep but no problem at all."

Antonia Helm had cleaned herself up and been supplied with fresh clothes which could have been her exact size. A WPC told Alexander that she had drunk frequently since his last visit – several cups of water and coffee. She had eaten well last night, but nibbled at her breakfast. A doctor had given her two paracetamol for her leg pain around 10pm. The doctor was satisfied both tablets had been swallowed. The prisoner had not requested any painkillers since then.

The two solicitors arrived together, chatting away like old friends. Peters had christened them the Gay Gordons. No consular official would be making the trip; the American Embassy was apprised of the situation and would take over at King's Cross.

Helm was silent, sullen almost, as DS Peters cuffed her hands then placed another set further up her right wrist and attached one side to herself. Helm glowered at the sergeant. Peters glowered back. The American won the private staring war.

Alexander then took hold of Helm's left arm, attaching her to him with a third pair of cuffs. Only then did she speak. "Nice and cosy. At last we are together."

He said nothing and made a point of avoiding her eyes.

They were driven in an unmarked van to the platform, Alexander flinching uncomfortably as Helm rubbed against him. Her actions were involuntary, caused by the motion of the van rather than an attempt to unsettle him. They were settled in their carriage half an hour before the other, paying passengers, all completely unaware there was a special carriage at the front with a very special guest.

The carriage sat four to a table. Peters took off her cuffs and pointed Helm to the window seat. Alexander was to remain cuffed for the journey. He was grateful for the arm rest which kept their bodies apart.

Helm was allowed to rest her wounded leg on the facing window seat; Peters sat herself opposite her boss by the aisle. Pierce and Burns were sat on the other side of the carriage, one facing her and one at her rear. The solicitors were furthest away, by the exit.

Don't speak unless spoken to. Alexander was desperate to talk to her. Capture was not enough. He needed to know more; he wanted to know everything, or as much as possible. It wasn't simply just the detective in him, it was the human being, striving to comprehend what makes a person do such cruel, wicked things. The detective would receive another notch on his belt; the promotion would go through. But the man in him wanted more; needed more.

Is this what people meant by evil personified? This pathetic creature next to him? Alexander had never encountered a serial killer outside the movies. Some vicious slashers. A pro hitman once. That guy had given him the creeps, or his little red book had. The book contained details of 27 successful 'jobs', complete with payment charges ranging from 250 quid to five grand. Alex Matthews would kill your husband or your wife, your mother or your father. If you could provide the money and wanted someone dead, anyone dead it didn't matter, Alex Matthews was yer man. Alex Matthews had been evil personified.

Alexander had solved his fair share of domestic murders, too. They always struck him as tragic or deranged rather than pure evil. Some he could even understand were truly acts of mercy, but that was for the courts to determine; he was just a copper doing his job.

None touched his insides the way Antonia Helm did. At least Alex Matthews, five years into a life term, could claim it was business. Antonia Helm was killing for kicks, and Alexander had not been sure what to expect or how he would react. He wanted, needed to get inside her mind.

Eventually the train creaked into action. Helm waved at a family on the platform. The groans of the engine tugging at the reluctant carriages broke the dreadful silence inside the carriage; the solicitors suddenly found their hushed voices once more.

Helm stared out of the window, but Alexander knew full well she was not focussing or thinking about the tawdry tenement blocks, the untidy backyards of terraced houses, or the overgrown allotments. A penny for your thoughts, Jake, Scarlet, Antonia Helm or whoever you really are.

"Just over four hours to London, they said. What shall we talk about?"

Her voice was soft, much softer than yesterday. It sounded like a pleasant normal voice. Perhaps it was her normal voice.

"Up to you."

"The strong, silent type, huh, Rory?"

She turned to look out of the window again; he wished he hadn't been so dismissive in his attempt to appear unconcerned.

Five minutes later. "How about a game of Monopoly?"

He smiled indulgently, shaking his head slightly at the same time. "I don't like your rules."

"Come on. Mine should still be in my rucksack unless someone's thieved it. You didn't take it for a souvenir, did you? A British policeman!"

He smiled again, and then turned to look at her rucksack on the luggage rack opposite. He was still struggling to formulate his opening question. No criminal had ever unsettled him like Antonia Helm had.

"Play with me and I'll tell you all about it. Could be the best offer you'll get."

Alexander licked his lips. Of course she noticed. "Check the game in the rucksack for me would you, DS Pierce."

"All looks clean, sir," said Pierce a few minutes later and handed over the open case. "Plastic pieces, magnets underneath."

Helm laughed, again more natural and warmer than the previous day's cackle. She held up a piece. "Did Rory think I was going to try and kill him with The Shoe? Ha! Ha! Ha! Or with The Hat? Ha! Ha! Ha!"

She leaned over to collect the cards and clear the board, ready for a new game. "You mind if I'm The Hat? Now, I guess you're a Car man, right?"

A shrug, signifying whatever you want.

No money was shared out but she was playing before he realised. Five and one; she moved The Hat to The Angel Islington and handed the dice to Alexander. Six and five; he counted The Car to Pall Mall.

"Did Rob like to be The Car?" As opening salvos went it could have been worse. The funny thing was, Alexander felt not the least funny asking it.

She never batted an eyelid, showed no surprise that he knew about Rob. "Oh no! Rob was not a car person. He didn't even drive. Waste of time and money, he said. He was right of course. Think about it. If you were driving us now we wouldn't be able to play Monopoly."

"Did you and Rob play a lot of Monopoly?" Alexander fought his simmering nausea.

"Not really. I mean we always had a game going. ALWAYS. But we could go days without going back to it. One game musta lasted two months. Rob kept hanging on. I had hotels on The Boardwalk and Park Place but would he land on them?" She stopped shaking the dice and smiled wistfully. "I wish he could have played the London game with me."

A shiver went right through Alexander and he caught Caroline Peters turning her face away. A murderous game, is that what she meant? Christ, this carriage felt cold!

"But he is happy; I know he is. He has seen London through my eyes. I promised him he would."

Her eyes were far away now. She was rolling the dice and moving tokens without concentrating. She was taking both their turns. And she was rambling. Her speech was fast but soft. Rob was this …Rob was that …Rob could …Rob …Rob …Rob …

All of a sudden she slowed down. "Rob could never strangle anyone, you know? His poor body. He simply didn't have the strength."

"Not even to kill a 72-year-old widow?" Alexander barely managed to keep the anger and disgust from his voice.

"That was so Goddamned funny!" She slapped her right thigh. "My strap broke! Ha! Ha! Ha! So I put that cushion on her head and just sat on her. Jeeze."

All the detectives were listening intently. They failed to see the funny side of sitting on top of a frail, helpless old woman while she breathed her last.

Alexander spotted Pierce taking notes. None of it could be used in evidence, of course. That was a risk Alexander was taking; she could deny the conversation ever took place no matter how many witnesses. The chat was for his own peace of mind.

"What did you do with the cushion? There seemed to be a cushion missing?" She didn't answer.

"So you strangled people to prove you were stronger than Rob?"

"No! Don't be silly. It was that sonofabitch on The Boardwalk. Sonofabitch."

It eked out, again more in a ramble. Alexander listened, fascinated and wondering if there were other murders they were unaware of. He guessed the confession had finished when she handed him the dice. He rolled and moved The Car a few places, not bothering to count.

"The next one was the guy in the casino, right? The African Queen?"

Again, no sign of surprise at his knowledge. "That was all Rob's idea. Wasn't it brilliant? Oh you should have been there." He didn't tell her that he felt as though he had been there. Another ramble burst from her mouth …Rob …Juichi …blowfish …fugu …roulette …pins.

She stopped as the train drew to a halt. They had reached Newcastle. She stared out of the window at people leaving, to be replaced by more passengers.

Alexander tensed, ridiculous though it was to contemplate an escape attempt. Helm waved again at people on the platform. A young girl waved back. Then Helm raised her handcuffed arm and blew the girl a kiss.

They rolled the dice and moved their pieces in silence for a while. Alexander's mobile rang, filling the whole carriage with an abrupt and unwelcome tide of noise. The screen displayed Christine Stevens's name. He hurriedly handed the phone to Pierce.

"How did you decide where to kill?"

"Just by playing." She tilted her head. "Why? How did you think I decided?"

He had no answer to that. DC 'Mensa' had been on the right lines, not that it would ever have been much use to them.

"Have you ever tried fugu?"

Her question took him aback; he was just about to ask her about the poison but had been unable to speak.

"No I haven't. Do you recommend it?" His voice was calm but his stomach was in turmoil.

"S'ok. If you like seafood."

"The fugu was Rob's idea I take it?"

"Yeah. Well it was Juichi that started it, telling us about this weird meal his dad had made him eat back home. That's where Rob got the idea."

Alexander probed gently and heard the full story of the three Harvard friends dancing with the feast of death.

"Was Juichi at the casino with you?" He made it sound as though Juichi was known to him.

"No way, man! Me and Rob – a private party. Most of our parties were private." She sounded so innocent, telling Alexander about the magic in Rob's voice whenever he read to her. Oscar Wilde was her favourite and she began quoting passages from The Selfish Giant.

"What about London? Why did you start using the poison in London?" Helm scowled at him, angry at having her pleasant memories unceremoniously interrupted.

"Rob told me to."

"Rob?"

"Yeah, who else d'you think?" A harsher snap to her voice.

Alexander was struggling for words. This was a job for a shrink. He tried to concentrate. Lucy came into his head; he had forgotten to call her last night.

"You see much of Rob?" He shivered inside as he asked the question; his stomach performed another somersault. He felt lousy, and noticed Caroline Peters was keeping her head bowed.

"Course I do. All the time. He always calls to say goodnight."

Alexander hadn't notice the train had stopped, not until it was pulling out of Darlington station: the home of the railways; the home of Lucy's parents.

"You used the last of it to kill those three men in the bar at Euston?"

"Tried to send you off in the wrong direction. Didn't work, huh?"

They weren't people to her. They were not human beings. If Alexander had ever wondered if they meant anything at all to her he now knew. They were nothing.

So Alexander let his next question pass. He was going to ask if the last three deaths were really necessary. The question would have been as pointless as the deaths.

"Why'd you send the notes to me?"

She held her right hand out in front of her. She appeared to be checking her fingernails were all the right length. "Rob's idea." As if that was obvious.

"Were they intended to annoy me? Rile me?"

"They were for my amusement, not yours. Did they annoy you? I didn't mean them to, honest."

She made it sound genuine. He almost believed her.

"May I use the bathroom?"

"How long to the next station?" Alexander looked at DS Peters.

"York, not long."

"After the next stop, OK."

"You coming with me, honey?" She raised her eyebrows and rattled the cuffs. York passed in a grey whirl; Alexander unlocked the cuffs and told Peters to go stand outside the toilet.

Alexander leaned over to Pierce. "What did Christine want?"

"Just to say all's ready at King's Cross."

"You get everything on this Jap student? This guy on The Boardwalk?"

"Think so. Not sure how to spell the Jap's name."

"OK. You run that by Lieutenant Preece soon as we get back. Have I missed anything important?"

The ISS solicitor was standing over them. "You know anything my client—"

"Yeah, we know. Please go back to your seat. If she wants you, she can ask. We're just having a chat."

The solicitor bristled but did as he was told. It would all go in his report.

"She's a fruitcake, Rory. You know and I know, this dead guy Rob's going to take the blame, voices in the head and all that. She's going to be banged up with the loonies."

Her return separated the officers.

"Shouldn't be long now," she said, shuffling into her seat and shaking the dice in her right hand.

"Couple more hours. We have some friends waiting at King's Cross. You know King's Cross well, don't you?"

"I didn't mean that, Rory." Her eyes burned into his face. "Doubt we'll still be playing by King's Cross."

She rolled one of the dice, the other remaining in her hand. She was flicking at it with her thumb. "Rob bought me these?"

"They didn't look like they came with the set, too big. Let me guess: he bought them in Atlantic City."

"Yes. Our special place." She looked out of the window then back to Alexander. "Loaded dice, they are?" Alexander could now see one of the sides had been tampered with – a corner grazed. "What d'you think this one was loaded with, Rory?"

He looked at her face; an innocent face wearing a slightly quizzical look which turned slowly into an uneasy smile. A wary smile.

"Oh Christ!"

"It won't be long now. I'm not that scared. Well, yes, I am a little scared. Wouldn't anyone be scared? It's supposed to be quite painful for a few minutes."

"Oh God!" He tried to stand but met resistance from the handcuff. Helm's left hand was gripping the armrest between them, her right hand gripping the other armrest by the window. She was strong, the Israeli agent had been right.

Peters and Pierce had got the message. Both were standing and staring and absolutely clueless as to what to do. No known cure, they all knew that.

"Won't be long now. I could have taken you with me. Easily. Yes, Rory, just remember that. I could have taken you with me, no problem at all. But I'm a good girl really. Ask Rob, he'd tell you. I am a good girl."

Burns had left his seat to find out what was happening. Why were they standing?

Helm closed her eyes and lay back as best she could in her seat. She started rambling again — about Rob, about Harvard, about Rob, Rob, Rob, Rob …

Gradually her breathing became laboured. A few seconds later the upper part of her body was thrust violently forward and her eyes forced wide open. She seemed to be trying to keep the bile in her mouth, and at first it just dribbled from the corners.

Then both hands suddenly flew to her throat. Alexander's hand followed and hung there helplessly. Two hands clawing at the skin as if trying to scratch out another opening, a release valve. Alexander was shaking his head from side to side and trying to pull his hand free. "No! No! No!" he cried through gritted teeth.

Helm's left leg began banging against the underside of the table, the pain from the wound now of no consequence. Her head was swinging so savagely it cracked the reinforced window. Splashes of liquid from her mouth splattered across seats and the detectives. She retched several times, a hideous bellow echoing off the carriage walls.

The two solicitors had left their seats; the Scot engaged by ISS was now watching and started gagging into his handkerchief and discovering its uselessness.

Alexander scrabbled for his key to the cuffs, but it slipped from his fingers. Pierce leaped onto the seat behind Helm, trying to hold her back by her shoulders but fighting a losing battle with her natural strength and the sheer violence of her convulsions. Her reaction seemed more violent than Jack Daniels in the video.

Two minutes passed before her body seemed to cave in. She slumped back at last between Pierce's hands, her chest heaving harshly. A gurgle — like a sink being drained — came from her open mouth.

Burns had been scrambling on the floor and emerged with the key for the cuffs. He unlocked a panting Alexander. The inspector sat back, his shirt covered with patches of Helm's bile, water streaming from his closed eyes. Blood trickled from a wound on the side of his head, caused by the American thrashing about. His wrist was bleeding, too, from the strain of the cuffs.

Peters's eyes were open, but she was crying. Crying and cursing into her handkerchief. Pierce was perspiring heavily, his head bowed.

They waited in silence, trying to recover as Antonia Helm slowly died.

Alexander knew she was dead when he reached for her arm, felt for a pulse and found none. At last he opened his eyes and saw the mess around him. Just as the train was pulling into Peterborough.

Pierce took his hands from Helm's shoulders and dashed to the toilet.

"Water, Rab. Pass the water." Burns handed out bottles of mineral water from the two cool bags they had been supplied with at Edinburgh. Alexander drank some and poured the rest over his face.

At last he managed to look across at Helm. Yes, a pathetic creature. A clever, good-looking American girl – not quite a woman somehow. A bright girl capable of pulling off multi-million pound contracts. A bright girl capable of multiple murders. A pathetic creature and now a dead one.

He had learned a little, but he still wasn't quite sure why. Not really. Voices in the head, perhaps there was something in that. His cynicism had diminished during the train journey.

And what had sparked his own reaction? After all, her death spared the country an expensive trial and an expensive lifelong incarceration. Lucy wanted it, too; dismissed and out of their lives.

It was the proximity, the violence and the sheer helplessness. No matter what she had done, she was still a human being – a clever one, a sick one, a weird one, and a truly wicked one.

Questions remained unanswered.

Berlin. It was crazy, but part of Alexander was desperate to discover which version she had been playing, European or the Berlin city game.

Her victims – how did she choose them?

But above all, why? Was there one pivotal spark that had sent her on this perverse killing spree?

There was something tucked under the cuff of her blouse. He leaned over and drew it out. It was a crumpled card.

A crumpled Get Out Of Jail Free card.

THE END

+

✝

70 NOT OUT

My daughter wafted in for lunch. It was a rainy day in late August, one of the rainiest days of a considerably rainy British summer holidays. She had been playing Monopoly at a neighbour's – the Essex version, she informed me, and she had bought Southend pier.

The Essex version was new to me, but not too surprising. There are versions for each and every occasion these days – the latest to catch my attention being a Simpsons one.

Monopoly has come a long way since the Depression years. It has come a long way since my granddad bought one for the family 30-plus Christmases ago.

To mark the 70th anniversary of the game in 2005, a limited edition 'Here And Now' version was produced. Many of the old London properties bit the dust to be replaced by the likes of Canary Wharf and the London Eye. Players received £2 million for passing GO, and the tokens included a hamburger and a mobile phone. Traditionalists will be pleased to know that the old version remains.

Monopoly possesses a remarkable longevity, even in the video-era. Long may it reign.

All the characters in The Monopoly Murders, if it at all needs saying, are entirely a figment of my own imagination.

The effects of blowfish are not; though, of course, I have used much licence. Rob's experiments are naturally just dramatic effect. If anyone doubts the toxicity of the fish, some news items on the following page may convince them otherwise.

T J Sandy

+

FATAL ATTRACTION

FUGU poisoning sparks a 'rapid and violent death,' according to the US Food and Drug Administration. Nausea, convulsions, paralysis lead to total respiratory failure. There is no antidote.

Puffer fish has been on FDA's Automatic Detention List since 1980, because the product 'appears to contain the poisonous and deleterious substance tetrodoxin.'

Death usually occurs within four to six hours, with a known range of about 20 minutes to eight hours.

Around 7,000 people died from fugu poisoning in Japan in the last century. The peak year was 1958 which witnessed 176 fatalities.

THREE deaths were reported in Italy in 1977 following the consumption of frozen pufferfish imported from Taiwan and mislabelled as angler fish.

FIVE PEOPLE died and nine others fell ill after eating puffer fish at a communal banquet on Flores Island, Indonesia, in July 2004.

"Those who died ate the innards of the fish while the others only ate the meat," said a police spokesman.

Mitsugora Bando VIII, a famous Japanese actor and gourmet, died after eating four bowls of Chiri, a soup containing fugu liver, in a Kyoto restaurant in 1975.

North Korean dictator Kim Jong Il regularly defied doctor's orders and demanded his personal sushi chef prepare fugu dishes for him.

ONE MAN died and 18 others, nine of them children, were hospitalised after eating puffer fish in Maguindanao, The Phillipines, in August 2004.
  The 22-year-old deceased was the one who cooked the two puffer fish that local fishermen caught off Bongo Island at dawn of the same day.

TWO MEN died in northwestern Cambodia after eating toxic blowfish bought from a local fisherman in August 2004.

Scientists in North America have been conducting research into the possibility of using blowfish toxin to help wean addicts off heroin. If the cause don't kill you …

MONOPOLY MISCELLANY

WADDINGTONS made special games for World War Two prisoners. Maps, compasses and files were inserted into the boards. Real money was provided to help escaping POWs.

A team of 300-plus divers from Buffalo, New York, in 1983 used a specially-manufactured set to play underwater for 1,080 hours.

Leeds was the first British city outside London to have a game made in its honour – in 1990.

American Lee Bayrd won the first world Monopoly Championship in New York in 1973.

Monopoly helped capture the Great Train Robbers in 1963. The gang left fingerpints on the board and tokens after playing with real money from their £2.3 million raid.

San Francisco jeweller Sidney Mobell produced a glittering set, featuring gold and 165 gemstones, in 1988. It was valued at $2 million.

Neiman-Marcus made a chocolate Monopoly set in 1978 which retailed at $600.

American game manufacturers Hasbro now own the rights to Monopoly.
To check out the versions available visit www.hasbro.com

Also by Tom J Sandy

Perverting The Course Of Justice

A senior detective is accused of being involved with a paedophile ring. Can Britain's most flamboyant barrister rescue his reputation? Who is the mystery man who tipped off the award-winning crime reporter? And why? No smoke without fire? Or innocent until proven guilty?

Many crime books are based around newspapers, but it's rare to find a look at life in a newsroom that's as realistic as this ....Refreshing and slightly offbeat.
YORKSHIRE POST

SCATE: Speed Cameras Are The Enemy

Gavin Lloyd is guilty as hell, but what's to stop him having a good rant? The source of his wrath soon becomes an obsession and brings him into conflict with the cops, the Government and the infamous Dr Glue - Britain's most wanted vandal.

Many motorists will empathise with the themes in the novel
BBC TV'S TOP GEAR

For the Eight

CONTENTS

Page

1.	Mission to a Faraway Country	11
2.	Personal Journey	20
3.	A Republic at Bay	42
4.	A Brush with the Gestapo	52
5.	A Castle – and Princesses	64
6.	Foreign Correspondents	70
7.	'The Truth Will Prevail'	78
8.	Betrayal	87
9.	The Great Munich Lie	96
10.	Beaverbrook	101
11.	France after Munich	111
12.	The Munich Lie Exposed	127
13.	Troubled Spring	132
14.	'There Will Be No War'	145
15.	Towards the Precipice	150
16.	War – and Phoney War	156
17.	Real War in Finland	171
18.	Belgium on the Eve	190
19.	Attack in the West	197
20.	Collapse Under Blitzkrieg	216
21.	Maytime in Paris	231
22.	Exodus	252
23.	An End and a Beginning	264
	As It looks Now	273
	Index	281

LIST OF ILLUSTRATIONS

Hitler taking the salute at the Nuremberg Parade, 1934
  (*Radio Times Hulton Picture Library*)
Foreign correspondents en route to the Anschluss
The Czechoslovakian army on manoeuvres, 1938
Hitler in Vienna, 15 March 1938
Princess Mara Scherbatoff
The view across Paris from the Rue de Calvaire
Chamberlain and Hitler at Munich
German troops crossing the Charles Bridge in Prague
The story which caused the police to raid the *Daily
  Express* (*Express Newspapers*)
The author with Finnish ski troops, December 1939
The battlefield of Suomussalmi
Edward Ward, BBC war correspondent (*Courtesy
  Viscount Bangor*)
George Millar when serving with the Rifle Brigade
  (*Courtesy George Millar*)

Illustrations in the Text

Map of Czechoslovakia at 28 September 1938

1

Mission to a Faraway Country

Punctually at 11.15 on 3 August 1938, in the pale steamy
sunshine of a Central European summer morning, the
Paris-Prague express crossed the German frontier and
drew into the Czechoslovak border station of Eger.

On the platform a group of customs and passport
officers, German and Czech, moved towards the five cars
which made up the train. In one of the first-class compartments a small, quiet man with thin grey hair, wearing a
wide wing collar and a pale grey suit, glanced out at the
platform, and then returned to his reading. Viscount
Runciman of Doxford, millionaire British ship owner,
personal friend of Mr Neville Chamberlain, had arrived
in Czechoslovakia on his mission, to mediate between the
Czechoslovak Government and its Sudeten German
minority.

In the dusty side street half a dozen Sudeten Germans
pressed against the goods yard railings, staring at the
train. There were no cheers, no marching throngs, no sign
of the heiling battalions of Storm Troopers which the
Neo-Nazi German Sudeten leader Konrad Henlein could
have summoned at will. Clearly he and his followers had
orders to lie low. Nor had any Czechoslovak ministers
come to the border to meet Lord Runciman. Their official
reception was to be in Prague – a clear sign that they had
not sought, and did not welcome, this intrusion into their
affairs. Only two burly Czech policemen in blue uniforms,

with broad red stripes down their trouser legs, and trailing long scabbarded swords, took up their positions outside Lord Runciman's carriage window.

Frontier formalities did not take long. There were few tourists heading for Prague in this troubled summer. Passports were quickly stamped, a Czech detective nodded an all clear to the stationmaster, pulled a set of overalls over his tweed suit, clambered into the cab beside the engine driver, and the express departed on its final lap to the Czechoslovak capital.

Beyond Eger Sudetenland lay in all its beauty. Rolling hills covered with dark pines; corn fields, half cropped where cloud shadows followed one another over the gold of corn and the brown of stubble; red-roofed, white-walled villages; peasants cycling home to their midday meal. Beauty and peace. How far any crisis seemed from all this – and yet how near it was.

The Victoria Hotel, outside Eger Station, was Henlein's headquarters, from which was to be unleashed before the summer was out the insurrection in which eighty people were to be killed. Into these quiet villages by which the train passed tins marked as containing fruit, which were really camouflaged grenades, and cans marked as bicycle oil, which contained high explosive, were being stored under barn floors or in pits in the woods – as the Czech police were later to discover. Only twenty minutes' car drive to the north, in his flat in a suburb of Asch, right on the German border, Konrad Henlein awaited Hitler's next orders.

Now the train was approaching Marienbad, a favourite resort of Edward VII in those days early in the century when the rich and the great had gone to a spa each summer to starve themselves for a month, drink the medicinal waters, and prepare themselves for a further eleven months of ten-course meals. The other famed spa of these Bohemian mountains, Karlsbad, lay a little to the south. The Emperor Francis Joseph had gone there regularly. Amongst its pre-Great War guests had been a slim young Englishman named Neville Chamberlain, who had taken its waters as a cure for the gout which troubled him, and in this way paid his only visit to the faraway country of which we knew so little.

Trout streams wound through the pine and beech forests: in the hay fields peasants scythed and raked their second cut of the thick grass matted with wild flowers; children bathed in small lakes; beyond the carriage windows the Bohemian countryside steadily unrolled itself. Then suddenly we were in the outskirts of Pilzen, and Lord Runciman was over another frontier, the unseen one between Sudetenland and the truly Czech areas. Here were the hundred chimneys of the Skoda arms works, their smoke mingling with the rain clouds which had suddenly blown up, and Czech names only on the railway station, and peasant women, handkerchiefs on head, queueing at the booking office.

Prague was now only an hour away. Soon we were running alongside the Moldau river, with thousands of brown-skinned bathers in the fields by its edge, waving to the train as it went by. Then the Hradschin Castle on the skyline, and at last the Wilson Station in Prague, named in that flush of post-war hopefulness after the American president who had been one of the main architects of this now threatened state.

On the platform waited representatives of the Czech Government, and the British Minister in Prague, Mr Basil Newton, in an Anthony Eden black Homburg hat. With him were two men, one middle-aged, stocky, with a black Hitler moustache, the other young, neat, fair. They were two of Henlein's chief lieutenants, and were presented to Lord Runciman by the British Minister.

That night Lord Runciman held a press conference – the only one he was ever to hold in Czechoslovakia. Into one end of the lounge of the Hotel Alcron, where the mission was staying, were jammed 300 Czech, German, British, American, French and Central European journalists. Cinema arc lights made the sweltering evening more infernal still. Lord Runciman, now in a black suit with a wing collar, looking like a Liberal front bencher from a Victorian sketch of the House of Commons, came quietly through the curtains and stood on a small dais. (It had been hastily moved from the other end of the room, where otherwise Lord Runciman would have been filmed against the bronze statue of a nude woman, her arms outstretched in supplication.) In a genial, low voice Runciman read a little speech. He said, 'I am the friend of all and the enemy of none. I have learned that permanent peace and tranquillity can be secured only on a basis of mutual consent. There is much to be said for the exercise of patience.'

It was generally agreed that the mission had made a good start. The Czech papers the next morning came out with welcoming headlines 'The Lord Arrives'. The French, availing themselves of the fortnight's annual holiday decreed by the Popular Front Government in 1936, swarmed in unprecedented numbers onto the Riviera beaches. The British people in their deckchairs by the seaside read optimistic messages in their newspapers. *The Observer*'s editor, the great J. L. Garvin, assured his readers that 'the nation is justified in packing up for the holidays with a free heart'. Neville Chamberlain departed to fish for salmon in Scotland and in Berlin Adolf Hitler finalised his plans, under the guise of manoeuvres, for assembling one and a half million troops, and putting the nation on a war footing, by the end of August.

*

The Runciman mission was the first positive British move to try to cope with Hitler's drive to absorb into the Reich all neighbouring areas which had inhabitants of German race. Ever since he had attained power as German Chancellor in January 1933 Adolf Hitler had been engaged in overturning those clauses of the Treaty of

Versailles which had been devised to clip the wings of the German Reich after World War I. The ban on conscription, and the limitation of the Reichswehr to 100,000 men had been the first to go. Controls on rearmament, and on the construction of an air force, had been the next to be disregarded. In 1935 Great Britain had condoned German naval rearmament in an Anglo-German Naval Agreement, in which Hitler agreed to keep the German fleet to one third of the size of Britain's. In 1936 came the reoccupation of the Rhineland, which had been declared a demilitarised zone not only at Versailles but in the Treaty of Locarno of 1925. Two years later, in March 1938, Hitler spread his power into an area into which not even the Kaiser's Germany had penetrated, when by the Anschluss he absorbed Austria into the Reich.

British policy in the face of those moves had been to protest – and to yield. A guilty feeling that the Treaty of Versailles had been too harsh on the Germans, coupled with a belief that the Nazi Reich was a bastion against Communist Russia, helped to shape this stance. But the main factor, particularly in the mind of Neville Chamberlain, who had become Prime Minister in 1937, was undoubtedly to avoid a renewal of the horrors of the war of 1914–18, to which had now been added the further danger of mass bombing from the air. But when, in the spring of 1938, Hitler, having absorbed Austria, turned his pressure onto Czechoslovakia, Neville Chamberlain realised that any further German expansion brought with it a very real risk of war. There were three million people of German stock within the boundaries of Czechoslovakia, mostly in the strategically important mountain ranges of Bohemia and Moravia. These Sudeten Germans, as they came to be called, had never been citizens of the Reich. Before Czechoslovakia came into being in 1919 they had been citizens of the Austro-Hungarian Empire. Some of them had long-held pan-Germanic views. Others resented being under the Slavonic domination of the more numerous Czechs and Slovaks in the new republic ruled from

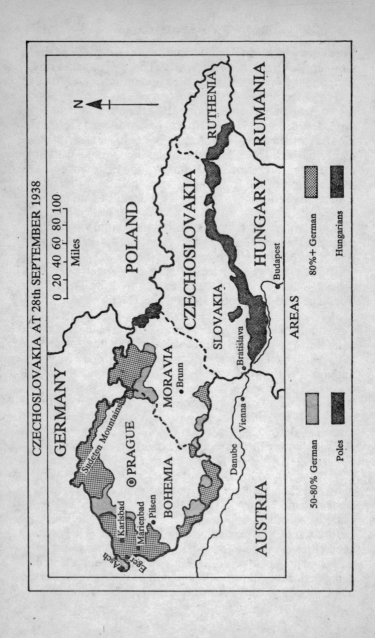

CZECHOSLOVAKIA AT 28th SEPTEMBER 1938

GERMANY

POLAND

Sudeten Mountains

Karlsbad
Asch
Eger
Marienbad
Pilsen

BOHEMIA

⊚ PRAGUE

MORAVIA

Brunn

CZECHOSLOVAKIA

SLOVAKIA

Bratislava

RUTHENIA

RUMANIA

HUNGARY

Budapest

AUSTRIA

Danube

Vienna

0 20 40 60 80 100
Miles

N

AREAS

50-80% German

Poles

80%+ German

Hungarians

Prague. Many Sudetens were therefore ready to support demands for at least autonomy with Czechoslovakia if not – or at least if not yet – for complete union with the Reich.

These demands were articulated by Konrad Henlein, of Asch, in the border area of Egerland. When, soon after Hitler came to power in 1933, the Prague Government suppressed the Sudeten Nazi Party, Henlein formed the Sudeten German Home Front, which rapidly showed itself to be simply a Nazi Party in disguise. In the elections in 1935 it won the support of two-thirds of the Sudeten Germans. Hitler at first restrained Henlein, who limited his demands to the granting of greater freedom to the Sudeten Germans within Czechoslovakia. But once however the Anschluss had opened up the southern frontiers of Czechoslovakia to attack by the Reichswehr from Austria, Hitler gave the signal to Henlein to turn up the heat. In a speech in Karlsbad on 24 April 1938 Henlein made eight new demands. One of these, a claim for Sudeten Germans to 'have full freedom to profess German nationality and the German *Weltanschauung*' amounted to a demand for a Sudeten German state within the Czechoslovak Republic – only one step from full union of the Sudetenland with the Reich.

A month later had come a real war scare on the frontier between Czechoslovakia and Germany. On the morning of 21 May two Sudeten German motor cyclists refused to stop when they were challenged by Czech frontier guards. Both men were shot dead. They were found to be carrying into Czechoslovakia large quantities of leaflets, printed in Germany, attacking the Prague Government. The Czechs reacted by carrying out a partial mobilisation, not large enough to defend their frontiers against a full-scale German attack, but enough to put down any Sudeten rising, should one be on the way.

It was a highly efficient military operation, and it lanced the boil in an instant. Half a million men, called up overnight, moved into the fortified lines along the frontier. Barricades were flung across roads from Germany, bridges mined, anti-aircraft guns set up round the big cities. For four days and nights fighter planes roared above Prague, searching the cloudy skies. Henlein's supporters, faced with this strength, showed no fight. Those of military age answered the call to mobilisation almost without exception, with among them Henlein's press officer in Prague, who had been assuring the foreign press that in a day or two 'You see big things from us'. White stockings, that unofficial Nazi badge, disappeared overnight.

Hitler waited four days before issuing a further series of indignant denials that anything like a thrust into the Sudetenland had been contemplated. Henlein was told to re-open the negotiations with the Czech Government. He was rushed into Prague by night to meet the Czech premier, Dr Hodza, travelling in a fast car, with Czech motor-cycle police screening him from any over-patriotic Czechs along the route.

This May crisis alarmed Neville Chamberlain and his Foreign Secretary, Lord Halifax. They realised that it was no longer practicable just to turn a blind eye to German expansion. For the first time a country which was prepared to fight stood in Hitler's way. Though Britain had no treaty obligations to Czechoslovakia, the French did. And if France got drawn into a war over Czechoslovakia, then Britain would inevitably find herself drawn in too. Faced with this danger, the British Government fell back on a traditionally British device – that of a Committee of Inquiry. If an investigator, proclaimed as fair-minded and independent, went to Czechoslovakia, and decided that Henlein – and Hitler – had a case, at least for the autonomy of the Sudeten areas, then perhaps the Czech will to resist could be weakened, and public opinion in France and Germany could be prepared for a withdrawal of the direct French treaty guarantees – and the indirect British guarantee – of the present frontiers of Czechoslovakia.

The Chamberlain Government chose a spectacular background against which to deploy this plan – the visit of the new British monarch King George VI and Queen Elizabeth to Paris in July 1938. The visit was a brilliant success. For four days the streets of central Paris were submerged in a sea of bunting and Union Jacks. Huge crowds lined the boulevards to cry *'Vive le roi – vive la reine'*, and went wild with delight when the royal couple broke with all precedent and appeared just before midnight on the balcony of their apartments in the Quai d'Orsay, to wave to the crowds below as they had done from the balcony of Buckingham Palace on their coronation a year before.

In the royal entourage had been the Foreign Secretary, Lord Halifax, who had arrived in the scarlet and gold uniform of a royal chamberlain, a bearskin helmet crooked under his arm. But he lost little time in exchanging these for the striped trousers and black jacket of the statesman and in settling down for discussions with the French Foreign Minister, the devious M Georges Bonnet. On the final day of the visit Bonnet summoned the press to his ornately gilded room in the Quai d'Orsay to announce that the French Government warmly welcomed the decision of the British Government to send Lord Runciman, a statesman with a high reputation for fairness, to Czechoslovakia. Runciman's role would be to investigate the Sudeten crisis, and to offer any appropriate mediation between the Sudeten Germans and the Prague Government. So was opened up the primrose path to Munich, to the agreement of 30 September 1938, which was to sacrifice Czechoslovakia to Germany in the hope of avoiding war – that war which was to come a year later.

2

Personal Journey

I travelled into Czechoslovakia on the same train as Lord Runciman, as a special correspondent of the London *Daily Express*, which was then at the peak of its influence as the daily newspaper with the largest circulation in the world. I had come to Europe from New Zealand six years earlier, as a Rhodes Scholar to Oriel College, Oxford. During my vacations I had set about learning as much as I could of this Europe which had been the setting for the events which had filled the newspapers and periodicals of my childhood and youth, the continent of the Great War, of the Bolshevik Revolution, and of the rise of dictators like Mussolini of Italy and Primo de Rivera of Spain, the place of the Great Slump and of Stalin's Five Year Plans.

In the summer of 1932 I had taken an Intourist trip through Russia, from Leningrad to Moscow and then down the Volga to Stalingrad, and across to the Ukraine. It had left me with some good impressions – the sense of fulfilment in the bearing of workers who had risen to manage great factories; hefty but eager young men and women athletes in a new sports stadium in Moscow; suntanned children, clad in red shorts, in a crèche amid pinewoods. Other impressions were less favourable – drunks lying inert in gutters along the drab, unkempt Nevsky Prospect in Leningrad; a mounted policeman breaking up a rioting queue outside a vodka shop; and in particular the massed crowds of peasants, many of them women and children, tearful and harassed, all carrying great bundles, fighting to board steamers on the Volga or trains in the Ukraine. Only later did I realise that we had witnessed the stampede of the peasantry from Stalin's man-made famine in the Ukraine. But there was no mistaking the meaning of another scene which we came upon suddenly – to the manifest embarrassment of our guides – in a dusty street in Kuybyshev on the Volga. A long column of peasants, great bearded men in bast shoes and bast leggings, were being marched off under the guard of troops with long, sword-type bayonets on their rifles, and wearing peaked cloth caps with a red star on the front, exactly as had been depicted in the sketches of artists at the time of the Russian Civil War.

I carried away from the Soviet Union the belief that if – as many of the pundits of the day assured us – the future lay with communism, it was going also to be a future of harsh political authoritarianism which would bear hard on the empirical reformism that I had adopted from the pioneering background of New Zealand. I had also come up against something quite unexpected – the realisation that war might come again in my lifetime. Warnings of war, training for war, preparations for war had been everywhere apparent in Russia, under banners calling upon all citizens to be ready to defend the Soviet Union. This was in jarring contrast to the belief inculcated in us in our schools and universities that the League of Nations and the Kellogg Pact had meant that our generation could, for ever, say goodbye to all that.

Later that summmer I saw something of Germany in the last few months of the Weimar Republic. I spent a month at Heidelberg, studying German, and came to know quite another aspect of those pre-Hitler days than that of the decadent Berlin which has become its hall-mark, that Berlin of *Cabaret* and George Grosz and Brecht. Side by side with this was a Germany of the open air and of the cult of physical fitness, a country where lithe, sun-browned young men and women swam in the as yet unpolluted rivers, where hikers sang as they made their way in bands, a guitar player at the head, along paths through pine forests, where families crowded into new sports grounds built with the loans American had thrust on Germany in the twenties. This was a Germany tasting freedom. It was the knowledge that this freedom would be crushed under the Nazis which made me an unhesitating opponent of Hitler from the moment he became Chancellor in January 1933, before it was clear that he represented an even greater danger to freedom not only in Germany but throughout the world.

This stance, ironically, led me to gain a close acquaintance with the Third Reich. In 1934 a German Rhodes Scholar at Oxford, stung by an anti-Nazi talk I had given to a discussion club, challenged me to serve a period during my next vacation in the Arbeitsdienst, the Nazi Youth Labour Service. There, he claimed, I would discover the true nature of National Socialism. I took up the challenge, and spent three weeks in a Labour Camp outside Hannover, wearing a khaki uniform, one of a squad drilling with spades instead of rifles, and working to drain marshland. We were told this was to provide land on which to grow more grain, but I suspect that a more likely use was for airfields from which to bomb London.

Another chance Nazi acquaintance, a school teacher from Nuremberg in England to improve his English, was equally shocked by my attitude. He was a sincere and long-time Nazi, typical of the many basically decent lower-middle class Germans who had turned to Hitler out of their fears of socialism and communism, and out of distaste for the decadence of Berlin. His family owned a bookshop on the main square in Nuremberg. He invited me to join them on seats they placed in the shop window, to watch the parade at the annual Nazi Party Rally. In the evening they would take me to hear Hitler address the Party faithful. The dais on which Hitler, flanked by the other main Nazi leaders, took the salute at a march past of the storm troopers and the SS, was only some fifty yards from the bookshop window. I found myself, as a result, with a front row seat at an occasion which found its way into the history books and – even more importantly for the later television years – into the film archives. For this was the Nuremberg Rally filmed by Leni Riefenstahl for her epic propaganda film *The Triumph of the Will*, a work which has been drawn on ever since by countless producers of documentaries about Nazism. Leni Riefenstahl was very much in evidence on that overcast September morning, a striking figure, in this most masculine of settings, in a cream-coloured suit and a close fitting hat. She stood with her camera crews at the side of the saluting stand, and on one occasion, when there was a pause in the parade, she appeared on the platform and took Hitler by the sleeve, drawing him to a point where she could get a better shot.

The old Market Square in Nuremberg, renamed only a few weeks earlier as the Adolf Hitler Platz, provided the type of historic setting beloved by Hitler and his propaganda chief, Dr Goebbels, for the opening parade of this week of marches and speeches. The reddish stone buildings, dating back to the fifteenth century, were draped with long red banners, each with a white circle within which was a huge black swastika. Other swastika flags and garlands and bunting hung above every shop and office. Only the front of Nuremberg's great church, the Frauenkirche, whose pinnacles, jagged shapes like stone pine trees, rose on either side towards the peak of its tall, triangular facade, was left unadorned.

Stands for dignitaries and for the press had been built around three sides of the square. The saluting base was in its centre: beside it a military band. As the bandmaster held up his gleaming, tasselled staff, the drums rolled, and the band struck up one of the Nazi Party's many rousing marching tunes. From a side street, in ranks twelve abreast, came column upon column of SA men in their brown uniforms, and SS men in black, their boots crashing in unison on the pavement as they passed their leader.

The bookseller had binoculars, and through them I studied eagerly this man who was to play such a huge part in the lives – and deaths – of so many millions. I did not envisage him then as a mass murderer, or even as someone bound to make war on Britain, but chiefly as the most formidable embodiment of dictatorship, of a form of government which, in those days of the great Depression, might engulf us all, even in countries where democracy was so deeply rooted as in Britain. Dictatorship was by no means a dirty word everywhere in the Western world. Mussolini had been in power in Italy for over a decade. Kemal Attaturk was widely praised for having used authoritarian methods to bring his country into the modern world. Primo de Rivera had been dictator of Spain from 1923–30. Poland was under the absolutist rule of Pilsudski, Portugal under that of Salazar, and Yugo-slavia under that of King Alexander. Mussolini had many British admirers. Even Churchill had some good words to say of him. As late as October 1937 Churchill was to write in the *Evening Standard* of Mussolini's 'amazing qualities of courage, comprehension, self-control and persever-ance'. Lloyd George was to say 'Hitler is one of the greatest men I have ever met'. D. H. Lawrence in *Kangaroo* had presented a picture of an Australian would-be dictator which had many sympathetic aspects. Written in 1922, it forecast a situation which, ten years later, seemed briefly to be a possibility, when a World War I veteran, Colonel Campbell, formed a para-military force, the New Guard, to oppose the left wing Labour Govern-ment of the New South Wales. Campbell had one brief moment of glory, when one of his sympathisers, an ADC on the Governor General's staff, galloped forward, sword raised, and slashed the ribbon across the newly built Sydney Bridge to prevent the Labour Prime Minister carrying out the opening ceremony.

In Britain itself Sir Oswald Mosley's British Union of

Fascists was, literally and metaphorically, on the march. 'Hurrah for the Blackshirts' Lord Rothermere had proclaimed in the *Daily Mail*. Only a few weeks before I had come to Germany, Mosley's Blackshirts, at a mass rally at Olympia, had demonstrated a sickening brutality in dealing with hecklers and interrupters of a rally at which their leader had spoken. Even though the disruption of the speech had been clearly planned, chiefly by Communists, the violence shown by the black-uniformed stewards, women as well as men, had been so ugly and wanton that it was to do lasting damage to Fascism in Britain. No doubt, coming as I did from a young, new country, I tended to see these complex European issues too sharply in terms of black and white, not to make sufficient allowance for the durability of British parliamentary democracy. Yet right wing totalitarianism was a real threat to Britain at this time, particularly if Fascism and Nazism became dominant throughout the Continent, isolating Britain and so helping to impose at Westminster an authoritarian government which would be Fascist in everything but name, a black jacket and striped trousers Fascism, if not a Blackshirt one. That at any rate is how I saw events at that time, and why I studied these men on the platform at Nuremberg as the enemies of personal liberty not only in their own country, but everywhere.

Hitler wore the brown uniform of the SA, but with a well-cut jacket, a collar and tie, a Sam Browne belt, knee breeches and knee-high leather boots. The Iron Cross hung on his left breast pocket, and on his left sleeve was a swastika armband. But for this, and the high boots, his uniform could at first glance have been taken for that of a British army officer wearing a rather odd shade of khaki. He was hatless, and his dark hair was brushed down closely and sleekly, except for one long lock which tended to slip over his forehead.

Seen in close-up through the binoculars, Hitler looked very much as he was portrayed in the newspapers and magazines of the time – a tribute to the effectiveness of the still picture in those pre-television days. I scanned his face eagerly for signs of the mystical powers of leadership which had won him such a grip on the German people. But they were difficult to detect. His face revealed a strange blend of ordinariness and strength. The nose was somewhat more prominent, the moustache a shade larger – and to that degree less comic – and the chin more determined than I had expected. Perhaps it was the low forehead, sloping back abruptly, and the fleshy cheeks which made it seem so ordinary, the kind of face one would not have glanced at twice in a crowd.

Hitler's stamina was remarkable. For four hours he stood, with only intermittent breaks, as the brown ranks of the SA and the black ranks of the SS passed in front of him. As the chromium-plated metal standard carried by each detachment came abreast of him, Hitler would swing his ring arm across his chest, then sweep it out in the Nazi salute. At the same time his eyes would fix on the face of the men in the ranks with an intent, concentrated stare. He would then move his arm slowly to the right, following the standard, through an arc of about fifteen degrees, and then cut it back abruptly to his side, hooking his right thumb into his belt until the next column approached. It was a skilfully designed movement, military and precise, which enabled him to alternate two or three minutes of saluting with a similar period of rest – without the rest appearing as slack or untidy. Even though the parade was organised to provide an occasional pause, the strength necessary for four hours of such activity was considerable.

Hitler was flanked by the other main Nazi leaders, their brown uniforms contrasting with the grey of Reichswehr generals and the purple and black of two bishops, one of whom wore an Iron Cross alongside the crucifix which dangled on a chain round his neck. There was an unmistakable air of relaxation, almost of jollity, amongst Goering and Goebbels and Himmler and the other Nazi chieftains on the dais. And well there might be. For the

Nazi Party had not only survived, but emerged strengthened at the end of three traumatic months, which had
begun on 30 June with the slaughter of Ernst Roehm, the
commander of the Storm Troopers, and some thousand
of his senior officers and men. Roehm, a homosexual
thug, had been one of Hitler's earliest associates in the
Nazi Party, and he had stood at Hitler's side on this very
spot a year earlier, as his Brownshirt battalions had
marched in pride past their leader at the first Party Rally
since Hitler had become Chancellor in January 1933. Now
Roehm was dead, shot on Hitler's orders by an SS
execution squad. Ostensibly Roehm had been accused of
preparing a putsch, but in reality he had been sacrificed
to placate the Reichswehr, who resented and distrusted
this alternative Brownshirt army.

The killings had created a sensation abroad stigmatis-
ing National Socialism as a grisly creed which devoured
its own leaders even more speedily than Bolshevism had
done in Russia. But within Germany it brought Hitler a
swift reward. On 1 August the aged President Hindenburg
had died, and the Reichswehr commanders acquiesced in
Hitler's demand that the posts of President and of Chancellor should be merged in the new post of Reichsführer.
Endorsed by a plebiscite in mid-August, this change gave
Hitler greater power than any previous leader of
Germany, including the Kaiser, had possessed.

The full impact of these events was not clear to me that
morning as I stared out from the bookseller's window.
But the fact that the Nazi leaders were very pleased with
themselves, and with the way events had turned out, was
plain to see.

Goering, whose flesh seemed to slop over at every point
within his brown shirt, was clearly in high good humour,
exchanging jokes with the burly and bald-headed Julius
Streicher, present in his dual capacity as party Gauleiter
for Nuremberg and as editor of *Der Stürmer*, the party's
virulently anti-Semitic journal. Goebbels, a small figure
under a wide, flat cap with a swastika badge, his club foot

disguised by long trousers – he was the only party leader not wearing jack boots – looked at first sight like a boy among adults. Only when one looked closely did one see that his sharp, wary expression was far from that of a youth. Even Himmler, his spectacles glittering in the sun, his black SS uniform standing out amongst the prevailing brown of the platform party, allowed himself an occasional smile.

Physically they were an ignoble lot, far from being the embodiment of the Master Race which they proclaimed Germany to be. Only Hess, erect and stern, like an overgrown boy scout in his brown shirt and black tie, had any physical presence, and that was marred by the deep-set, harsh fanaticism of his eyes under their heavy eyebrows. Even Baldur Schirach, leader of the Hitler Youth, was already running to fat within his calculatedly boyish uniform. Yet my bookseller host and his Nazi family and friends saw no such defects. To them these were demi-gods, the men who had protected Germany from Bolshevism and corruption by international Jewry. Any defects they might have were to be glossed away. Goering was to them a merry figure, a man who enjoyed life, to be admired now for his lustiness, 'Der Dicke' – the Plump Fellow. Goebbels, I was assured, was a clever man, 'the kind the Führer needs to combat the many enemies threatening the Reich'. And when Hitler smiled patiently as Leni Riefenstahl posed him for yet one more shot, my hosts were almost in ecstasy at these signs of the humanity of this Supreme Being, so understanding even with so many weighty concerns on his mind.

That evening Hitler delivered his main speech of the rally, in the vast new concrete exhibition hall on the outskirts of the city. We were there early to secure a good place in the body of the hall. Once again I had a better vantage point than that available to the foreign press, for I was part of the audience in the midst of the Party faithful, caught up in its reactions and its moods, not observing it from a place set apart. Around me were the men and women from whom National Socialism derived its basic support – peasants in dark suits, clearly their Sunday best; shopkeepers; small businessmen; clerks. Amongst them were many women. Behind the platform a huge metal swastika was ringed with red paper flowers, about the words '*Alles für Deutschland*' – All for Germany – painted in blood red letters six feet high. The pillars along the walls bore the swastikas, surmounted by the German eagle. High up in the wings electricians were busy with batteries of arc lights. From the rostrum in front of the platform a voice called, '*Achtung, achtung*, silence. We are testing the loud speakers.'

Slowly the minutes passed. A man in front of me ate tomatoes from a paper bag. A Storm Trooper walked up and down the aisle spraying the sultry air with eau de cologne. Then a sudden blare of trumpets, and everyone was on his feet. 'Yes, there he is, there. *Heil, heil.*' Through the thicket of outstretched hands the dark head of Hitler could be seen, as he made his way with his officers down the central aisle, and took his place on the platform.

The trumpets sounded again. In the entrance stood a black-uniformed standard bearer holding the 'Blood Flag', the banner carried in the first, abortive Nazi putsch in 1923. It was borne swiftly up the hall, in the glare of the arc lights. Behind came the SA section standards, three abreast, sweeping up the central gangway in a stream of gleaming metal, their storm trooper bearers hidden by the tasselled swastika banners.

One of Dr Goebbels' most astute techniques then came into play. Instead of the meeting launching immediately into vehement political oratory, an orchestra played the prelude to Act II of *Lohengrin*. It was mood music on a grand scale, preparing the audience's mind for higher things and deeper thoughts, and at the same time throwing a cloak of respectability and legitimacy in advance over whatever outrageous assertions or claims Hitler might make. Opponents of Nazism even argued that classicial music of this kind purged the audience of its better feelings, leaving its baser instincts open to exploitation by Hitler's oratory. Certainly an almost religious hush had spread over the whole vast audience by the time the prelude finished.

The mood then abruptly changed. Rudolf Hess, looking more than ever like a grown-up boy scout, strode to the rostrum, curtly declared the meeting open, and then cried, 'The Leader speaks.' In a tumult of cheering and heiling, Hitler's brown-uniformed figure took its place at the rostrum.

He spoke for an hour and a half. It was a speech aimed not for foreign consumption but at the German people, at emphasising that he now embodied Germany, that the Nazis had supreme power. His long, convoluted sentences, his addiction to high-sounding, abstract words and sudden bursts of slang were difficult for me to follow, so that I was not caught up in the emotions he roused. But the crowd clearly were. A mother in front of me turned to her teenage son, her eyes bright with tears. No one seemed to notice the stage management behind it all. As Hitler worked towards a climax the arc lights came on, one after another, until he rounded off his sentence, fist in air, in a blaze of purplish light. When he brought his fist down on the rostrum, and turned to his text again, every light would go out except one beside him, illuminating his face. At his feet crouched cameramen, and a film camera on a moving trolley moved up and down the aisle.

Whenever he made a deliberate pause, brushing back his thin, shining hair from his eyes, the crowd were on their feet shouting, '*Heil, heil.*' One woman broke into hysterics, and went on with a shrill, '*Heil, heil*' after the others had ceased, until she was pulled down into her seat. The tense, straining, menacing voice continued. 'The world outlook of the German people, the whole character of the German race demands . . .'

The Führer finished amidst a tumult of cheering, clapping, heiling. The SS guards smiled with pride. Hess mounted the rostrum. His voice sounded deep and calm after Hitler's: 'The Party is Hitler. But Hitler is Germany. All for Germany means all for Hitler.' The band broke into '*Deutschland über Alles*' and then '*Die Fahne Hoch.*' Hitler stalked out through the cheering throngs, the standards followed in their gleaming stream, the crowd surged to the doorway. Outside it was raining. By a corrugated iron refreshment shelter a child was looking for a dropped handkerchief. The trams were crowded, and it was late in the night before I made my way to the railway station.

None of this shifted me from my belief that Hitler was both dangerous and evil, a view which had been literally further hammered into me late one night in a street in Berlin. I failed to salute the swastika banner of a platoon of Storm Troopers marching off the railway station to take the train for the Nuremberg festival. Confident of my status as a foreigner, I was showing my passport to the squad commander when others of the squad came up from behind and hit me on the head. I came to in the gutter a few minutes later, to see the squad continuing their march in the distance. I was not seriously hurt, with only a few cuts on the scalp, and a throbbing head. My wounds were cleaned and dressed in a nearby chemist's shop where I was taken by a man who assured me – whether with sincerity or sarcasm – that I would understand such actions once Mosley won power in Britain.

My Arbeitsdienst experiences brought me the unexpected bonus of an entry into journalism. I emerged from my time in the labour camp to find that I had the answer to a question which was being investigated at the time by the foreign press corps in Berlin. Were these labour camps, as the Nazis claimed, a way of rehabilitating the unemployed youth and giving a sense of service, or were they a form of disguised military service? The answer was that they were a bit of both. Since I could provide first-hand information, the *New York Times* invited me to write an article on the camp. They made it the cover story in their Sunday magazine. The weekly *Spectator* in London took a similar piece from me. They printed it in the same issue as carried an attack by their art correspondent, one Anthony Blunt, on Salvador Dali's work as 'psycho-sexual exposition, not art'. Armed with my cuttings of these articles I was able, in the spring of 1935, to secure a toehold in Fleet Street. The Liberal *News Chronicle* gave me a trial as a reporter 'on space', as a freelance. This meant that I was paid only for such of the stories as I got into the paper.

In time I won my way onto the regular reporting staff, at first in the far from glamorous role of late-night reporter, sprinting off to cover fires and crimes in the small hours. But it gave me an invaluable apprenticeship in covering hard news, and brought me a footing within Fleet Street at a time when newspapers occupied the centre of the media stage in the way in which television does today.

Eighteen months after I had joined the *News Chronicle* the Spanish Civil War offered me a lucky break. In October 1936 Franco's forces were advancing on Madrid in a seemingly unstoppable fashion. The *News Chronicle* was an ardent opponent of the Franco regime. There seemed every chance that any *Chronicle* reporter who was in Madrid when the city fell would be arrested or held in detention – as indeed six months later Arthur Koestler, the *News Chronicle* correspondent in Malaga, was jailed when that city fell. The paper was reluctant to have one of its stars, like Vernon Bartlett or Philip Jordan, wasted in this way, so the editor, Gerald Barry, looked around the newsroom for someone more expendable, and his eyes fell on me. 'Sorry, Geoffrey, but you are for it' were the words with which the news editor told me to set off for Madrid.

I went with avidity, not only because it was a big story, but because I was passionately on the side of the Republicans. Not only was Franco an ally of Hitler and Mussolini, both now flexing their muscles in the face of what seemed the inert and frightened democracies, a Spanish dictator who had to be opposed if we were to prevent authoritarianism spreading to Britain, but there was also the prospect of a better and freer life which had opened up before the Spanish people. After the first rising of the Generals had been thwarted in Madrid and Barcelona, there emerged the hope of a new order in which the peasants could own their lands, in which schools and hospitals and freedom might be open to all. The egalitarianism in which I had been steeped since childhood in New Zealand led me perhaps to over simplify the issues, and to read too much into those early, exhilarating days of the summer and autumn of 1936 in Spain, the time which André Malraux wrote of as the Days of Hope. But I shared fully Malraux's view, expressed in the final passage of his book *Man's Hope*, that the Spanish people were hearing in those months 'the voice of that which is more inspiring even than the blood of men, more enigmatic even than their presence on earth – the infinite possibilities of their own destiny'.[1]

The immediate problems facing me in Madrid were, however, more practical. Early in November as Franco's troops reached the outskirts of the city the Republican Government fled to Valencia. Most of the foreign press went with them. I stayed, and found myself one of only two Fleet Street newspapermen in the capital. And Madrid did not fall. Instead of finding myself expelled or in prison, I found my report leading the front page of the paper day after day, particularly when Franco turned his German and Italian bombers against the city in a foretaste of the raids which the civilian populace in every European city dreaded – and about which they wished eagerly to read.

When I went back to London in December, after the first Franco offensive had ground to a halt, I had assumed

---

[1] Random House, 1938. Translated by Stuart Gilbert and Alastair Macdonald.

it would be for a short spell of leave before I returned to Spain again. But this was not to be. The other, senior correspondents on the *News Chronicle* now claimed their share of this major story. I would have to wait my turn in the queue. In the meanwhile, in the chastening way of Fleet Street, I found myself chasing late fires once again.

To offset my frustration I wrote a short book about that first battle for Madrid. Victor Gollancz published it in the spring of 1937 – books came out speedily in those days. It sold well, and attracted the attention of Arthur Christiansen, then at the peak of his fame as editor of Lord Beaverbrook's *Daily Express*. He offered me the post of *Express* correspondent in Vienna. This was one of the plum journalistic jobs of the time, for the whole of Central Europe and the Balkans was your bailiwick.

I was reluctant to leave the *News Chronicle*, not only because I was broadly in agreement with its political stance, and in particular with its staunch opposition to Fascism, but also because it offered its journalists a remarkable degree of editorial freedom. Having selected its correspondents, it trusted them, and printed their stories unchanged. The maverick Conservatism of Beaverbrook's *Daily Express* was much less to my taste, and there was always the fear that you might find yourself being called upon to dance to the tune of its subtle and powerful proprietor. But the attractions of a senior post as a foreign correspondent were strong, and the money was good. That loomed a larger factor now, for in 1935 I had married Cecily Turner, a student at Oxford with me, and our first child was due in the autumn. So I took the gamble, and in June 1937 set off for Vienna.

Austria was a country which I had come to know in my Oxford days, having spent the long summer vacation there in 1933. At that time it had been a blend of the vestiges of Habsburg grandeur; of a widely praised Viennese municipal socialism, which had given the city modern flats and crèches and schools and sports stadia; and of the Catholic Nationalism of Chancellor Dollfuss. But since then the Socialists had been hunted from power in Vienna, and the workers' flats shelled by artillery to dislodge the Socialist militia which had resisted the change. In turn Dollfuss had been murdered by the Nazis. Now the tall, arid figure of Chancellor Kurt Schuschnigg ruled over a state grey and drab with unemployment, whose people waited with either hope or fear – depending upon whether they were Nazis or not – for the day when Adolf Hitler would move to take Austria, his original homeland, into the Reich.

That merger, the Anschluss of Austria and Germany, did not come during my time as Vienna correspondent of the *Daily Express*. I had been there only six months, just enough time to begin to get to know the marvellously varied and fascinating lands which I had to cover, and to settle into a flat in Vienna, where our son Peter was born in September 1937, when Christiansen moved me to Paris. It was promotion, for Paris was the most senior *Express* post in Europe, but I went sadly, not only because I liked Vienna but because I wanted to be on the spot when Hitler began the thrust eastwards which was clearly his next move.

I did, however, manage to persuade Christiansen to let me go back to Austria to cover what, at the time in March 1938, was seen merely as a plebiscite being held by Schuschnigg to confirm the stand he was taking for the independence of Austria against Nazi pressure.

Many leading American correspondents were on the train from Paris on the night of 11 March, among them John Whitaker of the *Chicago Daily News* and the famed H. R. Knickerbocker, of the Hearst Press. There was also a young reporter from the *New York Herald Tribune*, Walter Kerr, with whom I was to share many assignments in the next few years, and who was to become one of my closest friends. It was a moment to savour as I sat with them round a table in the *wagon-lit* dining car into the night, as the pundits swapped reminiscences, and argued about the future of Europe.

We woke the next morning, in the brilliant light reflected from the snow-covered mountainsides, to astonishing news. Hitler had denounced the plebiscite, and was moving his troops into Austria. In the train corridor I was approached by a small, well-dressed, extremely agitated Austrian Jew, appalled at finding himself returning into the jaws of the avowed enemies of his race. Was it true, he asked me, that the great H. R. Knickerbocker was on the train? When I told him this was so, relief spread over his face. 'With the foreign press here they won't dare to do anything wrong, will they? Will they?' he kept asking. 'We will be all right with you there.'

It was an impressive reminder of the power which the press possessed in those days – or had possessed. I wished I could have shared in his confidence, even if there was more wishfulness than real hope in his words. But I knew in my bones that we were a very fragile defence indeed against the forces even then being released upon the people of Austria.

In Innsbruck Kerr and I hired a car and set off up the road towards the German border. In the hall of the hotel, the Jew who had spoken to me on the train, his face grey with fear, was frantically trying to get through on the telephone to Switzerland, whilst in the corner the radio blared out the cheers of the crowds waiting in Linz for Hitler's arrival.

It was a brilliantly clear morning, and the snow, still heavy on the mountainsides, lay in streaks across the black earth of the fields. The road wound alongside the River Inn. At one bend a peasant boy in *Lederhosen*, a tiny swastika flag in his hand, rushed to the roadside shouting, 'The German Army is coming: the German Army is coming.' We had just time to pull on to the road edge as, round the corner, came a dozen or so steel-helmeted motor cyclists, rifles slung on their backs. Behind them came a line of swiftly moving, camouflage-bedaubed military trucks filled with grey-green uniformed troops, sitting bolt upright, rifles between their knees. In some trucks a heavy machine-gun barrel pointed sky-wards; others hauled anti-tank guns, their barrels covered with canvas. Then came the sound of drums, and a long column of infantry marching three abreast, following along behind a regimental band. Then came a line of staff cars, some with skis piled on top.

It was a thrilling, chilling sight. Here in the bright spring sunshine were the machines of war rolling across frontiers, like the first falling rocks and shifting earth of a great landslide which could engulf us all. That morning, on that chilly mountain road, I was sure not only that war would come, but had already made its own remorseless beginning.

*

Scene after scene was etched into my mind as the day wore on. As the Reichswehr columns approached Innsbruck, from a side road a yellow sports car appeared and halted. A bronzed woman in an expensive coat jumped out, and flung her arms round the neck of the nearest German officer. At the Brenner Pass a German mechanised army unit and a straggling column of Austrian Nazi Storm Troops in white shirts, black trousers and swastika armbands halted a few yards from the Italian frontier post. A Reichswehr colonel, clicking the heels of his shiny, high leather boots together, saluted the Aus-trian customs official and assured him of the 'comradely feelings of the Germans'. The late afternoon sun glowed on the snowy slopes of the Dolomites as the swastika flag was raised on the Austrian customs post. In fields near Kitzbuhel children ploughed knee deep through snow to pick up yellow leaflets scattered from German planes, welcoming Austria into the Reich. The road behind was jammed with horse-drawn field kitchens, and horse-drawn machine guns. And in the streets of Innsbruck, as the foremost German units marched into the town, I found myself standing next to a grey-haired Jewish woman tremblingly holding out her hand in the Hitler salute whilst the crowd roared out the Horst Wessel Nazi hymn, the words of which she tried with her mouth but clearly did not know.

I got as far as Salzburg by midnight, and got a bed in an hotel which had Reichswehr sentries on the door, and the names of twenty-seven German officers, among them a major-general, in the register. By midday on Sunday I was back in Vienna making my way through streets where units of the Reichswehr rumbled through, not halting, but moving on towards the Czech and Hungarian frontiers.

That evening the press were summoned to the Federal Chancellery, where we were informed that the new Austrian Chancellor, the Nazi lawyer Seyss-Inquart, and his cabinet had declared that Austria had become a state of the German Reich. A monocled official, Dr Mazar, read the announcement to us in a room just down the corridor from that in which Chancellor Dollfuss had been shot dead by the Nazis three and a half years before. Through the windows came the shouts of the crowds, cheering the Reichswehr as they drove along the Ringstrasse.

The next day ecstatic crowds lined the streets to see Adolf Hitler drive in triumph into the city which had rejected him as a failed artist and casual labourer twenty-five years earlier. A huge crowd packed the space in front of the Imperial Hotel. When Hitler appeared on the balcony, a triumphant, smiling figure in the same type of brown shirt uniform he had worn at Nuremberg, every arm went out in salute. I raised my own with them. To have done anything else would have been suicide, for no passport, no claim to be a foreigner could have stood against the hysteria which filled the air.

All around me the chant of 'Sieg Heil! Sieg Heil!' rose like an insistent, gigantic drumbeat. Hitler's face flushed with pleasure as he looked down on this city where he had known failure, and which he now faced as Leader of a Reich more powerful than anything the Hohenzollerns or the Habsburgs had known. Despite the dangers which my mind told me lay ahead, I felt surge through me a sense of exhilaration at witnessing this moment when a page of history was being turned, however deadly the message written on it.

Already the mass arrests of Jews and Socialists and other opponents of Nazism had begun. In many streets Jews, old and young, men and women, herded by Storm Troopers with drawn truncheons, and surrounded by jeering crowds, were forced onto their hands and knees to scrub the Schuschnigg signs off walls and pavements. At SA barracks other Jews, including doctors and professors, were forced to clean out the latrines, in one case using for this the sacred prayer bands, the Tefellin, from a nearby synagogue.

Earlier that afternoon I had nearly been myself on the receiving end of attention from the local Nazis. The *Daily Express* office in Vienna was in a flat, which also served as the correspondent's home, in a small square, the Modenaplatz. I was standing by the window of the flat with Roland Bodchow, a Reichs German from Berlin who had become the assistant correspondent of the *Express* in Vienna, when I saw a khaki-clad squad straggling across the grass of the square. At the front was a tall, gangling Storm Trooper in a brand new khaki uniform. Behind him came a dozen or so other Storm Troopers in a variety of garbs. Some had khaki shirts and black trousers; others khaki shirts and *Lederhosen*; others the white shirt, black trousers and swastika armband which was the most easily adopted version of a Nazi uniform. Their leader was trying to get them into some form of marching formation, but they looked a sorry lot. I taunted Bochow with the bearing of his new allies. 'You'll never get Austrian Nazis even to march in step.' I said – and then I paused, for I realised the squad were crossing the road towards the entrance to our block of flats.

A few minutes later we could hear the clang of heavy boots on the stairs, and the doorbell rang. Bochow said quickly, 'I will see to this.' I could hear voices raised when he opened the door, then argument, and suddenly Bochow's voice, in sharp Prussian tones, ordering them away. He came back into the room, aggressive, but also a little shaken. 'These Austrian fools,' he said. 'That bloody janitor who looks after this building has been up to tricks. He had denounced you as an enemy of Nazis and a friend of Jews, and persuaded the local SA to come round and teach you a lesson. They were going to wreck the flat and beat you up. I gave them a piece of my mind, I can tell you. And as for that bloody janitor, I will see he is out of his job before the week is over.' From the window we watched the squad file dispiritedly away. They halted in the middle of the square, and gathered round, arguing. One man clearly wanted to return, and kept trying to get the others to follow him. But in the end they dispersed.

*

My journey back to Paris provided a strange postscript to this first Nazi conquest. On the train, on a hard wooden seat in an open plan third class carriage, was a girl in her late teens, manifestly British, with a swathe of blonde hair across her forehead, a delicate complexion, and cheeks which seemed to have still the fullness of adolescence. On her dress was pinned a swastika badge. I recognised her as Unity Mitford, friend and ardent admirer of Hitler, one of whose sisters had married Sir Oswald Mosley and another Esmond Romilly. She answered my questions angrily and disdainfully.

'I was heartbroken when I did not see Hitler when he arrived at his birthplace at Linz,' she said. 'Another English friend, who was with him there, said it was the most wonderful experience of his life. But I saw his entry into Vienna, and perhaps after all that was best. Afterwards I saw him for a few minutes in his hotel. He was tired, but seemed very moved by it all. I think it was wonderful.'

The other friend who had been with Hitler in Linz was G. Ward Price of the *Daily Mail*, the most prominent apologist in the British press for Hitler and Mussolini. At Linz he had stood on the balcony alongside Hitler, watching the Reichswehr march in, and had broadcast in English over the German radio, in their live transmission of the scene, his delight at it all.

With Austria in his grasp, Hitler was in a position to move against Czechoslovakia. When, therefore, in July 1938 Arthur Christiansen sent me to cover the Runciman mission I knew I would be reporting not only news but history.

3

A Republic at Bay

On his second day in Prague, 4 August, exactly twenty-four years since Great Britain had entered World War I, Lord Runciman put on a top hat and a morning coat, and went off in a heat wave, with temperatures of over 82° in the shade, to pay a series of formal calls on the leaders of the Czechoslovakian Government. As his car drove across the red sandstone Karlsbridge, with two police motor-cycle outriders in front, and mounted up through the winding, tree-shaded streets of old Prague, the scene was full of reminders of what was at stake for this young new republic.

The Hradschin Castle, with its sheer brownstone walls, and the high, pointed spires of St Vitus's Cathedral, which stood in its inner courtyard, had for three hundred years been the bastion from which the Germanic Habsburgs had ruled the Czechs. Along the road which wound downhill past the castle had come in 1620 the battle-stained but victorious Habsburg knights and their peasant levies who had overthrown the Czech nobles in the battle of the White Mountain, a pine-fringed tableland on the outskirts of modern Prague. It was a battle which brought to an end the ancient kingdom of Bohemia, which had been established a thousand years earlier by the Slavonic Czech tribes who had migrated here on their wild, shaggy ponies from the steppes of Central Asia. The good king Wenceslas of the carol had been amongst its early rulers, and his name was celebrated in the wide main boulevard of modern Prague. But Bohemian independence, like that of neighbouring Moravia, had been crushed at the White Mountain, and from 1620 until the First World War the Czechs were to remain under the Habsburg heel – or, as it appeared to the ordinary Czech, under the heel of the Habsburg German policeman, the German tax inspector, the German aristocrats whom the Habsburgs brought in, or promoted, to rule the Slav peasantry and the Slav workers. German was the official language, German the main tongue in the schools.

Then came World War I, and the winning of Czech and Slovak independence. One key element in the way independence was gained could be seen by Lord Runciman in the uniforms of the sentries who presented arms as his car swept into the courtyard of the Prime Minister's residence. For they wore, not the somewhat greenish khaki of the modern Czechoslovak army, but the World War I uniforms of the French, Italian and Czarist Russian armies. Czechoslovak prisoners and deserters in that war had been grouped into foreign legions to fight against their former rulers. Pale blue of the French *poilu*, with a floppy, dark blue beret; grey green of Italy, with felt hat upturned at one side; khaki, and flat-topped forage cap of Imperial Russia; each of these uniforms appeared in the three companies of the Legionary unit which provided the castle guard.

These wartime legions provided a strong reinforcement to the claims made by Professor Thomas Masaryk at the Versailles Peace Conference for the setting up of an independent republic for the Czechs, and the Slovaks, and the Ruthenians who lived on the borders of the Ukraine. The Allied leaders agreed, and since the natural western frontier of such a state was formed by the great curve of the Sudeten Mountains, three and a half million Germans of Sudetenland were incorporated into it. It seemed logical enough at the time. The Sudeten Germans had never been part of Germany, but had always, as

nation states emerged in Europe, been ruled from
Vienna. Only now, with Hitler demanding to rule not
only the Reich of the German Kaisers, but a new, greater
Reich into which all of German race, whatever their
present nationality, should be incorporated, had the presence of this non-Slav minority within the confines of the
young new republic become an issue to trouble the
Chancelleries of Europe.

Thomas Masaryk had been President of the Czechoslovak Republic from its inception until his death in December 1937 – his funeral in Prague had been one of the last
stories I covered before moving to Paris. He had been
succeeded by his close friend and collaborator, Edouard
Benes, a quiet, scholarly man whose lack of ostentation,
and stubbornness, and reasoned approach were characteristic of the Czech people. His prestige was great, and the
Czechs gave him their absolute trust. Benes had been in
his youth a good footballer, a fact I was careful to record
for the *Daily Express* readers, in my efforts to arouse
their interest in this distant land. He waited now to receive
Lord Runciman in the high-ceilinged room, with its tall
windows overlooking the long curve of the Moldau River,
in which he was to endure not only one but two betrayals
of his country – for he was again President when in 1948
the communists took over.

The Prime Minister, Dr Hodza, was a Slovak, the son
of a wealthy peasant. Stocky, well dressed, precise, with
pince-nez and a stubborn chin, he looked like a successful
bank manager. Hodza had in pre-war days been a representative of the Slovak minority within the Hungarian
Parliament, and had not that instinctive antagonism
towards the formerly dominant Germans which welled up
in the minds of most of the older generation of Czechs.
He was in favour of compromise towards the Sudetens –
if compromise rather than capitulation could be achieved.

The Foreign Minister, Dr Kamil Krofta, a white-haired
low-voiced man of sixty-five, was very much Benes's man.
He had resigned his professorship of history at Prague

University to join the government on Masaryk's death. He worked in the Czernin Palace, formerly the home of the Czernin family, one of whose members, Count Czernin, had been Austrian Foreign Minister in World War I, and had signed the Treaty of Brest Litovsk with the Bolsheviks. Part of the building was now a barracks, and as Runciman's car approached it was halted by a column of troops swinging past, without rifles, roaring a Czech peasant song. Krofta was a kindly, genial, unostentatious man who could be seen in the mornings taking his dog for a walk in the park at the back of the Czernin Palace, prepared to wait his turn at the corner stall to buy a bag of fresh apricots or strawberries from the peasant woman who ran it.

Back in the Alcron Hotel that evening Lord Runciman met leaders of the Sudeten Germans. Henlein was not among them. Hitler had instructed him to play it tough with Runciman, so he was to insist – and prevail in his insistence – that Runciman must come to him in Sudetenland, not he to Runciman in what he saw as alien Prague. His lieutenants were men cast very much in the Nazi mould. For a brief period their names and their faces were to be in the newspapers all over the world, until they slipped back into comparative obscurity once they had played the parts Hitler had allotted them. There was Ernst Kundt, the ex-front-line soldier, son of a washerwoman, whose pennies had gone to educate him before the war. Wearing a simple, ready-made suit and an old overcoat, his face was deeply lined, and he wore a dark Hitler moustache. His expression was cheerful, despite its aggressiveness. He was to win the confidence of the Runciman mission. 'Kundt is an honest man,' one of them said to me. When fighting had been started in the Sudetenland, he alone of the Sudeten leaders did not flee from Prague. He was more of a sincere man with a grievance than a blind, fanatical supporter of Hitler.

Another distinct Nazi type was Sebekowesky, a smooth, astute young lawyer, a relatively new recruit to the Party, but rising rapidly in it, sincere no doubt in his beliefs, but also in the belief that this was the way to advancement. Their propaganda chief was Oscar Ulrich, bald-headed, with a gold tooth and pale horn-rimmed spectacles which gave him a bland, semi-oriental expression. He had been at one time a chinaware salesman in Britain.

The toughest of them all, Karl Hermann Franck, Henlein's deputy (and perhaps the real Nazi driving force behind Henlein's more genial facade) was also absent this first evening, though he was to join in the formal talks with Runciman. Tall, gaunt, stern faced, he had the air of the fanatic. He too was an ex-soldier, who had fought in the Austro-Hungarian army in the Great War. A misfit after the war, he had set up a small printing firm in Karlsbad, which just managed to keep itself from bankruptcy when Henlein set up his Sudeten German Party in 1933. Franck became one of his first supporters. From his printing works he did the Party's early printing. As the Party expanded, and the sales of its pamphlets, its books and its posters greatly increased, Franck began to flourish, and now drove about in a big black Mercedes Benz.

These Nazis were not, however, the only leaders of the Sudeten Germans. The Social Democrat Party still existed in the Sudetenland. Its leader was a young, slightly built, friendly lawyer, Wenzl Jaksch. I took to him immediately when we talked after his first meeting with Runciman. His thin, humorous face lit up with a smile as he explained that the meeting had not gone very well. 'Lord Runciman emphasised that we Social Democrats were only a small party compared to Henlein's. I agreed. I told him our problem is that we are a party of peace and freedom, ideals which are not very popular these days, so we don't compete very well with parties which don't believe in such things.'

Jaksch had an easy, laughing courage, moving freely about Prague despite frequent threats from the Henleinists. He managed to escape from Czechoslovakia in 1939, survived the war, and returned to become a post-war leader of the revived Social Democrats, only to lose his life in a car crash outside Bonn in 1948.

When this first hot, steamy week which the mission had spent in Prague came to an end, Lord Runciman, true to the habits of his caste, departed to the country for the weekend, having accepted an invitation to the stately home of one of the country's aristocrats. The trouble was that the only aristocrats in Czechoslovakia were those left over from the days of the Habsburgs, most of whom were of German race, so it was to the castle of the Germanic Count Kinsky near Brunn that this impartial British arbitrator set off for the first break in his duties.

*

Runciman's weekend off meant time off for the press as well. I was able to start learning something about the people of this land whose fate was to bring us to the brink of war, and who were now living through the last eight weeks they were to know as a truly free people, before being trapped in a bondage which, in its differing forms, has lasted until this day. In those weeks which I shared with them I found Prague an easy city to come to love: modern, garish Prague as well as the old and handsome Bohemian city.

Impressions crowded in on my mind – crowds packing the wide pavements of the Wenchelas Square on a Sunday, strolling slowly up and down in their Sunday best; material well being, with shop after shop packed with cheap silk stockings, cheap dresses and suits, cheap shoes – cheap and good; delicatessen shops by the score, where a midnight snack might consist of half a roast duck, a plate of Russian salad, and half a dozen cucumbers; constant noise from trams, and constant grime from the smuts of soft coal which fell everywhere, from factory chimneys and household chimneys alike; taxis driving at breakneck speed; Slovak peasant women in brilliant costume selling piles of embroidery from stalls outside the international hotels; the gigantic sixteen-inch shell, and a host of smaller shells, with beside each the armour plating, suitably pierced, which it could penetrate, displayed in a shop window in a side street as if it were like any other merchandise, products of the great Skoda works so soon to fall into Hitler's hands; the rows of sexy French magazines, the elegant forerunners of *Playboy*, which appeared on every street bookstall, even in the hotel lifts, but which no one ever seemed to buy; the night club which claimed to be 'the only baroque night club in Europe', with ornate gilt balconies, and a pianist who looked like Aldous Huxley, and a troupe of dancers from Riga – itself another city tasting its last months of freedom.

When the crisis unfolded in September this club was to become an unofficial foreign press centre, for it served excellent food into the small hours. Many a late story datelined Prague was to be telephoned from its telephone booth, whilst in the background the dance floor was packed with people slapping their thighs and twirling their fingers in 'The Lambeth Walk', the dance the tune for which was to provide the background music for Britain as it stared war in the face that September. With its defiant if bogus Cockney tones, it was not a bad anthem for the times, and the Czechs took to it avidly, proclaiming that they too were determined to be.

> 'taking it free and easy
> doing as you damn well pleasy'.

I explored the narrow, cobbled streets of old Prague, where gateways gave you sudden glimpses of old, stone-banked gardens, and willow trees with the Moldau swift and brown beyond. Almost every house had its sign – here three violins, there a stork, or a pelican, or a lamb – painted above its doorway. From the old Karl Bridge I watched bathers in canoes shooting the rapids formed by the weir across the river. Old men fished from the base of the powder magazine tower where students had held back the Germans in the Thirty Years War, and where Elizabeth of Bohemia, daughter of James I of England, had sheltered with her husband from the attacks of the ruler of the Palatine. I went up the river on a slow paddle boat, to spend weekends in a cottage in pinewoods, where we bought milk from a great stone monastery whose farm was run by brown-robed monks. In the local inn we ate huge, butter-drenched meals, in which *Schweinscarre mit Kraut und Knödel* seemed to have the stature of a national dish. In the fields the peasants gathered in the rye harvest, the famous golden rye of Bohemia.

Of course it was not all milk and honey in this young republic. There were the unemployed – 100,000 of them – a big total for a small country; wages were low, if social benefits were high; there were ugly neon lights, and stark modern buildings, in a particularly hideous grey concrete, amid the old castellated towers. But there was a sense of vigour, and an absence of marked distinctions between wealth and poverty which reminded me of Australia and New Zealand.

As if aware that the days of freedom were numbered, people poured out to enjoy the sunshine of that fine August. Along the Moldau the brown bodies of the bathers seemed almost to hide the green of the fields. At Barandov, in the lovely cliffside restaurant, couples danced in the warm moonlight. In the nearby concrete and glass modern villa of a film producer, writers and directors and actors and actresses from the film studios which had made *Extase* and *Matricula* sipped Melnik wine, and worried about the future. On the villa's flat sunbathing roof an anti-aircraft gun had been placed during the 21 May crisis. 'The officer in charge was a Sudeten German,' our host told me.

A wine hall on the river's edge was packed and in full song. Troops in coarse khaki, men in shiny, tight-fitting

suits, fair-haired, sunburnt women in bright cotton dresses
sat at the long tables roaring out the words of a Slovak
peasant song, laughing, drinking the light golden beer of
Pilsen, or the sharp red wine of southern Slovakia. The
woman accordionist who led the orchestra changed suddenly to another tune, less rollicking, more military. The
crowd half sang, half hummed the refrain. It was clear
that the words were not yet familiar to them. But when
the chorus came, they were all in, with a crash of voices:

> Come on Adolf, we're ready.
> Come on Adolf, come ahead.

This audience was clearly not afraid of the German
divisions manoeuvring along their frontiers. They sang
with a lusty self-confidence and ease of mind which had
nothing artificial or strained about it. The song, written
after the 21 May crisis, matched their feelings. There was
no sign that they were singing to reassure themselves, to
screw up their determination. They were expressing their
feelings that, whatever might come, they were ready for
it. It reminded me of the happy-go-lucky, slightly jeering
but in no way false confidence of the Madrilenos in the
face of Franco's bombs.

Many times in the next few weeks I was to feel a
similarity between besieged Madrid and threatened
Prague. In both cities the dominant feeling was of people
who have made up their minds to risk death rather than
to yield, who have come to – and passed – a decisive point
from which there was no going back. Their minds were
easy, for their decision was made. Come what may, we
will fight, said the common people of Prague in their
every action in those days of early August 1938 – and
given the lead they would have kept their word. A middle-
aged man who sat by me in the train one day, when I was
on my way to riverside beach for a swim, had served in
the United States Marines during the war. 'It may be our

lot to go down to servitude again,' he said. 'But if we do, it won't be without a fight.'

This deep-seated confidence was not based on any misreading of the facts so far as they, the mass of people, knew them. Had not 21 May shown that if you stood up to Hitler, he backed down? Had not Britain and France stood by them on that day? Had not France repeatedly said she would honour her treaty obligations? And were there not always in the background the khaki-clad millions of the Russian armies, that Red Star in the East to which these fellow Slavs now looked eagerly? Again and again this defiance was expressed to me. There was the Czech mill owner from Sudetenland who said, 'We will all go, every old man, every boy, even the women if necessary, if he attacks us.' In the village inn, near the monastery where we got our milk a burly soldier on leave went further: 'We should start the fighting ourselves, and have done with it. I got two wounds in the last war, and I'll go again willingly'. The peasants at the other tables nodded their approval.

'And to think that your Government is planning to sell these people down the river,' said Maurice Hindus, as he lay in the sun at Barandov and read *The Times*. Hindus, whose books had brought us in New Zealand our first detailed, if slanted information about the Soviet Five Year Plans, proved to be a dark-haired, craggy-faced man in his forties. In his talk, if not yet in his writing, he was already showing signs of disillusion with Stalin, whose personality and policies he had in the past effusively praised. Though I agreed with his evaluation of British policy, his words and his tone irritated me, for he was only one of many American journalists who were very ready to urge Britain and France to stand and fight, but were apt to shrug their shoulders if we suggested that America might join in, and do the same.

4

A Brush with the Gestapo

As Lord Runciman settled down to the task of hearing formal evidence, working in the panelled, fussily furnished sitting room of his suite in the Alcron Hotel, Dr Goebbels gave him a striking reminder of Nazi propaganda skill. He built up the death of a Sudeten German in an inn brawl into a case of political martyrdom, and ensured that the dead man was given a hero's funeral. It was no doubt an easy enough task for Goebbels, for he had long since transformed the murdered pimp, Horst Wessel, into a German hero, and had made the Horst Wessel song into Germany's second National Anthem.

On the night of Sunday, 7 August, Wenzel Beyerl, a 28-year-old woodcutter was stabbed to death at Gasterwald, a lonely Sudetenland forest village. Beyerl was a Henlein supporter, and he had quarrelled, during a session of heavy drinking, with a fellow villager, another Sudeten, Robert Hoiden, who was a Social Democrat who had lived for many years in Austria. The facts were not in dispute. I checked most of them literally on the spot, where the sticky stain of Beyerl's blood still showed by the roadside. He had been followed from the inn by Hoiden, who had stabbed him five times in the back. Hoiden worked in a glass factory whose tall white chimney showed up incongruously amid the dark, bleak, deserted pinewoods – a factory whose workers formed a Socialist enclave in this Henleinist territory.

The German radio jumped on the story right away. 'More Czech brutality' it thundered. The broadcasters had one difficulty to overcome. They did not want to admit that Sudeten German had been fighting Sudeten German, that the support of the people of the Sudetenland for Henlein was not rock solid. They overcame that by arguing that since Hoiden had at one time lived in Austria, he was a dirty red from red Vienna, and therefore an honorary Czech.

Beyerl's funeral was turned by the Henleinists into a major propaganda demonstration. The body, in its white peasant coffin, was laid on a platform covered with red Henleinist flags and guarded by four men in the grey shirt uniform of Henlein's Storm Troopers, the FS, or Volunteer Defence Service. Three Henleinist deputies, members of the Prague Parliament, strode militarily to and fro in grey uniforms which were exact copies of the black German SS uniform. Local Sudeten Nazis, in white shirts, black ties, and black trousers held up sometimes by Sam Browne belts, sometimes by brilliant coloured braces from their Sunday suits, lined the rough forest road. In sharp contrast was the dark green greatcoat of the local gendarmerie commander, a short sword in a scabbard at his waist. Further back, their green uniforms brilliant against the dark hills, stood a squad of gendarmes, bayonets fixed on the loaded black Mausers, gleaming spiked helmets on their heads.

Onto this scene strode the tall, gaunt figure of Hermann Franck, Henlein's deputy. He saluted the bier perfunctorily, conferred with a plain clothes police officer and with the gendarmerie commander. The funeral cortège formed up, a choir sang the Henleinist song '*Wir Bleiben Deutsch* – We remain forever German'.

Suddenly from a wooden peasant house on the other side of the road came one of the most terrible cries I have ever heard. Beyerl's mother emerged, a bent figure in black, with a black handkerchief over her head, and a candle clutched in her hand. Rocking herself slowly to and fro she cried, 'My son, my son, my Wenzel.'

Slowly they brought her down to the bier. Beside her walked the dead boy's stepfather, a heavily moustached peasant uncomfortable in his rough best suit. Franck and the other Sudeten Nazi leaders shook the mother's hand, said some words to her. The village priest, a young man, nervous and seemingly uncertain of himself, began to intone the burial service, and the mother began again this terrible, heart-wrenching wail.

The ranks of the storm troopers stirred. You could sense the feeling running through them. 'These swinish Czechs. What brutality to bring this sorrow on this poor peasant woman.' Hatred glowed in their eyes as they stared towards the Czech gendarmes, who stared equally contemptuously back. The hatred which Goebbels sought to foster was growing with every moment.

The priest finished, the funeral procession formed up, and with drums rolling portentously in the forest, moved off towards the graveyard. There Franck delivered an oration in Henlein's name. He emphasised the Party view that the murderer was a deserter from the German people. 'In our eyes he was no German. He was a traitor.' He paused, and once again the mother's terrible cry, almost animal rather than human in its suffering, tore the silence. Below the churchyard were the rolling pine hills of the Bohemian forest, a dark brooding world as sombre and as full of foreboding as any forest in the tales of the Brothers Grimm. From country like this, further to the south, had sprung Hiter's forebears, the Schickelgrubers. Today, under the grey clouds through which the sun struggled, menace overhung it.

Down in the village the gendarmes, their faces still marked with scorn rather than fear, strode through the funeral crowd towards their headquarters in the village school, which was packed to the windows with their reinforcements. At the start of the ceremony I had thought their bearing was scornful to the point of provocation. I was less sure after I talked to the stepfather. He told me that Beyerl's mother, a Catholic, had wanted a simple Catholic funeral, but that all the comfort she might have gained from the quiet rites of her faith had been lost amid this panoply of scarlet banners, and grey uniforms and rolling drums. The Czech gendarmes certainly had no doubts. They saw this as a sordid local quarrel inflated by the Nazis into an incident to go all over the world as a breeder of further hatred. They knew their foe. And as they strode down the village streets the crowds drew back as if a leper were passing.

My reporting of the funeral at Gasterwald got me into trouble with the Henleinists. The next time I called at their offices in Prague their chief publicity officer, Herr Ulrich, had a cutting from the *Daily Express* in front of him, with passages in my story underlined in red ink. My reference to the funeral as a propaganda occasion had aroused deep resentment, he said. When I argued that this was a fair interpretation, he fixed me with a hard stare. 'You must realise, Herr Cox, that feelings amongst our rank and file are running high, particularly amongst our members here in Prague. If you continue to write in this vein you may find that some of the more rash of them take matters into their own hands. And that would be a pity.' The gold tooth in the front of his mouth glinted in a half-smile. It was, I suspected, a hollow threat, and indeed may have been partly animated by his personal annoyance at an earlier story of mine. I had described him not only as having been at one time a chinaware salesman in Britain, but as one who specialised in a particular line – chamberpots. I decided however that it would be sensible for me to move from my present hotel, the Esplanade, which had no security precautions, into the Alcron where police were always on duty.

I had also to bear in mind that an incident during my days as correspondent in Vienna, in which I had stumbled upon some of the Gestapo's secrets, could have got me, if

not onto a Gestapo black list, at least onto a dark grey
one. It arose from a story which involved Roland Bochow,
the refugee from the Nazis who had been appointed by
my predecessor as an assistant correspondent in the
Vienna office. A burly man in his forties, he had been
born in India of German parents who had been interned
and – he claimed – badly treated during the First World
War. Bochow spoke almost perfect English, which he had
learned when working as a planter in Malaya. He had
been forced back to Germany by the slump and had found
new employment as an official on the personal staff of
von Papen, the East Prussian landowner who had been
one of Hitler's main Nationalist rivals for the Chancellor-
ship. When Hitler became Chancellor in 1933, he had, in
order to reassure the aged President Hindenberg, had to
appoint von Papen as his Vice-Chancellor. When Hindenberg died in August 1934, and Hitler merged the offices
of President and Chancellor to become the absolute ruler
of Germany, he shunted von Papen aside to the post of
German Ambassador in Austria.

In Berlin during the pre-Hitler period Bochow had
become an important contact for Sefton Delmer, the star
Daily Express correspondent. That link had saved
Bochow's life during the turbulent days of late June 1934,
when Hitler had moved against the commander of his
storm troops, Ernst Roehm.

On the morning of 30 June 1934, the day on which
Roehm was arrested and shot, Bochow had been at work
in von Papen's offices in Berlin. He was well aware that
matters were moving towards a showdown not only
between Hitler and Roehm, but between Hitler and von
Papen, who, even though Vice Chancellor in Hitler's
Cabinet, had criticised the Nazis openly in a speech a
fortnight earlier, at Marburg University. A corridor,
which also served as a reception and waiting room,
separated Bochow's office from that of his immediate
superior on von Papen's staff, a young Junker called von
Bose. Suddenly Bochow heard voices raised, and then

two shots, from von Bose's office, which had its own separate entrance from another corridor. Bochow had only seconds within which to act. He hit upon a brilliant scheme. He took his hat off the hatstand in the corner of his office, walked out into the waiting room and took a seat, with his hat on his knees, on one of its chairs, as if he had come in for an appointment.

'My main worry was the commissionaire behind the reception desk,' Bochow told me. 'I had given him a rocket that morning about not keeping the place tidy. He could easily have given me away.

'The next moment the door of von Bose's office opened, and an SS officer appeared. He was stowing his revolver, which was still smoking, into its holster. Behind him I could see two other SS men rolling up von Bose's body in a carpet. The officer glared at me and asked who I was, and what I was doing there. I gave a false name, and said I had had an appointment with von Bose. I even managed a joke. I said, "But I seem to have chosen the wrong day on which to come." The commissionaire, thank God, said nothing.

'The SS officer told me to get out. I walked down the three flights of stairs, wondering if I would get to the door before the commissionaire changed his mind, and told the truth. I could see the sunlit street in front of me, and was just moving through the main doorway, when suddenly two SS men, who had, unseen by me, been stationed one on each side of the doorway, crossed their rifles in front of me and shouted, 'Halt.' I barked back at them in my most Prussian, commanding tones, 'I am from the Gestapo.' They hesitated, and then raised their rifles and said, 'Very good.'

'I took the underground to my home in the suburbs, reckoning it would get me there faster than the SS could move by road. At home I gathered my wife and my two boys, in order to drive them to the Swiss frontier. As I was backing the car out of the garage, I heard a shout from a policeman further down the street. I died half a dozen deaths in my seat as he hurried towards us. I assumed word had come for my arrest. But he had merely noticed that, in reversing, I had damaged a small tree which had recently been planted near the street verge. For what seemed an age he noted down my name and address, and told me I would be charged with damaging public property.

'I got my family to the border near Berne, where they were able to cross safely into Switzerland. I did not dare accompany them, because it was almost certain that by then instructions to arrest me would have been sent to all frontier posts. I left the car in the German frontier town, in the hope that the SS would assume I had crossed the frontier, and took a train back to Berlin. There I used the last of my money to pay the premium due on my life insurance, in the hope they would pay up if I was killed. Then I phoned Delmer, and borrowed some money from him. With that I took a train to a place on the Czechoslovakian border which I knew from former holidays, where the frontier line ran through thick forests. I was able to slip across it, and make my way to Prague, then on to Vienna.'

On Delmer's recommendation Bochow had been taken on as assistant in the *Express* office in Vienna. He had found himself a flat next door, where he lived with his wife Hansi and his two sons, aged six and nine. He found himself just round the corner from his old boss, von Papen, whom Hitler had rusticated to the post of German Ambassador to Austria. Bochow re-established his links with von Papen, but discreetly, as both men assumed they would be under the surveillance of Gestapo agents operating in Vienna. Bochow was in close touch with another member of von Papen's entourage, the Baron von Keppler, who had been on the SS's death list in 1934, but had got away to Switzerland, and now held a post in the Vienna Embassy under his old chief. A third trusted figure in this group was Keppler's secretary, a small darkhaired girl in her twenties, whose Christian name was Rosa, and who had a flat opposite us in the Modenaplatz.

I never really liked or trusted Bochow – nor, I suspect, did he me. But we worked together easily and well, for we shared a common fascination with the shifts and manoeuvrings of power, and a common relish in finding out about them. Bochow had some excellent sources – I assume through von Papen – and he took considerable risks in passing on information, much of which I am sure had been imparted to him on a confidential basis by the man whose trusted servant he had been.

It was this fascination with getting to the bottom of a story which landed Bochow – and myself – in trouble with the Gestapo. It arose over the most famous British traitor of the thirties. In November 1937 Lieutenant Norman Baillie Stewart of the Cameron Highlanders was released from Maidstone prison after serving a five-year sentence for handing over to the Germans secret information about British tanks and British tanks tactics. Celebrated as 'The Officer in the Tower', because the first news of his arrest had come when he was imprisoned in the Tower of London awaiting trial, Baillie Stewart had after his release suddenly disappeared from England. It was believed that he might have headed for Vienna.

The Viennese police followed a practice very helpful to journalists. All hoteliers and boarding house keepers had to report to the police the names and home addresses of anyone who checked in with them. If you wanted to track down a visitor, you had only to fill in a card at police headquarters giving the name and most recent address of the person you were seeking, and twenty-four hours later, if they were in Vienna, your card came back with the record of the place at which they had registered. Bochow filled in a card for Baillie Stewart. In the space marked 'Last Known Address' he put 'The Tower of London'. The system functioned admirably, and informed us that a Herr Baillie Stewart was registered at the Pension Minerva. I hurried round to the Minerva, which proved to be on the third floor of a large, gloomy nineteeth-century apartment block just off the Karntnerstrasse, in the heart of the city. When there was no answer to my ring on the door bell, I pushed open the heavy oak door and found myself in a well-lit, spacious lobby with, in one corner, a modern telephone switchboard, much larger than would usually be installed in such a place.

A young dark-haired efficient looking woman was dealing with a caller on it, and looked up with annoyed surprise when she found me standing by her. As soon as she saw me she swept with a single gesture the three or four telephone leads from their connections on the board. To my inquiry for Herr Baillie Stewart she retorted angrily that no one of that name was staying at the pension. The police record must be a mistake, she argued. As I turned to go, the door opened, and a tall, fair young man with a hurt and yet stubborn expression came in, accompanied by a good-looking woman in her late twenties, with shoulder-length blonde hair, and wearing a smartly cut raincoat. Since girls even more than money had been the chief bait employed by the German secret service to entice Baillie Stewart, this seemed all in character. I addressed the man in English as Baillie Stewart. He looked surprised, but nodded acknowledgement, and was about to answer my query about how long he planned to stay in Vienna when his blonde companion brusquely intervened. She drew him swiftly into the hall, and then turned on me and said in excellent English, with only faint traces of a foreign accent. 'That is not Mr Baillie Stewart. You are mistaken. I must insist you leave this place immediately.'

None of my protests that the man had acknowledged that he was Baille Stewart, and that I was a British correspondent, proved effective. So I made my way back to the Modenaplatz, and talked the problem over with Bochow.

We had at least half a story, and an exclusive one at that, in the fact that Baille Stewart was in Vienna, and we downed a few whiskies to celebrate the fact. These may have been the reason for the rash step which Bochow next took. He suggested that he rang the Pension Minerva, using not the office telephone, which might well be bugged, but the telephone which had long been installed in the hall of my flat, and which was listed under the name of the man from whom we leased the place. This was an old-fashioned apparatus, which had, in addition to the usual handpiece, a small round spare receiver on a cord, which could enable a second person to hear the conversation.

I listened through this whilst Bochow rang the Pension Minerva. A clipped, north German woman's voice replied, admitting that Herr Baille Stewart had stayed at the Pension, but had now left. Bochow, adopting his most abrupt, arrogant Prussian tones, demanded to know where he had gone. The woman refused to say more. Bochow, his voice increasingly imperious, insisted that he must know Herr Baillie Stewart's new address. His manner rather than his words proved effective.

'Who is speaking?' the woman demanded.

'Herr Baumgarten,' responded Bochow, 'and I want an immediate answer.'

There was a moment's silence, then a respectful reply. 'Just a moment, Herr Baumgarten.' A minute or so later, she was on the line again. 'Herr Baille Stewart has left for Budapest. He can be found at the usual address there,' she replied, and hung up.

Bochow put the telephone back on the hook, and turned to me, his huge frame sweating with strain. 'I have done something very foolish, very foolish,' he said. 'You must promise to me that you will never tell anyone the name I used then. It was stupid of me to use it. It is a name which is a password in the German Secret Service, a password I learnt when I dealt with the service on behalf of von Papen in Berlin. You must forget it, and forget this incident. Otherwise I could be in severe trouble.'

This conversation made clear to me that the Pension Minerva with its large switchboard and its female minders was a safe house for the German Secret Service. To cover

Bochow's tracks I confined my report to the facts that Baillie Stewart had been in Vienna, and had gone on to Hungary, where he went to ground skilfully, evading us all.

I thought no more of the matter until a week later, when I was engaged in one of the more pleasant aspects of a foreign correspondent's duties, that of reading the local morning papers in bed before breakfast. The bedside telephone rang, and a man, in sharp, clipped Prussian tones asked to speak to Herr Bochow. When I said he was not there, my caller demanded his home number. I explained that we never gave the home numbers of our staff. In icy tones the caller continued:

'I suggest you contact Herr Bochow and tell him to telephone me immediately at the Hotel Imperial.'

'Who is speaking?' I enquired.

'Herr Baumgarten,' came the reply.

I rang Bochow. Within minutes he had arrived from his house next door. He was grey and shaking. Early though it was, I poured him out a large whisky. 'This man has been sent from Berlin,' he told me. 'He demands that I see him at the Imperial Hotel at ten this morning. I am in real danger. This is the German Secret Service in action.'

We arranged that I would station myself in a café across the Ringstrasse from the Imperial. If Bochow had not emerged by eleven o'clock, I was to ring von Keppler of the German Embassy. Since calls to the Embassy would certainly be monitored, Keppler would be waiting at his home.

About ten minutes to eleven Bochow emerged from the Imperial accompanied by a burly man with a square, close-cropped skull – almost the cartoonist's prototype of a German. I could see from the relief on Bochow's face, as they crossed the road that all was, for the moment at least, going well. The newcomer introduced himself, not without relishing the irony, as Herr Baumgarten. In good if stiff English he came quickly to the point. Any reference by me either to the telephone call, or to this morning's events would bring me trouble. 'You could find Vienna a very unpleasant place if you do not agree,' he said. 'Unpleasant not only for you but for your wife and child. We may not be the government here – yet. But we have means of getting our own way in matters like this.'

His message delivered, Herr Baumgarten relaxed. He insisted that Bochow and I dine with him that night. It proved to be a long night, in which we all drank a lot, and in which Herr Baumgarten boasted that he had been in England recently on a special mission. It was to try to buy up the British news magazine *Cavalcade* (one of the British imitations of *Time* magazine, all of which were doomed to failure) with a view to making it a journal advocating the restoration of the Duke of Windsor as King. It was nearly three in the morning when Bochow and I finally steered our visitor back to the Imperial, and made our way through the cold autumn streets to the Modenaplatz. Of his interview that morning, Bochow would say only one thing. 'They have given me a further chance – but they've warned me it is my last.'

I took it upon myself to decide to keep my mouth shut, and my typewriter silent, about the events of that day. I did not believe the *Daily Express* would have appreciated my making a martyr of myself – as Christiansen confirmed emphatically when I later in London told him the whole story. Even less would they have appreciated it if I had got Bochow into a concentration camp for what had, after all, been a zealous piece of news gathering.

Bochow did not suffer in the long term for this indiscretion. Immediately after the Anschluss he was summoned to the headquarters the Gestapo had set up in Vienna, and there told he was in the clear. I do not know what actions he had engaged in to win this rehabilitation, but certainly he was the only one of von Papen's close associates in Vienna not to be either executed or sent to a concentration camp. But I had now, in this new land under threat by the Nazis, to work on the asumption that I had been noted down as certainly no friend of the Reich.

5

A Castle – and Princesses

If the Henleinists in Prague were not forthcoming with
information for the foreign press, nor were the members
of the Runciman Mission. Both the Foreign Office
officials on his staff were certainly no adherents to the
idea of open diplomacy. The senior of them, Runciman's
chief policy adviser Frank Ashton-Gwatkin, could not
hide his dislike of the press. He increasingly infuriated the
American correspondents by the tight-lipped disdain with
which he would refuse to amplify the daily communiqués,
which merely listed Lord Runciman's engagements. The
other official, Frank Stopford, though excellent company,
witty, full of anecdotes about strange happenings in
diplomatic missions in which he had served, was an expert
at escaping behind an enigmatic smile when pressed for
information. 'After all, war or peace may depend upon
what we are doing now. One false word, one mistaken
remark by us could bring the whole delicate structure of
mediation crashing down,' was the refrain. Nor was the
third member of the group, the Conservative MP Mr
Geoffrey Peto, any more help, though I discovered I had
a personal link with him. He was the present owner of
Sandford Park, the Oxfordshire manor house which my
forebears had sold after my grandfather had emigrated to
New Zealand. He was, alas, to emerge as an ardent
appeaser.

This secrecy brought a furious row with the press when,

on 18 August, Lord Runciman met Henlein for the first time. The day before it had become clear that Hitler had decided to step up the pressure. Henlein's Party had turned down the Czech offer of partial home rule, not just for the Sudetenland, but for all five provinces of Czechoslovakia — North and South Bohemia, Moravia, Slovakia and Ruthenia. This meant that the Germans would have had no one province which they could have dominated, for the boundaries of each of the two Bohemias, in which most of the Germans lived, though following natural geographical and economic lines, had been drawn so that almost as many Czechs lived in them as Germans.

Herr Kundt rejected these proposals as 'a mere phantom of home rule', and concluded on a menacing note — 'The patience of our people, which has seen no sign of good will on your part, is less than our patience.' As he and his men walked down the stone stairs of the Kolowrat Palace, after delivering their message, and came out into the evening sunshine, news of their decision was brought to Lord Runciman in the Hotel Alcron. He decided he must tackle Henlein himself about this attitude even if that meant a move of appeasement. When Henlein would not come to Prague (pleading his safety could not be guaranteed, which was nonsense, for the last thing the Czechs wanted was to provoke Hitler) he offered to go to Henlein. A meeting was arranged for the next day at Schloss Rothenhaus, the castle of Prince Max Egon von Hohenlohe, at Langenburg in the Sudeten mountains fifteen miles from the German border.

The Schloss was a great square country house set among beech and pine woods. The problem which Runciman faced — and which the Czech Government and the world faced — was writ large in the scene that morning, as Lord Runciman's car made its way westwards across the plains, past fields where Czech peasants were gathering in the harvest, to where, like a wall on the horizon, stood the mountains of Sudetenland. Sheer and definite on the

skyline, the hills looked that day just as Bismarck had
described them, as 'a fortress built by God in the heart of
Europe'.

Just before midday Lord Runciman and Lady Runciman in one car, and Ashton-Gwatkin and Geoffrey Peto
in another, turned off the main road into the castle drive.
Gamekeepers of Prince Hohenlohe's staff, Henleinist
badges on their coats, gave the Nazi salute as the cars
passed. Ten minutes later two open cars, travelling at
high speed, turned in through the same gates. The gamekeepers' salutes were even more emphatic. In the front
car were Henlein and Karl Hermann Franck. Franck was
in the grey uniform he had worn at the funeral a week
earlier. Henlein, bespectacled, suntanned, wore a brown
sports jacket and neatly creased grey flannel trousers, like
an English bank clerk on holiday. The cars moved on
through a gateway into an inner courtyard. The British,
American, French and Czech correspondents who had
raced after Runciman in a cavalcade of dusty cars, were
left outside this gateway, by the side of the castle drive,
to await events.

After lunch, just before the talks began, we could see
Prince Max and his wife and their guests sitting in the sun
on the castle terrace, sipping their coffee. Before them
was the rolling parkland of the castle grounds, like that of
a great British country house. Children played with a
brown retriever, laughing and tumbling on the lawn. The
gamekeepers, reinforced by grey-uniformed Sudeten
storm troopers, kept guard discreetly, hidden by shrubs
and trees. Voices and laughter rang out in the stillness.
Here was the Cliveden touch, the art of country house
diplomacy, being applied with skill in Central Europe.
Everything in this environment combined to convey
impression of peaceful, genial folk, with a real appreciation of life, people whose surroundings seemed to guarantee peace and reasonableness. The contrast with the
hot offices of politicians in noisy Prague was sharp. And
behind these tall windows, with their view over the green

and gold summer landscape, Konrad Henlein, Hitler's Sudeten lieutenant, was quietly demanding that the Czechs should hand over to his control these frontier mountains, which were the one safeguard which the Czechoslavak democracy had against German dictatorship, and which were the only true defensible frontier between Berlin and the Black Sea.

The talks lasted five hours. All that time we waited in our cars in the drive, though we could see clearly the correspondents of Sudeten Nazi papers and photographers in their grey Party uniforms in the castle courtyard, coming and going freely from the house. At six o'clock Lord and Lady Runciman drove off to Prague. A few minutes later Henlein left, sitting alone in the back seat of a car which swept past us at high speed. Then Mr Ashton-Gwatkin came out to read a press communique. It told us nothing more than that the meeting had taken place, and that Konrad Henlein had put his views to Lord Runciman. When Walter Kerr, in the name of the highly influential *New York Herald Tribune*, asked Ashton-Gwatkin how he expected us to write our despatches without any information, the British official answered short-temperedly, 'You can use your imaginations.' When we protested that Sudeten journalists and photographers had been admitted to the castle courtyard, whilst we had been kept outside, Ashton-Gwatkin snapped back, 'You ought to consider yourself lucky to be allowed within the grounds at all.'

All of this led me to an error in my story. Amongst the people we had seen from time to time in the castle courtyard was a dark-haired woman in an elegant summer dress. No one had identified her, but when we got back to Prague one of the evening papers was carrying a photograph of Princess Stephanie Hohenlohe, a cousin of the owner of Schloss Rothenhaus. Princess Stephanie was an ardent Nazi, a Viennese with wide contacts with England, who had launched a number of Nazis on London society. The woman in the photograph looked very like the woman in the courtyard. Perhaps because I was infuriated by Ashton-Gwatkin's attitude, I allowed myself to jump to the conclusion that this ardent pro-Nazi, also of the Hohenlohe clan, had been at the castle during these talks. It was the kind of gossipy angle which the *Express* loved, and they made the most of it. The next day the denials came in thick and fast, from Princess Stephanie herself, from Prince Max, from Runciman. But the story had attained a momentum of its own. It was picked up by *Time* magazine, and spread round the world.

It was the type of slip which could have cost me dear. But in the event it proved a protection rather than a danger. For the Princess Stephanie was, it seems, friendly with Lord Rothermere, and for some complicated reason which I never bothered to fathom, Beaverbrook was at that moment by no means averse to seeing Rothermere embarrassed.

This was as well, for the tone of my stories, reflecting as they did my belief that the British might be about to sell out the Czechs, was not finding favour. Christiansen raised this with me in a letter of 17 August:

> I think your despatches are very good indeed, as you know. But I get an undercurrent of depression from them which shows to me a foreboding of trouble that you have.
>
> Maybe you are right. But I tell you this: in the five years I have been Editor of the *Daily Express* there have been many, many nights on which the news seems enough to turn a man's hair white. We have gone on during those times, vigorously and cheerfully, saying 'Everything is going to be all right' and so far we have been right!
>
> The trouble is you sometimes get your nose too near the grindstone; things look a bit too gritty.
>
> I don't write this to you in order to ask you to alter the tone of your despatches, but to suggest to you that you should stand back and survey the possibilities and probabilities as though you were living in Wigan and not in Prague.
>
> Kindest regards.

I took it at the time as a sign that Christiansen was out of touch with what was happening in Europe, that it showed how limited, even if keen, was his perception of events outside the British Isles. But this may have been a misjudgement. I think it more likely that complaints were coming through from Beaverbrook, and this was a kindly move by Christiansen to warn me – and also to deflect that criticism. For he could always say, 'I have sent Cox a strong letter telling him to get back on course.' Whatever the reason behind the letter, I certainly made no attempt to change the tone of my reports, because I believed the facts would soon justify them.

6

Foreign Correspondents

The meeting at Schloss Rothenhaus marked the end of the first stage of Lord Runciman's work, that of establishing the facts. There was no doubt that Henlein would accept nothing less than the demands he had made at Karlsbad in April for the creation of what would be virtually a Sudeten German state within the Czechoslovakian Republic. Runciman now moved to his second task – mediation. Since there was no chance that Henlein, with Hitler at his back, would move an inch, mediation could only mean one thing – cajoling or forcing the Czechs to yield.

This Lord Runciman and Mr Ashton-Gwatkin set about doing, spurred on from London by a realisation that the Germans were gathering their armies on the Czech borders, and that the Nuremberg Rally, due to begin on 6 September, gave Hitler an ideal chance to inflame German opinion, and prepare it for war. The story of the four weeks in Prague which followed the Henlein-Runciman meeting of 18 August was therefore one of relentless pressure on the Czechs, with Runciman adopting indeed not so much the role of mediator as of arbitrator, ultimately ruling that Henlein was entitled to have what he demanded. The Czechs were caught between the twin pressures inherent in the nature of the Runciman mission. If·they resisted what he thought reasonable, they risked not only losing the support of the British Government, but of providing an excuse for the French not to honour their treaty with Czechoslovakia. If they gave way to Runciman's proposals, which increasingly took the form of Henlein's proposals, they risked breaking up their own country and opening its borders to Hitler. Sadly and bitterly they chose the second course: sadly and bitterly their Foreign Office spokesman made plain to us, each evening, what further retreats had been agreed to: sadly and bitterly each evening I reported these to London.

With each day, too, the Sudeten Nazi attitude became more arrogant. To deal with Henlein Mr Ashton-Gwatkin had to embark on a second journey to Sudetenland, this time to Marienbad. Henlein exploited the propaganda value of the visit to the full. Before he met the British official, he held a meeting of his senior leaders in the Hotel Weimar in Marienberg. No ordinary room would do for the occasion. He insisted that the room which Edward VII had occupied during his pre-war visits to the spa be opened up. It had remained closed ever since 1914. Now the dust covers were removed, the daguerreotype of the Emperor Francis Joseph came down from the wall. When the meeting was over, Henlein came out on the balcony to receive, Hitler fashion, the cheers of the crowd. The hotel proprietor had the scene photographed, ready for use in his publicity once the territory had passed to Germany.

Meanwhile at Nuremberg prominent Britons were gathering as Hitler's guests at the annual Party Rally. The guest list showed the kind of attention Hitlerism commanded in Britain at the time. Lady Stamp, wife of the powerful chairman of the LMS Railway, sat next to Rudolf Hess at a tea party for VIPs. Her husband was there, and Lord Clive, Lord and Lady Brocket, Lord and Lady Hollenden (he had been High Sheriff of London), and Lord McGowan, the chairman of ICI. Another guest at Nuremberg, the MP Sir Arnold Wilson, had long advocated appeasement of Hitler. He had asked me to lunch at the Athenaeum in in 1934 after my articles on the Nazi Youth Labour Camp had appeared, to chide me for criticising the Nazis. His pro-Nazism rested on a desire to avoid another war like the one in which he had served in 1914–18. When war did come, he took the honourable course, and though well into his forties enlisted in the RAF, and died as the air gunner in a bomber shot down over Germany.

As the crisis deepened, the journalistic stars of the day came to join us in Prague. Tom Driberg, then writing the William Hickey Diary column on the *Daily Express*, drove out by car from London. Under his hand, the Hickey column was far from being the collection of society gossip and scandal into which it later degenerated. It was for the most part an account of events witnessed or experienced by Driberg, combining meticulous observation with shrewd reflection, presented in clear, scholarly, at times pedantically exact prose.

Driberg was thirty-three years old. Tall, poised, wary, apart, with a remarkably large head, smooth dark hair and wide set, dark eyes, he had a curiosly sleek look, as if covered by a fine silken veil. Within Fleet Street he was widely known to be both a homosexual – a fact he admitted much later, in his autobiography – and a Communist, a fact which he readily acknowledged when, later that year, Beaverbrook carried out a survey of the political views of the staffs of his newspapers. What was not known was that he was also a member of MI5.

Driberg had his own chauffeured car. His driver, a stocky, bullet-headed ex-sailor dressed in a well-cut black suit, soon emerged as having another role than that of just a chauffeur. Obsequious to Driberg in public, in private he was curt and almost arrogant. In England they shared a house together, and, in one late-night drinking session in our hotel, confided to me their great wish was to adopt a child. They were angry that the law would not allow an all-male ménage to do that, and became even more angry when I made plain that I thought the law was right.

For me the most interesting new arrival was Vincent

Sheean. His book *In Search of History*,[1] recounting and analysing his journalistic experiences in the twenties and early thirties, reflected exactly my own fascination with news as instant history, and had reinforced my determination to get into international journalism. Known as Jimmy to his friends, Sheean was a tall man with greying hair, a wide, sensitive mouth and an amused, if sardonic, dignity. There was poetry as well as perception in his writing. It is illustrated in the closing sentences of his account of the defeat by the Spaniards of the Moroccan rebel leader, Abd-el-Krim:

> And the bones of my friend Mohammed ben Madj, after so many summer's suns, must long ago have added their pinch of dust to the dust that whirls and sifts across the Moroccan plain. The traveller in such regions, riding through it, does well to wrap his turban around his face to keep it out of eyes and throat; it will sting none the less for being the dust of an honest man.

Sheean, who was in Prague with his wife, Diana, a daughter of the actor Sir Johnston Forbes Robertson, was writing for an American news features agency, which syndicated his articles to papers throughout the States. Hemingway's reporting from Spain was for the same agency. It provided a valuable function, for writers were freed from the need to meet daily deadlines, and could report and interpret events in depth. Virginia Cowles, who had recently come to London from America, was to adopt the same technique for the *Sunday Times*, with marked success.

Two of my former colleagues in Vienna, G. E. R. Gedye of the *Daily Telegraph*, and Douglas Reed, formerly of *The Times* and now of the *News Chronicle*, had moved to Prague. Both had served in World War I, Eric Gedye in the infantry, Douglas Reed in the Royal Flying

[1] Published by Hamish Hamilton, 1935.

Corps. Both felt deeply that all that had been won in that war at such great cost was being thrown away by Chamberlain's misreading of the nature of Hitler and of Nazism. They were very different in character. Gedye was eager, extrovert, cheerful; Reed was reserved, living a secretive life with his Hungarian mistress. Each of them was to write books which had deep influence on public opinion – as could happen with books in those days when they could be quickly produced, close on the heels of events, and when the television picture had not crowded aside the written word. Douglas Reed had had to resign from *The Times* in order to bring out *Insanity Fair*, an account of the rise of Hitlerism up to, and including, the Anschluss. His policy towards Hitler was the direct opposite to that of the editor of *The Times*, Geoffrey Dawson, the high priest of appeasement. Gedye's book, *Fallen Bastions*, was to appear after the fall of Czechoslovakia. Though the *Daily Telegraph* had been wary of Hitler, and had acquiesced in, rather than advocated Munich, the contents of *Fallen Bastions* were too strong meat even for that paper. Gedye had to go off and work for the *New York Times*.

This list of correspondents had a major gap in it, though it was one few noticed at the time. In this crisis which was to bring Britain to the brink of war, no reporter or commentator for BBC radio was stationed in Czechoslovakia, or visited the country. This was so, even though Edward R. Murrow had demonstrated, during the Anschluss, the power of radio to provide its own vivid and instant, on-the-spot coverage of a big event. CBS was to repeat this process during August and September 1938, with over one hundred special broadcasts from Prague, Berlin, Nuremberg, London, Paris and other centres. Their main rival, NBC, also moved into direct news coverage, and enlisted my friend and colleague, Walter Kerr of the *New York Herald Tribune*, to do news talks for them from Prague. I went with him to the Czech broadcasting headquarters in Prague when he did the first of these, the first time I had been in a broadcasting studio.

Of the pressmen who crowded to Prague, the most influential was almost certainly Claud Cockburn whose cyclostyled weekly news sheet *The Week* was then at the peak of its influence, eagerly scanned by foreign diplomats, and eagerly drawn upon by every foreign correspondent in London. His description of the pro-appeasement group centring upon Lady Astor, Lord Lothian and Geoffrey Dawson of *The Times* as 'the Cliveden Set' – Cliveden being the Astor country house near Maidenhead – was not only a brilliant propaganda coup but a statement very close to the truth.

I had come to know Cockburn well during the siege of Madrid in 1936. Tall, bald, pale, with large, alert, sardonic eyes behind horn-rimmed spectacles, with jowls which managed always to look darkened by five o'clock shadow, and with an almost mockingly upper-class voice, Cockburn's utterly confident, intellectual assurance would have been intolerable had it not been offset by his sense of humour. Even the gravest of events had for him their comic side, and you were not likely to be long in his company without finding yourself caught up in a burst of laughter. This was a quality which made Claud Cockburn not only good company but which, skilfully interwoven with his doctrinaire Marxism, was to make him the most formidable propagandist of the Left in Britain in the thirties. A mocking adjective, a witty anecdote, a deft quip would ensure that key passages in *The Week* would be repeated in clubs and pubs and over dining-tables because they were funny, as well as shrewdly politically angled. Cockburn's humour was all the more politically effective because, though hard-hitting, it was seldom rancorous, owing more to the philosophy of 'what fools these mortals be' than to the usual scaffold-side jesting of the left-wing extremism. But he kept such light touches for *The Week*. His reports under the name Frank Pitcairn in the *Daily Worker* were cast in the sternness of Party orthodoxy.

Claud Cockburn viewed not only the Spanish Civil War, but all events in this turbulent decade from the Marxist standpoint that truth was not an absolute, but was what helps advance the class struggle. If this involved distorting or even faking events, he did so with gusto. In his autobiography (*I Claud*, Penguin Books, 1967, p. 192)[1] he describes with hilarity how he invented an anti-Franco revolt in Tetuan in order to affect a French Government decision on arms for Spain. In that same year he equally readily propagated false reports that the Trotskyist POUM in Barcelona had plotted a rising against the Republic, so justifying the imprisonment and execution of many members of the POUM by the Communist-dominated Spanish Republican police.

Cockburn later sought to justify his view that all journalism is in part propaganda in a passage in his autobiography which has been taken as Holy Writ by later generations of self-termed 'committed journalists', who have numbered in their ranks many television reporters and producers ready to use the privileged position accorded them to mingle opinion with information.

> To hear people talking about facts [Cockburn wrote] you would think they lay about like pieces of gold ore in the Yukon days waiting to be picked up – arduously, it is true, but still definitely and visibly – by strenuous prospectors whose subsequent problem was only to get them to market.
>
> Such a view is evidently and dangerously naive. There are no such facts. Or, if there are, they are meaningless and entirely ineffective; they might, in fact, just as well not be lying about at all until the prospector – the journalist – puts them into relation with other facts; presents them, in other words. Then they become as much a part of a pattern created by him as if he were writing a novel.

[1] *I Claud*, Penguin Books, 1967, p. 147.

But there are such facts, and common sense tells us we face them every day of our lives, when we learn on the news that snow has fallen across the country; that Club A has beaten Club B in a cup tie; that mortgage rates have gone up or down. These are plain unvarnished facts that do not depend upon the manner of their presentation by any journalist. All that matters is that they be stated accurately. If anyone doubts the validity of hard facts, he need only to serve on a battlefield. An enemy tank suddenly discovered on the far side of a hill is certainly not 'meaningless and entirely ineffective' to the troops on the spot, something which would have validity only if it were dressed up in some form as a 'tank of the reactionary imperialist forces' or of 'the terrorist insurgent forces'. It is simply a tank which might kill you, a fact if ever there was one.

Claud Cockburn remained a dedicated Communist until the 1950s. He swallowed the change in the Party line in September 1939, even though that meant putting his cause above his country, and he never openly disavowed his faith. Cockburn's various works of autobiography make plain that his experience of reporting the Wall Street crash of 1929, which he covered for the London *Times*, had convinced him that Marx was right, and that capitalism was doomed to crash and make way for communism. Given that, it made sense to align oneself with the future. That Cockburn proceeded to do with unhesitating vigour, and with scorn for lesser beings who failed to see the light. There was also in Cockburn a great deal of the autocrat, drawn to a system which he found not only intellectually satisfying, but which favoured élites, and particularly intellectual élites, amongst whom he instinctively numbered himself.

'The Truth Will Prevail'

On Monday, 5 September, the Prague Government finally gave way to Runciman's pressure, and agreed to a plan which gave Henlein the home rule he had demanded. Their reward was to find in the London *Times* two days later an editorial advocating, not home rule for the Sudetens, but outright cession of Sudetenland to the Germans. 'It might be worthwhile', the key passage read, 'for the Czechoslovak Government to consider whether they should exclude altogether the project, which has found favour in some quarters, of making Czechoslovakia a more homogeneous state, by the secession of that fringe of alien populations who are contiguous to the nation with which they are united by race.'

The English papers got to Prague in mid-afternoon, and the few copies of *The Times* were snatched from the hotel news stands by waiting foreign correspondents. Set in the neat clear typeface of Times New Roman the words in the leader column looked innocuous, like a sentence in an academic dissertation. But in Central Europe they seemed to be in lettering two inches high, a proclamation of the death sentence on a nation. Seven words made this impact – 'which has found favour in some quarters'. These were taken as an indication that *The Times* was relaying the British Government's view. It mattered little that the next day the Foreign Office denied that this editorial reflected British Government policy. The opinion was by then widespread that if *The Times* took this view, then dismemberment of Czechoslovakia was the aim, if not of the British Government, of powerful forces which sooner or later would sway the British Government, of people like the Astors and Lord Lothian and Dawson of *The Times*. I had met Lothian at Oxford, when he was head of the Rhodes Trust. He had scorned my intention to go into journalism. 'Real power rests with Government,' he said. 'We decide what to do, and then send for the newspapers and tell them to sell it to the public.' His mind, once made up, would take a lot of shifting. Claud Cockburn may have over-stressed the role of Cliveden, the Thames-side country house of the Astors, as the meeting place of the appeasers, but he had certainly not misjudged their intentions.

Cockburn's *The Week* for 8 September gives an interesting indication of his methods. Not content merely with underlying the significance of the *Times* editorial, he asserted that the leading article had been referred before publication to the German Embassy, in London, and had been approved by them. No evidence for this has ever emerged. This report was almost certainly a fabrication, a textbook example of Cockburn's view that truth is not an absolute, but is what helps your side in the class struggle.

Events now gathered pace. On 12 September Hitler was thundering from the tribune at Nuremberg his demands for the Czechs to hand over Sudetenland by 1 October, addressing himself to Benes and the Czech Government for the first time in this dispute. Until then he had spoken only through Henlein. Within minutes of the end of his speech, the Henleinists were out on the streets of towns and villages in the Sudetenland, chanting, '*Ein Volk, ein Reich, ein Führer*' and attacking the police with stones, glasses and chairs.

By the weekend, rioting in many Sudeten towns and villages developed into open revolt with shots fired at the police, Czech and Jewish shops looted, customs houses and police stations attacked. More than a score of Czech gendarmes were killed, many more wounded. In one battle, at Heberskirk, on the morning of 14 September, fourteen gendarmes and twenty-eight Sudetens were killed. The gendarmerie were seriously handicapped by orders from the Ministry of the Interior in Prague to 'do nothing to aggravate the situation', a policy urged on the Ministry by the British and French ministers in the capital. Yet when martial law was proclaimed in the Sudetenland on Tuesday, 13 September, the fighting quickly died away. The Henleinist squads took off their swastika armbands, restored their guns to their hiding-places, and withdrew from the streets. Henlein himself, and Prince Max Hohenlohe, Lord Runciman's host at Rothenhaus, decamped across the frontier in Germany, with Henlein proclaiming in a farewell message the new slogan: 'We want to go home to the Reich'.

The rioting put paid to the Runciman Mission, which may have been one of its aims. Runciman and Ashton-Gwatkin had been standing by for talks with Henlein on Monday, 12 September, when the Sudeten leader telephoned to cancel these, claiming that in Eger there had been 'a terrible massacre, with hundreds dead, mostly children'. This was a lie. Yet four days later Runciman and his mission left for London, claiming that the Sudeten problem could not be solved within Czechoslovakia. He was to recommend to Chamberlain that all frontier districts where the Sudeten population was in an important majority should be ceded to Germany – so providing the British Prime Minister with a justification to dismember Czechoslovakia. Chamberlain did not delay. On Thursday, 15 September, he flew to Berchtesgaden for the first of his fatal talks with Hitler.

During the weekend that followed, the last weekend of normal life which the twenty-year-old Republic was to know, the people of Czechoslovakia waited in a mood of stunned stoicism to learn their fate. Sunday was a day of brilliant sunshine; the pavements in the Wenchelas Square were thronged with the traditional Sunday promenade.

An outburst of cheering came from a group in front of one of the show cases in which newspapers were displayed for passers-by to read. A new turn in the crisis? No, just a win for Prague in a key football match. In the courtyard of the Hradcany Castle a great pile of sand had been placed, to be used against incendiary bombs. Children played on it in the sunshine, laughing as they shaped it into sand castles.

The next day Czechoslovakia learnt the contents of Chamberlain's betrayal. In mid afternoon the British Minister, Mr Basil Newton, and the French Minister, M Delacroix, drove to the Hradcany Castle. History allowed itself a grimace of irony, for the Legionary guards who presented arms as the French Minister's car passed were that day wearing the uniforms of the French Army in which their forebears had served. I hope M Delacroix averted his gaze, for the message he and his colleagues bore was a demand for the dismemberment of the Czechoslovakian Republic. France and Britain called upon Prague to hand over to the German Reich all areas of their country in which more than fifty per cent of the inhabitants were of German stock.

Though the portents for such a move had been clear ever since Chamberlain stepped into his plane at Heston, the news nevertheless came as a profound shock to the Czechs. They had never believed that the French, who were bound to them by a formal alliance, would desert them, even if Britain did. I was in Wenchelas Square when the first newspaper-seller came running through the crowds, shouting news of the plan. People seized the papers, and stood reading them on the pavement, turning to the first passer-by to comment. Small crowds gathered, arguing and gesticulating. One was at the foot of the statue to King Wenceslas, at the place where, thirty years later, the Czech student, Jan Pallach, was to burn himself to death as protest against yet another betrayal, this time by the Soviet Union. By now the British morning papers had arrived. The *Daily Express* carried across its front

page the words 'The *Daily Express* declares that Great
Britain will not be involved in a European war this year
or next year either' – that ill-fated slogan which was to
haunt Beaverbrook to the end of his days.

The first reaction of the people of Prague was disbelief,
followed by anger, and then defiance. That too was the
response of the Government, which next day gave a firm
though courteously phrased 'No' to the proposals. At the
same time they gave the army and police orders to deal
firmly with a new development – organised incursions
across the border into Sudetenland by bands of Sudeten
guerrillas, equipped with German arms and supported by
German Nazi units. Customs houses were attacked and
burnt, Czech police and officials killed or kidnapped. It
was the start of a carefully orchestrated cross-border
insurrection, designed to give the outside world the
impression that Czechoslovakia was breaking up from
within.

Late that Tuesday night, after I had sent off my story
to London, I walked to the Charles Bridge. In the
Government buildings on the hillside above lights still
glowed. In the chilly late summer night air, they seemed
a symbol of a country determined to fight rather than
yield. I woke the next morning to find that these were
illusions. At two o'clock on the morning of that day,
Wednesday, 21 September, the British and French ministers were back at the Hradcany, having demanded an
interview with President Benes. An exhausted President
dragged himself from his bed, and dressed to receive
them. They presented an ultimatum. Neither France nor
Britain would stand by Czechoslovakia should her refusal
to cede the Sudetenland to Germany lead to war. Mr
Chamberlain was off to Godesberg that day for his second
meeting with Hitler, and he wanted an immediate answer.

The weary Czech Cabinet were called to the Hradcany.
They argued and debated throughout the Wednesday
morning and afternoon. Finally at five in the evening they
capitulated.

By that time the wide thoroughfare of the Wenchelas Square was a great mass of waiting people. Loudspeakers had been placed on lamp-posts along its length, and over these, at six o'clock, came the news that the Government had yielded to this fearsome pressure. The crowd began to surge towards the Charles Bridge, and across it towards the Hradcany. It was growing dark now, and the castle rose dark against the sky, with only an occasional light showing. A black-out had been ordered on all Government buildings, in case Goering's air force struck without warning.

At the head of the crowd half a dozen people carried the Czech tricolor, the same red, white and blue of the French who had failed them. Singing the National Anthem, chanting, 'We will not give in: We will keep our frontiers', the huge procession surged on.

There was little fanaticism, only a mixed air of confusion and determination. Here was a man carrying a briefcase, on his way home from work. There a group of students. Behind them factory workers in black leather jackets, their hands still black from the work bench. Women led children by the hand. Well-dressed people came out of cafés to join the march. They all pressed on up the hill, under the blue-shaded street lights – another air-raid precaution.

At the foot of the narrow street winding towards the castle the way was blocked by fifty mounted police, and a double line of foot police. The crowd made one attempt to break through, and two policemen were pulled from their horses. But violence was not their aim. Instead they stood in the darkness, singing and chanting their slogans until after a couple of hours they began to drift away.

Above them, from the flagpole on the Hradcany, the President's flag still flew, with on it the words 'The truth will prevail'. They were proud words, which my grandfather had taken as the text of his inaugural lecture when he became one of the founder professors of New Zealand's first University in 1871. They are no doubt true – but even then they seemed sadly incomplete. Today any Czech must ask himself how long will it be before the truth does prevail in his country. He could indeed be forgiven if the ultimate blasphemy occurred in his mind, if he asked himself whether the truth might perhaps prove to be that of the torturer O'Brien in Orwell's *1984*, rather than of the hero-victim, Winston Smith?

The next day there was an even larger mass demonstration, as hundreds of thousands of people massed in the Wenchelas Square, and before the Parliament buildings, and moved slowly up and down, waving the Czech flag. Many were workers, their lunch boxes in their hands, carrying banners saying, 'We made the arms: let us use them.' They had marched in columns from the outer suburbs and even from surrounding villages. When at ten o'clock the loudspeakers announced that the Hodza Government had resigned, and that a Government of National Defence had been formed with at its head General Jan Syrovy, the cheering shook the windows of the Ambassador Hotel from which we were watching. Syrovy, with a patch hiding an old wound in his right eye, had been the legendary commander of the Czech Legion in Russia, the force which had battled against the Germans and then had fought its way to freedom, across Siberia, against the Bolsheviks.

The next day reports came through from Godesberg that Hitler had stiffened his terms still further, to a point at which even Chamberlain found them unacceptable – at least to a point at which Chamberlain feared he might not be able to get the British people to swallow them. The British Prime Minister returned sadly to London, and the British and the French advised the Czechoslovak Government that they could 'no longer take the responsibility of advising Czechoslovakia not to mobilise'. At twenty minutes past ten that evening a general mobilisation was proclaimed throughout the Republic.

It gave me – for what that was worth in such times – a scoop. At five minutes past ten that evening I had just finished dictating my copy to London when the Czech journalist who worked as assistant in the *Daily Express* office in Prague signalled to me to stay on the line. He was, like almost all fit Czechs of his age, an army reservist. A friend in the War Ministry had telephoned him to say that a general mobilisation was to be announced in a few minutes' time. His friend was warning him, not as a journalist, but to enable him to get home and say goodbye to his wife before rushing to his depot. I dictated then and there a further story to London, giving news of the mobilisation. I had just finished when all telephones were cut off, in readiness for war. No other newspaper correspondent got the story through to London that night.

The proclamation of the mobilisation was broadcast in Czech, then in Slovak, then in German, then in Hungarian, in Ruthenian, and finally in Polish – the many languages of the Republic. It precipitated an extraordinary spectacle. Men rushed wildly through the blacked-out streets to get to their homes for their equipment. Waiters in restaurants took off their aprons, late-night shop-keepers closed their premises, cars in the streets were halted by the police and asked to take men to their assembly points. Soon the streets were full of men, each with his small suitcase, hurrying towards barracks or the railway stations. One man walked with at his side his ten-year-old son proudly carrying his suitcase. With little traffic in the streets, the dominant sound was of hurrying feet, insistent in the darkness. At every street corner, in hotel lobbies, on station platforms, men and women were taking their swift farewells. Guards appeared in front of every public building, and in the Alcron Hotel the management produced a gas mask for each guest.

It was a night when a nation faced a supreme test, and found itself unafraid, when it thought it had a chance to fight for its freedom. Three years later, when I found myself with a Free Czech battalion on the outskirts of

Tobruk, I met two men who had been mobilised that night. Their faces lit up when they recalled it. 'We only wanted to fight,' they said. 'Why couldn't you have let us do so?'

8

Betrayal

We now had to make our own plans to deal with war, if it came. The experts predicted that Prague would be bombed flat within days of the outbreak of hositilies, so Kerr, Sheean and I set about finding a base outside the city from which we could work, should the need arise. We found such a place in house No 94 in the village of Seberov, just beyond the city outskirts – a neat brick peasant house overlooking a village pond, crowded with ducks and geese. The woman of the house showed us a painting of the pond with two photographs of young boys set in it, like a Surrealist picture, and told us that these were her sons, both of whom had been drowned in the pond three years ago, when ice had suddenly cracked under them. She was now pregnant again.

On the ridge outside Prague, on the way back, we paused to look down on the city with its grey roofs packed around the high walls of the Hradschin Castle, where the President's flag was a dot of red and white against a very blue sky. Sheean said, 'That's just how it will look to the bombers when they come.'

We never went to live at Seberov. We went there only once again, on the night of 26 September, when Hitler was due to speak at the Sportspalast in Berlin. If he was going to attack Czechoslovakia, this seemed the moment for him to do so. We listened to the speech in the kitchen of No 94, where they had their wireless set. Through the static we strained to follow the speech, waiting for a declaration that at that moment bombers were on their way to Prague. The pregnant woman sat with her hands folded round the child inside her, and with the picture of her drowned sons behind her, and when Hitler raved against Benes she said, 'He sounds just like our dog does when he's angry.' Her husband told us later that he was very worried about her, as she had had two miscarriages already, and the baby was lying the wrong way, and might kill her. He was very quiet and gentle with her, and she was rather cross with him, as pregnant women can be. It was on to such individual burdens, borne that night in millions of homes across Europe, that Hitler was now preparing to add, sooner or later, the terrible further burden of war.

But no declaration of war came that night, and we were able to drive back through the darkness to Prague, knowing that Hitler had confined himself to one final threat. 'Either Benes will accept this offer by October 1st, and give the Sudeten Germans their freedom at last, or we will come and fetch that freedom.'

This ultimatum left four days, time enough, as it proved, for the final betrayal at Munich to be arranged and executed. We used this time to further our plans to cover a war, buying winter clothing and some reserves of food, and arranging for special supplies of petrol. My main concern was that if war came, I would find myself cut off in Eastern Europe, separated from France, where my wife and son would be in the heart of one of the main targets for bombing raids, the city of Paris. We lived in a flat at St Cloud, on the southern outskirts of the city. It was just upstream from the great riverside Renault car factory at Billancourt, a military target if ever there was one. What is more, Cecily was pregnant – our second son was to be born in March 1939. We had agreed that if the French mobilised, and war seemed likely, she should take Peter, now a year old, into Central France. But that posed the nightmare burden of arranging evacuation by train in

Czechs now had to abandon. Across one field a line of khaki-clad Czech infantry, carrying light machine guns and boxes of ammunition as well as their rifles, were moving towards a lorry waiting to evacuate them. At the rear was a young officer, map case under one arm, field telephone under another. Tears coursed down his sun-burnt cheeks.

Back in Prague the hotel lounges were now thronged with new faces, those of taut, grey-visaged men and women, political refugees or Jews who had fled from Sudetenland, and sought now to flee from Prague. Amongst them was Gregor Strasser, one-time Nazi and former confidant of Hitler, against whom he had turned ten years before. Though he was probably the refugee from Nazism whom Hitler would most have liked to have seen dead, Strasser was undismayed by this huge defeat the forces against Hitler had suffered. A hardened soldier from World War I, his mind was on where the next stand could be made. Rumania? Turkey? He canvassed both with vigour. I learnt an important truth from Strasser that day, that the best antidote to defeat is to prepare for your next battle. It was something which I was to find, when I became caught up in soldiering myself, that came instinctively to all good commanders, whether they had charge of a platoon or an army.

One refugee had sold us occasional news stories in Vienna. Though Czech by race, he had an Austrian passport, and had fled to Prague when the Anschluss came. He felt the Gestapo closing on him, and when not only the British and Americans but even the Jugoslavs refused him a visa, he literally foamed at the mouth with fear – the only time I have seen such a phenomenon – as he walked agitatedly up and down the *Daily Express* office in Prague. He was a meagre figure, almost certainly a spy for several countries, but he was a human being. So I raided the *Express* cash reserves, and gave him fifty pounds – a big sum in those days – and told him to try to buy a visa on the black market. He got one to Yugoslavia only to be gathered in by the Gestapo there in 1941.

The time had come for me to leave Prague. I drove south with Jimmy and Diana Sheean. Along the road towards the Reich frontier in what had been Austria, we passed the Czech army in retreat. There were lines of field guns drawn up by the roadside, cavalry in village squares, lorry upon lorry filled with dejected men. At Bratislava the Czechs allowed us through their frontier barrier, but the German police officer on the other side would not let us pass. The frontier was closed until German troops had moved up into a newly ceded strip of land. 'I am sorry,' he said, when he saw my British passport, 'because you are on our side now.'

We turned towards the Hungarian frontier, which also ran up to the outskirts of Bratislava. It was dark now, and on the frontier road was a line of troops trudging dispiritedly through the darkness, leading horse-drawn carts piled high with equipment. A brilliant rim of flame broke from the windows and doorway of a concrete pillbox, whose wooden fittings had been set on fire.

I asked the troops if the Hungarian frontier was still open. 'They are all open. There aren't any frontiers any more anywhere around here,' their corporal replied bitterly. 'Everyone just takes what he wants now.'

The Czech customs station was deserted, its flagstaff broken, its door open. The red and white frontier barrier was down, locked into place. We drove around it, across an open, bumpy field, towards the Hungarian post. They let us through without argument, and we were soon on the main highway towards the Hungarian border and Vienna. It was a long drive, and Sheean kept himself going with draughts of neat whisky from a bottle he kept on the floor by the gear handle.

It was well after midnight when we reached Vienna. I spent that night in a gilded bed in a gilded bedroom in the Sacher Hotel. The next morning I took the Paris train from the Westbahnhof, the station at which I had arrived

so hopefully as a student five years before, on my first
visit to Austria.

In Paris I found that Cecily had just returned from
Limoges. When events reached their crisis on the weekend between the Godesberg and Munich meetings, she
had put into operation our plan for her to move away
from our dangerously placed flat at St Cloud. Though by
now three months pregnant, she had struggled aboard a
hideously overcrowded train with our one-year-old son
Peter, and had made her way to Limoges. Our Bretonne
maid Yvonne had returned to her home near Lorient, and
our Danish nurse Else followed Cecily to Limoges. In a
letter to her parents Else recorded those days:

> Limoges was an awful town, rather big and dirty. The hotel
> was untidy, everything was untidy and dirty. The only
> attractive thing in that town is *la patisserie*. I never tasted
> such wonderful *patisserie* as in Limoges.
>
> You ought to have seen us the evening we came back
> from Limoges. Mrs Cox went out to buy some food while I
> put Peter to bed. When Mrs Cox came back with the
> parcels we moved two arm chairs into the kitchen and then
> we started to cook and fry and we ate and drank half the
> night. We were awfully hungry.
>
> We went back to Paris on Monday. Yvonne arrived on
> Tuesday. Mr Cox arrived today, dead tired and terribly
> disappointed. He is only 28 years old but looked more like
> 40. And when we heard how the circumstances are in
> Prague today, and how the Germans rule, you can't but
> think that in spite of it all it might have been better to fight
> the Nazi regime now. Experts say a new crisis could take
> place in springtime and the war will break out within two
> years.

The Great Munich Lie

I returned to a France and an England where public life was dominated by the Great Munich Lie, by the assertion that the Munich settlement had brought, in Chamberlain's words, 'Peace for our time', and had marked the end of Hitler's aggression in Europe. Only events could prove whether this was false or true. If you argued that it was an illusion, that Munich had brought merely a respite, at huge cost, and that war would assuredly come, you were deemed to want war to come. Moreover, as the evidence began to mount, week by week, that Hitler was as belligerent as ever, the appeasers became all the more vehement in their defence of Munich, until at times their intolerance of criticism had itself undertones of totalitarianism.

This came across strongly when the Commons debated the aftermath of Munich early in November. I was in London on leave, and Guy Eden, the *Daily Express* Lobby Correspondent, got me a seat in the lower Strangers Gallery at the House of Commons. This small gallery (now a broadcasting booth) was on the floor of the Chamber, which made one seem part of the proceedings, rather than just an onlooker.

Clement Attlee from the Labour front bench attacked the Munich agreement as a great defeat for Britain and for the cause of law and order. Chamberlain was quickly on his feet, his voice cold with venom. 'If the Right

Honourable gentleman really believes that,' the Prime Minister said, 'then I am sorry he should say so publicly. It is not one of the characteristics of totalitarian states, at any rate, that they are accustomed to foul their own nests.'

To attack a fellow Parliamentarian for openly criticising the Government's policy was an odd attitude for the Prime Minister of a Parliamentary democracy to adopt. To cite the totalitarian states in support of that attitude was not only odd but sinister, when it was clear that the way in which Hitler ensured that no criticism should 'foul' Germany's nest was to use the truncheon and the concentration camp.

The absolute certainty of the appeasers that they were right, their bland refusal to contemplate that there had been any alternative but to surrender Czechoslovakia, was chilling to encounter. I came up against it in the heartland of appeasement, in the editorial offices of *The Times*. Ferdinand Kuhn, the chief correspondent of the *New York Times* in London, had been one of my earliest friends in Fleet Street. He had an office in the *Times* building in Printing House Square. He was so struck by my account of the injustices done to the Czechs, even down to the arbitrary course of the new frontier line, that he took me to see Robin Barrington-Ward, then assistant editor of *The Times* (he became editor in 1941). But Barrington-Ward had no doubts at all about what Chamberlain had done, or what *The Times* had advocated. I appreciated the forces which had led him to this view. He had served for more than three years in the trenches in the last war, winning a DSO and a Military Cross and three mentions in despatches. He was determined to prevent another generation from going through such wasteful horrors.

That evening Barrington-Ward rejected everything Kuhn and I had to say with such cold certainty that Kuhn was provoked into saying to him, very quietly, 'Should you not bear in mind from your own history books the words used by Oliver Cromwell to the Church of Scotland, "I beseech ye, by the bowels of Christ, consider ye may be mistaken."'

Since the *Daily Express* was in the front rank of those preaching that Munich meant peace, I felt deeply that I should resign. One major fact dissuaded me. Cecily was having a difficult pregnancy, afflicted by a skin rash which the doctor (but only after the baby was born) discovered was due to a food allergy. It irritated her by day, and tormented her with sleeplessness by night. To have called upon her, with another child just over a year old, to uproot herself from Paris, and set about rebuilding a new home in Britain, when we had no savings, and there was no certainty I would get another job, would not only have been unfair, but unreasonably dangerous. Sinclair Lewis, in his novel *It can't happen here*, written to warn of the dangers of creeping Fascism in America and Britain, makes one of his characters exclaim, 'What crimes are committed in the name of a man's wife and children.' But it is also a crime to endanger the health, perhaps even the lives, of your wife and children.

There was, too, another argument. Despite its editorial policy, despite Beaverbrook's memorandum to Christiansen, the *Express* had printed my stories from Prague unchanged and intact except when cut for reasons of space. The paper had done this, although on at least one occasion it had carried leaders virtually contradicting the deductions I was drawing. If I resigned, I gave up this chance to depict to millions of people events as I saw them, and would perhaps make way for someone who would present them from an appeaser's angle. I decided upon a compromise. I would stay with the *Express* until after the baby was born, and then make a move.

I took out some of my frustration by using part of my leave to canvass for Lindsay of Balliol in the Oxford by-election where he was standing as an anti-appeasement candidate in a contest with Quintin Hogg. One fellow canvasser was an old friend from my undergraduate days, a young history don at Merton called Bill Williams. So strongly did he oppose Munich that he had joined the Territorials. When war came he was called up into the King's Dragoon Guards, and in due course was posted to the Middle East. In March 1941, as an officer with an armoured car unit in Cyrenaica, he was in command of the armoured car which first sighted the vanguard of Rommel's forces advancing from Tripoli. After fighting in the open desert, and in besieged Tobruk, Bill Williams was posted to GHQ in Cairo as an officer in Intelligence. There he caught the attention in 1942 of the newly appointed General Montgomery, who promoted him to be Chief Intelligence Officer of the Eighth Army, setting him on the road which was to bring him, at the war's end, to the rank of Brigadier Williams, DSO.

Another man with whom I tramped the leaf-strewn streets of Oxford that autumn was my fellow New Zealander John Mulgan, who was working with the Oxford University Press after taking a first in English. For him too a hard war lay ahead. He joined the Territorials, and as an officer in the Royal West Kent Regiment was to fight at Alamein, and then to serve behind the enemy lines with the Greek Resistance for nearly two years, only to die suddenly in Cairo just before the war ended.

The areas in which we canvassed were solidly pro-Chamberlain. We received many rebuffs, and insults, some of which we brought upon ourselves, for we interpreted the role of canvasser as being not merely to ask people how they were going to vote but of urging them to vote our way. I felt a hatred for the beefy, sleek, loud-voiced Conservative officials, many from their Party HQ in London, who gathered in the bars of the big hotels at the end of the day's campaigning. They embodied for me the selfish shortsightedness of the abandonment of Czechoslovakia. I felt the same for Quintin Hogg, even though I knew him only as a distant, boyish figure on Union Jack draped platforms. Hogg was to prove himself a brave soldier. The next time I encountered him was when we were in the same war in an army hospital in Jerusalem, where he was recovering from a wound in the knee, received when he manned a Bren gun in the open desert against low-flying Messerschmitt fighters. And he was to prove himself after the war an equally doughty fighter for human freedom. But in October 1938 he was caught up in the wrong cause.

10

Beaverbrook

In mid-October Lord Beaverbrook paid his first visit to
Paris since the Munich crisis. One of the hazards of the
job of *Daily Express* correspondent in Paris was that the
city lay on the route between Beaverbrook's London
home, Stornaway House, and his Riviera villa at Cap
d'Ail. The rich travelled by train in those days, and
Beaverbrook and a small entourage of two or three would
travel by the Golden Arrow to Paris, and stay a night or
two at the Ritz before continuing by the Blue Train to the
Cote d'Azur. Whilst he was in the city, the Paris correspondent had to be ready to be summoned at short notice
to Beaverbrook's suite in the Ritz, to answer questions
about developments in France or give his views on whatever subject was uppermost in his lordship's mind at that
moment. I learnt quickly to brief myself fully on the state
of the rolling stock on French railways. One of Beaverbrook's hobby horses was to get wooden-walled passenger
carriages, of which there were still many on British
railways, replaced by metal-walled ones, which would be
less dangerous in accidents. The French were in the
process of making that change, and it was as well to have
the latest statistics at one's fingertips.

Soon after I had been transferred to Paris I was warned
of an even more alarming prospect. Beaverbrook was
considering acquiring an apartment in Paris, as a more
permanent base there. When he heard that Cecily and I

had found a superbly placed flat in a new block at St
Cloud he insisted on inspecting the block. The visit was
not without its problems. Beaverbrook was delighted with
the view from 32 Rue du Calvaire and by the fine series
of rooms on the front, and then demanded to see the
smaller rooms at the back. Cecily took him to look at
them. In one room our nine-month-old son was asleep in
his cot. He was a fine, strong baby, and he looked his
best, his fair hair outlined against a blue blanket. Beaverbrook swung round to Cecily and asked:

'Is that your child?'

'Yes,' she answered, with rightful pride.

'If it was mine I would take him out and drown him,'
came his retort.

Cecily was equal to the occasion. 'Lord Beaverbrook,'
she replied quietly, 'you must have been very unlucky
with your children.'

I was not surprised, but I was relieved to learn a day or
two later that his lordship had decided against buying
himself a Paris flat.

Lord Beaverbrook did not seem perturbed by Cecily's
riposte and as the weeks went by Christiansen passed on
to me occasional words of praise from him for my work. I
was however taken completely by surprise when, late in
June 1938, Christiansen telephoned me to say that Beaverbrook wanted me to be appointed as one of his leader
writers. It was a job which I was immediately sure I did
not want. I recoiled from it partly because I was increasingly concerned about the pro-appeasement stance which
the paper was beginning to adopt, but partly also because
I did not want to work in a post where my own judgement
would be swamped by that of the proprietor. Yet that was
something which was inescapably part of the role of leader
writing for a Beaverbrook paper. I wanted to exercise my
own judgement, as I could to a considerable degree in
evaluating and covering daily news. I did not want to put
my pen – or, more exactly – my typewriter, at the service
of someone else's ideas. This was not the outcome of

intellectual vanity or pride (though no doubt that came into it) but from a sense that if I once became Beaverbrook's man, in the sense which was implicit in being his leader writer, I might never become fully my own man again. I was later to observe that those who, by joining the Communist Party, agreed to abdicate their own judgement in favour of the Party line, seemed to be intellectually scarred for life, even if their Party membership had been relatively brief. The same could be true, I feared, if I toed the Beaverbrook Party line. It was not only that I realised that in journalism one's own power of judgement was an essential and invaluable asset, but I knew that unless I developed it as far as I could at this stage of my life, it might be dangerously blunted and damaged.

The pro-appeasement policy which also worried me had been detectable in an article in the *Evening Standard* as early as April 12 1938, a month after the Anschluss, an article which played down the dangers of Hitlerism. It was under the title of 'No War in Europe'. The astute Sir Bruce Lockhart, then on Beaverbrook's staff, noted in his diary that evening that though the article was signed by Frank Owen, it was 'obviously written by Lord Beaverbrook'.

On 23 May, after the weekend of alarms along the Czech frontier, Beaverbrook's policy became more explicit. On the front page of the *Daily Express*, over Lord Beaverbrook's signature, appeared this message:

> Britain will not be involved in war. There will be no major war in Europe this year or next year.
> The Germans will not seize Czechoslavakia.
> So go about your business with confidence in the future, and fear not.
> Provide us with aeroplanes, anti-aircraft guns, and ammunition.
> Develop our own Imperial resources, and give our races prosperity and happiness at home.

This was the first use of the 'There Will Be No War' slogan which was to become the hallmark of Beaverbrook's policy between then and the outbreak of war in September 1939. It was an exceedingly dangerous slogan, because it was a half truth, and a half truth can very often be more deadly than a lie. Fully spelt out, it should have read, 'There will be no war this year, or next year either, *if we let Hitler have his way*, or, alternatively *because Mr Chamberlain intends to let Hitler have his way*.' For there was no question of Hitler giving up his expansionist aims. Even a cursory study of his writings and his speeches ruled out that possibility. Yet the price tag of appeasing Hitler was carefully omitted from the *Daily Express*'s 'No War' slogan, so lulling the British public into a false sense of security at the very moment when they needed to be alerted to the dangers ahead. At the same time it encouraged the Nazis in their expansionist policy – for they quickly supplied in their own minds the missing second half of the sentence.

The slogan was, in fact, a skilful, though disguised advocacy of a policy of appeasing Hitler. Though the word appeasement had not yet passed into common currency, this message of 23 May 1938 aligned Beaverbrook as one of the first and one of the most formidable of the advocates of appeasement. Beaverbrook and his apologists have since defended his attitude by pointing to the fact that an integral part of his policy was British rearmament – or, as his lordship insisted that his leader writers phrased it, a policy of 'filling the gaps in our defences'. This was good so far as it went, but such rearmament could, if we abandoned our alliances in Europe, at most help us to survive a war when it came. If, however, we stood firm over Czechoslovakia, we had a chance – the last chance – of preventing that war by halting Hitler in his tracks, a process which could have led to his overthrow by the more cautious elements in the German High Command. And even from the point of view of rearmament, it made sense not to abandon an ally as well armed as Czechoslovakia. The armament of her thirty to forty divisions which, as the outcome of Munich, was in a matter of months to make its way into German hands, was equivalent to the output of British arms factories during the first two years of the war. Sir John Colville, who as Churchill's Private Secretary at 10 Downing Street, came to know Beaverbrook well, categorised Beaverbrook at this time as 'an arch-appeaser of the dictators'.[1]

I had not thought all these issues through at the time when the invitation to become one of Beaverbrook's leader writers came, but they were clear enough in my mind for me to be sure that I wanted no part in advocating this aspect of his policies. I had, too, another strong objection to moving into an editorial writer's sanctum: I had not become a journalist in order to tell other people what they should do. I was an historian at heart, not a preacher or advocate. I wanted to tell other people what was happening in the world around them, tell them as frankly and as clearly as I could, and leave them to make up their own minds about things. I believed that if people could learn the truth, they would act sensibly upon it.

I decided to base my case against becoming a leader writer on the second of these grounds. That left me some chance of remaining an *Express* reporter – a job in which I had been given a high degree of freedom. So I told Christiansen that I could not take the job. 'You realise it's the Old Man's wish; if you won't do it, you will have to tell him yourself,' was Christiansen's reply. 'He will be in Paris tomorrow.'

In his suite at the Ritz, with its pink silk-lined walls and gilt Louis XV furnishings, Beaverbrook was seated in a high-backed chair. On the table before him stood the dictaphone he frequently used, a machine on which messages, spoken into a small, trumpet-like mouthpiece,

[1] *The Fringes of Power*, Sir John Colville, Hodder & Stoughton, 1985, p. 733.

were recorded on a drum, like those of the earliest gramophones.

The wide mouth, which in a grin seemed to extend from ear to ear, the large head on the neat body, the wide-set, keen eyes which studied me had already been the subject of innumerable photographs, drawings and caricatures. In particular I was familiar with David Low's portrayal of him as a grinning, mischievous imp. I had, in my encounters with him, so far had no experience of this lighter side of his character. That he was to display only later, particularly during the war, when we met on a different basis. Perhaps I took life too seriously in the thirties – at any rate with my elders – for me to stimulate his mischievous wit. It was the tough magnate, not the Puckish jester, whom I faced that afternoon.

Yet he welcomed me warmly, indeed affectionately, and came immediately to the point. 'Christiansen tells me he's going to make you a leader writer,' he began – which was hardly the version of the proposal which Chris had given me.

'Yes,' I replied. 'And I've explained to him that I don't want to be a leader writer. I want to remain a reporter.'

He pretended to be surprised at my decision, though he clearly knew of it in advance from Christiansen. I explained I had come a long way from New Zealand to see and learn about Europe, and that I wanted to stay in the field, where the news took place, rather than retreat to an office to write about it. He deployed the contrary case – that leader writing was the way to power, power over people's minds, power and advancement within a newspaper. He argued the case always in my own interest, not at all from that of the paper, and argued it patiently, without anger or tension. I made my own case with, I hope, as much calm. Then he shook his head. 'Well, if your mind is made up . . .' and he picked up the speaker of the dictaphone.

'Memo for Mr Christiansen. Kaarx' – my name was drawled out in his Canadian accent into what seemed like polysyllables – 'Kaarx doesn't want to be a leader writer. Better let him ride.'

I returned home shaken, but confident that I had done the right thing. 'There's no doubt about these big men,' I told Cecily that evening. 'They respect you if you stand up to them.'

I would have been much less confident had I known the full terms of the memorandum which reached Arthur Christiansen the next day. I learnt of it only in April 1940, when I told Arthur Christiansen that I was not prepared to go to Norway as the *Daily Express* war correspondent, as I intended to join the army. We were drinking in a pub off Fleet Street, and he grew indignant. 'After I saved you from getting the sack in 1938, you owe it to me not to walk out on me now, when I and the paper need you,' he said.

How could he have saved me from getting the sack? I had heard Beaverbrook himself dictate a memorandum telling Christiansen to let me ride. Christiansen's answer was to take me through the black-out across Fleet Street to his office, where he dug out the file. The memorandum was there, neatly typed. It was a fuller message than the one dictated in my presence. It read:

> Cox does not want to be a leader writer. Better let him ride. Sack him within a month.

I had survived on the paper, Chris explained, only because he had won for me a short-term reprieve, on the grounds that I was needed to cover the Runciman Mission story. My work in Prague had then, he said, been good enough for him to avoid implementing Beaverbrook's command.

The leader-writer post which I had turned down went to Michael Foot, whose journalistic efforts until then had been confined to left-wing journals like the *New States-man*. A young, dark-haired, bespectacled figure, he was with Beaverbrook in the familiar suite at the Ritz when I was summoned there in that post-Munich autumn. I had had contact with Foot on only one previous occasion, at the War Memorial in Oxford on Remembrance Day 1932. The Oxford University Labour Club had organised a line of demonstrators to hold up anti-war banners when the official wreath-laying ceremony took place at the Memorial. I was in my first term at Oxford, and the dangers of another war of which I had become aware in the Soviet Union and Germany during the summer were fresh in my mind, so I decided to join the demonstration. Michael Foot was one of those organisers marshalling us into line amidst the jeers of passing motorists. For in those days Remembrance Parades were held always on November 11th, which that year was a weekday.

I do not know if this incident remained in Michael Foot's mind, but he gave no sign of remembering it when we met in this more exotic setting. Beaverbrook addressed Foot in warm, friendly terms, as if to indicate to me what a good job I had passed up. But I noted too that he also took care to dictate to Foot in my presence a couple of paragraphs for a future editorial, as if also to remind me – and Foot – who was the boss. Foot's main work for Beaverbrook was to be with the *Evening Standard* which, when war came closer, Beaverbrook allowed to take a non-appeasement stance.

Looking back over the years, I am not surprised that Beaverbrook should have wanted me to be fired from his employ once I had refused the leader-writing offer. For he was offering me not only advancement, but his friendship, admission to that entourage of intimates who formed his personal court. What Beaverbrook wanted from his lieutenants was not only that they should do his work, but that also they should become virtually his sons. He gained this from many of them, from Peter Howard and Frank Owen, and particularly from Michael Foot, who indeed came to love him like a son. That was a role I could never have played.

It is commonly believed that the influence of Beaverbrook on his close entourage was malign, that Sir Stafford
Cripps was right when he accused Beaverbrook of having
'an intentionally demoralising effect on his young men'.[1]
Yet those who did join Beaverbrook's court have not
shown many signs of regarding themselves as having been
corrupted by 'Robin Badfellow' – as Muggeridge termed
Beaverbrook when he worked for him on the *Evening
Standard*. Frank Owen, it is true, hád he not been drawn
into Beaverbrook's web, might have moved over from the
Liberals to Labour, and have taken his place alongside
Gaitskell and Evan Durbin, Douglas Jay and Hector
McNeil as a minister in the post-war Labour Government,
instead of ending his days as a hard-drinking literary
pensioner of Beaverbrook, hammering out a life of Lloyd
George which won few plaudits. But Owen was not the
first or the last Fleet Street figure to regard alcohol and
journalism as natural partners, and he did after all in his
lifetime edit with distinction two Fleet Street newspapers.
Michael Foot executed the leader-writing job with loyalty
and avidity, and yet emerged five years later with his
socialist principles apparently unscathed – certainly in
good enough shape for him ultimately to lead the Labour
Party.

Peter Howard, who accepted and shared Beaverbrook's
views more completely and more enthusiastically than any
other of his acolytes, did break with him decisively, and
went on to become ultimately the leader of Moral Rearmament. Others who served Beaverbrook for long
periods got as much as they gave. Sefton Delmer
remained faithful to the man who had brought him into
journalism until he was ultimately cold-shouldered from
the Beaverbrook court by a monarch who sought new
courtiers. Arthur Christiansen might well have found
himself hemmed in as a highly gifted chief sub-editor had

[1] Quoted by Cecil King in *With Malice Toward None*, a diary entry for 9
September 1942.

Beaverbrook not recognised and supported his talent. In return for the right to edit the *Daily Express*, Chris endured with equanimity many strains and even cruelties across the years. 'I never went on holiday without Beaverbrook ringing me just before I left, and planting some anxiety calculated to destroy my peace of mind whilst I was away,' Christiansen told me once. Beaverbrook's final words to Christiansen, after at last firing him from the *Express* Newspapers in 1953, were a classic of mischievous cruelty. He accompanied Christiansen to the lift in his apartment block, and as the lift began to descend said to him, 'Going down, Mr Christiansen, going down.'

It is true, as the diaries of Sir Bruce Lockhart reveal, that Beaverbrook could, apparently deliberately, humiliate those who worked for him by demanding their attendance at short notice and at all hours, and add the further indignity of dictating leaders or passages for the gossip columns to them whilst stalking about his room naked after a shower. But such callous indifference to the time or the habits of subordinates is a common characteristic of many men of power. Churchill had no hesitation in keeping the Chiefs of Staff up to the small hours of the morning, despite the enormous other pressures on them, often simply to have an audience for his reminiscences. Lloyd George heaped many petty indignities on his staff, not only in the discharge of his official duties, but in covering up the arrangements for the amours which gained him the nickname of 'The Goat'.

Beaverbrook was no more demanding than were these men of their close associates. The criticism of his actions may therefore have derived more from the nature of the ends to which he directed the talents of those who served him, ends which were not so much evil as mischievous. It is not surprising that those of Beaverbrook's contemporaries who were on the receiving end of this mischief should have seen as wicked the use of able young men for this purpose.

11

France After Munich

In France *le mensonge de Munich* was sustained with
fervour by the Foreign Minister, M Georges Bonnet, and
by the large section of the press which, for one reason or
another, wrote what the Government wanted. The general public was more cynical. 'See you again next time'
was a common farewell spoken to one another by the
reservists who had been called up to man the Maginot
Line, as they were demobilised in early October. But
relief that war had not come was widespread.

It endured even when, barely six weeks after Munich,
an event in the heart of Paris set in train actions which
were to reveal the true nature of the Nazi regime in which
both the British and French Governments were reposing
their trust. On 7 November 1938 I reported: 'At 9.30 this
morning Henschel Feibel Grunszpan, a 17-year-old Polish
Jew, shot dead Herr von Rath, a 32-year-old Third
Secretary, in the German Embassy here.'

Two days later came the Nazis' reply to Grunszpan's
deed, the pogrom of *Kristallnacht*, the night of broken
glass. Jewish shops, Jewish homes, synagogues were
smashed, burned and looted throughout the Reich.
Thirty-five Jews were killed, 101 synagogues destroyed by
fire, another 76 so badly damaged they had to be demol-
ished, 7,500 shops wrecked.

Faithfully, the bulk of the French press played this
down, as M Bonnet was in the midst of negotiations with

von Ribbentrop for a Franco-German declaration that neither side would in future resort to war against the other. The French Foreign Minister wanted a piece of paper to match that which Mr Chamberlain had so proudly flourished on his return from Munich, as proof that he had secured 'peace for our time'. Von Ribbentrop was prepared to come to Paris and sign such a declaration provided the French gave him a reception 'at least equal to that shown when the King and Queen of England came to Paris' (German Foreign Ministry Archives). The French matched this in at least one respect, by receiving him at one of the special inner railway stations not open to the public. In Ribbentrop's case, this was to be the Gare des Invalides, in due course to become familiar to millions of visitors to France as the post-war Paris air terminal. It had for the French the great advantage that, unlike the Bois de Boulogne station where the British King and Queen had been received only four and a half months before (though that now seemed in another age), it would not involve a drive of any length through streets where the German Foreign Minister might meet either hostile or at best indifferent crowds.

So on a morning of brilliant late autumn sunshine we of the foreign press found ourselves once more standing alongside a red-carpeted platform, where M Bonnet, smiling with real warmth, hurried forward to greet the former Pomméry champagne salesman, now returning triumphantly to Paris in the role of Foreign Minister of Hitler's increasingly powerful Reich. Von Ribbentrop allowed himself some cordiality. He saw the fine weather as a good omen for the talks. 'I saw France last night under the beauty of a magnificent moon,' he added. The Garde Republicane presented arms with their carbines, and in an oddly tense silence a group of Germans resident in Paris shot out their arms in the Nazi salute from where they stood under two swastika flags – the only ones apparent in Paris that day. Mobile guards and gendarmes lined the short route from the station through which the long black car carrying von Ribbentrop made its way across the Place de la Concorde. No crowds turned to wave. The few onlookers were silent, a silence accentuated by the halting of the traffic to allow the car and its motor-cycle outriders to pass. Its destination was the Hôtel Crillon, that hotel which had been the headquarters of Lloyd George and the British delegation at the Versailles Conference less than twenty years ago.

The Franco-German declaration, signed that night in the famous Clock Room of the Quai d'Orsay, may have removed France's anxieties about any future German demands on Alsace and Lorraine, but it did nothing to diminish French anxieties about a new problem which had suddenly surfaced. Just a week earlier Mussolini had suddenly made clear that he was going to take a leaf out of his Axis partner's book, and set in train his own revanchist demands. On 30 November the black-shirted Fascist deputies in the Chamber of Deputies in Rome had, in the presence of the French Ambassador, suddenly risen to their feet and chanted, 'Tunisia, Corsica, Nice' – all territories under French sovereignty or French control to which Italy was now laying public claim.

So, in early December, I found myself on the way to Tunisia, to report once again on a dictator's claim on a neighbour's territory. Tunisia, though still nominally ruled by its Bey, was a French protectorate. It had almost as many Italian settlers as it had French – indeed, Mussolini claimed the Italians were in the majority – but there was little chance that it would form another Sudetenland. Its military importance to France was too great. A French staff officer explained this to me on the shore of the Gulf of Tunis, just above the white-walled, minareted village of Sidi Bou Said, and close to the ruins of Carthage. Offshore the dark shapes of two French submarines showed up as dark dots against the brilliant blue sea that stretched away towards the Cape Bon.

'Twenty minutes' flying time from here is the Italian island of Pantelleria, which Mussolini has turned into a major military base,' said the officer. 'Another half hour's time by fast bomber lies Sicily. We are almost an extension of Europe here. If the Italians controlled Tunisia they would cut the Mediterranean in two.'

Five hundred miles to the south-east another officer drove with me to the frontier of the Italian colony of Libya. At the desert border post a sunburnt Italian Carabinieri officer and the two Libyan cavalrymen on duty gave us the Fascist salute, and chatted in a friendly way. On the Italian side the tarmac road doubled in width, forming the wide military Via Balbia which stretched from this border to the frontier of Egypt at Sollum. Along it an Italian invasion force could have moved rapidly from Tripoli towards Tunisia. But it would have made little progress inside the French-held territory. Forty miles from the border just south of the Mareth Oasis, the French had built a desert Maginot Line. Along one side of a rocky desert gully (the word 'wadi' had not yet passed into everyday English) the camouflaged cupolas of gun positions could be glimpsed, almost indistinguishable in the sandy ground. Barbed wire entanglements, five rows deep, and a triple line of upright steel rails formed a barrier to troops and tanks. The line ran in a forty-five-mile curve from the Mediterranean shore to the Matamata mountains, steep and grey against the hazy desert sky. It was a formidable line, and I reported confidently that it formed an impassable barrier against an army approaching from Libya. It was an accurate enough prediction, for when an army did advance against it four and a half years later, the Mareth Line held firm, in the battle in which Montgomery launched his desert Eighth Army against Rommel's Afrika Korps, who made at Mareth their first major stand after Alamein. But the rest of my prediction proved less sound. I wrote that the Mareth Line was protected to the west by the Matamata Mountains, 'roadless, waterless and impassable'. This was true, but what I did not foresee was that, with modern motor transport, these mountains could be outflanked by a wide sweep through the desert further west, a move which was to be carried out by General Freyberg and the 2nd New Zealand Division in 1943, forcing Rommel to withdraw from the Mareth fortifications.

For my work, those ten days in Tunis marked an important development. The *Daily Express* gave me space on the leader page to sum up and evaluate what I had seen and learnt in that time, not just to report but to delineate the underlying contours of events which I had reported from day to day. It was a satisfying form of journalism, which I was to develop further during the coming months. Of all my work as a writing journalist, it is by these leader page articles I would most want to be judged.

We were working – though we had no inkling of it at the time – in the final stages of the era of the descriptive writer in daily journalism. Within the next decade radio would oust the newspaper as the main means of conveying a picture of events – and radio would in its turn swiftly be thrust aside by the even more powerful reporting instrument of the television camera. We were amongst the last practitioners of the art of depicting in words, for the immediate information of the public, the events of the day. Once broadcasting, and in particular television, became dominant in this field, the role of the writing journalist was increasingly to be confined to interpreting, analysing and evaluating, rather than to depicting and describing. 'I am a camera with its shutter open,' Christopher Isherwood had written in the opening passage of *Goodbye to Berlin*, and in the field of daily news our eyes and our ears were the camera lenses and microphones of the time. We had the responsibility and the pleasure of practising the craft of instant history.

It was a fascinating and fulfilling, if harassing, task. There was the search for the event; the noting, amidst the tumult and confusion, of its salient features and of significant and vivid detail, the quickly scribbled interviews with participants; then, as often as not, the long drive back to base, slumped in the back of a bumping car, formulating the story in your mind, seeking similes and metaphors, groping for an effective opening sentence and a strong conclusion; the hasty typing on a rickety table or wash-stand; the race to the telegraph office or the anxious wait for the telephone call to London. It was an odd way in which to practise an art – for certainly the skill of capturing the essence of a fast-moving event, and trans-forming it into words which would convey the truth of it to millions of readers the next day was an art form. Descriptive written journalism went out, however, in a blaze of glory. These, its dying years, produced some of its best practitioners – Douglas Reed and de Caux of the London *Times*, George Steer of the *Daily Telegraph*, Alan Moorehead and Alan Wood of the *Daily Express*, William Forrest of the *News Chronicle*; and, in its last post-war phase, Patrick O'Donovan and Hugh Mas-singham of *The Observer*. It was a good company in which to serve.

This report from Tunis nearly got me into serious trouble with the Italian authorities. When I reached Rome on my way back to Paris I was greeted by Frank Gervasi, of the International News Service. 'I would get on to the train for Paris right away,' he counselled. 'The Propa-ganda Ministry are after your blood. They say you have insulted Fascist youth.' The trouble stemmed, I discov-ered, from a mishearing by the *Daily Express* telephonist who had taken down my article from Tunis over a bad, crackling telephone line. In describing how highly organ-ised, on Fascist lines, was the Italian colony in Tunis, I had said, 'This minute, as I write, thirty little Sons of the Wolf Fascist organisation are drilling in the school court-yard next door with little wooden rifles.' It had appeared in the paper as 'dirty little Sons of the Wolf'. I took Gervasi's advice and I was thankful when early the next morning I found myself safely on the French side of the border.

*

The winter of 1938–39 in Paris remains in my mind as a sour and dark period, a time of snow-bordered pavements, of low, ochreous skies, with overlying all a sense that what lay ahead was war, or, worse still, betrayal without a fight. Cecily was tormented and increasingly exhausted by the skin affliction brought on by her allergy. The *Express* news desk, with the international scene for the moment relatively calm, stepped up its demands on the Paris office for yet more stories of crime and scandal. When on New Year's Day 1939 it called for coverage of a cockfighting tourney in Calais, due to be attended by members of the British aristocracy, it seemed to me that news values had reached rock bottom. With war looming, the paper was prepared to devote space to this degrading and brutal occasion. Fortunately I was saved by a change of plan. A reporter and photographer were sent from London. When the story, full of vivid detail, appeared in the paper it bore the name of a relatively new recruit to the staff, George Millar. His disdain for the story, as he has since made clear, was no less than mine, but he had tackled the task with a more cheerful acceptance of the foibles of human nature than I could summon up that winter.

Early in the New Year it was clear that the Spanish Republic was nearing its end. On 26 January 1939, Barcelona fell, leaving only the beleaguered central zone around Madrid and Valencia in Republican hands. The progress of the war had been a constant background to the other stories on which I had been engaged during the previous two years, something never far from my thoughts. Day by day, once I had dealt with the news items of immediate concern to my duties, I had turned to the reports from Spain, to follow the ebb and flow of battle around Madrid and along the Ebro, in the Basque country and in the Asturias, reading these with mixed feelings of guilt that I was not still in the midst of the battle, and envy for those who had followed the long struggle at first hand.

In Paris the Spanish Civil War was close at hand. Through the French capital moved a steady stream of correspondents and propagandists, politicians and spies, on their way to and from Madrid and Barcelona. I spent many hours with new arrivals from Madrid and Barcelona on the terrace of the Café Flore or the Deux Magots, the two cafés on the Boulevard St Germain which were replacing the Dome and the Coupole in Montparnasse as the Paris meeting place for expatriates. From these travellers, more than from the newspaper reports, I gathered the sense not only of war weariness but of disillusion within the Republic. The discipline of the Communist Party, which had been so important in the defence of Madrid, had become a two-edged weapon, cutting against liberty within Republican Spain as well as against Franco's forces. Through their control of the police, and of the dreaded SIM – Servicio de Investigacion Militar – the Communists were able in 1937 to crush the Trotskyist POUM. George Orwell, who had served in the POUM militia, was lucky to escape with his life. The Spanish Communists also enabled the OGPU to extend to Spain the Stalinist purges then at their height in Russia. Kleber, the Red Army officer who commanded the first International Brigades, was one such victim. He was at first demoted to a lesser command in Spain, and then recalled to Russia, where he disappeared without trace. General Berzin, the senior Soviet officer in Spain, was also executed.

I was reluctant to accept the ever-increasing volume of evidence that things were going sour in Republican Spain, and clung hard to my belief not only that the Republic would win through, but that the bright new world which seemed to have dawned for the ordinary people of Spain in the summer sunshine of 1936, and had still been a glowing prospect that autumn in Madrid, might yet come about. My closest Spanish contact in Paris, a former press attaché·at the Republican Embassy there called Massip, who had been ousted from that post for being too liberal, constantly warned me that these were vain hopes. A slim, dark-haired Catalan, he felt that whichever side won in Spain, individual liberty would now be the loser. 'There are two enemies of man,' he would declare. 'Nature and the State. Both have to be tamed if man is to be free.'

By the end of January 1939 such discussions had been overtaken by events. With the fall of Barcelona some 400,000 refugees fled along the mountain roads and tracks into France, in a long terrible cavalcade of suffering, a nightmarish foretaste of what was soon to be witnessed on roads all over Europe. Alan Moorehead, who had become my assistant in the Paris office, went to the frontier, and his descriptions of this disaster, and of the brutally harsh treatment meted out to the refugees in France, demonstrated fully for the first time the capacity for vivid reporting which was in World War II to win him enduring fame. The story proved, too, to be a milestone in British broadcasting. The BBC sent Richard Dimbleby to the Franco-Spanish frontier near Port Bou. From there he broadcast an eye-witness account of the mass Republican evacuation, the first such account carried by the BBC from their own reporter of these events of the turbulent thirties.

On 27 February 1939, France recognised Franco's regime as the legal Government of Spain, though another month was to elapse before the Republican forces in Madrid, Valencia and Alicante were finally overthrown. In Paris the Spanish Embassy passed formally out of Republican hands at five that evening. All diplomatic staff had long since left the building in the Avenue Georges Cinq. Shortly before five o'clock struck on the clock of the nearby American church, a grey-haired porter emerged from the Embassy with a few belongings wrapped in a newspaper under his arm. He closed the gates, and walked slowly away towards the Champs Elysées, quickly swallowed up in the throngs of smartly dressed men and women hurrying along the pavements. A few minutes later a long black car drew up, and a burly

man in a black coat and homburg hat, accompanied by
two excited young women in furs, unlocked the Embassy
door and took possession in the name of Franco. It was
the end of an era, not just for Republican Spain, but also
for the hope which had flared brilliantly if briefly for many
of us.

During the post-Munich months I forged a friendship
with Madame Genevieve Tabouis, then at the peak of her
influence as a columnist. She was the wife of a former
diplomat, and her column in the radical daily paper
L'Oeuvre was regarded as a major source of inside
information, quoted constantly by the news agencies, and
relayed throughout the world.

Madame Tabouis was a small, neat, vibrant, handsome
woman in her mid-forties with grey, carefully coiffured
hair. She was passionately opposed to the Munich settlement, and to the policies of Georges Bonnet and liked to
bring together people who shared her views at the apartment she and her husband occupied just off the Boulevard
Haussman. It had been once a highly fashionable area,
but most of the *haute monde* had now deserted it for the
new apartment blocks and mansions between the Arc de
Triomphe and the Bois. I found myself a fairly frequent
guest at these lunches, many of which were attended by
army officers like General Juin who were deeply worried
by the shifting balance of military power in Germany's
favour. Tabouis and I fell into the habit of exchanging
information regularly. Frequently, often early in the
morning, my telephone would ring at St Cloud and the
now familiar voice would pour out a torrent of news and
rumours and interpretation. I had learned to cross-check
carefully anything she told me, but Tabouis not only put
me onto a number of usable stories, but also kept me
abreast of the way French informed opinion was moving.
I came to have a very real affection for her, particularly
because of her fierce patriotism and her determination to
see France stand up for itself. We were never on Christian
name terms – indeed in those days surnames could often

reflect as close a link as do the instantly used Christian names of today – but we worked easily together, sharing not only news, but laughter at the sardonic turns of events in those bitter days.

Paris had become a gathering place for exiles from Nazi Germany. Amongst them was a girl in her early twenties called Charlotte Reimer, whom I had last seen on that day in 1934 on which the Storm Troopers had given me a taste of their methods when I failed to salute the swastika. She had a German father and an English mother, and I had been given a letter of introduction to her from friends in London. Her parents had left Germany when Hitler came to power, but she had stayed because Karl, the young German to whom she was engaged, and who had been prominent in the Communist Youth Movement, was imprisoned by the Nazis.

Charlotte proved to be a small, dark-haired, vital figure, speaking perfect English. She surprised me by asking if I would take her to lunch the next day in a restaurant on the top floor of a leading department store, in the heart of Berlin's West End. It was a fashionable and costly place, the Fortnum and Mason's of Berlin, and my funds did not run to such luxuries.

'I will pay,' she explained. 'If we get there early, and get a table by the window, it is possible to see into a corner of the courtyard of the Moabit prison. The prisoners are allowed into the yard for exercise between midday and one o'clock. If I can see that Karl is amongst them, then I know he is still there, and has not been taken off to Dachau or some other concentration camp. The police have beaten him terribly, but so long as they hold him, he has a chance. Once he is handed over to the Nazis, they will destroy him.'

We were in good time, and secured a window table, from which it was possible to see, some blocks away, a small patch of courtyard surrounded by high grey walls, and to detect tiny figures moving across it. Charlotte sat, outwardly appearing nonchalant and talkative so as not to arouse the suspicions of the waiters or the people at other tables. Only one hand, clenched around her napkin until her fingers seemed almost bloodless, revealed the strain she was under. Around us women in the flowing gowns of the time, furs draped across the backs of their chairs, lacquered hair showing under expensive hats, laughed and talked to their escorts – many of whom were in well-cut Storm Trooper uniforms. As cover for her scrutiny of the prison yard, Charlotte pretended to be pointing out the sights of Berlin, spread out in the sunshine below us. We were half way through ordering our meal when I noticed her grip on the napkin suddenly relax. Her eyes softened with relief, and once the waiter had gone she nodded, and began to ask eagerly for news of London. Only when later we got to the relative privacy of the street outside did she say that she had seen Karl walking with two other prisoners, and with an apparently undamaged stride.

I saw her again that evening, and marvelled at her courage – for she was a German citizen, and constantly in danger of arrest – at staying on in Berlin when she might have fled to safety. When I left her at the doorway of the ponderous, old-fashioned apartment building in which she had a room, and watched her start briskly up the stairway, she looked vulnerable and very much alone. Her spirit of defiance may well have had something to do with the fact that when, a few minutes later, I encountered the marching Storm Troopers in the dark Berlin street, I deliberately refrained from saluting their swastika flag.

Now Charlotte appeared in Paris, together with Karl, whom I had glimpsed that day from the roof-top restaurant, as he trudged round the exercise yard of the Moabit Prison. He had been released after serving a five-year sentence, and he and Charlotte had managed to escape from Germany, and were now married, and in exile in Paris. But they were in trouble, and sought my help. The Stalinist purges had spread to the emigré world in France, and Karl and Charlotte, who had also become a Communist, were under suspicion from their Party colleagues, accused of having played in with the Gestapo to ensure their escape from the Reich. An emigré Communist tribunal was investigating them. It could help, they argued, to prove their case if I could certify to it that I had seen Karl in Moabit Prison on that particular day.

So on a bright summer afternoon in July 1939 I had found myself in an office in an old building just off the Boulevard St Germain, facing four men and a woman who sat behind a big oak desk piled high with papers. The air was thick with tobacco smoke, and through the tall windows came the familiar sounds of Paris, the blare of taxi horns, and the whistles of traffic policemen. Karl and Charlotte sat, anxious and intent, on two hard chairs at the side of the room, as I gave my account of that day four years earlier. I was cross-questioned for about half an hour. My evidence could not have been much help to them, for they were both expelled from the Communist Party, and their photographs printed in the emigré press as people to be shunned. This may have been fortunate for them, for they set about emigrating to North America, where Karl built up a new existence as a clothing manufacturer, his political days very much over. He was more fortunate than the members of the tribunal which had condemmed him. They were handed over to the Nazis when France fell, and died in concentration camps.

One mysterious Left Bank figure of this period was a German of Czech origin, born in Brunn, who went by the name of Andre Simone but whose real name was Otto Katz. Simone-Katz was a small pale man in his early forties, who appeared self-effacing, but was in fact skilfully self-assertive. One of his cheeks bore the scar of a street fight with the Nazis in pre-1933 days, a characteristic which led Edgar Mowrer of the *Chicago Daily News* to describe him as 'the Jew with a duelling scar'. After the rise of Hitler, Katz had escaped to Paris, where he led the Comintern propaganda on behalf of Republican Spain, exaggerating or fabricating pro-Republican news items for the left-wing French press.

My links with Simone (as I knew him), were not concerned with Spain, for which I had no news responsibility, but with French politics. On these he not only had good sources, but an avid interest in discovering what was happening, which made him a useful contact. In the twelve months leading up to the outbreak of war he not only put me on to a number of good stories, particularly concerning the flow of Nazi money into the French press, but had a hard shrewd mind against which to test the multitude of rumours and reports which swirled around Paris, where politics, society and journalism intermingled on several levels.

Simone preferred for us to meet on the Right Bank, well away from the Latin Quarter and Montparnasse cafés frequented by his fellow Communists. He favoured in particular the downstairs room of a large garish café on the Boulevard des Capucines, close to the Place de l'Opéra. It had red leather and velvet banquettes, black-topped tables, and bright strip lighting, and was frequented by vividly dressed and vividly made up prostitutes who plied their trade both in the café and on the pavements above. Into this gaudy setting would suddenly appear the incongruous figure of Simone in a pale khaki raincoat, with a bundle of newspapers under his arm. 'You can buy nice girls here,' he said to me the first time we used this rendezvous, in tones someone might have used in recommending the cakes on offer in a *patisserie*.

Our discussions soon fell into a set pattern. It was the period when the Stalinist trials were at their peak, and almost every day the papers would carry reports from Moscow of one more unbelievable accusation, one more unbelievable confession. I would challenge Simone on the latest of these. He would be ready with his riposte, often thrusting into my hand some lengthy cyclostyled statement from Moscow, badly translated into English, of a so-called confession. I still have the 800-page hardback copy of the official court proceedings *In the Case of the anti-Soviet Bloc of rightists and Trotskyites* which he gave

me. Each of us having in this way established our funda-
mental difference of political approach, we would settle
down to our scrutiny of the French political scene, about
which Simone could often be sardonically witty, for mixed
with his dogmatism was a sense of humour. Then, as
suddenly as he had arrived, he would gather up his papers,
mutter about an urgent further meeting he had to attend,
and disappear up the stairs. I used to wonder if these swift
entrances and exits were a skill imparted by the Comintern to their key operatives.

One story which Simone and I, by pooling our information, successfully cracked concerned the manoeuvre of
Daladier and Bonnet to do a secret deal with Italy, in
which they would make some concessions about Djibouti,
Tunis and the Suez Canal, whilst at the same time
outwardly taking a determined stand against the Italian
claims. Early in February 1939 Bonnet sent Paul Baudouin president of the French-controlled Bank of Indo-
China, to the Italian Foreign Minister in Rome, Count
Ciano, to offer a deal. The Italians loyally informed their
Axis partner. This alarmed the Nazi Government, who
had no wish to see France solve her problems with Italy,
and so be left free to face up to Germany. Ribbentrop
therefore leaked details of the secret talks to pro-Nazi
forces in Paris. I picked up a hint of these: so too did
Simone. I consulted Tabouis, and within twenty-four
hours both she and I were able to break the story.
Daladier and Bonnet denied it furiously, but the talks
were ultimately called off.

My problem, once I established the story, was to get
the *Daily Express* to use it. Their sub-editors, ever
sensitive to what would interest people in drab back
streets in the Midlands, had little taste for stories about
complex diplomatic manoeuvrings about remote places
with unpronounceable names. I had to sell the story not
only to our readers, but to the hard-headed sub-editors
who guarded their portals. To do this, I exploited the fact
that the three principal French figures involved all had

surnames beginning with the letter B – Bonnet, Baudouin, and a third emissary, de Brinon. So I built up the story as 'The Mystery of the Three Messieurs B'. It proved a selling line, and Arthur Christiansen's 'suburban house-wife in Walsall', at whom we were told to aim, was for several weeks kept well abreast of these developments. Remote though the places involved may have seemed in 1939, within the next few years men from Walsall and a multitude of similar towns in Britain were to move through Djbouti to free Abyssinia, and to fight fierce battles in Tunisia.

12

The Munich Lie Exposed

On 15 March 1939 the Great Munich Lie was at last exposed. At six o'clock that morning German troops crossed the frontiers of the rump state of Czechoslovakia and moved to occupy Prague, just three hours after the aged President Hacha had, in Berlin, signed away control of his country to the Germans. By mid-afternoon the *Paris Soir*'s front page was covered with photographs of the stunned crowds, tears coursing down their faces, watching German tanks and lorried infantry move down the Wenchelas Platz where, only six months before, I had seen the people of Prague demonstrate in their thousands their desire to defend their land. I could readily envisage the other scenes the cameras did not catch, as the squads of Gestapo and of the SS hustled people from their homes into the backs of vans, on their way to the concentration camp and the blood-stained interrogation cellar. I hoped that Jaksch, and Schafranek and Ripka and the host of others whose sole crime was to love their country had been able to escape. But at least in Britain and France the air was now clearer, and the lie had been given to the belief that Hitler had been sated at Munich, and that if we were polite to him peace was assured.

Yet I was not surprised when, that afternoon in the Commons, Chamberlain showed no sign of giving up his illusions about Hitler. Far from condemning this new

move, the British Prime Minister did not speak of Czechoslovakia as having been invaded. Instead it had 'become
disintegrated'. Sir John Simon explained that the guarantees which at Munich we had given to protect the frontiers
of reshaped Czechoslovakia could not be applied, as that
Czechoslovakia had ceased to exist. Chamberlain stressed
that he had no wish to associate himself with any of the
charges of breach of faith on Hitler's part which were
being 'bandied about'.

This speech was prominently displayed in the Swiss
newspapers which I bought the next morning on the
platform in Zurich, on my way by train to Bucharest.
Rumania, with its rich oil reserves, and its own homegrown Fascist movement, the Iron Guards, seemed set to
be the Nazis' next target. I broke my journey in Budapest.
Our correspondent there, an old friend from my Vienna
days, had been mobilised. But his young, dark-haired
wife was in their flat overlooking the Danube, and it was
there, on their short wave radio, that I heard the BBC
report of Neville Chamberlain's speech at Birmingham on
the evening of 17 March. It contained an astonishing
change of tone. Now he spoke of Czechoslovakia having
been invaded, of its independence having been lost, of
Hitler having 'taken the law into his own hands'.
Chamberlain promised to consult with France and with
the countries of the Commonwealth, who, like Britain,
were not 'disinterested in South-East Europe'. Were we
at last preparing to stand and resist? Was indeed this
speech intended to deter a further move in the Balkans,
with Rumania as its target?

Bucharest in the early spring of 1939 was an imitation
Paris, part flashy, part musty in a way which seemed
characteristic of those Balkan countries which had for
centuries been under the Turks. Along the wide tree-
lined Chaussée, a would-be Champs Elysées with its own
Triumphal Arch (which, on close examination, proved to
be made of concrete), stucco-fronted mansions stood like
stage sets in Hollywood. The side roads were muddy and

13

Troubled Spring

ring months which followed, though overhung by
reat of war, were at least free of the cant and
ods of the post-Munich period. Beaverbrook
d the *Daily Express*, after at first opposing the
tee to Poland, gradually to shift its position to one
ding firm against further German aggression. 'We
rty-nine million foreign secretaries in Britain these
it declared in a leader, 'and they all seem to want
e a stand.' So the paper went along with them, at
s far as ceasing to pretend that Hitler did not pose
it. I could work for it now in a much easier frame
d, no longer feeling that I was caught up in a
acy – however frank I might try to make my own
ng – to lull the public into an attitude of false
y.

personal lives were brighter too. On 8 March our
child was born in the American Hospital at
. It was a boy, and we gave him the name of
. It was the name of Cecily's younger brother, and
s our bid to offset the fact that two days after the
birth Lieutenant Patrick Turner of the Royal
s had died at sea, having jumped overboard from
Ramillies off Malta in an effort to save one of his
ho had fallen from the deck in a rough sea.
the baby's birth Cecily's allergy had disappeared,
was soon fit enough to live a full life again. Late

unpaved, ending abruptly in open country, and over it all
was the immense, arching sky of the Danube delta.
Droskies, wooden arches curving above their shafts, and
pulled by magnificent, long-maned horses, rattled through
the streets alongside modern cars and lorries. On the
crowded Calle Victorei you gathered at eleven in the
morning to take a glass of champagne and eat caviare,
served by the scoopful. In the early warm evening air you
dined in a garden restaurant where officers in sky-blue
uniforms, direct from the pages of a Ruritanian romance,
bent to kiss the hands of vivid-lipped women who strove
to emulate the chic of Paris, but somehow never seemed
to achieve more than a rather strident version of it. Even
the bronze of their gleaming hair, which those knowledgeable in such matters assured me was its true colour,
looked as if it was the product of a dye. Yet though so
much of this culture was ersatz, the place had an abound-
ing vitality, a sense of being the capital of a land of rich
natural resources – which it was – which overcame its
falsities.

The British Government had by now become convinced
(on the basis of what has since been shown to be inaccur-
ate information) that Hitler was indeed about to seize
Rumania, and King Carol was pressurised into mobilising
a substantial part of his armed forces. The order calling
up reservists was published on the evening on which I was
travelling by train towards Arad, on the Rumanian-
Hungarian frontier. I awoke to find that at every station
at which we halted the platforms were crowded with
peasants reporting for duty; tall, moustachioed men in
rough sheepskin jackets and high black woollen caps,
their legs bound with straps of bast, and often with bast
shoes on their feet. Their womenfolk, young and old, in
bright green and red dresses, with white kerchiefs on their
heads, talked and wept and gesticulated. As the train
drew out they gave way to a shrill, undulating wail which
struck straight at the emotions, the anguish of simple

people caught up in events which they feared – and rightly feared – would prove both painful and long.

As station after station yielded up its reservists, the carriages of the train became jammed with men and bundles. They spread into the *wagon-lit* carriage, filling the corridor and ultimately crowding into the first class compartment into which my sleeping berth had been transformed. The *wagon-lit* attendant protested at the door that they should not disturb 'the gentleman'. One big peasant answered swiftly in Rumanian. I asked the attendant what he had said. 'He says that this is war – and in war there are no longer gentlemen, only men.'

Throughout the Balkans that March, the last time I was to visit them until, two years later, I found myself as a soldier in Greece, there was a sense of dislocation, of stones loosening which would soon precipitate a landslide. In the black earth of the Danubian plain in disputed territory long claimed from Rumania by Hungary, troops in the yellowish khaki of the Rumanian army dug trenches and trained their machine guns on either side of the road leading to Budapest. They had to keep an eye to their backs all the time, for this was a Hungarian-speaking area, reft from Hungary at the end of the Great War, eager to be united to Hungary. Their spokesman was the Roman Catholic Bishop of Arad, who was extremely cordial to me, not only because he wanted to plead the case of the Hungarian minority but because he was an avid reader of the *Sunday Express*, an *outré* activity for a cleric in those days. His dark brown eyes glowed with excitement when I assured him that I had indeed seen Lord Castlerosse, the gossip columnist of the *Sunday Express*, in the flesh – a fitting phrase for this Irish peer, who must have weighed close on eighteen stone.

In Zagreb, Matchek, the Croatian leader, spoke warily of the need for self-rule for the Croats within Yugoslavia. Zagreb was a quiet city, Austrian in appearance (Croatia had been part of Austro-Hungary until 1918), with yellow stucco buildings and tree-lined streets where the sound of

horses' hooves outdid that of the occasio Brown-eyed, wide-browed girls walked the girls who had walked last summer th of Prague. The young men at the corner to catch their glances. Around the recep hotel crowded a group of Jewish refuge Prague, their luggage piled high beh middle-aged woman put on the desk a b passport and said in German, 'I go tomorrow.'

In Vienna camouflaged Reichswehr through the streets, and steel-cowled Re marched along the Ringstrasse with set ing, the boyhood home of Adolf Hitle banner, stained by recent snow, swung road. It proclaimed, 'A New Thousand Heil Hitler.' Beyond Munich red light darkness, warning aircraft to keep aw concentration camp.

in April we took a holiday at the village of Sils Maria in the Engadine in Switzerland, the last we were to have for many years. We climbed to the edge of the snowline. Where the white crust crumbled and melted, white crocuses sprang up amidst the flattened grass. There was still snow enough on the tops to provide a passage for the coffee smugglers, dark figures on skis making their way across from Italy, watched through binoculars by the Swiss frontier guards. The warmer weather brought landslides to the steep mountainsides, setting cascades of rocks tumbling and bounding down the bare screes, to splash like shell bursts into the blue waters of the lake. In a wooden chalet by its waters Nietzsche had written *So Spake Zarathustra*. Here he penned his picture of the man of the future, 'anti-Christ and anti-nihilist, conqueror of both God and Unbeing', a vision which had helped to inspire Adolf Hitler towards deeds the full horror of which we had in that spring of 1939 not yet envisaged.

Yet even in this remote valley in this most neutral of countries there were reminders of the threat of war. The Swiss had called up their reservists for army manoeuvres, and grey-uniformed troops, skis on shoulders, trudged through the village street at dawn. On the road which wound down from Maloja to Lake Como gun barrels showed in the slits of fortresses cut into the living rock. Across the Italian frontier Como lay benign and lovely, a stretch of pale blue silk in the spring sunshine. We drank apéritifs at a lakeside café just a kilometre or so from the spot where, six years later almost to the day, Mussolini and his mistress Clara Petacci were to be seized by the partisans, and taken off to be killed and hung by their heels from the awning of a filling station near Milan.

In May I took a late skiing holiday at Lac de Tignes, in the Haute Savoie. In those days you had to climb by foot for half an hour from the now-drowned valley floor to reach the plateau, ringed with mountain peaks, where one lone chalet stood, and where today a whole town has been erected. There were no ski lifts, and we climbed with skins tied under our skis to the tops of the runs, coming down in twenty minutes across a stretch which had taken three hours to ascend. Except for one other visitor, a Swiss, the hotel was occupied by a film unit making a feature film. A score or more of the world's foremost skiers were taking part in it, and at the end of the day's filming they would swoop down the slope carrying huge loads and cameras and other gear on their backs. It was late enough in the season, too, for avalanches to be a constant feature, roaring and thundering every half hour or so from the high peaks, during the heat of the day. I went back to Paris fitter than I had been for years.

That spring and summer gave us a last rich taste of a Paris which was never to be the same again. The rate of exchange made the pound worth a lot in francs. With the generous living allowances the *Daily Express* paid to its men abroad we could live well. Many mornings I rode in the Bois de Boulogne, cantering along the sandy rides which wound for miles amidst the oaks and beeches of that huge park. There were pleasant tennis courts at St Cloud, and good swimming at the Porte Molitor and even in a huge wooden swimming pool moored in the Seine close to the Quai d'Orsay, in river water as yet remarkably unpolluted by passing barge traffic. In the evening the highly efficient services of the French post office enabled me to dine out, and yet stay on the job. The telephone exchange would divert any calls coming in to your number to any other number you designated. Several of our neighbourhood restaurants became in this way out-stations of the *Daily Express* office. Two were our particular favourites – Pierre in the Place Gaillon, and the Roy Gourmet in the Place des Victoires. At their doorways trays of oysters and sea urchins and lobsters were ranged in straw baskets. Inside were coarse white tablecloths, and constantly bustling, ever friendly waitresses, and family parties with napkins tucked under their chins, discussing eagerly what they should eat, what they were eating, and – over the cognac *pour la dégustation* – what they had eaten. Wild strawberries sprinkled with white wine were a speciality of the Pierre, and *canard aux olives* and *ris de veau au Marsala* those of the Roy Gourmet.

On a Saturday evening we could go up market and up town, to Fouquet's which offered a *table d'hôte* dinner and a half bottle of wine per person for the then modest equivalent of ten shillings sterling, or Pruniers for *quenelles de brochet* of exquisite texture and taste. We used the great restaurants, like Maxims and the Tour D'Argent and Le Grand Vefour only sparingly, if we had guests to entertain who needed to be impressed. And Le Pré Catalan in the heart of the Bois on a warm summer evening was subtle luxury at its peak.

After dinner at Fouquet's we could cross the Avenue Georges Cinq to listen to the pianist at the Boeuf sur le Toit, the pleasantest bar in this part of Paris. Though the Boeuf had a reputation as a meeting place for homosexuals, they formed – at least to the outward eye – only a small part of the clientele, and in the custom of the day did not flaunt their tastes. Throughout the period from Munich to the outbreak of war one tune was to be heard in every Paris bar and nightclub, the slow, poignant lilt of 'J'Attendrai', fitting exactly the mood of fatalism, melancholy and yet hope of the time. Noël Coward's words, 'Ah, the potency of cheap music' were never more true than in the thirties. Perhaps because hit tunes were fewer, and held their place longer, perhaps because the tunes were in themselves more memorable, a handful of songs formed a constant background music to the march of events. Prague had gone valiantly forward in the summer and early autumn of 1938 to the tune which was sweeping London – and indeed New York – 'Doin' the Lambeth Walk'. *The Times* had even noted, in a fourth leader that if war were to come, 'Doin' the Lambeth Walk' might prove to be the equivalent of 1914's 'Tipperary'. So 'J'Attendrai', the tune to which the reservists had gone off in September 1938 to man the Maginot Line, was to remain the theme song of France in the last months of peace in 1939. It was indeed to be the most evocative tune of its period until Eric Maschwitz's 'A Nightingale Sang in Berkeley Square' was to catch exactly the mood of nostalgia and daring of the summer of 1940, when it became the favourite record played on their gramophones by young fighter pilots as they awaited the order to scramble during the Blitz.

Alternatively, on those summer nights of 1939, we could drive across to the Rue St Anne, near the Opera, to hear Suzy Solidor sing in the *boîte* which bore her name. The walls of its one long, narrow room were hung with modern paintings, some seascapes from her native Brittany, others portraits of the *chanteuse* herself by leading artists of the day – Domergue and van Dongen, Yves Brayer and Jean Dunard, even a drawing of her by Jean Cocteau. Suzy Solidor herself, tall, with a strong, curved Viking nose, wide-set eyes and ash-blonde hair in a page boy bob – *à la Jeanne d'Arc* as the French said – sang or recited in a warm, strong, mezzo-contralto voice which seemed to belong more to the outdoors than to this crowded Parisian room. Her voice was part of the ambiguity which surrounded Suzy Solidor, an ambiguity which was perhaps the secret of her attraction. It was partly sexual, but partly also that of the contrast between the wind-swept Atlantic coasts of her youth and this elegant and indeed decadent Paris. The *chanteuse*'s long gleaming Schiaparelli and Chanel evening dresses, often a metallic gold or silver or jet, were the highest of *haute couture*. Yet the bare shoulders which they fashionably displayed were the rounded, strong, sunburned shoulders of a swimmer, and her gaze, above the crimson curve of her sharply outlined lips was as much that of the mariner as of the *grande elegante*. And which she changed abruptly from the haunting rhythms of her famous 'Les Filles de Saint Malo' to Cole Porter's 'Night and Day', the contrast, and the ambiguity was a mixture which intoxicated Paris, and it became the fashionable thing for society hostesses to bring their dinner guests on to Suzy Solidor's to round off the evening.

One of the few people impervious to her personality was Lord Beaverbrook. At his request, I took him there on one evening. The visit was not a success. Beaverbrook did not have enough French to follow her songs, and though Suzy Solidor made a point of coming to our table (I had ensured that she had been advised in advance of his visit), and spoke to Beaverbrook in fluent English, each was too strong a personality for there to be any rapport. It was on this occasion that I first realised that what Beaverbrook demanded – at any rate in his leisure hours – was not so much friends, as a court.

There were also, in that Paris of 1939, excellent places for that most English of occasions, afternoon tea. Rumplemeyer's and La Marquise de Seville offered mille-feuilles and éclairs and surpringly good Indian and china tea, as well as a range of the tisanes loved by the French matrons who, dressed as if for Gold Cup day at Ascot, chattered eagerly at the tiny tables. Almost equally in vogue with Parisian society was the tearoom run by W. H. Smith's above their English bookshop in the Rue de Rivoli, which served good strong Indian tea, and crumpets and buttered anchovy toast.

More spectacular, and very much of its period, was the scene in the late afternoon in the huge gilded foyers of the two main tourist hotels off the Champs Elysées, the Georges Cinq and the Prince de Galles. Between five and seven o'clock, particularly on a Saturday, they saw an extraordinary parade of the rich and the would-be rich where the *grandes* – and not so *grandes* – *cocottes*, silver fox furs draped over the arms of their gilt chairs, mingled – without any apparent embarrassment to either side – with Parisian matrons and rich Americans. It was Veblen's theory of conspicuous consumption displayed in its most vivid form – and, it seems, for the last time in Western Europe. For when the rich emerged again after the war, they took care to keep the display of their wealth within their own increasingly guarded compounds.

The theatres too were crowded that summer. Cocteau's *Parents Terribles*, in the Theatre Marigny near the Rond Point, drew crowds whose elegance made the scenes in the foyer during the entr'acte as dazzling as anything on the stage, with the latest work of the great couturiers – Schiaparelli, Chanel, Worth, Paquin – being worn with a casual pride. A similar parade, where the faces rather than the clothes caught the eye, took place between acts at the Comedie Française, where Voltaire in marble sardonically watched from his armchair the crowd pacing the long broad hallway. In this throng one evening was a woman whose somewhat coarsened features exuded an extraordinary vitality and confidence, a quality emphasised by her hat. In the fashion of the time it was in gleaming black straw, fitting with a narrow brim, like the hat of a village curé, but decorated with a shaft of fur rather like a monkey's tail. She stalked around, talking animatedly, contemptuously indifferent to the fact that the appendage to her hat was apt to thrust itself into the faces of others strolling in the foyer. Pierre Lazareff, who was with us that evening, identified her. '*C'est la Comtesse Hélène de Portes, la maîtresse de Paul Reynaud.*'

Yet these pleasant times were overshadowed by the constant realisation that war could be on us before the year was out, a threat which loomed like a distant thunderstorm on a sunny day. It both sharpened and soured our enjoyment. We lived that summer in a way in which, I was later to experience, men and women live together during periods of leave from the battlefront, with gladness and sorrow intertwined. It was a sensation at its sharpest at the beginning and the end of the day. I woke to the superb vista of the Bois beyond our windows, with one sturdy son running across the sunlit room towards us, and another cheerful in his cot, only to feel the sudden pang of their vulnerability. At night when we came home the Bois would be black, with the Eiffel Tower outlined against a sky glowing with the city lights. The broad line of the Seine below us, gleaming in the moonlight, was not only beautiful but, one realised, a source of danger, a clear guide to enemy bombers, so easy to envisage sweeping in from the east, leading them to the new bridge under construction just upstream, and to the roofs of the huge riverside Renault factory, busy now on night shift building tanks and trucks for France's rearmament programme.

The *Daily Express* office in Paris was housed in two large rooms in the modern seven-storied building of the leading French popular paper of the day, the *Paris Soir*, in the Rue du Louvre. It was set in a mixed quartier of tall, grey-stuccoed, wooden-shuttered building where finance, newspapers, small workshops and good restaurants jostled one another. The Paris Bourse, a grey, columned building, like a discoloured Greek temple, was close by, and during dealing hours the clamour of its dealers, many of them bargaining on the wide steps of the building, brought echoes of penned animals in distant stockyards. The Bank of France, the National Library, and the colonnades and garden of the Palais Royale were at our back. So too were several of the most celebrated Maisons Closes of Paris, one, the House of Nations, offering its delights in bedrooms each decorated in the style of a different country.

Paris Soir was an evening paper, owned by a millionaire textile magnate turned newspaper proprietor, M Jean Prouvost, and edited by Pierre Lazareff, a small, eager Jew, with thick, pebble-lensed spectacles, whose family stemmed from Poland. Lazareff was a genius in news presentation – quite the equal, in French terms, of Arthur Christiansen. He used his front page largely as a billboard for the contents of the inside pages, with huge headlines dramatising the main story, and a lavish use of pictures. His wife, small, dark, and good-looking, was an equally successful editress in her own right and under her own name of Hélène Gordon. She had built up the women's weekly *Marie Claire* into part of the fabric of French life.

Under them the *Paris Soir* building, jutting like the rounded prow of an ocean liner on to the small Place D'Aboukir, pulsated with life, as motor cyclists dashed up with the latest copy or cans of film, as elegantly dressed reporters, overcoats slung like cloaks over their shoulders, moved gravely towards the lift. I relished the vitality of it all, enjoyed being greeted as '*cher collègue*' by Pierre Lazareff as, in his high-pitched, confident voice, he would call me into his office ostensibly to tell me some item of political gossip, but really to share with me his pleasure in the pattern of a page or the use of a photograph.

A central figure in the *Daily Express* Paris office was the secretary, a White Russian, Princess Mara Scherbatoff. Tall, dark, calm, with a rounded, Slavonic face, she glided rather than walked, moving with an erect, easy dignity no doubt acquired by generations of her forebears on the parquet floors of lofty palace rooms in St Petersburg and Moscow. She moves *comme la Reine Elizabeth*, the commissionaire in the hallway of the *Paris Soir* building would comment admiringly, going on to explain that the queen he had in mind was not the recently crowned Queen of England but the new great liner portrayed in newsreels of the time making its way serenely across the seas.

Mara Scherbatoff was the oldest of four equally beautiful sisters, one of whom was the head mannequin at Balenciaga. They lived with their old Swiss governess in a flat in Passy. Scherb, as she was called by everyone, had no shorthand, and her typing was slow, but she spoke English, French and Russian perfectly, and provided an admirably steady, as well as a glamorous centre to the swirl of a newspaper office.

My work was made the pleasanter in the summer of 1939 by the arrival in the Paris office of a new assistant who delighted in handling the sex and scandal stories so beloved by the London news desk. He was a sturdy, middle-aged, whimsical Scot called Donald Augustin Robertson – though no one ever called him anything but

Robbie – whom the paper had hurriedly posted abroad until a row he had had with the Metropolitan Police had died down. Sent to cover a story of a gang battle in London's East End, Robbie had seized a moment when the desk in the Poplar police station had been left unmanned. Posing as a detective, he summoned a suspect from the waiting room into a nearby interview room, grilled him and got the full story, and then departed before the station sergeant knew what had happened. His resultant story had produced demands for Robbie to be charged with impersonating a police officer. Christiansen suddenly remembered Robbie had learnt French during World War I, and attached him to the Paris office. He transformed my life. Not only did he take over all the so-called human interest stories, but he did them with marvellous gusto and humour.

Robbie had one of those varied backgrounds which characterised Fleet Street men in the days before journalists were mass produced from universities and schools of journalism. He had at one time been a violinist on the music halls. He played well, but it was his gimmick rather than his music which would bring down the house. Before each performance he would carefully pace out the distance between where he would stand to play, and the edge of the orchestra pit. As he reached the crescendo of his main piece, he would seem to be so wrapped up in the music, so carried away by his feelings and his concentration, that his gaze would turn upwards. At the same time he would begin to move forward, step by step, closer and closer to the edge of the stage, until with the next step it would seem certain that, with eyes averted, he must plunge onto the heads of the orchestra. The audience would watch, riveted, until with one foot outstretched, apparently about to step into space, he would bring the piece to a triumphant end. Relief from the tension – as well as appreciation for his playing – would ensure a tumult of applause, a fact which would delight as well as puzzle the music-hall managers.

Robbie's arrival enabled me to undertake some investigative journalism into the flow into France of Nazi money to be used for anti-Semitic and anti-British propaganda. The name of Bonnet, the Foreign Minister, kept cropping up in rumours about the distribution of these funds. My inquiries led me to some strange sights – to a flat in the fashionable Paris suburb of Passy where even the wallpaper had been stripped from the walls, leaving only the stained and scratched plaster, in a police search for evidence: to a frightened woman in Angers, south-west of Paris, who was so relieved to discover that I was not yet another detective coming to grill her that she poured out her story to me; the trail led from her to a blonde German au pair girl who left abruptly for Holland just an hour before I reached the home where she had been employed. I discovered that there had indeed been a Bonnet engaged in handling money from Germany. It was not, however, the Foreign Minister, but a nephew of his, who held a minor post in Pari-Mutuel, the French totalisator system.

The clues ultimately led back to Otto Abetz, the Nazis' chief agent and unofficial ambassador in Paris. Though he was a close friend of both Georges and Madame Bonnet, the evidence against him was strong enough for the French Sûreté to expel him from the country. I traced the blonde au pair to the Hague, and was about to go off to interview her there when J. B. Wilson, the *Daily Express* news editor, intervened. He had studied a photograph of the girl, with long hair falling over a sunburned shoulder, taken on the beach in Holland. 'Cox is not at all her type,' he opined. 'A dark sardonic type is likely to be much more her line. Send Montagu Lacey.' And so Lacey, from the London staff, departed for Holland, and proved Wilson's judgement correct by producing a lengthy interview – and photographs which delighted Christiansen.

This story gained me considerable publicity in Paris. The French papers, inhibited as they were from investigating too closely the affairs of their own ministers, avidly reprinted my findings. This was particularly the case with the left centre *L'Ordre*, for which Tabouis now wrote, and which was edited by a massive veteran of Verdun, Emil Buré. '*Cox, de la grande quotidienne anglaise, le Daily Express*' became a much-quoted source in his pages.

In July I visited Verdun, the World War I battlefield which to the French meant all that the Somme and Passchendaele meant for Britain – and indeed more, for it had been fought on French soil, and had its fortresses fallen in 1917 the way to Paris would have been open. The ruined Fort Douaumont was still surrounded by rusty barbed wire entanglements, overgrown trenches and mine craters. Behind it a huge ossuary presented a dignified, cathedral-like front but through the basement windows at the back could be seen the bones and skulls of tens of thousands of unidentified bodies. Beside it was the Trench of Bayonets, where the tops of twenty-four rifles, with long thin bayonets attached, showed in a ragged line above the earth which filled the trench. Beneath, it was claimed, the holders of the rifles stood, buried, engulfed by the earth thrown up by a land mine which had exploded as they prepared to go over the top in a charge.

Even the hideous concrete walls which had been built around the trench, making it look like a municipal water works, and the broken strings of rosaries, scraps of ugly purple wreaths, and stray bits of wood and paper which littered the trench surface could not destroy its poignancy. Even more moving were the mile upon mile of cratered ground which covered these rolling hills, pockmarked by countless shell holes. The green leaves on new, stunted bushes could not hide these craters, filled with stagnant water or churned gravel or rank grass. It made me think of telescopic photographs of the moon's surface. This was the outcome of a war fought only twenty years earlier – and a presage of what a new war could mean for us, the generation who would be called on to fight it.

On that sunny afternoon, with the larks singing high above these ravaged hills, it was almost more than the

mind could take in that such events could ever be deliberately set in train again. Yet even here the signs were
clear. Beyond Douaumont a new barrier cut through the
old, rusty barbed wire. The road, a notice said, was closed
to all but military traffic. Lorries carrying material for
new fortifications ground their way along the dusty track.

14

'There Will Be No War'

Towards the end of July Lord Beaverbrook paid his last visit to Paris before the war began, en route to the Riviera in the company of his close friend and employee, Viscount Castlerosse. It was to give me my friendliest contact with him in this pre-war period. I had expected it to be otherwise, for I had turned down as worthless a story which he had brought to the paper's attention. A titled English lady in Monte Carlo was gaining fame locally as a faith healer, claiming to be able to cure by laying on of hands. The fame may have been genuine, but our local correspondent could find no evidence of its being based on any genuine cures. The *Sunday Express*, however, thought otherwise. A few days after I had rejected the story, they sent a special correspondent down from London who found it all very true and very wonderful.

When I entered Beaverbrook's suite at the Ritz the *Sunday Express* lay prominently displayed. 'I see you were scooped yesterday,' said his lordship. Not so, I countered, the *Sunday Express* had got it wrong.

To my surprise, Beaverbrook did not show annoyance. Instead, he turned to Castlerosse. It was the first time I had met this Irish peer whom Beaverbrook ranked not only amongst his leading columnists, but amongst his closest friends. A tall, sleek, pear-shaped figure, superbly dressed in a dove-grey morning suit and black cravat, in which shone a jewelled tie pin, with shrewd eyes alert above long, close-shaven jowls, he allowed himself a slight smile as Beaverbrook said:

'We have an independent witness here. Lord Castlerosse knows the lady well. Tell me, Valentine, could Lady X cure you by laying on of hands?'

'It all depends where she laid them on,' came the Viscount's swift reply.

The main reason why Beaverbrook had summoned me proved to be more serious. With the threat of war ever closer, he wanted a candid survey made of the attitude towards a possible war of the ordinary people of France and Germany. This, he claimed, needed a fresher eye than a resident correspondent could bring to bear. Therefore, instead of my reporting on how the French felt, I was to go to Germany and find an answer to the question 'Will Germany fight for Danzig?' Castlerosse would do the same in France. We would meet in three days' time, here at the Ritz, to report our findings.

To assess accurately in three days the feelings of a nation living under a dictatorship, with security already tightened as it mobilised for war, verged on the absurd. I decided the best thing was to call on the British consuls in Düsseldorf, Essen and Cologne. If there was hostility to Hitler, it would be in this traditional working class heartland, the Ruhr. All three consuls proved to be sensible and helpful. They were unanimous that not only would the Germans fight, albeit reluctantly, but that they would go on fighting so long as they were called to do so. The anti-Nazi right were powerless so long as Hitler was successful. The Left was smashed to smithereens and could be revived only in a defeated Germany. I supplemented this with more direct research, chatting to workmen in small taverns close to the railway station in each of these cities, and in talks with a correspondent of the *Kölnischer Zeitung* I had come to know in Prague. Though there was no sign of the elation with which Germany had gone to war in 1914, and everywhere a sense of concern and apprehension, there was no sign either of opposition to Hitler. To the traditional German sense of discipline had been added both the constraints of Nazi terror and an unmistakable trust still widespread in Hitler as the Führer.

Three days later I reported at the Ritz at noon. As I waited in an anteroom Castlerosse arrived. 'I've a message to be here by twelve,' he said. 'Do you know what it's for?' I reminded him of our assignments. 'Hell!' he commented. 'I had completely forgotten about it. I've made no enquiries at all.'

I thought my findings would be unpalatable to Beaverbrook, as I expected him to be hoping for signs of anti-Nazi feeling in Germany which could curb Hitler. But he nodded his agreement. 'The German sense of discipline is bound to assert itself at a time like this.' Then he turned to Castlerosse. 'Now, Valentine,' he said, 'tell me of your findings. Will the French fight for Danzig?'

Castlerosse relied on candour. 'Max,' he replied. 'I haven't got much further in my enquiries than the bar of Fouquet's. But I can tell you one thing for sure. No one in the bar of Fouquet's is going to fight for Danzig.'

It was to prove a shrewder assessment than appeared at the time. For the rich who drank in Fouquet's, many of them very much the *nouveaux riches*, reflected accurately the views of their fellows who, when the crunch came in the summer of 1940, preferred to surrender to the Nazis than to continue a fight which could put their wealth and power at risk.

Early in August the old Adam of Beaverbrook's appeasement reasserted itself. He got Christiansen to conduct a poll of *Daily Express* correspondents in Europe on whether there would be war in Europe in 1939. I was convinced that the French would do everything possible to avoid fighting for Danzig and Poland, and that when the crunch came Chamberlain would find some means of doing a Munich on the Poles – as indeed he would have done had Hitler been prepared to accept a Polish surrender instead of yielding to the temptation to launch the first blitzkrieg. So I replied, 'The odds are now in favour of there being no war this summer and autumn – but only just.'

It was a view which, even as late as 15 August, was shared by the well-placed Canadian diplomat Charles Ritchie, later to be Canadian High Commissioner in London. He noted in his diary for that day: 'We are to sell out the Poles apparently . . . the advice going out to them from the Foreign Office over Danzig is just what we told the Czechs this time last year over the Sudeten crisis.' What neither Ritchie nor I foresaw was how the odds would be abruptly swung on 23 August, when Stalin entered into his pact with Hitler, the deal which enabled the Nazis not only to attack Poland without fear of Russian intervention, but to share the spoils with them.

Of the fourteen *Daily Express* correspondents in Europe (how many popular papers today have four, let alone fourteen correspondents in Europe?) twelve opted clearly for no war in 1939, whilst two hedged their bets. Beaverbrook had these findings trimphantly blazoned across the front page of the *Express* on 7 August. He was later to make much play of this poll. On it he justified the repeated use in the paper of the slogan 'There will be no war this year or next year either'. This was nonsense. The slogan had been in use by the *Daily Express* for fifteen months, ever since its first appearance in May 1938, before this poll of correspondents was conducted. The attitude it expressed had been implicit, and often explicit, in a multitide of leading articles and feature pieces from early 1937 onwards. It was Beaverbrook's view long before any of his correspondents were asked to give theirs. In the event, the 'No War This Year' slogan was used only once more in the *Daily Express*, on 11 August. By this time, in any case, it was too late for public opinion to be affected. What had mattered was Beaverbrook's appeasement stance over Czechoslovakia, when a tough stand might have prevented war, and even earlier, when the seizure of Austria made plain that Nazism was on the march. Even so, it stung when the opening sequence of Noël Coward's film *In Which We Serve* showed the front page of 7 August 1939. I was thankful that when I first saw this film, it was in an open-air cinema behind the front line in Italy, and I wore the khaki of a serving soldier.

This was not the first time Lord Beaverbrook had canvassed the views of his staff. In the summer of 1938 all the main members of the editorial staff were asked to state their political views. These would, it was stressed, be kept in the strictest confidence. I replied that I belonged to no political party, but had voted Labour at the 1935 General Election. Alan Moorehead thought this was a good formula, and recorded that he too had never belonged to a political party, but had voted Conservative in 1935.

The findings of this poll, held now in the Beaverbrook Library, show that Tom Driberg had answered without hesitation, 'I am a member of the Communist Party of Great Britain.' At a time when Communists working in Fleet Street were usually anxious – presumably on Party instructions – to keep their membership quiet, this was a surprising admission. The most likely explanation for it became clear only after Driberg's death, when it became known that he had been a member of MI5 throughout the thirties. Indeed he remained one until Anthony Blunt in his own MI5 role discovered the fact during the war, with the result that Driberg was abruptly expelled from the Communist Party in 1942. It is likely that Beaverbrook knew of Driberg's link with MI5, providing a good reason – and a good excuse – for him to keep this brilliant journalist in his team despite his Communist associations.

15

Towards the Precipice

By mid-August events began to move at a pace which made forecasting superfluous. From Danzig, from the Polish frontiers, and from Berlin appeared the signs we had come to recognise that Hitler was about to move against yet another country. Arms, including even armoured cars, were being smuggled into Danzig for the use of local Nazis. At border stations disputes began to erupt between Polish and German guards. The Swiss Dr Carl Burckhardt, who ruled Danzig as the League of Nations High Commissioner, was invited to Berchtesgaden and subjected to a tirade from the Führer. German press and radio each day printed more and more stories of alleged Polish atrocities against Germans living in Poland.

Then just before midnight on 21 August came the news which made war seem a virtual certainty. I learnt of it in the strident setting of the Café Coliseé, the biggest and brashest of the cafés of the Champs Elysées. We often dined or drank there now in the evenings, because it had a Havas ticker tape machine in its basement on which we could check on developments. It was this machine on which, amidst the perfumed and noisy setting of Parisians and Parisiennes making telephone calls and chatting, the news was spelt out just before midnight on 21 August that the Soviet Union and Nazi Germany had agreed to sign a non-aggression pact. Unbelievingly, I twice read through these few words, set out in the bright blue type of the Havas machine, my mind yielding only slowly to the knowledge that this meant only one thing – war.

I was thankful that Cecily and our two boys were at this time on holiday in England, with her mother in Sussex. I arranged for her to stay there until the Polish crisis either blew over or became war. I locked up the St Cloud flat, and moved into a small hotel near the office, the Hôtel St Romain in the Rue Saint Roch. It was in a pleasantly historic quarter. The walls of the church of St Roch still bore the marks left by the 'whiff of grapeshot' which Napoleon had fired from two 8-pounder cannons to disperse the last counter-revolutionary attack and consolidate the grip of the Convention on post-revolutionary France in 1795. The Palace of the Bourbons which the mob had stormed in 1789 had stood just across the way, on the far side of the Rue de Rivoli. The Tuileries Gardens, with their formal flower beds and gravel walks now occupied the site. They provided a perfect place on which to read the papers on a sunny day, with before one the finest city view in the world, the long sweep of the Champs Elysées rising towards the Arc de Triomphe on the sky line.

The St Romain had no bar, and provided no meals beyond coffee and rolls for breakfast, but its small rooms were scrupulously clean, and its proprietors, Monsieur and Madame Lamartine, came to be my friends, a friendship which was cemented in the next summer when the St Romain was my base during the Battle of France.

Paris in the closing weeks of August saw a strange pilgrimage, as those who loved it, particularly Britons and Americans, sought a final taste of its life before the deluge engulfed us all. Claud Cockburn was in the Dome, as ill-shaven and sardonically ebullient as ever, with a lithe young woman with a small head of jet black hair, who looked like a figure from a Scott Fitzgerald novel, and spoke with the most cut-glass English accent I had ever heard. As we came near to war, I thought, we all revert to type, and Claud's type, whatever his Communist beliefs, was that of a ruling class. Dan Davin, who had come to Oxford as a Rhodes Scholar in 1936, was in the Deux Magots, a first in Greats from Balliol under his belt, and a pile of saucers on the table in front of him proclaiming that war or no war there was always time for a drink and a debate with friends. John Mulgan and Jack Bennet from Auckland arrived in time for us to fit in a few days at a small riverside hotel on the bank of the Seine, west of Paris. John had with him the typescript of *Man Alone*, the only novel fate was to permit him to write. I read it in a small bedroom overlooking the village square, whilst in the café below the juke box thumped out the hit song of the moment:

> Jeepers, creepers, where did ya get those peepers?
> Jeepers, creepers, where did ya get those eyes?

and the reservists in cheap khaki uniforms danced the Lambeth Walk with girls in dresses of imitation silk and satin.

We talked of the trench warfare we assumed would be our lot, and of how well or badly we would face up to the moment when we in our turn, like the men buried at Verdun, would have to stand in a trench at zero hour ready to move out across a bullet-strewn no-man's-land. John's comment reflected the good humoured good sense which was his strength. In our time at university, boxing in the annual inter-university tournaments in New Zealand had been dominated by a middleweight from Fiji called Tom Dovi, a small, frizzy-haired man who seemed to be carved from granite. John brushed aside the debate about whether we would be afraid. 'I don't think that anything else could ever be as frightening as finding oneself alone in the ring with Tom Dovi after the gong had gone,' was his estimate.

As war came nearer, those who had served in the last

war could at times be persuaded to talk of their experience. Tom Cadett, the *Times* correspondent, had found himself within a few days of arriving in France as an eighteen-year-old lieutenant in the Argyll and Sutherland Highlanders, in charge of a platoon sent out in the darkness into no-man's-land to repair a barbed wire entanglement damaged by enemy shelling. It had to be repaired before daylight when a German attack was expected. The enemy had been using gas shells, and gas still lingered in the hollows and shell holes. But in their gas masks the men could make only slow progress. The only way to get the job done was to order them to remove their masks. One man refused to do so, and defied Cadett's repeated order.

'I took out my revolver, thrust it into his stomach, and gave him one further order. He still refused, saying he would sooner die than risk breathing gas. Then the very seasoned sergeant-major who was with us took a hand. He clenched his fist and said to the man, "If you don't take off your bloody mask and get on with the job, I'll knock your bloody head off." That threat was far more effective than mine. The man complied, and we got the job done just in time.'

Not all recollections of these veterans were gloomy. Martin Herlihy, head of Reuters' office in Paris, told me that what stayed most clearly in his mind was not the mud and strain of the trenches, but the pleasure of marching, in a column of well-trained troops, with larks in the fields beyond the poplars. 'Memory seems to blot out the awful bits,' he said, 'and leave the pleasant ones.'

By the last week in August huge placards, each with small crossed tricolours at the corners, had proclaimed the Mobilisation Generale, and throughout the day train after train of reservists pulled out from the Gare de l'Est for the frontiers and the Maginot Line. For the most part they went with dignity and sadness. '*Il faut en finir*' was the tenor of this mood. They ranged from youngsters barely out of their teens to grey-haired men who had been just old enough to serve in the concluding stages of the last war, some carrying suitcases, some with their belongings in a roll under one arm. Grimly they parted from their tearful wives and mothers and fathers and sons and clambered aboard the carriages marked Metz and Strasbourg. One couple in particular caught my eye, a young wife and her officer husband, locked in each other's arms at the barrier, standing silent, a silence which said more than any words could have done, until the officer tore himself away and strode off towards the train. The woman, beautiful under her tears, her hand resting on a bunch of violets pinned to her coat, watched until the last carriage of the train disappeared on the eastward line of tracks.

An hour later I was sitting on the terrace of the Colisée on the Champs Elysées when this woman appeared, easily recognisable because the bunch of violets was still on her coat. Her face was set, held high, almost as if in a trance. Once seated, she stared angrily around the café, her glance resting defiantly on the men in civilian clothes who crowded so many of the tables. Ten minutes later she drained her cup of coffee, paid her bill, and with an almost elaborate slowness moved towards the door. A man who had been seated a few tables away from her followed her out. I saw them talking on the pavement in front of the café, clearly two strangers making contact, before they called a taxi and got in. Had I misread the sincerity of that parting at the Gare de l'Est? Or are some partings so painful that they call for more human opiates than are provided by alcohol or drugs?

In the last week of August Otto Katz left for Mexico. He asked me to dinner, in a small restaurant near the Opera, shortly before he left. For the first time I met his wife, a small blonde woman with a pinched and anxious expression. At the end of the meal Katz stared across the table at me intently and said, 'During the next few years events will take many strange turns. But if you want the key to them, remember one thing – Stalin is always right.'

Thirteen years later Stalin had him hanged. As a key figure in the Czechoslovak Communist Party, Katz was caught up in one of the last of the Stalinist purges, and together with six other Ministers went to the gallows in Prague, condemned as Trotskyist deviationist and a spy.

16

War – and Phoney War

Came Friday, 1 September, and by breakfast time the agency tapes were clattering out the news that German forces were swarming across the frontiers into Poland and Danzig, and their bombers were striking at Polish towns. Widespread fighting was under way. Was France at war? The Quai d'Orsay could answer only that we must wait until the next afternoon, when Prime Minister Daladier would speak to the Chamber of Deputies. Was Britain at war? It seemed not. In the House of Commons Neville Chamberlain gave no indication that an ultimatum had been sent to Hitler. Only a warning message had been despatched. The smell of last-minute appeasement seemed to be in the air.

I got to the Chamber of Deputies only just in time to hear Daladier begin his speech. I had been held up by a phenomenon we were soon to become only too familiar with – the wartime queue. I had queued to get a gas mask from a stock made available by the Embassy for Britons living in Paris. Chief of the volunteer workers organising the distribution, in a hall near the Arc de Triomphe, was a cashier from the English bank where the *Express* kept its account. His manner at the bank counter had always verged on the obsequious. Now, dressed in the alas none too brief authority which war confers, he had great pleasure in ordering us all about.

In the lofty Chamber of the Palais de Bourbon the air

seemed even staler than usual, as deputies packed the semi-circle of seats, and journalists and visitors crammed the galleries. In this atmosphere of weary strain Daladier spoke with effective, blunt, peasant eloquence, a lock of hair falling from time to time over his wide red forehead. France, he thundered, must honour her obligations. If France allowed German aggression against Poland to go unchecked, it would earn her contempt, isolation and discredit. 'At the price of our honour we would be purchasing a precarious and revokable peace, and when the time came for us to fight, having lost the esteem of our allies and of other nations we would be a wretched people, doomed to death and enslavement.'

Powerful words, but of action there was no sign. The French Prime Minister ended his speech without any word of an ultimatum to Germany, or of a French and British declaration of war. Once the Chamber realised this, there was tumult, with deputies from the left and centre booing and hissing, and with derisive cat calls and whistles from the French press gallery. For good measure I added the whistle I had learnt for controlling sheep dogs in New Zealand. Out in the lobby Emil Buré gave his summing up. 'They are talking to the Italians, and hope to get a conference tomorrow. We will yet see a sell-out.' With Chamberlain having made a similar stalling speech in the Commons, I went to bed convinced that my prediction that war would not come to us in 1939 was well on its way to fulfilment.

For all my keen sense of history, I cannot record that I learnt in any memorable manner the next day of either the British or the French declaration of war. Exhausted by the work and strain of the recent weeks, I slept deeply, and woke late on the morning of 3 September. I was unaware of Chamberlain's broadcast when I joined Walter Kerr for coffee on the terrace of the Café Select on the Champs Elysées. Then I saw Edwin Hartrich of the *Wall Street Journal*, running up the Rue du Berri. He had a piece of agency copy in his hand. 'You're at war,

Geoffrey,' he said. 'A British ultimatum to Germany expired at eleven o'clock, without response.' I looked at my watch. It showed twenty past eleven. There was a chilling incongruity in finding oneself at war on this half-deserted boulevard in a foreign land. And though Kerr and Hartrich were my close friends, I felt suddenly a wide gap between us, the gap between those who are at war and those who are neutral.

France had also sent an ultimatum, due to expire at five that afternoon. I passed this news on to the driver of the taxi in which I was heading for our office in the Rue du Louvre. He reacted with fury, pouring out a stream of oaths and obscenities, and driving like a madman, weaving in and out of the traffic as if the Germans were already coming down the street in pursuit. 'Take it easy,' I pleaded. 'There are eighty million Germans trying to kill us now. There's no need for you to do the job for them.'

The moment of France's entry in the war passed for me even more anti-climactically. During the afternoon Alan Moorehead and I drove in his Ford V8 up to the heights of Montmartre. Alan was in Paris on leave, to take a last look over a Paris which we believed could before the night was out be reduced to a shattered smoking ruin under the attacks of the Luftwaffe. It was a grey, overcast afternoon, warm and humid, with a break in the clouds away to the east, the direction from which the bombers would come. I thought of Madrid under its bombardment, and tried to envisage these close-packed roofs, broken here and there by the lines of green from boulevard trees, and by church steeples and the dome of the Opera, being ripped apart and burning as had been the Gran Via.

Down on the Boulevard Montmartre, as we drove back to the office, the crowds were as thick as on a normal Sunday, but now their faces were tense and their steps hurried. I was studying them when Moorehead's car spluttered and stopped. There was nothing for it but for us to get out and push. We were doing this, in a stream of

Hitler taking the salute at Nuremberg parade, 1934.

Foreign Correspondents en route to the Anschluss, March 1938, in a photograph which shows the creases of the years. The author is at the far right: H.R. Knickerbocker in centre, in spectacles: Walter Kerr seated, far left.

The Czechoslovakian army on manoeuvres.

In Vienna after the Anschluss, Hitler proclaiming the incorporation of Austria into the German Reich.

Right: Princess Mara Scherbatoff in the Paris office of the *Daily Express*.

Below: View from 32 Rue de Cavaire, St Cloud.

Chamberlain and Hitler at Munich.

German troops crossing the Charles Bridge in Prague, March 1939.

Daily Express

WORLD'S LARGEST DAILY SALE

Tuesday, September 12, 1939

No. 12,265

One Penny

BLACK-OUT ZERO HOUR TO-NIGHT

Men in khaki lean from a train as it rumbles

through a village, revealing to the world—

BRITISH TROOPS IN FRANCE

French folk run to cheer the Tommies

'TOGETHER IN MAGINOT'

From GEOFFREY COX
Daily Express Staff Reporter

PARIS, Monday

IN A FRENCH VILLAGE THIS MORNING I WATCHED A LONG BRITISH TROOP TRAIN RUMBLE THROUGH. THE VILLAGERS RUSHED TO THE STATION AS A FEW WATCHERS ON THE PLATFORM SHOUTED "LES ANGLAIS!"

Infantrymen in khaki leaned from the carriages, waved cheerily and shouted to the French people. From the compartments at the end of the train officers saluted smilingly.

NO FLOWERS, BY REQUEST

No flowers may be thrown at Hitler during his visit to the front. Says an order from the "Fuehrer's headquarters," quoted in the German radio yesterday afternoon. The order added: "Flowers should be handed to the troops."

U-boat sinkings:

A row in the Nazi command

from FRANCIS DANTON

50,000 Germans killed

IT was reported last night on the high est authority that German casualties until Saturday mid day—after a week of war —— were 50,000 killed and 170,000 wounded.

WHY THE ADVANCE STOPPED

Daily Express Naval

The author's story which led to the seizure of the *Daily Express* by the police.

The author with Finnish ski troops, December 1939.

The battlefield of Soumussalmi.

Edward Ward,
BBC war
correspondent
in Finland,
1939.

George Millar,
newly
commissioned
in the Rifle
Brigade, 1940.

exceptional calibre, whom I would be able to lead if I made plain that my leadership rested not just on my position as head of the office, but on my ability. To do this the best way was to tackle a major story which remained uncovered – that of the arrival of British troops in France. All our requests for permission to go to the disembarkation areas had been refused. I decided to act without permission, and set out by car for Brittany with Eric Sevareid and Walter Kerr.

Sevareid was a tall, handsome mid-Westerner of Norwegian stock, in his late twenties, who could well have been cast for the film role of Abraham Lincoln when young. He had come to Paris a year earlier, to be a reporter on the Paris edition of the *New York Herald Tribune*, the journal of the considerable American expatriate community in France, and had been recruited for the Columbia Broadcasting System by Ed Murrow. Eric Sevareid was to come through quickly not only as one of the greatest of radio reporters, but was also one of the few in time to make the transition from radio to television news. His broadcasting skill rested on his ability to write, which not only enabled him to produce scripts of depth as well as vividness, but was also to make his book *Not So Wild a Dream* a classic of this period – and a best-seller when it was published in 1946.

On the outskirts of Cherbourg we found what we sought. In columns of threes (a formation which surprised me, as when I had done my territorial training in New Zealand eight years earlier British troops had still formed fours) a company of the Black Watch were striding up the hill from the port, their tartan kilts replaced by khaki, but their cap badges unmistakable. Down in the port Bren carriers and trucks were being swung ashore and other Tommies – the World War I word was in vogue again in the French papers – were stacking supplies on the quayside. When the port authorities discovered we were journalists, they hastily hunted us out of the place. But we had seen British fighting troops back again on French soil, and we hastened back to Paris to write our stories.

The French censor passed them, but in London the War Office banned my piece peremptorily. A few days later chance gave me another glimpse of the BEF. I had gone back to the riverside hotel where John Mulgan and I had stayed, to collect some shirts I had left there. I was standing on the station platform at Villennes when a long troop train came rumbling through. Leaning out of the vans portrayed in so many World War I photographs with their labels of '*8 chevaux ou 40 hommes*', were British Tommies, in the new battledress khaki, waving to the crowds on the roadside and singing in poignant imitation of 1914, 'It's a Long Way to Tipperary'. From a carriage at the rear two British officers saluted. The station master saluted back, tears pouring down his cheeks.

This story too I sent to London. It arrived on Christian-sen's desk at the same time as an official ruling from the War Office that British newspapers might now, after nine days of war, make public the fact that British troops had arrived in France. The other papers had no eyewitness material to add to the official statement, but Christiansen had my pieces from Cherbourg and Villennes. He made the most of them in a story which covered the whole of the front page.

This proved too much for the censors, who took the view that only the bald official communiqué should be published. The first edition presses were rolling when a police inspector, wearing a World War I DCM ribbon, and carrying a tin hat and gas mask, arrived in Fleet Street with an order for them to be halted. Chris raised hell with the War Office, who at 3 a.m. changed their minds, and let the edition go, with one excision. Any references to '*8 chevaux ou 40 hommes*' had to come out. The halting of the presses led to a furious debate in the Commons about censorship, skilfully fuelled by Christian-sen, who relished the publicity for this, the first scoop of the war.

I was able a few days later to provide him with a second one. Encouraged by the success of our Cherbourg venture, Sevareid, Kerr and I decided to make another excursion, this time towards the east, to the areas where the French and British armies were deploying. Chuck Findlay, a newsreel cameraman, came along with us, but just for the ride, as we thought the presence of his camera would be a certain way of our being turned back. We set out on a Sunday morning, expecting at the most to get no further eastward than Rheims, or perhaps Verdun.

We had no passes, other than our French police cards – those highly distinctive thin metallic cards, very aptly called *coupe file* – which could cut their way through red tape as well as the more literal white tapes with which the French police loved to bar access to areas where anything newsworthy was happening. Yet we found no difficulty at checkpoints along the way. Often we were waved on without even being stopped, perhaps because Sevareid and I, in the front seats, were both wearing brown belted raincoats which had a military look, perhaps because the Peugeot was of a near khaki colour. In any event military convoys of the time were full of requisitioned civilian cars and vans, still in their original colours. For kilometre after kilometre we passed the signs of the Allied forces deploying. Near Rheims RAF aircraftmen were setting up tents alongside a temporary airfield, with Gloster Gladiator fighters already hidden among cornstacks and barns. We drove into one village just as a bus full of RAF men arrived there. The men disembarked on the green in front of the church. Villagers pressed eagerly forward to see these men who had come to fight on their soil again. Soon they were talking to each other in broken French and English, exchanging cigarettes, and soon making their way to the small café on the corner, beyond which stretched the airfield.

Near Verdun columns of lorries carrying shining-faced Senegalese infantry bumped over the cobbled roads, along the Voie Sacrée of 1917. We still expected to be stopped, but even when we entered the clearly marked Zone Militaire around Metz, our passes were only casually scrutinised, and we were waved on. In the dusk we drove on through Thionville and out towards the frontier, our ears cocked for the sound of gunfire. Though we could not be far from the front, there was none of the crack of rifle shots which had marked even the quietest nights in Madrid, or of the staccato sound of machine-gun fire, or the flat crump of mortars, let alone the thump and thud of artillery fire. It was quiet – so quiet that at one stage we argued whether a sound we had heard had been a rifle shot, or the bark of a dog. Of the constant frontier skirmishes, let alone the raging battles featured by *Le Petit Parisien* there was no sign.

At the village of Sierck, only two kilometres from the German frontier, we finally caught up with the war. Down a lane came some thirty or forty Moroccan infantrymen, their khaki uniforms mudstained, their faces under the steel helmets weary and fringed with a dark growth of beard – the growth which brought French troops the name of *poilus*, the hairy ones. Their long bayonets were still fixed to their rifles, and behind them rolled two tanks, muddy also. It had every appearance of a fighting patrol returning from a stint in the no-man's-land between the two armies.

At the edge of the village the patrol came abreast of a column of fresh troops, with their own two tanks, waiting to take their turn on patrol. Men lay by the roadside amidst stacks of new haversacks and rifles. Some talked with a farmer and his wife at the door of their farmhouse. Others filled their waterbottles at the village well. On an order they formed up and swung forward into the growing darkness, followed by calls of '*bonne chance*' from the men who had returned.

When they had gone it was very quiet, except for the distant clanging of a church bell. Suddenly across the sound of the bell came a deep thump, thump from under the black hill which was Germany. I knew from my days in Madrid that it was the sound of artillery fire. But it died away as abruptly as it had begun. We turned round the car and made our way back to Metz.

We spent the night in an hotel there. The city was half evacuated, with little but military traffic in the streets. No one challenged our bona fides, and the next day we drove back to Paris. I was working on my story when the telephone rang, and a Frenchman, identifying himself as an official of Quai d'Orsay, told me that he knew of our trip, and warned me that we would all be expelled from France if we sent our stories. The threat was one Sevareid and Kerr could readily defy, as correspondents for the great neutral power whom the French were anxious to win over. But as a reporter for a country at war I could not afford lightly to disregard such a warning. I rang Sevareid, told him of the call, and arranged to meet him in half an hour's time outside his hotel, where we could talk without risk of being overheard. I was about to leave for this meeting when the telephone rang again. This time it was Ken Downs, head of the Hearst International News Service in Paris. He explained, with many chuckles, that the call had been a hoax. He had heard of our expedition to the front, and had set a Frenchman who worked in his office to the task of acting as the bogus official. What Downs claimed as a practical joke virtually killed my story. The delay caused by the first call meant that the story reached London in time to make only the very last and smallest edition of the paper.

Sevareid's broadcast, and Walter Kerr's story were, because of the time difference, unaffected by the delay. Yet the story had one further twist. Three days later another group of American journalists including Ken Downs followed in our tracks. By one of the quirks of fate, their exploit caught the attention of *Time* magazine in a way ours had not, and they were acclaimed as daring defiers of red tape, and as the first journalists to visit the Western Front. But it was Kerr's report which was to prove the most durable. He commented that this looked like being 'a pretty phoney type of war' – a phrase which was to pass into history.

The French authorities were infuriated by our stories, both because these showed how lax were their controls behind the lines, and how inactive were their forces on the front. They were unwilling to act against the Americans, but as a correspondent from a co-belligerent I was more vulnerable. I was berated by an army officer in the censor's department, and told that no official credentials to cover the front would be extended to me. The British Embassy also made a fuss, so Christiansen decided to move me to Brussels, and there I went late in September.

Neutral Belgium was drenched in highly effective German propaganda, including dramatic newsreel material showing the swift – and by now completed – blitzkrieg against Poland. Shot on 16mm film, using the lightweight Arriflex cameras which were still in use when we set up ITN fifteen years later, and obtained by daring cameramen up with the foremost troops (twenty-three of them were killed or wounded covering the Polish campaign) it was a revelation of the power of the moving picture. British propaganda was by comparison feeble, concentrating not on proving that we were winning – which was what the neutrals wanted to know – but on why we should win, because of the virtue of our democracy. Helped by Maurice Fast, a Brussels newspaper editor who was the *Daily Express* local correspondent, I wrote an article which began 'One German army has already invaded Belgium, an army of propagandists and they are achieving victories because they have the field almost entirely to themselves.' It seemed to have impressed Lord Reith, then Minister of Information, because he called me in when I at last got back to London, and questioned me at length in his room at the top of the University of London building in Bloomsbury.

From Belgium I went on to Holland, which throughout the rest of the autumn was to be the most newsworthy part of Western Europe. Holland provided the first major spy story of the war. On 8 November two leading members of the British Secret Service, Major H. R. Stevens and Captain S. Payne Best, were lured by the Germans to Venlo on the Dutch border, seized there, and taken off to Berlin to be interrogated and imprisoned. It was a coup which smashed the British Intelligence network in Western Europe. The Venlo frontier post was ideally suited for such a kidnapping. It was on a stretch of open heathland, with about five hundred yards separating the Dutch and German frontier posts. The only building on the road between the two was a restaurant and café, still formally on Dutch soil. It was here that the two British agents had agreed to meet what they thought were dissident SS and army officers prepared to mount a putsch against Hitler. It had been a matter only of a few minutes for the waiting Gestapo, once they had seen the two Britons arrive at the café, to raise the frontier barrier and send a truck full of soldiers to surround the building, make the arrests, and rush their captives back into Germany. The Dutch authorities, in their post two hundred yards to the west, had no time in which to react, even if they had been prepared to risk a border incident by doing so.

Two days later, when I visited the café to talk to the waitress who had witnessed the kidnapping, the place seemed very exposed, and I had a wary eye on the nearby German frontier guards throughout the interview. They left us alone, but another British correspondent had a narrow escape. German troops did surround the café whilst Ralph Izzard of the *Daily Mail* and a Dutch journalist were there. Izzard hid in the lavatory, ready to drop his British passport down the pan should he be found. But the Dutch waitress insisted to the Germans so vehemently that only one man, the Dutch journalist, was on the premises that they left without a full search.

The main and continuing story from Holland throughout that autumn, and into January, was the possibility of a German invasion. The Dutch plan to deal with this was to open key dykes and river locks, to form a series of water lines, flooded areas two or three miles wide, which would form huge moats, barring the way to German tanks and lorries and guns. It was a costly scheme, for it involved flooding valuable farming land, and the Dutch were not anxious to give the signal for it until danger seemed to be genuinely imminent. Yet on a number of occasions in November they were on the point of doing so, as information reached them from their agents in Germany of signs that Hitler was preparing to move against Holland.

From Amsterdam and the Hague we reported these fears, and the Dutch state of readiness, and we frequently drove out towards the German frontier to check for any signs of the water lines being flooded. Most military experts in Britain and France could not believe that Hitler would do anything so rash as to attack at a time of the year when bad weather could impede not only his troops on the ground, but above all the Luftwaffe, which had shown itself so deadly against Poland. We were in consequence accused of scaremongering and exaggeration. I felt confident of what I was writing, however, because my information came chiefly from the head of the Dutch Military Intelligence in the Hague, who adopted an unusual policy for a military man, that of trying to tell the press all that he could, within reasonable bounds of security.

The German archives captured at the end of the war have revealed that Hitler not only did plan an invasion, at first of Holland, and then, under a later scheme, of Holland and Belgium, but issued specific dates on which Operation Yellow, as it was code-named, was to begin. It was set first for 25 November. This was later brought forward to 12 November, and cancelled only after a furious row between Hitler and the Commander-in-Chief of the Reichswehr, General Brauchitsch. During December four more dates were set, but each had to be cancelled because of the terrible conditions of snow, ice and fog which settled over Western Europe. Even so, when fine weather brought clear blue skies in the New Year, 17 January was set as a new D-Day for an attack which was to be launched against both Holland and Belgium. This was cancelled only after an extraordinary stroke of fortune. At Mechelen, just across the Belgian frontier from Aachen, a light plane carrying two Luftwaffe majors to a conference lost its way in mist, and crashed. The majors had with them detailed plans for the invasion, part of which they were able to destroy, but part of which safely reached Belgian Intelligence. Fearing that all surprise had been lost, Hitler hesitated, and then, as the weather closed in again, abandoned the attack until the spring.

In one story about developments in the Luftwaffe, I went direct to the source – in Germany itself. Towards the end of November rumours spread that Professor Messerschmitt, designer of the fighter aircraft which were, in the Battle of Britain, to become as well known as Hurricanes and Spitfires, had fled the Reich and taken refuge in Holland. The French and. American papers made such play with these that Radio Berlin was driven to issue a formal denial, and added, 'Those who disbelieve our report can telephone the Professor at his Augsburg works.'

This seemed to me an invitation which should be taken up, so I placed a call from Amsterdam to the Professor, allowing myself the gloss of saying that it was 'from a journalist in Amsterdam'. To my astonishment I was put through immediately to his office. 'Hier Messerschmitt in Augsburg', stated his brisk voice. After he had denied the rumours of his defection, I put to him a query about the Me109. In the few aerial encounters which had taken place along the Western Front, the French had claimed to have destroyed several of these. 'Is it not true,' I asked, 'that the French have shot down a number of Me109s, and that they are not manoeuvrable enough?'

'I have heard rumours like that, but I have other information on the subject,' was his dry response. But when I pressed on with further questions about his new plane, the Me110, either he, or some security check, became suspicious, and I was cut off with an abrupt '*Gute Nacht*'. It cannot be said to have been a very productive interview, but *Time* magazine liked it, and gave me a chuckling pat on the back for the manner of my getting it.

17

Real War in Finland

Holland proved to be a stepping stone for me to another war – and very much a shooting war. The Dutch airline KLM still maintained a service to Scandinavia, its new DC3 airliners – the first civilian version of the Dakota – flying across the North Sea, parallel to the German coast, to Copenhagen. When therefore at the end of November the Soviet Union began to issue threats against the Finns, it was logical for the *Daily Express* to move me from Amsterdam to Helsinki, to cover what looked to be a brief war of nerves, in which tiny Finland would surely yield without a struggle to their giant of a neighbour.

That Amsterdam-Copenhagen flight, which I was to make four times in the next three months, was a strain, for it would have been very easy for the Germans to have sent up fighters to intercept the KLM plane and divert it to a German airport. I was thankful when, on 29 November, I saw the flat coast of Denmark moving towards us, under the wings of the Douglas. I had no wish to spend the war in a German internment camp.

The Russians had already drawn the Baltic states of Estonia, Latvia and Lithuania into their orbit through a series of mutual assistance pacts negotiated after they had overrun their share of Poland. Their demands on Finland were stringent, involving a rolling back of the Finnish frontier for some thirty miles to protect approaches to Leningrad, the leasing by the Russians of the Finnish naval base of Hango, and of the ice-free port of Petsamo in the north. The Finns refused, but did not break off negotiations. To their astonishment, and to that of the outside world, Stalin did not continue the negotiations. Instead on 30 November he launched the Red Army and the Red Air Force against Finland, and set up a puppet government under a Finnish exile, Otto Kuusinen, who had long been resident in Moscow, where he had been General Secretary of the Comintern. The Russian view was simple. Khruschev, who was present when Stalin took the final decision, set it out in his memoirs. 'All we had to do was raise our voice a little bit, and the Finns would obey. If that did not work, we could fire one shot and the Finns would put their hands up and surrender – or so we thought.'[1]

Stalin's one shot took the form of an all-out invasion of Finland. When I reached Helsinki on the evening of 30 November the red glow of burning buildings glowered against the thick darkness of the Arctic night. Black clouds of smoke were shot through by sudden spurts of red which could only have come from some great fire. They came, I was to learn, from the Technical High School and two nearby apartment buildings which had been hit by high explosive and incendiary bombs that afternoon, in raids which, the Finns claimed, killed 61 people and wounded 120.

These raids had been launched by the Soviet Union without warning, and without any ultimatum having been issued to the Finns. They were attacks on the capital city of a country with which Russia was still formally at peace. No last-minute chance had been given to the Finnish Government to yield to the Soviet demands, if they knew that the alternative was war. Even when, on the night of 30 November, the Finns made a further bid for the reopening of talks, the Russians would not listen. The Soviet Government's reply, sent through the Swedes on 2

[1] *Khruschev Remembers*, André Deutsch, 1971.

December, was that it recognised only the 'People's Front' Government of Otto Kuusinen as the true government of Finland. Not even Hitler, in his onslaught on Poland, had shown such a degree of callous cynicism.

The political as well as the military implications of this attack came home to me vividly when, on my second day in Finland, after a further nine Soviet bombers had attacked the centre of Helsinki, I tracked down the wreckage of one bomber which had been shot down by Finnish anti-aircraft guns. In a patch of pines on the western suburbs of the city the smashed remains of a two-engined medium bomber were on fire. The tail section, with the letters 'S.B.' and a huge dull red Soviet star, lay against a tree. Near by was a bloody, tangled mess which had been the pilot's head, and his khaki-clad torso. His hands were tightly clenched. I noticed they were surprisingly small. His uniform was the same drab khaki I had seen worn by the tank crews at the Hill of the Angels before Madrid, those grave-faced young men who had stood then as the defenders of a democracy, and of a small nation battling against the power of Hitler and Mussolini. These same red stars had been on the snub-nosed Soviet fighter planes I had seen swoop across the roofs of Madrid, cheered as deliverers by the people in the battered streets. This was the air force which only a little over a year earlier had seemed to us in Prague one reassuring final guard against a Nazi invasion. Now this boy had been sent to his death hurling bombs against a small people defending its own freedom.

The Finns had built a defensive line across the narrow strip of territory, south of the huge Lake Ladoga, which provided the main route from the Soviet Union into southern Finland. It had been given the name of the Mannerheim Line, after Field Marshal Mannerheim, who had led Finland in its struggles against the Bolsheviks in 1918–21, and had been recalled to take command in this war. True to the prevalent military theory of the time, we assumed that this line, like the Maginot Line in France, would be virtually impregnable to direct attack by any but overwhelming forces. This view seemed to be borne out by the events of the opening weeks of what came to be called The Winter War. The Russians launched massive attacks of infantry supported by tanks and guns against the Mannerheim Line, and were repulsed.

Other attacks launched in the heavily forested country north of Lake Ladoga, on all the seven main roads leading westwards from their frontier, were equally frustrated. So too was an attack from Murmansk towards Petsamo, in the very north. All these attacks were halted by fierce resistance by the highly trained and determined Finnish Army. In several instances Soviet formations, unable to move off the narrow, tree-lined and snow-bound forest roads, were cut off and annihilated. In the intense cold, the dead were frozen where they fell, sprawling or lying like waxworks in a staged spectacle of warfare. Photographs of these scenes were to provide a powerful visual impression of a Russian defeat, an impression which, as the weeks went by, was to give rise in Britain and France for demands not merely for assistance to the Finns, but for a declaration of war against the Soviet Union.

I was the first correspondent from Britain or America to witness these forest battle scenes. I did so by adopting the methods we had employed in France; that of not waiting for official permission, but instead of moving directly towards the front, of marching towards the sound of gunfire. The Finns had from the outset clamped strict controls on all foreign journalists. They would at first allow none of us to visit the front. When they relented, it was to allow only four agency reporters to make a one-day visit to the area behind the Mannerheim Line. The rest of us had to subsist on a diet of stale communiqués, or on what gossip we could pick up in the gloomy hall of the Hotel Kamp in Helsinki.

After a few days of this I decided to try the fronts further north. I teamed up with a Swedish woman correspondent, Babro Alving, who had been in Madrid during the siege. Without informing the Press Office in Helsinki and armed only with a letter of credentials from the Finnish Foreign Office, Babro Alving and I and a Finnish girl interpreter took the train north from Helsinki. Fuelled only by wood, the train moved northwards with excruciating slowness. After a journey of a full day and night, we reached Oulu, where – so a young officer travelling on the train had told us – there was a military base. The general in command was a sensible man. Instead of making a fuss about red tape, he had us escorted to the front in the forests of Kuhmo. Only patrol activity was in progress, but we had our first sight of the ski troops, moving almost invisibly in their white snow capes in the half light of the few brief daylight hours.

It was at Kemijarvi, further north, just above the Arctic Circle, that we encountered the first of the astonishing battle scenes of this war in the frozen snow. A Russian column of some six thousand men and twenty tanks had thrust across the narrow waist of this part of Finland, aiming for the top of the Gulf of Bothnia, hoping to cut Finland in two. They were met by Finnish troops under a tough, seasoned commander, General Wallenius. A former Chief of the Finnish General Staff, he had turned politician, and had tried to mount a military coup in 1932. Virtually exiled, he had worked as a war correspondent in Spain, and had reported the Nazi invasion of Poland. Recalled now to the army, he had been given command – though in his early sixties – of this crucial northern front. Half way across the country, on the frozen River Kemi, the Russians were stopped and then counter-attacked on the narrow, snow-covered roadway where they had halted for the night. Within a few hours half the Soviet force had been destroyed. The rest retreated.

It was just beyond the village of Kemijarvi, where the open fields suddenly narrowed down to one road edged with pines, that we found the first twisted corpses. Scattered in the ditches, or on the road itself, they were a ghastly trail that led us to the low cliff above the River

Kemi. Here the fight had been around a group of farm buildings. The log walls were shattered like the skeletons, where shells had smashed through. Horses, smashed wagons, and more dead lay twisted beside the road. The horses, their coarse blood spilled upon the snow, seemed almost more tragic than the men. They had certainly had no hand in this ghastly business, yet here they lay.

On the ice-covered river itself a lorry stood where the Russians had left it, right in mid-stream. Beside it lay the bodies of two men. Farther off, half-way to the shelter of the pines on the bank, was another crumpled figure, killed by some Finnish sniper's bullet as he ran. We drove on across the ice to the narrow entry of the Salla road that dropped, still and white, to the edge of the river.

The ruins of the column lay three-quarters of a mile farther on. We scraped past another great van, loaded with more bodies of the Finnish dead, being gathered up to take home to their families. For in Finland till the end all dead were sent home for burial. Then ahead I saw a line of what looked like junk cars drawn up in some empty allotment on the edge of a city. At the head was a staff car; behind it three tanks; then lorries, some straight on the road, others swung into the ditches.

Still gripping the wheel of the staff car was the driver, his forehead smashed by a bullet. Alongside lay the body of a Russian officer – the first of the dead who were strewn everywhere. How strange were these bodies, on this road where it was already so cold that if I took my glove off to write I could keep my hand in the air only a minute. The cold had frozen them into the positions in which they fell. It had, too, slightly shrunken their bodies and features, giving them an artificial, waxen appearance. The whole road was like some huge waxwork representation of a battle scene, carefully staged. Even the dark brown-red stain that was spilt on uniforms and on the snow was paint rather than blood. Dead that I had seen in Spain had usually been slumped, shapeless bundles of clothes and flesh, that still had about them the horror of decay as well as death. But this scene here struck in me, I found, no horror. It was hard to believe that these figures had ever been men. Yet men lay with hand grenades in their hands, poised to throw; one man leant against a wagon wheel with a length of wire still in his hands; another was fitting a clip of cartridges into a rifle. Until you got right up to him you could not tell that he was not still living. Others had spun into ditches, and fell there, still giving an impression of movement. It was this incredible effect of the cold which gave the Finnish battlefields their fake appearance, for the very action seemed to be frozen into stillness. It was as if in one moment of the battle time had suddenly stopped on this road near Kemi, halting the scene for all time.

There was a line of thirty-eight trucks, all Fords made in Russia, with hinged sides. The tyres, with chains on one rear wheel, looked of poor-quality rubber. They lay amid the spilled gear, the endless gear of war. Gas masks, telephone wires, machine-gun belts, sausages tied together like ropes, a spilled barrel of frozen fish, a pile of old leather shoes, a poster of a girl advertising a Red Cross fund, two curved swords, and amidst this, the dead, like so much more gear. Here a shattered arm; there a leg covered with snow. Wooden boxes that had held ammunition lay everywhere; horses, their guts smashed and open, artificially pink, lay under the high wooden arch of the sledges.

The Russians had apparently cleaned out anything left by the Finns in evacuated houses along the way. I saw an ancient sewing machine, a butter churn, even a bundle of silk stockings, two silver teapots and some girls' underclothes – the rather pathetic looting of men who have few consumer goods in their lives. Some of the Russian dead wore steel helmets; some peaked caps. They all had heelless felt boots, which are wonderfully warm when the snow is dry, but hopeless if it is wet. Some had overcoats that were adequately thick; others had thin coats, and I saw that their padded uniforms were rotted. Few looked adequately clothed for this terrible temperature.

You could follow the course of the battle as you walked from man to man. Here three men had spun and fallen as they charged for a machine-gun pit; there the horses were piled in one great hillock of flesh where they had been mown down, farther on half a dozen lorries were half turned, as their drivers had tried to get them round and move off. Other lorries were on their side. And everywhere I turned back from the material to the men. Russian dead lying face down, as if weeping, in the snow; curled on their backs, eyes closed, as if asleep; clutching stomachs, sides, heads; gripping the sides of lorries; stumbling forward, gun in hand; running back, gun thrown away; everywhere the dead. In one place two men, Russian and Finn, lay frozen together in their final death struggle. Over most of the bodies frost and light snow had already put a faint hoary coating.

The Finns were easy to distinguish. They all had white snow clothes over their grey uniforms, and their boots were of new, yellow leather. Every man's face had been covered by his comrades with a piece of cloth or a fir branch. I drew away the branch from the face of one man, huge in his grey uniform. It was the typical Finnish peasant face, rounded, with almost slit eyes and strong, curving sweep of jaw. In his death he looked very young – just in his twenties. I had seen enough of this uniform now, in my three weeks in Finland, to realise what this death was going to mean when word of it got back to some red-painted peasant shack in the forests of the south.

And the Russians? I went from body to body, staring at the faces of these men fallen here, in their peaked Soviet caps with the dull red star on their front. The faces underneath were Oriental, simple, a little brutish, those of peasants from southern Russia. One man, a huge fair figure, had completely Mongoloid features; another the dark, sharp look of a Tartar. But the mass had the broad nose, narrow forehead and wide dark eyes of the peasant.

I tried to think of what this slaughter would mean to their families and lovers in the collective farms and the dusty peasant villages from which they had come. But, though I had visited Russia, I found this difficult, for these people and their lives were, I realised, strange to me. Then, fallen across the body of a dead horse, I saw one man who brought it home to me abruptly. He clutched still in his hand a doll and two pairs of children's black gym shoes, and a child's frock. He had clearly picked them up from a Finnish peasant's house. The man was young. You could see how carefully he had gathered these things, thinking of the day when he would be able to go back to his home, and his daughter would run out to meet him, and he would give her this doll, and these precious clothes. Now here he lay, outstretched on this forest road in Finland, beside a horse with its entrails scattered in the snow.

The sun was already almost gone, and the sky behind the pines was a brilliant, lovely yellow that made the scene more fantastic than ever. Through the small pine trees on either side of the road patrols moved looking for survivors. A band of peasants were piling saddles, rifles and other gear together, and carrying corpses to the huge yellow wagon that had returned for yet another load.

In his nearby headquarters General Wallenius readily explained to me, in German, the course of the battle. A stocky man with greying hair, a deeply lined face, small blue eyes, a scarred nose and curiously bony handshake, he responded with remarkable frankness to my queries about his methods and his tactics. This may have resulted from his belief, which I was never able to shake, that I was not just a reporter, but a British officer in disguise. At times, in an effort to catch me out, he would suddenly address me as '*Herr Hauptmann*', and then chuckle loudly with disbelief when I would disavow the title. 'Now, now, *Herr Hauptmann*,' he would say. 'You British are our friends. It is good that the British Army should learn all about us.'

The *Express* made the most of my story from Kemi-jarvi, and within a few days many of the correspondents in Helsinki had made their way northwards to Rovaniemi. Amongst them was Edward Ward, the first BBC reporter I had encountered on a news story. Ward, who in time was to inherit the title of Viscount Bangor, was to pioneer with skill and success the new art of on-the-spot radio reporting. He had an easy, relaxed style, an eye for significant detail, and a command of clear and often vivid English. He sensibly decided to concentrate on providing eyewitness material of the scenes of battle, leaving the day-to-day progress of the war to be dealt with by the agencies. He faced formidable practical difficulties. He had no recording gear and his talks had to be delivered live from the nearest radio station.

At Rovaniemi we lived in considerable comfort in a modern two-storied hotel, the Pojanhovi, half of which had been turned into a military hospital. Rovaniemi was almost exactly on the Arctic Circle, a fact which enabled me to use a phrase which had been on the tip of my tongue ever since I got to Finland, 'It is reported in Arctic circles'. The only discomfort we endured was when we were from time to time hustled out of the hotel, into an eighteen foot deep trench in the grounds which served as an air raid shelter, and which proved necessary when Russian planes ultimately raided and damaged the town. From Rovaniemi the foreign press, now numbering a score or more, were taken on long bus or car drives to the widely scattered forest battle fronts. On one of these, at Suomussalmi, the Finns repeated the Kemijarvi victory on an even larger scale. Two Russian divisions, the 163rd and the 44th, were almost completely wiped out by Finnish ski troops, moving like shadows in the forests. The scenes at Suomussalmi, much photographed and much written about, brought home most vividly to the outside world the extent of the Russian defeat in the north. There was one significant difference from the scenes I had witnessed at Kemijarvi. There the Finnish dead had been still on the battlefield. At Suomussalmi they had all been removed before the press arrived. Only the Russians, in their peaked caps and thin uniforms, frozen in the lifelike or terrible contortions of sudden death, appeared on the pages of the newspapers and on the cinema screens of the outside world.

Rovaniemi was a small town, not much more than a village, almost entirely of single-storied wooden buildings. Even its sauna was no more than a hut in which an aged peasant woman poured water on to hot stones, and where the only way of taking a cold plunge was to leap into the snowdrifts outside. This smallness brought the advantage that in the weeks we were based in Rovaniemi we were able to meet and get some idea of the attitude of ordinary Finnish people caught up in this struggle. Since many of them spoke German, language was not an impenetrable barrier. This experience left met in no doubt that the Finnish people fought this war with unity and a deep-rooted patriotism. I felt this particularly strongly one day when I climbed to the top of the two hundred-foot wooden ski jump, which stood like some strange mechanical toy on the edge of a wood four miles from the town. A seventeen-year-old girl, her cheeks flushed with the wind, her fair hair thrust under a grey fur hat, stood wrapped in a great Robinson Crusoe goatskin coat. A refugee from the frontier city of Viipuri, she did eight hours' plane spotting a day, two hours on, two hours off, warming up in a hut at the foot of the structure. The top platform swayed in an icy, whistling wind which felt as if a fully grown man were tugging at your sleeve. A four-teen-year-old boy with a rifle stood by her, the only protection against a machine-gunning Soviet plane. Yet the two of them laughed and joked with the guide who was with us, and shouted a cheerful 'Huyva paivaa' – 'Good-bye' – to us as we climbed down. I was to think often of that pair when later pro-Soviet propagandists

assured me that the Russian army came to Finland as
liberators of an oppressed people.

*

Early in February I returned to England for a spell of
leave from what seemed likely to be a long war, with the
Russians halted at the Mannerheim Line and blocked in
the northern forests. I was astonished to find in Britain a
considerable degree of acceptance of the Soviet case that
the Red Army was intervening to rescue the Finnish
people from an oppressive, white Fascist Government. In
the train up from Dover a well-dressed man, learning that
I had just come from Finland, assured me knowingly that
he was not taken in by all this anti-Russian propaganda
being written from Helsinki. Letter writers to *Picture
Post* took the same view. A. J. Cummings, much cultivated by Maisky, the astute Soviet Ambassador in
London, lent his influential pen to throw doubts on the
bona fides of the Finnish Government. D. N. Pritt went
off to Finland to write a Penguin special strongly slanted
against the Finns.

    Left-wing friends sought me out, some to berate me for
what they saw as deliberate anti-Soviet bias, others – who
had made, or were about to make – a break with
Communism, to question me about what I had seen and
experienced. For many British Communists, and particularly many fellow travellers, the invasion of Finland was a
final blow to a faith which had become interwoven with
every aspect of their lives, in which not only beliefs but
friendships, contacts, even jobs were put at risk by their
change of mind. Other people, more to the right, wanted
to probe my views about the chances of continued Finnish
resistance once the snows melted, and General Winter,
the Finns' best (and only) ally, was no longer in the battle.
The Finnish defensive victories had encouraged a number
of politicians and military writers, particularly in France,

to develop what was surely the maddest of all the strategic
ideas which were to emerge in World War II – that France
and Britain should use the war in Finland as an excuse to
attack the Soviet Union, widening the struggle into one
not only against Hitler but against Stalin. Since we had
stalemate in the West, this argument ran, and since
neither the Maginot Line nor the Siegfried Line could be
breached, we should hit at Germany through the Soviet
oilfields of Baku. By capturing them, and moving on to
capture the Rumanian oil fields as well, we would then
cut off Hitler's oil supplies and bring Germany to her
knees.

This rested on one key assumption – that the Russian
defeats in Finland showed that the Red Army was rotten
through and through, its officer corps ruined by Stalin's
purges, and that therefore it could not withstand attack
from France and Britain. This seemed to me a very
dubious deduction, given the degree to which the excep-
tionally hard and early winter had aided the Finns, and I
threw my weight against any such idea of extending the
war wherever I could. The most we could do for Finland
– and this was a position I did support – was to help the
Finns secure a stalemate, and so protect their independence, by supplying them with the fighter aircraft, field
and anti-tank guns and ammunition which, we were
assured, both Britain and France now possessed in
abundance.

Even that policy depended, however, on the assumption that the Mannerheim Line, like the Maginot and
Siegfried Lines, could withstand direct attack. By the time
I returned to Finland late in February, this faith in
prepared positions, so deeply rooted in the military theories of the thirties, was being overthrown by events.
Frustrated in the forests in the north, the Red Army had
opted for a massive onslaught on the Mannerheim Line,
an onslaught which was to go on continually for forty-six
days. They ultimately smashed their way through the

Line, but the decisive move was a daring flanking movement in which armoured formations were sent across the frozen waters of the Gulf of Viipuri, and seized positions on the shoreline to the rear of the main Finnish line. The Finns had to sue for peace – and to buy it by conceding all Stalin's demands. At eleven on the morning of 13 March the fighting stopped.

The Finns, with their difficult language, their reticence and their pride, are not an easy people to get to know. Yet they showed in those three months of the Winter War that even when the odds seem to be stacked adamantly against you, it pays to fight. Their resistance between November 1939 and March 1940 cost them 27,000 dead – a high figure for a country which, with its two million people, was no bigger than New Zealand. They had not only bared their teeth but sunk them in so fiercely that the Soviet Union took care not to try any offensives against them when, in 1941, the Finnish Government sought the recapture of its lost territories by coming into the war on Germany's side. When Germany lost that war, the Finns could have faced a terrible retribution from the Russians. That nothing of the kind was exacted – except in terms of draconic reparations – must owe much to the reluctance of the Soviet High Command to get caught up in any more military operations in such terrain, and against such people.

It was not, of course, only their freedom as a nation which the Finns had protected in the fierce fighting in those bitter snows. It was their freedom as individuals, a freedom which today may have some limitations on it, but which is incomparably greater than that of any other people within the aegis of the Soviet Union.

When I left Finland in mid-March to return to Britain, Giles Romilly took over the Scandinavian coverage from me. He and his younger brother Esmond were celebrated figures of their time. Nephews of Winston Churchill, cousins of the Mitfords, they had, as schoolboys, started an anti-war, anti-Establishment magazine called *Out of*

Bounds. Both had enlisted in the International Brigade, and had fought in battles around Madrid. That war over, Esmond had married Jessica Mitford and gone to the United States. Giles had joined the *Daily Express*. We had worked together during the final stage of the Finnish war in an easy partnership. He had a Churchillian courage and gaiety and forthrightness. His courage was indeed to prove his undoing. A month later, when the Germans invaded Norway, he was in Narvik, in the far north of the country. The Germans had sent marines into Narvik in advance, hidden in the hold of a merchant ship. When these stormed ashore to seize the town, the porter at the hotel where Romilly was staying woke him and told him there was just time to get to the Swedish frontier, a mile away, before the Germans reached it. Romilly was half way to the border when he realised that he had left his overcoat behind in the hotel. 'I thought,' he told me after the war, 'why the hell should the Germans have that good woollen overcoat of mine? So I went back to the hotel, got the coat and was just walking out through the front entrance when a squad of marines arrived and arrested me.'

As Churchill's nephew, Romilly was deemed by the Germans to be a prize catch. He was imprisoned for much of the war in Colditz. When I saw him again in 1945 he looked much older, and battered – though the Germans had not used force against him. The loss of those years, made the harder because he felt he had contributed to his own capture, drained some of the vitality out of him, and he died when still in his early thirties.

When I arrived back in England in mid-March, President Roosevelt's Assistant Secretary for State, Mr Sumner Welles, was touring Europe exploring the possibility of a negotiated peace. Beaverbrook was taken with the idea, and invited me to a dinner at Stornaway House, at which the Welles tour was the main topic under discussion. It was not the only bid for peace which had interested Beaverbrook since war broke out. He had given some encouragement to the Clydeside ILP leaders, James Maxton and John McGovern, and to the Labour MP Richard Stokes, in campaigns they had mounted for peace by negotiation. Indeed McGovern even declared that Beaverbrook had offered them £500 to fight a by-election on the issue – a claim which Churchill had in 1941 to deny on behalf of Beaverbrook, who was by then Minister of Production.

The guest list of the dinner at Stornaway House in mid-March survives amongst Beaverbrook's papers. It was:

> Mr Christiansen
> The Duchess of Westminster
> Mr McCloughly (a Canadian businessman)
> Mr and Mrs Frank Owen
> Mr Cox

We wore dinner jackets, with the stiff shirts of the time, a practice still usual in many homes and restaurants, war or no war, in London's West End. After the meal, as we sat over coffee and port at the dinner table, Beaverbrook canvassed our views on the Sumner Welles mission. He posed the question in his own probing way. 'Are you for peace?' he asked his neighbour, and then went round the table asking each of us in turn. Most echoed our host's manifest preference for negotiation. But when he came to where Frank Owen and I sat he said, 'I'm not going to ask you. I know your views. You are both for war.'

Beaverbrook's appointments diary for that day gives not only the names of his dinner guests, but of the man with whom he lunched – Maisky, the Russian Ambassador. He is not likely to have got much encouragement from Maisky for a negotiated peace, for the last thing the Soviet Union wanted at this stage was for Germany to make peace in the west, and be free to turn east.

Hitler, in any event, soon demonstrated his reaction to talks about such negotiations. On 9 April, only a few days after Neville Chamberlain had assured a Conservative rally that Hitler 'had missed the bus', German forces invaded Norway and Denmark. I learnt this news in the Buckinghamshire countryside, near Princes Risborough, where Cecily had leased a house. In an upper room there, with a view stretching away from the Chilterns, where the white Whiteleaf Cross, cut into the chalk, was now covered with turf to lessen its value as a marker to German aircraft, I set about writing a book on the Winter War in Finland. I was determined to get on the record events as I had seen them, and probed them. This I did, though I finally had to complete the work in the barrack room of an Officer Cadet Training Unit in Droitwich six months later. It was published by Victor Gollancz in May 1941, was well reviewed and sold all that were printed in those days of paper rationing. I had sought another publisher, to be free of the propagandist stamp associated with Gollancz, but those to whom I submitted it rejected it, some in terms which made it plain that I was up against the network of fellow travellers within the publishing world, who were not going to bring into the bookshops a book recording this deed by the Soviet Union. A similar attitude within the New York publishing world could account for the fact that it was not published there. Gollancz had, however, now broken decisively with the Communist and fellow-travelling Left, particularly once they opposed the war against Hitler, and willingly devoted a considerable part of his quota of scarce paper to *The Red Army Moves* – not an ideal title, but the best we could devise to give the book timeliness in the swiftly changing pattern of events.

I had completed only the first couple of chapters when the Germans launched their invasion of Norway and Denmark. Christiansen recalled me to London, and asked me to go to Norway as the *Express* war correspondent – the proposal which triggered off our discussion about Beaverbrook's memorandum in 1938. I had long been clear in my mind that I would not become a war correspondent in my own country's war. In other people's war, the correspondent role was undoubtedly journalistic. Your task was to discover and tell the truth about what was happening. In your own country's war, your task was bound to be largely that of the propagandist, writing material which should sustain and encourage the war effort. You could still execute, to a considerable degree, the role of instant historian, by careful observation and clear portrayal of the scene and atmosphere of battle – a role which Alan Moorehead was to fulfil superbly, as were, in the new field of radio, men like Eddie Ward, Richard Dimbleby, and Robert Reid. But at the end of the day what you wrote or said had to be subordinated to the more immediate task of winning the war. This was a perfectly reputable role and one which, God knows, was to involve war correspondents in much danger. But it was not one I wanted to execute.

There were deeper reasons, too. In my reporting throughout the past four years there had been the message, implicit or explicit, that we should stand up to Hitler. Now that we were doing so, it seemed to me only right that I should carry my share of that task, that now that war was here I should fight in it, not just write about it. The time had come to fulfil the pledge I had made to myself on that September day in Prague. Perhaps, indeed, it was even simpler than that. Perhaps I just wanted to be able to look in the eye those veterans beside whom we had paraded, as school cadets, on Anzac Day in Invercargill.

I could not set all this out to Christiansen. Nor was it a simple matter, in that early spring of 1940, to become a soldier. New Zealanders in Britain who had volunteered at the outbreak of war had been formed into an anti-tank battalion, which was already completing its training on Salisbury Plain, and had no scope for new recruits. For the British army, I was told to wait until my time for call-up came, which – since I was now thirty years old – might not be until much later in the war. Nor did those of my friends who had joined the British army seem to have

fulfilling tasks. John Mulgan, commissioned into the
Oxford and Bucks Light Infantry, was guarding arms
dumps in Northern Ireland. Dan Davin, a private in the
Warwickshires, was in a training camp on Salisbury Plain.
Bill Williams had had the best break. He was in an
armoured car regiment with a prospect of action – if any
came. In these circumstances I accepted, as the best
interim alternative, Christiansen's decision to send me to
Brussels, even though he – and I – both saw it was
banishment to an apparent backwater.

Belgium on the Eve

Beyond the frontier bridge on the road to Aachen the jagged concrete teeth of the anti-tank barriers of the Siegfried Line curved away like the Great Wall of China across the swelling, smiling, green slopes to the north and into the depths of a wood to the south, white dragon's teeth of a modern sowing. Behind them, scarped white amidst the golden clay, were the turrets and loopholes of strong points. One, built beside a cottage, covered the road and the bridge.

With a Belgian frontier guard I walked down to the stone barricade which the Belgians had put across the road just this side of the border. A German sentry in grey-green uniform and cowled steel helmet walked to his edge of the bridge and stared at me. From a window of the German Customs Station an official photographed me. Out of the other windows leant young soldiers off guard, brown-skinned, laughing boys. Their voices and laughter rang in the still air of this April evening. Someone was playing an accordion. The Aachen tram clanged to its terminus by the bridge and a group of Belgians; girls and men, passed into the German Customs House, had their passports stamped, and came on towards Belgium. Two of them laughed back to shouts from the soldiers, who, stripped to the waist, called to them from the windows overlooking the road along which, three weeks later, the German tank columns were to roar into Belgium. When later in the Western Desert and in Italy I was to hear the refrain of 'Lili Marlene' from the Soldatensender in Belgrade, with its evocation of the scene 'underneath the lantern, by the barracks gate', this moment of early spring 1940 by the Aachen bridge would recur to my mind.

In a field only a few kilometres back the young grass was still scarred and rutted where the small plane carrying the two Luftwaffe majors had crashed in fog on the morning of 9 January. Scorched stems of bushes showed where they had tried to burn the documents they carried, detailing the German plan to invade Holland, Belgium and France. Enough of their papers had fallen intact into the hands of the Belgians to set their forces, and those of the French and British on the alert. The Allied armies in Northern France closed up to the Belgian frontier, ready to counter-attack. When German reconnaissance planes appeared overhead, photographing these movements, it was widely assumed that the crash had been a fake, skilfully organised to force the Allies to show their hands. I recorded in my notes at the time that it was probably 'a beautifully organised plant'.

Brussels, into which I had flown the day before, was garishly but attractively bright after the drab, blacked-out streets of London, Paris and Helsinki. On the Place de Brouchère, outside the Metropole Hotel, yellow letters twenty feet high burned in the darkness, calling upon Brussels to buy Cresta Spaghetti. Next to them a bunch of grapes, looking rather like a pineapple, gave another electric message for someone's port wine. Above Maxim's bar three neon chorus girls tossed a ball again and again above their heads, and moved shining feet in a flicker which lit up the ceiling of my hotel room. In the hall of the hotel, where ochre-coloured marble pillars rose towards a glass church-like dome, plump women in black satin and shining hats gathered in the afternoons to drink coffee or sweet liqueurs, and await the massive men who came in from the Bourse, smoking cigars and spilling provincial prosperity. One corner table was occupied regularly by a Spanish actress who claimed to be a refugee, but whom I overheard speaking excellent German to a man and a young woman who visited her every afternoon. I put her down as doing a watching job for the Reich, just as I assumed that a charming grey-haired English couple, he claiming to be a retired businessman, were doing the same job for the British.

The Metropole was a centre for the British, Americans and French. The Germans, dozens of them, journalists and Gestapo agents, were in hotels close to the railway station. Amongst them was the correspondent I had visited in Cologne nine months before. We passed one another in the street one evening, each restraining a half grin of recognition before we averted our gaze, and hurried on our ways.

The first clear sign of what was to hit us came less than a week ahead of the invasion. On Sunday 5 May, Maurice Fast, who had been so helpful to me in the autumn, asked me to come to his office. He told me that he had information direct from King Leopold's private secretary that Hitler had informed Mussolini that he had plans to make a simultaneous attack on Holland, Belgium, Luxembourg and France. Mussolini wanted to bring the Italians in on this but the Italian royal family were against it. The king of Italy decided, however, to inform the Belgian king of what was about to happen.

The information rang true to me. Fast, as the editor of a small but influential newspaper was in too exposed a position to risk exaggeration on a story of this kind. He would not have trusted me with knowledge of his source unless he was anxious to underline its reliability. Moreover a simultaneous attack against all four western countries along his border was the type of audacious move which Hitler had a genius for. Until now the military experts in Britain and France had been busy arguing which of these countries Hitler would attack. Few if any had predicted an attack all along the line. On the other hand, if the story was untrue, or a plant, I would be guilty of crying wolf, and so not only of giving a false alarm to the British public, but of weakening my voice when the real thing occurred.

I tried to check out the story with the British Embassy, without disclosing my source. They knew nothing which could confirm it. At a lunch at the Brussels Chamber of Commerce I managed to get a word with the American Ambassador, Cudahay. He said he had seen the king within the last week, and nothing of the sort had been mentioned. Even so, I decided to back my instinct, and wrote the story.

The *Express* published it, but in an obscure place on the back page – in sharp contrast to the lavish front-page presentation of a recent interview with General Ironside, who had said 'Come on Hitler. We are ready!' Even though mine was an exclusive report I could not altogether blame them, as I had not been able to disclose my source. I suspected, too, that the policy line coming from Stornaway House was that if we did not predict a flare-up in the fighting all might settle down again to stalemate. But *Newsweek* in the United States were less inhibited. I had been cabling them material, on a free-lance basis, since the previous summer. They ran my story with a flourish.

Next day provided some confirmation, with reports of pontoon bridges being assembled near the German frontier, and of big troop moves around Hannover. I decided that this was the real thing, and for the first time, in all the invasion scares since the war began, I wrote a further strong red light warning that a German D-Day was near. I held to this even though by Wednesday, 8 May the alarm, which by now was filling the Belgian newspapers, seemed to be lessening. I recorded in my notes that the British Embassy 'believed it was blowing over'. Marcel Fodor, who had been the astute and very well informed correspondent of the *Manchester Guardian* in Vienna, was now representing that paper in Brussels. He was convinced that I was wrong. He saw the reports of German troop movements as a bluff to distract attention from a German thrust into the Balkans. From Amsterdam my colleague Morley Richards telephoned to say that the Dutch too thought the crisis was past.

Thursday, 9 May was clear, blue, sunny. The morning BBC news reported that in the Commons the night before thirty-three Conservatives had voted against the Government. In the cautious fashion of the day, it did not however predict that this would bring down Chamberlain and pave the way for Churchill. In the afternoon I drove northwards through Antwerp towards the Dutch border to see what signs there might be of extra preparedness against invasion. I went with Bob Okin, of the Associated Press of America, and his lovely Spanish wife Pepita. He had married her during the Civil War, and was deeply worried for her safety, should the Germans overrun Europe, for she had been ardently anti-Franco.

It was an afternoon of complete spring beauty. In the big parks on the edge of Antwerp women wheeled children in the sunshine, pausing to watch, on one big open sports field, troops training to meet air attack. Belgian biplanes swooped, and the khaki-clad soldiers scattered and went through the motions of fighting back. The old city forts loomed behind new barbed wire barricades, the forts of which Winston Churchill, even though he was First Lord of the Admiralty, had impetuously taken command in 1914, with a young Lieutenant Freyberg among his officers.

When we reached the wide, straight line of the Albert Canal, which ran, a sixty-foot-wide natural anti-tank barrier, from Antwerp to the Meuse and the German frontier, the sentries were strict, noting details of our passports, our passes, our identity cards. It was the same at the forward defensive line north of the canal, where iron rails, set as a anti-tank obstacle, and a series of trenches stretched across the dead flat plain towards

Holland and the Ruhr. The trenches were solidly built, with revetted sides and in places strengthened with concrete. There was no sign of any special alert. When I had driven through here in October the trench lines had been manned. Now they were untenanted. In front of the barracks in one village three men raked a flower bed, bright with early pansies. Others strolled about the street in the sun, exuding boredom. Along the Canal, when we passed back southwards over it, anti-tank guns were in position, but were unmanned. So, too, were the weapon pits on the canal bank. Groups of troops, unarmed, waited by the roadside to hitch-hike into Antwerp on leave. Reliefs for sentries sunbathed beside the sentry boxes. It looked as if I had indeed fallen for an invasion scare. But I could check the situation at a high level the next day, for I was due to lunch with General Badoux, the Belgian general who had designed for Finland the Mannerheim Line defences.

On that grey gold spring evening I dined with the assistant press attaché of the British Embassy, a man who before the war had had the tough task of selling British beer in a country which could boast twenty-eight different brands of excellent beer of its own. He had, as an artillery officer, been a member of the first British party to enter Brussels after the Armistice. 'The Metropole had been a German officers' centre, and we ate in its dining room with officers in field grey all around us.' On our way up the hill to the little restaurant where we ate roast chicken and drank red wine he showed me the bullet marks on two houses where the Reichswehr had turned their machine guns in 1918 on Bolshevik mutineers in the German army.

I went on to have a drink with Okin and his wife at Le Boeuf sur le Toit, where the small dance floor was a crowded, bobbing turning mass of young Belgians, very much the *jeunesse dorée* of this wealthy city, the girls wearing wide short skirts in what was then deemed the American style. They were dancing to '*Sur le Pont d'Avignon*', adapted as a swing tune by Marius B. Winter and his British band. I had a final coffee with Marcel Fodor in a café opposite the Opera. He had already established there a *Stammtisch* like that over which he had presided in the Café Louvre in Vienna, where friends came to hear him talk and tipsters came to give him information. He smiled knowingly and relievedly behind his big spectacles when I told him of the peaceful scenes along the Albert Canal. 'The attack will come in the Balkans, not there. You will see,' he assured me.

I was in my pyjamas, writing a letter to Cecily in my room in the hotel, when the phone went, and the bottom dropped out of the world as we had known it. It was Fast's voice. 'You had better come round. They are on the move. This time it is the real thing.'

Attack in the West

I hurried into my clothes, and round to Fast's office. In the streets it was just another Brussels night. Outside the night clubs touts and commissionaires waited for any late pleasure seekers. Couples still strolled home slowly from the cinema. Waiters were cleaning up the cafés around the Opera, and taxi drivers stood by their cars, chatting. I found Fast, and his military correspondent, Colonel Piquard, and a group of sub-editors in the paper's newsroom.

'The Belgium secret service has been informed that German columns are now moving towards the frontiers of Belgium and Holland. All Belgian army leave has been cancelled, and the General Staff is leaving Brussels shortly.' I thought of grey-green tanks I had seen massed along the roadside outside Karlsbad, of the lorried infantry moving into Innsbruck, and envisaged them moving now through the villages of Western Germany, and the streets of Aachen and a score of other frontier towns, no doubt watched excitedly and apprehensively by people from their doorways and windows. Yet one thing seemed inexplicable. Why was Hitler, shrewd and successful as he had always been until now, hurling his army against the bastions of the west which, if not impregnable, were strong?

We tried the radio. From Europe, silence. From America, a mid-Western news announcer was summarising events of the day in Europe. Of Belgium he said, 'The Nazi invasion scare has died away. Every report from Brussels and Amsterdam shows that tension is easing there.'

I ran back to the Metropole, and got the old, old man who was night porter to put in a call to London, to the Ministry of Information through which all wartime press calls had to pass. The call was refused. The Ministry of Information censors went home at twelve o'clock, so no further press calls were accepted after that hour. It did not matter that the world was cracking under our feet, that I had information which could prepare the public for the shock which was to come the next day. Censors were respectable fellows who lived in Ealing, and had to take up their bowler hats and get the last tube home.

More news. A call from General Badoux's ADC. The General would not be able to keep our lunch date. He was leaving town. So it was definite that the General Staff was moving.

Hugh Greene of the *Daily Telegraph* hurried into the hall. His local correspondent had just rung with news that Pierlot the Prime Minister, and Spaak the Foreign Minister had hurried from a dinner party at eleven o'clock to the Foreign Office, and that a Cabinet meeting was going on there. I got a taxi and drove to the Foreign Office. Its lights were ablaze.

It was now close on one-thirty. As I got back to the hotel a police car drove up, and a constable came to the desk. Any army officers staying in the hotel, he told the porter, were to be woken up and told to rejoin their units at once. Other police cars were racing through the streets, their tyres screeching, on their way to wake up air-raid wardens.

But nothing else gave any sign of war – no black out, no guards. In the small, all-night café on the far side of the square two girls and two men in flashy striped suits were eating and laughing. On the pavement in front of the hotel a small man came up to me, 'Like a nice

American girl, mister? First class American girl, just round the corner from here.'

No, I didn't want an American girl. Why not? Well, if you really want to know, because there is going to be a war. He shrugged his shoulders. Of course there was going to be a war. But you couldn't hold up all life just because one day there might be a war, his manner implied.

I said, 'I mean it. I am a foreign newspaperman, and I tell you that at this moment the Germans are crossing the Belgian frontier. You will be at war in a few minutes.'

His face changed. The wheedling look of the pimp vanished and alarm took its place. 'No, not war,' he said. 'I've had enough of war. I was in the last one.' He pulled open his coat and showed me the medal ribbons on his waistcoat. 'You are fooling, eh?'

'Fooling? Wait till dawn,' I said abruptly.

The alarm on his face grew. He ran across to the concrete benches in the middle of the square, and shook awake a man stretched out sleeping on them. I could see the tout gesticulating, talking rapidly. The man on the seat was unconvinced. He waved his arm in scorn, and turned over to sleep again. The tout returned. 'My mate doesn't believe you,' he said. 'And anyway' – this part with a smile – 'what about that nice American girl?'

I went back and rang Fast. There was still no definite news that the invasion had begun. His paper was going to press with 'Serious New Crisis' as its headlines. But in the hotel army officers were now clattering downstairs and driving off in taxis. Two agitated businessmen, who must have been telephoned by someone in the know, appeared with their bags, paid their bills, and went off.

Into the midst of all this walked a tall, beautiful, dark girl, very well dressed, and a tall young man. The man asked the agitated night porter for a room. As he did so the girl slipped her hand into his. On her face was a look of shining contentment. They went off upstairs, key in hand. Did they know nothing of what was happening or perhaps did they know a great deal?

I decided I must try to get some sleep, and lay fully dressed on my bed. I slept and then suddenly I was awake, and guns were booming. I tried to reassure myself that perhaps after all these were just Belgian guns firing at British or German planes flying high overhead. They often did. Perhaps it had all been just one more crisis, one more huge false alarm.

But the scene outside my window destroyed these last illusions. It was dawn. The sky was clear, a pale bluish grey. Away in the distance, where the airport lay, heavy clouds of black smoke were rising. Above them, like minnows in a pool, long dark bombers were circling. Then the guns started again, and streaks of golden sparks crossed the cloudless, delicate sky. Ack-ack tracer shells. The roar of engines grew and grew. There must have been scores of planes about. Seven biplanes, which I knew to be Belgian fighters, rose in formation behind the towers of the cathedral, climbing steadily. A bomber, moving high above the roofs, climbed swiftly away from them. The chatter of machine guns broke through the flatter crump of the anti-aircraft fire. Belgium was at war. We were all now truly at war.

Down on the ground floor two charwomen, half cowering, half curious, stood by the glass fish tank at the dining-room door, staring out into the street as the guns thumped and as glass fell on the pavement. The glass dome of the hotel lounge looked suddenly lethal. Whistles and sirens sounded, and a small man in a bowler hat ran in through the swing doors shouting, 'Take cover, take cover. I am an air-raid warden.'

The lift-buzzer went incessantly, and the night porter, too old to show his fears or his weariness, set about bringing down the baggage of those wanting to leave. Fat Jewish businessmen from Amsterdam, fat Belgian businessmen from Liège and Bruges milled around the desk, paying bills, shouting for taxis, whilst their wives, hastily dressed, cried to them, or rushed for luggage. At windows all round the square outside pyjamaed people, night-dressed people stared skywards. Was a great city ever awakened into war in this way?

Down the stairs, down the lift people still poured. Into the middle of this uproar walked the two who had booked in the early hours, the tall beautiful girl and the tall young man. Quietly they went to the desk, he paid his bill, she smiled at him, and they walked out hand in hand. In the midst of the crowd battling for timetables and taxis, another young man and his girl wife stood, his arms around her, lips to lips, for seconds, minutes, long minutes. Then the porter called, '*Votre taxi, monsieur*', and she turned, with tears over her face like rain, as he moved towards the swing door, outside which the guns had taken up their thumping again.

In the streets Brussels was going to work, as if nothing had been changed. Sturdy workmen, hurrying charwomen and shop assistants moved along the pavement in droves. A boy was cleaning the windows of a shop at the corner whilst the guns went on roaring, and a plane darted across a corner of the sky. There was one macabre touch. Through the crowds darted a woman, her face deeply rouged, her stockings cheap, her eyes glazed. An old, old tart. She grabbed at the hands of workmen carrying their lunch boxes, at the hands of businessmen seeking taxis. They brushed her away, and she darted on through the crowd, her white handbag swinging.

I drove to the Foreign Office as the sirens wailed, and bursts of shrapnel showed like white roses in the pale blue sky, just as I had seen it above Madrid. With me was Mike O'Leary, correspondent of a group of mid-western papers, and very different from the other American correspondents I had known, who were either ardently liberal, like Mowrer or Gunther, or shrewdly sceptical, like Walter Kerr. O'Leary was anti-British to every corner of his Irish soul: 'Oh boy, this is the works, this is the works. I've seen what those monkeys did to Poland, and believe me they know their business. Those monkeys don't mess about once they've begun. You've really got it coming to you now.'

Guards stood outside the Foreign Office, big Flemish peasants who looked bewilderedly at our passes, and whose hands seemed too big for the light machine guns set up on the pavement. Iwens D'Eickhoute, head of the Press Bureau, told us that the German Minister in Brussels had called on Spaak at five in the morning and told him Germany was moving into Belgium to anticipate an Anglo-French invasion of the country. The king had issued an appeal to the nation, and had gone to take command of the army; the Dutch were resisting; there was no word from the fronts. Appeals had gone out to the Allies who were sending help at once.

At midday the first sign of that help appeared. Up the Rue de la Loi raced a khaki-coloured car, with a white-helmeted Belgian policeman standing up through the open sunshine roof, his whistle going like a fire-engine siren. Behind came a British military policeman on a motor cycle, the scarlet top of his flat cap brilliant, his steel helmet slung across his shoulder. He led another car in which sat four British officers, steel-helmeted, their scarlet staff tabs bright within the shadow of the car. The first part of the British Expeditionary Force was in the Belgian capital, on their way to plan the move through the capital of the British divisions which were to take up a position along the River Dyle, south of Louvain.

On the pavement the Belgians stared and clapped. I clapped with them – proudly. This was at last no Spain from which we had averted our gaze, no Czechoslovakia which we had betrayed, no Poland we were unable to help in time. This time we were meeting Hitler with the one argument he understood – force.

The BEF was part of a wide Allied sweep forward. The plan was that, like a great steel door hinged on Sedan, three French armies, with the BEF in their centre, would swing round to form a barrier, stretching from where the Dutch stood behind their water lines, covering the great port of Antwerp and across Belgium east of Brussels, lining up with the River Meuse, which in turn would link up with the Maginot Line.

Throughout this Friday, 10 May, the Allied armies poured into Belgium. On the frontier the customs barriers were cut down to let the tanks pass, and crowds waited in every village, hurling lilac at the troops in their lorries. By nightfall, when the sirens, which had wailed all day as the airfields around the capital were steadily bombed, were still going, the advance guard of the BEF rolled along the Chaussée de Mons, and made its way across Brussels towards the great avenue which led out of the city towards Louvain. In the dusk the Belgians stood cheering and the men in the trucks and Bren carriers and cars waved back. Every man was wearing lilac, purple on his steel helmet, in the barrel of his rifle, stuck in his web equipment. They smiled and saluted with thumbs up – a gesture which at first shocked the Belgians, to whom it had a very rude significance, but which they soon recognised as a sign of cheerful confidence, a thumbs up in the tradition of ancient Rome. Soon the children who ran or cycled beside the British columns were giving it in return. It was a great sight, one to bring tears to the eyes, as this military machine moved forward in all its strength, efficiently, quietly, with the British military police guiding it on at every crossroads as if they were dealing with rush-hour London. It was to prove itself a good fighting machine, too, whenever it was given the chance to fight during the next few weeks.

When dark fell I came out of the hotel with Okin to get dinner at a nearby restaurant. As we came into the Place de Brouchère I stared around, for the moment puzzled. It seemed completely changed. Then I realised that the spaghetti advertisement and the girls above Maxim's and the bunch of grapes were gone, and in their place was just the grey cliff wall of the buildings, with a few pale searchlights beyond. It was like being suddenly thrust into

a dark, narrow canyon. In one more country in Europe
the lights had gone out.

All through that warm night the sirens kept up their
noise, and over the radio came incessant alerts. 'Enemy
planes are moving over Anderlecht and Molembeek and
Koekelberg. Parachutists are believed to have been
dropped near the Jardin Botanique. Police cars take
note.' The guns continued their clamour, planes droned
overhead, and from time to time came the distant crump
of bombs – but chiefly on the outskirts, where the airfields
lay. Few fell in the city itself, though one did hit a building
thirty yards from the American Embassy, sweeping the
inside out of an old five-storied building as if with a great
hand. There was no fire, and the debris looked old and
dusty when we saw it half an hour later.

Parachutists was a word on everyone's lips. Though the
Germans had used them only to seize specific strategic
targets, chiefly bridges across the Meuse, and though their
military achievements were considerable – perhaps even
decisive – the indirect blow they dealt to morale was
equally important. In Holland, on Hitler's own orders,
some parachutists had been dropped in Dutch army
uniforms. Other German troops on the ground had
dressed in Dutch police uniforms, to seize a key bridge.
From this tiny seed of fact a monstrous growth of rumours
spread – and endured. Parachutists, it was said, had
descended dressed as nuns, though given away by their
hob-nailed boots; as commercial travellers with explosives
rather than samples in their bag. Poisoned chocolates
were being dropped from the air for children. Fifth
columnists were signalling, it was reported, from attic
windows. On that Friday afternoon I had seen Belgian
troops rushing to surround a block of buildings close to
the British Embassy where parachutists were reported to
have been seen. British Field Security troops raced round
the block on their motor cycles, keeping watch.

The first round-up of German civilians in the city had
taken place on Friday morning. Outside the Metropole a

crowd gathered round a large covered van. In a corner of the lounge a group of men and two women were guarded by half a dozen plain clothes policemen and other helmeted police in uniform. Two of the men I had seen daily in the hotel for weeks.

At a signal from the door four police gathered round one man and hurried him to the van. The crowd were at first silent, and then, with cries of '*Les salots*' a group of men and women tried to get at the prisoner. Police bundled him into the van, and two stayed to guard him whilst others went back for the next man.

With each prisoner the cries grew louder, mixed with laughter and shouts of sheer excitement until it formed a harsh, baying noise. It was ugly, and somehow artificial. The Belgians, were, heaven knows, soon to have reason enough to hate the Germans and their Gestapo. But at this moment some of the crowd gave the impression that they were showing a hostility they did not really feel, but which, from books and pictures of the last war, they felt they ought to feel. We had all in 1940 read of war so long, imagined it so long, that now that it had come it had an air of unreality. It was as if we were watching others looking like ourselves, and dressed like ourselves, playing parts in a film which would suddenly flicker to a close, and the cinema organ would strike up 'God Save the King' and we would come out into the open air of reality again. But this was the reality, as on this Brussels pavement yet another generation learnt to hate.

On Saturday, the second day of the invasion Hugh Greene and I drove out towards Louvain. Through the streets the British infantry were now moving. Brought up by rail, they marched through in platoons – bigger formations could have been more vulnerable to air attack – to their billets in schools, parks and big houses on the city's eastern edge. They were small compact units of men burnt brick red by the sun, a boy officer in front, stick under his arm, map case at his side, moving along at a steady, swinging pace from corner to corner where the

military police, rifles slung over their shoulders, directed
them on. The troops were bedecked with lilac. The
military police drank glasses of beer which people brought
out from the cafés.

Under the trees of the big avenue leading towards
Louvain line upon line of lorries and of twenty-five-
pounder guns, with their tractors and their ammunition
trailers, were drawn up, utilising the camouflage of the
thick green chestnut leaves. They must have formed a
tempting target to the Luftwaffe. Yet they went
unbombed – as indeed had been virtually all the long
British and French columns which had crowded the roads
from the frontier since Friday morning. For the first time
the thought occurred to me that perhaps this was not
where Hitler's main blow was going to fall, that the
spearhead of his thrust might be elsewhere, that the bulk
of French and British armies were being manouevred on
to the wrong foot. 'When I fight France,' Hitler had told
the German writer Hermann Rauschning,[1] 'I will lure
their armies out from behind the Maginot Line and
destroy them in the field.' British censorship would not
allow any such speculation in British papers, but I could,
and did set out, in my weekly cable to *Newsweek*, a
warning that we might be being lured into a trap.

Louvain was a name which, to my generation, spelt the
'Hun frightfulness' proclaimed by the propagandists of
World War I, when newspapers and magazines had been
filled with drawings depicting German troops burning the
historic library of Louvain, with its irreplaceable ancient
volumes, and stabling their horses in the city churches.
The road to it this afternoon lay through countryside of
great beauty, with the pale green of meadows, the dark
green of forest, and the bright green of young corn
stretching away under an arching blue sky. Convoys of
lorries, some Belgian, some British, moved under the

[1] *Hitler Speaks*, Rauschning, 1939.

young chestnuts still decked with their soft maroon candles. A Belgian biplane fighter rose from behind a wood, and soared away eastwards, and in the roadside fields British gunners were setting up Bofors and Brens.

In this setting we came suddenly face to face with a tragic procession, a long column of refugees making their way to Brussels, the first I had seen in this war. Cars, farm carts, even hand barrows were laden with baggage, mattresses, household gear, crates of fowls and ducks. Set-faced men, harassed and weeping women, bewildered or weary or excited children stared from vehicles or trudged in the dust. In this rich land this seemed an even uglier sight than the similar columns I had seen set against the background of the poverty of Spain or the austerity of Finland.

We could explain this exodus as that of peasants fleeing from fighting zones along the Albert Canal. What was harder to account for was the steadily increasing numbers of Belgian troops who intermingled with these civilians. Some were on foot, some on bicycles, others in lorries and carts. There were staff officers in cars, and lorries where troops in ribbed Belgian steel helmets held machine guns or sat amidst piled crates of ammunition. There seemed to be no units, no set order, just a great stream of troops which thickened steadily, jamming the roads against the advancing British convoys. These were unmistakably Belgians in retreat, an ominous sign in a battle not yet forty-eight hours old.

From a ridge outside Louvain we had a view across the city roofs and the spire of the church. From a wood some ten miles further east a column of black smoke rose, the only clear sign of war in this sunny countryside. Then steadily the air filled with the sound of planes. I could pick out, black gnats against the blue, seven bombers circling high above the countryside.

Suddenly one fell, dropping like a stone thrown from a cliff top, its engine wailing, wailing. 'Good God, what a shot,' I said to Greene. 'The ack-ack guns must have got a direct hit on it.'

I looked for the smoke which must come from its crash. Smoke there was from the ground, and a sudden roar, but the plane had not crashed. Steadily it was climbing up to rejoin the others, and another was diving down behind it towards the smoke marked target. The roar of the bombs came, heavy, clear. 'Stukas,' said Greene abruptly, drawing on his experience of the Polish campaign.

It was my first sight of dive-bombing, the tactic which was to prove so devastating in this campaign. All the bombing I had seen in Spain and Finland had come from bombers following a steady level course above their targets. This was a new method, in which the bombers were put into a steep dive aiming the plane towards the target before releasing the bomb, with a siren wailing to intensify the shriek of the falling bomb. Throughout that long afternoon we watched relays of planes circle, dive, bomb and soar away again, in attacks on what we later learnt were positions the BEF had taken up. The Germans had the air to themselves. Not an Allied plane appeared to tackle them. We drove back in sombre mood towards Brussels. The same mood had spread to the British troops in their lorries. They were no longer the smiling men who had shouted and waved to the crowds in the city streets. Set-faced, they were picking the lilacs out of their rifle barrels and throwing them away from their gear. The men at the Bren and Bofors guns stared keenly skywards.

The next morning there was at last news from the front – and it was bad news, shockingly bad. Not only had the Germans seized two bridges across the Albert Canal, but the mighty fort of Eban Emael, the most powerful in Western Europe, had been captured. Eban Emael had been built into the bank of a 300-foot-high terrace which ran above the River Meuse. One sunny Sunday afternoon in October Eric Sevareid and I had stood on that terrace close to the fort, and had looked out at the perfect field of fire its guns had, covering the flat land below which stretched to the Albert Canal, and to the Meuse with its mined bridges, and to the outskirts of Liège, with its black pyramids of coal debris. Eban Emael had seemed impregnable – and so it had been to everything except attack from the one direction in which it was unguarded – from the air. At dawn German sappers had landed on the unguarded top of the fort. At the time they had been described as parachutists, but they had come silently by glider – yet another new technique of war introduced by Hitler's Reichswehr. With new powerful hollow charge high explosives they had swifly knocked out the gun turrets, even destroying the largest guns by thrusting high explosives down their barrels. The troops inside, with the ventilation system damaged, could offer little resistance, and by midday on Friday, 10 May Eban Emael surrendered.

Its loss had not been announced when, at one o'clock on Sunday, 12 May, Paul Henri Spaak held a press conference at the Foreign Office. His plump young face was lined with weariness and worry. Most of the journalists present were Belgians, and it was to them Spaak spoke, 'I appeal to you, gentlemen, to help us support public morale. I assure you news from the front is not as bad as you hear, but these rumours flying round must be checked. Write that the situation is all right.'

This brought a white-haired journalist, whom Spaak addressed as colonel, on to his feet, his face white with fury. 'You ask us to support morale, M le Ministre, but what are you doing? Are you doing anything to stop desertion? Are you telling the public anything definite, to replace the rumours? Aren't you making all the same mistakes as the Government made in 1914?'

Back in the Hôtel Metropole many of the official war correspondents with the BEF had arrived. Among them was William Forrest, arrayed now in khaki, with war correspondent tabs, and J. L. Hodson, a World War I veteran whose novel *Jonathan North*, with its searing account of life in the trenches, had become a best-seller just before this new war was declared. Kim Philby represented *The Times*. It was another *Times* man, however, whom I remember most clearly from that day. I was about to take the vacant place at the table where they were lunching when someone pointed out that I would bring their total to thirteen. I am not usually superstitious, and more in jest than in seriousness I sat down at a table near by. A few minutes later Jerome Caminada of *The Times* took the place I had avoided. A few days later he was captured by the Germans in Ostend and interned in a German camp near the Polish border, from which he ultimately escaped.

To my delight that evening Edward Ward arrived at the hotel, the first time we had seen each other since we went our separate ways after reporting the battle of Suomussalmi. Not only was Eddie a good man to work with, but a man of nerve and judgement, qualities which, I suspected, were going to be needed in the days ahead. For I was about to face one of the most difficult choices which civilians confront in war – that of deciding when to leave a threatened city or country. For the military, that choice is made for them by their superiors. But civilians caught up in an invasion have to decide, usually on very little information, for themselves, whether they are being courageous, or rash, to stay at their posts a little longer, or prudent – or cowardly – to leave while the going is good. This dilemma, facing expatriate Britons first in Rumania and then Greece provides the dramatic tension in Olivia Manning's marvellous *Balkan Trilogy*. Sefton Delmer had confronted the same problem in Warsaw in September 1939 – and, as he later made plain in his *Trail Sinister*, felt he had made the wrong choice, and left too early. I sensed, after Spaak's press conference, that I might soon have to make this choice myself.

I had arranged with Cecil de Sausmarez, the British Press Attaché, that if the Embassy decided to leave at short notice, he would alert me. In order not to alarm the

hotel staff, we agreed on a form of code. A messsage
saying that he wanted to see me urgently at his office
would be the signal that the Embassy was off. To my
surprise, a message in exactly these terms reached me
that Sunday lunchtime at the Metropole. I could not
believe that events had worsened so dramatically, so I
decided to check with de Sausmarez. I found him in the
luxury flat which had been turned into a wartime press
office. There was no sign of any urgent departure. No,
the Embassy was not leaving, but the Ambassador had
given instructions that all non-essential British residents
should be got out of Belgium. Courtenay Young, Reuters
correspondent, was with me, as was O'Leary, who had
been drinking harder than ever since the German attack
began, and who, with the cunning of the drunken, had
followed us to see what was amiss. When I objected to de
Sausmarez that our task of keeping the British public
informed of what was happening hardly rated as non-
essential, he was dismissive. 'They don't need the newspapers in a crisis. They can take their news from the
BBC,' was his evaluation.

'But where,' I asked him, 'do you think the BBC get
their news from?'

He pondered that a moment. 'That's an interesting
question,' he said. 'I had never thought of it. Where do
the BBC get their news from?'

It was clear that the Foreign Office did not deem it
necessary for their Press Attachés to be familiar with the
workings of the press and broadcasting in Britain. When
I explained that it came mostly from Reuters and similar
agencies, he agreed we might have a case for staying
longer, though he could no longer undertake to warn us
if the Embassy left abruptly.

My advocacy of the importance of the press was not
helped by O'Leary. During this talk he had disappeared,
and we ultimately found him asleep in the flat's opulent
black marble bath. War, I had already discovered, is often
shot through with farce, but I had not expected to find

myself in the third day of the Nazi blitzkrieg in the West engaged in hauling a drunken Irish American out of a millionaire's bath tub.

Signs of mounting chaos multiplied that afternoon, even in the heart of Brussels. On the pavement in front of the Metropole a small crowd gathered round a young Belgian soldier, who was talking excitedly about '*les Boches*', and their terrible tanks and bombers. A Belgian officer, realising the dangers of such wild talk, asked Edward Ward, and a British officer from the Intelligence Corps who had come to Brussels with him, to drive the man home in his car. I went with them.

In the back of the car the soldier poured out his story. 'We were in reserve behind the Albert Canal last night and suddenly a motor cyclist came down the road shouting that the Germans were coming. They were only three miles away, and they were racing on, and we were only in reserve and our officers got up and grabbed a car and went off, so, *tiens*, we went off too. It was only reasonable, wasn't it, to go off if the officers went? We had been bombed all day. God, what bombs, all day. No man wants more than one day of that.'

His young, beardless face was tense. Reddened eyes showed that he had been weeping.

We dropped him outside an old apartment house close to the Midi station. An old man rushed out from a tobacconist's shop on the corner to greet him. The boy saluted us as we drove away, and then stood out on the roadway shouting to an upstairs window, '*Maman, maman, c'est moi, c'est Jean.*'

Maman. It was heart-rending, the cry of that frightened boy. But, as the intelligence officer commented, you don't win wars by calling on *Maman*.

That night we dined at the Savoy restaurant. With its oaken walls, its big mirrors, its massed flowers, it was one of the pleasantest restaurants of pre-war Europe. When I had been there four nights before, it had been crowded with women in evening dress and men in uniform. No doubt in just such places Wellington's officers had dined in the weeks before Waterloo. This night we were the only guests. The cloakroom attendant was in tears. 'Is it true that the Chasseurs Ardennes have been almost wiped out, that the Germans are right through the Ardennes? My husband is there, and my boys, both my boys, are on the Canal Albert.' All of which was true, though we did not know it until two days later.

Pierlot, the Belgian premier, had spoken on the radio at six o'clock in an attempt to check the flood of rumour. He said the Germans had penetrated some distance into the Belgian first line of defence, but were being held on the main positions. Which was as good a half truth as any, but it was not going to halt the flood of refugees from the north and east. They were still streaming along the boulevards as we drove back to the hotel that night, with the sirens wailing again, and the street lights dim spots of blue in the warm spring darkness.

All the next day, Monday, 13 May, this flood poured on into the city. It was now a vast column, streaming along the by-roads and main roads from Louvain, through the outer suburbs, and the parks on the city edge, on to the inner boulevards. They walked, they rode in cars and carts or on donkeys, were pushed in bathchairs, even in wheelbarrows. There were youths on bicycles, old men, old women, babies, peasant women, kerchiefs covering their heads, riding on farm carts piled with mattresses, furniture, pots. A long line of nuns, their faces red with perspiration under their coifs, stirred the dust with their long grey robes. Under a tree at the city's edge an old man sat, staring exhaustedly, as an equally old woman gathered sticks for a fire. A village priest in a black cassock and high black hat strode beside a donkey piled high with church gear. There were old creaking cars jammed with peasant women and children, and modern limousines, one with an anxious plump man and his anxious plump wife on the front seat, and the back seat and the roof loaded with their luggage.

Many headed for the railway station, hoping for trains to take them southwards. The stations were like drawings from those of Russia during the Revolution, with people sleeping on the floor, huddled against the walls, women with weeping babies, men pale and exhausted. You had only to glance at such scenes to know that Belgium could not long hold out, with this huge extra problem – unexpected and unprovided for – on its hands.

The Germans soon realised what a bonus these refugees were to their strategy, and from time to time machine-gunned or bombed the refugee columns to add to the chaos. Already on Saturday evening a young girl had been brought in to the Metropole wounded in the head by a machine-gun bullet. We drove towards the front that Monday morning, past mile upon mile of these columns, until I found my feelings becoming deadened by the sheer size of the tragedy, and I felt myself running out of pity, and instead, perhaps to maintain some sanity, I began to dwell on the military problem it presented, on the way it must clog up the roads for the troops.

Just beyond the edge of Brussels, on a ridge to the north of Waterloo, we caught up with the BEF. Gunners were placing their 25-pounders in orchards and farm yards, whilst officers with range finders worked out targets on maps spread on the ground amid the young corn. British voices rang strangely amongst the grey barn walls and the muck-smelling farmyards. Ahead the guns were roaring steadily, where battle had been joined along the line of the River Lyle. Planes moved constantly overhead, hard to detect or identify in the hazy blue sky. It looked as if the settled phase of the battle, which we had for so long been told to expect, was beginning.

The reality was very different. In ferocious fighting further to the south, near Dinant, a hitherto obscure German general called Erwin Rommel had forced a crossing of the Meuse. Even more significantly, under intensive bombardment by Stukas, the Germans had secured a bridgehead across the river at Sedan. In Holland

German tanks had reached the outskirts of Rotterdam, cutting off the Dutch armies from the advancing French. The Allied front in front of Brussels was soon to become untenable.

Collapse Under Blitzkrieg

Tuesday came and went swiftly, another sunny day with the sirens wailing, police on motor cycles dashing after parachutists, and everywhere the refugees. It was ideal bombing weather, and eighty miles to the north of us the Luftwaffe used it to deadly effect. Within twenty minutes, beginning at two o'clock in the afternoon, German bombers smashed to ruins the old centre of Rotterdam, even though the Dutch were at that time negotiating for peace. Working in relays from captured airfields on the outskirts of the city, Heinkel bombers pattern bombed the crowded and defenceless city, as they had learnt to do at Guernica. That evening the Dutch Foreign Minister announced that 30,000 people had been killed or wounded in the raid. These figures were to prove wildly exaggerated. The actual total of dead was 900. Even so it was the most terrible air raid in history up to that time. It dealt a final blow to any chance of Dutch resistance, and by ten o'clock that evening the radio from the Hague announced that Holland had capitulated.

Even more ominous were the German news bulletins the next morning, with their cold, triumphant, curt communiqué, announcing not only the Dutch capitulation, but that the Belgians had been pushed back, the French lines broken at Dinant, and the Meuse crossed above Sedan. How on earth had the Germans got through the Ardennes, that 'one great minefield' which the experts had told us was impassable to tanks? It was clear to me that I must now prepare my own lines of retreat.

I had arranged with our driver that he would hold himself ready at any time to take us to Ostend, where we believed the Belgian Government would go. An ex-soldier, of steady nerve, he had agreed. He was making a fortune, working by day for us, and running refugees to the French border at night. He usually reported at the hotel at seven-thirty in the morning. But by nine there was no sign of him. I went across to his garage. It was closed, and the man in the shop next door told me that the driver had gathered up his family, locked up his premises, and moved off early that day to Ostend 'for the duration'.

To hire another car, or even to buy one, was impossible. The wealthier refugees had taken the lot. In the centre of the Place de Brouchère a white-helmeted policeman had blown his whistle and was shouting to the crowd around him. 'Every man between the ages of eighteen and forty who has not been specially told to stay in the city must make his way as best he can to Ypres.'

Evacuation of all men of military age. The Belgians had at least learnt one lesson from the last war, when thousands of their men were taken off to work in Germany. This move showed foresight – but also that things were now very serious.

My search for transport was interrupted by a call from London, asking me to do an urgent task for John Fitzwilliam. He was a middle-aged freelance journalist who had appeared in Paris shortly before the war began and had later stationed himself in Brussels. He mixed little with the regular press corps, eschewing the comforts of the Metropole for a small hotel near the railway station.

London told me that John Fitzwilliam had left Brussels just before the attack, could not get back, and wanted me to go to his hotel and get hold of money and documents he had left in a deposit box there. It was not an easy task. All I had by way of credentials were the number of the

deposit box, and my own press card and passport. The
hotel manager at first refused point blank to give a
stranger access to any deposit box without written author-
isation. I argued and pleaded as outside the sirens wailed,
and police continued to blow their whistles and shout
orders for the evacuation. In the end I discovered a way.
Had Mr Fitzwilliam paid his bill? No, he owed a substantial sum, as he had expected to be away for only one
night. I offered to pay with the money I knew was in the
box. This – and perhaps the general sense that the world
was cracking beneath our feet, that the Germans might
well be in Brussels that night – did the trick. The manager
produced the key. In the box I discovered well over a
thousand pounds worth of Belgian francs, a very big
amount for those days. Beside it was a list of names of
Belgian people, each with a sum set against it. One name
I recognised as that of an official in the Belgian Foreign
Office whom I had often met: two others were Belgian
journalists; yet another a retired army officer. It did not
take any profound act of judgement to realise that John
Fitzwilliam had had other tasks than those of a freelance
journalist, and that this was the payroll of Belgians
helping British intelligence. I felt incensed at the utter
incompetence this revealed. Had I not been able to talk
the manager into letting me open the box, this list would
have remained, almost certainly to fall into the hands of
the Gestapo. Every man on it would have been lucky if
he ever reached a concentration camp alive, after monstrous torture. I took the money, paid the bill, and on the
pavement outside burnt the list and dropped the ashes
down a grating in the gutter.

It was now early afternoon. Eddie Ward and I were
debating on the pavement outside the Metropole whether
we should try to buy bicycles, and make for the French
border, since we could not get a car, when fate intervened. Up to the hotel drove a van, camouflaged in khaki
and green, belonging to the official French radio. In it

was M Masson, correspondent of Radio Diffusion Française. More realistic than the BBC, the French broadcasting authorities had provided their reporter with his own transport. Masson was very ready to offer a lift to his *cher collègue* from the BBC, and to that *cher collègue*'s friends. We could squeeze seven in all into the van. But Masson must leave by five that evening for Lille, in order to send off his report.

We had feared that might be too early for us, that after all the fighting front might yet stabilise, that we should not quit our posts too soon. At the headquarters of the Belgian Broadcasting Corporation, in an old red-brick château on the edge of the city, it was difficult to feel that matters were urgent. Its French windows looked over a garden which had been allowed to run wild, with untrimmed grass, and lilac and rhododendron bushes banked around great beech trees. Troops, mostly big Flemish boys, lounged under the trees. To the north-east the roll of guns from Louvain sounded almost reassuring, like breakers on a distant shore. On a poplar in a corner of the garden a thrush sang, its notes rising above the gunfire. Even when three Dornier bombers moved across the sky and a lone fighter soared towards them, its machine guns rattling, they were all soon out of sight behind the trees, and the springtime peace returned.

But this was a false oasis. Elsewhere there was ample evidence that it was time to go. At the French Embassy the grates were black with the charred remains of burnt papers. All over the diplomatic quarter scraps of blackened papers drifted down from the chimneys, falling over the long queues outside the banks. Fast had gone. At the War Ministry Colonel Piquard, now a member of the army press department, was hastily stuffing papers into a rucksack. 'Still here?' he queried. 'Get out as quickly as you can. We are going this afternoon, so too are the censors. The Government moves this evening. Head for Ostend.'

I asked him what had happened at the front. '*Mon*

vieux,' he replied, '*c'est bien simple, et bien tragique*. We have simply come up against a new type of war, one we cannot deal with. These dive bombers, these heavy tanks have changed warfare. We Belgians could not cope with it. But we do not matter. What matters is that you and the French cannot cope with it either. You are preparing to retreat. Worse still, it seems that at Dinant and Sedan a thousand tanks are across the Meuse, inside France. That's why we are going and why you had better go.'

The Metropole Hotel was now almost empty, except for the correspondents, and a few others. The staff watched us closely. These journalists know what is going on, their manner seemed to imply, and so long as they are here, things can't be too bad.

The lift man had lost an arm in the last war. His chest was covered with war medals. 'Tell me,' he said. 'Is it true that they have crossed the Albert Canal already? It can't be true, surely? The line there is so strong. They have always told us so. My boy is up there. It can't be true,' he said, pleadingly, as if after all he had known and suffered in the last war it could not be true that there would be Germans in Brussels again, that all the efforts of 1914–18 were to prove meaningless and in vain.

I reassured him. 'We have no exact news, but we will hold. Remember, our armies are big, and strong.'

I could not have told him the truth, for the life of me.

In the hall a woman, her face pale with agitation, came up to me. She was Dutch, but married to an Englishman, with an English passport. Could we help her to get out? The consul had told her he could do nothing. The last parties of Britons had left two days ago. 'I should have gone with them, I should have gone with them,' she said, her voice near to a shriek.

There was nothing we could do for her. We had no room in the van. I felt sorry for her, but also angry. She was only too typical of hundreds of people who have no direct concern with the waging of a war, but who stay out of foolhardiness, or out of excitement, or out of sheer inertia, despite all the urgings of consulates and embassies, until it is too late. We had to tell her that her only chance was go up by train, and that in fact she would take less risk by staying. Better be caught than take her two children out on the roads in their present state.

When we told the hotel to bring down our bags it was as if someone had fired off a revolver in the lounge. The cashier and the manager both paled. The porter, another old soldier, stared blankly, and the liftman looked at me with disbelief. The old luggage man went off muttering. Two businessmen in the lounge got up and asked for their bills too. Almost ashamedly we piled our luggage into the van.

We prised O'Leary out of a small bar round the corner, on the ground floor of a bordello. With the infuriating calm of the not-quite-drunk he insisted on finishing his half bottle of champagne. The young blonde madame sought my reassurance that she was right not to flee. 'My girls are frightened we will be bombed as Rotterdam was bombed. I tell them, go if you wish. I will stay. I am not going to start rushing madly all over the countryside.'

For the last time we drove up the big boulevards towards the Foreign Office. Under the trees lorries of Belgian soldiers waited, sad-faced in the sun. Lines of BEF trucks still moved through, the troops singing, waving cheerfully, unaware of the atmosphere that was steadily gripping the hearts of all the people who stared at them, silently now, from the street corners. The refugees still poured in in their ghastly stream. An old man sat calmly on a seat in the sun, watching it all. A boy and a girl on another seat had their arms around each other and their cheeks touching. They too seemed indifferent enough. Then out through the suburbs, with sirens going and ack-ack bursting to the south, on to the Mons road.

A Scots sentry at the main crossroads stopped us. '*Pas passer*,' he said, adding a Glasgow accent to the French. When he heard the English voices he grinned. 'All right, go on then. But ye'll have to tak' your chance. I canna guarantee anything further than yon corner.'

'Yon corner' was a mile further down the road. Here we were stopped again by a British patrol, but Masson produced a document hung with diplomatic seals and army stamps and we were allowed through on to the Tournai road, the one main road the army was keeping clear from the frontier to Brussels. The refugees were diverted on to side roads where they trudged now, one long cavalcade staring at us enviously as we entered the wide, empty highway.

It was not empty long. Soon we began to pass supply columns moving up, line after line of British trucks, camouflaged, with Bren guns mounted on top. A Lysander swooped low over us to see what we were doing and, uncertain of its markings, we stopped and dived for the ditch. O'Leary, suddenly waking to life, scrambled with astonishing agility up the roadside bank, and crouched in the hedge, his lips moving rapidly. His words were in a foreign tongue which seemed to me both familiar and yet unfamiliar. It took me a moment to realise that, for the first time in my fairly frequent experience of taking cover, I was hearing the Deity's aid being invoked in Latin. Then in the evening sunlight we moved on.

Luck was with us. Though the air-raid sirens were wailing in each of the three towns through whose narrow, jammed streets we had to make our way, no bombs fell whilst we were there, and we got to Tournai, seven miles north of the French frontier, just after dark. Here the four Britons – Ward, Hugh Greene, Courtenay Young and I – got out and gave our baggage to Masson to take on to Lille. We got beds in an hotel opposite the great jagged mass of the cathedral, and slept like children.

We were to need that sleep, for there was to be none for us the next night.

*

We woke to find Tournai full of refugees. They were massed on the railway station. They covered every inch of the huge square outside. They lined every street, and filled the Grande Place, with its gold-fronted Flanders houses and its great stone bell tower, till it was like the slopes of Tattenham Corner on Derby Day. Every café, every restaurant was jammed. Along the main streets, over the canal bridges, round the bell tower and on the road towards the frontier went one endless stream which never halted and yet which never seemed to ease the congestion in Tournai itself.

On to this town at three o'clock that afternoon the Germans launched their bombers. I heard planes and saw, behind the massive, pointed bulk of the stone medieval bell tower, line upon line of bombers, black against the blue sky. I ran for the doorway of the tower, which looked the solidest place in the city. But it was an ARP post, already jammed full. So I lay down at the foot of the tower, on the side furthest from the bombers, and pressed myself against the stonework. Ward and Courtenay Young did the same.

On the pavement corner opposite a Belgian soldier watched us, a sneering grin forming on his face. At that moment the first salvo of bombs sounded from the far side of the town, and his expression changed to sheer incredulous fear. In the square there were shouts, and a panic rush for shelter. As wave after wave of bombers came over they dropped their bombs in rows across the town, thudding, roaring, smashing their way closer, closer, until one line crashed just behind us and then another smashed into the square itself. A pause, and then another wave would start up on the far side of the town again, closer and closer, until the final salvo felt as if a bit of the sky itself was falling on us. The air was filled with dust and the stink of explosive and the sound of bricks and beams hurtling and breaking.

Then silence, except for the sound of falling beams, the crackle of flames, and cries. The Grande Place was hidden

in a cloud of dust through which showed golden, leaping
flames. Out of this a woman came running, blood streaming from her face, a baby clasped in her arms.

Gradually the dust cleared. Three cars were burning in
the centre of the square. Two of the golden-fronted
houses were on fire. Bodies lay strewn on the cobbles.
From a café opposite the belfry they were helping out
people covered with blood. There was glass everywhere.

The café had not been completely cleared of its
wounded when the sirens went again. This time we dived
for a cellar. There the explosions sounded less terrifying,
and most of the bombs seemed to fall on the far side of
the town, by the railway station. When again there was a
pause we hurried round to our hotel. In one corner of the
lobby a young Belgian soldier sat sobbing in a chair.

Again the sound of bombs. Hugh Greene had now
joined us, and we went down to the wine cellar. It was
crowded with the proprietor and his family. When at last
the bombing had died away the proprietor blocked the
doorway, 'I intend to have you arrested,' he said. Why?
Because we were suspicious foreigners. Tournai had never
been bombed until we arrived. We must come with him
to the British headquarters in the town.

Ward had the most sensible response. He suggested
that the proprietor might at least sell us a bottle of
champagne to settle our nerves. The proprietor did this –
and called the police while we were drinking it. A
gendarme and the proprietor then escorted us to the office
of the British Town Major, the army officer set up to
liaise with the local authorities. A small crowd began to
gather round us as we made our way through the bombed
streets, their attitude increasingly ugly. I could hear
mutterings of 'espions' and 'parachutistes'.

We got clear of these troubles by a coincidence no
novelist would have dared to invent. The Town Major
had been at Harrow with Edward Ward. They greeted
each other by their school nicknames. The Town Major
vouched for us, and the crowd dispersed – rather sadly.

He was indeed delighted to find himself with fellow Britons. He had been badly shaken up by the bombing. His car was one of those we had seen blazing in the square. He had leapt out of it, and flung himself on the ground just in time. The Duke of Gloucester, who had been in another army car just outside the city, had had his wrist cut when he too jumped for safety. Already eighty civilians had been brought in dead.

As we talked a BEF truck drove up, its sides splintered and torn by bomb fragments. A corporal stepped out and saluted.

'All OK?' asked the Town Major.

'OK, sir, but the sergeant stopped one in the neck. We picked a six inch strip of shrapnel out of his neck. But it went in just under the skin, and he seems all right.'

Self-possessed, alert, disciplined, that corporal made me feel good to be British – and stirred my feelings that it was high time I too was in uniform.

We made a quick tour of the town. One street, near the entrance, was smashed flat, its buildings burning. Smoke rose from a score or more other places. The big square before the station was cratered. But the bridges across the canals were intact, and the refugees were on the move again.

In the evening sun we sat on the terrace of the bombed café. The glass had been swept away. The burnt-out hulks of the cars stood in the square. A patch of blood was drying brown on the paving. Yet the evening sky was serene with yellow and turquoise, and the sun warm. It seemed as peaceful as if we were sipping drinks beside a beach in New Zealand, watching the late sun glinting on the long Pacific rollers.

The hotel proprietor came hurrying up. He had an air of grievance, as if he resented being denied the satisfaction of capturing a nest of spies. He went into a long discussion with the Town Major, who turned to us. 'Here is your chance to get a lift to Lille. Our boy friend here wants to get his wife away to France. She has two women friends with a car, but no one to drive it. If you offer to drive it to Lille you could all cram in.'

Outside the hotel stood a five-seater Chevrolet. Inside were three Belgian woman, massive, fleshy figures, and a great heap of luggage. The proprietor explained his plan. His wife began to weep. She didn't want to leave. One of the huge women said that with the luggage they could take only two of us, but not all three. The Town Major acted with admirable decision. In a heavy English accent he explained they would have to take us all. '*C'est votre bagage ou votre vie, Madame,*' he declared. Even there, in the dark, with the flames from the burning buildings behind us, it sounded so corny as to be comic. But it worked. Madame decided to sacrifice her *bagage* and save her *vie*. So we piled in, with Ward driving, and Greene and the least bulky of the women in front. Young and I settled into the back, each with one of the huge women on our knees. Even before we started I felt as if I had cramp, with every leg muscle being crushed. I did not know how long I could take it, but at least we were on our way. The Town Major told us to make for France, and give up any idea of getting to Ostend. The game was up around Brussels, the BEF was preparing to pull back, and the Belgian Government had gone.

The frontier was six miles ahead, a darkened roadside building with a gendarme who suddenly loomed up to halt us. We got out and looked round. Heavy clouds now covered the sky. Roaming them, brushing against them in pools of light, were searchlights round Lille. On the northern horizon guns flashed and from above came the steady drone of planes. Moving along the road, past the frontier post, on into Belgium was a long line of BEF lorries, their lights blue, shaded. They went on and on quietly, in the dark.

The frontier guards took little persuading to let us pass. Our journalists' passes were enough. As we turned to clamber back into the car, I looked back towards Tournai. Suddenly great flashes leapt into the air from where the town lay, followed by the glow of flames reflected against the sky. A few seconds later came the roar of explosions. The bombers were back.

At noon the next day we were in Paris. Between the frontier and Lille we had argued it out and decided to push right on to Amiens. We had a car now, and God knows when we would get another. There was an air raid on when we got to Lille, and the military picket was perfectly willing to let us go ahead. We drove out on the Arras road with the ack-ack lighting up the night. The clouds had gone now, and it was a clear pale green moonlit night. After many errors we found our way out of Arras on to Bapaume, where we stopped briefly. My legs were almost paralysed with the strain of our Belgian hostesses. One of them kept complaining bitterly that she would have done better to have stayed; she would lose all her furniture, and it was wonderful oak, genuine oak. Another was being noticeably, consciously calm and brave, with a soothing insistence that all would be well. She was very responsible and concerned. 'Are you on the right road, monsieur?' 'Ah, yes, monsieur, but I too am a driver and I know how easy it is to be on the wrong road. You are sure, yes?' Was the back tyre not flat? and the petrol, were we sure there would be petrol enough, and 'Oh, that back tyre, it felt so strange and my husband had always said, now you be careful of the back tyre when you drive. But monsieur was an experienced driver, wasn't he?' And monsieur, alias Edward Ward, hung on in silence cursing under his breath, and drove like mad. By two o'clock we were again able to call a halt, and I walked up and down the road getting some circulation back into my legs.

We went on, driving towards Amiens over the road which a week later was to be the main line for the German armoured columns' advance on their way to the coast. Here and there an occasional barricade of carts held us up, and peasants with shotguns looked at our papers.

We had just petrol enough to get to the railway station

at Amiens. We were luckier than most. The last ten miles of the way into Amiens the roadside had been dotted with dark shapes of cars around which people slept, exhausted. They were refugees who had driven till their petrol ran out.

At Amiens we left our hostesses and their car at an hotel opposite the railway station. The next day they were to go on to Normandy. They felt sure they could manage the driving now they were out of the danger zone. We got a cup of coffee and at five o'clock climbed aboard a train that, jammed with refugees, limped towards Paris. The three-hour journey took more then twice that time. On the way we passed a few trucks carrying tanks. Then the white shape of Sacré Coeur showed above Montmartre, and we were in Paris again.

I had seen it last in early February, on my way back from Finland. Then it had been a grey, wintry Paris, but still cocksure, cheerful enough despite the blackout. Now, in this same spring sun that lay over Flanders, it was a city terribly afraid. It had reason to be. Twenty-four hours earlier General Gamelin had told Daladier and Reynaud that between Verdun and Paris not a single corps of French troops stood in the Germans' path. What had saved the city – for the time being – was that Hitler was aiming first at the Channel ports, before he turned south towards Paris and central France.

George Millar, in a well-cut khaki uniform of a war correspondent with the French army, and looking like a boy of eighteen rather than the very experienced 29-year-old he was, had just got back from Sedan. We drove up to the Champs Elysées and sat in a café in the sun and talked. He had been with a party of correspondents up behind Corap's army, at Vervins, close to Sedan, on the fateful Tuesday. They were waiting in a village close behind the lines unaware that the Germans were anywhere near, when suddenly stragglers began to pour in, filling the cafés, ordering pernods, standing talking in the square. They all told the same story – of terrible bombing by planes against which they had no guns, of tanks from whose armour the French anti-tank shells bounded off '*comme les balles de tennis*'.

The village had been bombed, and bombed again, and then the press officers had hurried up and rushed them away from the front and back to Verdun. What was happening was something the French army was not anxious to have seen or written. In the streets of Verdun they watched the French infantry being thrown in to stop the gap. Boys with rifles and bayonets and grenades, sitting silent, set-faced in the long clumsily camouflaged Paris buses, going out to face the thirty-five-ton tanks and the dive bombers. 'And when we bought the Continental *Daily Mail* that morning the headlines told of the "Steel Ring Being Drawn Round the German Advance,"' said George bitterly.

As I listened to him I stared round the café. Here, as in Brussels in the last days, you could smell fear, alarm. A journalist can acquire an instinct for sensing a situation almost unconsciously, an ability to 'smell' confidence or defeatism or danger. All that weekend in Paris fear hung in the air. Many factors went to make it apparent – there were fewer taxis about and the streets were emptier and bleaker, because the taxis were being used to rush troops to the front and refugees to the rear; people talked tensely, their faces concerned, leaning over tables; you noticed, curiously enough, the whites of their eyes more. Perhaps these dilate with fear. They were more impatient, more nervy.

I had noticed it first when I droved to the Hôtel Saint Romain. When I had reached there in February from Finland, in the middle of the night, the proprietor, since the war his own night porter, had carried up my bags and got me supper, talking cheerfully all the time. Now he forced a smile for my welcome, worriedly said, yes, he thought he had a room, hurried down as soon as he had shown me to it, and contented himself, when he saw from my police form that I came from Belgium, with saying,

'*Alors, c'est bien fini la bas, eh?*' instead of breaking into his usual flow of questions.

This atmosphere was a shock. In our two days on the way from Brussels we had had no outside news. I had regarded Paris as well away from the war zone, a safe base city from which I could make my way back at leisure to the Belgians at Ostend. Yet here it was, grim if not determined, manifestly in danger.

21

Maytime in Paris

Paris had three weeks more of freedom before she began to serve her term of bitter imprisonment under the Nazis, years which were to leave scars which still remain. She had three weeks during which the Reichswehr was fighting its way to Dunkirk, and then reorganising and driving south across the Somme, until the French Government were to flee to Tours, leaving the capital to fall into the hands of Hitler. It was an extraordinary period to experience. Out there in Flanders, and to the north, the greatest battle the world had ever known was raging, with this beautiful city as one of its main prizes. Yet here inside Paris itself there was hardly a sign that this was different from any other spring. Like a beautiful woman, Paris waited, delicate, lovely, to see who should conquer, who should possess her. Not until the end was very near were there any signs of war in the city itself, and even then they were few – an occasional barricade, the thunder of guns at night, tanks in the streets at dawn.

Never was Paris so beautiful as in those last days of May and early June. Dawn came clear, tinted, gentle behind Notre Dame; midday was a blaze of sunshine on the chestnuts along the Champs Elysées, on the red umbrellas on the café terraces; in the evening the sun went down behind the Arc de Triomphe and the soft spring night came slowly over the boulevards. We walked across the Tuileries, where children played on the unscythed grass, to conferences at the War Ministry, where we heard of more German advances towards '*Le camp entranché de Dunquerque*' – Dunkirk, an inferno of fires and corpses rotting in the sand and long lines of men waiting under the bombers, and here the birds singing in the limes of the little square beyond the red, white and blue striped sentry box in the Rue Saint Dominique. We lunched in the shade at the Racing Club in the heart of the Bois, while overhead tiny white specks turned and fought for the possession of the sky above Paris, and the radio told of heavy counterattacks '*pour le saillant d'A-miens*', Amiens where men were being crushed under the caterpillars of the German tanks and where shells burst all day in the streets where the refugees cowered. We walked back from the evening conference, with its same tale of blood and steel and the ghastly noise of battle transformed and hidden behind brief words of *combat locales*, and the Seine shone like silk beneath the bridges and the old men sat and fished from the quays under the Concorde Bridge where Daladier's police had fired on the rioters of 1934.

I had taken charge of the *Daily Express* Paris office again, even though Sefton Delmer was now also based on Paris. Tom Delmer, as he was known to his colleagues and friends, was at that time one of the half-dozen best known figures in British journalism. A big, stout man in his early thirties, he was a blend of Friar Tuck and Prince Hal, with a commanding presence, a sharp eye for his own (and his paper's) advantage, and yet with a merry, boyish manner, in which there was even a hint of diffidence. The son of an Australian-born professor of English in Berlin, he had spent the First World War as a schoolboy partly at a German Gymnasium and partly at St Paul's in London, at both of which he had suffered because he did not fit the accepted norm. He spoke perfect German, a quality which had made him an outstanding correspondent in Berlin for the *Daily Express* – he had walked through the burning Reichstag with Hitler – and was to make him a formidable head of Black Propaganda in World War II.

In Paris this May Delmer had opted for the role of war correspondent with the Allied armies awaiting the German attack along the line of the Somme. George Millar, also in war correspondent's uniform, was ready to report from the French army's fronts. With the blinded hopefulness without which wars could not be endured, I allowed myself a faint belief that a line might yet be stabilised along the Somme, linking up with the still intact Maginot Line, that we might still get to the more static warfare for which our armies were trained. And with every day that passed I got increasingly restless, increasingly anxious to get back to Britain and to get some role, however minor, in which I could take a direct part in fighting this monstrous force. It was no longer a question of freeing other countries from Nazism. It was now a question of preventing it over-running our own country – and installing in its wake a British version of itself.

I scanned the British papers for signs that Britain was aware of the danger which faced it. They seemed disturbingly few. The papers were worried about the right name for what was to become the Home Guard. Should they be called 'parashots', or 'anti-parachutists' or 'paracops'? 'Vicar joins the parashots' ran one headline. Anyone would have thought it was a clay pigeon shoot. What we wanted, I felt, was a million tough, armed, determined men to back up the fighting forces. We were to get them, but in those lotus-eating days in Paris the chances seemed remote.

I was, at this distance, misreading the British mood, and I was underestimating what Churchill would do. He seemed to me too old for the task, however valiant his spirit. Old men like Gamelin had failed France. Even older men, like the 84-year-old Pétain and the 73-year-old Weygand were about to surrender her. I had shocked Mara Scherbatoff by declaring, when Pétain was appointed Deputy Prime Minister, that he was the one man famous enough to sack Gamelin and make peace with Hitler. That forecast was to prove true. But it was only when Churchill's first great speech to the House of Commons was printed in the Paris *New York Herald Tribune* that I realised that he was someone very, very different, someone at last who understood the nature of the enemy we were up against. One passage in particular caught my eye. In it he spoke of the 'dull, plodding masses of the German infantry, ever ready to stamp out with their jackboots the freedoms which they have long surrendered in their own land'. For the first time I became aware of the way in which, as Edward R. Murrow was to put it, Churchill 'mobilised the English language and sent it into battle to fight for democracy'.

The sense that Britain was not only in the struggle, but likely to become the next front line, subtly modified my relationship with the American correspondents with whom I had so long worked, and at least two of whom, Eric Sevareid and Walter Kerr, were close friends. Though I continued to work closely with them, I felt myself now increasingly in a world apart. They felt the tragedy of these defeats, they were heart and soul on our side, but they were not yet in the battle. They had another chance. If Europe fell, they could return to America, and prepare to fight on there. But for us this battle of France, and the battle of Britain which loomed ahead, were the last chance. The Americans could, however deeply they felt, watch this fighting as a spectacle, something to be reported in the coolly objective terms demanded by the American networks. I could not do that. Increasingly I found myself feeling as I was sure the Czechs and the Poles and the Finns had felt towards us: 'However much you sympathise with us, and want us to win, you are not caught up in it as we are, it's not quite your war – yet.'

I felt this keenly on Sunday, 19 May, two days after I had reached Paris, when Vincent Sheean took me to see Claire Booth Luce. I noted my reactions at the time in the diary notes I kept intermittently.

I had been to see Jimmy Sheean at the Crillon, and he said, 'Come across to the Ritz and meet the loveliest woman in France – the loveliest woman you ever saw. Haven't you met Claire Booth? But Geoffrey, she's the loveliest and wittiest creature you ever saw, and you must meet her. I'll take you over now.'

Behind the Louvre the sky was pale primrose and children played in the Tuileries around the half-finished ARP trenches. In the Place Vendôme sandbags had burst around the foot of Napoleon's Column. 'It's instinct that Hitler's got. He's got the most phenomenal instinct of anyone of our time,' said Jimmy. 'Not brains. Just instinct.'

We went in through the narrow doors of the Ritz, the doorway which never looked as if it led to an hotel, let alone to the grandest of hotels, and up in a gilded lift cage, where the liftman was dressed like a footman in livery, and along the shell pink corridor.

Claire Booth was indeed lovely, in her late thirties or early forties, with fair hair and a slightly worn, well pressed, well dry-cleaned American face, a little lined but still beautiful. There was no doubt about the sharpness of her mind. With her was a General in British uniform with red tabs. He was Lindemann, brother of the Professor I had met at Oxford. 'Jimmy, they're in Amiens and the advance guard is in Abbeville, and it's all up,' was her greeting. 'They're in Abbeville and the Channel ports will go.' Her voice was full of brave tones, as if to say 'I'll face the worst. No need to hide anything from me, even though it hurts me to hear it'. I felt suddenly savage, and cursed her, sitting there with a clipper ticket in her pocket, knowing you can get out when you want to, and it's all a great experience and good copy. But it's not your war, and it doesn't go right inside you as it does us. I know now what the Czechs felt about us, and why the porter in the Ambassador in Prague was so savage on the night of Munich, and said, 'You go away, but we have to stay here and live with it.' I knew that Claire Booth felt it deeply all right, but it was her playground which was broken up, not her life.

Lindemann was talking of the German tank columns. 'They spend the nights in a sort of korral with their transport in the middle. I can't understand why we don't take a few bombers and smash them at any cost. I'd take a bomber and crash it down on them if they would let me,' and I knew he would, and felt better.

The sunshine streamed across the ironwork on the balcony and into the room with its pale green furnishings. A cool wind stirred the curtains but I felt suddenly stifled, and said I must get away to the office. Outside in the Place Vendôme the pigeons wheeled around Napoleon's Column. In Schiaparelli's window three gold ornaments and a black handbag lay on the silk display cases. In the background was the flat where Noël Coward had carried out the hush hush mission which everyone seemed to know about, in those first foolish days of the war.

*

One evening a few days after my return to Paris Charles Gombaux of the *Paris Soir* took me to visit Paul Reynaud in his flat on the Left Bank near the Chamber of Deputies. It was a small, compact place, reached up a narrow flight of stairs, but Reynaud preferred it to the official residence of the Prime Minister in the Hôtel Matignon.

Reynaud was sitting in an arm chair by a low table covered with documents. It was the first time I had seen him since the war. He looked pale, his face puffy with fatigue, which made his high arching eyebrows seem almost artificially black. But he radiated a quiet defiance, and was confident that under Weygand the Germans would be halted when they thrust south. Hélène de Portes came and went from time to time, as we talked. I knew of her as Reynaud's mistress, but had no idea at this stage of the power she was exercising both in the choice of ministers and in the conduct of affairs, and I have to admit that I did not study her closely. I carried away only an impression of an active woman, expensively dressed, with an unusually athletic build for a Parisienne and with dark hair brushed into curls, giving an impression of tousled, restless energy.

Reynaud was Minister of Defence as well as Prime Minister, and meetings of his War Cabinet were held in the War Ministry in the Rue St Dominique, a five-minute walk from his flat. In the same building conferences to brief the French and the foreign press were held each morning and evening. We would gather in a long room frowsty with ornamented chairs, and with walls hung with suits of armour. They were wonderful suits of armour, chain and mail and sheet, with spears and lances and pikes underneath them, and they gave an appropriate touch of irony to the scene they looked down on. For they seemed only a little more out of date than the rifles and light anti-tank guns and inferior planes with which the French army was opposing the highly mechanised, highly trained Reichswehr. This lovely old rambling building, with its creamy walls, its courtyard peaceful as an Oxford college quadrangle, its red, white and blue sentry box that looked like something out of a comic opera set, was in atmosphere a building of another era, not of the twentieth century. This era, this war called for rooms with great businesslike desks and lines of telephones and swift lifts and radios and speed and machinery. The Third Republic, someone has pointed out, never succeeded in evolving its own style of architecture. It took over all the fripperies and ornateness of the Third Empire, as if it lacked confidence in itself. Now, like the Third Empire, it was crumbling to ruins.

So in the fresh morning sunshine, and in the warm evening sunshine, George Millar, Eric Sevareid, Walter Kerr and I would walk down the narrow Rue St Dominique, show our passes to the Gardes Mobiles in their shining black steel helmets at the iron gates of the War Ministry, and cross the wide hallway to the conference room. Often in that hallway we would pass the men who were ruling France – Weygand, striding up the stairs two at a time; Daladier, red-faced, glowering; de Gaulle, tall, stiff; Blum, grey, gentle, yet surprisingly robust in figure;

shaggy-moustached Louis Marin; the sly Bonnet; the thin-lipped pale figure of Georges Mandel, who had been secretary in World War I to Clemenceau – 'The Tiger' – and was now Minister of the Interior.

In the conference room the grey-haired old men of the French press and the younger British and American correspondents would gather. Everything had its set routine. On my first visit I sat on a chair near the door. But some old French correspondent had sat on it every day since the war began, and he raised as much fuss as if I had shouted, 'Heil Hitler'. There was Charles Maurice, pompous as ever, getting together a few scraps of fact for his long-winded articles in the *Petit Parisien*. There was de Caux of *The Times* with whom I had spent so many vigils in the Telefonica in Madrid, watching and listening with a calm I envied and admired. A liaison officer in the Great War with the British army, he sat now, tall and erect and quiet, recording philosophically the breakdown of this world which he knew and loved.

A stir by the doorway, and Colonel Thomas, the official spokesman, would stride in. A tall Norman with dark hair *en brosse*, pince-nez and a sense of confidence and strength, he was an excellent man for this job. True, he told us very little, but that was what the French High Command wanted. In a few incisive sentences he would outline the main shape of the struggle, answer or not answer a few questions, and the conference would be over, with the Germans a few score miles more across France, more towns bombed, the end a little nearer.

In the last week of May the Dunkirk evacuation was drawing to its close and our eyes and the eyes of all the world turned on the battle of France. On the line of the Somme, the Aisne Canal and Aisne the French at last had a front on which to stand. Here, Colonel Thomas told us, strongpoints, villages and woods defended with artillery and anti-tank guns, were being organised in depth. New tactics were to be employed. The tank columns would be allowed to pass, but these strong points, *points d'appui*, would hold up the infantry. The High Command were 'cautiously optimistic'. At Reithel, at the western end of the Maginot Line, the Germans had been attacking in old style, with infantry unsupported by tanks following an artillery barrage, and the French had held them easily. Once the speed of the war slowed down, all would be well.

But the main *point d'appui*, Paris, was not being put in a state of defence. Would Paris be defended, we asked? Of course, we were told. But there were few signs of it. Sevareid and Kerr and I drove out north eastwards, past Le Bourget Airport. Here and there on the roads that ran across the open country a tank waited by the roadside, a few troops guarding a barricade near by. They might have been some protection against parachutists or spies, but no more. Inside the city itself we had seen a few small sandbagged pillboxes being set up at the Rond Point, but in the outskirts there was nothing, no real barricades, no tank traps, no last-line defences such as Madrid built, such as England was to be covered with by late August.

The long, white French road, lined with poplars, wound over the plain. Paris, close at hand, was hidden by a curve in the ground. Then we came over the rise and there was Montmartre, with Sacré Coeur white and glowing on the top, and the tiny Meccano toy of the Eiffel Tower. How long would it be before the German tank crews were staring at it from this point? What a sight they would have of it, just as the Moors of Franco's army had when they first climbed the Hill of the Angels on the Castilian Plain and saw ahead the roofs of Madrid. In silence we drove on back to the city, past the old forts that had held the Prussians in 1870, which could help to hold them again if men with weapons were put along their ramparts. There were men there in plenty in those Paris streets, but they had no weapons.

On Monday, 3 June, I lunched with de Caux and his wife in a flat they had leased on the Place de la Madeleine. It was brilliantly sunny outside, with a whitish haze above the great squat mass of the Madeleine. Tom Cadett of *The Times* and I stood with the de Cauxs on their balcony and drank sherry before lunch. The room behind, the sitting room of the flat, was a museum piece. The woman who owned it was the daughter of a friend of Zola, and photographs of the writer and scores of knick-knacks and bits of bric-à-brac covered the walls and the tables.

Half-way through lunch the sirens went. We had had them often enough at night and morning recently, but this was the first daylight warning for a long time. In the streets the police whistles blew and the Place steadily emptied. We heard guns in the distance.

Throughout the meal we could hear overhead, distant, very high, the drone of planes, and roars that might have been bombs but might equally well have been guns. It kept up for a full hour. The All Clear had only just gone when I left just after two o'clock and went round to Pierre Lazareff's flat in the Palais Royale. His wife, Hélène Gordon, was there.

'What news have you?' she asked me. 'Of the raid, of course.'

Before I could reply the phone rang. Pierre was speaking from his office. I could hear Hélène repeating, 'Citroên works, Boulevard Souchet, Air Ministry.' So it had been the real thing – a full-scale bombing raid, the first Paris had ever known. I grabbed a taxi outside the door and rushed off.

We had had many *alertes* in Paris in the early days of the war, and some raiding on the outskirts this spring, but there had been no real attempt to hit the centre of the city. I drove along the quays to the Citroën works. A huge crowd blocked the last half mile. I went through on foot. Firemen were hosing a part of the factory that was blazing fiercely. Cars, half finished, were being dragged out on to the pavement; wounded were being carried from houses and cafés smashed near by. A line of bomb craters ran up the street towards the new, brick-red Air Ministry. All the windows were out of the main building.

One bomb had gone through the wall, another had gone clean through the Minister's study next door. Bullitt, the American Ambassador, who had been lunching there with the Air Minister, had missed death by feet.

I drove across towards the Porte de Versailles. Bombs had fallen haphazardly, tearing the innards out of flats and houses. It was the first bombing I had seen of an area I had known well in peace time. One bomb had fallen in the roadway outside the Auteuil flat where we lived in our first days in Paris. Houses along the street where Cecily had taken Peter for his morning walk were one line of destruction. One big crater lay in the Boulevard Suchet, five hundred yards from the house the Duke and Duchess of Windsor had lived in till the invasion began and – under advice from London – they had moved off abruptly to Biarritz. The French had not like that move, though enough of them had already gone to Biarritz themselves. 'Gone with the Windsors,' they used to say in Paris. It gaped now in front of the flats where the pick of the Hundred Families used to live, and maids and butlers in livery came out and emptied dust trays of broken glass into the gutter.

The main damage was on the outskirts. The railway junctions at Versailles and St Oye had been badly smashed. At Surennes the hospital was hit. One bomb at Versailles went through the roof of the courtroom where Weidemann, the German who had murdered six people in France in 1937, had been condemned to death in the last April before the war. It passed clean through the dock where he had sat. In all over eight hundred people were killed and injured in this raid.

The bombing of Paris had been the first move in the final battle of France. At the rail centres through which the French reserves and supplies would be moved, at the airfields from which the scanty French air force would work, the Germans had struck heavily. The next night, the night of 4 June, they made their final preparations.

With incredible speed they had turned their armies south-
wards from Dunkirk towards the Somme and the Aisne.
At dawn on Wednesday 5 June they began their attack.
That morning when we went to the War Ministry Colonel
Thomas came in, his face grave, and said simply, '*Alors,
messieurs, ça commence.*'

The attack came all along the line, but developed
chiefly at two points. From their bridgehead across the
Somme at Amiens one gigantic tank column thrust forward, trying to get to the lower stretches of the Seine and
cut off Paris from Brittany and the part of the coast
through which British aid could still come. Another hit
down towards Rheims, to cut down behind the Maginot
Line and isolate the troops there. Stubbornly in their
positions the French resisted, but they had not the organisation or the armament for this moving war. The break
came more rapidly than we expected. By Friday the
French were moving back. By Saturday June 6 they were
at Rouen, on the Seine, to the west of Paris.

I was determined that this time I would have my lines
of retreat prepared, and not left to chance, as in Brussels.
My luck had held there, but I was not going to rely on it
again. So I laid plans carefully, helped by George Millar,
who showed at this time that capacity for thinking ahead,
which was to make him a highly successful Maquis leader
in the Besançon area four years later.

The *Daily Express* already had one car, a Renault
convertible, which could seat three people. Sefton
Delmer, who was determined to wait until the last minute
and cover the fall of the city, needed this. For the rest of
us I bought a big Renault limousine which could, at a
pinch, carry seven people. My Belgian experience had
convinced me that we must carry our own reserves of
petrol. I secured a hundred-litre drum, a *bidon*, which I
managed to get filled from a special pump run by the
American Legion, the veterans association of World War
I. We hid the car and the *bidon*, in a locked garage. All
over Paris people were making similar plans, storing

petrol in cans in attics, in gardens, even in their homes. If the Germans had dropped incendiary bombs on the city, it would have been an inferno within a few minutes. But they didn't. They didn't need to. They were going to get the place intact.

We bought, too, sleeping-bags, and maps of Southern France, and laid in a store of tinned meat and pâtés, and of wine and mineral water. All of these arrangements, simple enough in themselves, seemed extraordinarily difficult at the time. As the danger increased, so too did a strange sense of lassitude and fatalism. The immediate future was so ugly that you hated to think about it, let alone prepare for it. This lassitude took many forms. Some of those who refused to contemplate the future excused their attitude as being one of optimism and courage, and my insistence on these preparations could bring mutterings of 'defeatisme' or 'paniquards'. Others laughed confidently, reproached me for worrying too much, and then at the last minute rushed round to see if they could get in on the arrangements I had made. But I had my experience in Belgium to spur me on, to enable me to fight the waves of laziness and irresponsibility which swept over me. It was so much easier just to drop in at the Crillon Bar, and chat with the war correspondents with the RAF, who made it their base, and who were the best informed of us all, or with American diplomats who had strolled across from the Embassy, than to continue to search for petrol or maps.

My visits to the Crillon Bar led to me being caught up in a dawn sweep to gather in Fifth Columnists. Though later research has shown that the Germans had no Fifth Column in Paris and other parts of France, that the whole idea that they had a widespread net of sympathisers and agents spreading rumours and creating panic was a myth, it was a myth almost universally believed at the time. Early on Thursday, 4 June, the day after the final German attack had been launched, I was towelling myself down in my bedroom at the Hôtel St Romain, after taking a shower, when the door was suddenly flung open and a British military police officer, his uniform ablaze with red tabs, and a French officer with gleaming Sam Browne came into the room and demanded my papers. I had been reported as a suspicious foreigner constantly in the company of British officers in the Crillon. My papers were not in order, as I had entered France from Belgium without a permit, and the Frenchman was all for arresting me then and there. But the British officer, who was no less a figure than the Assistant Provost Marshal, gave me the all clear, and went off calming down his furiously protesting French colleague.

As soon as the German attack began I had sent Stephen Charing, the assistant correspondent in the *Express* office, ahead to Tours, which we believed would be the place to which the French Government would move. He secured rooms for us at the Hôtel de l'Univers and set up an office there. Swiftly the remainder of the week passed. George Millar and I would work in the morning and then drive out to swim in the Racing Club pool in the Bois. Suntanned Parisiennes lay on the grass at its edge, or bought drinks from the open-air bar, or flirted with the RAF pilots on sick leave, many with newly healed wound scars on their legs and backs. Next week, we used to say to each other, Hitler's SS will probably be swimming here. We may as well enjoy it while we can. The sunburnt girls were usually rather bitter, for their boys of our age were *quelque part sur le front* and why weren't we mobilised? They had a right to be bitter, though there were plenty of young Frenchmen too hanging round this pool, men employed in 'essential services' at the rear.

In the evenings, after we had sent off the news from the evening conference and while we waited for any later developments, we would go to the Café Flore, just down the Boulevard St Germain. Every night there would be a visit by police with their capes rolled under their arms, who examined everyone's papers. It did not take them long, because most of the people at the marble-topped

tables were there night after night. In the Flore everyone
knew everyone else. There was a floating population of
girls, some mannequins, some shop girls, some typists,
eating meals with anyone who had the money, having
affairs with different people but always rather respectably
and with a direct simplicity that came from their peasant
origin. Lucienne, one of them, was typical. A Normandy
blonde, she posed for magazine covers, laughed, ate when
she had money or when her friends had, had a violent
love affair with a young RAF pilot on seven days' leave,
was heartbroken the day he left, and laughing and fatalis-
tic the day after.

There was little wild living in this dying Paris, little of
the reckless abandon, the last days of Babylon spirit that
one thinks of in times of crisis. The police regulations
were against this, for one thing. All the night clubs were
closed, all dancing prohibited. Half the big hotels were
shut. The cafes closed at ten-thirty. The city had already
half emptied, and the restaurants were sparsely filled.
Instead of wanting to live wildly, people seemed to desire
to savour quietly the small things which they found
enjoyable, like sipping an apéritif in a café in the sun,
walking in the Bois, talking, taking a quiet meal in their
favourite small restaurant. Troops back on leave took
their girl friends to dinner, walked home with them in the
warm black-out. The poet and novelist Antoine Saint
Exupéry, who was one of my heroes, we found and
interviewed one day on 48 hours' leave writing away at a
new book in the corner of a Montparnasse café.

These last few days we paid our farewells to places we
had loved. We drove up the Place du Théâtre in Montmartre and dined at the tables with their red and white
check tablecloths in the open square, cheerful despite the
black-out. A lone Russian violinist strolled round playing.
Before the war he had had a mate, like himself a White
Russian refugee, but when the Soviet-German pact was
signed the mate had been badly beaten up by a drunken
enthusiast who was looking for any Russian, of any type,

to hit. We motored through the Bois, where I had often ridden in the mornings in those distant pre-war days, to Saint Cloud park where the goldfish swam in the pond around which my son had played, and near which the first great German concentration camp in Paris was to be set up. Much of the park was fenced off, for AA guns – mostly old French 75mm field guns with their barrels set skywards – were in position to guard the Renault works below.

By Saturday night, 8 June, the guns from the battlefield could be clearly heard in Paris. We had got used to the AA now, but behind their roar came a new sound – the growl of the artillery on the front, a sign that that front was dangerously close. One tank column was reported to be across the river at Rouen; others were in the forest of Chantilly to the north, where a stone monument by the roadside still marked the nearest point that the Kaiser's Uhlans had got to Paris in 1914. In the blackout I watched the big dust carts and farm wagons being trundled out on to the Champs Elysées and the other boulevards running down from the Etoile, placed there to prevent these splendid wide streets being used as landing grounds for gliders.

In the grey dawn, too, tanks now patrolled the main streets, and the Place de la Concorde was a camp for troops all night. One enthusiast used to drive a peculiarly noisy tank up and down the Rue Royale just outside my window. Every now and then a new ack-ack gun in the Tuileries would roar out, its flash lighting up the windows of the hotel. Yet the crowds still went quietly to the cafés, and quietly home in the blackout.

By Sunday it was clear the end was near. At the morning conference Colonel Thomas looked tired and anxious. One German column, he confirmed, was definitely across the Seine to the west of the city. Others were drawing closer.

For the last time we drove out to the swimming pool. I was dressing at lunchtime when Ken Downs arrived. 'The

Germans are at Creil,' he said. That placed them only thirty miles from the centre of the city, a day's drive for a tank column.

That afternoon we made our final preparations to leave. From the *Paris Soir*, in whose offices we worked, we drew a stock of French francs; all spare papers we got ready to burn. M Prouvost, the millionaire proprietor of *Paris Soir*, was now Minister of Information. He had been put into the Cabinet when Reynaud made his last reshuffle. We knew if we watched *Paris Soir*, and moved when they did, we would have a good idea of the Government's plans. And at mid-afternoon this Sunday *Paris Soir* started loading cars and vans to take staff and equipment to Central France, where they were to print on Laval's presses at Clermont Ferrand. They offered to take Mara Scherbatoff and her sisters with them to Clermont Ferrand, but Sherb would not go. Nor would she come with us to Tours. Her family would stick it out in Paris. I thought it a wise decision. As White Russians they would have nothing to fear from the Germans, and they would be spared the turmoil and upheaval of quitting their home.

At five o'clock the phone rang. M Prouvost would like to see the British correspondents immediately in his room at the Hôtel Continental, which served as the Ministry of Information. Prouvost, tall, dark, urbane, well dressed, looked more the businessman than the journalist. He was the representative of a rich northern textile trust which had put its money into *Paris Soir*. Largely owing to the genius of Pierre Lazareff, they had built the paper into the largest and by far the brightest journal in France, and had built up *Match*, a French copy – and a brilliant copy – of the American illustrated weekly *Life*, to a huge circulation.

Prouvost, it soon appeared, did not want to see us because the Government was about to leave. He was new in the job and wanted to meet us because of the hard days ahead. That was all, he explained.

'Gentlemen, I can assure you the news is better tonight. I have just seen the Generalissimo and I can give you that assurance. There is no question of the Government leaving Paris. When it does leave, I will let you know and you will follow my Ministry, attached to me. Now perhaps you would like a few details of the impression I have gained of my talk with the Generalissimo.'

In clipped sentences, as if he were writing one of the inside story articles *Match* ran every week, he went on to give a typical French journalist's picture of Weygand. 'One enters by a courtyard, along a passage, and *voilà*, a little room, quite simple, that is the work room of this man who controls the fate of France . . .'

So on, and so on. Very interesting background, but a sheer waste of time to journalists waiting for one item of news and one only – where had the Germans got to?

The phone interrupted him. 'A cabinet meeting at seven, certainly.' He hung up the ancient bedroom phone which was still in use in this gaudy old hotel, and turned back to urge us to tell England that the situation was far from desperate, that we should send all the material, all the planes we could.

At that moment two burly porters in blue workmen's blouses came into the room, picked up a filing cabinet, and carried it towards the door. 'What are you about?' demanded the Minister.

One porter shrugged his shoulders. '*On part*,' he said. '*On part pour Tours. Nous avons nos ordres*'. It was clear that the new Minister of Information was no better informed than his predecessors had been.

At the back of the Hôtel Continental big lorries were drawn up, being loaded with documents and furniture. At the Ministry of the Marine Sunday afternoon strollers were watching sailors carrying out bundles of documents and stacking them into lorries parked beside the wall of the Ministry on which was kept, glassed in as a souvenir, the mobilisation poster of 1914, with beside it now that of 1939. The military press conference we learnt would in future be held not at the Rue St Dominique, but at the Quai d'Orsay – a clear sign that the War Ministry was also on the move.

Prouvost was to play only a very brief, but a very important role on the French political stage. He owed his appointment to Hélène de Portes, who had been one of many elegant women whom he delighted to have at receptions in his magnificent apartment overlooking the Trocadero. She had exacted a price for the appointment. The letter inviting Prouvost to join the Cabinet was brought to him by hand by an ex-mistress of his, who was a close friend of the Comtesse de Portes. She had the satisfaction of seeing the man who had spurned her accept Cabinet rank from her own hand. Prouvost had never been a Deputy or a Senator, and was to be a Cabinet Minister for only a few weeks. Yet in that time he was to have a decisive influence on the course of French history, for he was one of the strongest peacemakers when the final decision to surrender or fight on came to be made at Bordeaux.

With the irony in which history delights, the final War Ministry conference in Paris was held that evening in the ornate conference room of the Quai d'Orsay in which eleven years earlier Germany and France had joined other countries in signing the Kellogg Pact, renouncing war as an instrument of national policy. Colonel Thomas was late, and all his news was bad. The Germans were already at Forges les Eaux, a popular bathing place twenty-five miles from Paris. Indignantly the French correspondents asked for definite news, particularly about the Government's plans to move, rumours of which were already sending people stampeding in their tens of thousands on the roads to the south.

That night I sent a description of Paris about to fall, with gun flashes lighting the horizon, and smoke drifting over from fires on the outskirts. The smoke was still there in the morning when I drove to the office. The advance party of the *Paris Soir* had left. At twelve o'clock we were rung up by American Press Wireless, the only reliable speedy method of getting our news out – it all went to London via New York at three shillings a word. They were moving to Tours that afternoon. The roads were already one great traffic jam. At three o'clock the censorship closed down. Reluctantly the Ministry of Information admitted that the Government might be moving – it was in fact already hot on its way to Tours. We decided the time had come to put our plan of evacuation into action.

We loaded up the big Renault, destroyed all our spare papers, collected the office files, put aboard the *bidon* of petrol, and set out. At the St Romain, when I went to collect my bags, the proprietor and his wife were frantic with anxiety. They wanted someone to drive their two daughters, sixteen and fourteen, down to their parents' home in Central France. We tried by phone to find someone for them, but we could do nothing. Our route lay further east, and *Paris Soir* could not help. The younger daughter wept uncontrollably in the corner of the lounge, her sister trying to comfort her. The dry stench of defeat and fear was over everything.

Their quest had a tragic ending. When I returned to Paris for the first time after the war, in 1946, the proprietor and his wife broke into tears the moment they saw me. They told me the girls got away the next day with a friend, only for the older girl to be killed when a bridge south of Paris was hit by a German bomb.

We drove across the river and down the Boulevard St Germain. There was the Flore, with most of the regulars on the terrace. The blonde head of Lucienne gleamed in the sun. She recognised us and waved. Back up the Champs Elysées. Strange, there are those two refugee girls from Vienna who appeared just before the war and were always on the Champs Elysées in its first days, passing steadily from check tweed suits to prosperity and mink coats. There they sit, calmly waiting. Are they spies, or have they just got good nerves?

We drove out by St Cloud, across the new bridge which

I had watched being built, and which I had so often envisaged as the setting for this evacuation. The Seine, its water clean because there were few barges on it, gleamed under the willows. The tower on the Longchamps grand-stand showed through the trees of the Bois, and the white walls of 32 Rue du Calvaire glowed in the sunlight. The café to which I had run to summon the taxi driver M Audet to take Cecily to hospital when Patrick was about to be born was closed. Its owners must have fled with the rest.

On the bend of the road curving up the St Cloud hill we were suddenly no longer one car, but a unit in the great column of refugee vehicles pouring out of the city. I looked back over Paris in the late afternoon sun, over the view I had looked out over so often, morning and evening, and I realised I was leaving not only Paris, but a whole period of life, a period in which there had been time to play.

22

Exodus

George Millar's war correspondent's uniform and passes won us access to a road set aside for military vehicles, and for a time we moved swiftly along a wide road through a forest, where tanks stood hidden under trees, their crews stripped to the waist to wash in the streams, and ambulances waited near by. But south of Versailles we were caught up again in the main refugee flood.

Unlike the evacuation from Barcelona, which had been mainly on foot, or that from Belgium, which had been largely by cart and by bicycle, the flight from Paris was predominately by car. Wide, low-slung family cars, bought to carry people fishing or camping or bathing, now crawled along with mattresses and luggage on the top, blankets and cooking gear crammed inside, sometimes with a pram, often with one or two bicycles strapped to the roof or the back. Every variety of motor vehicle was there. Sleek limousines with uniformed chauffeurs; great lorries loaded with machinery; a tractor hauling a high, curved Norman farm wagon packed with women and children; vans bearing the names of laundries, perfume makers, greengrocers, clothiers, each crammed with people and belongings; Paris taxis, and many, many old cars which looked as if they had been taken from junk heaps or dusted down from garages where they had lain unused for years. Hens, sheep and cats rode in trailers, and every car seemed to have its dog. In and out of this column moved an accompanying stream of people on cycles and on foot, the swish, swish of their tyres and the tramp of their feet sounding amidst the noise of car engines.

Frequently the column would halt – something which brought new problems. To save petrol, drivers would switch off their engines. But many of the cars did not have self starters. Each time we moved on, drivers had to crank their vehicles to get the engine running – a process which could take time, and sometimes failed. Then the stalled car, its occupants wide-eyed with anxiety, would be forced to the roadside, or even into the ditch, to let the rest crawl on.

For miles we jolted and crept along behind a lorry loaded with machinery, where a sullen workman with tattooed arms caressed two black retrievers, in the intervals at glaring at our efforts to pass by. We crawled, stopped, crawled on again until dark came down. We were now in open country, where wide unfenced fields stretched away to the horizon. Every few yards now cars and lorries were halted, with mothers feeding babies and putting children to sleep in the fields. Just north of Chartres we turned into a field from which the hay had recently been cut, took out our sleeping-bags, and dined off crusty bread, sardines, cheese and red wine. It was a glorious night, aglow with stars. Only the moving line of black shadows on the roads, and the occasional glare of headlights told us that the evacuation was going ceaselessly on, or even hinted at war. Suddenly, an anti-aircraft gun boomed close by, a shell sang through the air, and burst high above us. The drone of a plane followed. Then the gun was silent again in the hay-scented night. Across the field came the sounds of children crying.

By three in the morning we were on our way again, part of a line of old cars and trucks which looked like the scene from the film of Steinbeck's *Grapes of Wrath*, when the Okies fled from the dust bowl of the Middle West to California. In every village, as the morning light came, people stood in queues before bakers' shops, hoping to buy something for their children to eat. Every food shop, be it a bakers or grocers or butchers or greengrocers or general provision sellers was stripped bare of produce, its windows empty. In farmhouse courtyards exhausted children slept under haycarts, whilst haggard women queued to get water from farm pumps. In one village a group of soldiers were carrying in a blanket the body of a seventy-year-old woman who had died of exposure when caught in a thunderstorm during the night. The storms had missed us, but had hit other regions, and continued throughout the next day, soaking the trampling columns, drenching the mattresses and the bags piled on the tops of cars.

The rest of the road to Tours was marked for me by dark-eyed, tired children staring from the interior of darkened lorries and of crowded cars as the line of traffic moved a few paces, and then jerked to yet another stop. At one place a girl of nine was watching over five other children in a broken-down car. Their mother had gone off two hours before in search of food and help. Every half mile broken-down cars had been tipped into ditches to clear the road. In one village I met a journalist from *L'Ordre*. He told me that in the wood where they had camped the night before they were awakened by shrieks from a ten-year-old boy who rushed towards them shouting, 'Mama is dying; Mama is dying.' They found the mother twenty yards away, lying under a bush, beginning to give birth to a child. They had walked the two miles to this village in search, but no doctor was available, and only now, nine hours later, was a midwife on her way. The woman had lain in her suffering all the night, whilst one air-raid alarm followed another, and anti-aircraft shells burst overhead.

In another village I caught up with a big car in which were travelling a Belgian senator and his wife and his beautiful, dark-haired daughter. I had last seen him in Brussels in April, when he had given me a lift from the

Senate in this same car. Now they had not eaten for forty-eight hours. When I gave them a tin of sardines and a loaf from our carefully hoarded stores they wept with gratitude.

As I spoke to them the column pressed on unceasingly past us, with the stench of petrol fumes filling the air, and the cries of whimpering children rising above the sound of the engines. Seen from the roadside, one aspect of it caught my eye. Many, if not most of the drivers were women. This was the women's evacuation. Their men were mobilised, and it was now the mothers and aunts and sisters who, set-faced and pale with exhaustion, tried to carry their families to safety. I began my story from Tours that evening – a story Christiansen, never one to underplay the work of his reporters, billed as 'the greatest and most moving of the war' – with the words, 'Through the green fields of the Loire and the Touraine today the mass evacuation from Paris produced scenes the world has not known since the days when Londoners fled the city at the time of the Great Plague, and roamed the countryside.' I concluded with this wording, 'When war hits England we must prepare schemes to avoid this evacuation ordeal for our people. For it is almost the ghastliest thing of modern war – worse certainly than any bombing I have seen.'

Tours was a madhouse. Into this provincial town, built beside the wide Loire, with its sandbanks and its brown swift waters and its narrow stone bridges, had poured – and continued to pour – hundreds of thousands of refugees. It seemed as if half of Paris had fled here. In the late morning we crawled, part of this endless procession, past the airfield where bomb holes showed in the nearby fields and as newly repaired patches on the field itself. We crept over the chief bridge, merely two traffic lanes wide, which spanned the Loire into the city, and which bore the name of President Wilson, whose ramshackle handiwork at the end of World War I was now crashing about our ears. Along the narrow main street we inched our way to the Hôtel Univers, where our one precious room was being guarded by Stephen Charing. The hotel lobby was crowded with deputies and senators, many of them old, grey-haired men who had never known a day's discomfort in their lives, and who whimpered and growled because there were no rooms available, and because they had to queue to get into the restaurant.

On the wide pavement of the boulevard outside mothers with children wept because the bakers' shops were sold out, the *crêmeries* had no milk, their cars had no petrol. It was like a mad transformation of Derby Day, with people everywhere, jostling you, imploring you, harrying you, and always with their eyes on the sky beyond the rooftops in case the bombers should come. We hardly cared, in the midst of this, when we learnt that Italy too had declared war. Yet it was against this background of suffering and confusion that the Government was expecting to function, and the Cabinet to deliberate on the conduct of the war.

The censorship and Press Wireless were installed in the old telephone building, a ramshackle structure in a side street which would have been knocked over by one puff of bomb blast. Havas were already installed on the ground floor, with Reuters alongside them, and the Belgian Government censors, still eager to function. Here too gathered our colleagues. Edgar Mowrer, his hair as ever tousled, his eyes ablaze, aghast at the collapse of yet one more democracy; the red-haired H. R. Knickerbocker, with his pale horn rimmed spectacles, calm, judicial, efficient; Alexander Werth of the *Manchester Guardian*; Cadett; and William Forrest – the BEF had got him and the other war correspondents away safely from Belgium. He had flown in that morning from London along with the pregnant wife of a British consul in the south of France, whom the Foreign Office had assured that all was quiet, and that she would be quite safe to come.

Through the crowded, chaotic streets of Tours drove that afternoon a small procession which looked as if it had been introduced by a Hollywood director who was determined that his war picture was going to have a touch of glamour, however improbable or unrealistic it might seem. Up to the Univers came a line of ambulances and cars each driven by a cool and beautiful young woman, her carefully made up face all the more striking because of her superbly tailored khaki uniform and her elegant khaki cap. This was the Mechanised Transport Corps, a British volunteer unit into which fashionable young London had flocked. Their commander, Mrs MacDonald, had been publicity manager for Elizabeth Arden in South America. Now, with pale blue hair, self possessed and competent, she might have stepped from one of her own advertisements. George Millar's wife Netty had joined the MTC during the winter, and we searched the column for her, but she was with a separate unit which had moved south on another road.

We had been unable to find rooms in Tours for ourselves, but had secured three in a village on the outskirts. We gave up two of those to MTC drivers who themselves had no billet, and slept in the other ourselves. Jerome Willis was unlucky. He lost the toss and slept on the wire mattress. Millar and I had the two kapok mattresses on the floor.

We woke in the morning to find ourselves in a yellow stone village with green lime trees, and a Mairie where the town clerk tried to have us arrested because we had not got our identity cards signed by the police before we left Paris. But we left him expostulating by the kerbside, and drove back to Tours. The village was on the north bank, which meant we had to cross on one of the only two bridges. It took us half an hour to make our way yard by yard across the bridge, caught in a target exposed to the enemy planes which droned in the hazy sky above. In the city itself the refugees were everywhere – on pavements, in parks, in doorways, under the trees of the boulevards, more numerous, more exhausted, hungrier, more desperate than ever. Yet in the hall of the Univers

Provoust was sitting, cool and confident, as if Tours had always been the capital, and the rest of us were all making a most unnecessary fuss.

We were falsely over-confident ourselves. On this Wednesday morning the Germans had not yet taken Paris, the Panzers were still one hundred and fifty miles to the north, and we assumed – as Churchill had done – that somewhere the French High Command still possessed reserves to throw into the battle, that *masse de manoeuvre* about which the British Prime Minister had queried Gamelin – only to meet the response '*Aucune*'. We had passed on our drive south British reinforcements, red-faced, confident boys, moving towards the Seine, and had seen reformed Belgian units waiting behind their Bofors guns by the roadside. So we settled down to write our stories at the desks provided for us in the shaky telephone building, and paperhangers came in and started to rede-corate the walls.

Came Thursday, and the bombers, and Churchill. He and Halifax and Beaverbrook (transfigured now into the highly belligerent Minister of Aircraft Production) arrived during the morning at the bomb-pitted Tours airfield, and spent the afternoon in discussions with Reynaud and French Ministers in the city's Préfecture. Churchill, we learnt, had asked for an undertaking that the French would fight on. Fight on? Was there any doubt that they would? Had events reached that stage? I found it difficult to believe, until in a corner of the lounge of the Univers I came across an old French journalist with whom I had often talked in the lobby of the Chamber of Deputies. As a young infantryman, he had been one of those brought out by taxicab from Paris to be hurled against the flank of the German army advancing on the city in 1914. Now he suddenly clutched my arm, and with tears pouring from his eyes said, '*Ah, mon cher Cox, la France est finie, finie.*' Half an hour later he sought me out, and apologised, no doubt lest he be accused of defeatism. But his apology was mere form. If old Max felt like that, how much more sure would these doddering senators and their fussy, over-dressed wives and their scurrying secretaries be that France was finished?

And in the press room the first of the anecdotes about Hélène de Portes' malign influence was being recounted. She had, it was said, slammed the door of Reynaud's office in Halifax's face with the words, 'Come in only if you want to talk peace.' There is no proof that anything of the kind happened, yet the story, though untrue in itself, expressed a truth – that the Countess was now harrying Reynaud at every turn to make peace.

I had had to deal with these stories in the intervals of grappling with an exasperating administrative problem. That morning I had been standing in front of the Univers when a Paris taxi drew up. Its top was loaded with luggage, and through its windows peered the faces of Mara Scherbatoff and her sisters. All four of them and their old Swiss governess-nurse had at the last moment decided to flee. They were a heavy extra responsibility, made the less easy to bear because had they accepted the alternative plans I had made for them with *Paris Soir* they would now be in safety and comfort at Clermont Ferrand. There was nothing for it but for me to offload them into the Renault – the taxi driver was determined to return to Paris – battle my way across the bridge with them to our village billet, find rooms for them there, and make the slow, dangerous return journey into the city, along streets paralysed now by air raids. I was in no mood that evening to provide an audience for Delmer, who had arrived from Paris with an account of the superb lunch he and Eddie Ward had had in Maxims before, as the last British correspondents to leave the city, they had taken the road to Tours. The walls of the crowded hotel bar seemed paper thin as the bombers roared overhead, and the explosions from yet one more raid on the airport shook the town.

The first official confirmation of the seriousness was the situation that came late in the afternoon, when a new

military spokesman, a young Chausseur Alpine officer,
Major Vautrin, set out the facts with remarkable frankness. The reason, we later realised, was that Paul Reynaud had appealed to Roosevelt for help, and wanted
France's danger to be made clear to the United States.
The Germans, Vautrin told us, had flung over 110 divisions into this new battle. The French had less than half
that number in the field. British forces were fighting
stubbornly on the French left, along the Seine. German
tanks outnumbered the French by three to one. Paris had
been declared an open city, and was to be surrendered
without resistance. On the Maginot Line the fighting was
very heavy. At last we had something definite to write,
and no longer to contrive to make our daily bricks without
straw. How much more sensible it would have been had a
comparable candour prevailed during the earlier days,
when rumour and half truths had fed panic, and set the
refugees stampeding from their homes.

On the morning of Friday the 14th Colonel Thomas
turned up again and confirmed that the Germans had
Paris and were advancing on Chârtres. By midday the
censors were packing, and Press Wireless was gathering
together its gear, and everyone was off to Bordeaux. The
Government had already moved there. Tours was too
exposed, too full of refugees. The folly of not going from
Paris to Bordeaux in one step was exposed. At Bordeaux
the Cabinet would have had the navy at their back, and
they would have been spared this endless, unnerving
spectacle of the nation in flight, the endless weariness of
waiting for meals in overcrowded restaurants, of the din
and shoving and thrusting of crowds, and the cries of tired
children and the faces of tired mothers.

I went to the telephone building at midday, in the hope
of getting away a message to London. It was deserted
except for the paperhangers. Futility of futilities, they
were still redecorating the walls.

We decided to leave for Bordeaux at seven that night.
Delmer took his wife and Jerome Willis in the smaller

car. George Millar and I and the four Scherbatoff sisters and their governess crowded into the big Renault, with their luggage tied on top and crammed into the boot.

This was a different type of withdrawal. We were no longer moving back to find a new base from which to cover the war. France, it was clear, would soon give up the fight, and we must now find a means of escape to Britain. It could only be by sea. Any other route except through Spain would be closed by the advancing Germans – and Franco's Spain would never give me a visa. Yet we first had to make it to Bordeaux. Though we had worked out a route on side roads which were remarkably free of traffic, it soon became clear that the car was heavily overloaded. It was well down on its springs, and we could move only slowly. More ominously, one tyre kept losing pressure, and we had to stop at intervals to blow it up. Finally at three in the morning, when we were halted by a police barrier on the outskirts of Poitiers, it blew out.

As we worked to change the wheel, I put the issue to Scherb. If she and her sisters wanted to be evacuated to Britain, I would keep going as we were, and get them through somehow to Bordeaux. But if they intended to stay in France once the fighting stopped, there was no point in them going further then Poitiers. They would be as safe there as in Bordeaux – safer, indeed, for the chances of bombing would be less, and they would be closer to Paris when the time came to return. In floods of Russian the sisters debated the question. Only when we reached the centre of Poitiers did Mara Scherbatoff suddenly say, 'We will stop here.' I found them beds in a large hotel in the city centre which had set up a dormitory in its ballroom. We reached it through a surrealist setting. The hotel was being modernised, and the long, glassed-in corridor leading to the ballroom was lined with row upon row of new lavatory pans, fifty or more of them, like parading troops.

Sherb had made a wise decision. She and her family were back in Paris within a month. Their flat was intact, and they spent the war safely there, troubled by food shortages – but no worse than they would have known in Britain – and free from bombing. After Paris was freed Mara Scherbatoff met and married an American general, went to the States with him, and became a journalist in her own right in the New York office of *Paris Match*. My final sight of her was tragically unexpected. In the summer of 1956, she was killed in a road accident whilst driving to report on Arthur Miller's marriage to Marilyn Monroe. A television news cameraman filmed her body by the road-side. Watching rushes in the projection theatre at ITN in Kingsway, I suddenly saw her face on the screen, on the grass verge of an American freeway, with cars moving swiftly in the background, sixteen years on from the early morning on which our working lives had parted in Poitiers.

Millar and I drove on southwards in the grey half light. All along the roadside cars were dotted, with families sleeping in or around them. As dawn came one after another gathered its belongings and started again on this seemingly endless journey. Traffic was as yet light, and the drivers drove at speed, with tired, set faces, racing to the next village to try to get petrol, to try to get food, housing, rest. On and on went this procession. We stopped ourselves to sleep for an hour. We fell asleep and woke to the roar of cars, leaving their stink of petrol over the fresh countryside. It was a nightmare of exhaustion, with people pressing on, on, uncertain where to go, leaderless, without news – for there were no car radios then – without advice, a nation disintegrating into a mass of squabbling, exhausted, desperate individuals at the one time when it needed cohesion in the face of an enemy.

As the sun rose, to bring one more glorious day, we found ourselves in rich, rolling country, lush with grass and trees and old farmhouses. With only ourselves now to fend for, I felt a sudden sense of relief, almost of exaltation, even though we had no certainty that Bordeaux might not prove a trap rather than a way of escape.

We got petrol from a roadside pump, served by a woman impressed by Millar's spick and span uniform. When she found that we had no certificates for it she was furious, but we thrust the money into her hand and drove on. By midday we were in Bordeaux.

23

An End and a Beginning

Bordeaux was another, larger, more crowded Tours. There were no rooms to be had, not even a sofa in an hotel lounge. On the steps of the Café Bordeaux in the centre of the town stood a familiar figure. It was Colonel Thomas, grey-faced, tragic. He nodded to us stiffly.

A few minutes later a big car drove up outside the Hôtel Splendide near by. Troops on motor cycles who had escorted it rushed to the hotel door to form a cordon. A small figure in uniform strode briskly into the hotel, his lean face set, unworried. A woman cried, 'Weygand, Weygand!' and the crowd clapped. The Generalissimo had arrived for the last two decisive Cabinet meetings.

Behind a cordon of sloppy, young Senegalese troops, their black faces vacant under their steel helmets, the first Cabinet meeting was held that afternoon. We waited in the Trade Union building, which had been made a press headquarters. Black clouds massed overhead, and suddenly peal after peal of thunder crashed out. An aeroplane flew across the storm towards the airport. It was a setting worthy of a Greek tragedy, worthy of these dying days of this France.

We knew that we must now plan our escape. The British consulate, close to the quayside by the wide River Garonne, was already besieged by people trying to get away from France. Frenchmen, Poles, Belgians, Britons crowded the staircase leading to the consulate offices on the first floor, packed the waiting-rooms and hallways, pleading for visas, for passages on ships, for information. Fear and despair filled the air. The consul could give us little help. A British destroyer, her grey masts and superstructure clear above the waterside warehouses, was in the Gironde, but would have space only for British diplomats and military men. Other ships had been called for, but there was no certainty when or even whether they would arrive.

Meanwhile the Cabinet meeting went on. We thought that this was to decide whether the French should fight on in France, or move to Algeria, which was legally part of Metropolitan France, and continue the battle from there. But events had already raced past that point. Now the argument was whether to fight on at all. Reynaud wanted to continue the struggle from North Africa. Against him now were ranged, we were told, not only the less resolute civilian ministers like Chautemps, but also Pétain and Weygand. Weygand, it was said, had at the start of the Cabinet meeting flung open his hands and started, 'Gentlemen, the armies are beaten.'

Throughout that afternoon the argument for peace grew steadily. Reynaud, supported by Mandel, hung on, and at seven o'clock the meeting agreed to defer a decision until the next day, when they would have before them a reply from Roosevelt to Reynaud's appeal for American help.

Meanwhile, by one of the extraordinary coincidences of war, George Millar had that afternoon come face to face with his wife in a street in Bordeaux, the first time he had seen her since Paris. Netty was tired, and her MTC uniform dusty and crumpled. The unit she had been with had been overrun by the Germans, and she and another girl had escaped through the German forward posts in a car which they hid by day and drove by night. But by evening, neat and elegant as ever, she was ready to dine with us at the Chapon Fin as if she had just arrived by air from London.

The Chapon Fin was one of the great restaurants not only of France, but of the world, and its tables that evening were thronged by Cabinet Ministers and ambassadors, generals and admirals, and the vivid women who in France never seemed far from the centre of power. A menu the size of a newspaper page offered the *specialités de la région*, and the incomparable red wines of the Garonne valley. Laval was there, swarthy and sinister, wearing his customary white tie, and looking far too pleased for our comfort. At a table in the centre of the room the British Ambassador, Sir Ronald Campbell, and the chief British Liaison Officer, General Spears, dined with their staffs. In another corner a noisy group of expatriate Britons had just arrived by car from the Riviera, where they had been helping the war effort by eating French food rather then returning to eat rationed foods in Britain. Now with Italy in the war, they were making a bolt for home. Gold, diamonds, pearls glowed and glittered against suntanned faces above superb Worth and Molyneux gowns. Arrogant, raucous voices rang out across the room, scorning France in defeat, and proclaiming that she had had this coming to her ever since the Reds got power during the Popular Front.

We slept well that night, underneath the wide stairway leading up to the British consulate. I had noticed a substantial, well-protected area there, in which we spread out our sleeping-bags. It was against the rules, but no one discovered us except a friendly RAMC sergeant who was acting as caretaker, and who rushed downstairs with a rifle when, in the dark, I broke a glass panel in the nearby lavatory door. Reasonably rested, washed and shaved, we came out the next morning into the overcrowded, sleepless city whose nerves were worn bare, almost bleeding.

On the terrace of the Hôtel Splendide deputies and senators, editors, army officers and businessmen, and their wives and mistresses, weary after broken sleep on hotel floors or in the backs of cars, waited still more wearily for coffee and news. Above all, for news. All

Paris seemed to be there. Pierre Lazareff, tired, mal-shaven, but still energetic, was talking to Prouvost – 'le patron' as they termed him on *Paris Soir*. It would be no fun for Lazareff if France surrendered. His name had been on a list of those who were to be the first arrested which had been found on the body of a dead German police officer outside Paris. Tabouis was there, for the first time looking elderly, very pale as she walked along on the arm of her young husband. Pertinax, monocle in eye, was talking tensely to the burly Emil Buré, that staunchest of supporters of Reynaud. Campinchi, Louis Marin, Admiral Darlan came and went. It was the last parade of the Third Republic.

Morning and evening the Cabinet met, while we searched the docks for possible British ships to get to England on, and harried the consulate to make arrange-ments for us. All sorts of British people were pouring in now. Under the trees outside the consulate waited a detachment of infantry in battle dress, cut off in the south. Half-a-dozen RAF pilots turned up, a group of naval officers, the whole of the MTC, more Riviera-ites.

Steadily but definitely during that day you could feel anti-British feeling grow in Bordeaux. Stunned by their sufferings and the steady realisation of defeat, the French looked round angrily at their Allies and particularly at those Allies preparing to get away. Opposite the consulate a small hostile crowd gathered, staring at the British refugees coming and going. We still had one more chance. Theirs was finished – unless they chose to risk everything and fight on. But the possibility that they would do so diminished with every hour that passed.

Against Reynaud the whole weight of Pétain, Weygand and M Lebrun, the President, was thrown. Pétain, already eighty-four, was physically and nervously worn out by the strain of this journey to Tours and Bordeaux. His mind, full from the days of Verdun with pictures of suffering, recoiled from the horror of the stampede from Paris. He had seen how Verdun brought a mutiny of 700,000 men.

This might bring revolution inside France. The business-men inside the Cabinet – Prouvost, Pomaret and their like – supported him. They wanted their property back, whether under the Germans or not. Weygand said the armies were done. A rigid, ascetic Catholic who detested democracy at bottom, he believed France must be purified by suffering, that she had been slack and godless since the last war. And he chose the sufferings of defeat rather than the sufferings of continued struggle.

He too believed in the dangers of a Communist revolt if the war continued. I did not see any evidence for this possibility. During the last days in Paris I had made contact with the underground organisation of the banned Communist Party. Though they were strongly against the war they knew that to try to revolt at the moment when the Reichswehr were spreading all over France was a pipe dream. Their main leaders were already in prison, arrested by the Daladier Government in the violent anti-Communist drive carried out in the early days of the war. Most importantly of all, Stalin was at this stage appeasing Hitler, and kept the brakes firmly on the French party.

Above all Pétain believed that if he became Premier and sued for peace, France would get better treatment and would retain more of her independence. Hitler the soldier would accord respect to Pétain the solider.

Just before ten o'clock that evening the final vote was taken. Fourteen members of the Cabinet voted for peace, for an immediate armistice. Reynaud and nine others voted to continue the struggle. When the final result was announced, the staunch old Conservative, Louis Marin, in tears, opened his hands and, staring at Pétain, said bitterly: 'Gentlemen, I am ashamed to be a Frenchman.'

A few minutes after ten I was eating supper in the Hôtel Splendide when Charles Gombaux appeared in the doorway. 'Reynaud has resigned. Pétain has taken over,' he said. We rushed round to the Préfecture and asked for Mandel. Cool, inscrutable as a buddha, he confirmed the news. He displayed no emotion, this man who from the innermost ranks of power had seen one war won and another lost. He had been the trusted aide to Clemenceau, the fiery old man who had held France together, and brought her to victory in 1918. Mandel had stood by Clemenceau's side at the Arc de Triomphe during the victory parade of 1919. On this sultry evening twenty one years later he must have known that, as a Jew, he faced great personal danger in a defeated France – and indeed, four years later, a prisoner of Pétain's Vichy Government, he was murdered by their Milices, their French storm-troopers. Yet at this moment I could detect no trace of fear on his pale, drawn countenance.

Exhausted, I returned to the consulate and settled down to sleep again under the stairs. I was woken an hour or so later by sounds of a row on the stairway. A voice, easily indentifiable as that of one of the most assertive of the refugees from the Riviera who had behaved so crudely the night before in the Chapon Fin, was shrieking, 'Your wife called me a drunken whore. Do you hear me? Your wife called me a drunken whore.' I could not see who replied, but his riposte was swift. 'And are you?' he queried.

An hour or two later, I was wakened again by the voices of naval officers seeking the consul. They cursed him heartily for not being on the premises – he had apparently a code they wanted – and for not leaving any official in charge at this moment of crisis. The officers' confident, cheerful voices were like music in this atmosphere of indecision. If the navy was here, and taking over, we should get away before the German army arrived. My guess was right. By nine o'clock the next morning the consulate was functioning like a new concern. We were told to get down to Le Verdon, at the tip of the southern peninsula on the Bordeaux Estuary, and embark there.

De Caux was breakfasting calmly on the terrace of the Hôtel Splendide. We stopped the car to say good-bye to him, and to Eric Sevareid, who was standing by to report to America the speech Pétain was due to make on the radio at noon, the speech in which he was to utter the chilling words '*il faut cesser le combat*'. We drove north through flat country rich with vineyards. Mouton Rothschild and Château Latour, Margaux and St Julien proclaimed themselves on roadside signs. At Le Verdon a naval cutter was waiting close by the memorial commemorating the first landing of American troops in the 1914–18 war. Netty and George and I piled our luggage into it, left the car on the quayside, and were ferried to where the SS *Madura* lay in mid-stream.

The *Madura* was a 7,000 ton P and O liner, a smaller version of the ship on which I had travelled from Sydney eight years earlier. She had been on her way from East Africa with 120 passengers, mostly Empire builders and Empire maintainers coming on leave, when she had been diverted to the Gironde. On to her in the next twenty-four hours were to be crammed a further 1,623 people. Ambassadors, ex-premiers, ex-cabinet ministers from France, Holland, Belgium, Poland crowded in with journalists, the Riviera gang, bank officials, stray Britons from all over France, and French men and women who either feared the Nazis or were, like Eve Curie, determined to continue the resistance. That evening bombs were dropped just to our stern, throwing up great white cascades, in a series of air raids in which, to the north, the Cunard-White Star liner *Lancastria*, with some 6,000 British troops on board, was sunk, with some 4,000 men drowned. There was another attack on the *Madura* the next evening, but it was beaten off by the guns of the cruiser HMS *Arethusa*, which had drawn in alongside us. An hour later we drew out into the Atlantic, followed by another P and O liner on which were Embassy officials, the MTC, a number of British troops, and some star refugees like Madame Tabouis – I could see her thin form leaning on the rail – and Pertinax.

We spread our sleeping bags on the boat deck. Every yard of deck space was covered with sleeping bodies. We mounted anti-U-boat watches in relays throughout the night, and again throughout the long sunny day which followed. In the intervals of taking our turn, George Millar and I discussed our futures. We were both sure we had to join the army. He would enlist in a Scottish regiment. With no New Zealand unit apparently open to me, I would opt for an English regiment.

'We have to accept that war is a much more normal part of life than we have been taught,' George argued. 'Mahbub the Pathan in Kipling's *Kim* had shot his man and begot his man by the time he was sixteen. Maybe we have to begin to think in those terms.'

At eleven that morning two grey shapes showed on the horizon, white bow waves racing with them. They were British destroyers. Gracefully they slipped into position ahead of us, weaving to and fro, a reassuring presence. The next morning we woke to see the coast of Cornwall, and soon Falmouth, its harbour crammmed with ships which had escaped from France.

It was a superb day of high summer, and on the green headland above the harbour they were stacking hay, loading it by pitchfork on to big wagons, as we had so often done in New Zealand. A grey church tower rose above thick green trees. Even the close-packed suburban roofs around Falmouth had a warm beauty. That afternoon England looked very much worth fighting for. Now that we were on our own, the war seemed not only a struggle against an evil creed but also a matter of straightforward patriotism.

We moored alongside in the late afternoon. There was still time for us to get our stories to the papers in time for tomorrow's editions if we got off immediately. The American correspondents, aware of their country's hunger for news about the last hours of France, were particularly anxious to get ashore. But the authorities were not to be hurried. Journalists could wait their turn, and that turn came well below those of the diplomats. First off must be the consul's party – amongst whom, I noted, many of the Riviera gang were now included.

Their luggage had to be sorted out from amongst the massed baggage on the deck. 'The little green hat case, and the pigskin suitcase next to it. Yes, that's it, old chap,' the clear, untroubled voice called as the slings slowly and carefully loaded. Minute by minute our edition times ticked away. I watched H. R. Knickerbocker's face. He was a good friend of Britain. What he had to write could help, at this crucial stage, to win or hold us vital friends in America. Weariness, and a scorn close to disgust showed on it. His edition times were going too.

At last we were ashore. In a Falmouth hotel that night I listened to the BBC News. France was suing for an armistice. Australian and New Zealand troops had disembarked in Britain, and were now stationed to help resist invasion. Here was my opportunity. A month later I was marching along a Surrey road in battle dress and steel helmet, with familiar New Zealand voices around me, a rifle slung on my shoulder, and live ammunition in my webbing pouches. For all the perils ahead, my mind was more at ease than at any time during these years when I had watched us slip into this gulf of danger.

As It Looks Now

The war which in that spring and summer of 1940 had got into its full stride was to last in Europe for five more years. Its aftermath of upheavals, suffering and minor wars was to continue over at least the next decade. Those who were caught up in it were too absorbed by its immediate problems and horrors to think much about how it had come about, and whether it might have been avoided. Yet one great issue of the time continues to tantalise historians. Of all the 'Ifs' of history, one will continue to pose itself to those who lived through the Thirties. If Britain had stood firm in September 1938, and had given the Czechs the support they sought, and given the French Government the backbone which they – but not the French people – lacked, would we have halted Hitler without war, or at least fought him on more favourable terms?

As the dust of events has settled in the intervening fifty years, it is clear that the last chance to have checked Hitler without risk of war occurred in March 1936, when he sent his troops into the demilitarised zone of the Rhineland. The obligation not to fortify the left bank of the Rhine, or to station troops within fifty kilometres of its right bank, had first been imposed upon Germany in the Treaty of Versailles. But it had been freely accepted by an elected German Government in 1925, as part of the Locarno Treaty, designed to avoid a new war breaking

out in Europe. Now Hitler had spurned these undertakings. His order to his troops to march into the Rhineland
on 7 March 1936 was the first occasion on which he had
openly repudiated an international treaty.

The first reaction of the French Government was that
they should order the mobilisation of the French army
and demand that Hitler withdraw his forces. At the time
the French army was overwhelmingly stronger than the
Reichswehr, and had it been mobilised Hitler would have
had no option but to withdraw, with damaging conse-
quences not only to his prestige but to his confidence. But
the British Government, under Stanley Baldwin, urged
the French to do nothing more than refer the matter to
the League of Nations – a League which was proving itself
impotent to halt Mussolini in Abyssinia. The opportunity
passed. The French did no more than protest, and Hitler
was left with his triumph.

Baldwin's attitude met with widespread public approval
in Britain, with Winston Churchill once again as almost a
lone voice warning of the dangers of letting the Germans
trample on their freely given undertakings. Most British
people echoed Lord Lothian's view that 'after all, the
Germans are only going into their back yard'. This apathy
and readiness to yield was in sharp contrast to the mood
the previous autumn, when Britain had strongly endorsed,
and indeed advocated, the League of Nations' plan for
sanctions against Italy for her invasion of Abyssinia. This
had tapped a vein not only of patriotism, but also of
idealism in support of a new international order. Those of
us who were of fighting age reconciled ourselves to the
possibility of being called up. In the news room of the
News Chronicle, for which I was working at the time, we
discussed which branch of the Services we might find
ourselves in. Veterans of the Great War, as we then still
called it, advised us whether we would have a better
chance of survival in the trenches as ordinary riflemen, or
as machine gunners. The office wit coined a recruiting
slogan. 'Join up and take a pop at a Wop,' he suggested.

But with the revelation of the Hoare-Laval Pact to carve up much of Abyssinia behind the back of the League of Nations, and the rapid failure of the half-hearted sanctions, cynicism spread. If Britain was not prepared to stand up against a blatant war waged against a primitive people, whose country was a member of the League of Nations, there seemed little reason to go to arms against the Germans for asserting themselves within their own borders. The opportunity to take this stand against Hitler whilst all the odds were still in our favour passed almost unnoticed.

But the Anschluss of Germany and Austria two years later was a very different matter. It was clearly the outcome of intimidation and of force, of the ruthless bullying by Hitler of the Austrian Chancellor, Kurt von Schuschnigg, and of the massing of German troops along the Austrian frontiers. Schuschnigg resigned rather than either yield to Hitler's demands for a merger of the two states, or shed German and Austrian blood by resisting them, and new, pro-Nazi Austrian Government gave way, providing a transparently thin cloak of legality for what Churchill termed 'the rape of Austria'. Once again Britain and France did nothing but protest. We had the excuse that Schuschnigg, hoping to the end to save something of his country's independence, deliberately played down to the outside world the nature of Hitler's threats – until it was too late.

Yet if the Anschluss provided no opportunity for us to intervene, even if we had been so minded, it did provide a striking opportunity for the British Government to warn the British people of the true nature of Nazism, and prepare the country for the dangers which lay ahead. For the incorporation of Austria into the Reich meant that Hitler had broken his word. He had solemnly declared, after he had seized the Rhineland, that 'Germany neither intends ... to annex Austria, or to conclude an Anschluss.' Here was the clearest proof that his assurances could not be trusted. The spectacle of the German army on the march, even in those pre-television days, had also provided vivid proof of Hitler's readiness to use force to impose his will. But Neville Chamberlain, who had taken over by then as Prime Minister, sounded no such alarm. Though he did something to speed up our limping rearmament programme, his main reaction to the Anschluss was to get ready to appease Hitler by clearing the way for him to secure his next objective, that of bringing the three million people of German stock, who lived in the Sudeten area of Czechoslovakia, within the borders of the Reich. Far from warning the British public of the dangers ahead, Chamberlain – and Beaverbrook – did their utmost to lull them into the belief that what happened in distant Czechoslovakia need not concern them. Only when, at Godesberg, Hitler's demands went beyond what even Chamberlain then felt reasonable (though he was to change his mind, and concede everything at Munich five days later) did the Prime Minister set about preparing the British public, almost overnight, for war.

Should we have stood firm, and refused to yield at Munich, even if that had meant war? At the time I had no doubt that we should have done so. My reasons were not based on any fine calculations of the relative strengths of either side, information available then only to the inner circles of the Military and of the Government, but on an instinctive feeling that Hitler would have to be faced, and it was better to do this sooner than later. An impressive volume of evidence has since emerged to show that this attitude made good sense. Much of this evidence came from the German files seized by the victorious Allies. Other material came from statements at the Nuremberg War Crime trials. Though in the year between Munich and the outbreak of war we improved markedly our armaments and our preparations, the Germans improved theirs even more markedly. In the field of weaponry much play is made by those who seek to justify Chamberlain's policy at Munich of the fact that in those intervening twelve months the Spitfire and the Hurricane fighters came fully into service. At the time of Munich only five RAF squadrons were equipped with Hurricanes: none yet had Spitfires. These were the planes which were to win the Battle of Britain in 1940. But no Battle of Britain could have been fought in 1938, nor any massive bomber raids mounted against English cities, unless the Germans had won airfields in the Low Countries and Northern France. To do that, the German army would have had to overthrow the France army. Yet in 1938 the Germans were not in a position to do this. They did not yet have enough tanks, of sufficient size and armament, to dominate the battlefield. In a war in the autumn of 1938 the French superiority in artillery, resting on the famous 75-mm guns of World War I, would probably have been decisive. Winston Churchill, writing in 1948, with all the experience of World War II to call upon, declared categorically, 'The German armies were not capable of defeating the French in 1938 or 1939.'[1] Another factor in the equation was the shift of Czechoslovak military might from our side to the Germans. By abandoning Czechoslovakia we lost the 35 Czechoslovak divisions, whilst the Germans gained not only the powerful Czech armament industry, based on the Skoda works, but laid their hands on Czechoslovakia's high-grade tanks. A considerable portion of the front-line tanks employed by the Wehrmacht to break through on the Western front in the spring of 1940 were drawn from the disbanded Czech armoured division.

The one gain which Chamberlain secured from Munich was that when war came in 1939 the British people, and those of the Commonwealth, entered it fully united, convinced not only of the rightness of their cause, but also of the fact that no other course had been open to them. We had leaned over backwards to meet Hitler's demands, in an effort to avoid war. When, despite all we

[1] *The Gathering Storm*. Cassell, 1948, p.304.

had conceded, war came, no one could have any doubt that it was not only right, but inescapable. This was of immeasurable value in uniting the country and in sustaining morale throughout the long, dark years of war. Such unanimity did not exist in September 1938. A sustained policy of educating the public in the reality of Hitlerism, in the fact that gathering all people of German race within the Reich was not an end in itself, but a means to domination of Europe, might have done much to convince people, by the time of Munich, that we should fight. But no such campaign was undertaken by the Government, and even Churchill's eloquence was not enough to convince the public that appeasement would not work. It took the Nazi seizure of Prague in the spring of 1939, and the invasion of Poland on September 1 that year, to demonstrate beyond doubt what Hitler and Nazism, truly were. Perhaps it is an inescapable fact that a democracy can only learn such lessons the hard way, by what happens rather than what people are told.

Yet it is the duty of the leaders of a Parliamentary democracy, equipped as they are with a mass of military and diplomatic information, to warn the public of what lies ahead, and to prepare the country to face it. On this count both Baldwin and Chamberlain failed the British people. Understandably reluctant to contemplate the horrors of another European war, and grappling with the problems of the Great Slump, Baldwin averted his gaze from the dangers of Hitlerism as long as he could. Yet the evidence of Hitler's aims was clear. It was set out in *Mein Kampf*. It was contained in his speeches, and in the reports of knowledgeable diplomats. But Chamberlain spurned all this. Confident he could do a deal with Hitler, and relying on the views of the British Ambassador in Berlin, Sir Nevile Henderson, who put a favourable gloss on everything the Nazis said or did, Chamberlain not only failed to alert the British people to what might happen, but refused himself to recognise the ugly possibilities of

Hitlerism, possibilities which his own actions were to help transform into probabilities.

This attitude led Neville Chamberlain, in the spring and summer of 1938, to spurn pleas which reached him from senior military men in Germany that he should stand against Hitler's pressure on Czechoslovakia. In 1945, when the long slaughter had ground to its close, and the enemies were free to speak, General von Halder, who had been Chief of the German General Staff in 1939, declared that he and a number of other generals had made plans to arrest Hitler, Goering, Goebbels and Himmler, and set up a military government in their stead, if Hitler persisted with his plan to seize the Sudetenland on October 1. Von Halder argued that they were on the point of acting when Chamberlain set out on his first mission to Berchtesgaden. If Hitler could gain a victory by bluff, without having to resort to war, then their plot had no point.

How valid this claim is can never be established. Sir Winston Churchill, in *The Gathering Storm* recounts it, and contents himself with describing it as a tale 'which the historians should probe'. The outlines of the plot were known to the British Government in September 1938, for the conspirators sent emissaries to London who were seen not only by Churchill but by the Foreign Secretary, Lord Halifax. The reports of these messengers were no doubt too insubstantial for British policy to be based upon them, but they were one more argument for a strong rather than a weak line.

In the end the British Government's decisions in September 1938 turned above all on one factor – an estimate of Hitler's true character and aims. Chamberlain misread both. It was to prove one of history's costliest mistakes.

INDEX

Aachen, 190–1
Abd-el-Krim, 73
Aez, Otto, 142
Abyssinia, 126, 274–5
Adolf Hitler Platz, 23
Alamein, 99
Albert Canal, 194–6, 220
Alcron Hotel, 13, 45, 52, 55, 65, 85, 90
Alexander, King of Yugoslavia, 24
Alsace and Lorraine, 113
Alving, Babro, 174–5
American Legion, 242
Anglo-German Naval Agreement, 15
Anschluss, 15, 17, 35, 63, 74, 275–6
Arad, 129
Arbeitsdienst, 20, 31, 72
Arethusa, HMS, 270
Argyll and Sutherland Highlanders, 153
Astor, Lord and Lady, 75, 79
Attaturk, Kemal, 24
Attlee, Clement, 96
Augsburg, 169

Badoux, General, 195, 198
Baku, 183
Baldwin, S., 274, 278
Balkans, 128
Barandov, 49, 51
Barcelona, 76, 117–9
Barrington-Ward, R., 97
Barry, Gerald, 32

Baumgarten, Herr, 61–3
BBC, 74, 119, 180, 194, 272
Beaverbrook, Lord, 34, 69, 98, 101–10, 132, 137, 145–6, 147–9, 185–7, 258
Benes, Edouard, 44, 79, 82, 88
Bennet, J., 152
Berchtesgaden, 80, 150, 279
Berzin, General, 118
Best, Captain S. P., 167
Beyerl, W. 52–5
Bismarck, 66
Black Watch, 161
Blum, Leon, 89, 237
Blunt, Anthony, 32, 149
Bochow, Roland, 39, 56–63
Boeuf sur le Toit, Brussels, 195
Boeuf sur le Toit, Paris, 135
Bolsheviks, 20, 27
Bonnet, Georges, 19, 111–2, 142
Bose, von, 56–7
Brauschitsch, General, 168
Brecht, 21
Brenner Pass, 37
Brest Litovsk, Treaty of, 45
Brinon de, 126
British Expeditionary force, 161–2, 202–3, 225–6
British Union of Fascists, 24–5
Brocket, Lord and Lady, 71
Bucharest, 128–9
Bullit, C., 241
Buré, Emil, 143, 157, 267

Cadett, T., 153, 256
Cameron Highlanders, 59

Caminada, Jerome, 210
Campbell, Colonel, 24
Campbell, Sir Ronald, 266
Campinchi, M., 267
Carol, King of Rumania, 129
Carthage, 113
Castlerosse, V., 130, 145–7
Cavalcade, 63
CBS, 74
Chamberlain, Neville, 11, 13–15,
    18–19, 74, 80–2, 84, 89, 96–7,
    104, 112, 127–8, 156–7, 276–9
Chanel, 136, 139
Chapon Fin, 265–6, 269
Charing, Stephen, 244, 256
Chautemps, C., 265
Cherourg, 161–3
Chicago Daily News, 123
Christiansen, A, 34–5, 41, 63,
    68–9, 98, 102, 105–7, 109–10,
    126, 139, 142, 160, 162, 187,
    189, 255
Churchill, Sir Winston, 24, 105,
    110, 194, 233–4, 258, 274–5,
    277, 279
Ciano, Count, 125
Clemenceau, G., 238, 269
Clive, Lord, 71
Cliveden, Cliveden Set, 66, 75, 79
Cockburn, Claud, 75–7, 79, 151–2
Cocteau, J., 136, 138
Colditz, 185
Comedie Francaise, 138
Comintern, 125, 172
Como, Lake, 133
Corsica, 113
Coupole, La, 118
Coward, Noël, 135, 149, 236
Cox, Cecily, 34, 88, 95, 98, 101–2,
    117, 132–3, 151, 187, 241
Cox, Patrick, 132, 151
Cox, Peter, 88, 151, 241
Cripps, Sir Stafford, 109
Curie, Eve, 270
Czenin Palace, 45

Dachau, 121, 131
Daily Express, 20, 34–5, 39, 55,

    63, 68, 72, 81–2, 85, 93, 96, 98,
    101, 103–5, 107, 110, 116–7,
    125, 132, 134, 139, 147–8, 166,
    242, 244
Daily Mail, 25, 41
Daily Telegraph, 73–4
Daily Worker, 76
Daladier, E., 89, 125, 156–7, 228,
    232, 237, 268
Dali, Salvador, 32
Danzig, 146–8, 150, 156
Darlan, Admiral, 267
Davin, Dan, 152, 189
Dawson, Geoffrey, 75, 79
de Caux, 116, 238–40, 269
de Gaulle, General, 237
de Portes, Countess Helene, 138,
    236, 249, 259
de Sausmarez, C., 210–11
Delacroix, M., 81
D'Eickhoute, I., 202
Delmer, Sefton, 56, 58, 109,
    232–3, 242, 259–60
Der Stürmer, 27
Deux Magots, 118, 152
Dimbleby, R., 119, 188
Dollfuss, Chancellor, E., 34–5, 38
Dome Cafe, 118, 151
Dovi, Tom, 152
Downs, Kenneth, 165, 246
Durbin, Evan, 109
Dutch Water Line, 168

Eban Emael Fort, 208–9
Ebro River, 117
Eden, Guy, 96
Edward VII, 12, 71
Eger, 11–12, 80
Eighth Army, 99
Elizabeth, Queen, 19
Elizabeth of Bohemia, 49
Engadine, 133
Esthonia, 171
Evening Standard, 24, 109

Fairfax, 98
Fallen Bastions, 74

Fascism, 25, 34, 98
Fast, Maurice, 166, 192, 196–7
Finland, 171–84
Fitzwilliam, J., 217–8
Five Year Plan, 20, 51
Fleet Street, 32–3, 72, 107
Flore, Café, 118, 244–5, 250
Fodor, M., 193, 196
Foot, Michael, 107–9
Forrest, William, 116, 209, 256
Fouquet's, 135, 147
Franck, Karl H., 46, 53–4, 66
Francis Joseph, Emperor, 12, 71
Frauenkirche, Nuremberg, 23

Gaitskell, Hugh, 109
Gamelin, General, 228, 233–4, 258
Gare de L'Est, 153–4
Gare des Invalides, 112
Garvin, J. L., 14
Gasterwald, 52, 55
Gathering Storm, The, 277n, 279
Gedye, G. E. R., 73–4
George VI, King, 19, 112
Gervasi, F., 116
Gestapo, 55–7, 127, 167, 205
Gloucester, Duke of, 225
Godesberg, 82, 84, 95, 276
Goebbels, Dr., 26–8, 52, 279
Goering, H., 26–7, 83, 279
Gollancz, Victor, 34, 187
Gombaux, C., 236, 268
Grand Vefour, 135
Gordon, Hélène, 139, 240
Grapes of Wrath, 253
Greene, Sir Hugh, 198, 205, 222, 224, 226
Grimm, Brothers, 54
Gross, G., 21
Grunzpan, H. F., 111
Gunther, John, 201
Gwatkin, F. Ashtoh, 64, 66–7, 70–1, 80, 89

Habsburgs, 34, 39, 42, 47
Hacha, President, 126

Halder, General von, 279
Halifax, Lord, 19, 258, 279
Hango, 172
Hartrich, E., 157–8
Hearst Press, 35
Heberskirk, 80
Heidelberg, 21
Hemingway, E., 73
Henderson, Sir Nevile, 278
Henlein, Konrad, 11–3, 17–8, 45–6, 52–5, 64–7, 70–1, 78–80, 89, 92
Herlihy, M., 153
Hess, R., 28, 30, 71
Himmler, H., 26, 28, 279
Hindenburg, President, 27
Hindus, Maurice, 51
Hitler Adolf, 12–15, 17–8, 21–32, 35–6, 38, 40–1, 44–5, 56, 70–1, 80, 82, 84, 88, 96, 104, 127–9, 132–3, 146–7, 167–9, 186–8, 192–3, 206, 228, 232, 232, 234, 273–9
Hitler Youth, 28
Hoare-Laval Pact, 275
Hodson, J. L., 209
Hodza, Dr, 18, 44, 84
Hogg, Quintin, 98–9
Hohenlohe, Price Max, 65–8
Hohenlohe, Princess Stephanie, 67–8
Hohenzollerns, 38
Hoiden, Robert, 52–3
Hollenden, Lord and Lady, 71
Howard, Peter, 108–9
Hurricane aircraft, 277
Huxley, Aldous, 48

Imperial Hotel, Vienna, 38, 62
Innsbruck, 36–7
Insanity Fair, 74
Intourist, 20
Ironside, General, 193
Izzard, Ralph, 167

Jaksch, W., 127
James I, 49
Jay, Douglas, 109

Kangaroo, 24
Karlsbad, 12, 17, 46, 91–2
Katz Otto (See Simone, Andre)
Kerr, Walter, 35–6, 67, 74, 87, 157–9, 161, 163, 165, 234, 237, 239
Khruschev, N., 172
King's Dragoon Guards, 99
Kinsky, Count, 47
Keppler, Baron von, 58, 62
Knickerbocker, H. R. 35–6, 256, 272
Koestler, Arthur, 32
Kölnischer Zeitung, 146
Kristallnacht, 111
Krofta, Dr K., 44–5
Kuhn, Ferdinand, 97
Kusinen, Otto, 172–3

Labour Party, 109
Lac de Tignes, 133
Lacey, Montagu, 142
Lamartine, M., 151
'Lambeth Walk, The', 48, 135
Lancastria, SS, 270
Lawrence, D. H., 24
Lazareff, Pierre, 139–40, 240, 247, 267
Le Petit Parisien, 159, 164, 238
League of Nations, 21, 150, 274–5
Lebrun, President, 267
Legion, Czechoslovak, 43, 81, 84
Leonding, 131
Leopold, King of the Belgians, 192
Lewis, Sinclair, 98
'Lili Marlene', 191
Lindemann, General, 235–6
Lindsay of Balliol, 98
Lloyd George, D., 24, 110
Locarno, Treaty of, 15
Lockhart, sir Bruce, 103, 110
Lohengrin, 29
Lothian, Lord, 75, 79, 274
Louvre Cafe, 196

Low, David, 106
Luce, Claire Booth, 234–5

Macdonald, Mrs, 257
Madrid, 32–4, 50, 75, 117, 158, 165
Madura, SS, 270
Maginot Line, 153, 183, 233, 242, 260
Maisky, I. M., 182, 186
Malraux, A., 33
Man Alone, 152
Manchester Guardian, 193, 256
Mandel, G., 238, 265, 268–9
Mannerheim, Field Marshal, 173
Mannerheim Line, 173–4, 182
Manning, Olivia, 210
Mareth Line, 114–5
Marin, L., 267–8
Maschewitz, E., 136
Masaryk, Thomas, 43–5
Massingham, H., 116
Massip, M., 118
Masson, M., 219, 222
Match (later *Paris Match*), 247–8, 262
Matchek, V., 130
Maurice, C., 238
Maxims, 135, 259
Maxton James, MP, 186
Mazar, Dr, 38
McGovern, J., 186
McGowan, Lord, 71
McNeil, H., 109
Mein Kampf, 278
Merton College, 99
Messerschmitt, 100, 169–70
Mechanised Transport Corps, 257, 265, 267, 270
Millar, George, 117, 160–1, 228–9, 233, 237, 242, 244, 252, 257, 261–3, 265, 270–1
Millar, Netty, 160, 257, 265, 270
Miller, Arthur, 262
Minerva Pension, 59, 61
Ministry of War, Paris, 159

Mitford, Unity, 40
Modenaplatz, 39, 58, 60, 63
Monroe, Marilyn, 262
Montgomery, Field Marshal, 99, 114
Moorehead, Alan, 116, 119, 149, 158
Morrell, W., 90
Mosley, Sir Oswald, 24, 40
Mowrer, Edgar, 123, 201, 256
Muggeridge, M., 109
Mulgan, John, 99, 152, 162, 189
Munich, 19, 88–90, 95, 96, 98–9, 101, 105, 112, 127–8, 131, 147, 277–8
Murrow, E. R., 74, 161, 234
Mussolini, Benito, 20, 24, 32, 113, 192

Napoleon, 151
Nazi Soviet Pact, 148
NBC, 74
New Statesman, 107
New York Herald Tribune, 67, 74, 159
New York Times, 31, 74, 97
New Zealand, 20–21, 33, 49, 64, 115, 184, 271
News Chronicle, 32, 34, 116, 274
Newsweek, 206
Newton, Basil, 13, 81
Nietsche, 133
Nuremberg, 22–3, 31, 38, 70–1, 74, 79

Observer, The, 14, 116
O'Donovan, P, 116
Okin, P., 194
Okin, R., 194, 203
O'Leary, M., 201, 211–2, 221–2
Olympia, 25
Operation Yellow, 168
Oriel College, 20
Orwell, George, 118
Owen, Frank, 108–9, 186
Oxford, 20, 34, 79, 98

Oxford and Bucks Light Infantry, 189
Oxford University Press, 99

Pallach, Jan, 81
Pantelleria, 113
Papen, von, 56, 58
Paris Soir, 127, 139–40, 236, 247, 249–50, 259, 267
Pertinax, 267, 270
Petacci, Clara, 133
Pétain, Marshal, 233, 265, 267–9
Peto, Geoffrey, 64, 66
Philby, Kim, 210
Picture Post, 182
Pierlot, M., 198, 213
Pilsudski, 24
Pitcairn, Frank, 75
Piquard, Col, 196, 219
POUM, 76, 118
Pritt, D. N., 182
Prouvost, 139, 156, 165, 247–9, 267–8
Prunier, 135

Quai d'Orsay, 19, 113, 134, 249

Radio, German, 41, 53
RAF, 72, 163
Rath, von, 110
Rauschning, H., 206
Red Army, 51, 172, 178
Red Army Moves, The, 187
Red Air Force, 172–3
Reed, Douglas, 73–4, 116
Reichswehr, 15, 27, 37–8, 41, 131, 129, 168
Reid, Robert, 188
Reimer, Charlotte, 121–3
Reimer, Karl, 121–3
Reith, Lord, 166
Reuters, 153, 211, 256
Reynaud, P., 138, 236–7, 247, 258–60, 265, 267–8
Ribbentrop, 112–3
Richards, Morley, 194

Riefenstahl, L., 23, 28
Ripka, 127
Ritchie, Charles, 148
Rivera, de Primo, 20, 24
Robertson, D. A., 140–2, 160
Robertson, Sir Johnston Forbes, 73
Roehm, Ernst, 27, 56
Romilly, Esmond, 40, 184
Romilly, Giles, 184–5
Rommel, E., 214
Roosevelt, President, 260, 265
Rothenhaus, Schlosss, 65–6, 67–8, 70
Rothermere, Viscount, 25
Royal West Kent Regiment, 99
Runciman, Viscount, 11–4, 19, 20, 41, 42–7, 52, 64–8, 70–1, 78, 80, 90, 107

SA, (Storm Troopers), 25–6, 29, 39–40
Saint Exupery, A., 245
Salazar, President, 24
Sandford Park, 64
Schrafranek, M., 90, 127
Scherbatoff, Mara, 140, 233, 247, 259, 261–2
Schiaparelli, 136, 138, 236
Schickelgruber, 54
Schirach, Baldur, 28
Schuschnigg, Kurt von, 35, 39, 275
Schmidt, Else, 95
Sebekowesky, 45
Sevareid, Eric, 161, 165, 234, 237, 239, 269
Seyss-Inquart, 38
Sheean, Diana, 73, 90, 94
Sheean, Vincent, 72–3, 87, 90, 94, 234–5
Siegfried Line, 159, 183, 190
Simone, André, 123–5, 154–5
Skoda Arms Works, 13, 48, 277
So Spake Zarathustra, 133
Solidor, Suzy, 136–7

Spaak, P. H., 198
Spears, General Sir, E., 266
Spectator, The, 32
Spitfire aircraft, 277
SS (Sturm Staffel), 22–3, 26–8, 30, 57–8, 127
Stalin, J., 21, 51, 148, 154, 172
Stamp, Lord and Lady, 71
Steer, George, 116
Steinbeck, J., 253
Stevens, Major H. R., 167
Stewart, Lt N. Baille, 59–62
Stokes, R., 186
Stopford, F., 64
Stornaway House, 101
Strasser, Gregor, 93
Sudeten Germans, 11–13, 15, 17–9, 43, 45–6, 52–3, 79–80, 82, 88–9, 91–3
Syrovy, General, 84, 90

Tabouis, Madame, 120, 125, 143, 267, 270
The Week, 75, 79
'There Will Be No War', 82, 148
Thomas, Colonel, 238, 242, 246, 260, 264
Time magazine, 63, 165, 170
Times, The, 51, 77, 79, 97, 135
Tour d'Argent, 135
Triumph of the Will, The, 23
Trotskyists, 76, 155
Turner, Cecily (see Cox, Cecily)
Turner, Lt Patrick, 132

Ukraine, 20, 43
Ulrich, Oscar, 46, 55

Vautrin, Major, 260
Vedun, 143, 152, 163
Versailles, Treaty of, 15, 43, 113
Villennes, 162
Venlo, 167

Wall Street Journal, 157
Wallenius, General, 175, 179

War Office, 162
War Scare, May 1938, 17
Ward, Edward (Viscount Bangor), 180, 188, 210, 212, 218, 223–4, 226–7, 259
Weimar Republic, 21
Westminster, Duchess of, 186
Wenceslas, King, 42, 81
Welles, Sumner, 185–6
Werth, Alexander, 256
Weygand, General, 233, 236–7, 248, 264–8
Whitaker, John, 35
Wilhelm, Kaise, 27, 44
Williams, Brigadier Sir Edgar, 99, 189

Willis, Jerome, 260
Wilson, Sir Arnold, MP, 71
Wilson, J. B., 142
Wilson, President W., 13, 255
Windsor, Duke of, 63, 241
Wood, Alan, 116
Worth, 138, 266

Yugoslavia, 24, 94, 130
Young, Courtenay, 211, 223
Yukon, 76

Zagreb, 130
Zurich, 128

MORE TITLES AVAILABLE FROM
HODDER AND STOUGHTON PAPERBACKS

	DAVID ROLF	
☐ 50820 5	Prisoners of the Reich	£4.50
	RICHARD BICKERS	
☐ 50824 8	The First Great Air War	£3.99
	DUFF HART-DAVIS	
☐ 42648 9	Hitler's Olympics:	£2.95
	The 1936 Games	
	ANN & JOHN TUSA	
☐ 50068 9	The Berlin Blockade	£4.99
	TREVOR ROYLE	
☐ 42213 0	The Best Years of Their Lives	£3.95
	WINSTON CHURCHILL	
☐ 41223 2	The River War	£6.95
	ALASDAIR MILNE	
☐ 49750 5	DG: Memoirs of a British	£4.50
	Broadcaster	

All these books are available at your local bookshop or newsagent, or can be ordered direct from the publisher. Just tick the titles you want and fill in the form below.

Prices and availability subject to change without notice.

HODDER AND STOUGHTON PAPERBACKS, P.O. Box 11, Falmouth, Cornwall.

Please send cheque or postal order, and allow the following for postage and packing:

U.K. – 55p for one book, plus 22p for the second book, and 14p for each additional book ordered up to a £1.75 maximum.

B.F.P.O. and EIRE – 55p for the first book, plus 22p for the second book, and 14p per copy for the next 7 books, 8p per book thereafter.

OTHER OVERSEAS CUSTOMERS – £1.00 for the first book, plus 25p per copy for each additional book.

NAME ....

ADDRESS ....

....

....